THIS
FALLEN
PREY

Also by Kelley Armstrong

Rockton
City of the Lost
A Darkness Absolute

Cainsville
Rituals   *Visions*
Betrayals   *Omens*
Deceptions

Age of Legends
Forest of Ruin
Empire of Night
Sea of Shadows

The Blackwell Pages (co-written with Melissa Mar)
Thor's Serpents
Odin's Ravens
Loki's Wolves

Otherworld
Thirteen   *No Humans Involved*
Spell Bound   *Broken*
Waking the Witch   *Haunted*
Frostbitten   *Industrial Magic*
Living with the Dead   *Dime Store Magic*
Personal Demon   *Stolen*
Bitten

Darkest Powers & Darkness Rising
The Rising   *The Reckoning*
The Calling   *The Awakening*
The Gathering   *The Summoning*

Nadia Stafford
Wild Justice
Made to be Broken
Exit Strategy

Stand-alone novels
The Masked Truth
Missing

THIS
FALLEN
PREY

A Rockton Novel

KELLEY ARMSTRONG

MINOTAUR BOOKS ✿ NEW YORK

THIS FALLEN PREY. Copyright © 2018 by KLA Fricke Inc. All rights reserved. Printed in the United States of America. For information, address St. Martin's Press, 175 Fifth Avenue, New York, N.Y. 10010.

www.minotaurbooks.com

The Library of Congress has cataloged the hardcover edition as follows:

Names: Armstrong, Kelley, author.
Title: This fallen prey / Kelley Armstrong.
Description: First edition. | New York: Minotaur Books, 2018.
Identifiers: LCCN 2017041314 | ISBN 9781250159892 (hardcover) | ISBN
    9781250159908 (ebook)
Subjects: LCSH: Women detectives—Fiction. | GSAFD: Mystery fiction. |
    Suspense fiction.
Classification: LCC PS3551.R4678 T482 2018 | DDC 813/.54—dc23
LC record available at https://lccn.loc.gov/2017041314

ISBN 978-1-250-29485-2 (trade paperback)

Our books may be purchased in bulk for promotional, educational, or business use. Please contact your local bookseller or the Macmillan Corporate and Premium Sales Department at 1-800-221-7945, extension 5442, or by email at MacmillanSpecialMarkets@macmillan.com.

First Minotaur Books Paperback Edition: November 2018

10 9 8 7 6 5 4 3 2 1

For Jeff

THIS
FALLEN
PREY

ONE

The season may have officially started two months ago, but it isn't truly spring in Rockton until we bury our winter dead.

Dalton and Anders are digging the shallow grave. I'm wandering, trying to calm Storm. As a future tracking dog, she needs to know the smell of death. I've read books that say cadaver dogs can't do the job for long because every "success" leads to a dead body. I dismissed that as anthropomorphism until I showed Storm the corpses . . . and she promptly set about trying to wake the dead.

We're walking in ever-growing circles around the grave. Dalton's occasional "Casey?" warns me to stay close, while Storm's insistent tugs beg me to let her explore and forget what she's seen. The tugs of an eight-month-old Newfoundland are not insubstantial.

"Switch?" Anders walks over and holds out a hand.

Storm isn't the only one who needs a break from this task. Every year, Dalton orders his deputy to stay behind. Every year Anders ignores him. As a former soldier, Anders might not need to see more death, but being a former soldier also means he refuses to grant himself that reprieve.

I give his hand a quick squeeze as I pass over the leash. "Remember, you gotta show her who's boss."

"Oh, she knows who's boss." The dog yanks, nearly toppling

Anders. "And it's not me." He plants his feet. "Fortunately, I'm still a whole lot bigger. Go help Eric. We'll be fine."

I walk along a narrow caribou trail bounded by towering spruce. Green shoots have snuck up in patches of sunlight, and the air smells of a light shower, the rain already evaporating. I see no sign of Dalton. The forest here is too thick. Endless forest, the quiet broken by the scolding of a red squirrel as I pass.

I stay on the trail until I find Dalton standing beside one hole dug down to the permafrost. Three bodies lie beside it. Two are long dead, partly mummified from having been stashed in a cave by their killer. The third looks as if she could be sleeping. Sharon was the oldest resident in Rockton until we found her dead of a heart attack this morning, prompting Dalton to declare the ground soft enough to bury our winter dead.

A shallow grave. Unmarked. As a homicide detective, I should be finding these, not creating them. But this is Rockton.

These three women came here in secrecy, fleeing threats from elsewhere. They came to the Yukon to be safe. And we failed them. One can argue it wasn't our fault. Yet we accept responsibility. To say "We did our best" is a slippery slope in Rockton.

We lay the corpses in the hole. There's no graveside service. I wasn't brought up in any religion, and our sheriff was raised right here, in this forest. I'm sure, if pressed, we could find a few lines of half-remembered poetry for the dead. But that isn't our way. We stand there, and we remember, and we regret.

Then we fill in the hole.

When we're done, Dalton rubs his face. He looks at his hands, as if thinking about what they just handled. I reach into my pocket and pass him a tiny bottle of hand sanitizer. He snorts at that and takes it, and when he's done, I lean against his side for a moment as he puts his arm around my shoulders. Then we both straighten, job done, moment passed, time to get back to work.

"Will?" Dalton calls. There's exactly one heartbeat of silence, and Dalton's face tightens as he shouts, "Will?"

"Over here," Anders calls back. "Pup found herself a rabbit hole and—" A grunt of exertion. "And she really wants bunny for dinner."

We walk over to find him only lightly tugging on the leash, his big biceps barely twitching. I sigh and yank the lead with a "Hut!" Storm gives me a look, not unlike a sullen teen, and walks over to brush against Dalton.

Anders chuckles. "If Mommy gives you shit, suck up to Dad. Nice try, pup, but—"

He stops as we all hear the whine of a small plane engine.

Dalton shields his gaze to look up.

"Does that sound way too close to Rockton?" Anders says.

"Fuck," Dalton mutters.

"That'd be yes. Come on, pup. Time for a run."

We kick it into high gear. Dalton scans the sky as he tracks the sound. It's not a supply delivery—it's exceedingly rare for anyone other than Dalton to handle those, and he's scheduled to head out later today, releasing a few residents. But from the sound, that plane is heading straight to our airstrip.

The pilot shouldn't be able to *see* our airstrip. No more than he should be able to see our town. Structural and technological camouflage means that unless the plane skims Rockton, we should remain invisible.

I look up to see a small plane on a perfect trajectory with our landing strip.

Dalton curses again.

"Has anyone ever found the airstrip before?" I ask.

"Ten years ago. Guy was lost. Rookie pilot. I fixed his nav, gave him fuel, and pointed him to Dawson City. He was too shaken up to question. I just told him it was an airstrip for miners."

Having anyone stumble over Rockton even by land is rare, but we have a pocketful of cover stories. Today, Dalton decides "military training base" will work. We're all physically fit. Anders keeps his hair stubble-short, and Dalton recently reverted to his summer look— his hair buzzed, his beard down to a few days' growth. Suitable for a backwoods military camp.

Anders pushes his short sleeves onto his shoulders, US Army tattoo more prominently displayed. Dalton snaps his shades in place. I put on my ball cap, ponytail tugged through. And we have our guns in hand.

We arrive just as the propellers creak to a stop. The pilot's door opens. A woman gets out. When I see her, I slow, the guys doing the same. We've donned our best quickie military costuming; hers looks like the real thing. Beige cargo shorts. Olive tank top. Dark aviator shades. Boots. Dark ponytail. Thigh holster. Arms that make mine look scrawny.

She doesn't even glance our way, just rolls her shoulders and acts like she has no idea three armed strangers are bearing down on her. She knows, though. She waits until we're ten feet away. Then she turns and says, "Sheriff Dalton?"

Her gaze crosses all three of us. She rejects the woman. Rejects the black guy. Settles on the white one as she says "Sheriff?" again. I could bristle at that, but she's right in this case, and the certainty on her face tells me she's been given a physical description.

Without waiting for confirmation, she steps forward and extends her hand. "I have a delivery for you, sir."

Dalton takes her hand. While he's doing a good job of hiding his confusion, I see the tightness in his face. He might rule in Rockton, but he's only thirty-one, two months younger than me, and new situations throw him off balance.

"We weren't informed of any deliveries," I say.

She hands me an envelope from her pocket. "The details are in here, ma'am. I'm just the courier."

Dalton walks over to the plane. When a hand smacks against the glass, Storm and I both jump. Anders says, "Shit!" Dalton just peers inside. A man's face appears. A man wearing a gag.

Dalton turns to the pilot. "What the hell is this?"

"Your delivery, sir."

She opens the cargo door and disappears inside, with Dalton following. Anders and I wait. A moment later, Dalton comes out, pushing the man ahead of him. He's blond, younger than us, wearing a wrinkled linen shirt, trousers, and expensive loafers. He looks like he's been pulled off Bay Street midway through his stockbroker shift. He's gagged with his hands tied in front of him; a cable binds his legs so he can't do more than shuffle.

"I was told not to remove the cuffs," the woman says as she follows them out. "I was also told to leave the gag on. I made the mistake of removing it. That lasted about sixty seconds. I have no idea what he's in for, but he's a nasty son of a bitch."

"In for?" I say.

"Yes, ma'am." She looks around. "There is a detention facility out here, isn't there? Some kind of ultra-maximum security?"

"Privileged information," Anders says. "Sorry, ma'am. You know how it is. Same in the air force, I'll wager."

The woman smiles. "It was. And it's no different in private security." She nods at his tat. "Cross-border job shopping?"

"Something like that. I appreciate you bringing the prisoner. We weren't expecting anyone new, so we're a bit surprised." Anders peeks into the cargo hold. "You wouldn't happen to have any beer in there, would you?"

She laughs.

"No, sir." She reaches in and pulls out a duffel. When she opens the zipper, it's full of coffee bags.

"Just this," she says.

"Even better," Anders says. "Thank you."

I look at the prisoner. He's just standing there, with Dalton behind him, monitoring his body language as Anders chats with the pilot.

"Thank you for bringing him," I say. "If you're flying back to Dawson City, skip the casino and check out the Downtown Hotel bar. Ask for the sour toe cocktail."

"There's an actual toe involved, isn't there?"

"It's the Yukon."

She grins. "I'll have to try that. Thank you, ma'am." She tips her hat and then motions to ask if she can pat Storm. I nod, and Storm sits as she sees the hand reach for her head.

"Well trained," she says.

"At her size, she needs to be. She's still a pup."

"Nice." She gives Storm a final pat. "I'll head on out. You folks have a good day. And remember, keep that gag on for as long as you can."

TWO

The bush plane has left, and we're standing by the hangar. I've opened the letter, and Dalton is reading it over my shoulder while Anders guards the prisoner. Storm lies at my feet, her wary gaze on the stranger.

As usual, Dalton reads faster than me, and I've barely finished the opening paragraph when he says, "Fuck, no. Fucking *hell,* no."

Anders leans over to see the letter—and the prisoner lunges.

Anders yanks him back, saying, "Yeah, it's not that easy, asshole," and the guy turns to see both Dalton and me with our weapons trained on him, Storm on her feet, growling.

"If you're waiting for us to get distracted and let you run, you'll be waiting a long time," Anders says.

"It wouldn't help anyway," I say. "You're hundreds of miles from the nearest community. Gagged. Bound. Your legs chained." I turn to the guys. "Can we let him go? Please? Lay bets on how far he gets?"

"Nah," Anders says. "Lay bets on what kills him. I vote grizzly."

"Cougar," I say.

"Exposure," Dalton says.

I look at Dalton. "Boring."

"Fine, rabbits."

"But the rabbits haven't killed anyone."

"Yet."

The prisoner watches us, his eyes narrowing, offended that we find his predicament so entertaining.

"On the ground," Dalton says.

The guy lifts his bound hands and extends both middle fingers. My foot shoots out and snags his leg. He drops to his knees.

"Boss wants you on the ground, you get on the ground," I say. "Practice your yoga. Downward dog. All fours. Ass in the air."

When he doesn't move fast enough, Dalton says, "Do you really think this is the time to challenge us? I just read that letter."

The guy assumes an awkward downward-dog pose.

Dalton holds the letter out for me to finish. I don't need to—my gaze snags on a few key words, and I skim the rest to be sure I'm not misreading. Then I look at Dalton.

"Fuck, no," I say.

"Uh-huh."

We've left our prisoner with Anders and returned to Rockton. As we enter town, I imagine bringing him back. Imagine how we might explain Rockton, how we'd pass it off. Wild West theme town would be our best bet. Seriously. That's what it would look like to an outsider—a place where rich people pay serious cash to pretend they live in a rougher, heartier time. Wooden buildings, all in perfect condition, each adorned with very modern, oversize quad-paned windows. Dirt roads swept smooth, not a scrap of litter or whiff of horse dung. People milling about in modern dress, because we wouldn't want to take the fantasy *that* far. Living without electricity, cell service, and Wi-Fi is primitive enough, thank you very much.

We drop Storm off at the general store, where Petra will dog-sit. Then we head to Val's house, which seems like old times, going to her and demanding to speak to the council. For my first four months in Rockton, I never set foot in Val's house except on business. And I swear she never set foot outside it unless she had to.

Since then, Val has come to realize the council set her up, that they

wanted their local representative isolated. She's finally begun changing that, which means that when I say there was an unscheduled plane
arrival, she doesn't hesitate to make the call. Phil answers right away,
as if he's waiting.

"A serial killer?" Dalton says. "You sent us a goddamn serial killer."

"For six months," Phil says. "Not as a resident, but as your prisoner. You are free to impose any restrictions on him. We will not
question your judgment. In fact, under the circumstances, we don't
want Mr. Brady to enjoy his stay in Rockton. That is the point."

"The point?" I say.

"Yes, hello, Detective." There's relief in Phil's voice as he realizes
I'm there. I am the reasonable one. Classic good cop, bad cop: the
hotheaded, profane sheriff and the educated, professional detective.
It's a useful fiction.

As Phil continues, his defensive edge fades. "Mr. Brady is in Rockton because he has refused other options."

"Like jail?" Dalton says. "Lethal injection? Because he's sure as hell
earned those."

"Possibly, but Mr. Brady's father believes society is better served
by saving the expense of a trial while removing him as a danger to
the public. He wants to keep Mr. Brady in what we would consider
luxurious isolation, on an island, with caretakers and guards. Mr. Brady
has refused. Which is why he is temporarily yours."

"So he'll come to see the appeal of a permanent Caribbean vacation," I say.

"Yes, and while we can argue that he deserves worse punishment,
that isn't our concern."

"Your concern is how much you make from this arrangement,"
Dalton says.

"No, how much *you* make. For your town, Sheriff."

Phil proceeds to remind us how expensive it is to run Rockton,
how the five-grand fee from residents hardly covers the expenses in-
curred during their two-to-five-year stays. How even the hundred
grand they get from white-collar criminals barely keeps the town
running.

Some white-collar criminals pay a lot more than a hundred grand, though, as do worse offenders. Rockton just never sees that money. The council keeps it. But with Oliver Brady . . .

"One million dollars," Phil says. "To be used at your discretion, Eric. And twenty percent of that is yours to keep personally as payment for the extra work."

Dalton glowers at the radio. "Fuck. You."

"Detective?" Phil says. "I trust you will speak to your . . . boss on this. Explain to him the benefits of a nest egg, should he ever decide to leave Rockton."

Explain it to my lover—that's what he means. Convince Dalton he should have money set aside in case he ever wants to leave Rockton with me. This is a threat, too. A reminder that they can kick him out.

I clear my throat. "I believe Sheriff Dalton sees that two hundred thousand as a bribe for endangering his town. While we could use extra money for Rockton, I think I can speak for both of us when I say we don't want it at the expense of endangering residents."

"People don't come here for feather pillows and fancy clothes," Dalton says. "They come for security. That cash isn't going to buy us a doctor, is it? Or radios that actually work?"

"We could certainly invest in better radios," Phil says. "Though I'm not sure that would be a wise use of the money."

The problem with the radio reception is interference. The same thing that keeps us safe and isolated also keeps us isolated from one another when we're in the forest.

Phil continues, "I'm sure if you asked the residents, there are things they'd like to use the money for."

"Yeah," Dalton says. "Booze. And more booze. Oh, and a hot tub. That was their request last year. A fucking hot tub."

"We could actually do that, Sheriff," Phil says. "It wouldn't be a Jacuzzi-style with jets, but a deep communal tub with fire-heated water and—"

Dalton cuts him off with expletives. Many expletives.

"There are always things we could use," I say. "And if we went to the residents and asked, they might take this offer. That's because they trust us to protect them from someone like Oliver Brady. But we are not equipped for this, Phil. We have one jail cell. It's intended as a temporary punishment. It's not even big enough for a bed. We can't confine Brady to it for six *days,* let alone six months. If you wanted to send him here, you should have warned us and provided supplies to construct a proper containment facility."

"And maybe asked us if we wanted this deal," Dalton says. "But you didn't because you knew what we'd say. Which doesn't excuse not giving us *any* warning. You dropped off a serial killer and a bag of fucking coffee."

"Tell us what you need to construct a proper containment facility, and we will provide it," Phil says. "Until then, your holding cell will be adequate. Remember, the goal here is to convince Mr. Brady to accept his father's offer. Show him the alternative. Let him experience discomfort."

"You want us to waterboard him, too?" Dalton asks.

"If you like. I know you're being facetious, Sheriff, but the residents of Rockton are not subject to any governmental constraints or human rights obligations. Which you have used to your advantage before."

"Yeah, by making people sleep in a cell without a bed. By sentencing them to chopping duty without a trial. Not actual torture, and if you think that's what I'm here for—"

"You're not," I say. "The council knows that. What the council may not understand, Phil, is exactly what they're asking. Even with a proper facility, we won't be equipped for this. We don't have prison guards. You saw what happened this winter."

"But Nicole is fine now. She's staying by choice. That alone is a tribute to you both and everyone else in Rockton. You can handle this."

"They shouldn't have to."

That isn't me or Dalton speaking. It's Val, who has been silently listening.

"Eric and Casey shouldn't have to deal with this threat," she continues. "The people of Rockton shouldn't have to live under it. I don't know what this man has done . . ."

She looks at me warily, as if not sure she wants me filling in that blank.

"He's a thrill killer," I say. "He murders because he enjoys it. Tortures and kills. Five victims in Georgia. Two men. Two women. And one fourteen-year-old boy."

Val closes her eyes.

"Oliver Brady is a killer motivated by nothing more than sadism," I continue. "An unrelentingly opportunistic psychopath."

"We can't do this, Phil," Val says. "Please. We cannot subject the residents of Rockton to that."

"I'm sorry," Phil says, "but you're going to have to."

THREE

For the first three decades of my life, I didn't understand the concept of home. I had one growing up, and outwardly, it was perfect. My parents were very successful physicians, and my sister and I lived a life of privilege. We just weren't a close-knit family. That may be an understatement. Before I left for Rockton, I told my sister that it might be a few years before she heard from me again, and she acted as if I'd interrupted an important meeting to say I'd be out shopping for the day.

I don't know if my early life would have doomed me to an equally cold and comfortless adult one. Maybe I would have married and had children and formed a family there. But my future didn't proceed in a direction that allowed me to find that out.

When I was nineteen, my boyfriend and I were waylaid in an alley by thugs who took exception to him selling drugs on their turf. I fought back enough to allow Blaine to grab a weapon so we could escape. Instead, he ran. I was beaten and left for dead, and he never even bothered calling 911.

I spent months in the hospital recuperating, post-coma. Then I went to confront Blaine. Shot him. Killed him. I didn't intend to, but if you take a gun to a fight, you need to be prepared for that conclusion, and at nineteen, I was not.

I spent the next twelve years waiting for the knock on the door. The one that would lead me down a path ending in a prison cell. I deserved that cell. I never pretended otherwise. Nor did I turn myself in.

Instead, I punished myself with a lifetime of self-imposed isolation, during which I threw myself into my job as a homicide detective, hoping to make amends that way. Create a home, though? A family? No. I gave up any hope of that life when I pulled the trigger.

Then I came to Rockton. I arrived in a place I did not want to be . . . and I woke up. Snapped awake after twelve years in what had been just another type of coma. I came here, and I found purpose and a home.

Yet my life in Rockton is an illusion. I know that. Our amazing little town exists inside a snow globe, and all the council has to do is give it a shake and that illusion of control shatters.

We do have options. We can refuse to accept Brady. And the council will send someone to escort Dalton to Dawson City. Ship him back "down south"—our term for anyplace that isn't here. Anyplace that Dalton doesn't belong.

You're on your own now, Sheriff. It might be hard to go anywhere when you don't legally exist. Might be hard to get a job when you've never spent a day in school. Might be hard to do anything when you don't have more than the allowance we paid. Oh, and don't expect to take your girlfriend with you— Detective Butler can't leave for another year. But go on. Enjoy your new life.

I'm sure Dalton's adoptive parents would help him. I could give him money—it's not like I've ever touched my seven-figure inheritance. The problem is that Dalton cannot imagine life anywhere else. Rockton is *his* purpose. *His* home.

We have a backup plan. If he's ever exiled, I will also leave, whether the council allows it or not. So will Anders. Others, too, loyal to Dalton and to what this town represents. We'll build a new Rockton, a true refuge.

Is that laughable idealism? Maybe, which is why we don't just go ahead and do it. For now, we work within the system. And under these particular circumstances, walking out is not an option.

These particular circumstances.

Oliver Brady.

Twenty-seven years old. American. Harvard educated. His father runs a huge tech firm. I don't recognize the family name, but I'd presume "Brady" is as fake as "Butler" is for me. Also, his father is actually his stepfather.

What does that stepfather hope to accomplish with this scheme? I don't know. Maybe saving his wife from the pain of an incarcerated son. Or maybe saving his corporation from the scandal of a murderous one.

"Murderous" doesn't begin to describe Oliver Brady. I told Val there were five victims, but in cases like this, five is just how many bodies they've found.

During that interview with Phil, I made him give me details.

The police believe Oliver Brady took his first victim at the age of twenty. I'm sure there were other victims, animals at least. There are patterns for this sort of thing, and Oliver Brady did not burst from a chrysalis at twenty, a fully formed psychopath.

Five victims over seven years. No connection between them or to himself. Just people he could grab and take to his hiding spots, where he spent weeks torturing them.

I'm not sure "torture" is the right word. That implies your tormenter wants something, and the only thing Brady wanted was whatever pleasure he derived from it. The detectives speculated that he never delivered what we might call a killing blow. He simply kept torturing his victims until they died.

This is the man the council wants us to guard for half a year. A man who likes to play games. A man who likes to inflict pain. A man who likes to cause death. A man who will not cool his heels for six months in a secure cabin. The first chance Brady gets, he'll show us how much he doesn't want to be here.

After we leave Val's, Dalton takes off to update Anders. I go in search of another person that needs to be told: the local brothel owner.

Yes, Isabel Radcliffe is more than the local brothel owner. I just like to call her that, a not-so-subtle dig at my least favorite of her positions. She owns the Roc, one of two bars in town. The Roc doubles as a brothel, and she and I are still debating that. I say it sets up dangerous and insulting expectations of the majority of women who don't moonlight in her establishment. She says it allows women to explore and control their sexuality and provides safe access to sex in a town that's three-quarters male. I'd be more inclined to consider her argument if "brothel owner" were a volunteer position. I mentioned that once. She nearly laughed herself into a hernia.

I find Isabel upstairs at the Roc, walking out of one of the three bedrooms that serve as the brothel—for safety, paid sex must take place on the premises. She's wearing a kerchief over her silver-streaked dark hair, and it may be the first time I've seen her in jeans. Her only "makeup" is a smudge of dirt on one cheek. We can't find room for makeup and hair dye on supply runs, which is a relief, actually, when that becomes the standard. With Isabel, it doesn't matter. She still looks like she should be lounging in a cocktail dress, smoking a cigarette in a holder, with hot young guys fetching her drinks.

She's carrying an armload of wood, and I look into the room she's exiting and see a bed in pieces.

"Whoa," I say. "I hope you charged extra for that."

"I would skin a client alive if he did that." She hefts the wood. "Well, no, if he could do that, I'd want a demonstration. I'm repurposing the room, so I deconstructed the bed."

"By yourself?"

"Yes, Casey. By myself. With that thing . . . what do you call it? Knocks in nails and pulls them out again? Ah, yes, a hammer. Kenny was busy, and I didn't want to disturb him when he was getting ready to leave."

"You mean he was going to charge you double for a last-minute job, and you decided to do it yourself."

"Same thing. Make yourself useful and grab some wood."

I do, and as I follow her down the stairs, I say, "You said you're repurposing the room?"

"It will now be for private parties."

"Kinky."

She glances over her shoulder. "Not that kind. However, if you're *interested* in that kind, I can certainly arrange them. I'm sure we'd find no shortage of buyers. Though I also suspect our good sheriff would snatch all the invitations up."

"Nah, he'd just glower at anyone who tried to buy one. That'd make them change their minds. Fast."

"True."

"And, just for the record, I'm *not* interested in private sex parties."

She stacks the wood onto a pile. "As I said, it's not that kind of room. We very rarely have three clients requiring rooms simultaneously, which makes it an inefficient use of space. Instead, this one will host private parties. Drink and food provided, along with a dedicated server . . . who will offer nothing *more* than drink and food. You may feel perfectly comfortable holding your poker games up here."

"With people banging in the next room for ambience?"

"I'm installing soundproofing. Now, what was a plane doing landing on our strip?"

"You saw it?"

"I see everything."

Her network of paid informants makes sure of that. Isabel not only runs the Roc, but controls the town's alcohol, which makes her—after Dalton—the most powerful person in Rockton. She's also the longest resident after him. She's passed her five years but has made an arrangement with the council to stay on. I suspect that "arrangement" involves blackmailing them with information gathered by her network.

In a small northern town, I'm not sure which is more valuable: booze or secrets. Sex comes next. Isabel owns all three, while holding no official position in local government. Kind of like the Monopoly player who buys only Park Place and Boardwalk and then sits back to enjoy the profits while others scrabble to control the remainder of the board.

I hand Isabel the letter that came with Brady. As she reads it, her lips tighten almost imperceptibly. Then she folds it and runs a perfect fingernail along the crease.

"This is one time when I really wish you were given to practical jokes," she says.

"Sorry."

She shakes the letter. "This is inappropriate."

I choke on a laugh. "That's one way of putting it."

"No, it is the best way of putting it. Springing this on Eric is inappropriate. It is also inappropriate to ask the town to accept it."

"They're paying us. A million dollars for Rockton."

"It doesn't matter."

"Did you actually say money doesn't matter?"

She fixes me with a look and heads back upstairs for more wood.

"We don't need a million dollars," she says as I follow. "People didn't come here for luxury accommodations. They came for safety. This trades one for the other. Unacceptable."

"That's what Eric said. So they promised him twenty percent."

"Imbeciles. Did he tell them where to stick it?"

"Of course. Doesn't change anything, though. We are stuck with Mr. Brady for six months."

"And you want my advice on how to deal with it?"

"If you have advice, I'll listen, but I'm here for your expertise on Brady himself. Use your shrink skills and tell me what we're dealing with."

She picks up the headboard and motions for me to grab the other end. "I was a counseling psychologist. I had zero experience with homicidal maniacs. Fortunately, you have someone in town who is an expert."

"I know. But he's going to be a pain in the ass about it."

"And I'm not?"

"You're a whole different kind of pain in the ass."

"I'll take that as a compliment. He is your expert with Oliver Brady. You need me for another sort of advice: how and what to tell the general population. That is going to be the truly tricky part."

FOUR

I pace behind the butcher shop.

"The answer is no." Mathias's voice floats out the back door. "Whatever you are considering asking, the answer is no."

"Good. Thank you," I say. Or *Bien. Merci.* Mathias's English is perfect, but he prefers French, and I use it to humor him. Or placate him. Or charm him. Depends on the day, really.

"Wait," he calls after me. "That was too easy."

"You're imagining things," I call back as I keep walking.

A moment later, he's shed his butcher's apron and caught up. "This is a trick, isn't it? You wish my help. You know I will grumble. So you pace about, pretending you have not yet decided to ask me, and then you leave quickly when I refuse. My interest piqued, I will follow you of my own accord."

"You got me. So, now, knowing you've been tricked, you should go back to your shop and not give me the satisfaction of victory."

"I could learn to hate you, Casey."

"Sure, you could. You could even find someone else to speak French to you. We're mostly Canadians here, so almost everyone knows rudimentary French. It's a little rusty, but I'm sure they—"

"Death by a thousand cuts would be less painful. As will whatever fresh torture you've dreamed up for me. I presume we have a rash of phantom chest pains in the wake of Sharon's demise, and you want me to assure them they are not about to die. William would be better suited to the task. He will tell the truth."

Mathias may be the town butcher, but he was a psychiatrist, which means he has a medical degree. He's just never practiced—the medical part, at least.

"No phantom chest pains." I glance around. Even if we are speaking rapid-fire French, I want to be sure no one is nearby. "We had a delivery today."

"I heard the plane."

"They dropped off a new resident."

"And he is ill?"

"In a manner of speaking."

I pass over the letter that accompanied Brady. As Mathias skims it, his eyes begin to glitter. By the time he finishes, he's practically beaming.

"I think I love you," he says.

"Fickle man."

"We all are. So, what does Casey Butler wish me to do? Assessment? Or assassination?"

"I haven't decided yet."

After talking to Mathias, I walk to the hangar. Inside, Kenny and Paul stand on either side of Brady, watching him so intensely I suspect they literally haven't taken their eyes off him.

"Hey," I say to Kenny. "You didn't need to be here. Your ride out of Rockton might be delayed, but you are officially retired from duty."

"Hell, no," he says. "As long as I'm here, I'm working. Especially something like this."

"We appreciate that, but for now, you can both head back to town. I've got this."

Paul looks over my shoulder. "Where's the boss?"

"Busy."

Paul opens his mouth to question, but Kenny shoulders him out, saying, "See you back in town."

They leave, with Paul casting regular glances my way. I wait until their boots tromp down the well-used path. Then I walk to Brady. His hands are still bound, feet chained.

I lower myself in front of him. He's watching me carefully. Analyzing the situation and struggling to hide his confusion.

I don't cut the most intimidating figure. I'm barely five foot two. A hundred and ten pounds. I just turned thirty-two, but the last time I was in the US, I got carded in a bar. My mother was Filipino and Chinese, and physically I take after her more than my Scottish father. In other words, absolutely nothing about me screams threat.

When I reach out, Brady draws back. Then he steels himself, shame flooding his eyes, as if he's been caught flinching from a Pomeranian.

I tug down his gag.

"I didn't do it," he says.

I shove the gag back up, and his shame turns to outrage. He doesn't move, though. Not one muscle. Still considering. Still analyzing. Still confused.

"Never been in prison, have you, Oliver?" I say.

He doesn't respond.

"If you'd like, you can blink once for yes, twice for no, but nodding and shaking will be easier. In this case, it's a rhetorical question. Guys like you don't go to jail. That's why you're here instead. But having probably never even spent the night in a drunk tank, you need some advice. Telling the guard you didn't do it is pointless. He doesn't care, and even if he did, he can't help you. No one here is your judge or jury. We're all just guards. Now, let's try this again."

Gag down.

"My goddamn stepfather—"

Gag up.

"Your escort was right," I say. "Best to leave that on."

His eyes blaze hate. Hate and powerlessness from a guy who has never known a moment of either in his life.

"Do you have any idea where you are?" I ask.

He doesn't respond.

"Nowhere," I say. "No place that exists. No place that falls under any law or jurisdiction. If I shoot you, the sheriff's just going to say,

Oh, hell, another body to bury. We buried three this morning. Our winter dead. And sure, it's easy enough to reopen the mass grave and toss your ass in, but I wouldn't do that. None of those people deserves to share their final resting spot with thrill-killing trash."

His mouth works behind the gag. He so desperately wants to tell me he didn't do it. I don't look forward to six months of hearing how this is all a big mistake. Could be worse, I suppose. Could be six months of him regaling us with the details of his crimes.

"My job here is to protect people," I say. "And you threaten my ability to do that. Yet killing you seems problematic. I'll have to give it more thought. I haven't worked out all the factors."

"In other words, don't give us an excuse," Dalton says as he strolls in.

"I wasn't going to say that."

"It's the truth."

"Far too Clint Eastwood for me."

"Which is why I'm the one who said it." He stops in front of Brady. "Did you take off the gag?"

"Twice. I got 'I didn't do it' and cursing about his stepfather." I turn to Brady. "Get up. We're taking you to town."

A press conference in Rockton is a strange thing. First, we don't have a press, which may make the entire endeavor seem rather pointless. Instead, it only makes it all the more critical. Without official media, the only way to disseminate information is word of mouth, and as anyone who's ever played telephone can imagine, that's a dangerous game when you're dealing with a matter of public safety.

In a Rockton press conference, I am the physical manifestation of the printed page. I climb onto the front porch of the police station, give the news, and take questions. Dalton stands off to the side, arms crossed, his expression warning that those questions better not be stupid.

Brady is safely ensconced in the station cell. We brought him in through the back door. So no one has seen him yet as I stand on that porch and tell them that the council has asked us to take custody of a dangerous criminal. I get that much out, and then I wait, knowing exactly what will come.

"How dangerous?" someone asks.

The first time I spoke to a community group, my sergeant told me not to give details. They don't need to know, he said brusquely, and I bristled at the implication that a frightened community didn't deserve to know the exact nature of the predator in their midst. Which wasn't what he meant at all. It wasn't patronizing; it was protective.

I must know what Brady has done to fully understand what I am dealing with. That's the nightmare I must welcome into my head so that I can do my job. No one else needs that.

Even Dalton, who'd insisted on listening earlier, now shifts behind me, porch boards creaking, that subtle movement screaming his discomfort at the memory. Whatever Dalton has seen, whatever tough-guy face he puts on, I know his overwhelming thought on Brady's crimes.

I don't understand.

I cannot fathom how one person could do that to another.

I can't either, but I must stretch my imagination there as much as possible.

For the town, I provide the roundabout blather of the bureaucrat, words that seem like an on-point answer.

He's dangerous.

Murderously dangerous.

While I understand that you may wish to know more, you must also understand that he comes to Rockton as a prisoner, to await a decision on his fate, which means we are not at liberty to discuss his exact crimes, for reasons of security.

Words, words, more words, spun out until I see nods of understanding. Or, at least, of acceptance.

I continue talking, imparting data now. He will be here six months. He will be confined for the duration. He is being held in the station until we can construct a special building to house him.

"How long will that take?" someone asks.

"We're assessing the feasibility of constructing a new one versus retrofitting an existing one," I say. "We're aware that the holding cell is far from ideal. That's why we want to move quickly on an alternative."

"Can't we just free up a house? Guard the exits?"

"No," says a voice from the crowd. Everyone follows it to Nicole. When they see who has spoken, a murmur runs through the assembled. They remember what happened to her.

"We understand that whatever this man has done, he is due his basic human rights," I say.

I feel that creak of the boards, Dalton recalling what Brady did and not convinced he concurs. I would agree. As far as I'm concerned, Brady can *get* comfortable in that cell. But that isn't an option, because the people of Rockton would not allow it without hearing the extent of his crimes.

I already see the crowd pulse in discomfort. I could tell them what he has done. *Do not let yourselves be concerned on his behalf.*

Just tell them.

Take the outrage and the anger and the impotence that Dalton feels. Multiply it by two hundred. An entire town, furious that the council has done this, furious that we have "allowed" it.

If we tell them his crimes, any civil rights we've accorded Oliver Brady will be held against us. Mob mentality will rise. Against him. Against us.

I love my town, but I do not trust them in this. So I remain silent.

FIVE

I'm in the station. It's a small building, with one main room and a door leading to the cell area. I've got that door open.

Brady is pretending to sleep. When I turn my back, moving about the station, I know he peers out to assess. I'm here alone, and again, he doesn't know what to make of that. But he is pleased. He gives that away in the curve of his lips. He's growing confident that this will be easier than he dared hope, that the alpha dog foolishly leaves the weakest in the pack alone with him time and again.

Kenny comes in while I'm settling behind the desk.

"No, Eric is not here," I say as he looks about.

He glances at Brady, slouched on the floor, knees up, eyes closed. Kenny lowers his voice and moves closer to me. "I know you can look after yourself, Casey, but maybe . . . You know."

I arch my brows.

"Look, I don't *want* to know what this guy did. If you say he's violent, that's enough for me. But whatever it is, I'm sure it involves women. Maybe leaving you here isn't . . ."

"Because I'm a woman?"

"No, just . . ." He makes this awkward motion, waving at me, top to bottom.

He's trying to come up with a respectful way to say that I'm attractive. When I arrived, Kenny was one of those guys who wouldn't see a problem with telling a coworker that a pair of jeans really showed off her "assets." He wasn't a jerk—he honestly didn't realize that was inappropriate. But as soon as someone points it out, he trips over himself to correct the behavior. Sometimes to rather comic effect.

"He's not that kind of killer," I say.

Kenny frowns, like he can't imagine any other kind. I could also tell him that *those* predators don't always target women they find attractive. At some point, though, that starts to sound like lecturing. So I just say, "He's an equal-opportunity killer, so watch yourself."

"Sure, sure. But then, maybe no one should be alone with him."

"Mmm, I'm not worried." Through the open doorway, I see Brady's lips twitch. "I am sorry it screwed up your departure, though. I know you were looking forward to getting out today."

Kenny shrugs and sits on the edge of the desk, positioning himself between me and Brady. "It's not like I have plans. I'm going to bum around, visit a few places before I decide where to settle. Which reminds me. . . . I know Eric got Storm because you like Newfoundland dogs. How about Newfoundland itself? You been there?"

I shake my head.

"You know much about it?" he asks.

"I had a detective partner who came from there. He said he spent his life waiting to leave . . . and now can't wait to retire and move back. City life wasn't what he expected, and he missed the open spaces, small towns, slower pace, friendlier people."

"That's what I'm looking for, I think. A place like here but . . ."

"With Wi-Fi? Microwave ovens? Real indoor plumbing?"

He chuckles. "All the twenty-first-century amenities, which are the only things I missed from down south. I might even build my own house. Never imagined that before I came here. I barely knew how to hold a hammer."

"Join the team."

"Yeah, but at least you had the muscles to lift one. I want to keep doing carpentry. Become that local guy people call if they need a new bed or cupboards."

He settles on the desk, gaze going distant. "Maybe I'll meet someone, have a kid or two. Never did that. I always figured I would—it just seemed natural, you know. Then it didn't happen. I'll try harder this time. Put myself out there. Find someone who might not mind settling down with a guy like me."

Jen walks into the station, saying, "You want my advice, Kenny? Skip Tinder and go straight to mail-order brides."

"Personal experience, huh?" he says. "Or is that the real reason you stay in Rockton? There are so many guys, even you can get sex. You can get them to pay for it, too. Not much but . . ."

She scowls at him.

I shake my head. "You walked into that, Jen."

She walks around the desk, where she can put her back to Kenny, and then shoots her thumb toward the cell. "I want to talk about him."

"Casey doesn't need—" Kenny begins.

"It's fine," I say. "We should refill the wood, though. We're going to need to run the fireplace all night."

Kenny hesitates, as if considering whether he can pretend not to get the hint. Then he says he'll grab some logs and be back soon.

Once he's gone, Jen looks around. "Where's the fur beast?"

"With Eric."

"So you're here doing paperwork alone while lover boy walks the pooch . . . and we have an allegedly dangerous killer in town?"

"When is the last time you saw us walking the dog during work hours?" I say.

Her jaw sets, like that of a petulant child countered with the indignity of a reasonable response.

"Eric is working," I say. "Storm is with him because she's a work dog."

"Then shouldn't she be here, guarding you?"

"Nah, if this guy escapes, I'll throw you into the line of fire."

Her snort awards me a point for the comeback. I'm trying to work with Jen, no matter how many people tell me it's a waste of time. I must be that idiot who keeps trying to pet the stray cat, knowing I'm just going to end up with bloody scratches. One could see this as a sign of deep compassion and the belief in inherent human goodness. It's not. As Dalton says, I'm just stubborn. Jen is an obstacle I will overcome. Which is not to say I'm winning the battle. We have reached an uneasy truce, though. I champion her continued role in the town militia, and she doesn't address me as "Hey, bitch." At least not in public.

Jen walks to the cell. She's spent her share of time in there, more than anyone else in Rockton. I first saw her at the Roc, Isabel having come by the station for help breaking up a bar brawl. There'd been no brawl. Just Jen, looking like a middle-aged schoolteacher enjoying a glass of wine with her significant other. Then Isabel tried to kick her out—for freelancing on brothel property—and that's when the brawl began.

I later learned that Jen really had been a schoolteacher. She still looks it to me—late thirties, average appearance, nicely groomed. When she walks to that cell, Brady cracks open one eye. He can't help it. He heard her talk—insulting Kenny, snarking at me—and he's looked, expecting to see a rough and bitter woman. Instead, she looks like the schoolteacher she'd once been, and his eye opens a little wider, just to be sure.

"How many?" she says.

I don't need to ask what she means.

"Five," I say.

"And you buy that?"

"I'm sure there's more. There always are."

"That's not—"

"You mean do I think he really did it. I don't give a shit. That's not my job, and after what we've been through, I'm not taking the chance."

"So the council—which I know you don't trust—tells you this preppy-assed brat has murdered five people, and you're just going to believe them?"

Brady's eyelids flicker, and I'm tempted to grab her by the arm and haul her onto the back porch. But it's too late, so I say, "And I'll repeat—I don't give a shit. If he was a citizen of this town, I'd care. He's not. And if I did decide he was innocent, you'd be first in line howling that I was putting your life in danger."

She looks at Brady again. "This just doesn't seem right."

"Well, considering I'd never expect you to agree with any choice I made, I'm not too worried."

Except I am. Jen is my Greek chorus—the voice that will never let me enjoy a moment of hubris. Every choice I make, she questions. So this should not surprise me. Should not concern me. But I expected her to walk in here and tell us we're *under*reacting, being too lax. When she instead says the opposite, I begin to worry.

SIX

I'm lying on our living room floor, fire blazing over my head. Dalton sleeps beside me. Storm whines, and I snap out of my thoughts and give a soft whistle that brings her bounding out of the kitchen. When she was a puppy, we'd barricade her in there whenever Dalton and I needed private time. Now we only need to kiss, and she'll give a jowl-quivering sigh and lumber off to the kitchen and wait for that whistle.

When she bounds in, I signal for her to take the exuberance down a few notches. She creeps over and sniffs Dalton's head, making sure he's asleep. I give her a pat, and she settles in on my other side, pushing as far onto the bearskin rug as she can manage.

As I rub behind her ears, I pick up on her anxiety. She knows something is bothering us, our stress vibrating through the air even now, as Dalton sleeps.

I don't think he has taken an easy breath since Brady arrived. So I may have intentionally worn him out tonight. But I'm wide awake, tangled in my thoughts.

I give Storm one last pat, head into the kitchen, and pull tequila from the cupboard. One shot downed. Then a second. I'm standing there, clutching the counter edge, when I hear a gasp from the living room.

"Casey?"

I jog in, and Dalton's scrambling up, eyes open but unseeing.

"I'm right here," I say, but he still doesn't seem to notice. He's on his feet now, looking from side to side.

"Casey?" Louder now.

I hurry beside him and put my hand on his arm. "I'm right here."

He turns, exhales hard. His arms go around me, and he's only half awake, as I lower us back to the floor. His head hits the rug, and he pulls me in, clutched like a security blanket, his heart rate slowing as he drops back into sleep.

An hour passes.

I'm still entwined with him, my head on his chest as I listen to the beat of his heart. That usually lulls me back to sleep after my nightmares. Tonight it doesn't. It can't.

I would get up and read a book, but if I leave, he'll wake, and he needs his sleep. So I lie there, listening to the dog's snores. Then Dalton's breathing hitches. His heart thumps, and he bolts up, gasping again.

"I've made a mistake," he says.

I don't answer. I just wait.

He says it again. Not "I fucked up," but "I made a mistake." His voice is soft, a little boyish, a little breathless. He's awake but with one toe in that twilight place.

I adjust so I'm sitting with him as he squeezes his eyes shut.

"With Brady," he says. "We need to do something else."

"Like what?"

He runs his hands through his hair. "I don't know. That's the problem."

Which is exactly what I've been lying here thinking. He says, "This isn't the way to handle it, but I don't know what is," and that articulates my thoughts as perfectly as if he's pried them from my brain.

"Fuck," he says, and I have to smile, hearing him come back to himself. He looks at me. "We're screwed, aren't we?"

"Pretty much."

Silence. When he speaks again, his voice is low. "I keep wanting to ask what we could do differently, but if you had an idea, you'd give it."

"I would."

Dalton's eyes shut. A sliver of moonlight bisects his face, half light, half dark. It's a lie. There's no darkness there.

Light doesn't mean carefree or easy or saintly, though. It's not even light so much as . . .

If the absence of light is dark, what is the absence of dark? To say "light" isn't quite correct. Even "good" doesn't work.

"If I knew for certain he was guilty . . ." He lets the rest trail off.

If I knew for certain he was guilty, I could kill him. To protect the town. To protect you. To eliminate any chance that he hurts someone here.

That's what he means, and maybe it should prove that he *does* have darkness. But this is sacrifice. It's a man saying he would take another life and suffer the guilt of that rather than let anyone else be hurt.

Dalton's lack of darkness, though, means he can never take that step as long as there's a chance that Brady is innocent.

We both know innocence is a possibility, but I wasn't lying when I told Jen it didn't matter. We cannot prove Brady's innocence or guilt. We cannot even investigate his crimes. He didn't kill here. We can't go there. Which reduces our options for dealing with Oliver Brady to two.

Keep him.

Kill him.

We can devise the most secure prison, staffed with our most reliable and loyal guards, while knowing we cannot truly guarantee safety.

Or I can conclude that we can't care whether he's innocent or guilty, but I must treat him like a potential patient zero and—without equipment to test for the virus—decide he must die.

"No," Dalton says, and I haven't spoken a word, but his eyes bore into mine with a look I know well.

Drilling into my thoughts. In the beginning, that look meant he was trying to figure me out. Now he doesn't need to. He knows.

"If you make that choice, Casey, you need to tell me first."

Which means I can't make it. I'd never allow Dalton to be complicit in Brady's death. Nor can I do it behind his back, for the purely selfish reason that it would be a betrayal our relationship would not survive. I'm not sure I could survive it either. I've had my second chance at a good life. I won't get a third.

He continues, "If it comes to that, it has to be both of us deciding." He settles back onto the rug. "I think we can handle him. Build a cabin like the icehouse. Thick walls. No windows. One exit. Only you, me, or Will carries the key. That door never opens without one of us there. Brady gets a daily walk. We'll do it when no one else is in the forest. At least one of us will accompany him, along with two militia. That's the only time he comes out. We'll gag him if we have to, so he doesn't talk to anyone, doesn't pull his innocence shit." He looks at me. "Does that work?"

It's the course of action we've already come up with. He's just repeating it, like worry beads, running plans through his mind, trying to refine it and seeing no way to do so.

"It works," I say.

And I pray I'm right.

Day three of hosting Oliver Brady in our holding cell. We're constructing his lodgings as fast as we can. The new building will serve as a food storage locker once Brady is gone. We have to think of that—construction like this cannot go to waste. That also keeps us looking toward the time when he *will* be gone.

I remember reading old stories of barn-raising parties, a building erected in a day. It's a lovely thought, but this is being built to hold something more dangerous than hay. We must have our best people on it. Which would be so much more heartening if we had actual architects or even former construction workers. We have Kenny . . . who builds beautiful furniture.

Dalton is the project foreman. Since he was old enough to swing a hammer, he's built homes meant to withstand Yukon winters. Solid. Sturdy. Airtight. He got up at four this morning to start work, after returning home at midnight.

It's ten in the morning now, and I'm waiting for Mathias so we can get Brady's side of the story. Part of me would rather not; I fear it will ignite doubt I cannot afford. But that gag can't stay on forever, and we must know what others will hear once it's off.

Brady is pretending to sleep. That's what he does for most of the day. He must figure the law of averages says that at some point we'll forget he's awake and say something useful.

When the door opens, I say, "I hope you brought plenty of anesthetic," in French. I'm kidding, while testing whether Brady knows French. He's American, but he's also a private-school kid.

Brady doesn't react. Nor do I get a rejoinder from Mathias . . . because the man walking through the door is Brian, who runs the bakery. He has a Tupperware box in hand and slows, saying, "Did you just ask if I brought a nest egg?"

I snort a laugh at that and shake my head.

"Yes, I failed French," Brian says as he comes in. "You must be expecting Mathias."

"I am."

He lifts the box. "I brought cookies, since I know you're stuck here with . . ." His gaze slides to Brady, and I tense.

The cookies are an excuse. With almost anyone else, I would have foreseen that, but Brian has been to our house for poker. We've been to his for dinner. I talk to him almost every morning as I pick up my snack. He's my best source of town gossip, but it's the harmless variety, local news rather than rumor and innuendo. He has never once asked me for information on a case.

But now he's here to see Brady. To assess the situation. And when his gaze falls on the prisoner, his lips tighten in disapproval.

"A gag?" he says. "Is that really necessary?"

I want to snap that if it wasn't, I wouldn't do it.

"Yes," I say. "For now, it is. We've replaced the original with something softer, and Will's watching for chafing. Given what this man is accused of, I'm okay with him suffering a bit of temporary discomfort. The gag will come off soon."

Brian eyes Brady. "What does he try to say when it comes off?"

"What would you say?" asks Mathias as he walks in. "If you were in this man's position, what would you say?"

"I-I don't know."

Mathias throws open his arms. "Look at where he is. Who he is with. He came to stay among strangers, accompanied only by a piece of paper accusing him of crimes. What is he going to say? That it is all a terrible mistake. That he did nothing."

"Then why not just let him say that?"

"Because it grows tiresome. For twenty years, I studied men like this. It is banally predicable. It begins with 'I am innocent' and escalates to 'You are a nasty human being for not believing me' and continues to 'Let me go, or I will slaughter you and everyone you have ever loved.' Tiresome. It is bad enough Casey has to sit here all day babysitting him. Does she need to endure that as well?"

"No, but . . ." Brian sneaks another look at Brady.

"The gag will come off," Mathias says, "once he realizes he wastes his breath with protestations of innocence and threats of terrible vengeance. Now go." Mathias waggles his fingers.

Once Brian leaves, Mathias makes a very indecent proposition to me *en français*. Then he watches for a reaction from Brady. There is none, confirming that if he does speak the language, it's probably limited to being able to order champagne in a Monte Carlo casino.

"Are you ready to interview him?" Mathias asks, still in French.

I make a noise in my throat. I'm unsettled by Brian's visit, seeing a friend and supporter question our decisions.

People want their monsters to look monstrous. At the very least, they want them shifty-eyed, thin-lipped, and menacing—a walking mug shot. But reality is that a killer can be a petite Asian-Canadian woman, well educated and well spoken. Or a killer can be a handsome all-American boy, a little soft around the edges, a young man you expect to see on the debate team and rowing team, but nothing overly rough.

When you look at Oliver Brady, you see wealth and privilege, but you don't really begrudge him that, because he seems innocuous enough, the type who'll attend a fund-raiser for the Young Republicans on Friday with friends and a Greenpeace meeting on Saturday with a girl.

Mathias opens the cell door. I'm standing guard, my gun ready.

"Step out," I say to Brady.

I don't tell him to put his hands where I can see them. It's not as if he's hiding a shiv in his pocket. He puts them up anyway and takes exactly one step beyond the cell door. Then he stops. Waits.

I motion to the door leading from the cell to the main room. "In there, please."

There's the slightest narrowing of his eyes as he assesses my *please*.

He walks into the next room and sits on the chair I've set out. He puts his hands behind his back. I ignore that. I'm not binding him.

When I circle around, Brady's head swivels to follow. I've holstered my weapon, but his gaze dips to it, just for a split second, as if he can't help himself.

"Detective Butler is going to remove your gag," Mathias says. "If you wish to scream for help, please don't restrain yourself on my account. It will give her the excuse to replace the gag, and me the excuse to get on with my day."

Brady grunts. I read derision in that. He looks at Mathias, hears his diction, and smells weakness. Mathias is twice his age. A slender build. Graying hair and beard. An air of the bored aristocrat, the French accent on precisely articulated English adding to that sense of the bourgeois. Brady comes from wealth, but it's new-world money, won by frontier ingenuity. In Mathias, he sees old-world rot and weakness. An old man, too, compared to him.

Brady's grunt dismisses Mathias, and the older man's eyes glint.

"Remove the gag, please, Detective. Let us begin."

SEVEN

I take off Brady's gag. He reaches up and rubs at his mouth, wincing as his fingertips massage a tender spot.

Mathias turns away as he pulls over a seat. It's a deliberate move. He could have placed the chair sooner, but he puts his back to Brady.

Brady's gaze flicks to me. He expects to see my hand resting on my gun. When it isn't, he looks back at Mathias, now tugging the chair over, his attention elsewhere. He sees that, and he frowns, as if to say, *I don't understand.*

Good.

Mathias sits. I back up to perch on the edge of my desk. Brady looks from me to the older man. As he does, his sweep covers the back and front doors.

His nostrils flare, as if he quite literally smells a trap, as if Dalton and Anders are poised outside those doors, praying he makes a run for it.

"Detective Butler says you have been very eager to tell your story, Oliver," Mathias says. "Now is your chance."

Silence. When it reaches ten seconds, I open my mouth, but a subtle look from Mathias stops me. Five more seconds pass. Then:

"Is there any point?" Brady says. "You don't want to hear it. You've all made that perfectly clear by the fact you've kept me gagged for seventy-two hours. I try to say a word when it's removed at meal-time and *she*"—a glower my way—"threatens me with starvation."

"*She* is Casey Butler. *She* is a detective who has been placed in a very frustrating position, forced to babysit you when she has other work to be done."

"And I'm supposed to, what, apologize for the inconvenience of my captivity?"

"No, you are supposed to recognize that Detective Butler has done nothing to deserve the inconvenience of your care. And recognize that she attempted to relieve the indignity and discomfort of that gag, and you called her . . ." Mathias purses his lips. "I will not repeat it. It is rude. Uncalled-for in any circumstances, but particularly these."

"I was pissed off. I vented." He glances my way. "I apologize." His gaze swings back to Mathias. "But you aren't interested in what I have to say. Neither of you is. You're treating me like a child throwing a tantrum. Let me get it out of my system, and maybe I'll shut up. Gregory Wallace has convinced you all that I'm guilty, and the only thing that surprises me about that is how easy it was."

Brady pauses. "No, I shouldn't be surprised. I've seen it my whole life. Got a problem? Drown it in money, and you'll drown all doubts. Don't look a gift horse in the mouth and so on. How much is Greg paying you?"

"Hot tubs," I say. "He's paying us in hot tubs and big-screen TVs. Oh, and diamond necklaces, to wear to the next town picnic."

Brady's eyes narrow.

I wave at the police station. "Look around. We don't have electric lights or gas furnaces, and that's not for lack of money. We have what we need. You're here because of what you did. Not because we're being paid to take you."

"No, I'm here because of what I know."

"Which is?"

"Does it matter?"

"Your plan is ill-advised," Mathias murmurs.

Brady turns to him. "And what is my plan? You obviously know, so how about letting me in on it. Maybe it'll be something I can use, which is a damn sight better than *my* plan—the naive one where I thought you people might be smart enough to question the lame-ass story my stepfather gave you."

"It does not seem 'lame-ass' to me," Mathias says. "Uninspired and unoriginal, and yes, that is the colloquial definition of lame, but I believe the word you meant was 'dumb-ass,' implying anyone who believes the story is not very bright, rather than that the crimes themselves suggest a lack of intelligence on the part of the criminal."

"What?"

"Is my accent impeding your comprehension? Or are you simply proving my point?"

"I'm not going to sit here and be insulted—"

"Yes, you will. We are not forcing you to speak. I spent my career interviewing psychopaths, sociopaths, and garden-variety sadists, and I always told them that they were free to cut the session short at any time. Do you know how many did?" Mathias holds up his thumb and forefinger in a zero. "But please, feel free to show some originality in this, if you could not in your crimes."

Brady seethes, and it is like watching a weasel in a cage, being poked with a cattle prod. All it has to do is retreat to the other side. Instead, it snarls and twists and snaps at the prod. That may feel like grit and courage to the weasel, but to an outsider, it looks like submission. Mathias holds the power; Brady is trapped.

"Ignore him," I say to Brady, and he starts at the sound of my voice, as if he's forgotten there's someone else in the room.

"He's baiting you," I say. "He gets little amusement up here, and you're his entertainment for the day."

Brady's lips tighten. He wants to smirk and lean back in his chair and say he isn't falling for the good cop, bad cop game. But my expression doesn't look like the good cop's.

Seconds tick by. Then he makes up his mind and twists to face me.

"I can't fight a bold-faced lie," he says. "I don't even know where to start."

"Try."

"How? We're not in San Jose right now. We're thousands of miles from it. So how exactly do I prove I wasn't the shooter?"

Mathias clears his throat, and I know my poker face has failed. Mathias's throat-clearing pulls Brady's attention away, and I recover.

"Try," I say. "Tell me what proof they had against you. What they were using to charge you."

Brady laughs. There's a jagged bitterness to it. The weasel has realized that attacking the prod does no good, but it can't help itself. It has no other recourse. Keep doing the same thing and hope for a different result, knowing how futile that is.

"Greg said I was being charged? Of course he did. It's not like you can call up the district attorney and ask. Not like you'd expect an honest answer if you did. *We can neither confirm nor deny*—that'd be the sound bite, and you'd take it to mean yes, they have a warrant out for my arrest, when the truth is"—he meets my gaze—"it's like me telling this old man that you think he's hot. You know it's bullshit. I know it's bullshit. But he'd love to believe it, and there's nothing you can say to defend yourself."

"Actually, no," Mathias says. "I find the thought rather alarming. I would have to disabuse Casey of it immediately, and inform her that, as lovely as she is, I really do prefer women who were born before I graduated university."

"Whatever," Brady says. "My point is that I wasn't even on the investigators' radar. Why would I be? What's my motive? Did Greg even bother to mention that? 'Cause I'd love to hear it."

"Haven't you asked *him*?" Mathias says. "Or are you testing us? Seeing if your stepfather's story changes, depending on the handler? That would be odd, given that we could simply compare notes, as they say."

"Do you think any of my 'handlers' were talking to me?" He shakes his head. "Everybody's looking for the shooter, so it was an easy story to tell. Greg just had to move fast, before they caught the real guy. Get me up into Alaska, some off-the-grid place where no one can check the news."

"But someone *did* tell you what your stepfather said."

"No, I overheard two guards talking about it. Couple of jarheads, must have thought gagging me also took away my ability to hear. When they fed me, I tried to reason with them. They gave me this." He pushes aside his hair to show a scabbed gash. "The gag stayed on for the next eight hours. No food. No water. That's what a guy who shot six kids deserves. Which is why Gregory used that story. The whole damn country wants that bastard to burn in hell."

"What's your stepfather's motive, then?" I ask. "You said you know something."

He eyes me. Sizes me up. Finds me lacking and eases back into his chair as he says, "That's my leverage, and I'm not giving it up until it'll get me somewhere. For now, let's go with the obvious motive. The one that's partly true. Money."

"From what I understand, it's his company. Your mother married into it."

"No, it was my father's company. My biological father. Gregory Wallace was his employee. After my dad died, Greg took his wife and his company. But my dad made sure no one would get their hands on my inheritance. On my twenty-eighth birthday, I get a trust fund of fifteen million. Do you know how old I am now?"

"Twenty-seven."

"Yep. Last year, I heard something that made me suspect there wasn't fifteen mil in that fund anymore. I tried investigating. Greg blocked me. Gave me some song and dance about the stock markets and poor investments my father made. He promised there will be plenty of money but . . ."

"Not fifteen million."

"Far from it, I bet. That's part of the reason I'm here. I'm not a stand-up guy. I'm a bit of an asshole. But I'm not a sociopath. That would be the guy who sent me here."

EIGHT

When I walk into the Roc with Mathias, Isabel is already pouring a shot of her top-shelf tequila. She holds it out for me.

"It isn't noon yet," I say.

"It is somewhere."

"And I'm on duty."

"True." She downs the shot herself. "I have a feeling I'm going to need that."

She pulls over a bottle of single malt and pours a shot for Mathias. He arches his brows. She points to the side.

"Glasses over there. Ice, too, if you insist on ruining good Scotch."

"I do not ruin it. I chill it. Two shakes around the glass and out it goes."

"Waste of good ice, then, which isn't cheap this time of year."

"Put it on my tab, and come winter I shall replace the cube with an entire block."

Isabel grants him a chuckle for that. She even gets him a glass, though she draws the line at adding the ice. Mathias still smiles, pleased with his victory, and then admires her rear view as she crosses the bar to start the coffeemaker.

"Eyes off my ass, Mathias," Isabel says. "I'll put that on your tab, too, and it's more than you can afford."

"Oh, nothing is more than I can afford, *chérie*. And I do not need to pay. You would be offended if I were not looking. I am simply bowing to your iron will."

She rolls her eyes.

The door opens. Dalton walks in and says, "Coffee ready?," as if this is his biggest concern, but his gaze slides my way, asking how it went with Mathias and Brady. I make a face. He grimaces and eyes the beer display but doesn't ask for one. The door opens again, and Val joins us.

"Gang's all here," Isabel says. "Before we begin, would you like a drink, Val?"

"Yes. Tea, please. Strong."

Isabel's lips twitch. From anyone else, that might have been a joke. Not Val. Strong tea *is* her equivalent of my tequila shot.

First, I tell them Brady's story about the shooter in San Jose.

"Bullshit," Dalton says. "Bullshit to make you do exactly what you're doing."

"Wonder if I've been misled."

"Right. He pretends he's been accused of an entirely different crime, and you start wondering if there are multiple stories going around, which makes it seem like we're being played."

That's the answer I like. I'm not sure it's the right one, though. I walk them through the rest of the interview.

When I finish, Isabel looks at Mathias. "Well, that was a mistake."

His brows shoot up.

"You just antagonized a man who viciously murders people for no provocation."

"Then perhaps, having given him provocation, I have removed myself from danger."

"You just can't help yourself, can you, Mathias? You are incapable of learning the lesson life has tried to teach you: don't piss off the psychos."

"I am stubborn."

"Stubbornly suicidal."

From that exchange, I presume Isabel knows why Mathias is here. One of those "psychos" accused Mathias of brainwashing him into emasculating himself and then managed to escape and come after Mathias, leaving dead bodies in his wake. Which should sound as if the innocent psychiatrist was targeted by a delusional psychopath spouting obvious nonsense. Yeah, I'm pretty sure that isn't actually how it worked. Not with Mathias.

Dalton cuts in. "I'll side with Mathias on this. Rattling Brady's cage might not be the worst thing. Get him worked up enough to snap, prove he's not Mr. Innocent. We just need to make sure his cage is locked tight. And if he does lash out?" Dalton shrugs. "He's got a target now."

"Thank you, Sheriff," Mathias says. "While I would think my approach is somewhat more nuanced than 'rattling his cage'—"

Dalton snorts and rolls his eyes at me, but Mathias continues, "—yes, that is part of my approach."

"Never learned the idiom about honey and vinegar, did you?" Isabel says.

"It doesn't work for me. Now, if *you* were to offer Mr. Brady honey, I suspect that would be an entirely different thing. He doesn't want mine."

"Should we do that?" Val says. "Should we allow Isabel to handle this instead? Or perhaps not *instead*, but in conjunction *with* Dr. Atelier. The honey and the vinegar."

"I can consult if you truly see the need," Isabel says. "But if you're hoping for me to charm and disarm, I suspect I'm twenty years too old for that. Brady seems like a classic narcissist, which implies he'll have no use for older women—they would not satisfy his self-image. He would only expect to charm *me*. To disarm *me*."

"Then he would prove himself a very poor judge of character," Mathias says. "Which I believe he is not, as evidenced by the fact that he has not attempted to charm Casey. He knows better. The same would go for you."

"But what about someone he felt he could charm?" Val says.

"That's actually a good idea." I make a face as I hear myself. "Sorry. I didn't mean it like that. But we could provide contact with someone we trust. Someone Brady will find an easy dupe. He needs an ally. He needs someone championing his cause and seeding doubt. Maybe even someone he thinks he can con into helping him escape.

A woman who will, at least to him, seem ripe for his charm. Lonely. Uncertain. Overlooked."

Mathias turns to Val. "I do hope you're volunteering."

I glare at him.

"What?" he says. "Have you not just described Valerie?" At a harder glare, he deigns to add, "In the sense that Valerie can *appear* to be all of that."

"No," I say.

"He's right," Val says. "I *wasn't* volunteering but . . ." She looks from me to Isabel, as if searching for an answer there. Then she squares her thin shoulders. "I *am* perfect for the job. We can even tell him I'm the town leader. That will make him feel as if he warrants special treatment. And he'll know I have power here, which makes me even more useful to him."

"Yeah, no," Dalton says.

"You think I can't handle it, Sheriff?"

He meets her gaze. "No, I think it's dangerous."

"And you think I can't handle *that*."

"No, Val. I think nobody should be put in that position. Don't pull this bullshit."

I know what he means. When Val first arrived in Rockton, she'd wanted to join a patrol. Dalton argued against it. She took offense—clearly he was discriminating against her because she was a woman. The council had backed Val . . . and she'd been attacked on that trip. Kidnapped by hostiles and almost certainly sexually assaulted, though she vehemently denies it. The truth is that Dalton has never let anyone—even Anders—into the forest so soon after arriving. But even now, Val hears only "*You* can't handle this," because she's been hearing variations on that all her life.

"Casey?" she says.

"No," Isabel says. "Don't do that, Val."

"Isabel's right," I say. "You're asking me to intercede with my *boss*, Val. This is a law enforcement issue. He's the sheriff."

I can feel Dalton studying me. Trying to figure out what my answer *would* be.

"You can still voice an opinion," Val says, and Isabel makes a noise, low in her throat, a warning that Val ignores.

"You think we should try it," Dalton says.

"I . . . I would rather not put Val in that situation," I say.

"In ideal circumstances," he says. "But under these ones, you think it's worth a shot."

I want to say no. Support him. He *is* my boss, and I never want to undermine his authority. That opens up a situation where residents will act like Phil, coming to me as the calm and reasonable one who can intercede with Dalton. Worse, they'll come to me as his lover, in hopes that I can use leverage.

So I want to just say Dalton's right. But he knows that isn't my answer, and he'll take more offense at a lie.

"I don't like the idea," I say carefully. "But if Val is willing—"

"I am." She straightens and meets Dalton's gaze. "I can do this. Whatever you think of me, Eric, I believe I am more, and I'd like the opportunity to prove it."

He mutters, "Fuck." It's like when Nicole asked to join the militia after her ordeal. I wanted to say no. Tell her to take more time. Not to push it. But I understood that need to push. Val is trying to step up. She's trying to be a valuable member of the community. Unless we are vehemently against her doing this, it's difficult to deny her that opportunity.

"Fine," Dalton says. "You have a week. If it doesn't go anywhere, I'm pulling you out."

Val wants to start right away. As hard as she fought for this task, once the meeting breaks up, I can tell she's having second thoughts. Yet when I offer her the chance to change her mind, that only solidifies it. She wants to meet him now. Before she loses her nerve.

Val and I walk into the station, talking town business. I give her some files. As she's preparing to leave, I ask her to send Kenny in to relieve me for lunch. She goes . . . and returns to say he's been called off and she'll stay instead. I hem and haw, but she insists.

I tell her I'll be back in thirty minutes. I actually do leave—I go for coffee at the bakery—but I've warned Kenny to keep an ear on that door.

When I return, it's with Dalton, and it hasn't been nearly thirty minutes. She knows to expect that, and when we walk in, she acts surprised, scurrying from the cell room.

"Sheriff," she says.

"Everything okay?" Dalton slows, his gaze moving from Brady to Val.

She stammers a response, and she overdoes it, but Brady doesn't seem to notice and comes to her rescue with, "We were just talking about my meals. I need more protein. And I'd like hand weights. Twenty-pounders."

"If you don't get the weights, you won't need the protein," Dalton drawls, but when Brady's lips tighten, he says, "We'll arrange trips to the gym later. We're not giving you dumbbells, though. We call those weapons."

"Oh, I think that's overstating the matter," Val says.

"Then you think wrong," Dalton says. "Now, if you'll excuse us . . ."

Val bristles. Dalton turns his back on her. Brady follows the exchange and allows himself the smallest of smiles.

NINE

It's now day five, and we need to get Brady out of that cell. Time for his first walk.

Anders, Dalton, and I lead Brady into the forest through the station back door. I've removed his gag, and he's trudging along, gaze down, docile and quiet. We make it three steps before he spots a woman by the forest's edge and raises his bound hands.

"Help me," he says. "Please. This is a mistake. They're going to—"

"Yeah," Nicole says. "You definitely want to keep that gag on."

She walks to Brady. "Oh, I'm sorry. Did I look like a gullible passerby? There aren't any of those here. You know what is here? People who'll take one look at scum like you and—"

He snaps forward to crack heads with her, but Nicole pulls back and their foreheads barely graze. Then she plows her fist into Brady's stomach, and he staggers, gasping in pain.

"Like I said," she says. "Don't bother."

She continues past him. Moving out of his field of vision so he doesn't see her flushed face and quickened breathing. I resisted bringing her on this walk. She's militia, which means she's trained for it, but she became militia after her ordeal. I understand her need to get past that, toughen up and move forward. I also know the dangers of doing it too fast, and that quickened breathing tells me that as badass as the encounter looked, she's quaking inside.

While Dalton replaces Brady's gag, I look over and Nicole mouths, *Please.* I know she means please let her come. I nod.

We've barely taken three steps when Dalton hears something, and we see a trio of residents, who just happen to have decided to stroll along the town border. Brady turns their way, his head bowed, bound hands lowered. He makes no move to get their attention, but he does, of course. He looks as pathetic as he had for Nicole.

Please help me.

They've made a mistake. You see that, don't you?

He says something against the gag, and I don't even think it's words. It's not meant to be. He's just drawing their attention to his situation.

This is the dilemma we face. Remove the gag, and Brady can plead his case. Leave it on, and the very gag pleads it for him.

Look at me.

Look what they're doing to me.

"You done gawking?" Dalton says to the trio. "Come over and take a closer look. See if Nicki has a bruise yet, from where he head-butted her."

Of course, there isn't a mark, but that's enough to make them decide to head back into town.

We set out. As we walk, Anders glances at me, as if feeling the urge to make small talk. I'm not sure that's wise, though. It feels too easy to let something slip, something that might suggest Brady isn't in Alaska.

Except that's not all he knows. He has seen faces. Heard names, even if they're fake. We are making an enemy here, one who does not seem like a stupid man. One who is not going to forget us.

I'm only beginning to realize the full extent of the danger the council has put us in.

We're a couple of kilometers into the forest when I turn to Brady and say, "Enough exercise?," and he looks around, as if he's considering, but it's more than that. He's processing his surroundings, and when he shakes his head, I know it's not that he wants more exercise—he wants to see more.

"We can go back and come out again," Nicole says.

"Nah," Dalton says. "We'll walk as far as he wants. He's enjoying the scenery. Plenty of it out here."

Endless scenery, that's what he means. Endless trails that go nowhere Brady will want to go. They lead to mountains and caves for us to explore. Lakes and streams for fish and fowl. Hunting blinds. Overnight campsites. Berry patches. Yes, one of those paths might hook up with a trail used by miners or trappers, which could ultimately get you to the nearest village. But Brady would still need to *survive* the trek with no weapons or skills.

As we continue, Nicole asks if anyone has seen our resident maneating cougar recently. It's a heavy-handed attempt to tell Brady what he'd face out here, but Dalton goes along with it, mostly for conversation. The silence is starting to smell of fear, as if we're too shaken by Brady to talk around him.

They're discussing the big cat when I see a figure around the next bend. My left arm flies up, stopping Brady. My right goes for my gun.

"It's just me," Jacob calls as he breaks into a jog. "I was about ready to give up on you guys. I thought we said noon . . ."

Jacob slows as he rounds the bend and sees us. His gaze travels over Brady, and I'm waiting for a *What the fuck?* Except he won't say those exact words. Dalton's younger brother does not share his propensity for profanity.

Instead, he just says to Dalton, "You forgot about me, huh?"

Now we get the "Fuck," from Dalton, and, "Yeah, sorry."

We're close to the spot where Dalton and his brother trade, and I'm guessing that's what they had scheduled for today.

I wave at Brady. "We had a situation."

"I see that. I heard Eric and Nicki talking, and I thought maybe she'd come along to help him carry supplies."

"Or to visit," Nicole says. "I hope I'd be more than a pack mule in that scenario."

"Course," Jacob says, his cheeks flushing over his beard, which I do not fail to notice has been trimmed short. His hair is tied back neatly, and he's dressed in the new jeans and new tee he'd requested at their last trade. Which isn't to say that Jacob *normally* looks like he's just crawled from a cave after a winter's hibernation. But he does live out here, without access to showers and department stores.

This extra effort was in hopes Nicole would accompany Dalton, as she often does, part of the slow dance between her and Jacob. They've been circling each other, not unlike a couple of fifteen-year-olds, trying to figure out if the other is interested before making any embarrassing moves.

"Eric did forget," Nicole says. "Otherwise, I'd have expected an invitation. But, yes, as you can see . . ." She nods at the man beside me. "We have a situation."

Jacob nods.

"You're not even going ask *why* we're walking a bound and gagged man through the forest, are you?"

Jacob shrugs. "Figure he pissed Eric off."

Nicole laughs at that.

Jacob looks at his brother. "You want me to store the game?"

"Nah, we'll take it off your hands."

We walk around the bend to the spot where Jacob left his trade goods—a brace of rabbits, one of ducks, and one of pheasants.

"Good hunting," Dalton says.

"'Tis the season, as Dad used to say."

Dalton nods, expressionless, as he always is when his brother mentions their parents. When Dalton was nine, the former sheriff of Rockton "rescued" him from the forest. And by "rescued," I mean kidnapped. So Dalton went from one loving set of parents to another. And the first set never came after him, while the second never realized that what they'd done was wrong. It's an impossible situation to reconcile, and Dalton refuses to even discuss it.

After Jacob mentions their dad, Dalton just bends to examine the game and discuss the price. If there's any haggling involved, it's Dalton trying to get Jacob to take more. Another impossible situation— Dalton wants to help his brother, and Jacob sees that help as charity.

Dalton has tried to get Jacob to come to Rockton. Jacob refuses. I wonder sometimes how much of that is choice and how much is fear that he won't fit in, that he will be seen as a freak. Dalton already feels that about himself. But if I presume Jacob chooses the forest out of fear, then am I any different from the women who presumed Dalton stayed in Rockton out of fear he wouldn't fit in down south?

Those women meant well, but in their way, they were no different from Dalton's adoptive parents. The Daltons found a boy living in the forest and decided no one could voluntarily want that life, so they rescued him. When Dalton and I look at Jacob's life and wish for better, we fall into that same trap of thinking what we have is clearly superior.

When Dalton and Jacob finally agree on a price for the game, Jacob says, "You can get me your stuff next week. If the weather holds, I want to head north for a few days. Got a spot up there that's all-I-can-haul hunting."

"Or all-two-can-haul," Nicole says. "Someone agreed to take me on a hunting trip once the weather improved."

When Jacob doesn't answer, Nicole quickly says, "Oh, I'm kidding. Maybe another trip."

Jacob shoves his hands into his jacket pockets. "No, this might be a good time. I could use the help. Let me check a few things. If it'll work, I'll leave a message in two days."

One might think it'd be easier for Jacob to just pop into Rockton, but very few residents know he exists, and while I'm uncomfortable adding Brady to that list, there's nothing to be done about it now.

Dalton says he'll check for the note. As they talk, Anders subtly directs my attention to our left, where I see another figure in the forest. My hand goes to my gun again, but slower this time. With Jacob, I could clearly see a human shape on the path. This is a big shape in a tree about fifty feet away. The only creature that size you'd find treed up here is the one we were just talking about. The cougar.

Anders's gaze shifts to Dalton, asking if we should tell him. I shake my head and take a step off the path, trying to see past a tree that partially blocks my view.

For the most dangerous creature in these woods, humans win hands down. But after that, the runner-up is a matter of debate. Grizzly or cougar? Pick your poison. One is seven hundred pounds of brute force. You'll see it coming. Question is whether you can stop it. The other? About my size. Much easier to kill. The problem is getting that chance—before it silently drops onto your back and snaps your neck.

Yet in this particular situation, a grizzly would worry me more. If this is a cougar, we see it, and that's really all we need. The question is whether it's the big cat we're looking for. She was the only one around—we're north of their usual territory—but we've seen signs that her cubs may have stayed. If it's the mother, I don't want to miss the chance to kill her. She's a man-eater, which makes her an indisputable threat. But her offspring?

Here is the question we face, not unlike our dilemma with Brady. If we see one of the younger cougars, do we exterminate it, just in case? That isn't our way. But if we let it live, and it kills someone, we have to take responsibility for that death . . . and *then* deal with a proven threat.

I edge around the tree. The figure is still too hard to make out, between the distance and blooming tree buds. All I can say for sure is that it's the right size for a cougar or a human, and it's lying on a branch watching us, which fits for either, too.

I glance at Anders. He gives a helpless shrug. We don't have binoculars—we were so distracted by Brady that we didn't grab our hiking pack. I survey that shape on the tree, and I know we can't walk away without seeing what it is. But we'll need to send at least two of us in for a closer look, and that leaves only two with Brady. No, wait, there's also Jacob. That'll work. Jacob and Dalton can go—

The figure moves and sunlight glints off—

"Down!" Anders shouts. "Everyone down!"

TEN

Anders's hand hits me square between the shoulder blades. Even as I fall, I look up to see Dalton spinning toward me. That's his first reaction. Not to drop, damn him, but to make sure Jacob and I are. Both of us *are* dropping, and I'm shouting "Eric, get down!" but he's already doing that. Then he sees that one person hasn't moved.

Brady.

Our sudden movement threw him into defensive mode, his hands rising as if to ward us off.

"Oliver, get—!" I shout.

Dalton lunges at Brady just as I see the distant muzzle flare. I shout "No!" and I'm scrambling up as Dalton knocks Brady out of the way. Then blood. I see blood.

Anders grabs my leg, but I yank away and lurch, bent over, toward Dalton as I shout, "In the woods! Roll into the woods!" Anders echoes it with his trained-soldier bark, and Brady, Nicole, and Jacob crawl off the path.

Dalton doesn't move.

He's on the ground. And there's blood. That's all I register. Dalton is on the ground, and there is blood.

Even when I see him rising, I think I'm imagining it. My brain has already seized on the worst possible scenario and refuses to let go.

"Down!" Anders says. "Both of you! Now!"

I'm close enough to grab Dalton, and then Anders is there, and we both get him off the path as Dalton says, "I'm fine, I'm fine."

There are no more shots. When Jacob tries to rise, though, Anders says, "Stay down! It's a sniper."

Jacob stares at him, uncomprehending.

"There's a shooter in the trees," I say. "Get off the path. We have Eric."

"I'm fine, Jacob," Dalton calls. "He winged me. That's all."

Which is a slight exaggeration. Dalton has been shot in the upper arm. A small-caliber bullet passed through what I hope is just muscle. It should be, but blood streams from the entry and exit holes, and I'm still fighting the panic that insists that it's more serious.

When I prod Dalton into thicker brush, he doesn't argue. I get my belt and shirt off and fashion a padded tourniquet around his arm.

"It's fine," he says. "We need to—"

"I know."

Anders motions. I peek around a bush and see what he's trying to show me—that the sniper's perch is empty.

"Go on," Dalton says. "You and Will."

I hesitate. I'd rather have Anders stay to properly assess him, but Dalton's stable and our shooter is on the move. He squeezes my fingers with his good hand and says, "Be careful."

"I'm not the one leaping in to save serial killers."

"Yeah, didn't think that one through. He'd better appreciate it."

I shake my head. Oliver Brady will consider rescue no less than his due. While Dalton can say he didn't think it through, I'm not sure that would have mattered. Brady is under his protection. Dalton isn't going to stand by and watch him die.

Anders and I slip from bush to tree to whatever will hide our approach. Every few moments, we stop to listen. There's nothing to hear, just the usual noise of the forest.

When we're about halfway to the tree, I pop up enough to scan our surroundings. Anders does the same. A shake of his head says he sees nothing either. When I frown, he jerks his chin, asking what's bugging me. The calm suggests our shooter has retreated, but I'd have expected to *hear* that—in the thump of a foot on hard ground, the crackle of undergrowth, the cry of a startled bird.

Our sniper hasn't beat a hasty retreat, crashing through the forest. Has he retreated at all? I whisper that possibility to Anders, and he nods, his gaze shifting to where we left the others. As much as we want to go back and warn them, Dalton will keep them safely hidden until we say the coast is clear.

We continue on, step by careful step. Listen. Step. Look. Step. *Feel.* Yes, that last one seems strange, especially if I admit I'm trying to catch a sense of someone nearby. Out here, I've learned not to be too quick to dismiss the raised hairs on my neck, the sense that I am not alone.

Dalton is the most pragmatic person I know, but he'd also be the first to tell me to pay attention to my sixth sense. He puts it into a context his brain understands—humans are both predator and prey out here, and so logically we might have something that is not quite premonition, but rather an awareness of another presence. Maybe it's vibrations underfoot or a scent in the air or a sound too soft to be identified.

I detect none of that.

We reach the tree and circle it, guarding each other while scanning the forest.

"Gone," Anders whispers.

I process the scene, but there's nothing to find. Not even a fiber trapped in the bark where he climbed. I shimmy onto that limb and find nothing. Then, as I'm climbing down, I catch the glint of metal in the undergrowth.

"Will . . ." I say carefully.

He's been circling the tree, searching. Now he halts, one foot still raised.

"Stay right where you are," I say.

"Can I put my foot down?"

"Very carefully."

He does that as I say, "There's something metallic on the ground to your left."

"Bear trap?"

"Not unless they come in long, barrel-shaped form."

"Shit. There's a gun pointed right at me, isn't there?"

"Yep."

"Of course there is." He curses some more. "Okay, if it's a trap, you're looking for a trigger. Presumably it would be tripped from the direction the gun is aimed. It could be a pressure plate under the soil."

"I don't see any soil disturbance around you."

"Good start."

I crawl out on the tree branch over him to conduct a full visual sweep. I don't see a trip wire, and I tell him that, adding, "But don't take my word for it."

"Oh, I'm not. Sorry. Can you climb out over the gun?"

"Yes, but I can already tell that won't help. It's nestled in the vegetation. I'm going to check it out. Just hold on."

I retreat down the tree. Then I circle wide. When I'm on the far side of the gun, I walk toward it, checking before putting each foot down. Finally, I reach the spot. I crouch. Then I swear.

"That doesn't sound good," Anders says.

"No, it's—Just hold on."

I swore because I know this gun. I'm temporarily putting that on the "not important" shelf, along with the ramifications of having a sniper in our forest.

I hunker down. Then I lie on my belly, getting a straight-on view of the gun.

"And . . ." Anders says.

"I don't see any sign of a trigger device. It looks as if the shooter just left it behind."

"That's actually kinda disappointing."

"At the count of three, I'll knock the barrel aside, and you'll dive for cover. We'll tell everyone else it was rigged, and you narrowly escaped death. Plus, of course, I saved your life, and you owe me forever."

"Yeah, no. But you *can* move the barrel aside. Carefully please."

I lean over the gun and take another good look, running my fingers along the perimeter for a trip wire. The trigger is clear, and the gun seems fine. I ease the barrel away from Anders.

"Thank you."

I start to rise, and he says, in a low voice, "Stop."

A low growl sounds behind me. I look over my shoulder to see a muzzle and eyes peering from a clump of weeds.

ELEVEN

"Is that a . . . ?" Anders begins.

He doesn't finish, but I know what he was going to say. It looks like a wolf—the size, the build, the ears, the muzzle shape, and the white and gray fur. But there are brown spots in that gray, and its face is freckled.

"Wolf-dog," I murmur.

"Shit," Anders says.

It's the dog part that worries me. I hear wolves almost every night, but I've only spotted them deep in the forest, as they catch wind of us and disappear like ghosts. Dogs are another matter. They're feral, descended from those either released or escaped from Rockton, back in a time when pets were allowed. Those canines don't always slip away like wolves. Even a few generations removed, they retain their fearlessness around humans.

I aim my gun. I don't want to. But this is Dalton's rule. If a feral dog makes an aggressive move, we must shoot to kill.

I can't tell with this one. It's watching me just as carefully as I'm watching it.

"Got your gun ready?" I ask Anders.

"I do."

"Count of three. Three, two, one—"

I lunge at the wolf-dog and let out a snarl. I'm hoping it'll run. It doesn't. Nor does it attack. It just hunkers down and snarls back, fur bristling. Anders curses some more, and I agree. We like our decisions cut-and-dry, and the universe isn't complying these days, not even with a damn dog.

"Protocol is to shoot," Anders says. "If it doesn't *back* down, we *put* it down."

I notice he doesn't actually shoot. He's waiting for me to say yes, that's what we have to do. When I say, "Wait," he exhales in relief.

I hunker to crouch.

"Good idea," Anders says. "Submissive pose. See if it attacks."

Which isn't what I'm doing at all. I'm taking a closer look at something I've spotted.

"She's nursing," I say. "Her cubs must be nearby."

"Right. Okay. So we leave her."

"As long as she doesn't attack, yes. I'm going to pick up the rifle, and we'll back off slowly."

The wolf-dog stands her ground, allowing me to get the gun and start backing up. Then she follows, stiff-legged.

"Making sure we leave?" Anders says.

"I hope so."

When we've made it about halfway to the others, I call, "Eric?"

"Here."

"Our shooter is gone. He left his gun. But we've got a wolf-dog backing us off. It's a nursing mother."

"Fuck."

I don't ask if he wants us to shoot. If he does, he'll say so. Instead, he calls, "Jacob?"

There's a murmur of voices. Jacob appears. He ducks to peer under a branch and gets a look at the canine.

"That's Freckles," he says. "She's not usually a problem. It's the cubs making her defensive."

I don't comment on him "naming" the wolf-dog. That's not what he's done. It's just a way to identify her, the same way people name ponds and hills and other landmarks.

Jacob tells us to keep backing away. When the canine continues to follow, he lunges and growls, and she freezes. There's a five-second stare-down. Then the wolf-dog snorts and stays where she is, letting us retreat.

"You need to be more intimidating, Case," Anders says.

"Nah," Jacob says. "You just need to learn the stare . . . and know which animals you can use it on. Do that to a boar grizzly, and you're dead where you stand. She was just making sure you got away from her litter."

We return to the others. Anders and I go straight to Dalton. That's when our sheriff sees the rifle.

"Fuck, no," he say.

"Fuck, yes," Anders says. "Now give me that arm."

"We need to—"

"Arm. Now."

Dalton lifts his arm for Anders to examine. Residents joke about Dalton being the alpha dog in Rockton. He is, and no one disputes that. But people aren't animals, and the idea of one person being in charge, at all times, in all situations, is bullshit. This winter, when Dalton contracted the flu in Dawson City, Anders happily turned to me and said, "You're up." *You play sheriff for a few days.* He didn't want the job. Yet all he has to do is adopt this tone, and Dalton shuts up and listens.

As Anders examines him, Dalton shoots glances my way. He's trying not to look at the rifle. Trying not to tip off Brady, who's watching us intently. He's also trying to hide the worry in his eyes.

"Does it matter?" I say. "Threat-wise? Six of one, half dozen of the other."

Brady's brows furrow. Dalton nods. He understands my verbal shorthand. This gun is from Rockton. That suggests our shooter is also from Rockton. On the surface, that's alarming, but what's the alternative? An external sniper would mean someone sent to kill Brady. Someone who came from Brady's world.

The two situations are equally dangerous.

Most pressing right now is Dalton's arm. Jacob and I are both hovering as Anders works. I see Brady watching, and I want to pull back, tug Jacob with me, but that's pointless. One glance at Jacob, and Brady can tell he's Dalton's brother. And if Brady hasn't figured out that Dalton and I are lovers, he's going to soon.

Dalton's injury isn't as serious as I feared, but it's still a bullet wound. It will be temporarily debilitating. Or so it will seem to a guy who agreed to stay in bed with the flu only when we warned he could infect others. It's his left arm, which is a problem.

When I say, "Good thing you're right-handed," there isn't even a moment of confusion. Instead, Dalton exhales, and says, "Yeah," and Anders agrees. Jacob looks up but covers his surprise fast. Having our prisoner realize that our sheriff has lost the full use of his dominant arm is the last thing we need. It really is.

In town, Dalton strides straight for Val's place. I catch his good arm. My gaze shoots to the station. He hesitates but nods, and we follow Anders and Nicole with Brady. When they head inside, though, we veer off to the supply shed.

The shed isn't part of the station—our building is too small to have the militia tramping in and out all day. Inside the supply building is a secure gun locker, which I examine for signs of tampering. There are none.

We have two sets of keys for this locker. Dalton carries one. Anders has the other. The militia use handguns on patrol, and they typically just pass their weapon on to whoever takes over their shift. Otherwise, they need Anders to open the locker. He never just hands over his key. Neither does Dalton.

Dalton reaches into his pocket with his left hand—force of habit—and then winces. With that wince comes a growl of frustration.

"As tempting as it is to play the tough guy," I say, "please remember that every time you do that, you pull at the wound, and it's going to take that much longer to heal. I'm going to suggest—strongly suggest—that you let me put your arm in a sling, if only to remind you to keep it still."

"Fuck."

"Yes, but it'll heal faster."

He nods. Then he switches his key to his right hand. When he fumbles to get it into the hole, I resist the urge to do it for him. The key goes in, and the cabinet opens, and sure enough, one of our rifles is missing.

I read the log. "It hasn't been checked out since last weekend, when we took the rifles for hunting."

"It was here yesterday, when I had to grab a gun for Kenny. So how the hell—?"

"Someone picked the lock," Anders says as he walks in. "That's the only explanation."

"Agreed," I say. "But it's not a standard lock. Whoever did this has some serious skills."

"So we go to the council and demand . . ." Dalton begins, and then trails off, grumbling under his breath.

"Yeah," Anders says. "You can demand to know if we have any thieves in town, but they aren't going to tell us."

"Do you know, for a fact, that there are only two keys?" I ask. "I'm guessing you didn't install that locker yourself."

Dalton shakes his head.

"So there could be a third key floating around . . . or the council has always had one."

Anders looks at me. "You think the council brought in a sniper?"

"I'm afraid to even start considering the possibilities. We'll need to report the attempt, but I'm going to suggest we don't mention finding the gun or realizing it's missing. If the council is responsible, their sniper could have brought his own weapon. Using ours suggests they wanted to frame us. By admitting it was ours, we set ourselves up to take responsibility if they succeed next time."

TWELVE

"I don't understand," Phil says after I explain what's happened.

"Someone tried to shoot Oliver Brady," I say.

"Yes, I understand that's what you're telling me, Detective, but I'm not sure I follow your reasoning. You presume Mr. Brady was the target."

"If Eric hadn't pushed him down, he'd have been—"

"And what proof do you have of that?" Phil cuts in, his voice edged with impatience. "I'm sorry to interrupt, Detective, but I am concerned that you are leaping to conclusions here. There is no way of telling that the bullet would have hit Mr. Brady. Even if there was, that doesn't prove he was a target. It may have been simply a random shot fired by a settler."

"The shooter was in a tree. That's a targeted attack."

"Perhaps because you were trespassing on territory the shooter considers his."

"So it was a complete coincidence that we were walking the prisoner in the forest when someone fired a shot from a tree—which has *never* happened before—and that bullet just *happened* to seem aimed at our prisoner. Presuming it was a random attack—"

"—is like seeing a grizzly barreling in your direction," Dalton says, "and standing your ground because there's a chance he's not actually charging at *you*."

"A colorful analogy, Sheriff," Phil says. "But I take your point. Obviously extra steps will be required to secure the prisoner."

"Like what?" Dalton says. "Keeping him locked up six months with no exercise?"

"I do not have an issue with that. Nor does his stepfather."

"Our residents will. They already think he's being mistreated."

"I'm sure you can handle that, Sheriff."

"I can. What I can't handle is the loss of respect they'll have for me—and Casey and Will—for a situation that is not our fault. We don't want Brady here."

"And did you take steps to rectify that?"

"Excuse me?" I say.

"Yeah," Dalton says. "We put one of our guys in that tree to shoot him. Stupid me forgot *we* planted the sniper and nearly got my ass killed trying to save the target. Whoops."

"What I mean, Sheriff, is that you might have let your dissatisfaction with the situation be known, and one of your citizens decided to relieve you of the responsibility. Are all your guns accounted for?"

"They're all in the locker," I say. Which is technically true.

"Then I don't know what to tell you, besides my suspicion that this was one of your forest people, and regardless of whether Mr. Brady was the target, you should reconsider walking him outside of town boundaries."

"On another subject," I say, "do you know anything about a shooting in San Jose?"

Silence. "A shooting . . ."

"In San Jose."

"There are many shootings in America these days, Detective. To the point, sadly, where they begin to blur."

"This was in a school playground, and the shooter is still at large."

"That does sound familiar. But I fail to see what . . . Are you suggesting that has something to do with *this* shooting?"

"Brady mentioned it."

"All right . . ." A long pause. "I'm still not seeing the connection. I seem to recall a sniper was involved in the playground incident, but I'm at a loss to even guess what the connection might be."

"I thought it was odd that he brought it up."

"Ah. What you're saying is that it's odd that he mentioned a sniper shooting . . . and then seems to be the target of one. You're wondering if Mr. Brady himself had something to do with the attempt this afternoon."

"Sure." That wasn't where I was going at all—I just wanted to verify that there *had* been a shooting in San Jose and see how Phil reacted to Brady mentioning it.

Phil continues, "You're asking whether Mr. Brady knew where he was going. Or if he might have been followed there by a confederate."

"Yes."

"There was no indication of a partner in his crimes. However, Mr. Brady has the money to hire someone to do what you are suggesting—appear to shoot at him, in hopes of bolstering his claims of innocence. He is proclaiming that innocence, I presume."

"To anyone who'll listen, which is why we're keeping the gag on."

"A wise idea."

"Yeah," Dalton says. "It really helps those who think we're mistreating him."

There's a pause, and Phil manages to sound borderline sympathetic when he says, "I can see that would be a problem. It will need to be dealt with very carefully."

Dalton snorts.

Phil continues, "Back to the issue, while I will agree that Mr. Brady could hire someone to do this, I don't see how he would carry it out. We were exceedingly careful with transport, funneling him through multiple handlers, none of whom knew the situation or the destination or had any experience with Rockton."

"*None* knew the situation?" I say.

"That is correct. They were told only that they were transporting a dangerous prisoner. We advised leaving the gag on, and we said they could not trust any story he told if it came off. The warning wasn't really necessary. For those we hired, this would go without saying."

"The woman who brought him here was ex-military," I say.

"Most were."

"Any with sniper training?"

He pauses. "I have no idea, but I will look into that, particularly with the woman who delivered him. That would be the only scenario I see working here—that he communicated with her and she agreed to help. She knew where he was being held. And she *is* a mercenary. Excellent deductive reasoning."

Or, maybe, just an excuse he can utilize. *Why, yes, Detective, it turns out she was trained in distance shooting, and we cannot track her current whereabouts. Good job, Casey. Gold star. Case solved. Move on.*

"What about the stepfather?" I say. "Does Gregory Wallace know where Oliver is being held?"

"Not specifically. And I can't imagine why he'd pay us to keep the young man safe . . . and then hire an assassin to kill him. That's hardly cost-effective."

Actually, it would be very cost-effective. If Oliver Brady is innocent, that will be proven when someone else is accused of the same crimes. Even if that never happens, his mother might begin questioning. It's far more convenient for Brady to be dead. *I'm so sorry, darling—I tried to keep him safe for you, and I couldn't.*

If Brady is guilty, there's still a reason to assassinate him. How long will Wallace want to pay to keep his murderous stepson safe? Whatever the scenario here, killing Oliver Brady is both efficient and cost-effective. The only reason Wallace wouldn't have done that right away is his wife. Better for her to think Wallace tried to save her boy, no matter what crimes he's committed.

I talk to Phil for a while longer, but there's nothing more to get. Before we sign off, he says, "Sheriff?"

"Yeah."

"I know we've put you in a bad position."

"The word you want," Dalton drawls, "is 'untenable.'"

There's a long pause, and then an almost reluctant "I'm not sure that's the proper term," as if he's loath to correct his uneducated sheriff, when the poor guy is trying to expand his vocabulary.

"Yeah," Dalton says. "It is. Untenable. A position or argument we cannot defend. We have a killer who has done seriously fucked-up things, yet I cannot explain that to people or they'll revolt. But if I don't tell them, they'll think we're mistreating a common criminal.

Or that he didn't commit a crime at all. Maybe we're afraid they'll discover the truth if we take off that gag. An untenable situation."

Another long pause. Then, "You'll work it out, Sheriff. I just need you to understand, particularly in light of this shooting, how important Mr. Brady is to Rockton. The cost of hiding the town against modern technology is skyrocketing. We need to take advantage of opportunities like Oliver Brady."

"Bullshit." Dalton's voice is low, nearly too low to hear, and there's a note in it that has the hairs on my neck rising.

"I beg your pardon?"

"That's bullshit, and you know it. You want to cover skyrocketing costs? Look at reducing your profit margin."

Phil's voice cools. "I don't like your implication, Sheriff. Anytime you would like to see our fiscal reports, I will have a copy sent to Dawson City for you."

Which wouldn't do any good. It's not the official income that counts. It's the hidden profits, from those who buy their way in under a false story.

"Oliver Brady is your responsibility, Sheriff," Phil says. "You only have to keep him safe for six months. I'm certain you can do that. If you can't, we'll need to find someone who can."

THIRTEEN

It's almost ten at night, and there's still enough daylight for me to squeeze in an hour of training with Storm. She's graduated beyond obedience lessons. We covered those as soon as she was old enough. We've passed manners training, too, which is particularly critical given her size. Greeting people by jumping on them ceased to be adorable about twenty pounds ago. By the time she's full-grown, even leaning in for attention could topple people. Roughhousing is for playtime and only with a select few people. For the rest, she must comport herself with queenly dignity.

Tonight's lesson is also critical for her breed: distraction and dominance training. She'll weigh more than me in a few months, which means I will physically be unable to restrain her. I'm putting her through her basic paces—sit, stay, come—while Dalton sits on the porch and tosses her favorite ball in the air.

"Storm . . ." I say when she looks his way.

Her ears perk, but her gaze doesn't move.

"Eyes on me."

Her head shifts, just enough so she can see me out of the corner of her eye.

"Uh-uh. *Eyes* on *me*. Both of them."

Her gaze shoots to me. Back to Dalton. He chuckles.

"*Storm.*"

She sighs, a deep one, her jowls quivering. Then she looks my way and keeps her attention there.

Dalton fake-fumbles the ball. As it thumps to the ground, her head whips toward him.

"Storm," I say. "Eyes on me."

Another sigh, as she looks my way with a glower, like a teen saying, *Happy now?*

"Stand."

She does.

"Sit."

She grumbles at that, having clearly hoped the stand meant she was about to be released.

"Down."

She flounces to the ground. Dalton pitches the ball. It springs past us, and her muscles bunch.

"Stay."

She hesitates, muscles still tense. Then she gives in and tears her gaze from the ball.

"Are you ready?" I say.

She whimpers, body quivering. But she doesn't rise. Doesn't look at Dalton. Keeps her gaze on me.

"Wait . . . wait . . . and . . . *go*."

She leaps up and tears toward Dalton . . . and I see that sling on his arm.

"Shit!" I say. "I mean, no, wait—"

He falls on his ass before she can get to him. As she pounces, I'm running over with, "Storm, no—"

"It's fine," he says. "We've got this."

He sits on the ground and rubs her with his good hand as she dances on his lap. Then he raises his arm for me to toss him the ball. I do, and I retreat to the deck to watch them play fetch. Except Dalton has never actually known a dog, so his version of fetch is, well, unique. He throws the ball, and they *both* run after it, which usually results in a football tackle. That's more his style, getting in there and working off energy, and Storm loves it, so I wouldn't argue . . . if he didn't have his arm in a sling.

When I try to intercede again, though, he waves me off, and he *is* being careful, so I settle on the deck. I watch him shrug off his day and become the guy he can be only in the relative privacy of our back-yard. The guy who slides on the grass and tackles a dog and gets a faceful of fur and comes up sputtering and laughing and crowing in victory, too, as he waves a slobbery ball over his head.

I think of Phil's thinly veiled threat to exile Dalton, as if he's com-mitted some terrible crime. That "crime" is devoting his life to this town, risking his life today to protect a man who did not deserve pro-tecting. Dalton might stride through Rockton like he owns the place, but it owns him, too, and it owes him better than this.

I never want to lose the guy I see tonight, playing with a dog. This problem isn't mine to fix, and it's patronizing to try, but sometimes I peer down Dalton's life path, to a future where he becomes the front he shows others—harsh, tough—and then continues along that road until he reaches bitter resignation, no longer even bothering to fight back, because he knows it won't do any good.

I fear for a future where Dalton is no longer Rockton's protector, its best advocate, its biggest cheerleader. A future where he's just a guy doing a job, putting in his time here because he has no place else to go, hating the town and himself for that.

I want to tell myself I'm overreacting. I see him playing with Storm, and I want to say, *See, even amid all this, he's fine.* But I know Oliver Brady will not be an anomaly. Phil hinted at that today. If Brady sur-vives his stay here, there will be others. If he doesn't? I don't know what happens then, but I fear that outcome would be even worse. For Dalton. For Rockton. For all of us.

FOURTEEN

That afternoon, I run fingerprints from the gun locker, which is a far cry from the way I used to do it down south. I'm a technology-era baby. From my earliest experiences in a police department—when I told my parents I was volunteering at the Y—I saw fingerprints run on computers. I remember my disappointment at that. It seemed so dull compared to what I'd read in old crime novels. I also remember, when I became a detective, looking back and rolling my eyes at my younger self, unable to imagine the work involved in manually processing fingerprints.

Now I can.

It might be possible to process them by computer. Dalton has a laptop for when he goes down south on business. It will run here if I charge it from the generator. I could buy a scanner and input the townspeople's fingerprints into a database and then find a program to compare them to crime scene prints. But honestly, with a small and constricted population, that's more work than manually processing.

So, in this, as in many other aspects of my job, I have become that Victorian-era detective. I have my fingerprint powder and my index cards of exemplars. And I love it. Sure, there's some misplaced nostalgia there. The public is better served by modern crime-solving methods. Yet I'm not sure that applies in Rockton, and I *feel* more like a detective when I dust prints from the gun cabinet, see whorls and ridges, and say "That one's mine, and that's Will's, and Eric's, and Kenny's . . ." without needing to consult my cards.

I've lifted all the prints and brought them home. I'm stretched out on my stomach on the bearskin rug. Storm has her head on my legs. She snuffled the cards once, withdrawing at an "Uh-uh" from me, though not before leaving a string of drool.

While I eliminated most prints at the site, I still lifted them to pore over here. Yet I'm not seeing any other than the ones I'd expect.

"The problem," I say to Storm, "is overlapping prints. A computer is so much better at analyzing those." I lift a card. "All I see is a mess of whorls. It's like a reverse jigsaw. A very imperfect science. I hate imperfect."

"Does she ever answer you?"

Dalton's voice drifts in as the front door clicks shut.

I wait until he appears and say, "She's not supposed to. She's my Watson."

He lowers himself beside me. "I thought I was your Watson."

"Watson is the guy Holmes talks *at*. A sounding board to hear his theories and tell him he's brilliant. You can do that last part if you like."

"Better stick with the dog." He reaches for the card I'd been examining. "Is it even possible to separate these?"

"With computers, there are algorithms. Even those are still works in progress. I can separate out the ones at the edges, but not once I get into the middle. I'm not sure this isn't just busywork anyway. I've got enough smeared prints to suggest whoever took the gun used gloves. The stock is totally wiped down."

"Which supports the theory that we're dealing with a pro."

"No, just a non-idiot. The fact fingerprinting works in any of our cases shocks the hell out of me. It's not like it's difficult to find gloves around here."

He stretches his legs. "Think there's any chance Phil's right? That this could be the woman who flew Brady in?"

"On paper, she looks good. Trained soldier. Mercenary. She admits she removed his gag. If he got the chance, he'd have offered her money. No doubt about that."

"Because he knows she's a mercenary."

"Right. But *how* mercenary? Adjective versus noun. Just because she uses her army skills to make a living doesn't mean they're for sale to the highest bidder."

"Yeah." He scratches Storm behind the ears. "And there's no chance she snuck into town without being noticed."

"Young, female, attractive . . . yep, they'd notice."

"Female's enough for this town."

I chuckle. "True. If the sniper *was* the pilot, why steal our gun? She'd have access to her own."

"But framing us would still help. Set us chasing our tails looking for a shooter internally."

"This is why you aren't Watson. You come up with good ideas."

Dalton rises. "Pretty sure Watson *had* some good ideas. Coffee?"

"Yet another good one." I watch him start the fire to heat water. "Does Tyrone have military experience?"

"Ty Cypher?"

I sit up, crossing my legs. "Sorry. Mental jump there. Thinking about the pilot made me wonder who in town has military experience. That's just Will and Sam, right?"

"Kenny was in Air Cadets."

"Which is a youth group. I don't think they train snipers. At least not in Canada. And Sam served in the navy."

"That's the one with water."

"It is."

"Any snipers?"

"The Canadian Navy has one destroyer, which is on its last legs. Lots of tugboats, though."

"Uh-huh."

"I think Sam was in peacekeeping."

"So . . . snipers?"

"That's one way to keep peace. But no. Not usually. I don't think a military connection is the answer. Marksmanship doesn't need that, though. Not by a long shot, pardon the pun. I'd like a list of our best shooters."

"That'd be Will."

I shake my head. "Good thing he was on the scene then. Otherwise, he'd be our key suspect, which is just awkward."

"After him? The best shooter is you."

"Even more awkward. Let me guess, you come after me?"

He taps his sling. "I am definitely out of the running. So that's top three. Next is the militia."

"Our boys like their target practice."

"As do Jen and Nicki."

"True enough. Are any of them good enough to make that shot, though?"

"Depends on what 'that shot' is," he says. "I hate giving Phil credit, but there's no way to say for sure that the bullet would have hit Brady."

"Are you thinking maybe he *wasn't* the target?"

"Who the fuck knows at this point? It seemed aimed at him. No one else was standing there until I got in the way. But would it have killed him if I didn't interfere?" Dalton throws up his hand.

"If it didn't kill him, would that have been intentional—trying to spook us rather than assassinate Brady? Or would it have missed because our shooter *isn't* a crack shot? We could just be looking at a decent shooter with an overinflated sense of his—or her—skills. So . . . Ty?"

Tyrone Cypher was sheriff of Rockton before Dalton's father. When the demotion to deputy rankled too much, he'd gone to live in the forest.

"Are you looking at Ty for this?" The wrinkle in Dalton's nose tells me what he thinks of that. He doesn't say it, though, just keeps making coffee in our French press.

"I'm looking at everyone for this. He was a professional assassin, though."

Dalton snorts. "Hit man. There's a difference."

Which is true. "Assassin" conjures up an image that is *not* Tyrone Cypher.

"What's his firearm prowess?" I ask.

"On a scale of one to ten? Negative three."

I give him a look.

"I'm serious," Dalton says. "The guy prides himself on not using guns. You know that."

"So when he says he worked with his hands . . ."

"If Ty says it, it's true. He's serious about *that,* too. I've never actually caught the guy in a lie. Which, like you said, might not mean he never lies—just that he saves the falsehoods for the big stuff."

"Has he ever *said* he can't shoot? His comments about the military make Will think he served."

"Tyrone doesn't volunteer information. He's never said he can't shoot—he just chooses not to. The problem is motive."

I rub my fingers together and then I realize the gesture means nothing in Dalton's world.

"Money," I say. "Ty killed for money before, and he doesn't seem to have any moral qualms about doing it again."

Dalton shakes his head. "I see where you're going, but Tyrone doesn't give a shit about money. Now, if they offered him a barrel of coffee creamer, maybe. But even then, it'd mean working for the council, and you know how he feels about that."

"So you trust Ty."

He makes a face as he passes me a filled mug. "I wouldn't say trust . . ."

"We've been trading with him since last winter."

"The man works for coffee and powdered creamer. Can't beat the price. But trust him? He's . . . What's the scientific term? Loony tunes."

I have to laugh at that. "True. He has his own special brand of crazy. But you trust him enough to trade with him, send him on scouting missions, and let him into Rockton."

"As long as he's escorted."

"Only because you don't want to freak out the locals."

"Yeah, okay, sure. I trust . . ." He stops. "Fuck. I just stepped into it, didn't I?" He sighs. "Where is this leading?"

"I'd like you to deputize Ty for a few days. I need information I can only get from the internet, and the only person who can fly out of here is you. It's a lousy time for you to leave, but I think the need outweighs the danger. I'd like you to take an overnight trip to Dawson City, with a list of what I need researched. I'll stay here and Ty can help guard Brady."

Dalton snorts. "Because he'll scare the ever-loving shit out of Brady?"

"Possibly." I smile. "Ty won't buy Brady's stories. He might even be able to give us some insight into how likely it is that he committed these murders. Mathias knows one side of killers. Tyrone knows another."

"It'll take a day or two to find Ty. By then, Brady's permanent residence will be done so I won't mind leaving. What do you want online?"

"Everything you can get on these crimes he supposedly committed. Including whether they actually exist."

"Actually exist?" He looks at me, his mental wheels turning fast. "Fuck."

"Yep. I need information on the San Jose shootings, information on the Georgia murders, plus anything that can help us figure out whether Oliver Brady is responsible for either."

FIFTEEN

It's the next afternoon. Val has conveyed Dalton's message to the council. They're "considering" letting him go to Dawson.

I'm the sole officer on duty right now. Dalton and Nicole have gone into the woods to get Jacob's message and look for Cypher. An hour ago, someone from the logging party came running back to say there's been an accident. Nothing serious, but a hatchet injury always requires immediate attention, so Anders has left with his first-aid kit.

I'm on Brady duty, all of our militia having been repurposed into construction workers. That's fine—Brady's cell is secure, and it's not as if he's going to ever talk me into letting him out for a walk. Still, Petra has come over to keep me company, and we're on the rear deck.

I haven't accidentally left Brady unattended. I'm testing him. He knows Dalton and Anders are gone. He knows the militia are doing construction. And now his sole guard has just wandered outside to chat with her friend. I want to see what he'll do. So far, the answer is "Nothing."

Petra has her sketchbook out. She was a comic-book artist down south, and up here, she draws art as a sideline—people buy it to decorate their homes.

"Looks like someone's hungry." Petra nods at a raven, who keeps circling to the deck railing and then pulling up before landing. "That's yours, isn't it?"

"It's not really—"

"Yeah, yeah," she says. "Wild animals are not pets. I once made the mistake of asking Eric if I could adopt a bear cub. I was kidding. I still got the lecture. Since he's not within earshot, though, this is your raven, right? The one you've trained."

"It is." I take a piece of muffin from my pocket. "It won't come close to Storm, so you'll need to hold her."

"Have you thought of training them?"

The raven swoops past, but it knows better than to snatch the muffin chunk from my hand.

Petra puts her sketchbook aside. "I grew up rural. We had chickens, and we had dogs that we didn't want devouring the chickens. You can train them both. Teach Storm not to go after the raven, and teach the raven that the dog is safe."

Petra explains how to start, and then she puts her hand on Storm's collar, while I set the muffin on the railing.

The raven lands at the far end and begins inching along, while croaking at me, telling me to move it farther from the dog.

I start to pocket the muffin chunk. The raven lets out a loud squawk.

"Oh, it doesn't like that," Petra says with a laugh.

I put the muffin down again, and the raven waddle-walks as fast as it dares—

The station front door slams, and the raven flies off. Storm growls. Petra glances through the rear door and pats Storm.

"Good baby," she says. "Excellent instincts."

The back door slaps open, and Jen barrels out.

"What the hell?" Jen says. "You're leaving him unguarded now?"

"We're on the back porch," Petra says. "And he's locked in a cell. We aren't concerned."

"I see that. I guess maybe he's not such a dangerous criminal, huh?"

"Jen?" I say. "Don't."

"Why? Because you're busy chatting with your buddy and playing with your dog? Are you even trying to find out whether this guy is guilty?"

I don't answer that. I remember a time when I'd check out online articles for crimes I was investigating. I'd read the comments section, in hopes of getting a lead or a fresh angle. Instead all I got were complaints. The cops are lazy. The cops are incompetent. The cops are corrupt. Why can't they just run DNA? Why can't they arrest the guy everyone knows did it? I'd log in under a fake name and try to explain, but those commenters didn't want explanations. The same goes for Jen.

Before I can speak, I see a paper in Jen's hand.

"What's that?" I ask.

"A petition."

"Oh, for God's sake." Petra reaches to snatch it.

Jen yanks it back with, "Hey!"

I put my hand out. Jen holds the paper up but doesn't pass it over.

"I have fifty names," she says. "Residents who demand a public inquiry into the department's handling of this situation."

"An inquiry?" Petra says. "Do you even know what that is? Or is it just something you heard on TV?"

"Tell me exactly what you want," I say. My voice is calm, but my heart's hammering.

Fifty names. One-quarter of the population doesn't trust our handling of this.

No, only a quarter agreed to sign Jen's petition. How many others disagree and fear saying so?

"Give me the list—" I say.

I'm stepping toward her, but she swats at my outstretched arm. Storm lunges at her. That's all she does. It's a feint, with a warning growl, nothing more, but Jen kicks Storm. Her foot slams square into the dog's chest.

If asked what I would do in this situation, I would say that I'd go after Jen. I'd be unable to help myself. But the thought does not cross my mind. Instead, I throw myself between them, stopping Jen, and then all my attention is on Storm. She's only staggered back, with a yelp that is more confusion than pain, but I'm on my knees, cradling her.

Then I hear a snarl and a thump and a gasp, and I turn to see Jen pinned against the wall. And the person pinning her is Petra. She has Jen against the wall, shirt bunched in her fists. The look on Petra's face is exactly the one I would have expected on my own. Blind rage.

"You do not ever touch that dog," Petra says between clenched teeth. "You do not ever touch Casey."

"I-It was a mistake," Jen stammers. "I'm sorry, Casey. Is she okay? Should I get someone?"

I ignore Jen as I check Storm. She's breathing fine. My finger prods make her flinch but not whimper. She's rubbing against my legs, looking for comfort, and that upsets me more than the kick itself. My dog has known nothing but kindness from humans. People here fawn over her, sneak her treats, pet her, offer to take her for runs. As the only pet in town, she's a pampered princess. Now someone has hurt her. She keeps sneaking glances at Jen.

"Just go," I say without looking up.

"Is she—?"

"You *kicked* her. Whether she's physically hurt or not, she isn't okay."

"I'm sorry. I really am. When I was a kid, a dog attacked . . . I'm sorry. I just reacted."

I pat Storm and get to my feet.

"I was trying to accept your petition," I say, my voice cold. "You brought it. I was taking it. We all know there's a problem. We know people aren't happy. And we're trying like hell to figure out what to do about it."

"I was afraid—"

"That I'd burn the petition before Eric saw it? Tell me, Jen, what have I *ever* done to make you think I'd do *anything* except present it to him?"

"I—"

"Use your goddamn brain for once. I know you have one. Fifty people can swear they signed your petition, so how the hell could I make it disappear?"

I shake my head. "Just go, okay? Take the petition or leave it. I don't give a damn. Just—"

A crash sounds inside the station.

SIXTEEN

I race for the door, and I don't even have it open before I hear voices. I throw open the door to see a half dozen people bearing down on Brady's cell.

"What the hell?" I say.

The guy in the lead—a new resident named Roy—points at me. "You, stay back."

"What the *fuck*?" I barrel in. "You do not ever tell me to do anything. Get the hell out of here. All of you."

Everyone except Roy stops. They don't leave, though. They just stop. He keeps going, barging into the cell room.

"Talk to me," Brady says, gripping the bars. "Please just talk to me."

I march past the mob. "Roy? You have ten seconds to get out of there or you are under arrest."

"Yeah?"

He steps up to me. He's at least six-two and probably two hundred and fifty pounds. It's not muscle, but he's still more than twice my size.

"Try that again, girlie," he says.

I reach for my gun. Then I stop. I see myself pulling it. I see myself pointing it. I see him laughing. And then I see Blaine, hear *him* laugh. A drop of sweat trickles down my hairline. I leave my gun holstered.

"Yeah, I didn't think so," he says. "Get out of my way."

I cannot get angry. Cannot get defensive. Cannot show this asshole what a mistake he's making, because if I do, I know how this ends up. With a bullet through his chest.

At a noise behind me, I glance to see Petra. Her eyes still blaze with that fire from earlier, and I put up a hand to stop her.

"Go get the boys, please," I say. "We seem to have a situation."

She stands her ground. I meet her gaze. She nods, abruptly, and then shoulders past the others.

"Yeah," Roy says. "Run and get 'the boys.' Their girlie needs some help."

"What do you want?" I say.

It's Brady who responds first. "These people see what you're doing to me, the injustice, and they aren't going to stand for it."

"Yeah, he's right," Roy says. "We see the injustice here. The injustice of being forced to live with a killer."

"No one said he—" I begin.

"I haven't killed anyone," Brady cuts in. "I didn't shoot those people. I'm being framed."

"See?" Roy says, his voice rising for the others. "Told you it was murder. *Multiple* murders, like I said. That's the only reason they'd build him his own private jail. He's a fucking psychopath."

"What? Wait," Brady says. "No. I didn't—"

"We want a trial," Roy says. "Now."

"How?" I say. "He didn't commit any crimes here."

"See?" Brady says. "I haven't done any—"

"Shut. Up." I glower at him. "These men aren't here to set you free, you idiot."

"Hell, yeah. We'll set him free," Roy says. "Swinging from the end of a rope."

"Are you fucking nuts?" It's Jen, shoving her way through.

"What the hell?" Brady says. "Did he say—"

"It's called a lynch mob," I say. "But if you want them to let you out and give you a trial, just let me know."

I turn to Roy. "Get the hell out of my station."

"*Your* station?" He snorts. "You're the sheriff's playmate, little girl. Now hand over those keys and let us clean up his mess."

"I'm going to count to three. When I finish, if you're still here, you'll be sharing the cell with this guy, and I really don't think you want that."

He laughs. Then he lunges. I duck, grab him by the arm, and throw him down. He hits the floor with a thud. I'm on him in a blink, pinning his arm behind his back.

"Holy *shit*," Brady says.

"I'm making the same offer to everyone else," I call. "Three seconds to get out. Which doesn't mean I won't remember all your faces."

Two leave as Roy rants and writhes beneath me. A guy named Cecil sidles into the cell room.

"Just let him go, Casey," he says. "We don't need to get Eric involved."

Jen laughs, "Seriously? Hell, yeah, Casey, just let that asshole walk away. No harm, no foul." She moves up to Cecil. "You cowardly piece of shit."

"Cecil, get out of here," I say. "You—"

I notice the knife at the last second. I'm distracted, pinning Roy's arm, his other one free to pull a penknife from his pocket. I see his arm move. I see the knife flash. But I'm too late to stop it, and it rams into my jacket. It gets caught there, and only the tip sinks into my side, but my reaction gives him the leverage he needs to throw me off. Before I can recover, he plows his fist into my jaw.

I fly backward. Jen lets out a squawk of alarm. Outside, Storm is going crazy barking. I barely hear her, just like I barely notice the remaining mob surge forward. I see only that knife coming at me again.

I am on the floor, pain throbbing through me, looking up at Roy, and I don't see him—I see four thugs in an alley. It's like I'm back there, and it's happening again, only this time I know what's coming. This time, I will not go down under a hail of blows and kicks. This time, it's *one* guy, and I am prepared, and he is going to pay.

Roy slashes at me. I catch his arm, and I wrench. He drops the knife. I kick it away, and then I throw him down. He falls and I'm on him, my fists and boots slamming into him.

A hand lands on my shoulder. I wheel, fist flying up. I see Jen's face. See her eyes widen. I manage to divert my blow, but then

Cecil has me by the collar, dragging me off Roy, saying, "Hey, that's *enough*."

"Fucking hell it is," Jen says.

She goes at him, and I see Roy crawling for the knife. I lunge and land on it, and he slams his fist into the side of my head.

I grab the knife from under me and flip over, brandishing it, and he lunges at me with a snarl . . . just as Kenny and Sam race in. They manage to haul him back.

I'm getting to my feet when I see Brady out of the corner of my eye. He's grinning. When he catches my glance, he shoots me a thumbs-up.

"That was fucking awesome," he says. "I gotta say, I've been complaining about the entertainment here, and you guys delivered. Hey, big guy, that 'little girl' kicked your ass, huh?"

"Shut the fuck up," I say as I rise. "Kenny? Secure—" Blood trickles into my mouth. I wipe it away. "Secure Roy. And—" I hear the slap of the front door. "Hey! No one leaves—"

The thunder of running boots cuts me short. Dalton barrels through with, "What the hell is going . . ." He sees me, staggering, blood dripping.

His eyes go wide. Then he pulls himself up short and wheels on the remaining mob. "You heard Casey. None of you fucking *moves*. Anyone who does will spend the rest of the *year* on shit duty."

"We—" one begins.

"You witnessed an officer being assaulted, and you stood and fucking watched it happen. I don't want to hear a word from any of you. Sit on the floor. Shut your mouths. And pray that when it comes time to pass sentence, I'm not *half* as pissed off as I am right now. Sam? Get out there and watch them."

As soon as Sam leaves the cell room, Dalton kicks the door shut with, "Better if I don't see their fucking faces right now."

He strides to me.

"I'm fine," I say. Which is a lie. I'm seeing double, my nose is streaming blood, and my lip is split. But I'm upright, and that's the important thing. I'd seen the look in Roy's eyes when he came at me with that knife, and I know I got off easy.

Dalton takes my chin in his hand, and he's checking my injuries when I catch his eye and shake my head. His lips tighten. He knows what I mean. It's what stopped him on his way in—made him tend to the mob before me. The job comes first, as long as I'm standing.

"Where's Will?" he asks Jen.

I answer, "Hatchet mishap with the lumber party. Nothing serious."

He grunts and tells Jen to get the backup first-aid kit from the clinic. She takes off. Then he strides into the next room, without a word to anyone there, and returns with a wet cloth. He hands it to me, and I press it against my lip as he walks to Roy.

"What the fuck happened here?" Dalton asks.

Roy blinks, as if surprised he's asking him first.

Before Roy can answer, Brady says, "These rednecks formed themselves a lynch mob, Sheriff. Took advantage of you and the deputy being gone and tried to storm the station. Your detective stopped him. He pulled a knife on her. Knocked her around. But she took him down. Too bad she wasn't carrying her sidearm."

"She's got her fucking sidearm," Dalton says, his gaze on Roy. "She knew she didn't need to use it on a useless piece of shit like you."

"I wanted to try him," Roy says. "A trial. Not a lynch—"

"You said you were going to string me up," Brady says. "We call that a lynching where I come from."

"Can you add anything to contradict what I just heard?" Dalton asks Roy.

"She went off on me. Started beating the shit out of me."

"*After* you stabbed and punched her." Brady glances at Dalton. "The stabbing was unprovoked. She took him down after that. There was a commotion, and he got free and started hitting her. That's when she went off on him." He smiles. "It was awesome."

No, it wasn't. I lost control. I don't say that now. I've been a cop long enough to know this is a situation I discuss with my superior officer . . . alone.

"Feel free to correct him," Dalton says to Roy.

"You're listening to a murdering—?"

"Feel free to *correct* him."

Roy glowers.

"Yeah, that's what I thought." Dalton returns to the main room and comes back with a handcuff strap. He tosses it to Kenny. "Let him chill in the icehouse until I feel like talking to him. Better grab him a parka, too. It'll be a while."

SEVENTEEN

Dalton deals with the mob. None of them may have thrown a punch, but in Rockton, witnessing a crime and doing nothing about it is a punishable offense. This law of Dalton's wouldn't fly down south, but up here, with such a small police force, we can reasonably expect better.

I've let Storm in, and I'm consoling her while Dalton chews out the mob. When Jen comes in with the first-aid container, I point to the back porch. She hesitates, but I march her out.

"Here's—" she begins, holding out the kit.

I thrust the discarded petition at her. "You set this up. You knew Eric and Will were both gone. You chose that moment to hit me with this."

"Yes, I did. I wanted to talk to you alone because you're the only person who actually listens to me."

"You took advantage of that to distract me while the others—"

"What? My petition was for a public inquiry, not a trial. Sure as hell not a lynch mob."

"Bullshit. You kicked Storm, knowing that was a guaranteed distraction—"

"*No.*" Guilt flits over her face as looks at the dog. "I'm genuinely sorry about that. If Eric wants to come up with a punishment for animal abuse, I'll take it. I kicked her, and that was uncalled-for. My past experience with dogs isn't an excuse. I reacted badly." She eases back and eyes me. "I think you know something about that, considering those scars on your arms and the way you went after Roy."

"That—"

"In your case, it was justifiable anger. Mine was not."

She's being reasonable, and I'm not sure how to handle that. I feel as if I'm being set up, and I'd prefer the old Jen, someone to snap back at me, someone I can rightly vent my rage on.

"You guys need to do something about Roy." Before I can snarl a response, she lifts her hands. "Yeah, I know, you don't need me giving you more work right now, but he's a nutjob."

"We've had a few run-ins with him already. He has issues with authority."

She snorts a laugh. "That's putting it mildly. What you just saw didn't come out of nowhere. I can tell you stories . . . and he's only been here a month."

"If you can tell stories, you should. As part of the militia."

"I did not have anything to do with what happened in there," she says, ignoring my comment. "You aren't going to find any of those names on my petition. I knew you were alone here, and Roy knew you were alone here. Two totally separate incidents."

I open the first-aid kit.

"People don't like what's happening with this Brady guy," she says.

"Really?" I scrunch my nose. "Personally, I can't see it, but that may be because I'm seeing two of everything right now, after getting clocked by a guy who . . . Wait, *he's* upset about Brady, isn't he?"

"I'm just—"

"You're pointing out the obvious, as usual." I yank out a bandage and lift my shirt. "You have your petition because you think we're overreacting. Roy tried to lynch Brady because he thinks we're *under*reacting."

"You need to clean that wound first." She picks up my discarded wet cloth from the railing.

Dalton peeks out the door.

"She's fine," Jen says.

Dalton ignores her and says to me, "I'm still dealing with these idiots, but if you need anything . . ."

I manage a smile for him. "I can stitch myself, remember?"

"Yeah, but don't. You need me, shout. Otherwise, I can help in five minutes."

He retreats inside.

I turn to Jen. "I know how you feel. You've made that abundantly clear. I'm fucking up, as usual. Now just go."

"I just think it's a dangerous situation. Especially after this. Whatever Brady did, does it really deserve this treatment?"

I stare at her. Then I march inside.

Dalton stops lecturing the coconspirators and arches his brows. I wave for him to continue. Then I unlock a drawer and remove the letter that came with Brady. I walk outside and hand it to Jen.

After she's read it, I give her the details.

When I finish, she's pale. Then she says, "Maybe Roy has the right idea."

"Really? That's your takeaway from this?" I throw up my hands. "I try to share information with you, so you understand why we're keeping him locked up, and you do a total one-eighty. Now we're wrong for not lynching him."

"I never said lynching."

"We are doing our best here," I say. "We need people to trust us. Like I trusted you with that letter. If I find out that anyone else knows those details? I know where it came from."

"I don't like this," she says as I walk away.

"No one does," I say, and take Storm inside to help Dalton.

The council has decided not to let Dalton go to Dawson. After what happened today, the situation is "too precarious." I can bitch about that, but they aren't wrong.

We're on Dalton's balcony, which is our bedroom in good weather . . . and sometimes in bad. I've been here nine months, and the allure of falling asleep to the howl of wolves and the perfume of pine hasn't worn off. We have a mattress out here, and we're lying on it, with Storm at our feet as we talk.

Roy is still in the icehouse. We gave him winter gear and a sleeping bag. He'll be fine. One of the militia guys is in there with him, just in case he decides to sabotage the ice. I wouldn't put it past him. Jen's right that he's been trouble. What happened today, though, was worse than I expected. Far worse.

"He's going back," Dalton says. "As soon as we figure out the shit with Brady, Roy is going home."

"Is that . . . a good idea? They made Diana stay because she posed a security threat."

"Nah, they made Diana stay because they're assholes. They've kicked people out before. They have blackmail to make sure they keep their mouth shut about us. We'll work it out. He's not staying, though. He could have killed you. His so-called backstory says nothing about violence, meaning his file is bullshit."

I don't pursue this. After Dalton finished dealing with the mob, he'd gone to the icehouse, and then Roy got to see how Dalton really felt about him attacking me. It wasn't physical. Dalton isn't going to rough up a bound man. But he managed to scare the shit out of Roy without lifting a finger. So while Dalton's calm now, I'd like to back-burner the issue of Roy.

We discuss the mob. Dalton's furious about that, too, especially since they waited until I was alone at the station. That is unacceptable. They've each been sentenced to six months of chopping and sanitation duty, the worst punishment I've seen Dalton inflict since I arrived. This was an uprising. A revolt. We cannot afford that in our little powder keg of a town.

The petition doesn't help. The fact that we have residents complaining that we're erring too far on *both* sides means we're, well, screwed. We can't inch in either direction without pissing someone off.

"Stay the course," I say. "That's my advice, if you want it."

"Course I do."

"Then we continue on as planned. Ignore those who argue that Brady deserves more freedoms. The bigger threat is Roy's gang. If that continues, we clamp down."

"Martial law." Dalton shakes his head. "I saw it done when I was growing up, and I was kinda proud of the fact that I've never had to resort to that. Thought that meant I was a better sheriff. Bullshit. It just means I got lucky."

"Rockton has never dealt with anything like Brady before. Right now, I think we're just in the unsettled phase. People are on edge. Once his cabin is built, they'll settle." I stretch out on top of him. "We'll be okay."

His arms go around my waist. "We will be."

Which is true. We'll be okay, as both a couple and as individuals. We'll weather this, however it plays out. The problem is everyone else. Everyone we are responsible for.

EIGHTEEN

"That is *not* perfect," Anders is saying early the next morning. "Casey cut the board backward."

"I was just—" Kenny says.

"Being supportive. Encouraging." Anders puts the board in place, and the angle is indeed the wrong way. "Well, at least it's straight. A for effort, Case."

I take back the board, with my middle finger raised.

As I carry it to the sawhorse, Anders says, "Casey *hates* the effort award. She wants the honest A-plus overachiever award."

"Ignore him," I say. "But yes, Kenny, you can tell me I did it wrong. I'll survive. And I'll do it right the next time."

"Overachiever," Anders calls.

Kenny comes over and helps me line up the cut. I don't tell him I can handle it. He means well. While I've chopped wood, even that was a new experience for me six months ago. When I was growing up, we never had so much as a saw in our garage. My parents would say sharp tools were unsafe, but part of it was also the mentality that such tasks were meant for people who lacked a surgeon's IQ.

Brady's new quarters are almost done, and we're spending every spare minute building.

I hand the fixed board to Kenny.

"Now it'll be a half inch too short," Anders says. "It'll leave a gap, and Brady will get his fingers through and pry it open and escape."

"It's for the bathroom interior wall."

"He'll still escape through it. Just watch. All because you cut an angle backward."

"Didn't we have to take down half a wall because someone put the damn door on the wrong side?"

"You said the door went on the west wall, and you know I'm directionally challenged."

"The sun was setting. It doesn't set in the *east*."

Jen walks by with a bucket of nails. "You two keep bickering like that, the sheriff's gonna get jealous. Sounds like someone has a crush."

"Only if you're twelve," Anders says. "Grown-ups bicker 'cause it's fun."

"The word you want is 'annoying,'" she says.

"You only say that because you feel left out. Hey, Jen, can I have a few of those screws?"

"They're nails."

"I know, but yesterday I asked you for screws, and you brought me nails."

She shakes her head.

"That's an opening," he says. "You're supposed to make a sarcastic retort."

"The only ones I can think of are puns on screwing and nailing, and every woman in Rockton knows not to mention those words around you, Deputy, or you'll think it's an invitation."

"Ouch."

"Good one, though," I say. "A little below the belt, but it's an A for effort."

Kenny snorts at that, and he starts to say something when I hear "Will? Will!" and Paul races around the neighboring building, pulling up short when he sees us. "Will *and* Casey. Perfect. I need you both at the station. There's something wrong with the prisoner."

Anders takes off ahead, Storm follows at my side.

"You didn't leave him alone, right?" I ask as Paul runs a pace behind.

Silence. Then, "He was sick, and I had to get Will, and there was no one else—"

"Is his door locked?"

"The station door?"

"*Cell.* Did you open his cell?"

"I don't have the key. Eric took it. He got called across town. As he was leaving, the prisoner said he had to take a shit, and Eric said to hold it or use the bucket. He wasn't leaving the key."

I send up a silent thanks to Dalton.

I yell ahead to Anders, "Careful! I think it's a trap," and he raises a hand, as if to say he's already figured that out. The medical emergency is a hackneyed escape ploy. The fact that it happened while Dalton was out? And after Brady tried to get him to leave the key? Yeah, this screams setup, and not a very clever one at that.

I race into the station to find Anders outside the cell. Inside, Brady is on all fours, vomiting. Vomiting hard, as if he's going to puke up his stomach lining. His back arches like something out of a horror movie, his body convulsing before he spews more of his stomach contents onto the floor.

Paul looks at me. "Should I go find Eric for the key?"

I take mine from my pocket. Then I proceed with measured steps toward the cell. Paul stares at me, and I see that once again, we are trapped in this dilemma, where caution seems callous.

Anders looks at me, his mouth set in a tight line. He knows this can be faked. Stick your finger down your throat to start the vomiting and then act out the rest.

"Guys?" Paul says.

"Lock the back door," I say, and then I do that with the front. As Anders holds open the back door, he says, "Out," to Paul . . . who hasn't moved.

"But he—"

"—could be just hoping we throw open the cell door and let him make a run for it."

"You think he's faking?" Paul says.

I say, "I think every second you debate whether to do as I said, you delay us helping him if he's *not.*"

Anders shuts and locks the rear door as he says, "Stay here then. And don't expect me to forget that you disobeyed an order."

We don't hear Paul's protest. I'm at the cell door with my key in one hand, gun in the other. Storm stands beside me. I hand Anders the key, and he unlocks the door. Brady is still doubled over, dry-heaving now, panting hard and letting out whimpers of pain between breaths. The stink of vomit fills the room.

Anders opens the door and steps over a puddle. His gaze goes to something behind Brady. He motions to me that he's going to bend over the heaving man to retrieve it. I stand poised while he crouches. What he lifts is Brady's breakfast tray. He backs out of the cell to set it on the floor. Then he starts in again.

Anders makes it one step. Brady lurches. I shout "Will!" but Anders is already on him, pinning him to the floor, a slap as Brady's body hits the vomit pool. Brady's arms fly out to the sides, as if in surrender.

"Dog," he rasps. "The dog."

He points in my direction, and I'm not sure if I'm mishearing, but he just keeps pointing. Then he starts heaving again, his body jerking and convulsing under Anders.

"Lock the door," Anders says.

I hesitate—I'm loath to lock Anders in there with Brady—but it's only a split second. Then I lock it and train my gun on Brady as Anders rises off him.

Brady stays facedown, racked with dry heaves.

"I need you to put your hands behind your back," Anders says.

At first, Brady just moans. Anders repeats the command, and Brady complies. Anders snaps on a wrist strap. He looks from me to the puddles to the food tray. It's mostly empty, the water and coffee drained. If Brady just finished his meal—including two drinks—that could account for the quantity of vomit. That tray, though, also suggests he might *not* be faking.

"Here?" Anders says, and I know he's asking whether we should attempt to care for Brady in the cell.

If it is poison, we need him at the clinic. He can't even lie flat in the cell, and it's such a mess that it'll impede our efforts.

"He's secured," I say.

"Can you walk?" Anders asks Brady.

The younger man puts one foot out and begins to rise. It's slow, unsteady, but even if he forced the vomiting, he will be weak.

Anders helps him to his feet. Then, "Paul?"

"Yes, sir." Paul hurries over from where he's been watching in silence. "I can help you carry him."

"Not you. Get Kenny."

Paul flushes. He knows Anders is saying: *I don't trust you.* He bobs his head and runs out the front door. I relock it behind him. Then I move to the cell and unlock that. Anders has Brady up, supporting him. I open the door and move in to help, but Anders says, "I've got it. Just stand point, please."

I step back and keep the gun ready as they walk out of the cell. A key scrapes in the front door lock. Then it stops.

"Casey? Will?"

I call for Dalton to come in, and he finishes unlocking the door. He steps through, sees Brady, and curses. Then he hurries over to help.

If there is an advantage to having parents who raised me to be a doctor, it is that I don't need to consult our medical texts to recognize the signs of poisoning. I assess Brady as Dalton and Anders carry him to the clinic.

He has a fever. He's struggling to breathe. His heart is racing.

Oliver Brady has been poisoned.

At the clinic, we pump his stomach. It's only our second time using the procedure. In Brady's case, after all that vomit, there really isn't much to pump, but it's all we know.

Brady is thankfully unconscious by this point. I say thankfully, because we would not have earned his confidence if he'd been awake, hearing Dalton reading aloud from a chapter on emergency poisoning treatment as Anders and I worked.

And he really wouldn't want to hear us concur that pumping his stomach is the extent of what we can do. After the pumping, we put him on an IV to replace fluids. Then we wait.

It's two hours before he wakes. I'm collapsed in a bedside chair. Anders sits on the floor beside me. Dalton has gone back to the station to secure the scene.

Brady wakes, and the first thing he says is, "Dog."

I remember him saying that in the cell, and again I think I must be mishearing.

"Doug?" I say. We do have a resident named Doug . . . who also works as a chef.

He shakes his head and rasps, "Dog. Your dog food."

Anders rises. "You think someone served you dog food?"

More head shaking, Brady's face screwing up in frustration. "Your dog. The food. Poison. Did she eat—?" He coughs and winces as the cough sets his raw throat aflame. "Did your dog eat the food? Tried— tried to warn—"

"You were trying to warn us that your food was poisoned," I say. "Before my dog ate the rest."

He nods, eyelids fluttering as if even keeping them open is too much effort.

"Is she okay?" he manages.

"She doesn't eat anything without permission. The sheriff got your tray out of there. We'll be analyzing it for poison."

He gives a harsh laugh, wincing again. "Pretty sure it'll come back positive."

NINETEEN

I've lied to Brady. I have no way to analyze his food. Down south, we'd just ship the sample off to the lab. Up here . . .

Before I requisitioned a Breathalyzer and urine-testing kits, Dalton used the old-fashioned methods—walk in a straight line, recite the alphabet backward, let me see your eyes . . . I need something more scientific. To be honest, though, I've never used the formal tests and gotten a result *different* from his assessment. It just stops people from protesting their innocence when I have hard evidence.

Our poison-testing method is not unlike Dalton's sobriety testing. Someone finds berries or mushrooms in the forest, brings them back to town, and he says, "Yeah, don't eat that." Food spoilage is a bigger poisoning risk, but Rockton has very stringent food-handling rules, and the problems occur only when someone says, "I'm sure that meat I left out of the icebox is fine."

The one person who might have been able to help us here is Sharon—the woman we just buried. Not only was she a gardener—familiar with poisonous plants—but for Sharon that was more than theoretical knowledge. She was one of the residents the council snuck in, a wealthy woman who'd poisoned her husband and his pregnant mistress. Even in that case, though, we could hardly have gone to her and said, "Hey, you wouldn't know anything about poisons, would you? Random question."

We don't have any chemists either. The two residents with that sort of experience are both dead, which has at least temporarily fixed Rockton's drug problem.

So I'm not sure what to do, beyond saying, yes, Brady was poisoned, and it seems unlikely that it *wasn't* in his food. As for what it could have been, I'm stumped. We don't use pesticides in our greenhouse. We certainly aren't spraying our yards to control "weeds." Nor do we use poison for vermin. That's just too dangerous.

I'll need to dig up all the chemicals we *do* have. I'm hoping to narrow the field by figuring out suspects and what sources of poison they have access to. The obvious place to start is by tracing the path Brady's breakfast took.

Dalton was the last person to handle it. He took the tray from the delivery person and gave it to Brady while Paul stood guard and the delivery person waited. So two people were watching the whole time, meaning I can eliminate Dalton, should anyone else suspect him.

Who delivered the food? That'd be Kenny.

Then I need to consider those who prepared the food. There's Brian, who made the muffin and poured the coffee. Before that comes the person who brought the tray—with scrambled eggs and sausage—from the kitchen. Then the person who made the eggs and cooked the sausage, as well as everyone else who was in the kitchen at the time.

Finally, the chain goes back to the guy who made the sausage. Mathias.

"I did not poison the sausage," Mathias says when I walk into the butcher shop.

"Yes, I know."

That stops him, bloody knife in hand. He wipes it on a cloth, slowly, as if awaiting a punch line.

"You delivered that batch of sausage yesterday," I say. "There was no way of knowing which links would go to Brady, and you wouldn't poison innocent people."

"Thank you." He sets the knife aside and removes his apron. "I did not shoot at Mr. Brady either. I was expecting to see you after that."

"It was the wrong kind of murder."

He chuckles, pleased. When Brady first arrived, Mathias had asked if I wanted him to assess or assassinate the prisoner. If I'd pursued that, he'd have claimed he was joking. He wasn't. I have no doubt that Mathias has killed murderers. He has a modus operandi, though. Poetic justice. What Brady is accused of requires a more fitting punishment than a shot in the head.

"Also," Mathias says, "you are not convinced he is a killer."

"Are you?"

"No. But I am rarely convinced until they confess. Even that is never a guarantee. In Mr. Brady's case, though, I require more interviews to make an educated guess. Which would still not be enough to warrant capital punishment. One must be absolutely certain. Hypothetically speaking."

"I should have you speak to Roy and his crew about that."

Mathias sniffs. "Roy is a cretin. I would like to interview him."

"That can be arranged. We'd appreciate it, actually."

"So if you did not come to question me . . ."

"Even if there's no way you poisoned the sausage, I must be seen coming in here to question you. Otherwise it'll seem as if I'm excusing you because we're acquainted."

"'Acquainted'?" His brows rise. "That is an odd word to use, and I will presume you choose it because you have temporarily forgotten the French word for *friend*. Otherwise, I would be insulted."

"If I said we were friends, you'd make some comment about *that*. Now, I do need to get back to the business of finding who poisoned the prisoner. If you have more of that batch of sausage, I'll take some for analysis."

"You mean you'll eat it."

"That's the best way to test it. Also, I missed lunch."

He walks into the back, leaving the door open. "So it *was* poison." I list the symptoms.

"Interesting," he says as he returns with a package of sausage. "Did Mr. Brady say anything?"

"Sure." I make retching noises.

He shakes his head.

"At the time, he only mentioned Storm. When we removed his food tray, he was worried she'd eat what was left and get sick."

His lips purse in thought. "Or worried she would eat it and *not* get sick, proving the food was not the source of the poison."

"If so, he could just say it must have been in his water or coffee. That was also the first thing he said when he woke. He was concerned that she'd eaten his food."

"Interesting," he says again.

I eye him. "In what way?"

"Just . . . interesting. I would like to speak to him later."

"I don't think he'll be in the mood for your brand of conversation."

"We will discuss dogs."

"Uh-huh . . ."

"He apparently has a fondness for them. It would be a topic of conversation—other than himself—that he might respond to."

I have a suspect for the poisoning. I'm just trying not to fixate on him, because, well, he couldn't have done it, considering he was locked in the icehouse at the time. Roy is the most obvious possibility. Less than twenty-four hours ago he wanted to try Brady, a sham trial that I'm sure would have resulted in a guilty verdict and a death sentence.

Obviously Roy didn't do it. But he didn't act alone yesterday. When I track the path that Brady's food took, I'm looking for one of those names, somewhere along the line. When there are none, I start to investigate the whereabouts of those five residents who'd been with him.

I've found a possible lead. Cecil was supposed to work at the main food depot this morning. He would have prepared Brady's breakfast . . . if Dalton hadn't yanked him onto chopping duty. It would be easy, though, for Cecil to pop into the food depot and wander around a bit, poison Brady's tray . . .

I'm heading to the depot when Val hurries up alongside me.

"It seems I've been trailing one stop behind you," she says. "I wanted to ask if I can sit with the prisoner."

"Hmm?" I catch a glimpse of Diana up ahead, coming out of the bakery.

"Take a turn playing nursemaid," Val says. "I think Diana's up next. Looks like she's got a coffee to keep her awake."

"Right." I'm distracted, and it takes effort to follow what Val's saying. "So you want to take her shift?"

"Oliver was awake when I went by earlier. Nicole refused to talk to him, so I think he's getting bored. If I go in when he's feeling lonely and groggy, it will help establish me as an ally." She gives a look, like a five-year-old whispering plans to eavesdrop on her parents' party. "I've managed to establish a rapport that I feel will be useful."

"Uh-huh."

I could tell her that I'm no longer convinced we need this. But that look really is childlike, her eyes glittering. Val wants to be helpful, and the idea of playing spy with Brady makes her feel both happy and useful.

"Sure," I say. Then I call, "Diana?" When she stops, I say to Val, "Tell her you're taking her shift. I'll swing by in a couple of hours to see if he's ready to go back to his cell. If not, Diana can take over then."

TWENTY

No one at the food depot saw Cecil there that morning. It's still possible he was—he'd have access. It's also possible there were more than five people following Roy's madness. I'm going to need a complete list of everyone who could have come in contact with Brady's food.

First, I want some idea of what kind of poison could have been used, in hopes of linking the two—who had access to both the food and the poison. Dalton's helping me compile a list of potential toxins. We're walking around Rockton checking labels on everything he can think of. We're in the brewery at the Roc, where Isabel is explaining that not only is this the most secure location in town, but the only poison there is methanol.

"He'd have spit it out," she says. "He's not going to think we just brewed a batch of cheap coffee."

"We *don't* brew cheap coffee," Dalton says. "He'd know that by now."

Which is true. Supply issues in Rockton are a matter of transport and storage rather than cost. Our milk might be powdered, along with most of our eggs, but when it comes to dry goods, we can get the good stuff. Which is one reason why the money Brady brings us won't impact our basic lifestyle.

"Are we sure he *was* poisoned?" Isabel continues. "I treated enough bulimic patients to know how easy it is to make yourself sick."

"He had symptoms other than vomiting. They were consistent with poison."

She's not the first person to mention this possibility. Each time someone suggests that Brady faked it, I feel a nudge at the back of my mind, the one that says *You're missing something.*

"Could it be environmental?" Isabel says. "God knows, there's enough in our forest that can kill you."

"We do have water hemlock and false hellebore," I say. "Which vie for the title of most poisonous plant in North America."

Isabel sighs. "Of course they do."

"Hey, at least it's not Australia. Everything's poisonous there."

"I would rather face a kangaroo than a grizzly. Or a cougar. Or a wolf. Or a wolverine. Or a feral dog, feral pig . . ."

"There are no feral pigs in the Yukon."

"Just the ones Rockton released. Like the dogs, the cats, the hostiles . . . Because our forest really needed *more* threats."

"Water hemlock's rare," Dalton says. "Only seen it twice this far north. False hellebore is the problem. Which is why I don't tell folks that real hellebore is edible. Can't take the chance. The symptoms fit, though."

"But it'd be tough to get and mix into his food or drink," I say. "That's why we're looking in town for poisons—"

There's a shout from outside. Then what sounds like . . .

"Is that the bell?" I say.

We installed a bell this winter. Another of my suggestions, after a fire burned down the lumber shed. Dalton resisted—there hadn't been a problem alerting people for the fire, and I think he didn't like the intimation that he needed a bell to make residents listen. A bell wouldn't have saved the lumber shed, so I didn't get one . . . until after Nicole was taken and rousting searchers five minutes faster might have helped.

"If that's another goddamn prank . . ." Dalton says as he strides from the brewery.

Shortly after we installed the bell someone rang it in the middle of the night. Drunk, obviously. Rang it and ran . . . leaving boot prints in the snow, which I matched to a perpetrator, whom Dalton then sentenced to go to each and every person in town and say, "I'm the fucking idiot who rang the fucking bell at two in the fucking morning. I'm sorry."

No one has touched the bell since.

As Dalton jogs out, I hear "Eric? Eric!" from several directions.

Jen races around the corner and sees us. "Finally. The lumber shed is on fire."

Dalton stops so abruptly that I bash into him. I know exactly what he's thinking. That the lumber shed cannot possibly be on fire nine months after we rebuilt it. Jen must be making a very bad joke. And yet one sniff of the air brings the smell of wood fire.

He shouts for everyone to "get to the goddamn fire," infuriated that they went looking for him rather than tackling the actual problem.

As we run, Jen explains that Anders is already at the shed, with as many people as he could gather. He sent her to find Dalton and me.

People join us as we run. They hear the bell and smell smoke and see us running, and they fall into our wake. This is Dalton's success as a leader. People don't smell that smoke and retreat. They join the fight.

As we run, Dalton barks questions. How did the fire start? *When* did it start? Who saw it first? How bad is the damage?

Jen doesn't know. She wasn't first on the scene. Dalton keeps questioning; I retreat into my head, into my own questions.

There is no chance that the lumber shed accidentally caught ablaze. We are a town made of wood surrounded by a forest of the same. Whatever dangers lurk in the wilderness, none approaches that of fire.

On the drive up from Whitehorse, one of the most memorable sights I saw was the markers by the roadside, memorials to past blazes. Each was labeled with a year, and I hadn't really understood the power of fire until I saw those signs and the forest they marked. Vast swaths of wasteland left by flames that had blazed before I was born. Dalton would point out the signs of rejuvenation in that seeming wasteland. He'd even say that fire served a purpose in the forest: rebirth. He saw hope and new life; I saw death and destruction.

The precautions we take against fire border on insane. Smoking is prohibited. Only a select few can use kerosene at night. Candles are restricted to certain areas, like the Lion and the Roc, where the staff can ensure they're put out at night's end. Fireplaces are inspected weekly. Bonfires are permitted only in the town square, only on designated days, and only with supervision and sand buckets. The list goes on. Before the lumber shed, the last fire had been years ago, when lightning struck a building.

This is arson, as it was before. That fire had been set to cover a crime. This time . . .

There is only one explanation.

"Eric," I call as I jog up to him.

He looks over as if startled, having been too busy to notice that I'd fallen behind.

"I need to . . ." I trail off. "To check something." Which is not an excuse at all, and any other time, he'd call me on it, but he's focused on that burning shed.

"I'll be right back." I turn to Jen. "Make sure he watches his arm."

A nod from her, and she will, if only because she's one of the few who'll tell him off. Whether he listens is a whole other matter, but the risk of him injuring his arm is minor compared to what I fear.

I'm running as fast as my bad leg will allow. I tear down the narrow passage between two buildings, and I fly out onto the street just as another figure heads the opposite way.

"Kenny?" I call.

He looks over but doesn't stop. "There's a fire."

"I know, but you're posted at the clinic."

"Val's there." He keeps running. "Brady's secure. She said I can go help . . ."

The rest is muffled as he runs into the passage between buildings.

"No!" I shout. "Get back to your post!"

He's gone. I slow, torn between running after him and—

A bang comes to my right. From the direction of the clinic. My brain screams gunshot, but as I spin, I see it's just a door slamming shut as Diana runs from her apartment.

She sees me. "Casey?"

Come with me. That's what I want to say. *I need you. Come with me.*

I can't, though. Both because I don't trust her, and because I can't put her in danger.

"I need someone at the clinic," I say. "Get . . ." I trail off. Get who?

"Mathias," I say. "Get Mathias for me."

She nods, no question, presuming it's a medical emergency. Also, she's happy to avoid going near the fire. I don't blame her for that—she nearly died in the last one.

I run for the clinic. I know what this is. A diversion. Everyone in town is dealing with that fire. No one is paying attention to Oliver Brady.

Even Kenny is gone, because Val wants to prove herself. As soon as Kenny asked Val what she wanted him to do, she would tell him to go help with the fire. Brady's hands were secured. He was weak from the vomiting. He was no threat.

The possibility that he was *under* threat? I could not trust her to realize Brady had faced two assassination attempts, and Kenny wasn't only there to make sure Brady didn't escape.

As soon as I dash into the clinic, there's a crash in the examination room. I already have my gun out. Now I put my back to the wall. The door is beside me. I watch the knob. When it turns, I aim, take a deep breath—

The door opens, and Val appears, stumbling through. A hand on her arm propels her forward. She sees me. "Case—"

She's yanked back before she can finish. The door slams shut.

"Lay down your weapon, Detective," a voice says. "Or I slit Valerie's throat."

TWENTY-ONE

When I hear that voice, my gut clenches.

"Put your weapon on the floor. Open the door. Kick the gun through. Then follow with your hands up. Otherwise, I'll kill her. You don't want to call my bluff."

I glance at the exterior door. Hoping for what? Divine intervention? Even if Diana finds Mathias, he's not going to get me out of this. There are exactly two solutions.

I do as I'm told.

Or Val dies.

And here is the terrible truth: I should stand my ground.

It is the coldly correct answer to this dilemma. The only way out of the clinic is the door behind me. When a suspect escaped through the back last winter, Dalton ordered that exit boarded up. I thought he was overreacting. Now I am glad of it. There's one way out. I'm blocking it. If I do not respond to the threat, it ends here.

I should let it end here.

I cannot let it end here.

I put Val in that room. I need to get her out of it and stalling won't help because there is no magical third solution.

"I want to trade," I say. "Val and I will switch spots. You can take me hostage."

"I don't want you, Detective. Val here will do as I say. Won't you, Val?"

"Casey?" Val's voice quavers. "Just do what he wants. Please."

I set my gun in front of the door. "My weapon is down."

"Good. When I open the door, you'll kick it through." A pause. "Step back first. I want to see you across the room. Then on my signal, you'll walk forward and kick it through. If I see you charging the door or doing anything other than giving me your weapon, Val dies."

I back up across the room, within the sight line from the door. It creaks opens just enough for me to boot the gun inside. The waiting figure makes no motion to bend and retrieve the gun. That would give me an opening for attack.

"Walk my way," he says.

I reach the door, pull back my good leg, and . . . kick the door with everything I've got.

It flies wide open, and Brady falls back.

"Knock him down!" I shout to Val as I go for my gun.

Val flies at Brady. She swings, and her fist connects with his jaw, and her eyes widen as if in surprise at actually making contact. But it's not enough. Not nearly enough.

Brady barely staggers, recovers fast and lunges at me, and I see a knife raised and twist out of the way just as it comes down. But that twist lands me out of reach of the gun. He scrambles for it. I kick. My foot strikes his jaw.

"Val!" I shout. "The gun."

She runs and snatches it up. Brady comes at me again. My fist plows into his jaw, in the same spot my foot had. He falls back snarling, but it's only a moment and then he's charging me with the knife.

I dodge his slash and dive over the hospital bed. There, on the floor, are the remnants of his wrist restraints. He cut them free with the knife. Where did he get—?

He circles around the bed, advancing as I retreat.

"Val?" I say. "Can you shoot?"

Her eyes round, as if I'm asking her to turn backward cartwheels. Shit. That means the gun is useless—Brady knows she won't fire it.

At least it isn't in *his* hand.

Brady keeps coming. I grab the rolling medical tray and fling it. The clatter startles him. I leap over the bed to get the gun from Val and—

She's backed across the room, and now she's by the door, weapon raised.

"If you can't shoot that," I say, "then run. Just take it and run. Get Eric."

"Val?" Brady says. "If you leave, I'll kill your detective."

"I can handle this," I say. "Just—"

He flies at me. I stand my ground, and he doesn't expect that and stops short. I slam my hand into his arm. The knife goes flying. He hits me, and I can't avoid that. The powerful blow slams into the side of my head. I stagger. Fall to one knee.

The knife. Damn it. Get the knife.

I see it. I lunge as he walks over, confident he's put me down. I slam my hand into the back of his knee. It buckles. I dive and hit the floor, shoving the knife along with me. I pick it up and—

I recognize the knife.

It's a pocket one. That's not unusual here. If you want one, you can buy it. The only reason I don't have mine is that I took it out on the jobsite to pry open a can.

"Here, Case, let me get that for you." A pocketknife appears.

"Got my own," I say. "But thanks."

I see the hand that grips the knife in my memory. I want to tell myself I'm wrong, but I have seen this knife too many times. I know who owns it.

Kenny.

I have Kenny's knife in my hand, as I'm backing into the wall. Brady keeps coming at me. I'm ready for him, ready to—

A muzzle flash from across the room. I swear I feel the bullet whiz past my head.

Val gasps in alarm. "Casey!"

"I'm fine."

"Oliver?" she says. "Stop or I'll—"

"Shoot?" he says. "Please do. With that aim, you're going to hit your own detective."

"Val?" I say. "The door is to your left. It's open. I want you to step left and back out. I've got this."

"If you leave, I'll kill Casey," Brady says.

"I'm the one holding the knife," I say.

"Doesn't matter. We both know how quickly that can change. I'm fighting for my life here. I will get that knife. I will stop you. I might kill you, but I don't want to. I just want to walk out of here."

"Do you really think I'd let a serial killer—"

"Serial killer?" He chokes on the words. "Is that what Greg told you? Figures. He didn't even keep his story consistent. Had to adapt it for the audience. A salesman to the core."

"You threatened to kill Val. You're threatening to kill me. And you're still proclaiming your innocence?"

"Because I *am* innocent. I'm fighting for my life. My actual life. I was shot at two days ago, nearly lynched yesterday, poisoned this morning—"

"Your accomplice gave you the poison."

That's the possibility that I failed to see. The niggling question in my head. I kept coming back to the possibility he'd faked it when I knew that couldn't be true. Yet faking it wasn't the only way he could be complicit.

"You're saying I knowingly put myself through that hell?" he says.

"It got you what you wanted, didn't it? And like you say, you're a desperate man."

"An innocent man, desperate to escape a death sentence. I will kill you if I have to. I don't want to. Just let me—"

He lunges, hoping I'm distracted. I feint to the side and slash. The knife slices his arm. He lets out a hiss and slams his fist into my gut. I double over, and he grabs my arm, trying to get the knife, but I grip it.

Val runs at us. She kicks at Brady, but he twists out of the way. He bodychecks her, and she goes flying. The gun fires.

I see the muzzle flare, and I dive, but Brady still has my arm. He yanks it and the knife falls. I manage to smack it away. That's all I can do—get the knife where we both can't reach it. But that move costs me a split second and in that second, Brady is on my back. He has my ponytail wrapped around his hand, wrenching my head. Then he stretches toward the knife.

"No!" It's a woman's voice, but not Val's. I manage to turn just enough to see Mathias and Diana behind Val.

Diana tries to get past, but Mathias pulls her back and shakes his head, and she turns on him with "We need—" but he silences her. Mathias is hoping Brady *will* go for that knife. It's just far enough out of reach that he'll need to shift his weight to stretch for it, and that will give me what I need to throw him off.

Brady reaches, but as soon as he sees how far it is, he stops.

"Give me the gun please, Valerie," Mathias says, his voice as calm as if he's asking her to pass the salt. "I can shoot him. You cannot."

Val steps toward him, gun outstretched. Before she reaches Mathias, Brady says, "If you take that gun from her, old man, I'll break this bitch's neck."

Val stops.

"That is misguided," Mathias says. "That *bitch* was the one keeping you alive. The one who was injured trying to save you from a lynch mob. The one attempting to determine whether or not you were guilty of your crimes. I suppose now she has her answer."

"I'm *not* guilty. I—" He stops, unfortunately, as if realizing he's about to go into a rant that could distract him. He settles for, "Damn you. Damn you all."

"Valerie?" Mathias says. "The gun please."

"Give it to me," Brady says.

Mathias chuckles. "Speaking of misguided . . ."

"I just want to get out of here," Brady says. "Either I take Casey as my prisoner, or I take the gun. Your choice."

"Take Casey," Mathias says. "Please. That will go *so* much better for you."

Brady scowls at Mathias. "Shut up, old man. I know it's a fucking strain for you, but shut the hell up." He looks at Val. "I don't want to take your detective. I know she fights to win. She will not come quietly, and I'll have to kill her. I do not want to do that. I just want to leave. Put the gun down and push it into the middle of the floor. To get to it, I'll have to let her go."

Val looks at me.

"No," I say.

Mathias echoes it. Diana says nothing, as she looks anxiously from me to Brady.

"Just give the gun a push," Brady says to Val. "If I get it, I'll walk away. If anyone else goes for it, we'll be right back here again, and I won't get out of this goddamn town without killing someone. Let me leave. Please just let me leave."

Val takes a deep breath. I can see her steeling herself. Then she exhales and pushes the gun into the middle of the room.

"Count of three," he says. "I'll let Casey go. No one moves."

He counts down. At two, he lunges for the gun. I can tell I have no chance of getting it, so I dive for the knife instead and come out in a roll. I leap to my feet, holding the knife. Brady is already across the room with the gun.

"Yeah," he says. "Don't even bother, Detective. Now, Val? I need you to come over here."

"No," I say. "She did what you asked, Oliver. You have the gun. We'll escort you to the edge of the forest. Then you're on your own."

Except he's not on his own. Never has been. Someone in this town betrayed us, and the knife in my hand tells me who that is, but I don't want to believe it.

Forget that for now. Focus on this.

Brady shakes his head. "I don't trust you."

"Then you are a fool," Mathias says. "Casey stopped that cretin from lynching you. Eric took a bullet for you. William pumped the poison from your stomach. These are not your enemies."

"Right now, they are. They won't let me walk away. They only want me to think I'm home free, so they can come after me the moment I turn my back. I need a guarantee. Val will come with me. If no one follows, I'll leave her at the spot where the sheriff got shot. If I hear anyone in pursuit, I'll have to shoot Val. Otherwise, she's yours. I just need a head start."

"And you expect us to believe that?" I say. "You told us that all you wanted was the gun. You lied."

"All I want *is* the gun. I'm borrowing her. You'll get her back. Now come over here with me, Val."

"Don't," I say. "We can't trust him."

"I'm going to count down now. Walk toward me, or I shoot."

I discreetly motion for Val to stay where she is. The moment he begins counting, I'll charge. I'm far enough to the side that it'll take him a moment to realize it. I will charge, and Mathias will get Diana and Val out and shut that door. That's all we need. I can handle Brady.

"Three."

I charge. Brady fires. I dive and the bullet hits the wall behind me. When I roll up, Val is walking toward Brady.

"Val, no," I say.

"I have to," she says. "I can do this. I'll be fine."

The gun swings in my direction.

"Val made her choice," Brady says. "The smart choice. If no one comes after me, I'll leave her at the spot where Greg's assassin shot your boyfriend. Give me one hour. She'll be fine."

Val reaches Brady. He has her turn around and raises the gun between her shoulder blades.

"Everyone step outside," Brady says. "Do not test me. If you do, you'll see exactly how desperate I am. Please. Just let me go."

Mathias and Diana retreat. I back out of the building, one slow step at a time.

TWENTY-TWO

As I back through that door, I'm torn between wanting to see someone out there . . . and praying no one is. Dalton, yes. Anders, yes.
Even some of the militia could be trusted to keep a level head and
help me end this. Sam, Nicole, Jen, Kenny . . .

Kenny.

I squelch the reminder.

There is no one outside. Not everyone will be helping with the
fire. We aren't a town of saints or heroes. Given what we actually
are—criminals and victims—it is a testament to Rockton that so many
put aside fear and self-interest to help. Those who have not, though,
certainly aren't going to come out now, as Brady steps onto the street
with a gun at Val's back.

"If you're truly innocent—" I begin.

"Trust the system?" Brady gives a harsh laugh. "There is no system here. There's just my stepfather and a mountain of money. That
old man there tells me to remember that you guys saved my life.
That's a lie. You saved an asset. If I die, you lose your share of Mount
Fortune."

"And what would we do with it?" I wave at the town. "We have
nothing to spend it on."

"Sure you do," he says. "You can spend it on the only thing that
matters. Freedom. You're trapped in this hellhole, same as me. For

money, I presume. Like guys who work on oil rigs. No one does that for fun."

I keep arguing, but I keep moving backward, too, because I know my arguments are pointless. A rich kid like him looks around and sees the wilderness equivalent of a ghetto. No one would choose to live here.

In talking, I'm only hoping that my raised voice brings Dalton or Anders running. It does not. I hear shouts over at the lumber shed, and I know they're still fighting the fire.

The fire that Brady's accomplice set.

I want to seize that as proof it isn't Kenny. He'd been outside the clinic door when it started. But it's easy to delay a fire. Start it small enough, and it could take an hour or more to be spotted. He's our carpenter. He's in charge of the lumber shed. In charge of the fire-wood stocks.

"Val?" I say.

She looks at me. Her eyes are fixed wide, and I know she's praying for me to save her. I cannot. Unless something startles Brady, I can't get the jump on him, and even if he is startled, it's just as likely he'll squeeze the trigger accidentally. I must let him take her and hope he is telling the truth. That he will free her.

I tell her that. Reassure her. *Do as he says. We'll be there within the hour. Don't leave that spot.* I'm not sure she hears any of it.

Then I ask what I must ask, as cruel as it seems to speak of anything except her immediate situation.

"Did you tell Kenny he could leave earlier?"

"W-what?" she says.

I repeat the question.

"*Tell* Kenny he could leave?" she says. "Why?"

"He was guarding the door."

"No, I—"

Brady prods her in the back. "Enough talking. I know you're hoping someone will hear us, Detective, but you also know that's not a good idea. Just let me leave. An hour from now, you'll have Val back."

———

I ask Mathias and Diana to go home. Diana hesitates, but Mathias says, "Casey fears we will raise the alarm, however unintentionally. Valerie may not be our town's most popular resident, but if people hear she has been taken hostage, and we are not running to her rescue . . . ?"

"Someone will decide to play hero," Diana says. "And he'll shoot Val." She looks at me. "You did your best, Case. Brady will let Val go—he knows if he doesn't, you'll chase him to the end of this damn forest. You can hunt for him as soon as she's safe. And it's not like he's going to get very far. Not alive, anyway. You made the right choice."

"All completely true," Mathias says. "But at this moment, Casey does not need reassurances. She needs to inform Eric. And we need to get into our homes and stay there until she requires us."

"Thank you," I say.

I take off at a jog, my expression neutral, so no one sees me running in a panic.

When I reach the shed, the fire is almost out. I can't see much damage from here. Just spirals of smoke that people with blankets are desperately trying to squelch. That smoke is a beacon for anyone who sees it, as dangerous as the fire itself.

Dalton is giving orders to wet more blankets and put them over smoldering wood.

"Save what we can," he says. "The shed's fine, but that's a shitload of wood at risk."

I look around for Anders. He's treating a burn. I walk up as he's saying it's not serious, just keep it dry.

"Will?"

He sees me. "Good. I was about to go look for you. Eric asked me to send someone ten minutes ago, and I kinda ignored him. We needed all hands. But I was getting worried."

"I'm fine. Just had to take care of something." I motion for him to follow me and walk out of earshot. "I need you to keep an eye on Kenny."

He starts to turn, but I say, "Don't look. He's supervising people carrying out wood. I need you to watch him while I talk to Eric. Do not let him out of your sight. If he even needs to go to the bathroom, make some excuse why he can't. I need about fifteen minutes."

"He isn't the one who poisoned Brady, is he?"

I pause. "I'll explain when I can. Just watch him, please."

"I will."

Dalton has spotted me, and he heads over with a quiet "Everything okay?" and a look that says he knows it's not.

"If you're done here, Storm's acting a bit off. I don't think she'd go into Brady's food, but I'm worried. Just come, and tell me I'm being paranoid."

Storm is in the station. We left her there what seemed like a lifetime ago. She whines as soon as she catches our footsteps.

We go inside, and I drop to a crouch to pet her and reassure her.

"She's fine, isn't she?" Dalton says.

I nod. Then I straighten. "The fire was a diversion."

"What?" He winces before the word is even out. "Someone tried to kill Brady. Shit. Tell me he's okay."

"It wasn't that kind of a diversion. I thought so, too—that's why I went to check—"

"No." He spins to the door. "Fuck, no. Do not tell me—"

I grab his arm. "Yes, I'm telling you he's gone, and that there's a reason why I didn't come running to get a search party. Just listen. Please."

He nods, and I explain.

TWENTY-THREE

You did the right thing.

That's what Diana told me. That is, I know, what I will hear from Anders, from Nicole, from everyone else who believes in me and wants to offer support.

That is not what I get from Dalton.

Fucking impossible situation.

That's what he says, and it's what I need to hear. Acknowledgment that there was no right choice here. There were only choices.

He doesn't tell me he'd have done the same. That goes without saying. Because what is the alternative? That I raised the alarm and hoped someone took Brady down before he could shoot Val?

Fucking impossible situation.

I put Val in that situation, so I could have done nothing that would end in her death. Even though what I *have* done might still kill her.

I don't trust Brady to let her go. Like Diana, Dalton argues that Brady has no reason to kill her and no reason to take her with him. But he says that because, to him, this is logical.

To Dalton, if Brady has no reason to kill Val, then he won't. He understands that we may be dealing with a man who kills for pleasure, but he cannot comprehend the implications because they don't exist in his world. Even with the hostiles, he presumes they attack us for a reason.

When I correct him, though, he says, "Yeah, but will he endanger his life for the enjoyment of taking hers? I like sex, but I gotta warn you—if our house catches on fire midway through? I'm leaving. Taking you with me, but leaving. If Brady kills Val, we're going to be all over his ass. Far as I'm concerned, if he gives us Val back, I'll do a rudimentary search—that's it. I'm not risking lives to recover him. But if she dies . . ."

"You'll hunt him down."

"*We* will."

Back at the shed, Dalton tells people to carry on. Then he asks a few to help him tackle "security shit—'cause it doesn't stop even for a fucking fire." He takes Anders, Nicole, Sam, and Kenny. Paul feels the sting of being passed over. Paul is core militia, and Nicole is not yet, but Dalton's commitment to women in the militia means showing that they won't be tokens, left off the front lines when situations get serious.

Anders runs Storm over to Petra's. Our first stop is the station, where Dalton asks Nicole and Sam to wait outside. We take Kenny in.

Dalton closes the door behind us.

"I'm going to ask you to step into the cell," Dalton says.

"Sure," Kenny says. "You need me to check something?"

"No, I'm going to lock you inside until I get back."

Kenny lets out a strained laugh. "Is it something I said?"

"When you showed up here three years ago, I thought you were useless. Couldn't hold a saw. Sure as hell couldn't fire a gun. Nothing I could do with you except make sure you didn't get your damn ass killed before you could go home. Then you decided to apprentice in carpentry, and I thought, huh, maybe . . . Still, when you asked to join the militia, I thought, fuck no. Another desk jockey fancies himself a lawman. Gonna shoot yourself if I give you a gun. But you proved you could handle it. You became Will's right-hand man. You still drive me fucking crazy sometimes, but I came to respect you. And that respect is why I'm not throwing you in the cell. I'm asking you to walk in yourself."

"I don't under—"

"The only thing to understand right now is that I gave you an order. Either you do it or this gets uglier than I want."

Kenny walks into the cell. Dalton closes the door.

"Oliver Brady is gone," I say.

"What?" Kenny says. "Someone killed—"

"He escaped."

Kenny's mouth works. Then he stops. "Because I left him un-guarded. Shit. I'm sorry, Eric. He was secured and the fire—"

"He got himself unsecured," I say. "With this." I hold out Kenny's knife.

Kenny pats his pockets. "No. *No*. He must have—I know this looks bad but—"

"You told me Val let you leave. She says she didn't. After you told me that, I called you back. You kept going."

"I didn't hear—Wait. Val says she didn't tell me to leave? I heard the bell, and then I smelled smoke, and I told her and she was freak-ing out over the fire, and maybe she didn't understand what I was asking. You know how she gets. Bring her here. Let me talk to her."

"Brady took her."

"Wh-what?"

Dalton says, "He took Val hostage. You're staying in that cell, and we'll talk when we get back. Just hope we have Val with us to straighten this out."

Before we go, Dalton changes his mind about bringing Anders. That would leave Rockton exposed. The fire was a distraction, and Dal-ton failed to see that, so now he's madly spinning out all the possi-bilities we might be missing. One is that Brady expects we'll do exactly this—gather our law enforcement and troop into the forest, leaving the town with a guard or two on fire cleanup. He could take more hostages, steal an ATV, even try to steal the plane.

I explain the situation to Anders, Sam, and Nicole as we walk. Then Anders runs back to town, where he'll have the remains of the militia guard the vehicles and patrol the town while citizens handle the fire fallout.

We move at a brisk walk. Val will be alone in the forest, which she has not set foot in since she was attacked here shortly after she arrived. Now she's about to be abandoned in these woods after being marched in at gunpoint. I cannot imagine what that will be like. Nicole can. She's moving faster than any of us, and Dalton has to call her back, saying, "If Brady thinks we didn't give him an hour, that gives him an excuse."

An excuse to kill Val.

We're approaching the final curve when Dalton's gait catches. A split-second hesitation as his chin lifts and his nostrils flare, finding some scent in the breeze.

"Eric?" I say as I come up beside him.

His nostrils flare again. His gaze fixes on the path, and when Sam whispers, "What's the plan?," Dalton doesn't seem to hear him.

"You two stay here," I whisper to Sam and Nicole.

I slant a look at Dalton, giving him the chance to contradict the order. He just keeps moving, his gaze fixed on that corner.

"Guns out," I whisper to the other two. "Watch the forest. Do *not* fire."

I jog to catch up with Dalton. He's rounding that final curve to the place where we should find Val—

The breeze hits, bringing with it the unmistakable coppery smell of blood.

I cover Dalton. He doesn't have his gun out. His arm isn't good enough for that. Instead, he reaches his right hand into his pocket for his knife.

I have my gun ready as we continue around the curve . . .

There's something on the path. Dalton stops short, but he doesn't look at the object. He's scanning the forest. I give the object one quick glance, and then pull my gaze away after I'm sure it's not a person.

As I survey the forest, though, I recall the image. A bloodied heap. Something brown.

What was Val wearing?

It's too small to be her body. Too small to be her *entire* body.

I don't pursue that thought.

I know why Dalton is ignoring the heap—he can't be distracted from a potential trap. But the unknown pounds at my head, my mouth going dry, and all I can think about is Val agreeing to be our spy with Brady.

And me letting her, despite Dalton's reservations.

So I look. I suck in breath. Dalton tenses, shoulder blades snapping together under his T-shirt.

"It's not Val," I say quickly.

His gaze drops then. And he lets out a quiet oath.

It is a dog.

No, it's a puppy.

On the path lies what looks like a shepherd puppy, with brown speckles on its muzzle. As soon as I see those, I remember the wolf-dog, the nursing mother.

The cub is dead.

Slaughtered and left on the path.

I pull my gaze from the cub and wrap both hands around my gun. Dalton steps over the tiny corpse.

I lift my foot to follow. Then I stop. Eyes on my surroundings, I crouch and lay my fingertips against the side of the cub's neck.

Still warm.

I hurry to catch up with Dalton, continuing around the curve and—

He stops and lets out a string of curses under his breath.

There is another heap on the path.

We don't stop for a better look. I see bloods and entrails, and my stomach churns. I've seen plenty of dead animals up here, often in worse shape, half devoured and rotting, but this is not a predator's kill. These cubs have been planted—a trap that Dalton and I are expected to fall for because we have a dog of our own. So we will see these poor dead cubs and stop, and then—

A whimper sounds in the bushes, and Dalton lets out another curse, this one softer, almost an exhalation.

Fuck, no . . .

What will be worse than seeing dead wolf-dog cubs in the path?

Seeing one that is not yet dead.

TWENTY-FOUR

We take a step. Then the sound comes again, that deep-throated whine, from the brush beside the path.

Dalton glances back at me. It's the briefest of glances, no more than a flicker of eye contact.

We should keep going. We're suckers if we don't, playing right into the trap Brady has set. A third cub has been left alive, horribly injured, as the cruelest of taunts. Punishment for the fact that we are not monsters.

Can you walk by this dying dog? You know you should. It's a wild thing, a feral beast. But I saw how you left the wolf-dog alone. I heard you say that she must have pups nearby. Heard the relief in your voices when she didn't attack, an excuse to let her live.

Suckers.

I'll leave Val by that spot where the sheriff got shot. You know the one. Just go there, and you'll find her.

The cub whines again.

"Fuck."

"Val?" I call. Then louder. "Valerie?"

She doesn't respond, and I know she won't. She isn't here. It would make no sense to kill these cubs and leave her with them, where she can warn us of a trap.

Brady is out there, in the forest, with my gun.

He's watching us. Figuring out how to put us both down before we can fire back. And this is the way to do it. Get us to lower our guard as we go after the wounded cub, because we will do that, of course we will.

Suckers.

I remember reading folklore that said one way to escape a vampire was to throw rice on the path, and it will be compelled to stop and pick up every grain before continuing on. I remember shaking my head at the absolute ridiculousness of it. But that is what Brady has done. He has thrown rice in our path, knowing we must stop to gather it up.

"Sam?" I shout. "Nicki?"

"Here!" Nicole calls back.

"Stay where you are, and stay alert. Brady's set a trap. There's no sign of Val. We're fine. Just hold there while we look for her."

"Got it!"

I cover Dalton as he takes another step. Then he bends to grab a stick with his bad hand, his knife still clenched in the good one. He pokes the stick around the brush where the noises come from. He jabs the cub by accident, and it lets out a startled yelp. Then it growls, and when he withdraws the stick, a pair of tiny jaws come with it, clamped on the wood before they fall away.

"Well, that's a good sign," he murmurs.

Confident he's not about to step into a literal trap, Dalton walks to the undergrowth, bends, and pushes fronds aside. Inside is a cub. I catch one glimpse of it before I remember what I'm supposed to be doing.

Don't be any more of a sucker than you need to, Casey.

I stay back and let Dalton handle it. The cub whines and whimpers and then—

"Fuck!"

I look over sharply. He's pulling back his hand, puncture wounds below his thumb welling with blood.

"It attacked you?"

"Nah, just snapped at me. It's caught in something."

"How badly is it injured?"

"I see blood where it's caught, but otherwise nothing. Looks like a snare wire. I'm probably going to get nipped again, so ignore the cursing."

"Got it."

I survey the forest. I know this is a trap. It must be. But there's no sign of anyone. Dalton works on the cub, swearing as he's nipped. Then there's a sound from the forest.

"Eric . . ."

"I hear it."

He backs away from the cub, who begins whining and yelping in earnest. However much freeing it hurt the cub, it's even more worried about being abandoned again, and it's making enough noise that I can't hear what's happening in the forest.

Dalton retreats to me, knife still in his hand. "Sound came from that way."

"Could you tell what it was?"

"Footsteps maybe? Hard to say."

The brush crackles, loud enough for us to catch it between the cub's cries. I see it, too, a wave of movement, branches pushed aside, something big crashing toward the path . . .

I aim my gun.

There's another movement. A dark shape *below* where I'm aiming.

The mother wolf-dog staggers onto the path. Her gray fur is matted with blood, and she moves with a stiff-legged gait, breath coming so hard I can hear it.

Dalton says, "Fuck, no," and that seems odd. Yes, it's a tragedy that the wolf-dog has also been mortally wounded, drawn back by the cries of her cub, but there's a note of fear in his voice that I do not understand until I see what hangs from her jaws.

Saliva.

Bloody, foaming saliva.

"Rabies?" I whisper.

"I hope not, but presume yes. We're going to have to take her down. You got a bead on her?"

I nod.

"Okay, take the—"

The wolf-dog charges. One second, she's shambling along, seeming a heartbeat from keeling over. The next she is in flight, jaws snapping, bloody froth flying.

I fire.

The bullet hits her. And she doesn't care.

I fire again, and Dalton stays right there, beside me, and I want to shout at him to *move*. Get out of the way. Dive for cover. Run!

But he just waits as I fire more rounds, and by then she's so close I can see the proverbial whites of her eyes as they roll.

"Eric!" I shout as I fire one last time.

He pushes me to the side. It's not a shove, just a push, and I'm scrambling out of the way, and he's just moving aside and . . .

The wolf-dog falls. Midflight, she collapses, this weird movement, almost like she's dancing as she folds in on herself. Then she drops, and when she hits the ground, those wild eyes are frozen open in death, a bullet hole between them.

"Nice shot," he says.

"Next time, can you *not* stay in the path of a charging wild animal?"

"I knew you'd get her."

"Just humor me, okay?" I walk over to see I *did* get her—with every bullet. Two to the chest, both of which would have been fatal, but she'd been too far gone to care.

"Got another one here where the blood's drying."

It's the spot I'd seen on her flank, matted with blood. Dalton pokes at it.

"Bullet's . . ." he says.

He uses his knife to cut it out. I've stood in on countless autopsies without flinching, but I swear Dalton makes me look positively squeamish. There is a question to be answered here, and he digs that bullet free without a moment's hesitation.

He holds the bullet up, his fingers red with blood.

"Nine-mil?" he asks.

"Yes."

One of the perks of being on the Rockton police force is that we get to choose our own sidearms. Mine's a Sig Sauer P226. Dalton is a revolver guy—the product of growing up here and using older guns. He carries a .357 Smith & Wesson. Anders prefers a gun that might actually stand a chance of taking down a grizzly: a Ruger Alaskan .454, which requires more wrist strength than I currently possess.

The bullet Dalton found fits my weapon . . . the one Brady took.

"Yes," I say. "It is possible we've misread the scenario. Brady shot this dog, which appears to have rabies or some other infection that drove it mad. It might have killed its own cubs. That one"—I nod toward the third—"could have gotten tangled in a settler's snare. Then Brady comes along, finds the mad dog and shoots. Even if it was a trap, it only seems to have been designed to slow us down, because he's missed the chance to attack."

"Or he was setting a trap. He killed the cubs, and the mother unexpectedly returned and attacked. He shoots her and takes off."

"Possible. Right now, though, we have two problems, leading in polar opposite directions. Finding Val and getting that cub back to town."

He frowns at me.

"No," I say. "As much as I love dogs, I'm not equating that cub's life with Val's. But this is about *yours*."

His frown deepens.

I wave at the wolf-dog. "If she had rabies, there's a chance her cub is also infected. The cub that bit you. We need to quarantine it."

"Yeah." No curse for this one. He hasn't considered this possibility, but now that I raise it, he doesn't freak out. *Huh, you're right. I could have a terrible and deadly disease.*

"Casey?"

I jump at Nicole's voice. I'd forgotten we've had two militia around the corner. The only reason they haven't come running is that they know how much shit Paul is in for disobeying an order. So they stayed put, our voices assuring them we aren't lying in agony, shot on the ground.

I tell them to approach, and I warn about the cubs, but when they appear, both are obviously rattled.

I'm standing point while Dalton continues freeing the cub. Nicole sees what he's doing and jogs over with, "Here, let me—"

"No," I say. "The mother may have been rabid. Eric's already been bit."

"*Rabid?*"

I struggle to keep scanning the forest. Dalton may not be freaked out about the possibility, but I sure as hell am. I feel him glance at me.

"It's unlikely," he says, his voice softer than usual. "Highly unlikely. There's never been a confirmed case in the Yukon. But, yeah, I've seen reports of it. We'll quarantine the cub. First sign of trouble, I'll get my ass south."

I don't answer, just keep looking for trouble, hoping that if it exists, it's out there, not here in the form of a small and terrified cub.

"Casey?"

"Hmm?"

"There's *never* been an incidence. Not one. The mother could have had a seizure. Could have been poisoned."

"I vote poisoning," Nicole says. "If that bastard did this, poison is your answer."

Dalton continues, "Even if, by some very slight chance, it was rabies, I'm not seeing any sign that this little guy was bit by his mother. His leg's messed up from the wire, so yeah, we have to consider the possibility that wound hides a bite. But what are the chances that she's got rabies—in a territory that doesn't have it—and she bit him . . . on the leg that he then got caught in a snare?"

"One in a million," Nicole says.

"We'll still take this guy back to Rockton to be sure."

He hefts the cub as he stands and holds it out. The wolf-dog lies over his hands, as if too exhausted to squirm.

"Male," he says. "Probably more wolf than dog. Which means it's not a pet. But, yeah, we gotta take it back. Sam, give me your jacket. You and Nicki will run him to town. Casey and I need to search for Val."

Dalton puts the cub inside Sam's jacket and pulls up the sides. "Carry it this way, like a bundle. Keep it tightly closed, and he won't escape. He can breathe—don't let him try to tell you otherwise. He stays in there until you're back at Rockton. Then take him to Casey's house. The door's unlocked. Put the whole jacket inside the door like this"—he demonstrates—"and then give it a push, and get that door closed before he escapes. Leave him be. His leg's bad, but it'll hold until we come back."

Sam takes the bundled cub.

"Nicole?" Dalton says. "While he's doing that, tell Will to announce what's happened. Minimal details. Arrange search parties. Let's get them out before dark."

TWENTY-FIVE

We search for Val. Call for Val. There's no sign that either of them was here except for that bullet in the wolf-dog, and even that's hardly ballistic proof. It just means someone shot her with a 9 mm.

I don't know what's going on here. I can speculate, but the whole thing is just fucked-up. There's no other term for it. Too many puzzle pieces could fit the hole, and yet none are exactly right.

Did Brady set all this up? That's the answer I both like and hate. My gut likes it for the lack of coincidence. My head hates it for the complexity of the plan.

Also, do I like it a little too much because it proves Brady is a monster, which makes this easier? If it wasn't for Val, having Brady escape might be the best possible solution—let him die out here, no longer a threat to Rockton. But if he is indeed innocent . . . ? Then he is like any other resident, and we failed him. He ran because we failed. He took Val because we failed. We put his back to the wall, and he lashed out.

Do not test me. If you do, you'll see exactly how desperate I am.

Please. Just let me go.

Val is the priority here. But she's nowhere to be found.

We return to the dead wolf-dog, and I examine the site. I find traces of footprints, but the ground is hard enough that they're only smudges, too faint to even tell if they're ours. Hell, even a perfect print of Brady's sneakers could be from our first time here.

When we're finished, I check Dalton's hand. The puncture wounds are red and inflamed.

"'Cause it's a bite," he says. "Trust me, I've had them. Gotta get it cleaned and then bandaged so it stays clean."

I nod.

"I'm okay, Casey."

I nod again. He puts his fingers under my chin and tilts my face up and bends to kiss me. It's a very sweet kiss, and when it breaks, I say, "You do realize that's an invitation for us to be attacked."

"I'm setting a trap."

I smile at that, and he kisses me again and then feigns stretching a kink from his neck.

"You gotta get taller," he says.

"I'll work on that."

I smile again, because I know he's trying to coax one from me.

He rests his forearms on my shoulders. "This sucks."

I do laugh at that. He's right, though. It might not be the most erudite description of the situation, but it's completely apt. There is nothing we can do about this. Maybe not even anything we could have done to prevent this. It just sucks.

"I should have gone looking for you during the fire," he says. "Should have realized something was up. Fuck, I should have realized *what* was up—obviously someone set that fire for a reason. We might have stopped him."

"Or gotten Val killed. Gotten me killed. Forced Brady into a panic and sent him over the edge. In hindsight I should have told you what I was doing. But I was playing a hunch, and my hunch was that someone was using the fire as a distraction to *kill* Brady. While I wasn't going to sit back and let that happen, it wouldn't be the biggest tragedy in the world. Even if he's innocent. That's a shitty thing to say, but he was a threat either way."

"Impossible situation."

I nod.

He looks out at the forest. "Still plenty of daylight left. You okay with walking another hour or so? Gives us a chance to get farther in while heading for a destination."

"Jacob's camp?"

He nods.

"You're worried?"

"Nah. Brady's not going after anyone out here. I still want to warn Jacob, though. I also want to let him know what's going on, get him to talk to Brent, maybe Ty, set them looking for Val."

"Good idea."

Jacob's camp is empty. That's no cause for alarm. He's packed it up, which means he headed off on his hunting trip. I feared that after he didn't leave the note yesterday. I know Nicole will be hurt, and I hate seeing that.

On our way back to town, we take a different route to widen the search. There's still no trace of Brady or Val. Tomorrow we'll visit Brent and swing by the cabin that Cypher used for the winter, see if he's still lurking about. Brent's easy to find, though, and he's a former bounty hunter, which makes him as good a tracker as Jacob.

Back in Rockton, the first thing I do is treat Dalton's hand. He's right that it just looks like a bite, but that won't keep me from worrying.

Anders has explained the situation to the residents. Oliver Brady used the fire as a distraction to escape. He took Val hostage, with a promise to leave her at a set location in an hour. If we hadn't agreed, he'd have killed her on the spot. Val was not at the promised location. We are currently searching for them.

He doesn't mention that we suspect the fire was deliberately set. That implies an accomplice, and people might jump to the conclusion it's the guy we locked up. We won't do that to Kenny. After Roy's bullshit, we don't trust people not to take justice into their own hands.

We passed a search party as we were coming in. Dalton told them to keep at it for another two hours and then switch off with a fresh group. We have the advantage of daylight at this time of year, and we can keep hunting until nearly midnight.

Next stop is the wolf-dog cub. When we enter my house, Dalton blocks the exit, expecting the cub to charge for freedom. He doesn't . . . because he's hiding behind the sofa.

I pull him out. I'm dressed in long sleeves and gloves, but he doesn't try to bite. Just shakes and whines. I've brought sedative, and he yelps at the needle, but a few minutes later, he's limp in my arms.

I work on his injured front leg. It's not as bad as I feared. It's just messy, flesh ripped as he'd struggled against the snare wire.

I bandage the wound. Then Dalton covers the cloth in a goop we use with Storm, when she insists on licking a cut or sting.

Once I'm done, I lean back on my haunches. He looks more like a lion cub than a wolf or a dog, with thick tawny fur, gray and dark brown striping, and an even thicker mane around his head. He has the same freckles as his mother, though.

"Do you think the father was a dog?" I ask.

"Probably not. Take away the coloring and those freckles, and he's wolf."

"Which is a problem."

"Either way, it's a problem. I'd rather face a wolf, but dogs have the genes for domestication. Wolves don't." He looks down at the cub and sighs.

"We'll keep him until we know he isn't rabid," I say. "Then we can . . . do whatever."

He slants me a look. "Do you really think either of us is going to be able to 'do whatever' after we've nursed him back to health?"

I don't answer.

"Yeah." He heaves to his feet. "We'll wait and see. But if anyone comes looking to adopt a puppy, the answer is fuck no. This isn't a pet. We can't turn him out into the woods at this age, though. Can't raise him and then release him after he's lived with humans. That's just as cruel. Dangerous, too." He runs a hand through his hair and sighs again.

"We'll figure it out," I say. "You and I both understand this isn't a pet wolf. But it's not a rabid dog either." I pause and look down at the sleeping cub. "Or so we hope."

"He's not. Just gotta wait to be sure and then we'll . . . figure shit out."

Figure shit out.

That's what we're doing, on so many levels, over the next twelve hours. There's still enough light for us to get to Brent's that evening, but Dalton doesn't want to leave town. We'll go at first light.

Dalton joins the last evening search. That's where he's best right now, as our top tracker.

He takes Storm. We're hoping to make a search-and-rescue dog out of her. That's what the breed is used for, though more commonly water-based, given their webbed feet and double coats. But her sense of smell is excellent, so that's our plan. She's only eight months old, just entering doggie adolescence, with the attention span to match. This is the one area of her training where I've discovered I can't push. I've introduced her to the concept of tracking, and we work on it weekly, but it's mostly play at this point—I give her the scent of someone in town, and if she can find her target, she gets a treat. If the trail's too convoluted, though, she loses interest.

Still Dalton takes her, along with Brady's and Val's dirty clothing. Storm has spent enough time around Brady that we hope that helps—she's definitely better at finding residents she knows. She knows Val less well—big dogs make Val nervous—but Storm only takes a quick sniff at Val's blouse, as if to say, "Okay, I know who you want." Which is promising.

They leave, and I stay behind to "figure shit out."

Some of that is investigating, some is talking to people, and some is just staring into space and thinking, and then jotting those thoughts into my notebook.

Brady had an accomplice in town. That is a fact. There is absolutely no way someone coincidentally set fire to that shed when Brady was out of the cell. His accomplice put poison in his food, enough to make him violently ill. That gets Brady out of the cell and into the clinic, which was exactly the scenario I expected the moment I saw him throwing up. *Not this old chestnut—prisoner fakes illness to get to a less secure environment.* Except he hadn't been faking. He'd gone the extra step and let himself be poisoned.

From there, I'd supplied Brady with a hostage. A nurse at his bedside. Then his accomplice sets the fire and Brady grabs Val as insurance to get him out of town.

Next Brady knows the wolf-dog is near that spot. He poisons her—and kills her poor cubs—to slow us down. It also gives him an "excuse" for Val not being there, in case we catch up with him. He couldn't exactly leave her with a frothing canine, right?

And the sniper? It could very well have been his accomplice, hoping to convince us Brady was in danger. Or hoping to scatter us so he could rescue him.

As a hypothesis, this solidifies Brady's guilt. He is a monster. A killer.

But it's only a hypothesis. The assassin might have come from his stepfather. That would give Brady reason to panic. Then Brady enlisted a local mercenary of his own, with promises of a rich reward.

Was Kenny that local mercenary? He *is* just about to leave, and he'll need money. Still, when I consider him as a suspect, I feel sick. I won't interview Kenny until both Dalton and Anders are back. The point is that Brady has a confederate in Rockton, and it doesn't matter right now if it's Kenny or . . .

There's another possibility. One person that I know suspects Brady is innocent. The one who delivered that petition. Also the one who came running to notify us of the fire. Jen.

Too much to think about. It's a puzzle of configuration, and each piece in it has two sides—guilt or innocence—and the meaning changes depending on which side I place up. If Brady is innocent, then x. If he is a monster, then y. Two ways of looking at everything, leading to two ways of investigating.

Stop. Focus.

Take it apart. Look at the trees, not the forest. That's what my first detective partner taught me. There are times when, yes, it's good to step back and see the whole. But there are also times in police work when you must focus on the minutiae. On the trees. On one puzzle piece. Figure out where that fits and that'll help you find where another goes. Get a few of those done and then step back, or you'll go crazy with possibilities, each configuration sending the investigation spiraling in a new direction.

Focus.

Start with the fire.

The problem with determining the cause of a fire? The evidence has gone up in smoke. Which is why there are trained experts for this—experts who are *not* police detectives. But I am every investigator in Rockton, and this is one of the many areas I've been researching. I've always been a believer in lifelong learning. I took every course my department would send me on. Learned every new technique. Subscribed to every journal. Attended every local conference on my own dime, even as my colleagues rolled their eyes and said, "We hire experts for that, Casey." True. I did not need to know anything about forensic anthropology, because I wouldn't ever be the person analyzing buried remains. But I wanted to know. And now I *am* that person. Jack-of-all-trades, feeling truly master of none.

Arson investigation.

I evaluate the scene. Document it. Process the evidence.

This time, the building has been saved. There's damage, but it can be repaired. And it doesn't take much investigating to know it's arson. The smell of kerosene gives it away, as it did the last time.

It is an arson easily set by anyone with any knowledge of wood and access to kerosene. Which really doesn't narrow it down in Rockton.

Dalton comes back ahead of the others. A dripping black rug trails behind him with a look that is unconvincingly contrite.

"Got too close to the lake, didn't you?" I call as I walk toward them.

Dalton only sighs.

"We need to take her there more often," I say, "so the siren's call of water is a little more resistible."

"I'm not sure it ever will be. Been thinking of buying one of those pools."

"The plastic kiddie ones? She's a little big for that." I gingerly pat her wet head, and she slumps happily.

"I mean the ones you set up," he says. "The bigger pools."

"Then we'll have to keep the humans out of it."

"If they want to swim in dog fur, they can go ahead. Just make a rule: you use it; you clean it."

He walks over. I take his hand to examine it, but he wraps his fingers around mine, holding tight. His expression is calm, as if he's just returned from a walk in the woods, but his tight grip tells me the rest.

"Not a trace," he says. "Storm did well. She found the trail out of town and followed it along the path. They turned off before the spot with the wolf-dog."

"Turned off or doubled back?"

"That's the problem. The trail left the path, and Storm followed it awhile, but the undergrowth thickened and hit a whole warren of rabbit holes. She went nuts and lost the trail. I couldn't get her to focus. So I took her backwards, in hopes she'd pick it up again."

"And?"

"And I don't know. She kept finding the same end point. I moved higher up the path in case he rejoined it, and then we were too close to the dead dogs."

He looks down at her. "She smelled those, and she was upset. Really upset. She got away from me and kept nosing the first cub and . . ."

He exhales. "It wasn't good. I got her out of there. Which means I can't answer the question. All I know is they left the path at one point and neither of us could figure out where they'd gone from there."

TWENTY-SIX

It's time to notify the council. Except we can't. Without Val, we don't know how.

We have a radio receiver. We understand the basics of how to use it, and Anders knows specifics. But we don't have a frequency. That's top secret, need to know only, and no one other than Val, apparently, needed to know.

We move the radio to our house and wait for Phil to call in. That's all we can do.

We're up at four. I play double nursemaid, first tending to Dalton's arm and his hand. The former is healing well; the latter shows no sign of infection. Then, while he cooks breakfast, I go to see the cub.

Storm comes with me. I'm not about to let her into the house—I'm still worried about rabies—but she smells him from outside and seems to think it's another dead wolf-dog. Her whines escalate to howls. So I lift the cub up to the front window . . . and then she goes nuts because there's another canine in town and I'm keeping him from her.

I try to calm her by cracking open the front door just enough for her to snuffle him. The poor cub sees this massive black nose and he freaks. I shut the door and Storm starts howling again. The cub stops quaking in mortal terror . . . and begins howling back.

It's an interesting way to start my morning. I don't think my neighbors agree.

The cub is otherwise fine. I'd left a bed and food and water. I have to clean up piddle and poop, but I'm not taking him out for a walk until that leg is better. I moved all my blankets and cushions and rugs upstairs, so the damage is minimal. I tend to his leg, replace the food and water, and then I return home for my own breakfast.

At dawn, we're off to visit Brent. It's a long hike to the mountain where Brent has his cave. Before we leave, we remind Storm of Brady and Val's scents, and every time the path branches off, we have her sniff. She finds nothing. As we draw near the mountain, though, she starts getting excited. Which *would* be exciting . . . if we weren't on the path Brent uses daily. Storm is very fond of Brent, who always has dried bones for her.

When we reach the cave entrance, she plunks down with a sigh. She still fits, but she won't for much longer. Once we get through, we shove a rock into the opening, the last thing we need is her wedging in and getting stuck. She sighs again and then sticks her head into the remaining opening to watch us mournfully.

Or that's what she usually does. This time, when she sticks her head through, her nostrils flare, and she sniffs wildly as she whines.

"Storm, no," I say. "Brent will come out. He'll bring your bone."

She keeps whining, but I've told her to stay and she obeys.

We're going down the first passage when my light catches something on the wall. Dalton is ahead of me, and as I stop for a closer look, he glances back.

I have the penlight between my teeth so I can crawl. Now I take it out and shine it on the wall to see . . .

A handprint.

A red handprint.

"Eric . . ."

"He's been hunting," Dalton says. "Must have butchered up top. That's what Storm smells."

He says that, but he still moves faster, and I remember Storm whining on the path, getting excited, presumably she smelled Brent.

And if it *wasn't* Brent? What if, instead, she picked up the very scents we asked her to find?

As we crawl, I tell myself I'm overreacting. Brady doesn't know anything about Brent. He has no reason to come for him. No idea where to find him. The chances that Brady would just happen to take shelter in the same cave where Brent lives? Infinitesimal. The opening isn't even visible from down the mountainside.

We reach the cavern that Brent calls home. There's blood on the floor, large drops, some smeared. A shelf has been pulled down, contents spilled, another bloody handprint on the wall.

"Brent?" Dalton's voice echoing through the cavern. "Brent!"

I'm following the blood. More smears here, like drag marks. They lead to the smaller cavern Brent uses for storage. I pull back the hide curtain. And there is Brent, lying on the floor, curled in fetal position, blood soaking his shirt, one hand pressed against it. His eyes are closed.

I bend to clear the low ceiling. Then I crouch beside him. My fingers go to his neck, and he stirs.

Dalton's figure fills the entrance.

"He's alive," I say.

Barely. Brent's eyelids flutter, but he can't open them. His face is almost as white as his hair. He isn't breathing hard enough for me to even see his chest rise. Then there's the blood. A pool of it under him, his shirt soaked with it.

We get him out of that small cavern. That wakes him, crying in pain. Dalton wets a cloth as I gingerly peel up Brent's shirt. I take the cloth and clean as carefully as I can. Brent whimpers, his eyes still shut, and Dalton tries to rouse him.

There's a bullet hole through Brent's stomach.

"Diagnosis dead?" a papery voice whispers.

I turn. His eyes are barely open, but he's trying to smile.

"I know the diagnosis," he says. "Dead from the moment the bullet hit. Body just hasn't realized it yet."

He's right. If he'd been steps from a hospital when he'd been shot, he might have survived. Even that is unlikely. And now . . .

Tears well. I blink them back hard.

"Casey?" Brent says. "I already know."

"I can try—"

He reaches for my hand and squeezes it. "Let's not waste my time. Not much left."

"You want a drink?" Dalton asks.

Brent manages a hoarse laugh. "I would *love* a drink."

Dalton takes a bottle from the backpack we brought. A gift for Brent, in return for his bounty hunting services.

Brent cranes his neck up. "Is that . . . ?"

"Scotch. I'm told it's the good stuff. Bought it a while back, in case you ever had anything better to trade than skinny-assed bucks. Never did. But I guess you can have it now."

Brent laughs, knowing full well that Dalton would have bought this on his last trip, after Brent and I argued over the merits of Scotch versus tequila.

Dalton pours him a glass full.

"Trying to get me drunk?" Brent says.

"Yeah, hoping those conspiracy theories of yours might make more sense if you're loaded." He hands him the glass. "Got any theories on who did that to you?"

"It's the bastard you were keeping in that town of yours. Kid told me you think he's some kinda killer. Insisted he's not." Brent looks down at his gut. "Seems he lied."

"Okay," I say. "Just rest and—"

"I'm not resting, Casey. I'm helping you catch my killer. And drinking. Heavily. If it starts spilling out my guts? Don't tell me."

He takes a deep drink. "I was down the mountain, shooting grouse at twilight. Kid got the jump on me, the fuck—" He stops. Apologizes to me for swearing, as always. "He got me dead to rights. I was picking up my game, had put my gun down. He wanted to know where to find Jacob."

"Jacob?" Dalton tenses.

"Relax, Eric. You think I told him?" Brent slurps more Scotch. "Said he wanted to hire Jacob. As a guide. Get him out of here. I said I could do it. He said no, had to be Jacob. That's when I knew something was up."

"He didn't *just* want a guide," I say.

"Right. So I confronted him, and he told me that story about being a prisoner in your town, falsely accused. Says he needs Jacob as a guide and as insurance, but he won't hurt him. Offers to pay me to take him to Jacob. I say no. He threatens to shoot me in the shoulder. I go for the gun. We fight. I get gutshot instead. Maybe that was an accident, but the bas—the jerk put his fist on my gut and pushed down. Made me howl, I'm ashamed to say. But I got the gun away from him. Fired a shot. He took off. I hauled ass back here. Lost the damn gun on the way, pardon my French. But I made it. Holed up with my rifle, in case he came back."

"He didn't?"

"Nah, ran and kept running. Little pri—prat."

"Was there anyone with him? Any sign of a hostage?"

Brent shakes his head. "He was alone. Never mentioned anyone else. It was all about him. How everyone done him wrong." Brent coughs and then gasps in pain with the movement. "Damn country song, he was. You don't need to worry about Jacob, though. I don't even know where he's camping right now. Left his last spot a couple of days back."

"So he's gone duck hunting," Dalton says.

"Not yet. Came by to say he was holding off—he was tracking a bull caribou and wanted to get that first. And he was trying to decide if he should ask that girl from your town to go duck hunting. Came to me for advice." Brent gives a weak laugh. "Like I'd be any help. I faked it, though. Told him yes, he should do it."

"So he's mobile right now?"

Brent nods. "Until he gets that caribou."

I help him lift the glass to his lips. His hand is trembling. He takes two big gulps. When he speaks again, his words are slurring, exhaustion and alcohol mixed.

"Eric?"

"Right here, Brent."

"You gotta bury me in my jersey, okay?"

"The Maple Leafs one?"

Brent raises his middle finger. Then he drinks more Scotch with my help. "You know how I want to go, right?"

"I do."

"Up in one of those platforms. Like the Indians used to do it."

"I know. I'll do it just like you wanted."

Brent's eyelids flutter. Then they open. "Almost forgot. Eric? You gotta get something for me."

His words are slurring badly now, and it takes a while for Dalton to interpret his directions and bring what he wants. It's two carved wooden figurines.

"Give it to me," Brent says. "You'll do it wrong."

He takes the figures and arranges them on his palm. It's a woman in a ponytail, kneeling in front of a rolling ball of fur.

"That a bear cub?" Dalton says.

Brent raises his middle finger again.

"It's me and Storm," I say. "When she was a puppy."

"First time you brought her here. I remember you two playing in the grass. Been a long time since I heard a girl laugh like that. I wanted to capture it. She's not so little anymore."

"Yeah, Casey, gotta watch what you're eating."

We both raise our fingers for that. Then Brent hands me the figures. Up close I see the detail, the hours spent carving them. I thank him, and we talk for a little more. He's flagging, and I tell him we'll build that platform and put him in his beloved Canadiens hockey jersey. And I say we'll get Brady for him.

"I'm sure you will," he says, "but I'm not too worried about that. I'm just glad you came. Not a bad way to go. Good Scotch. Pretty girl."

I squeeze his hand and bend to kiss his weathered cheek as his eyes close.

"Eric?" he whispers, voice barely audible.

Dalton bends by Brent's head.

"I figured it out," Brent says. "The secret behind that town of yours. This is what it's for, isn't it? Harboring the worst criminals. The ones the government wants to make disappear. Save folks the expense of a trial and hide them up here, let their sorry asses rot." His eyes half open. "I'm right, aren't I?"

"Took you long enough."

Brent smiles and his eyes close again. A few more breaths, and then he goes still.

TWENTY-SEVEN

I make Brent comfortable. I know exactly how ridiculous this is, but I do it anyway, arranging his body on his sleeping mat and pulling up a blanket, as if tucking him in for the night. Dalton doesn't say a word.

Then I stand and march to the exit. "I'm going to find Brady. I'm going to find him and put a bullet through his gut and leave him out there. Let him drag his ass to shelter so he doesn't get eaten by a pack of damn wolves. I will *watch* him drag his ass, and I will pray that the wolves come. Wolves or a wolverine or ravens. I hope it's ravens. I hope they find him, gut-shot, and they rip out his . . ."

I don't go further. Dalton knows what I mean, and he doesn't need to hear the details.

I stoop for the passageway, and Dalton grips my arm.

"Casey . . ."

"I'm going to find him."

"You will. But Brady's not waiting outside this cave."

I wheel on him. "You think I don't know that?"

"It's been twelve hours."

"I need to process the scene."

"Twelve hours."

The crime scene isn't going anywhere. That's what he means. He glances back at Brent's body.

"No," I say. "We're not doing that right now. We need tools."

"He has everything."

"Later. He's fine. He'll be . . ."

Fine. He'll be fine.

Brent is not fine. Brent is dead, and I don't want to lay him to rest because it feels like acknowledgment. Feels like acceptance. Feels, too, like I'm stalling when I need to be acting.

"We need to—" I stop myself.

Find Jacob. Warn Jacob. That's what I want to say, and that's where I must draw the line. I can't remind Dalton his brother is in danger, as if he doesn't know that, as if he's not holding himself back from running out to find him.

It has been twelve hours. Another hour won't matter. Not for finding Jacob. Not for examining the crime scene.

For Brent, though . . .

"We made a promise," Dalton says, his voice low.

"I . . . I . . ."

I look over at Brent's body. And I burst into tears, and Dalton's arms go around me, holding me tight as I sob against him.

We lay Brent's body to rest, the way he wanted it, on an open platform, with him wearing his Canadiens jersey, a reminder of the season he'd played for the team, fifty years ago.

Afterward, I examine the crime scene. That's what Dalton insists on for the next step. Jacob can wait—the crime scene could be disturbed.

Storm easily tracks Brent back to where he'd been shot. Blood and trampled grasses mark the exact spot, as do the grouse Brent shot. There's a bow and arrows there, and I remember he was new to bow shooting, having finally agreed to let Jacob teach him.

Too old for this, he'd said, *learning new tricks at my age. But it saves on ammo.*

Dalton said he could bring more ammunition with his trades, but Brent had blustered that he needed the other items more. Which was a lie. He *wanted* to learn something new. Wanted to challenge himself.

Dalton takes the grouse. When we first met, I'd have been horrified by that. Stealing from the dead? Now I know better. It is a sign of respect. Brent killed these birds, and his efforts should not go to waste. Nor should the lives of those birds. We'll eat them, and we'll remember where they came from.

Dalton takes the bows and arrows, too.

"Jacob made these," he says. "I'll give them back when we catch up to him."

Not *when* we find him. Certainly not *if*. There's very little chance Jacob is in any danger, and it really is just a matter of catching up to him. I know that. Dalton knows that. *Feeling* it, though, is another matter.

Brent said he got my gun away from Brady, and he's right. It's there, hidden in the grass.

I see nothing at the crime scene to contradict Brent's version of events. Not that he'd deliberately mislead us, but maybe he misunderstood. Maybe I'll find something that proves the gunshot *wasn't* an accidental discharge.

"What would prove that?" Dalton says when I admit what I'm hunting for.

"I have no idea. But I want it."

He wisely says nothing and just lets me keep scouring.

"Brady is still culpable," I say. "He held Brent at gunpoint. Whatever happens after that, it's still murder, even if it's second-degree."

"It is."

"And he ground his *fist* in the injury. I don't care how desperate he was to find Jacob. That's sadistic."

"It is."

I crouch and stare at the bloodied ground.

"You want proof he's exactly what his stepfather says," Dalton says. "Proof Brady is more than what he claims—a desperate man driven to desperate measures."

"Yes."

I want justification for my rage. I do want to see Brady gutshot for this. Gutshot and left in the forest. And that scares me. It's the sort of thing Mathias would do, and I tiptoe around the truth of what Mathias is, alternately repelled and . . . Not attracted. Definitely not. But there's part of me that thinks of what he does and nods in satisfaction. I could not do it, but it doesn't horrify me nearly as much as it should.

"I should have come out last night," Dalton says.

I look up at him, as I stay crouched.

"I decided not to come see him last night. I waited until morning."

I rise and walk to him. "Doesn't matter. This happened at twilight. We wouldn't have made it here before Brent got shot."

Dalton says nothing, and I know that will weigh on him. Like my poor choices with Val weigh on me. We haven't discussed that yet. It's not time. Not time for this either, as he pats Storm and then peers into the forest.

"Should see if she can find Brady's trail."

She can't. The blood seems too much for her. It's upsetting or confusing, and she grows increasingly anxious until I release her from the task.

Next we try to "catch up" with Jacob, while continuing to search for Brady and Val. We put up the markers, telling Jacob we need to speak to him. There's no way to warn him otherwise. Despite Dalton's best efforts, Jacob is functionally illiterate. Their parents taught them the language of the forest, the one they needed to know. I get the sense that Dalton had learned how to read and write before he came to Rockton, but presumably he sought that teaching from his parents and Jacob had not.

We head to the cabin Tyrone Cypher has been using as a base. There's no sign of him. We leave a note, though I'm not sure that will do any good either. Cypher can read; he just might choose not to.

Back in Rockton, there's been no word from the council. Petra and Diana have been taking turns with the radio. We aren't even sure how often they make contact with Val. Maybe, with us being pissed off over our unwanted prisoner, they'll just wait until we call and hope we don't.

THIS FALLEN PREY | 151

The search for Brady and Val didn't stop while we were off with Brent. We join that, and by the time we return home, it's after nine at night. Dalton and I are exhausted. We have one more task, though. Kenny has been in the cell over twenty-four hours, as Dalton lets him stew. We need to talk to him, as much as we're both dreading it.

Kenny was the first true Rockton resident I'd met. My first taste of what to expect in this town. I'd spent time with Dalton, in my admission interviews and then over twelve hours of travel together, yet I had no idea what to make of him. There was so much about Dalton that reminded me of the worst kind of cops—swaggering through life, a bully with a badge. He seemed to fit that slot . . . and then he'd do something to pop him out of it. That was uncomfortable.

I'd met Anders, briefly, and he seemed more my kind of colleague, competent and personable. But after maybe five minutes in Rockton, they'd both had to rush off to an emergency, and I'd made my way to town alone.

Go in the back door of the station. Stay there. Anyone comes into the office? Tell him to come back when we return.

Those were Dalton's orders, which seemed a little disconcerting, as if the locals were wolves who might pick me off while the alpha was away.

It was Kenny who came into the station. As I discovered later, a bunch of the militia guys had drawn straws to see who got to introduce himself to the "new girl" first. That's what I'd been to them. Not their new superior officer. Not the new detective. A new woman in town. An addition to Rockton's meager dating pool.

Kenny had exactly two minutes with me before Isabel showed up and shooed him off. I remember her asking if I could guess what he'd done in his former life. Given the size of his biceps and the perfume of sawdust, I'd guessed carpenter or construction worker. High school math teacher, she said.

When he arrived eighteen months ago, he'd never have worked up the courage to talk to you. People come here, and it's a clean slate. A chance to be whoever they want for a while.

What Kenny wanted to be was one of the cool kids. For a guy like him, cool meant tough. Except he lacked that edge and wasn't terribly invested in finding it. So he settled for hitting the gym and joining the militia. He became the guy he wanted to be. And now he'd been about to leave his new life. Had he panicked at that? Worried he'd end up back in a job he'd hate because his new skills wouldn't pay the bills? Had he been an easy target for Oliver Brady? I desperately want to say no. But the evidence must be acknowledged.

When we walk in to question Kenny, the first thing he says isn't *I didn't do it* or *Guys, come on, you know me.*

"I know how bad this looks."

"Good," Dalton says.

We pull up chairs outside the cell. Kenny has one inside. We've granted him that, in recognition that he's had to wait a very long time for this interview.

"Your knife was found with the prisoner," I begin.

He starts to speak, but Dalton says, "Be quiet and listen."

"Brady used that knife to cut his bindings," I continue. "He used it to take Val captive. You were his guard at the time—and you were in charge of the guarding schedule."

"I—"

A look from Dalton silences him again.

"You assigned yourself to that time slot. You abandoned your post. The prisoner was left unguarded, with a weapon, while a fire brought everyone else running. A fire set in the lumber shed, which you know very well. It was a delayed-start fire, giving you time to go on guard duty."

"I—"

"You brought Brady his breakfast. You offered to bring it. We realize now that it was poisoned—not to kill him, but to get him out of that cell. So Brady is in the clinic with his wrists tied and under guard. Fire breaks out. Everyone runs . . . including his guard. He is left with a knife and the perfect hostage."

He slouches in his seat. "Shit. I'm not even sure where to start."

"Well, that depends," Dalton says. "If you'd like, you can start with explaining why you were the one bringing that food tray."

"I took it from someone. She was in a hurry and complaining about her workload, and I wanted to be nice." He lowers his voice to a mutter. "Even if she'd never do the same in return."

"Jen," I say.

"I'd rather not name names—"

"You have to," Dalton says. "But in this case, you don't need to. That description says it all."

"So you volunteered to take the tray," I say. "Then you volunteered for guard duty at the clinic."

He shakes his head. "I was scheduled for guard duty with Brady here at the station. Will asked me to make up a twenty-four-hour schedule, with me and Sam alternating four-hour shifts. Will picked us two for it."

He pauses and then hurries to add, "Which made sense. Paul's in the doghouse right now, and Will wanted his best two guys. His two most experienced. That'd be me and Sam."

"And the knife?" I say.

"After I offered to help you open that can, someone asked to borrow it, and I said sure, just leave it on the sawhorse when you're done. When I went back to get it, it wasn't there."

"Who borrowed it?"

"I'm not even sure. I was cutting wood, and someone asked behind me. I never turned around. I barely heard him over the saw."

"Tell me about leaving your post."

"I heard the bell. I went outside, and someone said it was a fire. I ran back in. Brady was sound asleep. Val was doing one of her algebra puzzles. I'd talked to her earlier about it, said I remembered giving those to my students. She assured me this one was much more advanced."

An eye roll and a slight smile. "You know Val. Anyway, when I came in, she was absorbed in that. I said there was a fire at the shed, and I should go, and she said, 'Yes, yes.' Those were her exact words.

'Yes, yes.' She never even looked up. I double-checked Brady's restraints, and told Val I'd send someone to take my place. But then I saw you coming, Casey, so I thought it was covered."

Kenny shakes his head. "I made a mistake. A big one. But my mistake was leaving my post. *Not* helping Brady escape. I'd never do that."

TWENTY-EIGHT

We place Kenny under Dalton's version of work release. He'll do the lumber-shed repairs during the day and spend his nights in Brady's new residence, as we give his cell to Roy instead. As for our suspicions with Kenny, we will say nothing to the council. As far as they'll know, we are punishing him for letting Brady escape on his watch.

Kenny will be leaving as soon as this is over, and we will let him go, even if that means he's going to collect a reward down south for helping Brady. Otherwise, if the council knows, we cannot trust he'll survive the trip south, and whatever mistake he's made, it doesn't deserve the death penalty.

We spend the next day combing the forest for Val and Jacob. Dalton's trying not to freak out about that. There is no sign that anything has happened to his brother, and this *is* how Jacob lives. He moves with game and the seasons and whatever whim strikes him.

Jacob's life, though, means Dalton can't pick up a phone and call to warn him about Brady. Jacob comes and goes, and that stresses his brother out at the best of times. The fact we can't find him means absolutely nothing. It's just driving Dalton crazy.

We take an ATV out the next morning. We have three of them—two smaller ones that can take a passenger on the back and a side-by-side that only travels on the widest trails.

I've been trying to talk Dalton into dirt bikes for getting deeper into the forest. In fact, when the council told us we'd get a windfall from Brady, that's what Dalton said to me, trying to find an upside—*we'll get a couple of those bikes you've been talking about.* Which apparently isn't happening now.

We're riding one of the smaller ATVs. I'm on the back. We'll switch at some point—Dalton knows there's no way I'm taking the bitch seat for the whole trip.

Storm runs along behind us. We aren't going that fast, and we don't really have a destination in mind. We're just covering ground and making a lot of noise doing it, in hopes that if Jacob is around, he'll pop out. Or that Val will come stumbling from the forest, having been abandoned by Brady three days ago.

We're zipping along a straightaway. I have my visor open as I scan the forest. Dalton's turning to say something just as a massive shaggy shape tromps onto the path.

"Bear!" I yell.

Dalton hits the brake. The figure in front of us shouts, "Bear? Do I look like a fucking bear?"

The man is over six feet tall. Massive shoulders. Grizzled shaggy hair and beard. Dressed in a brown jacket that he's pieced together from skins and fur.

"A fucking bear, no," I say as I hop off the ATV. "A standing one? Absolutely."

"Ha!" Cypher jabs a finger my way and says to Dalton, "See, boy? That is what we call a sense of humor."

"You get our note?" Dalton says.

"Good to see you, too," Cypher says as he bends to pet the dog. "I'm fine, thank you for asking. Weather's been clear. Hunting's good."

"We have a problem."

Cypher plunks his ass down right on the path and then pulls a kerchief full of jerky from his jacket. One piece goes to Storm. He holds out another for me.

"I said—" Dalton begins.

"That you have a problem. I was hoping you'd say something new and original. You want to know how to solve your endless problems? Take your girl here and leave that piece-of-shit town. I did not get your note. I haven't been to the cabin in days. I heard the ATV and thought I'd say hi. Beginning to regret that."

"Brent's dead," Dalton says.

Cypher stops. He looks at me, as if checking whether he's heard wrong.

"He was shot by a prisoner who escaped from Rockton," I say. "Gutshot. We found him the next morning. He lived long enough to confirm who killed him."

"Fuck." A moment's pause. Then, "*Fuck.*" Another pause, this one followed by a knitting of his brows as he looks up. "Did you say *prisoner?*"

When we finish explaining, he says, "You let the fucking council—"

"We didn't *let* them do anything," I cut in. "You know how it works."

"Yeah, which is why I got the hell outta Dodge. You couldn't stop them from dropping off that guy, but you didn't need to accept the delivery."

"Yeah," Dalton says. "Coulda just left him there, a few hundred feet from town. A guy who tortures people to death for fun. What could possibly go wrong?"

"Okay, fine. You had to take him—onto the back of your ATV there, and then head to the swamp and dump his ass. I'd give him three days. If swamp fever doesn't kill him, the mosquitoes will."

When we don't answer, he looks from me to Dalton. "Fuck, no. Do not tell me this guy said he was innocent. No, scratch that. Of course he told you that. The *fuck no* is *fuck no, tell me you didn't consider the possibility.* Well, I guess you know better now."

"Because he ran?" Dalton says. "Yeah, if I was brought up here, held prisoner for crimes I didn't commit, I'd just plop my ass down— like you on this damn path—and sit it out."

"My ass is on the damn path because I'm tired. So is your puppy. I'm resting for her."

"We entertained doubts about his guilt," I say. "Those doubts had no impact on our treatment of him."

"Except that they kept you from dumping him in the swamp. Or taking him behind the hangar and putting a bullet through his skull. That's why you're in this situation, kids. You don't have what it takes to run that town properly."

"No, we don't have what it takes to *be* run out of that town," I say. "If we killed Brady, the council would have put Eric on the next plane out."

"Not if you did it right. Hire an expert. I'd have taken him out cheap. You could even blame me if you wanted—we took that kid for a walk, and Ty Cypher came roaring out of the forest. You know what he's like. Fucking certifiable. Dragged the poor kid off, and a hail of bullets couldn't stop him."

"What we *should* have done doesn't matter," I say. "The point is that he's out there, and he took Val, and he killed Brent, and I don't care if that wasn't what he had in mind, if I see him, there *will* be a hail of bullets. Our priority right now is twofold. Find Val and warn Jacob."

"Well, I can't help you with the first. If I'd seen a lady out here, I'd have noticed. I'd have come to her rescue right quick, hoping she'd have been grateful."

"Uh-huh."

"Don't give me that look, girlie. I mean I'd have hoped for a reward of the material variety. I'm not a perv."

"Didn't you tell me that you came to Rockton because you slept with a mark instead of killing her? And you slept with her because she was grateful for your warning?"

"Which means I have learned my lesson about gratitude. It is safer in tangible form. However, I can help you with Jakey. Saw him yesterday morning, carving up a bull caribou over by Elk Ridge. He let me have the heart. I am very fond of hearts. Builds strength."

"You ate a raw caribou heart?"

"Fuck no. I cooked it." A grunt as he hefts himself to his feet and hands Dalton the last piece of jerky. "I'll take you to the site. You gotta leave the wheels, though. I'm too old to run behind it with the dog."

"You need more caribou hearts," I say.

"Evidently."

TWENTY-NINE

Dalton is calmer now. Cypher has seen Jacob, and he's doing exactly what Brent said, which explains why he left his last camp and why he hasn't been easy to find. Elk Ridge is north, and we haven't searched in that direction. Brady will head south to find civilization. Actually, the nearest village is west, but he doesn't know that. South makes sense. North does not.

We hide the ATV. It wouldn't have done us any good anyway. The fastest trail to Elk Ridge isn't more than a footpath, soon cutting through sheer rock. As we walk, Storm has a blast, tramping through the mountain streams.

"I want a dog," Cypher muses as she whips past, water droplets flying.

"Well, we do find ourselves in possession of a very young wolf-dog cub," I say. "His mother seemed like she might have been rabid, and the cub bit Dalton, so we're holding him under quarantine."

He glances at Dalton. "Doesn't look like he's quarantined."

I roll my eyes. "The cub."

"It's not rabies anyway. Never seen that in all my years up here." He walks a few more steps. "Wolf-dog you say? How much of each, you figure?"

"More wolf than dog. Just your style."

He gives me a hard look. "Do I strike you as an idiot? Only a fool

thinks he can domesticate a wolf. You should give him to your boyfriend there. Seems *his* style. Raised by wolves, weren't you, boy?"

Dalton ignores him.

"If there's a decent amount of dog in the pup, you might be okay,"
Cypher says. "Too much work for me, but at least dogs are domestic
animals. Wolves aren't. Can't be."

"They probably *can* be," Dalton says. "The root genus is the same.
The question is time frame. It takes generations."

"You letting him read again, kitten?"

Dalton continues, "There was an interesting study using silver foxes
in Siberia. They keep breeding them with human contact. After forty
generations, they had domesticated foxes. That's *forty* generations.
Going in reverse, with dog DNA already in the cub, it should be easier. You still have the wolf to contend with, though. The question
would be mostly one of dominance. Not domestication so much as
establishing a leadership position."

"I like you better when you act stupid, boy."

"I like you better when you don't."

"Who says I'm acting? You keep your wolf-dog. Getting too old
for that dominance shit. Had that already with a dog like yours. Bull
mastiff. Took it in partial trade on a job. I liked the dog. Didn't like
the way its master was treating it—the guy figured he'd beat the dog
into submission. So I persuaded him to part with the beast."

"Uh-huh."

"It was a civil conversation. I asked nicely. The guy laughed, said
the dog was a fucking purebred, too rich for my blood. So I asked
again, said he could take five hundred off my pay. He agreed. Well,
he nodded. Had some trouble talking dangling two feet off the floor
with my arm crushing his windpipe."

"You're very persuasive."

"You have no idea, kitten." He looks at Dalton. "I want a dog. You
got this fancy purebred for your girl. I don't need anything that nice,
but I don't want some mangy mutt either. If I find this Brady guy
and take him off your hands, I get a dog, okay?"

"If you find *Val,* you get a dog," Dalton says. "After Brent, the other
bastard can die out here. If he hasn't already."

Cypher keeps us entertained on the walk. Or I'm entertained. When it comes to Tyrone Cypher, I can never tell how Dalton feels. If asked, he grumbles and rolls his eyes and grumbles some more. I believe he sees Cypher the same way one might view the grizzly the big man resembles—potentially dangerous, potentially useful, trustworthy enough if you know how to approach him but, really, you should probably avoid it if you can.

I like Cypher, but I respect Dalton's wariness. Cypher is the only person here who knew Dalton when he was brought to Rockton. When we first met, Cypher mocked Dalton by calling him "jungle boy" and making his "raised by wolves" jabs. Having gotten to know the man better, I think he was teasing. But those jabs cut deep. Dalton might not be that boy anymore—and he was never the half-wild savage Cypher claims—but he feels like he was, like he still is in some ways, and that's the sharpest needle you can dig into someone, piercing straight into their best-hidden insecurities.

There's more to it, too. I've never met Gene Dalton—the former sheriff—but I used to presume Dalton inherited his personae from him. The profanity. The swagger. The creative punishments. The hard-assed sheriff routine that is fifty percent genuine and fifty percent bullshit. Then I met Cypher, and I realized it wasn't Gene Dalton the boy from the woods had admired and emulated.

That boy wouldn't have necessarily admired the man I've since realized Gene is—quiet, thoughtful, fair and reasoned. No, if that boy was going to look up to someone, it'd be Cypher, larger than life, everyone scurrying from his path, a man both feared and respected.

The problem is that Dalton didn't stay a boy. He grew into a man who sees Cypher's shortcomings. Who realizes Cypher was more feared than respected and that maybe he enjoyed meting out his creative punishments a little too much.

But the die had been cast. Dalton still subconsciously emulates his first role model.

We're nearing Jacob's camp.

"He should be here," Cypher says. "When I talked to him yesterday, he said he wanted to finish butchering the caribou. If he's gone, he won't be far.

"Jake!" Cypher booms. "Yo, Jakey!"

There's a sound from up ahead, and through the trees I make out the side of a hide tent. Another sound comes, a grunt, and Dalton's arm shoots up to stop me.

Cypher swears under his breath. Storm catches a smell in the air, and her fur rises as I grab for her collar. Dalton pulls back a branch.

"And *that*, kitten, is a bear," Cypher whispers.

It is indeed, and it's right there, next to Jacob's tent, ripping through a pack on the ground. It's not a grizzly, which is some relief. It's a big black, though. A boar in his prime, maybe three hundred pounds. When he stands to sniff the air, he stretches to my height.

I cast a quick look around the camp. There's no sign of Jacob, and I exhale. While black bears aren't nearly as dangerous as browns, they can kill if provoked. Jacob knows better than to provoke one. Cypher on the other hand . . .

"You got a clear shot at it, kitten?" he asks.

"Only if it attacks," I say.

"If you've got a clear shot, take it."

"No," Dalton says. "She won't. We can't skin it here, so we're not taking it down unless we have to."

"Fuck, don't tell me you're one of those. Doesn't like killing things unless they need killing."

"Weird, I know," I say.

"Life's a whole lot less dangerous if you just take out everything in your path. Kill or be killed. It's the way of the jungle."

"We're not in the jungle," Dalton says. "This is boreal forest."

"Stop reading, okay? Just stop." Cypher sighs. "Fine, so how you want to do this, nature boy? Ask the bear if we may approach?"

"We're going to spook it. Casey can cover—"

Storm growls.

"I think your pup wants in on the fun," Cypher says.

Storm growls louder. She's straining at my grip, every hair on her body raised, head lowered. The bear rears up again and looks our way.

"Fuck," Cypher says. "Can we shoot it now?"

"Well, that depends," Dalton says. "Unless you've actually learned to aim a gun, you'd have to hold the dog while Casey shoots. And pray that Casey's nine-mil will take the bear down in one shot from this distance."

"You've got a three-fifty-seven."

"I'm left-handed."

Cypher glances at the sling on Dalton's left arm. "Can't just be right-handed like normal people. Fucking inconvenient, you are."

"Eric?" I say. "As fun as this debate is, I'm going to back Storm up before that bear decides to charge. Ty, take my gun. Eric, if you need to shoot, even with your right, you'll probably do better than him."

"Guns are unsporting," Cypher says. "I fight with my hands."

"You do that then, and I'll keep my gun."

"I'd rather you kept it anyway," Dalton says.

I start backing Storm up. It's a tug-of-war, but she allows me to inch her away. Dalton lopes off to the side, making just enough noise to pull the bear's attention.

I continue backing off until we've lost sight of them, and that's when Storm finally settles. She grumbles and grunts, not unlike a bear herself, her shaggy head turning from side to side as she sniffs the air. I manage to get her lying down and park my butt on top of her.

I hear a "Hie! Hie!" from the camp. That's Dalton. Cypher uses more colorful language to convince the bear it's time to go. Both crash through the undergrowth, making as much noise as they can. When a shot fires, I tense and Storm whines, but it's a warning shot, followed by crashes heading the other way and accompanied by the grunts of a fleeing bear.

"Casey?" Dalton calls.

"Right here!"

"He's taking off. We're going to check out the camp. Are you okay where you are?"

"I am."

"Then stay there with Storm in case the bear circles back."

"Got it."

I listen to the forest, gun in hand, but all I can hear is the rustle and murmured talk of the men at Jacob's campsite.

And then Storm leaps up. Leaps up, toppling me off her, and by the time I realize what's happened, she's a black blur disappearing into the forest.

I race after her. It happens so fast that I presume she's heading for the campsite, and I'm not too concerned about that. Then I realize we're heading in the opposite direction.

I should have shouted. If I'd even just yelled for Storm, Dalton would have heard it. I do now. I call for her, and I call for him, but I'm still running, stumbling through thick undergrowth, and I can tell my voice isn't loud enough to carry back to Dalton. But I cannot stop because in that moment, I am absolutely certain that if I do not catch Storm, I've lost her. She's running, and I see her, and as long as I can do that, I still *have* her.

I stop shouting for Dalton and call to her instead. *Storm. Get back here. Stop. Come. Wait.*

It's too many commands. I know that. I'm panicking and shouting whatever comes to mind, and she is not stopping. Goddamn it, she is not stopping. I should have her on a leash. She isn't ready for this, not well enough trained, and my hubris has failed her.

The ground opens up as we veer toward the mountain base. I can see her easily now, bounding over the rock. She's chasing something. I catch a glimpse of brown fur. Tawny. A deer? It leaps over rock, and as it jumps onto one, I see . . .

I see that it's not a deer.

THIRTY

When I realize what Storm is chasing, I scream at her. "Stop! Storm! Stop now!"

She just keeps bounding after a massive tawny brown cat.

A mountain lion.

"Stop!" *Please, please, please, baby, stop.*

She does not stop. Does not seem to hear me. She scrambles over the rocks, letting out a happy bark as she closes in on her quarry.

Quarry? No. Storm has no sense of other animals as prey. We have not taught her that.

We *should* have taught her that.

We didn't get her as a hunting dog, and we don't want her chasing down animals. She's had exposure to many—foxes, deer, rabbits. But they aren't prey. They're chase toys. They run, and she pursues until they take cover, and she loses the game. She's never caught anything bigger than a mouse that she once surprised, and then she just tossed it about until we got it away from her.

In failing to teach her, I have been, in my way, like my parents, failing to prepare me for life's dangers. Because what she is chasing right now is not a chase toy. It will not take cover. It is a predator, and when it turns on her, she will not flee. She will not attack. She'll think the game has taken an exciting new twist—not a chase toy, but a playmate. An animal her own size who is turning around to say, "Tag, you're it," like her human playmates do.

I'm screaming at her, and I know she can't hear me. There's a sharp wind coming off the mountain, blowing my shouts away. I'm not even sure she'd hear me without that. Her ears are filled with the pound of her oversized paws and the heave of her panting breaths and the thump of her adrenaline-charged heartbeat.

I have my gun out. I've had it ready since I realized what Storm is chasing. But I can't get a shot. She's too close to the big cat.

The cat is drawing her into its territory, its comfort zone. Cougars are death from above. The silent plunge from a tree or a rocky overhang. A deadweight thump on your back. Powerful jaws clamping around your neck. Spinal cord severed, you're dead before you hit the ground.

This cougar is luring Storm in. It will make one incredible leap onto a rock—a leap that requires feline hindquarters—and will leave the canine scrambling at the base. Then it will pounce. And that will be my chance. I'll see it spring onto that rock where Storm cannot follow, and when the big cat turns around, I will shoot. I will empty my goddamn gun if I have to.

We're scrambling up the mountainside. The cougar looks back a couple of times, obviously shocked that such a massive canine is keeping up. Storm is big, but she's young and agile, not yet the lumbering Newfoundland she'll become.

The cat veers suddenly. I see where it's going—the perfect overhang. But it has miscalculated. That rock is at least twenty feet above the path. The cougar can't possibly make the leap. Yet it intends to try. Still running, it hunkers low, gaze fixed on that spot. It slows, and Storm is gaining and oh, shit, no. Storm is gaining, and the cat will realize it can't make that jump. Storm will leap and—

The cougar jumps. I see it crouch, see its hind muscles bunch, see it spring, and as terrified as I am for Storm, I cannot help but mentally freeze-frame the sight, awed by the beauty and perfection of that huge cat in flight.

It lands squarely on the ledge. The shock of that freezes me again.

Then the cat disappears, turning around, and I jolt from my surprise to remember my shot.

I raise the gun and look down the sights. The moment the cat appears, I will fire.

At the base of the overhang, Storm barks, jumping and twisting, as if she can reach it.

The cat's ears appear first. Tawny black-rimmed ears. Then the top of its head, dark line down the middle, perpendicular dark slash over each eye. When the pink nose emerges, I start to squeeze the trigger. A chest shot would be better, but any shot at all should spook it, and if it runs the other way instead of pouncing, Storm will be safe, stuck below—

Storm gives one last bark . . . and tears off. I glance away from the gun just in time to see her racing along the rock. Looking for another way up.

Damn it. This is one time when I really wish I had a dumber dog.

"Storm!" I call. She has to hear me now. The cougar does. Its gaze swings my way, and I'm close enough to see those amber irises. Close enough to make eye contact and feel a stab of regret and a hope that my bullet will miss, and the big cat will be frightened off—

Another bark. The sound of paws scrabbling on rocky ground. The sound of paws finding purchase, finding a path, pounding up the mountainside . . .

Shit!

The cougar's head disappears. I fire anyway. Fire and hope the sound will send it running. But I only take that one shot, and then *I'm* running, tearing in the direction Storm went. I can see her, black against the gray rock, making her way up the mountainside, determined to win this game of catch-me.

"Storm!" I call as I run.

She hears me then. Looks back and gives a happy bark. *Mom's playing, too, this is awesome!*

"Storm, come—"

I stop myself. Focus. Breathe. I'm cold with panic. Literally icy with it, cold sweat dripping down my face as I shiver, each breath scorching my lungs, my heart pounding so hard my vision clouds. This is terror. Like seeing that sniper in the tree, Dalton lunging, Dalton falling— but that was a mere second of panic, the thin space between seeing him fall and seeing him alive and breathing. This seems to go on forever.

When I saw what Storm was chasing, I knew she could die. I realized death was a very real possibility and maybe even a probability, and it was all my fault. She trusted me, and I should have known better, and who the fuck—who the *fuck*—was I to think I could protect anything. I have never in my life been able to do that. I've spent years barely able to keep myself moving forward.

Don't rely on me. Just don't. I will do what I can, *everything* I can, but please do not rely on me. Do not give me that responsibility. I will fail.

I am about to fail.

Stop. Focus. I have one last chance. Storm can hear me, and any moment now, that cougar will appear and leap from a rock I can't even see down here.

"Storm? *Stop.*"

I don't shout it. I say it. Loud. Firm. Angry even. Let her know I'm angry. That is the key here. She doesn't understand fear. She doesn't understand shrieking panic. That is not the language I have taught her.

"*Storm. Stop.*"

She skids to a halt and glances over her shoulder and in her eyes, I see confusion. Hurt and confusion.

"Storm. Stay. Storm? Bad girl."

Her ears droop at that, muzzle dipping. She knows she has misbehaved. Knows she has run from me. I must use that.

"Storm? Come."

I'm still walking, as I extend my hand, reaching for her, my gaze on the rocks above. She's almost to me when I see a flash of tawny fur. That's all I see—a blur, as the cougar leaps and shit, oh, shit, no, the big cat is in flight, dropping toward Storm, who is making her way slowly to me, her head and tail down.

I fire. Shot after shot, I fire as the cougar is in flight. The big cat jerks, bullets ripping through its underside in a burst of blood. But it is still falling. Still on trajectory to hit Storm.

"Storm!" I yell, and that only confuses her, and she slows, her head lifting.

The cougar lands square on Storm's back, and I'm flying forward. A voice in my head shouts for me to stop, just stop. It's Dalton's voice, not mine. Mine is silent, accepting, and I'm sailing at the cougar, gun dropped, hands out as if I can physically wrench the big cat off Storm.

The dog bucks, her eyes rolling in terror. The cougar's jaws open. I hit it, both hands slamming into its side. One massive fang slices into Storm's shoulder. Slices in and rips as the big cat falls. I'm on it then, and a memory flashes, Cypher telling me he wanted me to teach him aikido so he could take down the man-eating cougar out here. I remember rolling my eyes at that. He was joking. Had to be joking. No one would attempt anything so stupid.

I'm falling, my hands wrapped in brown fur. Fur slick with blood, blood pumping from multiple shots in the cougar's white underbelly. We go down, and I'm atop the big cat, and all I can think is *What the hell are you going to do? Wrestle it to death?* I grab for my knife. I'm still pulling it out as we roll, and I rear up, knife raised.

The cougar stays on the ground.

I'm poised there, adrenaline pounding. The big cat lies on its side, flanks heaving, blood pumping from the bullet wounds. The cat's mouth opens, and it is breathing hard. Its eye rolls to look at me, and in it, I see a look I know well, from Storm when she is injured.

I don't understand.

I hurt, and I don't understand.

Storm moves up beside me. Blood seeps from her shoulder, but she's walking fine. She sniffs the cat's injured belly and whines. Then she lowers herself at my side and lays her big muzzle on my foot as she watches the cat.

I tentatively reach out and place my hand on the cougar's shoulder. That amber eye meets mine, but the cat just keeps breathing hard, gasping for air.

Dying.

When I shot Blaine, I saw him die. It took only a moment, but I had to watch it—the outrage, the anger, the disbelief. While he had not deserved what I did, he was not blameless. The punishment simply did not fit the magnitude of his crimes.

This cougar *is* blameless. It ran from a predator. It tried to stop a threat. It did what it needed to survive. And I shot it. Emptied my gun into it.

It's a young cougar. I see that now. A male, the size of Storm, which means it isn't more than a couple of years old. One of the man-eater's cubs. A beautiful creature, covered in blood, dying and confused.

Storm whimpers, and I know I have to tend to her, but I can't leave the cat to die alone. Maybe that's overly sentimental, but I feel I owe it something.

No, I *know* what I owe it. The question is whether I can do it. I don't want to. I have to. It is gutshot, like Brent, and if I walk away, it will lie here for hours, slowly dying.

I steady my knife. Then with my left hand, I rub the fur behind its ears. I half expect it to snarl, to tense, but that eye closes and the big cat relaxes under my fingers. I grip the knife firmly in my right hand, find its jugular, and slice, as quickly as I can. The cat's eye flies open, but it doesn't lift its head. With the pain from its stomach, it barely notices the cut. I keep rubbing its head, and that eye closes, and after a moment the cougar goes still.

THIRTY-ONE

I take only a second to regroup. Then I'm checking Storm's shoulder. There's a gash where the cougar's fang pierced and then sliced, and that, too, is my fault—I'd hit the cat as the fang caught.

Of course, if I *hadn't* hit, all four canines would have ripped out the back of Storm's neck. But I'm good at taking blame. Two seconds faster, and I could have saved her from any injury at all.

I have a rudimentary first-aid kit on my equipment belt. When I was a constable, I hated the equipment belt. Gun, baton, radio, cuffs, flashlight . . . The damn thing weighed fifteen pounds, and I consider myself in good shape—need to be in my profession—but I was still half the size of my partners, and my belt was just as heavy as theirs. I would long for the day when I could trade my belt for a shield. It came quickly—my education fast-tracked me to detective—but I still remember the damn belt. Now I must wear one again, and I'm fine with that. I've actually added items to what Dalton considers essential for venturing into the wilderness. The mini first-aid kit is one of my extras. God knows, we need it often enough.

I clean and suture Storm's shoulder. She is remarkably good about that. Part of it is that she's been stitched before, more because her owners are anxious new parents than because her wounds actually required stitches. I suspect her stillness is also because she knows she's in trouble. And part is, I fear, shock. Shock that this beast hurt her.

Shock that her attacker now lies warm and motionless and bloody on the ground.

I don't understand.

I hurt, and I don't understand.

I rub her ears and pet her and talk to her. She nudges the cougar a few times, as if seeing whether it will rise. Nudges. Sniffs. Lies down with her head on its foreleg and sighs.

I'll come back for the cougar's hide. While that sounds callous, it is the opposite. I don't want this hide. I want to say it's ruined and leave it here. But only the belly is shot, and this is what Dalton has taught me, that if we must put down a wild animal and there is any use to be made of its remains, then we must do that. Leaving it to rot is a last resort when, as with the mother wolf-dog, there is nothing to be taken.

I heave to my feet, and maybe I'm in a bit of shock myself, because it's only then that I think, *Oh, shit. Dalton.*

In everything that has happened, I've forgotten how it started. That Dalton and Cypher were checking Jacob's campsite while Storm bolted, and Dalton never realized I'd taken off. He's certainly realized it by now.

I need to get back to him.

I look around, and . . .

Which way is back?

Down the mountainside. I know that much. But from there . . . ?

I ran after Storm, focused only on her, paying no attention to my surroundings.

Shit.

No, I'm fine. There's a damn mountain here, a massive landmark. I know Jacob's encampment was near the base. It's just a matter of orienting myself.

I tell Storm to stay. She doesn't appreciate that, but when I insist, she wisely decides she has disobeyed me enough for one day, and she plunks down with only a grumble.

I climb up to where the cougar had leapt from. I walk to the edge and look out to see forest. Endless miles of forest.

"Eric!" I shout. My voice echoes over the woods below.

I scan for any sign of Jacob's campsite. Of Dalton. Of Cypher. Of anything that doesn't belong in this forest.

I see trees.

Lots and lots of trees.

Forget landmarks, then. I know I am on the proper side of the mountain. We approached from the south, to the southeast side of Hawk Peak—so called because it resembles a hawk's head, with a jutting rock for a beak.

The problem? From where I stand, I can't tell if I'm *on* Hawk Peak. I'm too close to see the rock formation.

If this is Hawk, then I should be able to see a smaller unnamed peak to the east and . . .

I do see rock to the east. Is it the smaller peak . . . or just rock? Damn it. I'm just too close to judge.

I know my way home. That is the main thing. The problem is that Dalton won't go home until he's found me.

I see a stream below. Possibly a small river. I didn't cross one, but I do recall running through marshy land. There's mud on my boots, so that seems to be the generally correct direction.

I unwind a strip of bright yellow cloth from my belt. Last winter I got lost in the woods during a snowstorm, and I'd been grateful for a particularly ugly scarf Anders gave me. So Dalton now insists everyone carry a strip of bright fabric. I fasten it to this rocky ledge to mark the spot where I've left the cougar. I also attach a note for Dalton.

We're fine. I'm going to try to find the campsite again. If you aren't there, I'm heading for the ATV. I know where I am. I won't wander.

Except, of course, I have already wandered, and by saying I know where I am, I mean only the rough geographic area. Rockton encompasses about fifteen acres. It seems a huge and exposed parcel of land, but it is tiny in this massive forest. It isn't as if I can just keep heading in a compass direction and not miss it.

I won't worry about that. I have my gun and extra ammo. I have energy bars. There's plenty of fresh water. It's good weather. Storm and I will be fine. This is the mantra I repeat to myself as I make my way back to my dog.

She's where I left her. I give her a strip of dried meat and a pat, and we set out. I watch her movement. Going downhill isn't easy with her shoulder. She takes it slow, growling now and then, as if frustrated by the impediment. I know exactly how she feels—I do the same, as old injuries in my leg protest the steep downward climb.

As we near the base, I know this isn't the spot we went up—it's too steep. I'm looking for an easier route down when Storm goes on full alert. She starts to whine, her tail wagging.

"Eric?" I ask her.

Her whole body quivers as she dances from paw to paw, her nose raised to catch a scent.

I say "Eric?" again, to be sure. She whines louder, giving me this look as if to say, *Well, obviously. What are we waiting for?*

"Slow," I say. She bounds forward. I call, "Slow!," and she gives me a reproachful glance as she takes it down to a walk.

We make our way down the steep incline. I hope it's Dalton she smells. Names are something she's learned only from general usage. If I say "Where's Eric?" she'll look for him. And one of Dalton's favorite games is to hear me coming up the steps and hold the door closed, saying to Storm "Is that Casey? No, I don't think that's Casey. Are you sure it's Casey?" while the poor puppy goes nuts. I've said one of these days, she's just going to get fed up and bite him, and I won't blame her. If she doesn't, I will—especially if he's holding the door shut when it's thirty below.

I test Storm, saying "Is that Eric?" as we walk, but that only makes her pick up speed, leaving me stumbling over rocky ground to keep up. I quit that before I lose her again. Another thing to add to my duty belt—nylon rope for a temporary lead. I search for something else to use, but I'm not wearing a regular belt, and I have gauze pads, not strips. So, I just keep calling "Slow!" when she bounds ahead, and then I get those looks, like she's humoring Granny with the bad hip.

We're definitely not going the same way we came in. I try not to worry about that. I still have my landmarks, and Storm is on a scent that is almost certainly Dalton's. When I hear something in the trees ahead, I call, "Eric? Tyrone?," and the long muzzle of a caribou rises from a grassy patch. The caribou sees us. Storm sees it.

"Stop!" I say.

Wrong move. The sudden shout sends the doe running, crashing through the trees. I dive for Storm, and I land on her, my hands gripping her collar. But she hasn't moved. She's quaking, watching that fleeing caribou as if fighting the urge to turn tail and run, the memory of the cougar still fresh.

I pet her and tell her it's fine, and I'm fretting about that, whether one bad encounter will now have her terrified of every creature in the forest. But as the caribou bounds off, Storm's shaking turns to another kind of quivering, the kind that says she wants to give chase, and it's a good thing I have both hands on her collar and my deadweight holding her back. The surge of fear has passed, and now all she sees is yet another fleeing play toy.

I sigh, shake my head, and say, "Stay, stay," and then I'm the one fighting an urge. A horrible urge to touch her shoulder, that raw line of stitches, a quick jolt of pain to remind her why she cannot chase things in the forest.

I feel sick even thinking it. Here I was worrying that this bad experience will traumatize her . . . and then I'm struggling against the urge to *reinforce* that?

I finger a tiny scar on my jawbone. Compared to all the other scars on my body, this one is invisible, but for so much of my life, it was "the scar." A permanent reminder that I had disobeyed my parents, and this was the price I'd paid—that my face would never be "perfect" again.

I got the scar rollerblading. I wasn't allowed to rollerblade, of course—looking back, I'm surprised my parents let me own a bicycle. But I'd been at a friend's place and borrowed her blades, despite knowing I was not allowed. I'd fallen and this scar, maybe a half inch long, was the result. After that, whenever I complained about not being allowed to do something, my mother would take out her compact mirror and hold it up for me, and I knew what that meant. *Remember the scar.*

In my head, a barely noticeable blemish became hideously disfiguring. A guy I dated a few times in high school touched it once, when we were sitting on the curb, and he told me it was cute, kinda cool and badass. I dumped him after that, convinced he'd been mocking me. As a child, though, when my mother showed me that mirror, I never felt angry at the reminder. It meant she loved me. It was the only way I knew my parents did. They might not hug or kiss me or call me endearments, but they cared about my safety. Now, as an adult, I'm not sure that was love at all, and yet, when I feel that urge to touch Storm's wound as she watches the fleeing caribou, *that* is what goes through my head. I will touch it and remind her of the danger because I want her to be safe. That is love.

I swallow hard and squeeze my eyes shut. That's not me. That will never be me. But even knowing I'd never do it, the urge still hurts. And on the heels of that comes the reminder that maybe it's a good thing my attack meant I can probably never have kids. I have no experience of how to be a proper parent, and so perhaps it's a decision that *should* be taken out of my hands.

I shake off the thought. Clearly not appropriate—much less helpful—at this moment.

Storm twists and licks my face, whining softly.

"Sorry," I murmur, giving her a pat. "Let's get on with it. Take me to Eric. That's who you smelled, right? Eric?"

Her tail thumps, and I nod, relieved that it wasn't the caribou.

I carefully release her, ready to lunge and grab her back, but she stays at my side for a few steps before venturing into the lead again. As she walks, she lifts her muzzle to catch the breeze, snuffling it, and I call "Eric!" each time to reinforce that's who we're looking for. There's no sign or sound of him, though, and I'm getting nervous. Nothing here is familiar, and there's no way to be sure he *is* what Storm's tracking. We just seem to be wandering deeper into the forest.

When a distant sound catches my ear, I home in on it, thinking, *Eric*. It's not the sound of people, though. It's water. The rushing water of the river I'd seen from the ledge.

Good, I'm on target. We'll go another couple of hundred steps, and if Storm doesn't track down Dalton, we'll swing east and try to find our way back to Jacob's camp.

Storm gives a happy bark and looks at me, tail wagging.

"You smell Eric?" I say.

She whines and dances.

I smile. "Okay then."

She takes off like a shot. I jog after her. The ground is more open here, and I can easily track her as she runs. I don't see anything ahead, but she very clearly does, tearing along, veering to the left, me jogging behind, my footfalls punctuating the burble and crash of water over rapids—

Water.

River.

To the left.

That's what Storm is running to. Not Dalton, but the one thing she can resist even less than fleeing prey: the siren's call of water.

I shout, calling her back, but she keeps running. I don't know if she literally can't hear me, being too far away, or if she figuratively can't hear, the call of that water too great.

Damn it, we need to work on this. Buy a whistle and train her to come to it.

We also need to seriously consider that pool. It might help with her water fixation. I can't blame Storm—Newfoundlands are water dogs. She'll even try getting into the shower with us if we don't close the door.

I'm chasing her at full speed, but I'm not worried. We'll be delayed for a few minutes while she splashes and plays. Then I'll continue on with a very wet but happy dog.

I hear the crash of the water over rocks, and I realize I know where I am. We came this way a couple of months ago with Anders, just as the spring thaw was setting in. He saw this river, rock-filled and fast-running, and said it'd be perfect for white-water kayaking. Dalton said sure, if he could—

My steps falter as I remember the rest . . . standing on the edge of rock and looking down at the river as Dalton said, "Yeah, if we can airlift you down there."

Down into the canyon river, fifty feet below.

THIRTY-TWO

"Storm!" I shout. "Stop!"

She doesn't slow. I yell louder. She keeps going.

I need a whistle. I need a leash. I need to do more goddamn training with her.

All of which is a fine idea, and perfectly useless at this moment.

We reach the rocks, and she's leaping over them, heading for that gorge.

"Storm! Stop!"

I shout it at the top of my lungs.

Less than a meter from the edge, she stops. Then she looks back at me . . . and begins edging forward, like a child testing the boundaries.

"No!"

Another step. A look back at me. *But, Mom, I really want to go this way.*

"No!"

I'm moving at a jog now across rocks slick with moss. Storm has taken one more careful step toward the edge. Her nose is working like mad, picking up the scent of the water below.

"No."

Please, no. Please.

She whines. Then she takes another step, and she's almost to the edge.

"Storm, no!"

Goddamn you, no. Damn you, and damn me for the idiot who didn't bring a lead.

She's stopped mere inches from the edge.

As she whines, I hunker down and say, "Come."

Whine.

"Come. Now!"

She looks toward the edge.

"Storm, come!"

I hear a noise. At first I think it's the water below. It must be. It cannot be what it sounds like.

Storm is growling. At me.

She growls again, jowls quivering.

My dog is growling at me.

I know it can happen. I've read enough manuals to understand that a growl is communication, and not necessarily threat. What it communicates is a clear no. A test of dominance. Yet it feels like a threat. Like I have failed, and she's questioning my authority. Telling me she's not a little puppy anymore.

"Storm," I say as firmly as I can.

Don't show fear. Don't show hurt.

She lowers herself to the rock in submission, as if I misheard the growl.

"Storm. Come here."

Still lying down, she begins belly-crawling toward the edge.

"Goddamn it!"

I don't mean to curse, but my words ring through the canyon. She whines. Then she continues slinking toward the edge.

My heart thumps. There are only a couple of feet between us, and I want to lunge and grab her by the collar and haul her back from the edge. Yet if she resists at all, we'll go over.

I keep moving, as slowly as I can, trying to figure out how to get her back without turning this into a deadly tug-of-war.

Please, Storm. Please come back. Just a little. I can grab you if you come a few inches my way.

She puts her muzzle over the edge, and I have to clamp my mouth shut to keep from screaming at her, from startling her into falling. She lies there, looking down. Then she glances back at me. From me to the river below. Her nose works. She whines.

"I know it's water," I say as I get down onto all fours. "I know it looks wonderful. If we keep going down the ridge, there's a basin. You can swim there. I promise."

I'm talking to myself. I know that. But I hope my voice calms her, even casts some kind of spell luring her from that edge.

Again, though, she looks from me to the river. Sniffs. Whines.

I form a plan. It's dangerous, but there's no way I'm taking a chance she'll go over the edge. I creep along on all fours. When I reach Storm, I rub her flank. My hand travels up her side, still petting, aiming for her collar. I carefully hook my fingers around it.

I won't pull Storm until I'm farther from the edge, with a better footing. Before I inch backward, I glance down into the gorge. I'm getting a look at what we face, so I will be prepared should we go over. And the moment I look down, I know I do not want to go over. Glacial ice coming off the mountain has been wearing away rock for centuries, and the walls go straight down. Below, there isn't even a safe amount of water to drop into. It's a shallow mountain river, more of a stream, filled with rapids and—

There is something in the water. An unnatural shape, unnaturally colored. Long and slender. Black on the bottom. Purple and yellow on top. It's the purple and yellow that I focus on. It's a pattern of some sort, and it jogs a memory of me thinking:

I haven't seen that shirt before. It's pretty. Far more colorful than usual. Did she bring it with her, tuck it at the back of her closet, an unwanted reminder of a time when she hoped for a brighter future in Rockton?

This is Val's shirt.

It is the blouse I last saw her wearing.

I tell myself she's lost it, that maybe she removed it to wash in the stream and it floated away and that's all this is. *All* this is.

That's a lie. An obvious, blatant, ridiculous lie.

I see that blouse trapped on the rocks. I see the black below it—the dress trousers she always wore. I see one shoe. One bare foot, pale against the dark water. I see her arms, her hands, equally pale. I see the brown and gray of her short hair.

I am looking at Val.

At her body.

Battered against the rocks below.

Storm whines. I glance over, and she has her muzzle on the edge, her dark eyes fixed on Val. That is why we're here. Not because she smelled water and wanted to go for a swim. She has located her target. We set her on a scent, and she has tracked it to its source.

I reach to pet her and whisper, "I'm sorry."

She nudges me, and then looks at Val again.

Well, there she is, Mom. Go get her.

I can't, of course. Not from here. I'm not even sure I can get to her from below. It's a narrow gorge, and she's trapped on the rocks.

Sure, Val, go ahead and play spy.

It's okay, Val. Just go with Oliver. You'll be fine. We'll get you back.

My fault.

My responsibility.

There is no surge of grief. No tears. I move slowly, looking around for a way to get down, my body numb, the crash of the rapids muted. Storm's muzzle against my hand feels as if she's nudging me through a thick glove.

I nod, and I murmur something to her. I'm not even sure what it is. All I know is that I need to get Val out of the water for a proper burial.

Like Brent.

How would you like to be buried, Val? Before you go, just answer me that. In case I fuck up and get you killed, how should you be laid to rest? Any final words you'd like said?

Tears do prickle then, but they feel like self-pity, and I swipe them away with the back of my hand.

I will get her out of the water. I see jutting rock down there, with sparse vegetation, a bit of windblown soil and a place for me to lay her body, safely out of the water. We'll come for her later. Just get her out before the current dislodges her body and whisks it away.

I survey the cliff. It's impossible to climb down right here—it really is an edge, with a straight drop below. But if I travel farther down, I see a route with a bit of a slope.

I head to it. Storm follows. I reach the spot and tell her to lie down and then, firmly, to stay. She does, head on her paws.

I crouch at the edge. From here, the route looks steeper than it did farther up. But I can do this. Just a bit of rock climbing. I see the first stone to put my feet on. It's a half meter down. Easy. Just back up to the edge and lower my feet over.

I do that. I'm holding on to a sturdy sapling with one hand, the other grabbing the rock edge. The rock should be right . . .

It's not right there. I'm past my waist, and I don't feel anything underfoot. I glance down. I'm about six inches short, that rock farther than it seemed. I take a deep breath and lower myself until my toes—

My foot touches down and keeps going. I grab my handholds as tight as I can and find my footing before I carefully look. I see my boot and the rock beneath it. A sloping rock. Okay, that's not what I expected but—

No.

I hear Dalton's voice in my head.

Hell and fuck, no, Butler. Get your ass back up here now.

I look over my shoulder and see Val's body.

You feel guilty? Fine. You're going to risk your own life to get her out of there? Not fine. Stupid. Unbelievably stupid, and you know it. You aren't saving her. She's dead. She doesn't give a damn if you bury her body or not. Get your ass up here, come find me, and we'll see if there's a way to do this safely.

He's right, of course. This is unbelievably stupid.

The second time I met Dalton, he called me a train wreck, hellbent on my own destruction. I corrected him—that implied I was a *runaway* train, not a wreck. I didn't argue with the principle, though. After killing Blaine, I never contemplated suicide. I never tried to die; I just didn't try to live, either. Didn't try to stay alive or enjoy that life while I had it. I felt as if I'd surrendered my future when I stole Blaine's from him.

Now, seeing Val's body below, I feel as if I have pulled that trigger again. If anything, this is worse, because I didn't act out of hate and rage and pain. It was negligence. Carelessness. But when I think that, I hear Dalton's voice again, telling me not to be stupid. Yeah, he understands the impulse—fuck, yes, he understands it—but we *aren't* shepherds with our herd of not-terribly-bright sheep. Mistakes were made. Mistakes will always be made. But I didn't throw Val to this wolf. I tried everything I could to keep Brady from taking her into that forest.

I still accept responsibility for Val's death. Yet I have to take responsibility for my life, too, for not doing something stupid because I feel guilty. That leaves Rockton without a detective and Dalton without a partner. I have made compacts here, implicit ones, with the town, with Dalton, even with Storm, and those say that I won't do something monumentally risky and stupid, or I will hurt them, and they do not deserve that.

I dig my fingers into the soil, and I test the sapling I'm holding. It's sturdy enough. I brace and then pull myself—

My hand slides on the sapling. It's only a small slip, but my other hand digs in for traction and doesn't find it and . . . And I'm not sure what happens next, it's so fast. Maybe when the one hand loses traction, the other loosens just enough to slide off the sapling. All I know is that I slip. I *really* slip, both hands hitting the ravine side with a thump, fingers digging in, dirt flying up, hands sliding, feet scrabbling for that rock just below. One foot finds it. The other does not. And the one that does slides off, and I fall.

I fall.

Except it's not a clean drop. It's a scrabble, hands and feet feeling dirt and rock and grabbing wildly, my brain trapped between *I'm falling!* and *No, you're just sliding, relax.*

The latter is false hope, though. It's that part of my brain that feels earth under my hands and says I must be fine. I'm not fine. I'm falling, sliding too fast to do more than notice rock under my hands and then it's gone, and I try to stay calm, to say yes, just slide down to the bottom, just keep—

I hit a rock. A huge one. My hands manage to grab something and my feet try, but they're dangling, nothing beneath them, kicking wildly, and *why can't I feel anything beneath them?*

I've stopped. Both hands clutch rock—a shelf with just enough accumulated dirt for my fingers to dig in and find purchase. There. I'm fine.

No, you're not. Where are your legs?

I'm fine.

Look down.

I don't want to. I know what's happened, and I've decided to pretend I don't.

See, I stopped falling. No problem. I've totally got this.

I look down. And I see exactly what I feared. I am holding on to a ledge. Dangling from a rock thirty feet over the water. No, over a thin stream and more rock.

The wind is howling, and I think, *That's just want I need.* But the air is still, and I realize I'm hearing Storm.

Newfoundlands have an odd howl, one that makes them sound like a cross between a dinosaur and Chewbacca. It's a mournful, haunting sound that has scared the crap out of every Rockton resident. It's been known to wake me with a start when she begins howling with the wolves.

"I'm okay!" I call up to her. "Storm? I'm fine."

Even if she understood me, she'd call bullshit, and rightly so. I am not fine. I'm dangling by my fingertips over a rocky gorge.

I flex my arms, as if I might be able to vault back onto that ledge. My fingertips slide, and my heart stops, and I freeze, completely freeze. My left hand finds a rocky nub on the ledge. I grip that and dig in the fingers of my right hand until they touch rock below the dirt.

Then I breathe. Just breathe.

I glance over my shoulder. Even that movement is enough for my brain to scream for me to stop, don't take the chance, stay still. But I do look, as much as I can without loosening my grip.

It's a drop. There is no denying that, no chance I could just slide down. I will fall. At best, I will break both legs, and even as I think that, I know that is extreme optimism. Death or paralysis are the real options here.

I'm going to die.

If I don't die, if I'm only paralyzed, I won't be able to stay in

Rockton, and when I think that, it feels the same as death. I want to tell myself I'm being overdramatic, but I know I'm not. Leaving this place would be death for me, returning to that state of suspended animation. I don't think I could ever return to that. I've had better. So much better. If I can't stay here . . .

I squeeze my eyes shut.

Breathe. Just breathe.

My arms are starting to ache. One triceps quivers. I strained it last week in the weight room with Anders, twisting mid-extension as he made a joke. Now it's quivering when it should be fine.

It is fine. It will be fine.

Breathe.

I don't breathe. I can't. That quivering triceps becomes a voice, whispering that even holding on is foolish. I can't hold on forever, and there's no other way to go but down.

The triceps is quaking now, and my right hand slips. I grip tighter. The rock edge digs into my forearms. Blood drips down my arm.

I look left and then right. Maybe that's the way to go. Perpendicular. Get to a safer spot and then slide. I can see one possibility, maybe ten feet to my left. Between here and there, though, the rock is smooth, and I'm not sure I could find hand grips.

Well, you're going to have to try, aren't you?

My left hand has a good hold on this rocky nub. I release my right a little and begin inching it left. It's slow going. Millimeter by millimeter it seems, excruciatingly slow as my dog howls above.

I'm almost there. Get my right hand wrapped around that nub and then—

My right hits rock. Solid, slick rock. My fingers slide. I try to dig in, but there's nothing to grasp, and my nails scrape rock and there's a jolt, excruciating pain shooting through my left arm and . . .

THIRTY-THREE

I'm dangling by one arm. My left hand still clutches that jutting rock, but that's the only thing keeping me on the rock face, and the pain, holy shit, the pain.

I grit my teeth and focus on the fact that I'm still holding on. Not how *barely* I'm holding, or how much that jolt hurt. I'm still okay.

Well, relatively speaking.

I make a noise at that. It's supposed to be a chuckle, but it sounds like a whimper.

Still hanging on. Still alive.

I need to find purchase. Whether it's my right hand or right foot or left foot . . . Just find purchase somewhere. Being slightly lower means I have fresh places to check.

Optimism. Awesome.

I start with my right hand. Reach up and . . .

All I can do from this angle is scratch the edge of that rock ledge, and my nails are already torn. I reach down instead. There's a rock there, a nub that I can at least grip to brace myself and take some of the pressure off my left arm. I do that, and then I try with my legs, but of course, that would be too much to hope for.

I'm still hanging off a ledge, my dangling legs nowhere near the cliffside.

I'm okay. I'm okay. I'm okay.

Two fingers on my right hand twitch. I'm holding them in an awkward position trying to keep some semblance of a grip, and they have had enough. Two fingers twitch. Then a third joins in.

No, no—

My right hand slips. That jolt again, my left shoulder screaming as my right hand clamps tighter and—

"Casey? Casey!"

I am hearing that, right? Not hallucinating?

Fresh pain stabs through my arm.

"Casey!"

The voice comes from right above me, and I peer up to see Dalton on his hands and knees, looking over the side, his face stark white. He pulls back, and I want to scream, *No, don't leave me.*

I remember my nightmares after finding Nicole in the cave, nightmares where I'm in the hole and everyone leaves me, and Dalton stays the longest but eventually he, too, gives up on me.

I'm hallucinating. He's not really here. It's the pain and the shock and that memory finding a fresh variation to torture me with.

Even Storm has gone silent above.

Pebbles fall, pelting my face. "Are you crazy, boy?" a voice bellows. "Get your ass back . . ."

The words trail off, and I see a foot over the edge. A boot. Dalton's boot. Vanishing as Cypher hauls him up.

"You want to *knock* her down into that gorge?"

Dalton reappears, looking over the edge. "Casey? Can you hear me?"

"Course she can," Cypher says. "The whole damn mountain can. Now stop panicking and get back from that edge. Your girl is fine."

Dalton snarls something at him. Cypher's bearded face appears over the edge.

"Hey, kitten," he says. "How are you doing?"

He gets a string of obscenities from Dalton for that, but I say, "I've been better," and Cypher laughs.

"Okay," he says. "I'm going to ask you to try something for me. Take your right hand and bring it up on the *other* side of your left. You need to reach maybe four inches to the left of it."

I do that, and I find a crevice in the rock, one I can dig my fingers into. It's an even better grip than I have with my left, and I ease a little of my weight that way.

"Don't get too comfortable, kitten. I'm going to make you switch hands. Which will be tricky, but a whole lot easier to maintain. Okay?"

"Okay."

He guides me through it, and a few minutes later, I'm still hanging, but in a far more secure position.

"I'm going down—" Dalton begins.

"No, Eric, you aren't," Cypher says. "I'm not rescuing both of you today. How about you help me figure out how Casey can rescue herself?"

"I'd rather—"

"I know you would. But if you try, I'll throw you down there with that poor drowned woman and save the trouble of having to rescue you."

As he says "poor drowned woman," I turn to see Val's body, directly below. Her one arm is stretched over her head, the current catching it in a macabre wave.

"Yeah, she's still there," Cypher says. "Still dead. Like she was when you apparently decided you had to go after her."

"I wanted to retrieve her body."

"Why? She doesn't give a damn." He shakes his head, grizzled hair hanging. "You almost kill yourself for a dead woman. Your boy here tries to turn this into a double suicide mission. And people say I'm crazy."

"Casey?" Dalton calls. "Don't move just yet, but I'm going to have you keep shifting left. Once you get past that overhang, you'll be able to get footholds."

"Oh," Cypher says. "You're back with us, are you?"

"Have to, or you'll *talk* Casey to death." Dalton leans out. "You're going to be fine, but if at any point you feel yourself slipping, or if a hold doesn't seem as safe, I want you to stop. No heroics. I *can* get down there. Got it?"

"Yes, sir."

Dalton guides me. Whenever he hesitates, Cypher points out possibilities, and they debate them quickly, before coming to a consensus. I move about five feet left and then I'm clinging to the cliffside, hands and feet secure.

"Up or down?" I ask.

"You can make it up," Cypher says.

"I'd rather you went down," Dalton says. "Please."

When I pause, he says, "It's a crawl with no serious obstacles. It's safer."

I start down. Once I'm securely heading that way, Dalton heads along the cliffside to find a more gradual decline. He'll join me, and we'll see if we can get back to Val. Cypher grumbles about that, but we outvote him.

I make it down. It is not an easy trip. Nor painless or even remotely graceful, as I slide down the last ten feet on my ass, try to put on the brakes, and land in the icy stream.

"It's not a waterslide, kitten," Cypher booms down the gorge.

I wave at him as I get to my feet. Dalton is already down, picking his way along the stream. I wave to him, too, as I start toward Val. She's still bobbing, her shirt hooked on a rock. I can't get very close. She's on the other side, and the stream is a good ten feet across and moving fast with spring runoff. One wrong foot placement, and I'll hurtle downstream.

"Wait," Dalton calls.

"I am."

I sit on a rock. He's discarded his sling, not surprisingly. He's almost there when his foot slips, and I leap up, my hand swinging out. He grabs it, but only gives it a squeeze and says, "You okay?"

"I am."

He nods, and I feel his assessing gaze, stopping on every gash and rising bruise, his lips tightening.

I hug him. Throw my arms around his neck and squeeze, and that's meant to reassure him, but as soon as I feel him against me, my knees wobble and every muscle unclenches, and if he didn't hug me back tight, I'd have been on the ground.

"You're okay?" he says again as he releases me.

"I'm fine, Eric. But Val . . ."

"Yeah, I know. Bastard." He looks over at Val's body. "I don't see the point, Casey. I really don't."

"With people like Oliver Brady, I don't think there needs to be a point. He killed her because he could."

He nods, as if he understands, but I know he doesn't. He can't.

"Let's just take her . . ."

I'm about to say "home." Rockton is *our* home; it wasn't hers. I'm not sure it ever could have been.

"Is there some other place to . . ." I'm being foolish when I need to be practical, so I don't finish voicing the thought.

"We'll figure something out."

He looks over at her. "All right. Trick will be getting her free without losing her. I'm going to grab her leg closest to this side." He starts untying his boots. "It looks about a foot deep. I'll wade. Safer than rock jumping."

"There's a clear path just above that rock. Stick to it or even in water that shallow, you can get your foot caught, and the current will take you down."

"I know. If it feels too strong, I'll drop."

He means that he'll fall on his ass and crawl. That's the way to do it. Twelve inches of water *does* seem like a simple wade, but between the current and the slippery rocks below, it's treacherous. He takes it slow, placing one foot down and making sure it's secure before lifting the other. Twice he just stops and waits until he has his balance.

Seeing Val's body this close up leaves little doubt she's been dead and in the water since not long after she disappeared. Her thin face has bloated, and her slender body strains against her clothing. That amount of water retention suggests he killed her on the first day. I can't see *how*—there's no obvious sign of injury—but I will once I can examine her body.

Dalton is close enough to reach Val's leg. Then he looks about, assessing.

"If you're considering whether you should drop," I say, "the answer is yes."

He lowers himself. A quick gasp as the icy glacial runoff soaks him. He's on his knees, stable now and less than a foot from Val.

Dalton reaches for her trouser leg. Her corpse rocks, as if even his body mass disrupts the rush of water. He lets out a curse and grabs for her, but that movement unsnagged her blouse and her body shoots off downstream.

I take a running leap along the rocky path, but Dalton shouts "No!" and he's right. The water is moving fast, and Val's body is hurtling faster than I can run along this uneven shore.

"She'll come to rest farther down," he says. "It lets out into a small lake. We'll get her there."

We're up on the cliffside with Cypher and Storm. Dalton has explained that he saw my yellow flag, and they'd been by it when Storm started howling. Which means I suspect she really *had* initially scented Dalton and only diverted when she smelled Val—the target I'd set her on. Doing as she'd been told, while her master freaked out, mistaking her for a feckless puppy.

When we reach them, Cypher has something for me. The young cougar.

"You went back for that?" I say.

"Fuck no. I was busy watching you two fools, in case you needed grown-up help. We found him"—he hefts the carcass—"up by your flag. When your pup started yowling, I grabbed the cat and . . ." He swings the cougar over his shoulders to demonstrate.

"And ran down the mountain with a hundred-pound cougar on your back?"

"Wasn't going to leave him for scavengers. That's some fine shooting. I'm guessing by the placement of those bullet holes the cat was midleap when you put them in him."

I nod. "They didn't kill him, though."

"Disabled him. That's all that matters. And you knew what to do next. Put the kitty out of his misery. See, now *that's* what I need."

"Someone to put *you* down?" Dalton says.

Cypher rolls his eyes. "I mean a girl like Casey to keep me company. Smart and pretty, a good conversationalist, knows how to take care of herself. If I found one who could cook and clean, too, I'd be set." He looks at me. "What do you figure my odds are?"

"Excellent," I say. "If you're twenty-five, gorgeous, have a Ph.D., and can bench-press triple your body weight."

"Two outta four ain't bad."

"Never knew you had a Ph.D.," Dalton says.

"And the boy makes a proper comeback. The next step? Make one that's actually funny."

THIRTY-FOUR

Shortly after that, Cypher leaves us. He'll drop off the cougar at his camp, where he insists on preparing the skin for me. We continue on to retrieve Val's body, but we can't find it. She's out of sight by the time we reach the top of the cliffside, and we follow the stream along until we reach the lake where Dalton is certain her body will stop. We don't see her there. At some point, her clothing must have caught again and submerged her body.

I'm not sure what we'll do about this. I want to find her, obviously. But someone else is missing, too, someone who is almost certainly still alive: Jacob.

Dalton tells me his brother's campsite seems to have been abandoned before the black bear found it. It's a hunting camp—a basic tent, sleeping furs, and the backpack we saw the bear rummaging through. The only thing missing? Jacob. That could suggest he was just out hunting . . . if he hadn't left his gun. And the food bag he'd hoisted into a tree was full.

"That makes no sense," I say as we walk. "If Brady found Jacob at his camp, he'd take the gun and food."

"Then he must not have found him at camp. Jacob could have been out scouting."

"Without his rifle?"

Dalton shrugs. "Getting water then."

"And you're sure it was Jacob's site?"

"One hundred percent. His gun. His pack."

I want to say that I don't think Jacob could be captured so easily. Or that Brady would have forced him back to take his supply stash. But, yes, Brady could have surprised Jacob, and he might not have realized Jacob would have food nearby.

"We'll stop at Rockton," he says. "Get Will and a couple of others and head out to look for Val."

Which seems to be the right move. But it's not. This winter, when we had a fatality in town, Anders had said, "I can't fix dead." It wasn't just a gibe, though. It was hard truth.

We can't fix dead.

Val is dead. Brady killed her. We know those two things; so autopsying her body will only tell us how he did it. Brady won't ever see the inside of a courtroom, though, especially for anything he does up here.

I do want to put Val's body to rest, but how much of that is about me and not her? She's gone, and I blame myself, and I want to do something for her, and the only thing I can do is retrieve her remains. Would she care?

No. The only thing she'd care about is justice. If we think Brady might have taken Jacob, that's all the more reason to focus on him.

We retrieve the ATV and return to Rockton. With everything that has happened, it feels as if it should be nightfall by now. Instead, it's two in the afternoon, and we're still able to grab a late counter-service lunch.

Dalton takes Anders, Jen, and another militia member and heads back on the ATVs to search for Val.

I stay behind. One of us should, and Dalton wants me to tend to my various scrapes and bruises and pulled muscles. When I don't argue, he gives me a look, as if to ask what I'm up to, but I tell him I don't want to slow them down, and someone *does* need to be here in case Brady circles back.

Plus, I have to tend to the wolf cub, change his dressings and look for signs of rabies. I think it's the last excuse that convinces him. I'm still worried about Dalton's bite, so that makes sense.

I put Storm in the house. I hate locking her in but the alternative is a recap of pup versus cub.

When I open the door to my old house, I hear the scrabble of claws as the cub races behind my couch. This time, I can lure him out with meat scraps. I haven't proven dangerous so far, and that monster isn't howling and scratching at the door.

I replace his dressings and check for signs of rabies. I see none, and by this point, I'm starting to agree he isn't infected.

As I change his dressing, I resist the urge to scratch behind his ears or cuddle him. That is oddly difficult, more than it would be with a human patient. We're already crossing a line by feeding him—associating humans with food. Yet we aren't sure what else to do, besides declare him rabies-free and dump him into the forest to fend for himself. Abandon him to die. That's what we'd be doing, and neither of us suggests that.

When the door opens, I grab for the cub. I'm accustomed to Storm as a puppy, where an open door meant freedom. Instead the wolf cub dives back behind the sofa.

Mathias walks in. Before I can give him shit for not knocking, he says in French, "I want the wolf-dog."

"Uh, yeah . . . no. He's not a—"

"Pet. I realize that. No one else will." He purses his lips. "Except Dalton. And of course, you, but you already have Storm, therefore giving you guardianship of another animal would be unfair."

"No one is taking this cub. The whole 'not a pet' issue."

"Which is why I am requesting guardianship." He crouches to peer at the cub. "Australian shepherd."

"Hmm?"

"The dog blood is Australian shepherd. I am familiar with the breed—my family owned several. It's a working dog, like all shepherds. I believe that will help counteract the wolf blood and the combination of the two will produce an excellent guard dog. Possibly even an acceptable hunting dog, given the wolf instincts."

When I say nothing, he looks over. "What is the alternative? It cannot be returned to the wild at this age. It cannot be released once it is grown. It cannot be given to anyone in town who will, despite all protestations, expect a dog like Storm. I have scraps to feed it. I have the time to train it. I am bored. It will be a project for me."

"I'm not sure an animal should be a cure for boredom, Mathias."

"Then consider it a favor. To you. Otherwise you will be placed in an impossible situation. You'll never euthanize an animal you have rescued and cared for. So you will be forced to add it to your household, which introduces a dilemma. It cannot sleep by your bed like Storm, or roam freely as she does. Yet if Storm bonds with the cub as a pack mate, you must treat them the same, which means either restricting her or being dangerously lax with him."

I hunker back on my haunches. "Did you hear about Val?"

"All right. You are not outright refusing me, which means you are changing the subject so you may consider my request. Also you are reminding me that this might not be the time to make such a request. Yes, I heard she is dead. I also know you will feel responsible. If you wish to discuss that, I would remind you that Isabel is the therapist."

"I'm not looking for therapy. Or absolution. You were there. You know what happened. I chose to let Brady take Val because that seemed the best chance for her survival."

"True."

I carry the wolf cub's bowl into the kitchen for fresh water. "The question I want to ask you is *why*. Why would Brady kill her? Yes, we suspect he's a serial killer, but his MO suggests he likes torture and captivity. Would a quick kill serve the same purpose?"

"No," he says as I return with the water. "But the urge to kill is . . . People often use the analogy of hunger or thirst. I prefer sex. Most of us enjoy it, and it satisfies a need, yet we can survive without it. For a murderer who likes to torture his victims, a quick death is akin to shower masturbation with someone banging on the door telling you to hurry up. It won't scratch the itch, but it does the job in a pinch."

I set the bowl down along with more meat scraps. When the cub comes out from behind the couch, Mathias crouches and takes a piece, holding it out.

I make a noise in my throat, and he says, "That is an excellent Momma Wolf impression, Casey."

"You know what I mean."

"Oh, but I do. The same thing Momma Wolf would. Watch myself because you have not yet decided whether I pose a threat to your little one." He feeds the cub. "Are we certain Brady murdered Val?"

"He murdered Brent."

"Which is not the same thing. And yet it is to you, isn't it? If he murdered your friend Brent, then you are not wasting time wondering if he is also responsible for Val. You will determine that when you have the body, but for now, it does not matter."

"Should it?"

"I suppose not."

I want to snap, *Then why bring it up?* I don't. He's only nudging doubts I don't want nudged. Brent is dead. There is no question that Brady shot him. But the question of *intent* is murkier. The gun went off during a fight. I want to say that doesn't matter. Death as a result of an armed robbery is still homicide. Brady also failed to do anything to help Brent after he'd been shot. He ground his *fist* into the injury. Therefore, he must be the monster his stepfather claims he is.

Yet I keep hearing him in the clinic, telling me not to test him, not to underestimate his desperation.

Desperate enough to take a hostage. Desperate enough to threaten to kill me. Desperate enough to waylay Brent in hopes of finding Jacob.

And Val?

When I realized she'd been in the water for a while, I jumped to the conclusion that this proved Brady killed her. Of course it doesn't. In fact, if I'm being brutally honest, the location of her corpse suggests he might not be the culprit. While it's possible that Brady led her up the mountainside and then killed her, I don't see the point of that. My theory was that her body had been dragged upstream by a large predator.

Yet is it not equally likely that Val herself fled in the wrong direction? That she escaped Brady, or he let her go, and she ran toward the nearest landmark? Climbed the mountain hoping for a good vantage point and then slipped into the gorge?

I don't want to think that. I need the simple answer for now—that Brady murdered her and therefore, if I see him, I am free to shoot.

He killed Brent. He killed Val. He is a killer. The end.

THIRTY-FIVE

Dalton returns at dinner hour. They didn't find Val. The stream is too narrow and shallow to miss her body, but there are several pools along the way. We have no equipment for diving, and the glacial water is still too cold for sustained searching. So they return, tired, frustrated, and empty-handed.

Dalton finds me in our house. I'm taking a shower with Storm—kind of—having trained her to lie with her head inside the partially open door so she can enjoy the spray without actually getting in with me.

Afterward, I'm dressing while packing a bag. He's too preoccupied to notice the latter.

"I've decided you're right," he says as he lounges on the bed, watching me scurry about in my bra and panties.

"Am I?"

"About Jacob, that is. There are other reasons he might abandon camp temporarily. Bears for one. And I didn't see his bow. He might have been out with that, got led off by good hunting."

"Uh-huh." I tuck one of his shirts into the bag.

"Even if Brady did get the jump on him, that doesn't mean he *kept* him. Jacob isn't some kid wandering the forest. He knows how to take care of himself."

"He does." I grab toothbrushes and paste from the bathroom. Then I start pulling on my jeans and shirt.

"But if it wasn't easy—or safe—to escape, Jacob would do the smart thing and give Brady what he wants. Lead him in the general direction of the nearest community. It'd take a fucking week to walk there. But that's a week for Jacob to escape."

"True." I heft the bag. "Needs marshmallows."

"Marshmallows?"

"For the bonfire," I say as I head downstairs.

I'm on the first level by the time he calls down, "What bonfire?"

"The one we'll have when we stop to camp. We should get going, though, while we still have light. You grab the marshmallows and bring Storm. I'll meet you at the stables."

Dalton doesn't argue with my plan, which is that we're going hunting for Jacob—immediately. All the self-talk in the world won't keep us from worrying. At least searching eases the tension, making us feel as if we are accomplishing something productive.

First, we check the marked tree and find the flag to tell Jacob we want to talk. Next we travel to a spot he sometimes uses for a temporary camp. There's no sign he's been there. He has a more permanent site where he hides his gear, but Dalton has no idea where it is.

He grumbles about that tonight, like he always does. Usually, that's just hurt feelings, and I tease that it's like when the brothers were little and Dalton had hiding spots to escape Jacob. Now Dalton knows what that feels like. It's a good analogy, too. Jacob avoids questions about his main camp because he doesn't particularly want his brother there. Part of it might be privacy, but I think more is fear of being judged.

Dalton is physically incapable of keeping his opinions to himself, particularly when those opinions relate to how others are living their lives. We occasionally need that blunt honesty and hard push toward what we secretly know is the right path. But there's a limit to how much honesty—and pushing—anyone wants, and Dalton struggles to find that line. I think Jacob imagines his brother seeing his permanent camp and finding all the faults with it, all the reasons he should make Rockton his base camp. Better to just firmly draw that line for Dalton. *I love you, brother, but this is my space, and thou shalt not pass.*

Now, though, not knowing where to find that permanent camp gives Dalton a real reason to complain.

We return to the abandoned camp to search it better. We confirm that, yes, Jacob's bow is missing. While he has the rifle, that's mostly for protection. It's the bow he keeps strung across his back in case he spots dinner.

We set Storm to work here. I pull a sweater from inside the tent and let her sniff, and she does a little dance of joy. On the long list of people she adores, Jacob is near the top, and she's been racing about camp already, sniffing and looking for him. Now realizing that *he* is her target makes her far happier than when we gave her Val and Brady.

The moment I let her sniff Jacob's sweater, she's off like a flash. Fortunately, I learned my lesson with the cougar. She's on a lead now, and Dalton is holding it—she can't take him butt-surfing, no matter how hard she pulls. She snuffles around the campsite for about three seconds and then zooms into the forest. She doesn't go far. Apparently, she's found the path Jacob uses for his latrine, which means it's well traveled . . . and goes nowhere useful.

When she comes back, she takes it slower, unraveling scent trails. She follows the one we came in on and then pauses, as if considering. We've been working on teaching her to "age" scents—parse older ones from new.

She circumvents the camp again. Then she takes off on a trail leading into the forest. She commits to this one, which makes things tricky when it goes through trees too dense for the horses. I go back for them, climb onto Cricket and take Blaze's reins. Dalton's gelding isn't thrilled with that plan, but he follows and we circle around while whistles from Dalton keep us going in the right direction.

We spend an hour like that. I ride and lead Blaze while trying not to stray too far from Dalton's signals. Twice Jacob's path joins a trail, which makes it easier, until he cuts through the bush again.

Dalton finds no sign of trouble. No indication of an ambush or a

THIS FALLEN PREY | 203

fight. But eventually we hit a rocky patch, and Storm loses the scent. She tries valiantly to find it again, grumbling her frustration when she can't. We have some idea of the general direction Jacob was headed, though, so we continue that way, both on horseback now, while Storm runs alongside, her nose regularly lifting to test the air.

"Satellite phones," Dalton says after a while.

"I know."

I've been advocating sat phones. I remember when I first moved here, I thought that's what Val used. When it turned out to be some kind of high-tech dedicated radio receiver, I presumed that was because nothing else would work. But Dalton and I did some research when we were down south, and we discovered there was no reason sat phones *shouldn't* work. We just don't have them, because they'd allow us to call out, which is against Rockton rules. Also, even calls between phones in such an isolated region could trigger unwanted interest.

We have discussed getting them anyway, for emergencies, and now is the perfect example of when a satellite phone could be a lifesaver.

"We'd need to know whether they could be detected," I say. "And figure out how to get an account without a credit card and ID. They aren't like cell phones. You can't grab a prepaid."

"Yeah."

"It might be possible to buy one on the black market. Yes, I'm talking about that as if I have a clue how to get *anything* on the black market. But I might be able to figure out . . ."

I trail off as Storm stops. She's sniffing the air. Then the fur on her back rises, and she reverses toward me . . . which means toward Cricket, making my horse do a little two-step before snorting and nose-smacking the dog.

I pull Cricket to a halt and swing my leg over, but Dalton says, "Hold," and I wait. Storm growls. I resist the urge to comfort her. If she senses trouble, I *want* her warning us.

Storm is sitting right against Cricket's foreleg. The mare exhales, as if in exasperation, and nudges the dog, but there's no nip behind it, and when Cricket lifts her head, she catches a scent, too.

"Step out."

Dalton's voice startles me. The animals, too, Storm glancing back sharply, Cricket two-stepping again. Only Blaze stays where he is, rock-steady as always.

"We're armed," Dalton says as he takes out his gun. "I know you're there, just to the left of the path. Come out, or we'll set the dog on you."

THIRTY-SIX

Silence answers. I haven't heard whatever Dalton and the animals must.

Then he says, "Storm? Get ready . . . ," and there's a rustle in the undergrowth ahead.

A boy steps onto the path. He can't be more than twelve. I see him, and the first thing I think of is Dalton—that this boy is already older than he would have been when the former sheriff took him from the forest.

The boy looks so young. It's easy to think of twelve as the cusp of adolescence, but it is still childhood, even out here, and that's what I see: a boy with a knife clenched in one hand, struggling to look defiant as he breathes fast.

Dalton looks at the boy, and his jaw hardens. Then he aims his glower into the forest.

"That's a fucking coward's move, and you oughta be ashamed of yourselves, pushing a kid out here. Did I mention we have guns? And a dog?"

The boy's gaze goes to Storm. He tilts his head, and I have to smile, remembering how Jacob mistook her for a bear cub.

"Storm?" I say. "Stand."

She does, and her tail wags. The boy isn't the threat she smelled, proving Dalton is right about there being others.

"If you're planning an ambush," he calls, "you do realize that the person I'm going to shoot at is the one I see, which happens to be a *child*."

"I'm not a child," the boy says, straightening. He pushes back his hood . . . and I realize he's not a boy either. It's a girl, maybe fourteen.

"And I'm alone," she says. "I came hunting and—"

"Yeah, yeah. There are three other people over there, who obviously think my night vision sucks."

"Sucks what?" the girl says.

I chuckle at that, and she looks over at me. "You're a girl," she says.

"Woman," Dalton says. "And a police detective. Armed with a gun. Now sit your ass down."

"You can't tell me—"

"I just did." He points the gun.

The girl sits so fast she almost falls.

I say, "Storm, guard." Which is a meaningless command, but I pair it with a hand gesture that means she can approach the girl to say hello. The girl shrinks back as the big canine draws near. Storm sits in front of her and waits to be petted. Patiently waits, knowing this is clearly coming.

"Three people," Dalton calls. "I want to see you all on this path by the count of ten. Your girl seems a little nervous, and if she runs, I can't be held responsible for what our dog will do."

Storm plunks down with a sigh, her muzzle resting beside the girl's homemade boot, as if resigned to wait for her petting.

"Just don't move," I say to the girl. "You'll be fine."

Dalton begins his countdown. By the time he finishes, a man and a woman have emerged from the trees. Both are on the far side of fifty.

"It's only us," the woman says. "You have miscounted."

"And you have mistaken me for an idiot incapable of counting." He raises his voice. "I see you coming around beside me. Do *you* see the gun pointed at your fucking head?"

Silence. Then a dark figure appears from the shadows, heading for Blaze.

"Yeah, no," Dalton says. "If you're planning to spook my horse, thinking he'll unseat me?" Dalton lowers the gun a foot over Blaze's head and fires. Cricket does her two-step and whinnies, but Blaze only twitches his ear, as if a fly buzzed past.

"Now get up there with the others," Dalton says.

A young man steps out. He has a brace of rabbits over his shoulder.

"Good hunting?" I say.

He only stares. Keeps staring, his gaze traveling over me a little too slowly.

"Answer her, and keep your fucking eyes on her face," Dalton says. "She asked you a polite question, as a reminder of how civilized people behave when they come across one another, each out minding their own business in the forest."

"You his girl?" the young man asks.

"She's . . ." Dalton hesitates, and I know he wants to say "my detective" because that is the respectful way to introduce me. But it might imply I'm single, and from the looks this kid is giving me, we'd best not go there.

"I'm his wife," I say, and Dalton's gaze cuts my way, but he only grunts and says, "Yeah. My wife *and* my detective."

"What's a detect—" the girl begins, but the older woman cuts her off with a look.

"I was a police officer down south," I say. "Law enforcement."

"Down there and up here," Dalton says.

"Here being Rockton," the older man says. "I know you. You're Steve's boy. Jacob's brother."

"And you're from the First Settlement."

The man nods.

"We're looking for Jacob," Dalton says. "You seen him?"

The older man and woman nod. The younger man's gaze alternates between me and Blaze, the look in his eyes suggesting we are of equal value, both chattels he covets. When he glances at Dalton, I see the dissatisfaction of a child looking on an older one, wondering what he's done to deserve all the good toys.

The girl is busy staring at Storm, and while Dalton talks to the woman and older man, I murmur, "Storm? Up."

The dog rises, and the girl falls back. No one else notices, and I tell her not to worry, the dog is safe unless I give her a command.

I lean over Cricket's neck and murmur, "Do you want to pet her?"

The girl frowns, as if "pet" is as foreign a word as "detective."

I say, "Storm?," and she bounds over to me. I bend as far as I can and scratch behind her ears.

"This is petting," I say. "She likes this, as you can tell."

The girl rises and approaches carefully.

"Put out your hand," I say. "That gives her a chance to sniff you, and it warns that you're going to touch her."

The girl lays down her bow first. It's a beautiful one etched with wolves. Then she lets Storm sniff her fingers and lays a tentative hand on the dog's broad head. As she strokes Storm's head, she says, "It's soft."

I smile, and as Dalton continues talking with the older settlers, I show the girl where to pet Storm, and I point out her black tongue and webbed feet. She runs her hands over the dog, fingers in her thick fur, and smiles when Storm licks her arm. She asks questions, too, like whether Storm hunts and if she ever runs off. I tell her about the cougar, and her eyes round at that. I may give Storm a little more credit for "rousting" the cat than she deserves, but it makes for a better story.

By the time Dalton is done, the girl is throwing sticks for Storm, fascinated by the dog fetching them back.

"Harper?" the woman says. "It's time to go."

The girl pats Storm again and gives her the stick.

The younger man says to Dalton, "If you're looking to camp, there's a good spot just west of here. Follow the path and take the first left. You'll see the clearing."

"Sounds good," Dalton says. "Thank you."

I straighten on Cricket. "Jacob isn't the only one we're looking for out here. There's a man. Young, maybe your age." I describe Brady. "He's dangerous. He doesn't look it, but he is."

The young man curls his lip, and even on the faces of the other two adults, I see contempt. Sneering at me for warning them.

"We will be fine," the older man says. "No one out here is a threat to those of the First Settlement."

I want to say no, he doesn't understand. *Do not underestimate the danger. Please.* But I can tell that would be interpreted as weakness. If I fear Brady, that means I am simply not as strong as they are.

Dalton says, "If you see him, the same reward applies. We want him alive, but in his case, we're more concerned with catching him than keeping him healthy."

"Understood," the older man says. Then he calls to the girl, still lingering by Storm, and they return to the forest.

THIRTY-SEVEN

We head off in the direction where the young man suggested we camp. We won't be stopping there. Dalton veers off on another path and cuts back to our initial route. We continue along for another couple of kilometers before we make camp, well off the trail, in a spot sheltered by rock on two sides.

We brought a small tent—a simple pop-up—and we tie the horses right outside it. The clearing is large enough that nothing will get the jump on them, and they are capable of looking after themselves. Storm will sleep inside, on our legs, which makes the tent a bit crowded, but I can't rest if she's outside alone.

Once the tent is ready, Dalton rigs up a simple intruder alert system. Rockton has never had problems with the First Settlement. Its elders are from the town, and while they may have chosen to leave, they respect what Rockton stands for. The problem, as I know Dalton fears, is that those who settled the community are getting old. The girl—Harper—is likely third generation. The farther removed the settlers get from the originals, the easier it will be to look on our town and covet its relative riches.

It's not just Rockton's horses and women they'll want—the differences in our standard of living are clear right down to our store-bought boots and fresh-scrubbed faces. Once the hold of the first generation relaxes, Rockton can expect raids. We both fear that day, and we know it's coming fast.

I start a fire while Dalton sets up the alert system. I'm still a fire-building novice—it really is a skill—but I manage to have one going by the time he finishes. Then we settle in, sitting on a blanket, his arm around my back. From his pocket, he pulls a flask.

"Tequila?" I ask.

"Of course."

He passes it to me for the first slug. There's not much in the flask. I max out at two shots—always. He'll go to two, if we're alone, but tonight he won't, not with settlers in the woods. So he just takes a long sip and hands it back.

"I've got vacation time coming up," he says.

"Do you?"

"Yeah, apropos of nothing except the fact that it's been a shitty day, and I'm trying to think of something good."

"Vacation time is always good."

I feel him shrug, and he says, "Guess so."

"You go to visit your parents, right?"

"Normally." Five seconds of silence. "Think it's okay if I skip that?"

"I think a guy who works his ass off is entitled to do what he wants with his vacation time. They'll want to see you at some point, but not all your breaks need to be family visits."

"Yeah." He pauses. "You like Vancouver?"

"Sure, and if you want me to suggest some places you can visit, I know it well enough."

He glances over. "I'm not going on vacation without you."

"Uh, I don't qualify—"

"Already worked it out. Before all this shit started. I get a week. I agreed to cut it to five days if you can come. I sure as hell wouldn't go to the city by myself." He shudders.

"Too many people?"

"People. Concrete. Noise. When I go to interview newcomers, if it's in a city, sure, I'll go sightseeing. Museums. Galleries. Libraries. Theater. But . . ." He makes a face. "I feel like people look at me and wonder if I took a wrong turn. Like everyone can tell I'm a country mouse in the city. I know that's bullshit. They're too busy to even notice me."

He pauses. "Which isn't how this conversation is supposed to go at all. I think I'd like the city a lot more if you were there, and I'm sure you'd like a civilization break. The way city people take a camping break."

"Am I allowed to suggest alternate vacation plans?"

"Sure."

"Down south, we have what's called staycations, which means you don't travel far from home. That's what I'd like. A five-day hike or horseback trip up here. Would that be okay?"

He looks over. "Is that what you want? Or what you think I do? Because it sounds like backpedaling to me."

He means "backpedaling" to the old Casey. The one who frustrated him because she never *wanted* anything. No likes. No dislikes. Every choice weighed according to practicality and the needs of others.

I scoop up the marshmallow bag and put one on a stick I've set beside us. When it's in the fire, I say, "If it's just five days of camping, then I might prefer a trip to Vancouver. But if it's five days of scouting for a potential site for a new Rockton, then that's what I want. Not a place to start building right away, but a place we know we *can* build at. A spot maybe a day's ride away that we can visit over the seasons and see how it seems, for water, game, other inhabitants, and so on."

"That would work."

"Then it's a date?"

"It is."

I pop the roasted marshmallow in my mouth. As I'm moving back, he pulls me into a kiss. Then he licks his lips and says, "Tastes like marshmallow."

"Shall I roast you one?"

"Hmmm." One brow lifts, his eyes glinting. "Tell you what. You roast one. Wherever you put it, I'll take it off."

"Oh?" I take another marshmallow from the fire, blow it out, and tear off one crisp corner. Then I put my finger in and pull out a dollop of gooey marshmallow. "So if I put this someplace . . ."

"On *you*."

I laugh. "Okay. Well, let's see."

I lick the marshmallow off my finger. Then I have him hold my stick while I slip out of my shirt. My jeans follow in a striptease. Bra. Then panties. Then I'm kneeling beside him, naked, his breath coming fast. I reach out for the marshmallow, take another fingerful, and lower it down. Then I slowly draw it up, over my belly, past my breasts, careful not to let it drip.

"Anywhere?" I say.

"Uh-huh."

"Hmmm, how about . . ." I streak it across my chin. "There?"

He laughs and his arms go around me as he does indeed lick it off, while toppling us onto the blanket behind.

THIRTY-EIGHT

We're sleeping soundly when a scream cuts through the night. Dalton scrambles up with, "Casey!" as his hands wildly pat the blankets. I've rolled just far enough away that he's panicking, and before I can say anything, the scream comes again.

"Casey!"

"Here," I say. "I'm right here."

I fumble in the darkness and find him as he turns on the flashlight. He's looking around, eyes still wide, as if getting his bearings. Storm is on his legs, whining.

"Is that a cougar?" I ask.

A moment's pause. Then he nods. "Could be."

The night has gone silent again. I replay the sound. I know what a cougar's scream sounds like only from anecdotal evidence.

"Have you ever heard one?" I ask.

"Once." Another pause. "I'm not sure that was it."

"Vixen then?"

I *have* heard those screams—female foxes at mating time—and they're chilling, but not quite what I just caught, and Dalton agrees.

"Do you think it's a trap?" I ask.

"Maybe."

A woman's scream to bring us rushing out. Riding to her rescue, worried and still sleepy. Ripe for theft.

"We shouldn't ignore it," I say. "Even if it's a trap, that means those settlers are looking for us. Better to confront them, while we're prepared."

"Yeah," he says, and I can tell he's relieved. Neither of us wants to be the chump who falls for a trap, but we can't ignore it, either.

We dress and then step out carefully, in case the "trap" was just to have us race—weapon-free—from our tent.

The horses are uneasy, Cricket stamping her feet, Blaze casting troubled looks in the direction of the screams. I glance at Storm. She's gazing about, on alert but calm enough that I know no one is nearby.

We gather our valuables—that's another potential trap: lure us away and then raid our camp. We leave only the tent and sleeping blankets behind. Then we set out, leading the horses.

There's been no other noise, and we take it slow. Dalton goes first. He'll have a better idea of where that scream came from. We follow the path to a spot that has Dalton pausing and looking about. He bends to check something at ground level. A grunt of satisfaction before he leads Blaze off the path, following a trail only he can see.

We've only gone about twenty paces before Cricket whinnies. She flattens her ears, her nostrils flaring, eyes rolling. Blaze snorts and shifts uneasily. Storm gives a long-drawn-out whine, her gaze fixed on the forest ahead.

Dalton motions for me to tie Cricket to a tree. He leaves Blaze untethered. His horse has been known to wait half a day by a stream. Cricket is too young and temperamental for that.

After I've tethered my mare, we proceed. Soon I smell campfire smoke. All is silent, though. We go another twenty paces. Storm stops. Just stops dead, and when I try to nudge her, she digs in and gives me a look, as if begging me not to make her go on.

I hesitate. Dalton takes the leash and sets it on the ground. Then he prods me to keep going. I do, with reluctance, but after a few steps, Storm follows. She may not want to continue, but she wants to be left alone even less. Dalton gathers up the leash, and we move slowly through the trees.

The first thing I see is a hide tent. Small and low, shelter for one person.

Dalton's arm springs up to hold me back. I survey the campsite, and after a sweep, I spot what he did—someone sitting by the embers of a fire. The figure is perched on a log and leaning back against a tree. A guard for the night. When I peer, I see the light brown beard of the younger man. I can't tell if he's resting or fallen asleep.

Storm growls, the sound vibrating through her. I bend to reassure her that all is well, and yes, praise her for the growl, proof that these are the settlers who unnerved her earlier.

I take the leash and tell Storm to sit while Dalton moves closer. As he does, I survey the camp again. One tent. A couple of leather pouches hang from trees, along with the brace of rabbits. That tent is much too small for three people, and I'm wondering where they all are when I make out the shape of sleeping blankets, just barely illuminated by the dying fire.

I follow one set of blankets up to the graying hair of the older man. He's sound asleep. I think I spot more blankets beyond him, but they're too far from the fire to be more than dark blobs.

If this is a trap, it's an odd one. I see both male settlers. They could be faking sleep, but it would make more sense to be lying in wait while leaving the woman and girl in sight.

The younger man is across the campsite. Dalton motions that he's going to circle around. Then he stops. Considers. Hefts his gun, held in his left hand, his arm far from healed. He shifts the gun to his right and lifts it. Considers some more.

"Let me," I whisper. I motion at my dark clothing and hair, better able to blend into the shadows.

He nods.

I give him back Storm's leash and whisper, "Stay."

Dalton says, "I will," and then gives me a smile, tight and anxious. I squeeze his arm and set out.

While it's only a quarter moon, the sparser forest here means I can see where I'm putting down my feet. It's mostly bare dirt, and the windswept puddles of conifer needles are damp from spring showers; even when I do touch down, they make no sound.

I head behind the young settler. As I pass the camp, I squint at a second set of sleeping blankets. I think I see a smaller figure. There's no sign of the older woman's white hair, so this would be the girl, Harper.

That means the woman is inside the tent. Where I can't see her and confirm she's fine.

She *should* be fine. The others wouldn't have slept through those screams. Either this is a trap, then, or they woke hearing the screams, recognized them for an animal, and went back to sleep.

I can see my target now. The tree is just inside the clearing. I have my gun out. And then . . .

Well, I'm not quite sure what I should do next. For the sake of a good night's sleep, I'd like to reassure myself that the woman and girl are both fine. I can't do that without marching into camp. I would also like to reassure myself that this isn't a trap. But how do I do that without the risk of waking the settlers, who'll think *we're* raiding *them*?

I circle behind the tree where the young man rests. Then I keep going so I don't emerge behind him, which is never the way to say "I come in peace."

I draw alongside him, close enough to see that he seems to be sleeping, his head bowed. Then I whistle. It's not piercing, but it's enough that even if he's asleep, he should jump up.

He doesn't budge.

Damn it.

Either my whistle is softer than I think, or this *is* a trap, and he's wide awake and waiting.

I whistle again, louder.

No reaction.

I get a better grip on my gun and then retreat behind the tree. From there, I creep forward, no longer worried about startling him. This is a trap. That or . . .

I know what the "or" is. I have from the start.

I slip up behind the tree. I can see the young man's arm, hanging at his side. I take a deep breath and count my steps. Three. Two. One.

The last brings me to his shoulder. I sidestep. Moonlight shines into the clearing, glistening off his half-closed eyes. Glistening off the blood soaking his dark shirt.

THIRTY-NINE

A slash bisects the young settler's throat. It's ragged at one side, cutting upward on an awkward angle. Rushed. But a single slice, deep enough that I see his spinal column. No hesitation cuts, no sign that the killer paused or reconsidered or had to steel himself to do the job.

The killer crept up while the young settler watched the fire. One deliberate slash to end his life before he had time to react. Blood covers the young man's hands as if in his last moments he'd reached up, unable to breathe, grabbing his throat. Too late to even rise from his spot.

I turn to call Dalton, but he's already making his way into the clearing. He sees me bent beside the young settler and knows he is not asleep.

Dalton ties Storm to a tree. She whimpers, but at a firm "Quiet" she lies down. She doesn't want to come closer. She knows what's here. She has always known what's here.

I crouch beside the older man. His eyes are open just enough for me to know he isn't sleeping. The top blanket has been drawn up to his throat, as if the killer tucked him back in. Not an act of contrition— the killer was hiding his work. I tug down that blanket to see the old man's throat has been slashed. There are other cuts, too, on his bare arms, and a clump of gray hair by my foot.

The killer tried to murder the older man in his bed, but something gave him away, an ill-placed footstep or the death gurgle of the younger man. The old man bolted up, maybe getting tangled in his blankets. Rising fast enough to fight, not fast enough to win.

There's a knife by his head. No blood on the blade. As if he'd grabbed it from under his blankets, but it was already too late. The killer had grabbed the old man's hair, yanked back his head and slit his throat. Then he laid him down and tucked the blanket up under his chin.

Dalton is at the tent, sweeping open the front flap. Even from here, I can see it's empty, the old woman gone. Then I remember the second set of blankets by the fire. The small form within. I stumble over to it and yank back the blanket to see . . .

A pack. There's a large deerskin pack under the blanket. The girl is gone, but someone has made it look as if she's asleep. What's the point of that?

Dalton stands in the clearing. He's peering around, gun in hand, but this doesn't seem like a deliberate trap. The first body wasn't staged in that position. The second was covered, but only—I presume—in case the woman or girl saw a body and panicked.

Kill the two men. Take the woman and girl.

Dalton's circling the camp, scanning it. He walks to the tree where the food has been hung. There are rabbits missing from the brace. Two food packs are missing, too, the cut ropes dangling. Two others remain, and scrapes in the trunk bark suggest someone tried to climb and reach them but couldn't.

"Hostiles?" I say.

Dalton shrugs. He knows I'm just avoiding the obvious conclusion. I don't want to give Brady that power, make him our bogeyman— everything terrible that happens must be him.

Dalton circles the camp. I realize what he's looking for: items the settlers wouldn't need to secure in trees. I spot cups, some cooking tools, and blankets. No weapons, though, other than the knife the old man grabbed.

On a second circuit, Dalton finds two bows propped by a tree. I check the pack hidden in the girl's bed and find a small knife, a sling with stones, a waterskin, and a pouch of dried meat.

I look again at the girl's sleeping place. There's no sign that the killer went through the pack before putting it there.

Why wouldn't he search the pack for supplies?

Why make it look as if the girl was asleep at all?

I walk to the two bows. Neither has the wolf etching.

"She snuck off," I say.

"Hmm?" Dalton is examining tracks and looks over.

"Harper snuck out." I motion to the bed. "A classic kid's trick. Make it look like you're asleep in case the grown-ups wake and look for you. She took her bow."

I back onto my haunches and survey the scene. "Intruder kills the lookout first. Then the old man. He leaves the girl because either he doesn't see her blankets or she's too small to be a threat. He decides not to bother with the tent—maybe the woman didn't wake up so he ignored her. He takes what supplies he can. But the older woman *does* hear him. She comes out . . ."

I move to the tent and shine my light on the flaps and then inside. "No sign of blood. Does she scare him off? Go after him?"

Dalton points at the forest's edge. I see signs of wild flight, trampled undergrowth and broken branches.

The woman woke and ran.

She did not run far.

We find her body ten meters from the campsite. I would have passed close to it when I'd been circling around, my attention fixed on the campsite, oblivious to the rest.

She is on her stomach. One hand stretches out, fingers dug into soil. Dragging herself away from her killer. A trail of blood smears the ground and undergrowth.

When I see that outstretched hand, I run to her. But she's gone. Long gone, body cooling fast, her eyes as glazed as the two men's. Eyes wide open. Fixed in horror and determination, as if she only needs to get a little farther, and she will be fine.

Stab wounds in her back. Her killer finishing the job as she crawled away.

Dalton turns the woman over.

More wounds there. She was attacked from the front and ran. Realized she could not escape. Turned to fight. Weaponless. Powerless. A dozen stab wounds perforate her chest.

I'm lifting my head to say something when I see a blur of motion. Dalton does, too, spinning, his gun rising. The running figure gives a roar of rage . . . and then skids to a halt.

It's Harper.

"You," she says, and there is disappointment in her voice. Her brandished knife wavers for a moment. Then it falls.

"They're dead, aren't they?" Harper says. "They're all dead." She looks down at the woman and her voice cracks. "Nonna."

"She was your grandmother?" I ask gently.

She nods.

I motion for her to turn away, but her jaw sets.

"I have seen death before," she says. "I am not a child."

I would like to say this is different—and it is—but she can already see the body, and she's not going to listen to me.

"You weren't in your sleeping blankets," I say.

"I wanted to see your dog again." She kneels beside her grandmother's body. "I was heading to where Albie told you to camp. I was almost there when Nonna screamed. I ran back. I . . . I saw him. The man who . . ."

She looks at her grandmother again. Rage flashes in her eyes.

"You saw their killer?" I say.

"I didn't know that. It was just a man on the trail. He had blood on his face, and I . . . I should have done something—I know I should have stopped him but all I could think about was that scream. I raced back here. Then I saw someone in the camp, and I thought the man had circled back. So I hid." She bites her lip and then straightens. "But not like that. Not hiding *from* him. I was preparing for my attack. Waiting until I could see who it was. Only it was just you."

Dalton murmurs to me that he's going to get Storm, whimpering back at the campsite. When he's gone, I say to the girl, "You saw the man who did this?"

"Yes."

"Where was he? How far from camp?"

"A quarter mile southwest," she says, with the assurance of a girl who may not know her times tables but must be able to relate distances and directions accurately, a matter of basic survival in the forest.

"How far away were you?"

"From here to the campsite. I was in the forest, and he was on the path. He was walking away with some of our stuff."

"What stuff?"

"I saw a rabbit and a food pack."

"Can you describe the man you saw?"

"I wasn't that close, like I said. But he was on the path, and there was moonlight. I could see light-colored hair. Straight, I think. Longer than . . ." She gestures toward Dalton, in the clearing. "But not long like yours. No beard. He had pale skin. That's how I saw the blood on his cheek. I couldn't tell his height, but he looked normal-sized. And he was wearing clothing like you people."

She's describing Brady. Oliver Brady killed these settlers. Slit a guard's throat. Slaughtered an old man in his bed. Chased down and brutally murdered a fleeing old woman. There is no way I can say these were acts of desperation.

Also, there was no sign of Jacob with him. Brady was seen a half kilometer from the scene alone.

Brady is not an innocent man.

Brady does not have Jacob.

That is everything I need to hear. Everything I want to hear, too.

FORTY

We hide the bodies under evergreen boughs, which should help mask the smell from scavengers. Then we escort Harper to the First Settlement. She walks while we ride slowly. I offered her a spot behind Dalton, but pride won't let her attempt to ride as a passenger. And, I suspect, it wouldn't have let her ride Blaze alone and risk looking foolish.

Harper walks holding Storm's lead. Now that I'm certain we are dealing with a monster, I cannot risk Storm taking off after her target. I explain that to Harper, who has never heard of using a dog to follow a smell, and she peppers me with questions, distracting herself from the memory of what happened tonight.

We don't talk about what happened. That is how, as a homicide detective, I handled dealing with a victim's loved ones so soon after the deaths. Let them set the tone. If they want to talk about it, I will, while giving away nothing about the investigation. More often, when it's this soon afterward, they either haven't fully processed the death or they are desperate to discuss anything else. For Harper, that distraction is talking about how dogs track scents. Every now and then she'll trail off and look back the way we came, only to shake herself and keep talking about Storm.

It's 4 A.M. when we near the settlement. We don't take Harper inside. We don't even take her to the edge. Three settlers are dead.

Edwin—the leader of the First Settlement—will figure out that the killer came from Rockton. That puts us in danger.

The First Settlement is like many splinter groups that break away over issues with its parent organization. They don't hate us. They don't wish us ill. But there is no warmth there either.

I once asked why Dalton doesn't trade with the settlement. We don't need their game, but we can always use it, and what they'd want in trade is paltry to us—some coffee, a new shirt, a gun or ammunition. More important, though, is the bond it would forge. The goodwill it buys. Trade links provide us with valuable partners in this wild life. While Ty Cypher might not tell us that ducks are particularly plentiful on a certain lake, he will mention if he's spotted strangers or a worrisome predator.

To the First Settlement, though, such a partnership would smack of weakness. If we initiate trade, that suggests they have things we need, and that we may be weaker than they think. Weak means ripe for raiding. I will admit I didn't fully believe that until I saw the way the settlers looked at me when I suggested they watch out for Brady. I may have been right—tragically right—but to them, Brady was just a lone outsider. No match for them.

We leave Harper about a kilometer from town. Dalton tells her to explain everything to Edwin and let him know that we had to hightail it back to Rockton, in case the killer heads there. He promises that we'll come by later to discuss the situation. By "later" he means "after we catch Brady."

We don't return for our tent and sleeping blankets. We'll get them another time. Right now we *do* need to hurry back to town. Jacob doesn't seem to be with Brady, and we'll willfully interpret that to mean Jacob is safe. We must return to Rockton, regroup, and organize a full manhunt for Oliver Brady . . . before he *does* circle back to Rockton, once he realizes that escape isn't a simple matter of a half-day hike to the next town.

As we near Rockton, I hear a sound that must be an audio hallucination. I've been working through the case as we ride, and I was analyzing the beginning to figure out what we could have done better. Then I hear the very sound that started this whole mess. Therefore, I am imagining things. Or so I tell myself until Dalton says

"What the fuck?" and I glance back to see him squinting up at the midmorning sky . . . as a prop plane flies into view.

Once again, we reach the landing strip just as the plane touches down. Cricket hears the racket and declares she's not going a step closer, and if I insist, then she'll send me there by equine ejection seat. Even Blaze flattens his ears and peers at the steel monster with grave suspicion.

We leave our horses and walk down the airstrip just as the passenger door opens. Out steps the kind of guy who'd seem more at home on a private jet. He's tall and trim, in his late fifties, with silvering dark hair. He has a magazine-cover smile that's dazzling even from fifty meters away. Dressed in pressed khakis and a golf shirt, he looks around with the grin of a big-game hunter, ready for his first Yukon adventure. When he spots us, the smile only grows, and he strides over, hand outstretched.

The pilot climbs from the cockpit. He looks like the passenger's personal assistant, a guy maybe my age, dark-haired and chisel-jawed, wearing stylish glasses that I suspect don't contain prescription lenses. *He* is not smiling. Instead, he bears down on us like we're about to contaminate his boss with our dirt-crusted hands.

"Sheriff Dalton," the younger man says. "Detective."

I know that voice. I can't quite place it, but it's one I've heard . . .

It clicks. Yes, I have heard this voice many times, and I've imagined the man it belongs to so often that I'm sure I'm misidentifying him now. In my head, the voice belongs to an older man, maybe fifty, another middle manager, like Val. A fussy little man with a potbelly and a comb-over.

The younger man passes the older one and puts himself slightly in front, as if shielding him from necessary interaction. Then he extends a hand—to me.

"Phil," he says. "It's good to meet you, Detective."

Phil. The council's spokesperson.

He takes my hand in a firm but perfunctory shake. And for Dalton? A curt nod. Then he turns to the older man.

"This is—"

"Gregory." The silver-haired man steps past Phil. "Gregory Wallace. I've come to see my stepson."

FORTY-ONE

I glance at Dalton.

Gregory catches the look and says wryly, "Yes, I suspect I'm not your favorite person right now, which is why I'm here. I insisted Phil bring me to see what can be done to make Oliver's stay less taxing."

"Yeah?" Dalton says. "You know what would make it less taxing? If it never happened."

Phil makes a noise in his throat, one manicured hand rising in the gesture you'd give a child, telling him to calm down before he embarrasses you in front of company.

Dalton continues, "I don't know what the hell your understanding of the situation up here was, Mr. Wallace, but we were not equipped to deal with a prisoner of any variety. This town is for *victims*. It is safety. It is sanctuary. It is not a fucking maximum-security prison."

"What Sheriff Dalton is saying—" Phil begins.

"Oh, I believe he's saying it just fine," Wallace says, and while he's smiling, the steel in his voice warns Phil to silence. "Please continue, Sheriff."

"We were not equipped for this," Dalton says. "We were not warned in time to become equipped. Your stepson was dropped off with a fucking bag of coffee. *Here's a serial killer. Please take care of him for us. Oh, and enjoy the coffee.*"

"I don't think this is productive," Phil says.

Dalton turns on him. "You want to talk about productive? How about giving me a damn method to communicate with you when everything goes to hell up here?"

Phil straightens, bringing himself to Dalton's height and looking him square in the eye. "You have a method, Sheriff. Valerie is—"

"Dead."

A moment's pause. Then Phil says, "What?"

"Val is dead." Dalton waves at Wallace. "His stepson took her hostage. Killed her. Dumped her in a river. Casey almost died trying to retrieve her body 'cause a proper burial seems the least we can do. Oliver Brady also murdered Brent, one of our key scouts and local contacts. Shot him and left him to die. Then he massacred three settlers, including an old woman trying to escape. Her granddaughter managed to avoid the carnage, though not without witnessing her grandmother's bloody corpse. We escorted the kid home, but we didn't dare take her inside the settlement and explain what happened, or we might not have walked out alive, considering the killer was one of ours." Dalton pauses. "That's our day so far. And yours?"

Phil's face hardens. "Your insubordination—"

"*Fuck* my insubordination. Go tell the council I was rude to you, Phil. See which of us they declare the more valuable asset."

I turn to Wallace. "I'm sorry we don't have your stepson. Despite the fact we weren't prepared, we do accept responsibility for his escape. I'm also sorry if you were misled about the appropriateness of this solution to your problem."

Wallace rubs his chin. He looks sick, and it takes him a moment to regroup.

"The blame, I'm afraid, is as much mine as anyone's, Detective," Wallace says. "I failed to properly warn you about exactly the sort of monster you were dealing with. I erred on the side of caution, fearing the truth would limit my options drastically. And in doing so—" He inhales sharply and then shakes his head. "Let's get someplace quiet, where we can come up with a solution."

We ride the horses to town, letting Phil and Wallace walk the short distance. When we're out of earshot, Dalton mutters, "Fuck," and I agree, and that's all we say, all that can be said. This wrinkle is the absolute last thing we need to deal with.

When we enter Rockton, Anders and Isabel are striding toward us. "Did we hear another plane?" Anders says. He notices the two men behind us. "What the hell?"

I jump off Cricket and call Storm over. Dalton wordlessly reaches for my reins, and I hand them over.

"The younger guy is Phil," I say when Dalton leaves for the stable.

"Our Phil?" Anders says.

"Yep."

"Huh. Not what I expected."

"But a not unpleasant surprise," Isabel murmurs as she gives Phil the kind of look I haven't seen her give any guy since Mick died.

"The other one might be more your style," Anders says.

She gives him a look. "More my *age* you mean?"

"Nah. I know you like them young."

He gets a glower for that. Wallace is looking about Rockton, his gaze here and there, taking everything in. I can almost see his thought processes—looking for electricity lines, noting the piles of lumber, checking the construction of the buildings and the layout of town, and nodding throughout, as if intrigued and impressed. Phil glances about in mild horror, and I can read his thoughts even better. *Dear God, I had no idea it was this bad.*

"And the older gentleman?" Isabel says, her voice lowered as the men approach. "Judging by his attire, clearly a man of means. An investor, I presume."

"You could say that. He's Gregory Wallace. Oliver Brady's step-father."

"Oh, hell," Anders mutters.

"Yep."

The men draw close enough for me to say, "Phil? Mr. Wallace? This is our deputy, Will Anders, and one of our local entrepreneurs, Isabel Radcliffe."

Isabel's eyebrows lift at the introduction. I mouth, *Brothel owner?*, asking if she'd prefer *that* introduction, and she rolls her eyes and extends her hand. Phil accepts it with a perfunctory shake, having seen and dismissed her in a heartbeat. Wallace's gaze lingers, and he smiles, as if she is much more than he expected out here.

"Gregory, please," he says, taking her hand and then Anders's. "Detective? If I might speak to you alone, I believe Phil would like to talk to the sheriff."

Phil gives him a clear *What the hell?* look, but Wallace only smiles and says, "I believe you and the sheriff have a few things to discuss. Or *he* has a few things to discuss with you. Detective . . ."

"Casey," I say.

He nods. "Casey and I will be at the police station."

I leave Storm with Anders. As Wallace and I enter the station, he says, "You are correct that I didn't know where I was sending Oliver. I understood the basics, of course. A remote, northern community. Hidden. Untraceable. Designed to conceal and contain those who need concealment and containment. That seemed enough. I made the mistake of presuming this was for people like my stepson."

"It's not."

"I see that now. I should have asked more questions. An associate told me this was the perfect solution, and I suppose, given what I was willing to pay, Phil's employers had every incentive to agree with me."

"Like Eric said, we just weren't equipped for it." I stoke the fire to start a kettle. "Our police force is just myself, Eric, and Will. We're all experienced law enforcement but none of us has done correctional work. We have a volunteer militia. We have one cell." I cross the room and open the door to show him, and then shut it before Roy can speak. "We couldn't leave Oliver in that for six months, so we were quickly building him a fortified unit. He escaped just before it was completed."

"Can you take me through—?" The door opens and Dalton comes

in, Phil following. Wallace says, "That was quick. Casey was just about to tell me what happened. I'm sure you'll want to hear this, Phil. Please, continue, Detective."

I tell the story.

"The poisoning was real," I say. "Oliver had inside help. He was, as you might expect, protesting his innocence. That's very easy to do when no one here can look up his alleged crimes on the internet. He claimed to have been accused of a shooting spree in San Jose."

Phil's head jerks up, as if he's remembering I'd asked about the shooting.

I continue, "It was far too easy to plant doubt under the circumstances. Yet the alternative was to keep him permanently gagged, which raised suspicions among the residents—they wondered if he had something he wanted to say. We tried to walk a middle line—no gag but limited access. That failed. He found an ally, who got him the poisoned food. We had to take him to the clinic to pump his stomach. We had him restrained while recuperating, but his accomplice provided him with a knife."

"And set the fire," Wallace says. "As a distraction."

"Helluva good one in a town made of wood," Dalton says.

Wallace nods. "As his accomplice knew. I am so sorry this happened. The loss of your town leader . . ." He shakes his head. " 'Sorry' doesn't begin to cover this."

"What was Val doing with the prisoner?" Phil asks.

"She hoped Oliver would see her as a potential ally, possibly even someone he could charm. She was trying to take a more active role in the community."

"Which was her first mistake," Phil says. "The leader of this town cannot become involved in such a way. It blurs lines."

Wallace looks at him. "Are you implying that by trying to *help* her town, she made a fatal error?"

Phil has the grace to color. "Of course not, sir. I misspoke. Val made a questionable choice but what happened was not her fault."

"It was Oliver's," Wallace says. "He is responsible for his actions, something he was never able to grasp, and that is our . . ." He shakes it off. "No blame. Not now. For now, we need to find him before anyone else dies. And then . . ." A pause as he glances away, his voice lowering. "And then we will have to make sure this never happens again, that he never poses a risk to anyone else again."

Wallace squares his shoulders. "That's for later, and whatever needs to be done, it will not involve anyone in this town. I am truly sorry that this happened. I will make it up to you. I know the town was counting on the added income."

"Income?" Dalton snorts. "That's *their* concern." He jerks his thumb at Phil. "We don't give a shit. Not like we were going to see more than a fraction of it anyway."

Phil bristles. "Of course you were. Beyond basic administrative costs—"

"Don't," Wallace says. "I have worked with enough foreign governments to understand the concept of 'basic administrative costs.' Roughly ninety percent, in my experience." He looks at Dalton. "When we get Oliver, you'll tell me what you need for this town. Supplies, infrastructure improvements, and any wish-list items that will make life here easier. I'll pay your *administrators* a reasonable fee for their work, and I will personally take care of everything on your list. Plus I'll pay you and your detective and deputy a bonus."

"Fuck, no," Dalton says.

"He means the bonus isn't necessary," I say. "We'll take the rest, but we don't need added incentive to find your stepson. What he's done is enough."

Wallace dips his chin. "I apologize if I implied otherwise." He looks at Phil. "You can run along now. Fly back to the city, and leave me here with these people to find my stepson."

Phil's jaw sets. "I will be staying and helping."

"Yeah," Dalton says. "Because if you leave, you have to tell the council how badly you all fucked up. Then they'd just order your ass back here anyway."

"If you're staying, stay," Wallace says. "But you damn well better make yourself useful. Now, let's talk about how to get Oliver back."

FORTY-TWO

Our plans? We're going to look really, really hard for Brady. What else is there to do? We could call in the Mounties with a full search team, blow Rockton's cover to hell for the sake of stopping one killer, and it wouldn't ultimately achieve anything more than we can do on our own, which is, in short, frustratingly little.

I remember hearing once that Alaska is the serial killer capital of America—not for the number of active ones, but the number who have disappeared there. That is, obviously, an urban legend. It's not as if serial killers leave behind a "gone to Alaska" note. Instead, the so-called fact is an acknowledgment that there are likely many people hiding there, who have done something terrible and then fled where they cannot be found.

The same goes for the Yukon. In Whitehorse, I've heard people joke that the most common question asked of newcomers is "So, what are you running from?" The answer for most is "Nothing." People run *to* places like Whitehorse. They come on a job placement or a vacation and fall in love, like I have. Whitehorse is a city of transplants. Willing transplants. But yes, everyone knows there are people in the wilderness who are hiding. Asking questions is frowned upon, both for safety and as a courtesy.

We don't know what—or who—might be in these woods. And we don't really care to find out, because the point is moot. Modern tracking equipment can't reliably locate hikers who wander off the Appalachian Trail. It sure as hell won't locate fugitives up here.

We must find lodgings for our unexpected guests.

"I will take Casey's old house," Phil says. "I know it's vacant."

"Yeah, no," Dalton says. "The guy paying the bills gets the house. Casey just needs to move something out first."

"No need," Wallace says. "I won't disturb any of her belongings."

"Thanks," I say. "But there's one item you'll definitely want relocated."

We take Phil and Wallace to my house with their luggage. I open the door and slip inside with a quick, "Give me a sec."

A few minutes later, I emerge with a duffel bag and a sleepy cub.

Phil sees the wolf-dog and turns on Dalton. "We allowed special dispensation for a single canine. Casey's dog, which is a working—"

"This isn't a pet," I say. "It's the remaining cub from the wolf-dog we had to put down."

"And so you brought it here? This isn't a wildlife refuge, Detective."

"This cub bit Eric. We feared it was rabid, and I needed to monitor it."

Phil steps back so fast I have the very childish urge to dump the cub into his arms. I do hold it out toward him. I can't resist that.

"It's fine, see?" I say.

"Then why is it still here?"

"As opposed to dumping it in the forest? Or killing it?"

As he opens his mouth, I spot a familiar figure passing and shout, "Yo! Mathias!"

Mathias makes his way over and arches a brow. "Did you actually hail me with 'yo'?" He speaks in French as his gaze touches on our guests, testing their comprehension. Wallace gives no sign of understanding. Phil squints, as if he recognizes French from long-ago classes.

"We have guests," I say in English. "I'm sure you've already heard that."

"Our illustrious council liaison, and the poor man who married into the family of a serial killer."

Wallace blinks, but then chuckles. "That's one way of putting it." He shakes Mathias's hand as I introduce them properly.

Then I say, "Your timing is perfect. I was just about to tell Phil that you've volunteered to take and train this cub as a guard and hunting dog. But I'm afraid he's going to tell you no."

"No?" Mathias says, as if he doesn't recognize the word. He turns to Phil and fixes him with a smile that has sent many a resident skittering from the butcher shop. "You wish to tell me I cannot have this cub, Philip? That is unfortunate. I was very much looking forward to it."

"I never said—"

"Excellent. Then we are agreed. I will quarantine and then train it properly, as a working beast." He hefts the cub from my arms. "The next serial killer must escape the jaws of a wolf if he wishes to flee." He pauses. "Or she. I would not wish to be sexist."

"Let's just hope we don't have to guard more serial killers, okay? Now Mr. Wallace is taking my old house while he's here, so you'll need to care for the cub."

Mathias says in French, "You realize you cannot take it back now. You have committed to the course. All for the sake of tweaking poor Philip."

"I couldn't resist."

"A cruel streak. This is why I like you." He takes the bag of supplies from my hand and switches to English. "Do you know where Philip will stay? I do not believe we have empty apartments."

"We can move Kenny out and place him under guard," I say. "Then let Phil take the house we built for Oliver."

"The windowless *box* you built for Oliver?" Phil says. "I am certainly not—"

"Yes," Mathias says. "That would be wrong. You must stay with me. Ah, no—I mean us." He hefts the canine. "Please. I insist."

Phil's jaw works, as if he knows he's being played here. Then he says, his voice tight, "Oliver's intended residence will be adequate."

We leave the men to settle into their lodgings, and we resume our search for Oliver Brady. We're out until dark, and I'm putting my extra gear in the locker when Isabel comes in and says, "We need a fourth for poker."

I laugh. Hard.

"I'm serious," she says.

I close the equipment locker. "I'm exhausted, Isabel. I'm going home with Eric, to a hot meal, a warm bed, and as much sleep as I can get."

"Eric won't be joining you for a while. There's a problem with the lumber-shed reconstruction."

"Of course there is."

"So, poker?" she says.

I shake my head. "If Eric's busy, I'm going to have that hot meal waiting when he's done."

"That's very domestic of you."

"No, it's considerate."

"I'm not sure that's the word I'd use, having heard Will and Eric discuss your cooking." She follows me from the equipment shed. "One of the cooks at the Lion owes me a favor. I'll have her prepare something to put aside for both of you."

"Then I'll rest—"

"That word is not in your vocabulary, Casey." She keeps pace alongside me. "If you want a rest, you'll find it in our poker game. It's an all-estrogen event. You, me, Petra, and Diana."

"Since when do you play poker—or socialize with Diana?"

"Since I requested her presence at this particular game. I know you and I both would have preferred Nicole, but she's busy with the search. Diana is joining us in a wake for the loss of one of our own."

I slow. "Val."

"Yes, and while you might not want the reminder, I think we owe it to Val."

I nod and follow her.

FORTY-THREE

We're in the Roc. Isabel has closed it for the night, both the bar and the brothel. There would normally be two women on "duty" in the evening. There are about six on staff. I say "about" because the number fluctuates, as women come and go from the ranks, most just deciding they're going to give it a try for a few months, for fun.

Isabel argues there is sexual liberation in that, and it isn't so much monetizing their bodies as experimenting with a traditionally more masculine form of sexuality, taking partners where and when they want, without emotional risk. Sounds great. The reality, though, is that if one of them refuses an offer, she has to deal with the prospective client outside these walls, and having a woman refuse *paid* sex is apparently more of an ego blow than just refusing sex. I dealt with an incident recently where the rejected john found a way to retaliate.

When we arrive at the Roc, there's a hopeful client walking inside just ahead of us, and Isabel pulls open the door just in time to see him sidling up to Petra and Diana, with a "So, are you ladies looking for—"

Then Petra turns and he sees who it is and stops short with an "Oh."

"Yes, oh," Isabel calls. "Have I spoken to you about this before, Artie? You do not ever presume that a woman drinking here is looking for *anything* but a drink."

"No harm in asking, Iz," he whines.

"Yes, actually there is. If a woman here wants your company, she will approach you. That is the new rule, as you have been told. If you're looking for company, you'll find it in the search parties. That's where tonight's staff is, and that's where you should be."

"Can I get a drink?"

"Yes, absolutely. I'll get you your drink, and you'll sit on your ass and enjoy yourself while everyone else searches for the man who murdered Val. I'll make sure all my girls know that's what you were doing tonight. They'll be terribly impressed."

Artie leaves. Quickly. I sit with Petra and Diana, and Isabel brings over tumblers and Irish whiskey.

"I don't think Val was Irish," I say.

"Do you have any idea what her heritage *was*?"

I shake my head.

"Then in the interests of a proper wake, tonight she was Irish. And we are playing poker."

"Never been to an actual wake, have you," Petra says.

"I'm improvising. Otherwise, we'll sit here and try to come up with things to say about the dearly departed, and it will get very awkward, very fast." Isabel pours the whiskey. "Have any of you ever attended one of those funerals? Where it's very clear that no one actually has anything interesting to say about the deceased?"

"Or anything nice," Diana says as she takes her drink.

"The lack of anything nice would be far worse than the lack of anything interesting. That's what I want for my funeral. I don't give a damn if anyone tells a single story that reflects well on me. Just tell stories."

"Val liked tea," I say.

Diana snickers and then sobers with, "Sorry."

"The point being," Isabel says, "that we have not a single interesting thing to say about Val."

"We didn't know her," I say.

"Not for lack of trying."

"Shortly after she arrived, she got lost in the forest and was attacked."

Isabel nods. "I know."

"She came to you?"

"Val ask for help? Never. But I have counseled enough survivors to know she did not wander out of that forest unscathed. I tried to broach the subject once, to offer support, and she shut me down. Nothing happened, and I should go practice my 'mediocre skills' on real victims." She raises her glass to me. "Kudos on being the one to break through."

"I didn't. When I confronted her, she said that to have 'allowed' herself to be attacked would have been a sign of weakness. Strong women don't do that."

"Ouch," Petra says.

"An unfortunate—and unfortunately common—belief," Isabel says. "Also monumentally wrong and stupid, but that goes without saying."

We take a drink.

"Val, however, was not a stupid woman," Isabel says. "She'd been a mathematician."

"I didn't know that," I say. "I'd seen her doing math puzzles. Not the kind you get in a paperback book, but real puzzles. Theoretical ones."

"Even if she didn't open up to you about the attack, Casey, you *were* the one to break through. To get her out of that house and into the community."

"Yep." I take a slug of my whiskey. "And look where it got her."

Three mouths open in simultaneous denials. I beat them to it with, "This morning, Phil said Val made a mistake trying to join life in Rockton. That her place was separate and apart from us. He may have had a point."

"Phil is an idiot. Gorgeous, but an idiot. And I don't just say that because he looked at me like I was a bag lady blocking the steps to his brownstone."

"It wasn't that bad," I say.

"Oh, yes it was, but since he wasn't checking you out either, I won't take it personally."

"You both might be the wrong gender," Petra says.

"He didn't give Will more than a passing glance."

"The sneer wasn't a physical assessment," I say. "It was disdain. For everyone and everything here. But I still wonder if he was right about Val. We couldn't afford to lose our leader, and involving herself in our affairs endangered her."

"Well, if that's your reasoning, you'd better tell Eric he has to stay in the station from now on. He's the one we can't afford to lose. Val was . . ." Isabel swirls her drink and shakes her head. "This isn't the proper way to conduct a wake, is it?"

"Does anyone have anything nice to say?" Diana says.

"She liked tea," Petra quips. Then she adds, "The truth is that none of us knew her well enough to eulogize her. But a year ago, no one would have been holding a wake for her either. She was coming out of her shell. She was starting to care. We were starting to care back."

Isabel raises her glass. "Then let's drink to that. A woman we didn't always understand. A woman we didn't always like. But a woman we were looking forward to getting to know better. A missed and mourned opportunity."

We clink glasses.

"Now, poker?" Petra says. "For credits, I hope, because I will clean you all out."

The door opens, and Isabel calls, "Closed!"

Dalton walks in. "Got a situation, Casey. I need you."

I'm getting to my feet when Diana says, "Can't you handle it alone, Sheriff? Casey deserves a rest."

"So does he," I say. "And he hasn't been sitting here drinking whiskey."

She opens her mouth, but a murmur from Isabel stops her. A quiet reminder, I'm sure, that harping on Dalton does nothing to bring Diana back into my good graces.

When we get outside, I say, "We were attempting to eulogize Val. It wasn't going well."

He slows. "Shit, I'm sorry. If you want to go back—"

"The eulogy part was over. It was booze and cards henceforth. Somehow I don't think Val would have approved."

He takes my hand as we walk. I might joke, but he knows that wake wasn't easy. Any reminder of Val is a reminder of how she died. But Isabel is right—Val deserved a few quiet moments of our time.

"So what's up?" I say.

"Kenny's missing."

"What?"

"He was out searching with a party. I wanted him at the lumber shed to deal with the reconstruction issues. When it was definitely dark"—he points at the night sky—"I went to see why he wasn't back yet."

"And?"

"His group returned fifteen minutes earlier. He had to use the bathroom. Someone stood outside waiting, not wanting to rush him."

"Let me guess—he's not in the bathroom."

"Yep."

FORTY-FOUR

There are three levels of occupancy here in Rockton. At the top is having your own house. At the bottom is apartment living—bachelor-style apartments. In the middle, you get the full level of a house, which still only nets you about six hundred square feet. Yes, we aren't exactly living in mansions here. We can't afford the energy costs or the footprint.

Kenny has a ground floor. Which means it was very easy to sneak out the window while his guard was watching at the front.

And his guard? Jen.

"Which is why you should have put a guy in charge of him," she says. "Someone who can stand in the bathroom while he takes a shit."

"Yeah, not even the guys are going to do that," Dalton says. "But next time someone's in there that long? Knock. Ask if he needs medical care."

"He took a book. I knew it was going to be a while."

"A book from the library?" I say.

"Everyone does it."

"Which is why I don't read books from the library," Dalton says. He stands in the bathroom and looks at the window. "Fuck."

"Eloquent as always, Sheriff," Jen says.

"Yeah, well, I'm saving time on a lengthy response." He strides for the door. "Time better spent catching his ass before he rendezvouses with Oliver Brady and gets his fool throat cut."

I join the search for a while, with Storm. The problem? Kenny knows what Storm can and cannot do. Which means he runs straight to the nearest stream.

We lead Storm up one side of it for about a kilometer, as far as we figure he could walk in the icy water. Then we take her down the other side and another kilometer in the opposite direction. Either Kenny managed to steal waterproof boots and three pairs of wool socks or Storm misses his exit spot.

Dalton takes her on a wider circle in the area while I return to town. There are a few things I want to check, and with both Dalton and Storm hunting, I really am a third wheel.

I want to look for a note. Even with what seems like an obvious betrayal, I still can't write Kenny off just yet. I find it much easier to believe he was duped by Brady's protests of innocence rather than jumping at a huge bribe to help a serial killer. If so . . .

If so, I have an alternate theory for his disappearance. One that paints Kenny in a better light. One that fits better with the man I know.

I find the note in the station. Paul said Kenny came in here earlier, to return a flashlight that he claimed belonged to me.

I find the note in the drawer, along with a spare flashlight.

The note is addressed to me. And when I read it, I discover I was wrong. Very, very wrong.

Dalton comes home at three in the morning. From the kitchen, I hear the door open, the solid *boom-boom* of his boots stepping inside and then the skitter and scrape of Storm's nails as she zips past him. After that double boom, his footsteps go silent. He's looking for me in the living room. When he doesn't see me, there's a sigh, and his boots come off, thumping to the floor.

Steps move into the living room. Not the solid boom of his initial ones. Not even his usual purposeful stride. These are dragging and whispery, socks skimming the hardwood. Then the thud of him collapsing onto the sofa.

He doesn't hear me come out of the kitchen, and I catch that first unguarded glimpse of him, forearms on his thighs, shoulders bowed, gaze empty as he stares at nothing. The floorboard creaks with my next step, and he looks over and his face lights in a smile.

I know he thought I'd gone to bed, and while he'd never complain about that, yes, he was disappointed. Now he sees me and smiles. Then he gets a whiff of the dinner I'm carrying, and his gaze goes to it.

"Don't worry, I didn't cook it," I say. "Isabel wouldn't let me."

He shakes his head.

I take the plates of rewarmed dinner onto the back deck, and we eat in silence.

I wait until he finishes before I say, "Kenny left a note."

Dalton's head jerks up at that. Then he snorts and says, "What? Telling us we were fucking idiots for not keeping a closer eye on him?"

Which isn't what he expects at all. He's just bracing for the worst. This was a person Dalton trusted. He feels betrayed, and so he wants to believe Kenny was not the man he thought. It makes this easier than any of the alternatives.

Tell me he betrayed us. That he deserves whatever happens to him in that forest.

I hand him the note. As he reads it, I watch him, his cheek twitching, gaze skimming the first time through and then slowing to reread. When he finishes, he crushes the paper and whips it across the back lawn.

"God-fucking-damn-it, no," he snarls, pushing to his feet. "Is he an idiot? Yes, obviously he fucking is. The biggest goddamn idiot . . ."

Dalton can't even seem to continue, and he starts pacing instead. Storm scratches at the back door. I've left her inside, and I know she's hurt and confused, certain we've accidentally forgotten her, patiently waiting for us to realize our mistake. Now she hears Dalton curse and she scratches, a tentative whine seeping through the wooden door.

Dalton wheels on me. "This is what I need. Exactly what we both need. Because clearly we're not doing fuck-all here. *Hey, why don't I just take off into the goddamn forest and give you guys something to do.* Or maybe no, we won't chase him because we don't give a shit. That's why he had to take off. Catch this murdering asshole himself. Because we aren't trying. So he'll do it for us and prove he wasn't Brady's accomplice, because otherwise, we'll just punish him and not bother with a fucking investigation."

I let Dalton rant. Let him express my own frustration and my fear and my rage. I still recall every word of that note.

Casey,

I'm going to fix this. I'm going to find Brady and bring him back for you. It's my fault he escaped and killed Val and your friend and those settlers. I didn't help him. I swear I didn't. But I'm going to bring him back. I'll catch him, and he can tell you who was his real accomplice.

I'm sorry for all the trouble I've caused.

Kenny

"Trouble he's caused," Dalton says. "He's sorry for the fucking trouble he caused, so the best way to fix that is to cause more. Poor Kenny feels guilty. Blames himself. Fucking awesome. Let's share that blame. Let Jen have some when Kenny dies, for letting *him* escape. Let you have some for suspecting he was the accomplice. Let me have some for trusting him enough to let him out of that cell. Let's all take another helping of the fucking blame pie, because it's clear we haven't eaten enough of it already."

He spins on me. "What am I supposed to do here, Casey? I feel like we're spending this whole damn case searching for people. Brady, Val, Jacob, now Kenny. I tell them not to go into the forest. I regulate every damn step out there until I feel like a paranoid parent. But they keep doing it. They walk out of this town, and they die. Do I need to build a fucking wall? A barbed-wire fence? Post armed guards? Shoot anyone who tries to leave? These are supposed to be responsible adults, but they come here and they act like fucking children, which means we have to be the fucking parents. No, not children. Teenagers. And we're just obstacles standing between them and whatever shit they want to pull. Well, if that's the way they want it, then fuck yeah, that's what they're getting. Prison guards."

My gaze flicks from Dalton as I notice something to the side. A figure stands just around the rear corner of our house. Watching Dalton rage. Listening to him rant. Observing and judging.

I get to my feet. "Can I help you, Phil?"

Dalton spins with a "What the fuck?"

"I wished to speak to you both," Phil says as he walks into the yard.

"It's almost four A.M.," I say. "We're on our own time, and our own property. This is a private conversation."

"At that volume, no, I don't think it is."

There's more judgment in his voice, and I want to snap at him, but I only say, "Then I'll repeat that we are on our own time. We'll speak to you in the morning."

Phil walks over as if I haven't spoken. "I take it you didn't find Kenny?"

"No," I say, as evenly as I can. "We will resume the search tomorrow."

"I don't think that's necessary."

"Excuse me?" Dalton says.

"I understand you suspected him of being Oliver Brady's accomplice."

"We did," I say. "The evidence fit, but it was all circumstantial. That's why we let Kenny out of the cell on work duty. If you wish to debate that decision, I'll suggest it's unnecessary. We already realize that might not have been wise."

"I don't care what choice you made regarding Kenny's incarceration. My point is that the only reason to pursue him is in hopes he'll lead you to Oliver. That is unlikely. Oliver has staff, not partners. He conned this man into helping him, and now he will have abandoned him as unnecessary. Otherwise, Kenny would have fled with him. Correct?"

He doesn't even wait for a response before continuing. "Kenny left because he realized his guilt had been uncovered, and it was only a matter of time—"

"No," Dalton says.

Phil sighs. It's a familiar sigh, one I've heard countless times underscored by the feedback from a radio receiver. "I know you—"

"He left a note." Dalton points at the wadded paper on the lawn. "He blames himself for Brady escaping and wants to bring him back. Kenny accepts responsibility because he left his post. Not because he was in cahoots with Brady."

Another sigh, the sort a supercilious teacher gives a student he considers not terribly bright. "Just because Kenny *claims* that doesn't mean it's true, Sheriff. Of course he'll defend himself. My point is that he isn't your concern. He has made his choice. He might hope to find Oliver. Perhaps even kill him, to cover his own crimes. But he's unlikely to succeed. His flight proves his guilt and therefore, whatever justice the forest metes out . . ." Phil shrugs.

"It saves the council from doing it?" Dalton says.

There's a warning note in Dalton's voice, but Phil only says, "Yes, it does. Casey no longer needs to waste time proving his guilt, and you can both focus on Oliver instead. Take this as a reprieve; do not turn it into a cause for extra effort."

"A *reprieve?*" Dalton says. "Extra *effort?* Kenny was a valued member of my militia, and whatever you might think of what he's done, he deserves my—"

"He deserves nothing. If you feel guilty, take this as an order. You may not search for this man. If you happen to find him, all right. Do what you must."

"Do what I must?" Dalton says, his voice lowering. "Kill him, you mean?"

"Of course not. Bring him back."

"If I must. Because, you know, the alternative is to just let him die out there. Which is worse than killing him. And it's not like, if I bring him back, he's going to live much longer anyway. Maybe I *should* just kill him."

I see where Dalton's heading, and I try to get his attention and cut him off, but before I can, Phil says, "What are you talking about?"

"Sure, yeah, let's pretend you don't know."

"Eric . . ." I say.

Dalton advances on the other man. "Tell me, Phil, what happens if I bring Kenny back and put him on your plane. What happened to Beth after I dropped her off?"

"Beth Lowry is fine, and to suggest otherwise only proves you are exhausted and need—"

"What if I want her back? We need a doctor. Let's bring Beth back for a while. Can we do that, Phil?"

"Certainly not. After what she did—"

"Forget about bringing her back. We have medical questions. How about the council hires her for satellite consultations?"

"We cannot—"

"Do you know where she is, Phil?"

"I don't care, and neither should you. But she is alive. We are not executioners—"

"No? Then tell me about the deal you tried to make with Tyrone Cypher."

Phil's face screws up. "Who?"

"The sheriff before Gene Dalton."

"That is long before my time, as you well know."

"The council tracked him down in the forest. Tried to cut him a deal. Ty says he knows what it was, because he has one real talent. His former occupation. A hit man."

Phil bursts into a laugh. "Is that what he told you? I'm sure whatever this Cypher man did in his past life, he was not a hired killer. The council would never put such a man in Rockton."

"No? Then tell me about Harry Powys."

"Eric," I say sharply.

"No, please, Casey," Phil says. "It seems the sheriff has a few things to get off his chest. If you are suggesting Harry Powys was a hired killer—"

"Worse," Dalton says. "He was a doctor who drugged illegal immigrants and removed their organs. Sometimes they lived; sometimes they didn't. Being in the country illegally, though, it wasn't like they could complain."

Phil stares at him.

"What Eric means—" I begin.

"Please, Casey. There is no alternative interpretation you can come up with to explain that away, however embarrassing I'm sure you find it."

I bristle. "I don't find it—"

"The sheriff's exposure to our culture is limited largely to his books and videos. Dime-store novels and fantasy television shows."

"That's not—"

"And from those, he clearly has a distorted view on the world, one that someone has exploited by feeding him ridiculous stories. Black-market organ sales are the stuff of pulp fiction and urban legend, Sheriff. Whoever told you Harry Powys did such a thing was pulling a prank."

"Look it up," Dalton says.

"What?"

"Harrison Powers. That's his real name. Google it. You'll find news articles—*legitimate* news articles—about a doctor suspected of exactly what I said. A warrant was issued for his arrest. He disappeared. Check the dates. Check the photograph. Compare it to Harry Powys."

Silence. Three long pulses of it. Then Phil says, "Whoever told you they found this online—"

"I found it. I'm not illiterate, you pompous jackass. I can use the fucking internet and read the goddamn evidence, which I verify against alternate sources."

Dalton steps closer to Phil. "You let a man like that into my town. For profit. And he murdered Abbygail. They chopped up her body and scattered it for scavengers. That's who you let in here. Because it was profitable."

"I'm sorry, Sheriff. I don't know how you came across this information, but it is wrong. Completely and utterly—"

Dalton hits him. A right hook to the jaw. Phil flies off his feet. Dalton steps away. Then he follows me into the house, leaving Phil on the ground outside.

FORTY-FIVE

We're upstairs in our bedroom. Phil is gone—I checked out the balcony window. I've let Storm upstairs, only because it would be more upsetting to keep her out and listen to her cry. Dalton is in the chair by our bed, and she's at his feet, her muzzle on his boots, which he's forgotten to take off. I bend to untie them, and he removes them silently. Then he says, "I fucked up."

"Yes."

He looks at me.

"This is the one time I'm not going to argue," I say. "You opened a hornet's nest that we should have left alone."

I take his boots and set them outside the door. "It was going to happen sooner or later. Probably best that it happened when it's just Phil, without the council listening in. That will make it easier for us to control the damage."

"Our word against his?" He makes a face, and I know he hates that. It's underhanded and dishonest.

"No, I have another idea. But first I have to ask if you *want* this damage controlled. Or is this scorched-earth time?"

He exhales and leans forward, both hands running through his hair. Then he shakes his head. "There's part of me that says 'fuck, yeah.' Just throw it all out there and end this. Pack our things and go. But that's me being pissy."

"Which you'd regret about twelve hours later."

"Yeah. As much as I'd like to confront the council, what good does it do? They'll pull a Phil—pretend they don't know what I'm talking about, treat me like a delusional idiot. Then they'll shut me up. Exile me. Exile you. Or worse. So, no, this isn't scorched-earth time. This is 'Casey fixes Eric's fuck-up' time. And you have an idea about how to do that?"

"I do."

After Dalton is asleep, I slip over to Anders's place to ask him to take the first search shift this morning. I know he's only been to bed for a couple of hours—and me waking him doesn't help—but when I explain what happened, he offers before I can ask. Then it's back home to make sure the blackout blinds are closed, reset the alarm, and ease into bed.

When the alarm sounds at nine and I admit my subterfuge, Dalton grumbles . . . until I point out that I would much rather *not* trick him and just be able to ask him to stay in bed until he's rested enough to search properly. He agrees. Even apologizes. Whether he'll voluntarily sleep in when I ask is another matter. I can't say I'm any better, though.

Phil is at the station when we arrive. He's waiting by my desk, his arms crossed, as if we're tardy children. Dalton sees him and slows to an amble, perversely acting as if he's just strolled in whenever he feels like it. He walks right past Phil and puts on the kettle for coffee.

"I believe we have an issue to discuss," Phil says.

"Yeah," Dalton says as he stokes the fire. "I'd like to explain."

Phil's voice chills even more. "I don't think that's possible."

Dalton straightens, still holding the poker. "You were right about Powys."

"I should certainly hope—"

"It's entirely possible the council didn't know what he was. I know that, which is why I've never said anything until I lost my temper last night." Dalton puts the poker back. "As for whether he did that shit, the answer is yes. Like I said, it's online. I suspected Powys was involved with making the rydex, especially with his background. According to his entry papers, he was a pharmacist."

"Correct."

"So I went looking online . . . and dug up more than I bargained for."

"Perhaps, but that hardly proves we let him buy his way in."

"Agreed. If you don't know anything about it, then obviously he faked his admission file."

Phil's eyes narrow, as if he's waiting for the punch line.

"I don't like the council," Dalton says calmly. "Never made any secret of that. But, yeah, accusing them of that went too far. So I apologize. Good?"

"No, Eric, it is not good. When I said I wanted an apology, I meant for this." He gestures to the bruise on his jaw.

"Fuck no," Dalton says. "You deserved that."

Phil's sputtering as the door swings open.

"Good, you're still here," Wallace says as he walks in. "I was afraid I'd been left behind. So, when do we start searching for Oliver?"

Dalton does not want to take Wallace into the forest. He argues. Vehemently. Profanely. Loudly. He is overruled by Phil. Both Wallace and Phil are coming along, and there's nothing we can do about that.

We fill thermoses with coffee and grab breakfast to go at the bakery. I think Dalton's hoping that our speedy departure will change Wallace's mind. It doesn't. Within the hour, we're deep in the forest, with the two men and Storm.

Dalton takes the lead with the dog. I hang back with Phil and Wallace. That's deliberate, allowing our trackers to work. I chat with Wallace. Phil tries several times to pull Wallace's attention his way, with topics I can't possibly address—American election issues, a stock-market roller coaster—but Wallace only answers politely and then steers conversation back to include me.

Phil surrenders with a sniff and once-over of me, as if suggesting

Wallace is only paying attention to me because I'm female. I get no such vibe from the older man, though. Wallace is just politely keeping conversation on things I can discuss, like the forest itself. When Phil falls back, I warn him to please stay close, but he dawdles just enough that I need to keep shoulder-checking to be sure he's with us.

When Wallace realizes both Dalton and Phil are almost out of ear-shot, he lowers his voice and says, "I would like to speak to you about something." He pauses. "Or perhaps not so much a discussion as a confession."

"Hmm?"

"About Oliver. I know how this looks from your viewpoint. You are a detective. You're supposed to catch people like my stepson and put them in prison. That is what should have happened to Oliver. And yet it did not. Why? Because we're rich. We can afford alternatives, and the alternative I chose resulted in the death of five more people."

"Yes."

He gives a strained chuckle. "Not going to sugarcoat that for me, are you?"

"I grew up with money. Not your tax bracket, but my parents had very successful careers, and we enjoyed all the privileges that come with that. So I won't rage about the inherent evil of the upper class. But nor do I agree with anyone using their money and their privilege to keep a serial killer out of prison."

We walk in silence for a few minutes. Then he says, "I told myself I was doing the right thing. The responsible thing. I'm embarrassed to say that now, but it's true. I thought that by incarcerating Oliver, I was saving my country that expense. Doing my civic duty by removing him from the population while not charging the taxpayer for our mistakes."

"It doesn't work like that."

"Oh, I know. The truth is . . ." He exhales. "I love my wife. I wanted to protect her—not only from a trial, but from ever knowing what Oliver did. As soon as the police started questioning, I hired an investigator. I found evidence and confronted Oliver. When I threatened to turn my evidence over to the police, he confessed. So I whisked him away and told my wife that he was innocent, but we couldn't trust the justice system. I said they'd convict him on the grounds of being a spoiled, rich white boy. But my wife wasn't the only reason I did that. I wanted to avoid the business ramifications of having a serial killer for a stepson. It was a sound business investment. Whatever this costs, it is not nearly the blow my finances would suffer if Oliver was arrested."

Storm barks, and I tense. It's just a quick bark, though, with a response from Dalton. I can see them through the trees around the next curve, and while I can't make out what Dalton's saying, there's no alarm in his voice.

Wallace has gone quiet, and I think he's waiting for me to respond. This is, as he said, a confession. A safe one, too—it's not as if I can tell the newspapers what he's said.

If he wants absolution, he has to look elsewhere. I do, however, credit him for the confession, which is why I just stay quiet.

"I wanted to be clear that I understand my position here," Wallace continues. "I am the interloper who brought this on your town. I realize now what I've done, and I'm sorry it took five deaths for me to understand that." Another few steps in silence. "I really did believe this solution was a valid one. But the hard truth is that anyone who comes into contact with Oliver is at risk. The only truly viable solution is one that doesn't put him into contact with anyone. Ever."

Execution. That's what he means, and I stiffen, fearing he's hinting that we should resolve this with lethal action. But his gaze is straight ahead, distant.

Jail is no longer an option. We both know that. It ceased to be an option as soon as Brady came here. Put him into custody, and he'll cut a deal any way he can, including talking about Rockton.

I don't know where to go with this, what to say, so after I glance back for Phil, I change the subject with, "You say it'd be a blow to your personal finances, but Oliver claims your family money comes from his father—from a business he started."

Wallace nods. "Yes, that's his version of history, and it's our fault. His mother's and mine. We wanted to keep his father alive for him. Honor him with a legacy of success."

"And the truth?"

"I worked for Oliver's father. At one time, we were partners, but when we formed the business, the money came from his family, so his name went on it. That seemed fair. The problem was that while David was an incredible inventor, he didn't have a lick of business sense. I lacked the clout to overrule him, and at the time of his death, the company was floundering."

"You brought it back."

A sharp laugh. "There was no place to bring it back *from*. We had investors—David's ideas were incredible—but we'd been scrambling to stay afloat from the start."

"With Oliver's father gone, though, you turned it around."

"Oliver's mother and I did. Together. Yet David's name remains on the company, and we have allowed Oliver the fiction of his brilliant inventor father who launched a billion-dollar corporation. Which led, unfortunately, to Oliver beginning to demand more than a trust fund. When his mother had enough, she showed him the financial records from the year of his father's death. He accused us of forging them. By that point . . ."

He shrugs. "By that point, I knew there was no arguing with him. He was never happy, never satisfied. Everyone was conspiring to keep him from his due."

I check for Phil again and—

The path behind us is empty. Then I spot him, stopped off the path with his back to us. It's obvious from his stance what he's doing.

I turn to give him privacy and call, "Eric? Hold up." I have to shout—he's too far ahead to see on the winding path. Then I say, "Phil, please let us know if you are stopping. The absolute last thing we need—"

At a rustle behind me, I turn. But it's not Phil. It's a man holding an old rifle, trained on me. Two men armed with knives step out in front of Wallace. Behind them, Phil stands frozen, staring at the men. Their backs are to him, and I tear my gaze away before they spot him.

One glance tells me these men are settlers, not hostiles, and I relax at that. I'm cautious, though, gauging the distance to my gun, ready to pull it if that rifle barrel swings out of my way.

I open my mouth to speak. Then I hear:

"Let them go."

As I turn, Dalton appears at knifepoint, his hands on the back of his head. Two men and a woman follow at his rear. The woman holds Storm's lead. My gaze drops to the dog.

"Take Storm and our friend there back to Rockton, Casey," Dalton says. "I've got this under control."

If my heart wasn't thudding so hard, I'd laugh. He said the same thing when Jacob had a knife on him. His brother was drugged and ranting and threatening . . . and Dalton's biggest concern was reassuring me that he could handle it. They'd talk it out. Yeah, just talk it out. No big deal.

"We are not letting your girl go," one of the men says.

"She's my wife," Dalton says, "and if Edwin has one drop of respect for me, he will let her walk away with our guest and the dog, and I will come willingly and answer any questions you have."

Edwin. Questions.

The First Settlement. The massacre.

Oh, shit.

"The girl comes," the man says. "That is what Edwin says. He wishes to speak to the girl."

I swear Wallace snorts softly. He's already realized that, given the choice, *everyone* prefers to speak to me instead of Dalton.

"All right," I say. "Let Eric take our guest and dog home to Rockton. I'll talk to Edwin."

Dalton mouths *Fuck no,* his jaw setting in a way I know well. But before he can speak, the man says, "Edwin will talk to the girl, but he says to bring Steve's boy. That was the order. Do not let him leave. If he tries"—he looks at Dalton—"shoot him."

FORTY-SIX

We walk to the First Settlement. They were willing to let Wallace go, but he refused.

"I don't know my way back," he said.

"Just follow—" I begin.

"Somehow, it seems safer to stay with you two. I've heard quite enough about this forest."

As for Phil, he's gone. Fled without ever being spotted.

I try to talk to the settlers. Defuse this situation. But they have been warned not to speak to us, and they are already wary. So I fall to silence, walking beside Dalton, armed settlers in front and behind.

We're nearing the First Settlement when the men in front of us turn and point their guns.

"Hands behind your back," one says, taking out a length of rope.

"Fuck no," Dalton says.

The woman steps forward. "Get your hands behind your back, boy, or we'll put a bullet through your damn skull."

Dalton wheels on her. "Excuse me?"

"Enough." One of the men turns to Dalton. "We are not letting you walk into our village after what happened. You will be disarmed.

You will have your hands bound. People are angry. If we bring you in like guests, there will be trouble."

Dalton grumbles, but puts his hands behind his back, and then lets them disarm us. Wallace silently follows our lead.

The woman glowers at Dalton's grumblings. "You're lucky we don't shoot you and drag your bodies through the settlement."

"What the hell?" Dalton says.

She steps up to him. "Albie. Nancy. Douglas."

"The people who died," I say. "Yes, we take full responsibility for letting their killer escape."

"Escape?"

"What do you expect?" one of the guys says. "They're going to blame this on someone else."

"No," I say carefully. "We acknowledge the killer was one of ours."

"So now you're blaming some innocent person from Rockton?" the woman says. "Was that your plan? Bring us a body and say 'There's your killer'?"

"Or is it him?" The man turns to Wallace. "Are you forcing this old man to take the fall?"

"What the hell are you talking about?" Dalton says.

The woman steps right in front of him and spits up in his face.

I move between them fast. "We don't know what's happening here—"

"Harper told us who killed our people," the woman said. "Your husband. She saw it, and she barely escaped with her life."

FORTY-SEVEN

We cannot even begin to speculate on what's happened here, which doesn't keep Dalton from demanding answers. But our captors are not talking.

We enter the village at gunpoint. The First Settlement is composed of about ten cabins, spread over a couple of acres. As people emerge from homes, the palpable weight of their rage pulses through the air.

If I had any idea what they thought we'd done, I'd have fought our captors. Allowing a dangerous Rockton resident to escape was one thing. We could have handled that, though. Made promises. Made apologies. Made concessions. Now . . . ?

I glance at Dalton. His face is taut, gaze straight ahead, jaw set as if he's outraged, but the vein throbbing in his neck tells me he is afraid.

"In here." One of our captors prods Dalton toward a dilapidated building.

When I see Harper, I try to catch her eye, not accusing but confused, concerned. I gesture that I would like to speak to her, but she's pretending not to see me. She circles to a man behind us and says something. He shakes his head. She gestures my way and I think it's at me, but then I realize she's pointing at Storm. The man shakes his head and reaches to squeeze her thin shoulder, but she throws him off and stomps away.

Dalton's captor prods him again.

"Yeah, no," he says. "I'll wait here for Edwin."

"You aren't talking to Edwin." The man nods at me. "She is."

"Fine, then I'll sit my ass down right here and wait."

The man points at the building. "You will wait there. She will wait at Edwin's."

Dalton opens his mouth, but I shake my head. He hesitates, and I know this makes him nervous—it makes me nervous, too—but we cannot give them any excuse for using those weapons to *force* us to obey.

Dalton stalks off toward the building, muttering the whole way. Our captors prod Wallace to follow Dalton. I let them take me to Edwin's place. They open the door, and I walk in, as calmly as I can, as if this is an obvious misunderstanding that I know will be cleared up.

Edwin isn't there.

I turn to ask where he is, but they've shut the door behind me.

I take a deep breath and sit on the floor. Storm lowers herself beside me, leaning in hard, panting with nervous tension. I pat her and tell her it will be okay, it will all be okay.

I hope it will be okay.

I've been there about ten minutes when I hear a noise in the next room. The door swings opens, and Harper stands there, an open window behind her, a knife in her hand.

"Put that down," I say.

"I just came here to talk."

"Good. Then you don't need a knife."

She shakes her head. I ask her one more time. Then I take it. She doesn't see that coming. She tries to slash, but I already have her by the forearm. I squeeze just tight enough to hold her steady. Then I pluck the knife from her hand. When I release her, she swings at me. I grab her arm, pin it behind her back, march her to the open window and drop the knife through it.

When I let her go, she backs off, rubbing her wrist.

"That hurt," she says, and there's genuine shock in her voice.

"You attacked. I defended."

She eyes me as if this calm response isn't what she expects. "It was my knife. I was defending *myself*."

"One shout will bring the guard to your aid. I only put your knife outside. I didn't keep it."

She's still eyeing me. She says, again, "That hurt," and there's a tremor of outrage, as if I should be ashamed of myself hurting a kid. But like she said the other day, she is not a child, not out here.

"What's going on?" I say.

I'm waiting for the look of worry, of guilt. The one that says they've made her blame us. Someone has forced her to make a false statement. Someone she respects. Someone she fears.

I'm waiting for her to apologize. To say she had no choice.

When she says, "I told the truth," my heart sinks. But I am not surprised.

"The *truth*?" I say.

"Eric killed them. I was there."

I could blame post-traumatic stress. Confusion. Even fear.

Instead, I say, "Why?"

"Why what?"

Now I'm the one eyeing her. Sizing her up. There's no point in Harper coming here to talk.

"What do you want?" I say.

I follow her gaze to Storm. "No."

"Yes."

"She's town property."

"She's yours," Harper says. "I heard Eric say that he got her for you."

"Are you sure?"

Her face scrunches up. "That he got her for you?"

"No, that you overheard it. When? As you were running for your life? After Eric killed three of your people?"

"I want her."

She says it as if this is a simple matter. As if she is indeed a child, one too young to have realized that a wish is not a command or an obligation.

But I'm not sure it *is* childlike to her. Out here, it's a very normal

THIS FALLEN PREY | 261

thing, at least for some of the settlers and probably all of the hostiles. *I want this thing. You have it. So I will take it from you.*

I remember the young man—Albie—checking out our horses. Suggesting where we might camp, and Dalton being sure *not* to camp there.

You have this thing that I want, and I will take it from you, and that's nothing personal. It's just the way it is.

Harper steps toward Storm, who leans against me, whining.

The girl looks at me. "Tell Eric that you're giving me the dog, and I'll tell Edwin I made a mistake."

"Little late for that, isn't it?" I say.

"What?"

"How exactly do you tell him you made a mistake? Say that you hallucinated Eric murdering your people? Or that the event was so traumatic you forgot what happened and made something up? How will that make you seem?"

I see her mental gears whirring madly as she looks for the trap here. There must be a trap. Why else would I ever advise her *not* to rescind her story?

"You want a new husband," she says.

"What?"

She nods, satisfied. "You have met someone new in your town, and you want him. Or you never wanted Eric, but he is the leader, and you cannot say no to the leader."

"Yes," I say. "He is the leader. My boss. But if he's gone . . ."

"You want his job."

As she says that, I get a glimpse into the woman behind the girl's mask. When she speculates I simply want a new lover, she is dismissive. Now, as I claim it is ambition, respect flashes in her eyes.

"Can you help me?" I say.

"For the dog?"

I nod. "For the dog."

"What do I need to do?"

"Just stick to your story. *Exactly* to it. Can you do that?"

She nods.

"Tell me everything you told Edwin."

FORTY-EIGHT

You can learn so much about a person by how they react to others. In the forest, my view of Harper was formed almost entirely by how she responded to Storm. I love my dog, and Harper found her fascinating, and that made me happy. It made me open up to her, engage her, see her as more than just some settler kid. I never suspected there was darkness in her.

I don't believe she actually realizes what she's done. She is incapable of realizing it. She wants Storm. I have Storm. Therefore she must get her from me, and if Dalton is endangered by her actions, well, he's a stranger, a meaningless bit player in her life drama. And so was I . . . until I "admitted" that I'd like my lover out of the picture so I can take his job. With that, I became someone interesting to her. In her strengths, she also shows me her weaknesses.

After Harper leaves, I wait for Edwin to finally show up. He'll bring Harper with him, and I'm prepared for that.

The door opens, and my guard walks in.

"Edwin is ready for you," he says.

"Good. I'm here."

The man shakes his head. "*He* is waiting out here."

I tell myself this will still work. Then I step outside, and Storm starts whining, and I look over to see Dalton being led—bound and gagged—across the village.

Wallace follows, bound but not gagged, and he's glancing about, taking everything in, and I don't think he really understands what's at stake here. How can he? He doesn't come from a world where strangers can grab you in the forest, accuse you of murder, and string you up from the nearest tree. To him, this is just an interesting cultural study, a blustering show of force, all sound and fury, signifying nothing, because there's no way these people would actually *hurt* us.

Dalton is being Dalton. Chin up, shoulders squared. He's not worried. Nope, not worried at all. When he sees me, the facade cracks, but only for me—am I okay? He can see I am, and he nods.

Don't worry, Casey, I may be gagged and bound, but I have everything under control.

I could shake my head at that, but he's really just saying that he trusts me to have a plan. Trusts that I will get us out of this.

No pressure.

We are all led to the village square. Where the village waits. I skim-count thirty heads, all adults.

Edwin stands at the front. Someone has brought him a chair, but he's ignoring it. He's a small man, not much bigger than me, wizened by age.

The guard starts leading Storm away, and she digs in her nails, growling.

"She knows Harper," I say. "Let Harper hold her."

The girl takes Storm's lead.

I turn to Edwin. "What do you want?"

"Due process. This is a trial. A murder trial."

"And you're the judge. No lawyers, I'm guessing."

"I was one," he says.

"And one lawyer is quite enough."

He doesn't quite smile, but the glimmer in his eyes awards me a point for that.

I continue, "I'm presuming, though, that if you've gagged Eric, I'm acting as *his* lawyer. Witness and counsel."

"Correct."

"As a former lawyer, *sir,* you'll recognize the predicament I'm in here," I say. "All I know is that Eric has been accused of killing your people. I don't know what Harper told you. I don't know what you might have found at the scene. There's been no discovery. No formal laying of charges. So I'll skip straight to the biggest missing piece. Motivation. Why did Eric do this?"

Harper tenses, but I nod for her to trust me.

Edwin waves the question off. "As you well know, Detective, motivation isn't important. Fact is what matters."

"Yes, motivation gets in the way of an investigation. It clouds fact. But this is a trial. Unless Eric has confessed, we need motive."

"We have an eyewitness."

I give him a look. Just a look. He grants me another point. Juries love eyewitnesses, but a lawyer knows how unreliable they are.

"Fine," I say. "Set motive aside for now. What is the evidence *beyond* your witness? You returned to the scene to collect your dead, I presume."

"Our people did."

"And you saw how they died? Albie killed at his guard post. The older man in his sleeping blankets. Harper's grandmother running for her life."

A grumble runs through the crowd. This reminder does not please them.

"What evidence do you have that Eric did this?" I ask.

"He fled the scene, which means we can hardly search his belongings for bloody clothes or a weapon."

"What you need then is a second eyewitness."

I glance at Harper. Her face is glowing now. She sees victory— I will be that witness for her.

"I believe I have your motivation," I say, and then I switch to Mandarin with, "Keep your eyes on me, please, sir."

His brows lift, but he does as I ask. I nod discreetly to Harper, who is fairly quivering with anticipation. I do not dare implicate my lover when he stands right there, so I am using another language to do it, a language I share with her leader.

"Motivation," I say to Edwin. I speak slowly, carefully—my Mandarin is rusty and probably the equivalent of a four-year-old's. "You know Eric doesn't have one. You can't even think of one."

His mouth opens. I continue, while sneaking looks at Dalton. Worried looks. Maybe guilty looks. For Harper's benefit. Dalton doesn't even frown. He trusts me.

"But I have a motivation for you," I say. "A motivation for Harper to lie. That is right in front of your eyes. I have something that she wants."

"The dog? That's . . ." He doesn't finish.

"I have something she wants," I say.

He shakes his head. "Then she would know you're telling me the truth now. She would be arguing."

"Not if I've convinced her I want Eric's job. And that she can have the dog if she sticks to her story."

"What happened out there?"

I tell him. When I finish, I say, "Which story makes logical sense?"

Edwin says, in English, "So you were tasked with imprisoning a killer. You failed to do that, and we suffered. Is that your story, Detective?"

Oh, shit. I haven't fixed anything. Edwin never believed Dalton did it. This was all for show. We haven't dodged a bullet . . . we just stepped back into the path of the one that's been coming at us since we fled the massacre.

"Yes," I say. "We accept responsibility—"

"You did not. You walked away. You failed to show the basic respect due my people."

"Yeah," says a muffled voice.

I look to see Dalton has managed to get the gag down just enough to talk over it. He twists, and it drops further, and he shakes it off, saying, "Yeah, I did. That was my choice. Because I knew there was no way in hell we'd come in here, confess to our mistake and you'd let us walk away. And there was no way in hell I was putting up with your bullshit while I've got a killer out there."

"My *bullshit*?" Edwin's voice lowers, heavy with warning.

"Yes, and don't give me that tone. You're in charge here. I'm in charge in Rockton. We're equals. Which means you should have shown me the *basic respect* of marching me in here for a private audience. Not tying me up. Gagging me and talking to my detective instead. You *know* why I didn't come here right away. I wish I could have. Would have saved us all a shitload of grief. But I couldn't, and this is all fucking theatrics, so cut the bullshit and let me get on with my job."

"I think perhaps we should put that gag back on."

"Sure." Dalton meets his gaze. "Go ahead and try."

"He killed—" Harper begins.

Edwin spins on her, snapping as he finds a target for his frustration. "I don't know what you thought you saw out there, girl, but no one from Rockton is going to murder our people for a few bows and supplies. You lost your head in those woods, and you won't be going back out there anytime soon. Turn in your bow and hunting knife. You'll help Mabel with the cooking now."

Rage fills Harper's eyes. Impotent rage. She tried to step out of her assigned role, and she is being smacked right back into it. I want to sympathize, but she accused an innocent man of mass murder because she wanted a dog. Sympathy is a little hard to come by after that.

"Give Casey her dog," Edwin says with an abrupt wave.

Harper grips the leash. "She's mine. In forfeit, for what they did."

"You think we'll share our food so you can have a pet?"

"It's not a pet. It can track and hunt and—"

"The only animals in this town are the ones we cook on a fire. Give Casey her dog. Now."

Harper looks at me, her eyes blazing. Then she drops the leash and knees Storm. The dog falls back in shock, and I race over, and whatever Harper sees in my face, she decides not to stick around.

I crouch beside Storm and pet her, soothing her as she keeps looking at Harper's receding back in confusion.

"We demand justice, Eric," Edwin says behind me. "We demand this killer."

"When we catch—"

"You will not bring him to me. I know you won't. Casey would promise to convey our demand to the council, but you know they'll refuse. So you will tell me only that you'll catch him, and justice will be served. That's not what I want. I am keeping Casey until you bring me this man."

"What?" I rise.

"Hell, no," Dalton says. "Do not even—"

"Casey stays. With the dog if that helps. She will be our guest until you return."

"Guest? We call that a fucking hostage."

"She is *my* guest."

"Yeah?" Dalton strides toward him. "If you keep her, this psycho is never going to *be* caught. She's the goddamn detective. You want a hostage? Take me."

"That is far more trouble than—"

"I remember how my mother was treated here." Dalton stops in front of the old man and lowers his voice. "A child does not forget that. He does not forgive that. The answer is *Fuck, no.*"

"I realize Casey is now your wife and—"

"I would not let *any* woman from Rockton stay here. Casey is a fucking *detective,* which means she needs to be out there hunting for this guy."

"So do you." I turn to Edwin. "I understand what you're trying to do, but you need to come up with a solution that won't hinder the actual hunt for this man."

"Take me," says a voice behind us.

I look to see Wallace, who has been so silent I've forgotten he was there. Now he steps forward.

"This is my fault, not theirs," Wallace says. "I hired Rockton to imprison the man who killed your people. They weren't equipped to do so, which the council failed to tell me. Eric and Casey had nothing to do with that. I made the mistake here."

"And who are you?" Edwin says.

"The father of the man who did this to your people."

FORTY-NINE

If I could have stopped Wallace before he said that, I would have. But once the words are out, there is no taking them back. And there is no way of walking out of this village with him.

We must leave Wallace behind. Leave him, and trust that no harm will come to him. He is a smart man. He didn't interfere as we dealt with Edwin, so I feel confident he's not going to do anything that will endanger him in our absence. It just won't be the most comfortable way to spend his Yukon trip.

They don't let us speak to Wallace in private. All we can do is talk to him, within earshot of the others, reassuring him.

A group of settlers escort us into the forest. Then they put our weapons on the ground and tell us to stand with our backs to them while they retreat. We do. Only when they give us the signal do we pick up our guns. Then we walk in the other direction.

"Can we go back to the scene of the massacre?" I say when we're out of earshot.

Dalton nods. He leads me there. The bodies are gone. Even the blood has seeped into the ground and disappeared, and when we arrive, the only thing that tells me this is definitely the right place is a red fox. It's in the clearing, so busy sniffing around that it doesn't see or smell us. It's snuffling madly, smelling death and seeing no sign of it.

When Storm spots the fox, she lets out a bark of greeting. The fox's head jerks up. It sees her. And it bolts into the undergrowth, leaping logs and ripping through dead leaves while Dalton digs in his heels and clenches the leash in both hands.

Once the fox is gone, I pat Storm and head into the clearing. Then I search. After a few minutes, Dalton says, "Tell me what you're looking for, and I can help."

I shake my head, as if I don't know, too distracted to answer. That's not entirely a lie. I don't know specifically what I'm looking for. But I'm here with a purpose, a question niggling the back of my mind, not ready to be voiced. Maybe never ready to be voiced. Not unless I find evidence to support it. So I just look. Then I hunker in the middle of the clearing and observe.

When I finally start to rise, Dalton says, "You gonna tell me what happened?"

"Hmm?"

"With that girl. She lied, didn't she. Outright lied."

"Yes."

Silence.

I take another look around before answering his unspoken question. "She wanted Storm."

More silence. I glance over, and he's just standing there, brow furrowed.

"The dog?" he says finally.

I drop to all fours and peer about near ground level, still searching. Then I say, "An error in judgment on my part. When she was interested in Storm, I jumped on that as a topic of conversation. Of connection."

I rise and brush off my knees. "I told her how we've taught Storm to track. I showed her how well trained she was. I said how gentle she was. How much bigger she'd get. Apparently, that was like showing off your new vehicle's special features to a car thief."

"You're serious?"

I nod.

"That's fucked-up."

"It is."

I stand in the clearing. Think. Think some more. I'm so enrapt in my thoughts that I don't realize Dalton is right there until I turn and bash into him.

When I lean against him, his arm goes around me.

"You okay?" he says.

"I wasn't the one accused of murdering three people."

I feel him shrug as he says, "It was all for show. Just pissed me off."

I chuckle and shake my head. His arm tightens around me. "Something's bugging you."

"Everything's bugging me," I say as I step back. "We've left Gregory Wallace with people who know his stepson murdered their friends. To get him back, we need to turn over Brady. Which means finding Brady. Which we've been trying to do since this whole damn thing started and—"

Another squeeze as Dalton kisses the top of my head. "We'll get Wallace back. In the meantime, they won't hurt him. No point in it. If we'd left Storm, that'd be a whole different matter, apparently. But no one's going to want Wallace."

I give a strained laugh.

Dalton continues, "This just raises the stakes. Motivates us. Because, you know, we were just sitting on our asses before, trying to decide if we wanted to bother looking for this Brady guy."

I shake my head.

"Let's get to Rockton," Dalton says. "See if Phil made it back okay."

"Phil . . . Oh, *shit*."

"Yeah, I know. Come on. We'll—"

"One last thing. Sorry. I just want to check . . ."

I trail off as my brain finally homes in on the source of that niggling thought.

As Dalton follows, he says, "Something's up."

"Just . . . I just want to check this."

A grunt says he isn't happy with my answer. He doesn't ask again, though, just lets his dissatisfaction be known.

"This is where we found Harper's grandmother, right?" I say.

"Yeah." He points, and I see that some scavenger has rooted through the dirt, looking for the source of the blood.

"Harper came from . . ." I turn. "This direction."

Dalton nods.

I walk that way and find a spot where vegetation has been crushed. "She watched us from here. Which means . . ." I look around.

"She came that way," Dalton says, pointing. "That's what you're looking for, right?"

"It is. Thanks."

"The path where she saw Brady is over there. We can follow it, but if I thought that would do any good, we'd have tracked him from there right away."

"I know."

A soft growl of frustration. "So what the hell are you looking for, Casey?"

"I don't know exactly."

Three beats of silence as I backtrack on Harper's trail. Then he follows. He wants to demand answers, but he knows that's not how I work. My ego needs proof before I'll voice any outlandish theories.

Harper's trail doesn't lead directly to the path. She meandered, and when Dalton sees that, he says, "She was trying to decide what to do. Follow Brady or go back to the camp."

I'm nodding when I spot something on the ground. I walk over and bend. It looks like the shredded remains of an animal. I prod it with a stick, expecting to see a head or leg or tail. I don't. It's just hide.

"A food pouch," Dalton says.

A hide pouch that must have held food, now ripped apart, with no trace of what it once contained.

He lifts and turns it over in his hand, examining the craftsmanship. "First Settlement." He peers into the forest, both toward the camp and out in the direction of the path. "So Harper saw Brady on the path and then followed his trail back to the camp. That's why it meanders. He was making his way in the direction of the path but didn't quite know where it was. He dropped this." He shakes the pouch. "So . . ."

He peers up and down the path. Then he goes still. His head jerks up. Storm's muzzle does the same, her nose wriggling madly.

"Back up," Dalton says.

"Wha—?"

His hand wraps around my wrist as he starts propelling us backward. I take each step with care, rolling it, but Storm's paws crunch down on dead leaves. Dalton whispers a curse just as she starts to whine. *Loudly* whine, while straining at the lead.

Dalton stops. His gaze swings across the landscape. Storm dances and whines.

"What did you see?" I whisper.

"Movement. Something big."

Something big that Storm desperately wants to get to. Dalton has the leash wrapped around his hand, but he's distracted, looking about. When I see Storm hunker down, I know what's coming.

"Eric!" I say, and I lunge to grab the lead.

Storm leaps. A powerful leap that catches Dalton off guard, and he stumbles, the leash whipping free, my fingers grazing it, wrapping around it, only to feel the leather burn through my hand as the dog takes off.

"Storm!"

I run after her. I am aware, even before Dalton shouts, that I'm making the exact same mistake I made when she went after the cougar. But that doesn't mean I stop. I can't.

I hear Dalton coming after me, and I double down, terrified he's going to stop me. The messed-up muscles in my bad leg scream for mercy but—

Dalton shoots past.

"Gun," he snarls. "Get your damn gun out."

I do. Ahead, I can still see Storm, her black rump bobbing. Then I spot a figure with its hands out to ward her off. Dalton shouts. The figure says "Whoa—" and Storm takes him down. Then laughter rings out. Sputtering laughter.

Dalton slows, shaking his head. As I jog over, Jacob struggles to get to his feet while pushing Storm off.

"No one can sneak up on you guys, can they?" Jacob says.

"Yeah, because sneaking up on people who have these"—Dalton waves his gun—"is such a good idea."

"Cranky." Jacob grins my way. "That's the word you use for him, right?"

"Yes," Dalton says. "I'm cranky because my damn fool brother just tried to get himself killed by sneaking up on me when I'm in this fucking forest looking for—"

"The guy who killed all those people?"

Dalton eases back. "Yeah. He escaped and—"

"Found him."

"What?"

Jacob's grin widens. "Does that make you less cranky, brother?"

"Depends on how much longer you stand here instead of taking me to him."

FIFTY

We'd speculated that Jacob might have abandoned his camp because he got wind of irresistible prey.

And he had. His prey was Oliver Brady.

Jacob was camping after taking down the bull caribou when he spotted the man he'd met with us a week ago, and he knew Brady ought not to be out wandering the forest alone.

Jacob had his bow and knife and a waterskin, and that was all he needed. He followed Brady for two days, waiting for an opportunity to take him down. He didn't get one. The first night—when Brady massacred the settlers—Jacob lost him late in the day. He managed to find him again yesterday afternoon and planned to capture him that night but . . .

"He met up with a guy," Jacob says.

I glance at Dalton. He says nothing but shoves his hands deeper into his pockets.

"Can you describe the person?" I ask.

"I didn't get too close, but I could tell he was smaller than your guy." Jacob moves a limb from the path. "No, not smaller. Shorter."

Jacob goes on to say the guy had short, dark hair, maybe graying, but he wore a hat so it was hard to tell. Clean-shaven. Dressed in jeans, boots, and a bulky jacket. Carried a gun.

I reach for Dalton's hand, our fingers interlocking. Jacob notices and says, "He's one of yours?"

I nod. "Our lead militia. He took off last night. He was due to go home the day Brady arrived. We suspected he helped Brady escape, but we hoped Brady had just conned him into it, convinced our guy he was innocent."

"That could still be the case, though, right? Brady tells your guy he's innocent, and gets his help escaping, and then they meet to get through the forest. Paid escort."

"Yeah," Dalton says, "but if we keep telling ourselves there's a logical explanation, we're going to end up on the business end of a gun, finding out there isn't."

"I guess so."

We keep walking. I ask Jacob where Brady has been, what he's been doing. Jacob first encountered him over by the mountain, where we found Val's body. From there, Brady wandered. Or so it seemed to us, but as Dalton points out, without wilderness navigation experience, he probably thought he was getting someplace.

It's even possible that he climbed the mountain to get a better vantage point and in the distance spotted the First Settlement. Because that's the direction he seemed to head. From the mountain, he must have met up with the hunting party and killed them. When Jacob found Brady's trail again the next day, he saw him *watching* the First Settlement.

"He scaled a tree on the far side. He kept his distance, but he stayed up there until early evening before he came down and took off."

Had he seen the village from the mountain, thought it was a town, and made his way there, only to realize those people lived even more primitively than we did? That they had no ATVs or motor vehicles or horses he could steal?

But the First Settlement was only two hours' walk from where Brady massacred settlers for their belongings. Why do that if he thought he was close to the end of his journey?

So many questions. All of them unanswerable until we have Brady. Jacob had spent today tracking his quarry. Plan A had been to capture him at night and march him back at knifepoint. Plan B had been to wound him from afar and do the same. But Kenny's arrival kiboshed that.

Then, as Jacob tracked them, he heard the First Settlement men who'd escorted us into the forest. He overheard enough to realize we were in the area. So he'd made note of Brady's current location and hurried to find us.

We reach Brady's camp. He's not there. That's only mildly disappointing—we figured he'd only pulled over to rest. But he's been here, very recently, so we'll find him.

There are two wrappers in the clearing where Jacob had seen Brady and Kenny sitting on logs. Protein bar wrappers. The kind we keep stashed in the militia equipment shed.

I pick one up and examine it.

"Yeah, that's ours," Dalton says.

"I know." Something about the wrapper nudges at me, though, telling me to look closer. I see these bars almost daily—Dalton insists we inventory any pack before taking it out.

This flavor is my personal favorite—chocolate peanut butter. Or it used to be my favorite. The company revamped the recipe lately and changed the packaging, sticking on a *New & Improved Taste!* band, which I'd grumbled should read *New & Cheaper Ingredients!* because it definitely did not taste better.

"This is old stock," I say, confirming as I check the expiration date.

Dalton shrugs. Jacob has already headed out to find the trail, and Dalton's struggling against telling me to put the damn wrapper away and come on before the trail gets cold.

"We ran out of these months ago," I say.

"Yeah, okay." He peers into the forest, head tilting as if he's listening for his brother. Storm tugs at the leash, seconding his impatience.

"Did we have old stock anywhere?" I ask.

"I don't know," he says. "Is that important?"

It isn't. Not right now. But it's bugging me, like so many things.

I fold the wrapper and put it in my pocket as I follow him from the clearing.

Jacob finds the trail easily. Brady is no outdoorsman. Once he got far enough from Rockton, he stopped using even amateur methods of hiding his trail. He's walking along what he probably thinks is a path, but it's really just a deer route. That means it's narrow, and we find freshly broken twigs and crushed vegetation, and even footprints when the ground gets marshy.

Jacob is in the lead, maybe twenty paces ahead. It's impossible to walk silently with an eighty-pound Newfoundland panting and lumbering alongside us, so we're hanging back. When Jacob finds the footprints, he gives a birdcall and, through the trees, I see him gesture at the ground. Then he keeps going.

We reach the spot, and I see what he was indicating and crouch to examine footprint impressions in the soft ground. Some of the prints are partials, just a toe or heel squelching down, the rest of the foot on harder ground. But I count five nearly complete and distinct shoe impressions. Three come from sneakers. Brady had been wearing sneakers the last time I saw him.

When I motion for Dalton, he puts his foot beside one print and I can confirm it's the same size, a nine. Average-size feet from an average-size man. Yet they give me that now-familiar niggle. I didn't expect Brady would still be wearing sneakers. Why not, though? That's what he fled wearing, and it's not as if he'd have been able to find other footwear in the forest.

"Those are his," Dalton says. "Since you seem to be wondering."

"I am."

"They match the prints he left when he first ran. I remember thinking they're shitty shoes. The kind of fancy sneakers that wear out after a month out here."

I nod. He's right. But something . . .

I turn to the other prints. These are boots. Rockton boots. We don't exactly have a shopping mall of selection in town. Dalton finds a couple of styles that fit his criteria—good for outdoors, readily available, durable, and reasonably priced—and that's what you get. These are the type I wore until I went down to Whitehorse with Dalton and bought a pair better suited to my small feet.

I flash back to last month, in the station, waterproofing my new boots. Anders came in with Kenny and picked up the boot I'd already done.

He whistled. *"Nice."*

"Yep, I'm spoiled. Perks of sleeping with the boss."

"You mean compensation for sleeping with the boss."

Kenny chuckled at that and took the boot from Anders. "These *are* nice. Good arches. That's the problem with mine. Not enough support for high arches. Hurts like a bitch after a daylong hunt."

"How long have you been here?" Anders said. "And you're just telling us now?"

Kenny shrugged. "I didn't want to complain."

It'd been too late to get him special boots, and when Dalton said we had a stash of other ones—different designs for those who couldn't wear the usuals—Kenny had brushed it off. That's how he was. Never wanted to make waves. Never wanted to ask for anything special. Like the bullied kid who found his way into the cool clique and just wanted to ride that out, behave himself in case the others decided he was a pain in the ass and kicked him out.

Which is why helping Brady doesn't—

I rub my neck. Stop making excuses. My flashback does prove something: that I know Kenny left Rockton wearing boots like these.

Dalton moves his foot beside one print without prompting. It's smaller than his. Smaller enough to be noticeable, and yet significantly larger than my ladies' size five. A men's seven maybe.

I remember Anders joking that Kenny should try on mine—that they might fit. Which suggested Kenny's feet were small.

"Casey?"

I nod and straighten. This is the worst part of community policing—investigating a crime when the person responsible is someone I know, someone I like. I need to remind myself that beyond the few people I associate closely with, I don't *really* know anyone in Rockton. I cannot know their pasts. Even people without that past can come here and commit horrible crimes.

I grieve for the loss of the Kenny I thought I knew. I'm deep in my thoughts, following Dalton, and—

"Stop right there," a voice rings out. "Hands on your head, you son of a bitch, or I swear I'll—I'll fucking shoot you and drag your . . . fucking ass back to Rockton."

I know that voice. I even know the diction—a poor imitation of Dalton by a guy who wants to be him.

"Kenny?" I whisper. I was just thinking of Kenny, and therefore I must be mishearing or—

Dalton is running. Doubled over, running full out. I'm taking off after him, my gun out as he pulls his. We pass a tree, and ahead I see Kenny holding a gun at Jacob's back.

FIFTY-ONE

"Turn around," Kenny barks.

Jacob says something I can't hear, his voice low, words calming. He turns, and Kenny gives a start.

"Eric?" Kenny says to Jacob.

Jacob lowers his hood.

"Who the hell are—?" Kenny begins.

"Kenny!" Dalton thunders.

Kenny wheels, gun lowering, the perfect opportunity for Jacob to grab it, but he just stays with his hands on his head. Kenny realizes he's lowered his weapon and corrects his stance, but Dalton sees that gun go up, trained on his brother, and he lets out a roar. When he snarls "Drop that fucking—" he doesn't even need to finish. Kenny literally throws the gun aside.

The gun hits the ground hard enough that I half expect it to fire, but it only bounces into the undergrowth as Dalton knocks Kenny flying.

Kenny babbles something from the ground. I reach them, but I still can't make out what he's saying.

Then Dalton has his gun trained on Kenny, saying, "Get your ass in the air," and when Kenny doesn't obey within 1.5 seconds, "Get your fucking ass in the air!"

Jacob says, "Eric . . ."

"You think I'm being an asshole?" Dalton snarls. Then he turns to Jacob. "*This* is the head of my fucking militia. The man who let Brady get away and then came out here to join him."

"Wh-what?" Kenny says. "No. I mean, yes, I let him get away. I didn't do my job right. I screwed up. But I didn't come out here to—"

"Get in position," Dalton says. "Now."

Getting in position means assuming the position that's like a downward dog, feet and hands on the ground, butt in the air. The first time I saw Dalton make a guy do it, I thought Dalton was trying to shame the guy, make him look ridiculous. And while it does, that's just a bonus. The beauty of the position is that the average person cannot leap out of it and attack. If he tries to rise, a foot on the ass will put him down again.

It is also, as I later discovered, a trick Dalton learned from Cypher.

Kenny gets into position, saying, "Just listen to me, Eric. I left a note. Didn't you get—"

"Yeah, Casey found it. Covering your ass, in case we found you alone. You weren't alone a couple of hours ago, were you."

"What?"

"You were seen with Oliver Brady."

Kenny starts sputtering denials, which only pisses Dalton off, and Jacob is trying to interject until finally I step in, arms waving for silence. Dalton gets the last word, of course, but then backs down, a jerk of his chin telling me to handle this.

"Kenny?" I say. "Just be quiet and listen, okay?" I turn to Jacob. "Is this the guy you saw with Brady?"

"I didn't get a look at the guy's face," Jacob says. "This *could* be him. That's all I can say."

"It wasn't—" Kenny begins.

"Wait," I say.

"He's the right size," Jacob continues. "Jeans. Boots. Jacket. All the same or close enough to what I remember."

"Which is town-issue clothing," I say, and Kenny nods, relieved.

"Eric? Can you give me one of Kenny's boots?"

I train my gun on Kenny while Dalton removes a boot and hands it to me. It's the one I expect. Town-issue. Same tread as the prints I saw with Brady's.

"Have you been tracking Brady?" I say.

"I've been trying," Kenny says. "But I'm not Eric. I made a lot of noise, and I figured maybe Brady would see me and think I looked like easy pickings, and then I'd get the jump on him. It was a stupid plan. I haven't even heard anyone until this morning, and that was you guys." He glances at Jacob. "You're . . . one of Eric's contacts?"

The inflection tells me he knows full well Jacob is more. The resemblance is undeniable. But I only say, "Yes, Jacob is a local scout."

"I thought he was Brady. He's about the right size. And he's got light hair. His hood was up or I'd have noticed his hair's too long. Plus, uh, the beard." Kenny exhales. "I'm sorry. I heard someone, and then I saw a guy the right size, and I jumped the gun."

I compared Kenny's boot to Dalton's. Kenny's is a couple of sizes smaller.

"Have you been on this path?" I say.

"I was on a bigger one over there." He points left. "I might have been on this one earlier, but I don't think so. I've been heading for that mountain." He points to our right.

I look at Jacob. "The person you saw with Brady . . . He was definitely *with* him. Talking to him? Sitting with him?"

"I heard voices. They seemed to be talking. They sat together, and I saw the guy pass Brady food."

"Eric? Can you empty Kenny's pockets and backpack?"

He does. There's a waterskin and basic tools. For food, he's brought dried meat and a handful of protein bars.

"You took these from the supply cabinet?" I say, waving the bars. Kenny nods. "I'll repay them."

"Not my biggest concern right now." I go through the handful of bars. "You already ate the chocolate peanut butter ones?"

"I didn't take any. I know those are your favorite, so I leave them for you. The cookie ones are good, though."

"She's not asking because she's hungry," Dalton says.

"Right. Sorry. I didn't take any of the chocolate peanut butter."

"What about old stock?"

THIS FALLEN PREY | 283

"Old stock?"

"There was a box of chocolate peanut butter that went missing a while ago. Do you know anything about that?"

Dalton's gaze cuts my way, but he says nothing. I'm bullshitting about the missing box. The truth is that we don't monitor the bars that tightly, figuring if the militia want to sneak a few extras, that's a perk for their help.

When I say that, though, Kenny looks uncomfortable.

"Kenny . . ." I prod.

"Someone took a bunch of old stock," he says. "I don't know what flavors. I just know that when I did inventory a while back, we had out-of-date bars and I put them aside to ask Will what to do with them, and they went missing. I decided not to say anything. They *were* old stock."

"You have no idea who took them?"

That uncomfortable look again. "I . . . No. I don't."

He's lying. I don't know why, but I need this answer. I study Kenny—the set of his jaw, the look in his eye—and I see it's not time to press the matter.

"Eric?" I lift Kenny's boot, and he nods.

When I pass Storm's lead to Jacob, Dalton's ready to argue, but I say, "I'll be quick," and I get a reluctant nod.

I take off at a jog back to the footprints. They're just around the corner, and when I reach them, I look back to see Dalton. He's moved about ten steps from Kenny, his gun still on the suspect but staying within sight range of me.

I crouch with the boot in hand. First, I confirm, beyond a doubt, that the tread is correct. Eyeballing it, I'd also say the size is, but when I lower the boot below the prints, I see that the ones in the soft earth appear to be a size smaller.

I prod the edge of the print. While the ground is damp, it doesn't seem wet enough for the print to have contracted a size. That's possible, though. Soft ground shifts. If the boot is the right type and almost the right size . . .

Wait.

It's not the same boot. Closer examination shows that the wear pattern doesn't match. Kenny's are worn, with an uneven tread, maybe the result of unsupportive boots and high arches. The prints look like new boots, the tread very distinct.

I check the tag inside Kenny's. Then I look at the prints again.

New boots. Rockton-issue. Size-seven men's. Small for a man's shoe.

Not small for a woman's. Not unreasonably large either. That works out to maybe a nine. While we have women's boot sizes, many choose to wear the guys', finding them sturdier.

I work through Jacob's description of the person he spotted with Brady. Clean-shaven. Shorter than Brady. A bulky jacket, which would hide breasts.

There is a person with Brady. This person showed up at some point between day one and last night. This person is from Rockton, as evidenced by the clothing and the bars.

Someone has betrayed us. That person does not seem to be Kenny.

One name keeps coming to mind.

My other suspect for the poisoning, for Brady's accomplice.

Jen.

I'm working through how much of it fits when Dalton calls, "Casey?"

I've been bent over and out of his sight too long, and it's a testament to his self-control that he didn't shout "Butler!" the second I disappeared.

I rise and see him farther down the path, anxiously straining to spot me, resisting the urge to run and check. When I wave, I swear I hear him exhale from thirty feet away.

I glance down at the prints one last time, but they aren't telling me anything new. I'm turning from them when I see a flicker in the bush. I drop Kenny's boot and raise my gun.

Dalton gives an alarmed "Casey?" and his boots thump as he runs toward me. In the bushes, I can see a form big enough to be dangerous, and I back against a tree, my gun raised.

A woman steps out. She's filthy with snarled hair and ragged clothes, and I think of Nicole. A woman, lost in these woods or taken captive, escaping and hearing voices and making her way toward us.

Then I see the knife. A rusted one with a broken blade and a make-shift handle. When I see that, I realize I'm looking at a hostile.

I have not seen one since I arrived in Rockton. I have heard some stories from Dalton and read others in the archives, but I am still not prepared. This woman could have just crawled from a pit after a decade of captivity. Matted hair. Dirt-crusted skin and clothing. When she draws back her lips, I see chipped and yellowed teeth. But she has not crawled from a pit. She has not been held captive. She has chosen to do this to herself.

And yet . . .

And yet I am not certain she has chosen. Deep in my brain, tucked away into the morass of "things I will pursue later," I have a theory. A wild theory that I used to joke sounded like I'd been spending too much time with Brent. I will never make that joke again, but the truth of it remains—that I have a theory about the hostiles that I am ashamed to admit to anyone but Dalton because it smacks of paranoia.

A theory for which I have zero proof, and that only makes it worse, makes me fear it is truly madness arising from hate and prejudice, a place no detective can afford to draw from.

My theory is that the hostiles are not Rockton residents who left and "went native" in the most extreme way. That such a thing is not possible, not on such a scale, because that is not what happens to humans when they voluntarily leave civilization. Jacob is not like this. The residents of the First Settlement are not like this. To become this, I believe you need additional circumstances. Mental illness. Drug addiction. Medical interference.

My theory is that the council is responsible for what I see here. I don't know why they'd do that. I have hypotheses, but I won't let them do more than flit through my brain or I may begin to believe I truly am losing my mind in this wild place.

I see this woman. I see what she has done to herself. And it's not just dirt and lack of care. Those only disguise what Dalton's stories have told me to look for. The dirt isn't from lack of bathing. It has been plastered on like war paint. Under it, I see ritualized scar patterns. And the teeth that appear chipped have actually been filed.

I see a woman who should not exist outside of some futuristic novel, a world decimated by war, ravaged by loss, people "reverting" to primitive forms in a desperate attempt to survive, to frighten their enemies.

Which would make perfect sense . . . if people up here *had* enemies. If there was not enough open land and fresh water and wild game that the only force we need fight is the fickle and all-powerful god of this world: Mother Nature.

I stare at this woman . . . and she stares back.

I point my gun; she brandishes her knife.

Dalton is running toward us. Running and paying no attention to anything except me and this woman. Movement flashes in the trees, the bushes rippling.

"Eric!" I shout. "Stop!"

He sees something at the last second. He spins, gun rising, but his back is unprotected and there is another movement behind him. Then something white flying toward him. I yell "Eric!" and he dodges, and what looks like a sliver of white flies past his head.

It's a dart. A bone dart.

He's turning, and then there's a figure, in flight, leaping from a tree.

Dalton lashes out with his gun. A *thwack,* and the man goes down, howling. Another figure lunges from the forest. Jacob races around the bend, and Storm barrels past. And I fire. I lift my gun over my head and fire.

FIFTY-TWO

When I fire overhead, everyone stops. Even Storm.

The man who was charging at Dalton sees the dog, and he raises something in his hand, and Jacob drops on Storm, covering her.

"Stop!" I say.

I don't know if it will do any good. I believe they are capable of understanding the word; I do not believe they are capable of caring about it. I'm not even sure the guns matter, if the shot didn't just startle them.

Then I hear a voice, and the words are so garbled, it doesn't sound like English.

"Get on the ground," one of the men says again, slower, clearer, as the man Dalton knocked down rises.

Two others step up beside Dalton. Two men armed with clubs. One raises his and barks what I am certain is not a word, but the meaning is clear.

"Do as he says, Eric," Jacob says. "Please just do as he says." He glances over his shoulder and says, "You, too," and that must be for Kenny, sneaking up.

Dalton holsters his gun, and I wait for someone to tell him to hand it over instead, but no one does.

Dalton kneels and puts his hands on his head. His expression is blank, but I see the rage in his eyes. This is the second time today we have been ambushed, and that feels like failure, as if we are characters in a bumbling-cop movie. But the truth is that this is the Yukon wilderness, and we are always one step away from ambush, by human or beast. The forest swathes her threats in bush and shadow, and we can walk all day and see no more than hares . . . or we can be forced to lower our weapons twice.

In all this, the woman before me has not moved. When I fired, she flinched, but now she stands exactly where she was, watching me, studying. No one else pays me any mind. I'm standing with my gun out, but they don't seem to care. They have assessed our party and dismissed me. One man watches Jacob—still atop Storm—but makes no move to go closer.

Four men surround Dalton, and something tells them that this is all that matters.

Which is not wrong. Not wrong at all.

The man who spoke before prods Dalton with his club. "Jacket."

Dalton glowers, but even before Jacob can speak up, Dalton takes off his pack and tosses it aside. The jacket follows.

"Gun."

He lays that down.

"Shirt."

"What the hell—?"

"Eric?" Jacob says, and there's a quaver in his voice.

Jacob has spent his life avoiding the hostiles. There was an encounter years ago, when he'd been a young teen, after his parents died. I don't know details, but he's said enough for me to suspect it was not unlike the ordeal Nicole faced . . . in every way.

"We'll be fine," I say. "We'll be fine."

Dalton grunts and strips off his T-shirt. "There. If you want the rest, you're gonna need to—"

"We will take the rest."

The leader grabs Dalton's gun and swings it up.

I shout "Eric!" and lunge.

Dalton drops to the ground. The gun fires. And I fire.

I shoot the leader. I do not think about what I'm doing. I saw that gun rise on Dalton, and I knew what was happening. They made Dalton remove his jacket and shirt so they didn't ruin the garments when they put a bullet through him.

The leader falls. Dalton's gun drops from his hand, and Dalton scrambles for it. It takes only a split second, and then we're back-to-back, our guns raised.

The leader lies on the ground, blood pumping, his hands over the hole through his chest. His mouth works, his eyes wide. And not one of his own people even looks his way.

He is defeated. He is useless. He is forgotten.

"Jacob! Kenny!" Dalton shouts. "Go!"

There is a pause, and I know Jacob and Kenny are both assessing. Waiting for one of the remaining hostiles to turn on them, to raise a weapon, let loose a dart. But they do not. All they care about is us.

"Jacob," Dalton says again.

Then there's a rustle in the undergrowth, and while neither of us dares look that way, I know Jacob and Kenny are retreating. That's the smart move. This is bad enough already, with Dalton and me back-to-back, guns drawn, three armed men surrounding us, a woman with a knife just a few feet away.

"Back the fuck up!" Dalton says to the men.

The one with the club steps toward us.

"That is *not* backing the fuck up," Dalton says. "I know you understand English, so do not pull this bullshit caveman routine on me. I know where you are from. The same place I am, and you will not pretend you don't fucking understand me."

One of the other two men raises a knife.

"Drop that!" Dalton barks. "If you take a step toward us with that—"

The man draws back as if to throw the knife. I shoot his hand. He lets out a howl, blood spraying, knife dropping. Then he charges.

I kick. I don't aim for his groin, but that's where my foot connects. He falls back yowling, and the two other men run at us, weapons raised.

Dalton fires. I kick again and then swing my gun, hitting my attacker in the face. I hear Dalton snarl for the men to stop, just fucking stop before we put fucking bullets through their fucking heads. We do not want to do that. To them, though, that does not make us merciful. It makes us weak.

It makes us vulnerable.

I kick. I pistol-whip. Dalton shoots, aiming to wound, not kill. My foot makes contact. So do my gun and Dalton's bullet, and the three men are bleeding. Bleeding and enraged, club flying, knife slashing. I hear an *oomph* as the club strikes Dalton in the chest. I wheel to fend off his attacker, and a knife slashes my jacket.

I remember a story Brent told once, about a wolverine. He'd watched it defend its kill from a grizzly. Defend it to the death, the wolverine knowing it had no chance of winning against the bigger predator but unable to surrender. That's what this is. Only we cannot walk away. Cannot just say, "You win—take our stuff and go." That is not an option; it never was an option.

The hostiles can't win this fight against our guns. It doesn't matter. Our reluctance to use those guns is like blood in the water. The smell of weakness drives them into a frenzy, even if they *must* realize we won't let them beat and stab us to death while we hold loaded guns. They will force our hand.

The club blow winded Dalton. He lowers his gun, and his attacker is pulling back to strike him again. Dalton raises his gun, but he hesitates, and I know he will not pull that trigger. Something in his brain says he doesn't need to just yet.

He will not use lethal force until he is moments from death himself.

I can fix this.

Don't worry. I can fix this.

Dalton diverts his aim to the man's arm. His finger moves to the trigger, and I fire. I must fire. I will not gamble on his life. I have already killed one man today, and if I have to kill three more to walk away from this, then that is what I must do. They leave us no choice.

I fire.

My aim isn't perfect. This is not a slow dance. Only a few heartbeats pass between Dalton being clubbed and me realizing I must shoot before he is hit again. I pull the trigger, and my bullet hits Dalton's attacker in the shoulder. It is enough. He goes down, and I spin on the other two men.

Dalton shoots one in the leg. The other is coming at me, and I raise my gun and Dalton has his up, yelling, "Stop, you stupid son of a bitch! Just stop!"

A shot fires. The man flies sideways, and Kenny stands there, gun gripped in both hands, his eyes wide. The hostile slumps to the ground, shot through the chest. Kenny stands frozen, breathing hard.

"Eric?"

I hear the voice, and I think it must be Jacob. It isn't Kenny, and it comes from off to the side. It's pitched high, but I am still sure it is Jacob—he's frightened. Then there's a movement on my right as Jacob and Storm cautiously approach from the left.

I turn toward the voice.

The woman stands on the path.

I have forgotten the woman. She's gripping her knife, and there are four of her people on the ground, two dead and two injured, moaning and bleeding, and she doesn't seem to see them. She's staring at Dalton.

"Eric?"

FIFTY-THREE

Even before Dalton says "Maryanne?" I know who this is. A woman who left Rockton years ago. A biologist who'd mentored Dalton, taught him, shared his insatiable curiosity about the world around them.

When Maryanne left with others, his father made the militia pursue. Rockton did not allow residents to become settlers. Dalton had been the one to find their camp, with evidence they'd been attacked by hostiles. A year later, he saw Maryanne again, and she *was* a hostile—did not recognize him, tried to kill him, almost forced him to kill her. Maryanne is one of those pieces that makes me think my theory is not so far-fetched after all.

I look at this woman, and I try to imagine a biologist, rapt in conversation with a teenage boy. A brilliant woman with a doctorate who decided to go live in her beloved natural world, and who made that choice willingly. Chose that and ended up as this.

She looks at me, and she's squinting, studying me as she did before, when we faced off and she did not attack. She squints as if trying to place me, too. Or maybe it's more than that. Maybe she's looking at me and seeing a mirror, reflecting something that sparks forgotten memories.

I used to look like that. Used to dress like that. Talk like that.

"Maryanne," I say carefully, too aware of that knife in her hand.

"I'm Casey. This is Eric Dalton. You remember him, right? From Rockton."

Dalton gives a start, as if snapping out of the shock of seeing her. "Right. It's Eric." He pauses for a second. "Eric Dalton. Gene was my father. We talked about biology. You specialized in black bears. I found papers you wrote, on vocalizations and body language. I read them a few years ago. You were a professor at a university in Nova Scotia."

Her brow furrows, as if she's trying to understand the language he speaks. Intently trying to understand. She might even be struggling to hear—I see the blackened ear he mentioned, lost to frostbite. But there's more to her expression than incomprehension. It is as if she's peering deeper into that dark mirror, catching wisps of shadows that look like people she once knew.

"Bears," she says.

Dalton nods. "Right."

"Eric?" Kenny says.

Dalton lifts a hand to tell Kenny to stay where he is. He never takes his eyes from Maryanne. "I found your camp after you left Rockton. I know something happened to you."

"Eric," she says. "The boy with the raven."

"Uh, right." He shoots an almost sheepish glance at me and then looks back at Maryanne. "I was trying to train a raven. I wanted to see if it could be taught to use tools. You told me there'd been studies on that, and you thought it might be possible."

Dalton has never told me this. That look says he finds it a little embarrassing now. But I remember when he first caught me training "my" raven. He rolled his eyes then, but I'd gotten a sense that my experiment pleased him.

"Eric with the raven," she says. Then she pauses. "Eric with the gun."

"Yes. You wanted to learn to shoot. I showed you, but you couldn't actually do it. You couldn't shoot anything."

He's giving as much as he can, trying to prod those memories, like speaking to someone with amnesia, but I can tell it's not quite getting through. It's like talking to a small child, one who is listening mostly to the sound of your voice and picking up familiar words. She is making connections, though. She is remembering.

And she is not attacking. That is the most important thing, because in her restraint I see hope. The others attacked. The others now lie, bloody, on the ground. And yet it isn't fear that holds her back. She could have attacked. She could have fled. But she sees Dalton, and something has changed from the last time. The rage is gone.

"Do you remember Rockton?" he asks. "Where we lived? Where you met me?"

"Eric. The boy with the raven."

He nods. "I'm going back to Rockton. I would like you to come with me. You'll be safe there. We have . . ." He pauses, as if struggling to remember something. "We don't have ice cream. That's what you said you missed most from down south. Ice cream. But we've shaved frozen milk before. You can have that. It's *like* ice cream."

There's no sign that she understands what he's saying, but when he says, "You'll come with me?," she tilts her head, listening. I put out my hand, and she stares at it.

"Come with us?" I say.

She looks at Dalton. He moves my way, a sidestep, motioning for her.

"It's okay," he says. "It's your choice. You can come with us or . . ."

He doesn't say "or not." He glances at me, and we exchange a look that says that isn't an option. We want her to come willingly, but what is the alternative? To leave her out here, with her people dead?

There is opportunity here. So many opportunities. For her, to return to what she had been. For Dalton, to exorcise this particular ghost from his past. And yes, for me, to answer my questions about the hostiles. Both Mathias and Cypher have said we need live subjects, and while the very concept has horrified me, Maryanne is the perfect subject—not a lab rat but a woman we can help.

We walk a few steps. Then we motion for her to come with us. She looks about. She sees the men on the ground. Sees the two bodies. Sees the two wounded. Then she nods, and I can't tell whether it's acceptance or satisfaction. Whether she sees her comrades fallen through their own mistakes . . . or her captors finally getting their comeuppance. Either way, she nods. And then she follows. One step. Another.

There's a noise behind us. Kenny or Storm must step in undergrowth, and it crackles beneath their feet. Maryanne wheels. Dalton says "It's okay. We're—" and I don't hear the rest. I see her face. I see her reaction, as pure and unthinking as my own.

There is a noise in the forest. There is a threat.

She catches sight of Jacob and Storm on the path and lets out a howl, barely human. She charges. I'm right behind her as she runs, knife raised. Jacob only yanks the dog back behind him, no panic, knowing he's fine. He realizes she's just startled, and he can stop her, or I will, or his brother will, and she is no threat.

Dalton shouts, "Maryanne! It's okay!"

That's when she sees Jacob. Sees his face. Sees the resemblance to Dalton and begins skidding to a stop, a few feet from him and—

A shot fires.

For exactly one second, I think it's Dalton. Then I know it is not. Maryanne may have been running toward his brother with a knife, but Dalton has both a brain and a conscience. He will not shoot until he is absolutely sure his brother is at risk.

"Case—" Dalton begins, and then stops, having the exact same reaction as me. One moment of thinking I am shooting at Maryanne before realizing I am not.

Another shot. A half shout. Then Maryanne spins sideways. I run, and Jacob runs, and I hear Dalton's strangled cry and the thud of his footsteps.

Yet another shot. This one whips right past me, and I stop. I see Maryanne. There's blood. She's standing against a tree, and there's blood.

"Mary—" I begin.

She runs. She races into the forest, and I go after her, and there's a fourth shot. I feel pain. Then I'm falling.

"Casey!" Jacob yells.

Dalton hits me, and I drop as he's shouting his brother's name and I have no idea what the hell is going on, and the next thing I know I am on the ground under Dalton and Jacob is on top of Storm.

I twist, ready to leap up. That's when Dalton's eyes round, his mouth forming my name as he grabs my chin. I feel a hot burn, and my fingers rise to my cheek. There's a bullet graze across my cheek.

"I'm fine," I say quickly. "It just . . ."

Just grazed me.

Just about killed me.

"Who—?" I begin.

Another shot. This one hits the tree near our heads.

"Kenny?" I say as I try to twist.

That's all I can think. It isn't me shooting. It's not Dalton. Jacob doesn't have a gun. So it must be Kenny.

Dalton's gaze flies to Jacob and Storm. His brother is crouched and pulling Storm along with him, his free hand motioning to us. Behind them is Kenny, hunkered down, gun lowered at his side.

I look up and scan the treetops and . . .

There's a figure in a tree. A dark figure.

Sniper.

"Off the path!" Dalton shouts. "Get off the path. Into the forest."

We creep into the undergrowth. Dalton has one hand wrapped in my jacket, not unlike Jacob with Storm. I only need to see Dalton's face to know not to argue. He tugs me to a clump of bushes, and we crouch behind it, both of us breathing too hard for the minor exertion, both of us fighting panic.

The forest has gone quiet except for the moans of the dying hostiles. The sniper has his—or her—position and is holding it.

I look up into the trees. It's dense enough over here that I won't spot someone on a limb. It's *not* dense enough, though, that we can just run, certain of cover.

I glance to my right. Jacob has Storm behind a cluster of tall undergrowth. He's gesturing. Dalton is looking that way now, and they both motion, pantomiming a retreat plan.

I know what I want to do. Tell them to stay where they are while I make my way *toward* the shooter. Attack the problem.

Stay here, Eric. Stay there, Kenny. Jacob, hold Storm. Be safe. Please, I need you to be safe. Let me handle this.

Let me finish this.

If I even mention that to Dalton, he won't hold me here by force—he'll realize this is indeed the correct plan . . . and go to take down the sniper himself.

So when he taps my shoulder and nods to our next point of cover, I force myself to creep to that spot.

We reach it, and we make sure Kenny, Jacob, and Storm reach theirs.

Then we set out for the next point of cover. And the next. Each takes us deeper into the forest. Farther from the path. Farther from the sniper and the groans of the dying.

There is no sound except those moans. One turns to soft sobs. I hear a woman's name choked in those sobs, and I think of the men we are trying so hard *not* to think about. The dying hostiles. Just hostiles. That's what I want to think. Not people. Not men who may have been no different from Maryanne once upon a time, no less deserving of mercy and salvation.

The dying man keeps saying the name, over and over. A wife? Lover? Child? Sister? Someone he remembers in his final moments. Someone he calls for. And then there is a shot, and the crying stops.

The crying stops, and the other man lets out a string of unintelligible babble. The crunch of undergrowth. A thump, as if he's rising, and that babble keeps coming. He's begging for his life. Begging someone who is not in a distant tree but standing right over him and—

Another shot. Silence.

I hear a click beside me and turn to see Dalton topping up his gun. I do the same with mine after he's finished, and I can see that makes him nervous—he doesn't want my weapon unusable even for a second. When I finish, he nods, and I lean against him for a moment of comfort. Then I look out again.

I can see nothing. No one. Instead I listen, and I catch the telltale crinkle of dead foliage under a careful foot. It is off to our left, the sniper attempting to circle wide and surprise us that way.

Dalton taps my shoulder. He points as his brother does the same, both of them indicating rocks to our right. The foothills. Dalton nods. Then Jacob motions that we are to go, and he will stay. In explanation, he gestures at his side, where I know Storm lies.

He cannot run with her. We can't tell her to be quiet or careful, and if she runs with him, they will be spotted.

Dalton swallows hard. I squeeze my eyes shut and make a choice. A choice I know I have to make even if every fiber in me screams against it. Even if this might be the one thing I do that I will never forgive myself for. If I am a good person, if I love Dalton, if I care for his brother, then I must make a monstrous suggestion.

"He should let her go," I whisper in his ear.

Dalton's gaze swings to mine.

I force the words out. "Tell him to drop the leash and run, and she'll follow but . . ."

But she won't be right at his side. She will be ahead or behind and that makes her a target, and I can hope to God the sniper decides not to bother with a dog, but this . . . This is what I must suggest, isn't it? I cannot risk Jacob's life to save my dog.

Dalton shakes his head. I shake mine harder, giving him a look that tells him I will not back down. His jaw sets. Then he motions for Jacob to drop the leash. Even from here, I see Jacob's face screw up, like he must be misunderstanding.

Dalton motions more forcibly, and Jacob looks at me.

I nod, and mouth, *Please.*

He slowly and carefully lays down the lead, watching us for any sign that he has misunderstood. Once the leash is on the ground, Dalton gestures for Jacob to run into the rocky foothills. One final moment of hesitation, and a glance at Storm. Then Jacob runs.

Kenny takes off behind Jacob, and Dalton gives me a shove, making me go before I can even see what Storm does. When I also hesitate, he pushes harder, and I take a deep breath, and then I run.

I run as fast as I can, veering away from Jacob and Kenny so we separate, giving multiple targets, multiple sources of noise and movement. And I do not look at Storm. I do not try to see where she is and what she's doing.

I have never prayed in my life, but at that moment, I send one up. Wherever the sniper is, let him realize what he sees is a fleeing dog, and there is no point in wasting precious ammo on it.

I run, and I know Dalton follows, but his footsteps fade fast as he heads in another direction. He must, same as I did with Jacob and Kenny.

Dalton has run to my left, which I don't like. It takes him closer to the sniper's likely location. But there's nothing I can do except curse him—

A whistle. A bark.

No. Fuck, no. Eric. Tell me you are not . . .

Of course he is. Of course he will, and I'm a fool if I thought otherwise.

Another whistle. Calling Storm to him as he runs. I glance over to see him bend in midstride and grab her leash and then run with her at his side, with all the noise an eighty-pound Newfoundland makes running through the forest.

You fool. You goddamn fool.

That's what we are, isn't it? We are those vampires who cannot continue until we have picked up every grain of rice. The shepherds who cannot ignore a sheep in danger. The law keepers who cannot shoot to kill if there is room for mercy. The humans who cannot put their dog at risk, cannot let their lover suffer the loss of her pet.

No matter what the cost to ourselves, we keep making these damn mistakes, and we know they are errors in judgment, but we truly are no more able to stop ourselves than those vampires of lore. Compelled to help, to protect, to save.

It is weakness. I know it is weakness. I hate that weakness. But I know we won't overcome it, no matter how many times we are shown that it's a mistake.

We keep running, and I try not to think about Storm being with Dalton, Storm endangering Dalton. Try, try, try . . .

A shot hits the tree above my head.

"Cover," Dalton yells. I'm already diving. I hit the ground just as another shot passes over me. I roll fast. Keep moving, keep moving. That is the trick here. Do not try to hide and hope for the best. Present a moving target.

I roll and then leap up and weave through trees. Jacob and Kenny are safe—they've reached the rocks and gone behind one, disappeared from sight. Dalton sticks to thicker forest with the dog, opting for safety over speed. I can see a rock ahead. I just need to—

A shot passes so close that I swear I feel it. I'm not going to make it. I'm too exposed, and the sniper has gauged my speed and is refining his shots.

I can't go faster. I don't dare go slower.

Just a little closer, a little closer . . .

"Hey!" There's a shout behind me. "Hey, you! Over here!"

I think it is Dalton—it's exactly the kind of fool thing he'd do. But I can see him, and I know where Jacob and Kenny went, and there's no way either of them has circled behind me.

Another shot, and it goes nowhere near me. The sniper accepting the newcomer's invitation.

"Here!" someone calls ahead, and Jacob peeks out.

He's gesturing at a rock. It's farther than the one I chose, but bigger, and while the newcomer distracts the sniper, I cross the last few paces and dive. Then I twist to see who is helping us.

I am almost afraid to see who it is. Afraid it is Anders or Sam or Paul come to find us. Afraid it is Cypher or some other settler who has come to our rescue and may pay the ultimate price for it. I even think it may be Wallace, that he has escaped captivity.

It is not any of those.

It is the absolute last person I expect.

Oliver Brady.

FIFTY-FOUR

It is a trap. It must be. But at this moment, all I care about is getting
Dalton out of a sniper's sights, and if this is a trap, we'll deal with it
later.

I wave for Dalton. He's running my way, aiming for another rock.
A shot fires. A tree behind him splinters, and I leap from my hiding
spot and wave my arms, shouting, "Hey!"

Dalton motions for me to get the hell back under cover. Then he's
diving, and I withdraw. I make sure Dalton and Storm are safe, Dalton crouched behind the rock, his arms around her.

I spin toward Brady. He's coming straight at me. Running at me.
Motioning for me to stay where I am, remain hidden.

I aim my gun.

Behind me, Dalton snarls, "Stay the fuck away from her or I swear
I'll shoot your ass—"

Brady goes into a slide. The moment he does anything the least bit
threatening, I will shoot him. If he gets within a foot of me, Dalton
will shoot him.

But he does neither. He slides behind a smaller rock, one that barely
hides him. Then he pokes his head out and says, "We're sitting ducks
here. There's a spot farther down."

Dalton says, "If you think, for one fucking minute—"

"I just saved you, Sheriff. You and your girlfriend. I risked my *life* to save you two. What the hell else do I need to do to prove myself? Take the bullet?"

"Depends on where it hits," Dalton says. "And whether you survive."

Brady's eyes narrow, but Dalton is right. We know Brady has an accomplice. Of course that accomplice wouldn't kill him. Which means he could easily pretend to draw fire while leading us to our deaths.

Jacob whistles. He's gesturing toward a spot we can't see, presumably big enough for the three of us and the dog. He's ignoring Brady, his gaze going between me and Dalton, making sure we see where he's pointing. Then he disappears.

"Go," Dalton murmurs.

I do. Behind me I hear, "You stay where you are, Oliver, or I'll blow your fucking head off."

"Head or ass. Make up your mind, Sheriff."

"Whichever presents the bigger target. Right now, I'm figuring it's about fifty-fifty."

I run from rock to rock, and wherever the sniper is, he doesn't see me. Or he doesn't care, now that I'm with his partner.

I find Jacob disappearing into a crevice. By the time I reach it, he's turned and pokes his head out. Then he waves and retreats. I look in to see Kenny inside, safe.

I gesture for Dalton to drop the leash. He does, and I whistle for Storm. She comes running. When she reaches me, I pass her leash to Jacob and turn back to wave for Dalton. He's already on the move, and I curse him for that, because for a few seconds there, I didn't have my gun trained on Oliver Brady.

I remedy that, and when Dalton arrives, I make him go into the cave, which means giving him a shove. He gets halfway in before realizing that leaves *me* outside. He balks. I may kick his ass, possibly literally. Because here's the thing: we can't all crawl into this cavern and sit there, with Brady knowing exactly where we've gone. So I get Dalton inside, and then I look up to see Brady hightailing it our way.

I meet him with my gun drawn. I've plunked myself in front of that opening, ignoring Dalton's pokes from within. I'm crouched there, gun trained on Brady when he arrives.

The first words out of his mouth are "Oh, come on . . . " like we're kids on the playground, and I'm being terribly unreasonable.

He even rolls his eyes, and I swear he's lucky I don't put a bullet between them for that alone.

"I saved—" he begins.

"You lured us in. Diverted fire to convince us you're innocent. After you massacred a hunting party of settlers."

"What? Wait. What?"

"Casey?" That's Dalton. I'm about to ignore him, but he yanks on my jeans leg and says, "Back door."

He means there's a second way out. We won't be trapped in this cavern.

When I hesitate, Dalton sticks his head through and says, "You do realize you're arguing with this asshole while there's a sniper out there."

Point taken.

I twist and get my legs into the opening. Then I'm wriggling backward while trying to keep my gun trained on an exasperated Brady.

After a moment, Dalton just drags me inside. It is indeed a cavern. Not a big one, but there's a passage big enough for Storm to get through, evidently, because I don't see her . . . or Jacob and Kenny.

Dalton wants me to go through first this time, and I grant him that, but not before I say, "That stunt with Storm—"

He cuts me off with a kiss, and that startles me enough to stop talking, which may be the point. It's not just a quick smack of the lips, either, but a deep one, dark with residual fear and confusion, a kiss that says he was scared shitless out there—for all of us—and may still be.

When it breaks, I rest my head on his shoulder and I breathe. Just breathe. Then I inhale and say, "Onward?"

"Yeah," he says.

I'm turning to go, and I see Brady, his head and shoulders pushed through the opening, paused there, watching us.

Dalton turns on him. "Get the fuck—"

"You're going to kick me out there to get shot?"

Dalton meets his gaze. "Yes."

"Fuck you, Sheriff." Brady pulls through into the cavern and crouches in front of us. "I had nothing to do with what happened to those people. Yeah, I saw it—the tail end of it, when I heard voices and came to investigate. But if you're saying I massacred—"

"Not them," I say. "The others."

"What others?"

"A hunting party two nights ago."

"I have no idea—"

"Of course you don't. So where's your partner?"

"What partner?"

Dalton squeezes my shoulder. "Go with Storm. I'll handle this."

"Handle this?" Brady says. "By what, shooting me?"

"If I have to. I'd prefer if you just came along quietly. Saves me having to drag a corpse back to Rockton."

"And they call *me* a psychopath? You—"

I grab Brady's shirtfront, my hand wrapping in it, yanking him forward, and the surprise of that nearly topples him onto me. He tries to jerk back, but he's crouched in this cavern and can't get the balance to do more than weakly pull against my hold. I lift my gun and point it at his temple, and that gets him struggling hard, but I have a good grip.

"The person you need to worry about shooting you?" I say. "It's not Eric. I watched a good friend die in agony because of you. Saw a woman I cared about dead in a river because of you."

"No, not Val. I did not hurt Val."

"You took her hostage, you son of a bitch."

My finger moves to the trigger, and the only reason I don't pull it? Because another gun barrel flies up. Dalton lifts his gun, and his finger is on the trigger, and I know that if I shoot, so will he. That has nothing to do with agreeing that Brady deserves to die. He cannot stop me from killing Brady, so he will join me. Do something he would never do on his own, and do it to keep me from being the one who kills Oliver Brady, as I killed Blaine Saratori twelve years ago.

I see that gun rise, and I see the resolve on Dalton's face, and I release my trigger.

"Oliver Brady," I say. "You're under arrest. Get your ass through that hole"—I point at the opening where Kenny, Jacob, and Storm have gone—"and if you scream or fight or do *anything* that calls the attention of that sniper out there, I will shoot you. I swear I will."

We lock gazes. Hold them. When he tears his away, I see his outrage, the look that says he won't forget this, that no one treats him this way.

He goes through the hole after me. Dalton follows. There isn't any sign of Kenny, Jacob, and Storm until we go through another passage. I watch Brady come in, so I witness his first glimpse of Kenny. He sees him . . . and reacts no more than he does to Jacob.

They're crouched in a cubbyhole not big enough for all of us, and Storm is whimpering. She has no idea what's going on or what to make of this cave-crawling business. Dalton takes the lead and her leash, and Jacob falls in behind.

The exit is a tight squeeze, and my poor dog cries as she's being tugged by Dalton and pushed by his brother. But she trusts us and she doesn't fight, just lets herself be propelled through.

We come out a couple of hundred feet from where we went in. We move as quickly and quietly as we can, through the forest, getting at least a kilometer away. Then Dalton wheels and grabs Brady so fast that Jacob and Kenny dive for cover. But Dalton just puts Brady up against a tree and says, "If you fucking ever tell us you haven't killed anyone again—"

"I did accidentally shoot your friend. The old man. I'm sorry. I know you don't believe that, but I am."

Brady looks my way, still pinned to the tree.

"I told you before, Detective, whatever I do comes from desperation. My stepfather wants me dead. He has the money and the power to make that happen. I've run out of options. I will do pretty much anything to stay alive. That includes intimidating an old man. But I did not mean to shoot him. We fought for the gun, and he got shot, and I ran. Panicked and ran."

"You ground your fist—"

"I *panicked*. I needed to know where to find the sheriff's brother, and I did a horrible thing in my desperation to get that information. When he still refused, I didn't try again. I ran."

"And Val?" I say.

"If Val is dead, then I am sorry for that, too, but I didn't kill her. I took her to that spot. That wolf was there. Only it was rabid." He gives a ragged laugh. "Of course it was. It's not enough to just have wolves out here. They need to be rabid, too."

"So you saw the wolf . . ." I say.

"I saw it. Shot it. And it kept coming, like something out of a damn horror movie. So I ran. At first, Val was behind me, but then she apparently realized I wasn't holding her at gunpoint anymore. So she took off. I have no idea what happened to her after that."

"Then you did what?" Dalton says. "Wandered around hoping for fucking signs to the nearest town?"

"Yes, Sheriff, I kinda did, okay? Not an actual signpost—I'm not that naive—but I figured if I just kept walking, I'd reach a road, and I could hitchhike to town."

"Yeah, good luck with that. You hear any cars out here?"

"I've realized my mistake, okay? Which is why, when I heard voices, I just said 'screw it' and headed toward you. I've been out here for days, and I feel like I'm walking in circles—hell, I probably am. I'm exhausted. I have no supplies. No weapons. I saw a grizzly bear yesterday. A fucking grizzly bear. I may have pissed myself, but by now, I stink so bad, it's not like you're even going to notice. I give up, okay? I throw myself on your mercy. The only thing I'm going to ask is that if my stepfather orders you to kill me, you walk up behind me and just do it, before I know what's happening. I can't win here. Can't escape. I get that now."

I slow clap. He turns on me, but Dalton still has him pinned, and all Brady can do is glower.

"Just applauding the performance," I say. "It's really good. Unfortunately, while you can explain away Brent and Val and just play dumb about the settler massacre, we have an eyewitness who has seen you out here. Eating bars from Rockton." I take the wrapper from my pocket. "And you weren't alone."

"What? No. Just . . . Look, I have no idea who this eyewitness is, but if someone told you that, then my stepfather got to him—or her. Bribed him. Blackmailed him. *Something*."

Brady turns to Kenny. "It was you, wasn't it?"

"No, it was me," Jacob says.

"What?" He turns to Jacob. "You're the scout. The one I met on the walk with the wolf and the sniper. The sheriff's brother, right?"

"Yeah," Dalton says. "And he lives out here. Which means he's not working for your daddy."

I wave at the forest. "This isn't the big city. Your stepdaddy can't post on Craigslist for a spy."

"I realize that," Brady says coolly. "I presumed that whoever he paid off was a resident of your town." He glances at Kenny. "You or one of my other prison guards."

"It wasn't me," Kenny says.

"I saw you eating that bar with someone," Jacob says to Brady. "I saw you walking with someone. Heard you talking with someone."

"I don't even know what to say to that, except that I wasn't. Flat-out wasn't."

"So you're calling my brother a liar?" Dalton says.

"No, I'm actually not. I grew up with the biggest liar you could hope to meet—my stepfather. I know when someone's bullshitting, and I can tell your brother isn't, which leaves me . . ." A helpless shrug. "I don't even know. I just don't. Obviously he saw someone out here who looks like me. Same size or whatever."

"It was you," Jacob says. "Those jeans. Those shoes. That shirt."

"Then I . . ." Brady trails off and looks over at me. "I do not know what to tell you, Detective. I just don't know."

"Any identical twins we should know about?" I ask.

His lips tighten. Then he says, "I realize you're being sarcastic, but at this point, I'm starting to wonder myself. The only thing I can even think of is that my stepfather sent someone out here who resembles me, dressed like me. Which makes me sound like a raving lunatic. So I've got nothing, Detective. Absolutely nothing but my solemn word, with a promise that if you find out I'm lying, you don't need to shoot me. Walk me to one of these mountain gorges, and I'll swan-dive. Save you the bullet."

FIFTY-FIVE

Jacob leads the way. Brady is right behind him, with Dalton and Kenny following. I'm lagging back with Storm. I've given her food from my pack, and we've found water, but she's exhausted. Like a small child who senses this is not the time to complain, though, she troops silently beside me.

We're heading toward the First Settlement. That's what Dalton told me, murmuring, "I'll work it out," and, "Only thing we *can* do." Which is correct. We cannot risk Edwin finding out that we have Brady and didn't bring him. He would execute Wallace for that—he must, to keep the respect of his people.

So I'm lagging behind, and I'm thinking. I'm not thinking of how to get out of this without handing our prisoner over to people who'll execute *him*. I need to work through something else first.

We've been walking in silence for about thirty minutes when Dalton falls back with me.

"You know one of the best things about having you?" he says quietly, and I have to replay his words, so out of context here.

"Having *someone*," he continues. Then he pauses. "Yeah, that didn't come out right. Sounds like I'm one of the guys from town, desperate for a woman, any woman."

I manage a chuckle. "You've never had that problem."

"Yeah. But you know what else I've never had? A partner. Not just for sex. Not just for work. Not just for friendship. Someone who is all that and more. Lover. Colleague. Friend. Even using those words to describe other people? Seems like they should have different definitions altogether."

"I know."

And I do. I'm just not sure where this is coming from, if he's unsettled by what's happened and looking for distraction.

He continues, "Even 'partner' is a shitty word. Sounds like a business arrangement. The other day, when you said you were my wife, that . . ." He shoves his hands in his pockets. "It sounds lame, but that means something to me. We don't get that in Rockton. My parents—the Daltons—they were a couple, but I've never heard them use the vocabulary much. To me, husband or wife means . . ."

He takes his hands out of his pockets and flounders, as if looking for a place to put them, finally settling for taking Storm's lead in one and my hand in the other.

"My dad always used it," he says. "My, uh . . ."

"Birth father."

"Right. In the First Settlement, he used it a lot, and my mom would call him her husband. That was because they were reminding people—warning the men to leave her alone—but I didn't realize that at the time, so husband and wife, that seemed like their special words. And they were . . ." He shakes his head. "Fuck, they were in love. The kind of stupid, crazy love that makes you run into the forest when someone tries to separate you. Dumb kids. But they made it work, and they were partners—real partners—in everything. I told you Jacob says they died together, in a dispute with hostiles, but I wonder if maybe just one was killed and the other didn't . . ." His hand clenches mine, reflexively tightening. "Just didn't try very hard to get out alive after that."

We walk a couple of steps, and I say softly, "I don't know much about your parents, but from what Jacob has said, I don't think they'd have left him alone if they had a choice."

A moment of silence. Then he nods. "Yeah, you're right. If one could have made it back, they would have. For him. For their . . ." He swallows. "Fuck."

His hand grips mine so tight it hurts. Here is the discrepancy he cannot resolve: that the parents who didn't rescue him from Rockton were not parents who would ever shrug and say, *Well, that's one fewer mouth to feed.*

"The point," he continues, "is that this is important to me. What we are. You and me. One of the best parts is that I don't have to do this on my own anymore. Yeah, I know, I've always had help. But it's just been that: help. People who listen to me and do what I tell them because they trust my judgment. But fuck, you know what? Half the time I'm not sure *I'd* listen to me. Now I have you. Someone I can talk to, share with, confide in, ask for advice and, yeah, someone who'll tell me if I'm full of shit."

"Uh-huh."

"So my question is, Casey"—his gaze slides my way—"is that just me?"

"I don't understand."

"I want to be that for you, too."

"You are."

"Am I? Or am I the junior partner here?"

I look over sharply. "What?"

"The trainee. A promising one, but still new at this detective shit, and not ready to work at your level."

"What—?"

"I don't think that's it. But I like the alternative even less—the feeling that if you're holding back, it's not because I haven't proved myself, but because you want to protect me. I'm a little bit naive. A little bit idealistic. You like that. You want to preserve that. Which might seem fine to you, but I feel patronized. Like I'm years younger than you, not just a couple of months."

"I—"

"When we got Nicole back, I know Mathias left that asshole in a hole somewhere. Poetic execution. You know it, too, and I'm sure you confronted him. But you kept that from me."

"No, I did not, Eric. Yes, I confronted Mathias and didn't tell you—because he wouldn't admit to anything. He knew if he did, I would tell you. I have to. Not just because you're my boss, but because keeping it from you *would* be treating you like a child."

He relaxes at that. But he has a point, one I'm not going to admit right now. I *would* have told him if Mathias confessed, and I'm glad he didn't, because that would have meant Dalton needed to launch a hunt for a man who deserved his horrible fate.

I didn't push Mathias because I wanted to protect Dalton. And that is wrong. Not wrong to protect him, but wrong if, in protecting him, I'm trying to preserve his innocence, to shield him.

It is patronizing. It's what you do to your children and, at one time, it was how you treated your wife, presuming she didn't have the fortitude to face life's ugly truths. It is *not* what you do to someone you consider an equal, however good your intentions.

"I'm sorry," I say. "If I've done that, I apologize."

"So we can stop protecting Eric's delicate sensibilities?" he says.

I manage a smile. "We can."

"Good. Then tell me what you were thinking."

"Thinking . . . ?"

"Right before I came back here and gave you a hard time. What you've been thinking all day . . . whenever we haven't been trying to stay alive, which has been, admittedly, the bulk of our morning and afternoon."

"It's only afternoon?"

He shows me his watch. It isn't even 3 P.M. I curse, and he chuckles.

"I'm working on a theory," I say.

"Kinda guessed that."

"It's not one I like."

"Yep."

"If I've been keeping it from you, it isn't to protect your sensibilities. It's to protect your opinion of my mental health. And maybe your opinion of *me*."

"Because if you tell me what you're thinking, I'll wonder what kind of fucked-up person even imagines something like that."

"Yes."

"Then let me help. Are you wondering whether Harper killed the settlers?"

I blink over at him.

He continues, "She claimed to have seen Brady there but gave little more than what might be extrapolated from our description of him. She was the one found with blood-soaked clothing, explained away by trying to save her grandmother. Then there's the shredded food pack. If Brady killed the hunting party for their supplies, he'd have taken much better care of that. Instead, it was abandoned and ripped apart by animals. You just don't want to admit you're considering her because you're afraid it reflects badly on you, thinking a kid could do something that horrific."

He looks over. "So, am I close?"

"Uh, dead-on, actually."

"Good. Proves I'm making progress with this detective thing. And that maybe my view of people is a little more jaded than you'd like to think."

"Or just that I'm rubbing off on you."

He puts his arm around my shoulders. "Sorry, Detective. I'm pretty sure it's not possible to have lived my life up here and be completely unaware of what people are capable of doing to each other. I just don't like to jump to that for the default. Innocent until proven guilty. Good until proven evil. And there's a huge spectrum between those two poles. What matters is where you *want* to sit on that spectrum, and where you *try* to sit if you have a choice. Like when you need to shoot a hostile who's about to kill me."

I say nothing.

He glances at me. "You think I don't know that's bugging you, too? I'm the one who screwed up back there. I tried to avoid killing that man, and all I did was sentence him to a slow death. They had no chance of crawling back to their camp. No chance of being rescued. No chance of surviving. The sniper who shot that hostile did him more of a favor than I did in trying to just wound him."

"You—"

"I'm not looking for redemption, Casey. Just stating facts. I learned my lesson. Doesn't mean I won't leave someone alive if they *can* get to help, but I won't make that mistake again. Either way, I killed a man today, too."

"Have you ever . . . ?"

"No," he says, and shoves his hands in his pockets. "No, I haven't."

We are back in the clearing where the three settlers were massacred. I have watched Brady's expression the whole way, waiting for the flicker of recognition, of concern, of worry. Why are we returning him here? Is there something we might find that will prove he's guilty?

He must be guilty, right?

No. That is the hard truth I've come to accept. The likelihood that Harper killed these settlers. That Brady's claim of innocence is correct. At least in this.

As we approach, he gives no sign that he recognizes the location. We enter the clearing, and he's looking around. Then he's checking his watch, as if wondering whether we're stopping for the night.

"Turn around," I say.

He does. He's been quiet. Past the point of denials. Past the point of anger. Just exhausted and resigned to whatever his fate might be.

Earlier, I patted him down for weapons and found only Kenny's knife, which I have returned. Brady claims he had a stick, too—he'd sharpened it with the knife, as a spear, and he'd been proud of his ingenuity in that. He'd been unable to find anything to eat out here, but at least he had a sharp stick. Or he did until we crawled into that cave and he had to abandon it outside.

Now I more thoroughly pat him down, and he has nothing but crumbs in his pocket. Apparently Devon had delivered cookies to Val while she sat with Brady, and before Brady escaped, he shoved them into his pocket. A survival plan as pathetic as that sharp stick.

Those crumbs clearly came from sugar cookies rather than our protein bars, and Brady seems as weak as one might expect after three days. That does not mean I accept that Jacob made a mistake about seeing him with another man, eating our old bars. I'm just not sure how to reconcile that, so I've put it aside.

The lack of food isn't ironclad proof that he didn't kill the hunting party. Yet there is also the most damning evidence for a homicide detective. His clothing.

Brady is wearing what he left Rockton with. Right down to his socks and boxers. As filthy as his clothes are, I see no more than a smear of blood on his shoulder, as if he'd wiped a bloodied nose after fighting Brent.

Whoever killed the settlers had slit one man's throat. Stabbed another. Brutally murdered a woman. That much blood won't come out by rinsing your shirt in a mountain stream.

I would not take this evidence before a court of law—not unless I was a defense attorney, desperate to get my client exonerated. Brady might have taken off his shirt for the attacks. He might have hidden whatever food and supplies he stole from the settlers.

But I cannot continue to say he even makes a good suspect.

Which leads to a very uncomfortable admission. That he might actually be telling the truth . . . about all of it.

Brent's death was manslaughter, rather than murder. As for Val, I don't know how she died. I wasn't able to recover her body to autopsy it. I wasn't even able to get *to* her body for a closer look. I can only say that she was dead in that river, with no obvious signs of trauma.

Yet there are other things that don't fit.

Who did Jacob see in the forest, if not Brady? I trust Jacob implicitly, and I can't imagine he was mistaken, so what is the alternative? If it was Brady, wouldn't he come up with an excuse? *Why, yes, I did meet someone on the trail—a stranger who took pity on me and shared his stash of protein bars.*

Who the hell shot at us? Executed the two wounded hostiles? Tried to kill the rest of us?

It makes sense that it was the same person who shot at Brady a few days ago. Was Brady really the target, though? He was nowhere in sight when the sniper executed the hostiles and opened fire on us.

There are too many loose ends that "Brady is innocent" does not explain.

Yet none stamp him as guilty either.

We're missing a piece of the puzzle here. A huge one. And I'm starting to think I know what it is—or at the very least, I know where to begin this trail.

A few words from Brady, dismissed as the rantings of a killer, determined to lay blame anywhere he could.

Words that could have come straight from the serial killer handbook.

I'm being set up.

Why?

Because I know a secret.

FIFTY-SIX

"We're taking you to Edwin," Dalton says to Brady as we leave the scene of the settler massacre.

"Who?" Brady says.

"We need to get Gregory back," I say.

"Greg—? My *stepfather*? He's here?" Genuine fear spikes Brady's voice.

"He's being held hostage," I say. "In exchange for you."

"What?"

"You massacred three people from a settlement out here. They wanted a guarantee that we'd hand you over. Your stepfather volunteered."

"Volun . . . ?" He stares at us. Then he laughs. "Oh, that's funny. I know you don't mean it to be. You're trying to scare me into thinking you're handing me over to these crazy mountain men. I don't know why you'd bring Greg into this, but telling me he voluntarily turned hostage in exchange for me?" He shakes his head. "That bastard wouldn't *voluntarily* piss on me if I were on fire. He doesn't do anything for anyone except himself."

"Well, he did. Unless you're suggesting the guy we left as a hostage is an imposter."

I describe Gregory Wallace, and Brady's ashen complexion answers for him.

"No," he says. "That's not—He has an agenda. Goddamn it, no. He's up to something and . . ."

"And what?"

"And I have no idea what it is, but I can promise you—Wait. Hell, yes." He wheels on us so fast he startles Storm. "What are you about to do?"

I glance at Dalton.

"Didn't you just say you're taking me to trade for Greg?" Brady says.

"No, we're taking you to work this out," I say. "We aren't going to turn you over for execution. That's not—"

"But it's what Gregory expects. That in order to get him back, you'll need to hand me over. Which means he doesn't need to kill me. You guys handed me over. Some crazy mountain men killed me. Not his fault."

"So he wants you dead."

Brady stares at me, eyes bugging. He blinks. Stares some more. "Have you listened to a word I've said since I got here? Yes, Greg wants me dead. Why the hell did he send a sniper to shoot me? Why did he show up himself when that failed? To make sure—one way or another—that the job gets done."

"For the money." I turn to Dalton. "Seems a little overcomplicated, doesn't it?"

"Just a little," he drawls.

"I've never even been down south," Jacob says. "And that sounds crazy to *me*. Accuse you of killing a bunch of people, ship you off into the wilderness, and *then* execute you?"

"Gotta be easier ways of killing an inconvenient heir," Dalton says.

"At the risk of sounding like a rich prick lecturing the local rednecks, it's not that easy to get rid of me. My mother loves me more than she *trusts* Greg. If I died down there, she'd suspect him. In a few months, he'll tell her the so-called truth. By then, he'll have fabricated all the evidence he needs to convince Mom that her darling boy was a psychotic serial killer. Then he'll show her all the steps he took to keep me safe . . . only to have me die in these woods, through no fault of his own."

"There must be more to it," I say.

Brady growls under his breath. "I don't want to call you stupid, Detective . . ."

"Then don't. And please remember that I *am* a detective. Your story stinks. Back at the start, even *you* said there was more to it. A secret you knew, about your stepfather."

"It doesn't matter. What matters is—"

"Eric, can you cuff him? We really need to get him back to Edwin. We may need to find a gag, too."

Brady wheels . . . to find my gun pointed at his face, Dalton's at the side of his head.

"Hands behind your back," I say.

"You think you want my secret, Detective? Actually, you don't. Because if there's any doubt in your mind that I'm a lying son of a bitch, this will erase it. The only person who gets to hear it is my stepfather. One final card I can play to beat him at his game. It's my ace in the hole, and I'm not letting you take it away from me."

"Then I guess you're going to get the chance to play that ace very soon. Put your hands behind your back."

We are marching Brady to the First Settlement, and I'm trying to figure out what the hell to do about that. He's called my bluff, and right now, the only solution I can think of involves showing him it's not a bluff. Handing him over to Edwin and seeing what Brady plans to do about that. Which is a shitty, shitty plan.

It shouldn't come to that. Brady's smart enough to realize that no secret is going to fix this solution. His leverage is with Wallace, who has no power here.

So how does Brady think he's going to get out of this?

He doesn't. He really is calling my bluff, and he expects me to cave. *Okay, fine. Forget the hostage exchange. Let me take you back to town, and we'll work this out.*

I already know his secret. I've figured that one out. But if I confront him with it, I lose ground.

I need him to tell his secret. Break down and confess. Hand me that ace in his pocket. Give me what he thinks is his power.

I need it before we reach the First Settlement.

I look at Dalton, walking behind me, but he's deep in thought, also trying to see a way out of this predicament.

I pause to let him catch up. We need to talk. I'm not sure how but . . .

Dalton stops. He's looking to the side. I go still and listen. I don't need to focus very hard to hear the distinct clomp of boots on hard ground. Kenny's looking over, too. Brady opens his mouth, but at a sharp wave, he shuts it. Dalton motions for Jacob and Kenny to take Brady and Storm, and for me to follow him.

The boot steps continue along the path. There's no attempt to be stealthy or to avoid the path. That makes me hopeful—hopeful that as we sneak up through the trees, I'll see Anders. Or any familiar face from Rockton.

Instead, I catch the guttural tones of a settler.

Dalton lifts a hand, sees I've already stopped, and grants me a nod of apology. We both go still as we listen.

"We'll split up here," a man says. "You go left. I'll take right."

"Edwin said to stay together."

"We're tracking a southerner. An unarmed southerner."

"Didn't stop him from almost killing Martha."

"But he failed. He couldn't even take down a woman. He's soft. Old, too."

"He didn't seem that old. And he still got away. He's smart—"

"Not as smart as us."

Gregory Wallace has escaped the First Settlement. There's no other way to interpret this, but I still mouth the words to Dalton. He nods—he's come to the same conclusion.

I creep back to Brady, who's looking the other way, gazing into the forest. I slip up to him, put my gun to his chest, and whisper, "One word, and I pull this trigger."

His glare is icy rage. He hates me. I don't know if he would have hated me no matter what the circumstances. I don't know if my actions thus far have led to this. But whether he's a killer or not, I suspect

that if Oliver Brady got hold of a gun, his first bullet would go between my eyes.

We wait until the settlers are out of earshot. Then we wait a little
more, before Dalton nods, telling me they are gone.

"There is no exchange," I say to Brady, and he smirks.

Called your bluff, Detective.

"There's no exchange because your stepfather has escaped."

His lips form a curse, quickly swallowed.

"He'll return to our town," I say. "Which is where we're going.
We're done with this bullshit. We've lost two friends, and I don't care
if you murdered them or not, they would still be alive if you hadn't
shown up. This ends now. We are taking you back to your stepdaddy,
and we're putting both your asses on the plane. Eric will fly you within
a day's walk of the nearest town. He'll point you in the right direction. He'll give Gregory a gun. What your stepfather chooses to do
with the gun is up to him."

Brady's eyes widen, his mouth opening.

"You say you have a secret for his ears only?" I whisper. "You'll
have plenty of time to confront him with it, after Eric kicks you both
off that plane. Until then? You're gagged."

"No," he says, and there isn't any defiance in it. Only fear. "You
can't—"

"Can. Will. You may say you aren't a killer, but people die a little
too often around you, Oliver. So we're terminating the contract that
brought you here. This is family business. Yours, not ours."

"I didn't kill—"

"Like I said, we don't care. We did, once upon a time. But then
you went and escaped, which led to the whole 'two dead friends'
issue."

His face hardens. "You had no intention of listening to me—"

"You never gave us a chance to dig deeper. So off you go. Tell
Gregory your secret. Maybe you two can work this out." I pause.
"Unless it's a secret you plan to threaten him with . . . when the two
of you are alone in the forest, and only one of you has a gun. That
would be inconvenient."

I lift my gaze to his. "Yes, flare your nostrils at me, Oliver. Give me that look that says you're considering all the ways you could kill me. Relishing the options. In fact, why don't you just tell me what you'd like to do? Get it off your chest."

"I have done nothing." He can't even unclench his jaw to speak clearly. "I made mistakes out here, and your friends died. But that was desperation. I did not kill those people in Georgia. If you can prove otherwise, you would. You can't. So go ahead and put me and Greg on a plane. Let us go in the forest. But I want a gun, too. I deserve a fighting chance."

"Like those people you shot in . . ." I frown and look at Dalton. "Wait, did he just say Georgia?"

"Yeah," Dalton says. "Weird. I coulda sworn he said he was being blamed for a shooting in San Jose. You slip up there, Oliver?"

Another nostril flare. "No. I'm cutting through the bullshit. You know he's not accusing me of the San Jose shooting. He's saying I murdered five people in Georgia. Fucked-up, psychopath serial killings."

"Which you did not commit."

"No, I did not."

"Yet you know who did. Who would do . . . ? Wait. Don't answer. Let me guess. Could it be . . . your stepfather?"

Brady jerks forward. Dalton's gun barrel slams into his temple. Brady reels. Dalton catches him by the arm and presses his gun against the young man's forehead.

"You gonna call Casey a lousy detective now?" Dalton says.

"So you figured out Greg is the real killer," Brady says. "Fine. Now you see—"

"I see you're a desperate man," I say. "Desperate enough to accuse your own stepfather of the crimes you committed."

A string of obscenities follows, his face contorting with rage. "This is exactly what I knew would happen. See? See?"

As his voice rises, I say, "Do you want that gag? Or do you want the chance to keep talking?"

"Why bother? This is how it is. How it will always be. You want me to play nice, Detective?" He leans toward me. "I don't know how. Never learned the skill. Or maybe I lack the genes. You look at me, and you see a spoiled white boy. Self-centered. Entitled. An unpleasant son of a bitch. And you know what? You aren't wrong."

He eases back. "I'm an asshole. But that doesn't make me a killer. I'm probably not a good person. But that doesn't make me evil. I don't think that's such a difficult concept for you to understand, Detective. You're a stone-cold bitch. Doesn't mean you aren't good at your job. Doesn't mean you don't care about your people. The sheriff here doesn't bat an eye when you threaten me, and it doesn't stop him from looking at you like the sun shines out of your ass."

He locks gazes with me. "I *am* responsible for your mountain-man friend's death. Court of law would lock me up for manslaughter. I accept that. I am also responsible for Val's death. I promised you'd get her back, and you didn't. But those murders back home? Those were committed by a guy who makes me look like a saint."

"Gregory Wallace."

"You liked him, didn't you? Of course you did. Everyone does. Let me guess how it went. He showed up, apologized for all the trouble he put you through, promised to compensate you for it, while being clear he knows money won't fix this. Am I close?"

Brady doesn't wait for an answer. "I know I am. I know him. He was charming and gracious and humble. Probably confided in you, too, Detective. He wouldn't bother with the sheriff. He decided you were the brains of the operation. The moral compass, too, he'd presume, because he's a sexist asshole, and you know the problem with being a sociopath? You're so busy acting your role that you can't see through the performances of others. He bought the sheriff's redneck routine and your quiet-but-thoughtful one. Am I right? Did he confess to you? Admit he made mistakes? Of course he did."

I say nothing.

Brady continues, "I bet he volunteered to help search for me. Insisted on it. He feels *so* bad about the situation that he wants to help find me. Take the risks alongside you two. The truth? He doesn't trust you. He wanted to be there when you caught me, to make sure you brought me in and maybe use the opportunity to stage a tragic accident."

"Yeah," Dalton says. "That explains why he *offered* to stay behind as hostage. In Casey's place."

"Because that guaranteed you'd turn me over to those savages."

"Except he escaped," I say.

Brady finally goes silent. At least a minute passes.

"Can't explain that away?" Dalton says.

"No, Sheriff, I can't. I could speculate that he overheard something that made him think he might not survive the exchange. But that's speculation. I only know something happened in that camp, and he decided he'd overstayed his welcome. I bet he took out a few of the locals on his way, too."

"Actually, no," I say. "He hurt a woman, but he left her alive and made his escape."

"Okay, that makes sense. It's hard to keep pretending you're a good guy if—"

"Down!" Dalton shouts.

He falls onto me and, for a moment, I think he's been hit. Then I realize he's pinning me down. There's a shot. Then Storm lets out a yelp of pain.

FIFTY-SEVEN

My dog has been shot. There's a sniper in the trees, and Storm has been shot. I try to scramble up, but Dalton holds me fast, whispering, "I'm sorry. I'm sorry, Casey."

I fight the urge to snarl at him. To get free of him. To get to her.

I dig my fingers into the ground to hold myself still, and I listen, as hard as I can. After a moment, I hear a labored pant, each breath ending in a whimper.

She's been shot.

Definitely shot.

As I twist toward her, I catch a blur of motion. It's Kenny rolling into the undergrowth, his arms around Storm.

"I've got—" Kenny starts.

Another shot. Kenny's whole body jerks.

Dalton starts to leap up. I tackle and yank him into the undergrowth.

"Careful," I say. "We have to be careful."

He nods, and we creep on our bellies. We're on the same side of the path as Kenny and Storm, and I can see their shapes ahead.

As we move, I hear Jacob whispering, "You're okay, you're okay, just stay still. Play dead."

"Kenny?" I whisper, as loudly as I dare.

"I've got him," Jacob whispers back. "I have Kenny and Storm.

Stay down. Casey. Keep Eric *down*. Stay where you are. Do not move."

He's right. Any movement we make is going to draw fire. I reach out for Dalton's hand and clasp it, and we lie there, listening to Kenny's ragged breathing.

That's when I see Brady crawling away.

Dalton squeezes my hand hard, getting my attention, and then he shakes his head.

Let him go.

Don't take the risk of going after him.

But I have to, don't I? As long as Oliver Brady is out there, people will keep dying.

I look in the direction of the shots. I see nothing. It isn't like the city, where I could scan the buildings and know which is most likely to hold the gunman. This is a forest filled with towering trees, all perfect for a sniper.

And as long as this gunman is out there, we are sitting ducks. Eventually we need to come out, and all the sniper has to do is track us and wait for us to stop moving.

So we can't stop moving.

We can't wait for the shooter to figure out where we are. We have a wounded man and dog, and we need to get them someplace safe.

I watch Brady sneak off, and I wait for Dalton to relax, convinced I'm giving up on my prey. Then I leap up to a crouch, call, "Get them someplace safe!," and break into a run.

Dalton grabs for me. His fingers brush my leg. But I'm gone.

I zigzag. One shot fires into a tree several feet away. Another does the same. I'm careful, though, moving up, down, left, right, zipping behind every tree and bush in my path.

Behind me, Dalton whispers urgently to Jacob. I can't slow enough to focus on words, but I know Dalton's trusting that I'm okay while he gets the others to safety.

Brady hears me coming. He straightens to run faster. A shot hits a tree, clearly intended for me, but when he hears that hit, and he sprawls into a home-plate slide. I sprint and leap on his back. He bucks. I grab his still-bound wrists and wrench them so hard he howls.

"Shut the hell up," I say, slamming his head into the dirt. "I'm doing you a favor. Exactly how long do you think you'd survive out here with your hands tied behind your back?"

He glowers over his shoulder.

"Yeah, yeah," I whisper. "I'm a stone-cold bitch. I've heard it already. You would do well to note that you're still alive, when it would be a hell of a lot more convenient for me to change that. I *will* kill you, Oliver, but I need a reason. So don't give me one."

I wait until I'm sure the shots have stopped, the sniper trying to find targets again. I'm checking whether we're hidden enough to move when something thumps in the trees to my right. A family of ptarmigan explodes from the bushes, startled by whatever Dalton must have thrown at them.

The sniper fires toward the birds.

I prod Brady forward with "Move!" and "Stay down."

He does both. I steer him through the clearest patch of forest floor, where we don't make enough noise to draw the sniper's attention. The forest has gone silent again. Then there's a shot, one too loud to be the sniper. A tremendous crash. Brady dives. I grab him by the collar and propel him forward.

"That's Eric providing cover," I say.

This time, he's fired his gun at a dying sapling or dead branch, something that will break and fall, the noise again drawing the sniper's attention.

I get Brady behind rocks. We're back in the foothills. There's no conveniently located cave this time, but we wind through the rocks and tree cover until I see Dalton ahead, flagging me. I arrive to see he's found a sheltered spot where he's moved the others.

I spot Storm first. Dalton whispers, "She's fine. Bullet grazed a hind leg. She can't run, but she's fine."

I crawl to her and rub her neck, and she whines but stays lying down, muzzle on her paws, her gaze on . . .

Her gaze on Kenny.

I see him, and I stifle a gasp. He's lying on his stomach, his head to the side, eyes closed. Eyes closed, not moving.

As I scramble over, Jacob says, "He's unconscious, but he's . . ."

Jacob looks at Dalton.

"Where did he . . . ?" I trail off as I see the answer.

Kenny has been shot in the back. The lower back, the bullet passing through near his spine.

I forget that there's a sniper out there and a possible killer beside us. That doesn't matter. Kenny has been shot, and this is not a graze or a bullet passing through soft tissue. This is . . .

I drop beside him. I check his vital signs first. They're strong enough to suggest he's only fainted. He isn't in shock, not from internal bleeding or neurogenic shock—the injury is too low on his back for that.

I peel up his jacket and shirt, as carefully as I can. It's soaked with blood, front and back, but the bleeding is slow.

I tend to the injury as best I can while Dalton stands guard. It's quiet out there. Our sniper seems to have a remarkably short attention span. He—or she—is not the trained professional we first thought. With the exception of Kenny, everyone has suffered only minor injuries. Given Kenny, though, the intent does *seem* lethal. The sniper just doesn't have the skills to pull it off without a perfect target. The wild shots support that theory, as does the fact that it's been easy to draw his fire.

This is still someone who knows distance shooting—knows how to find a good perch and hit a clear target. That's more than I could manage with a rifle, but it's no better than Dalton or Jacob could do, with their hunting experience.

As for the sniper's intentions, I have no idea. Initially, Brady seemed to be the target. But he hasn't actually hit Brady. Nor has he fired only at those standing nearby. By this point, I'm almost wondering if the sniper is a completely separate situation—that we have a settler with a rifle who's decided to kill himself some Rockton residents. Because that's just what we need.

We must get help for Kenny. The best plan seems to be to leave Jacob and Storm with the remainder of our supplies and a sidearm. Both Dalton and I must take Brady back to Rockton, to guard each other from the sniper. That's not even considering the fact that we have settlers hunting for Wallace, who'd be quite happy to vent their outrage on us.

And then there's Wallace himself. Could he be the real serial killer? At this point, I'm beyond guessing. If someone lined Brady and Wallace up and told me I had to pick which one to shoot, I might as well make them play rock-paper-scissors to decide who gets the bullet.

With no knowledge of the crimes, no evidence to consider, no way of *getting* any evidence swiftly, it comes down to "Which man do I believe?" And the answer right now is neither.

Dalton and I scale the mountain partway to get a better look at our situation. We've climbed about a hundred meters up when a voice drifts over from the forest. A voice that has me thinking I'm clearly hallucinating, because it makes no sense in this context.

"Is that . . . ?" Dalton looks over at me. "Diana?"

She stops talking, and a man answers. I hear him speak, and I grin.

"Will," I say. "They're out searching—"

Oh, shit. Anders and Diana are out searching for us. In the forest. With a sniper and Wallace nearby. And some really pissed-off settlers. If we can hear Diana and Will, then others will, too.

FIFTY-EIGHT

"I'm going to go to them," I say. "Can you cover me?"

Dalton nods.

I slide down the mountainside as Dalton positions himself, gun ready. I reach the bottom and scamper from one point of cover to the next. I hear Anders again, but his voice is muffled now that I'm on ground level, and I can tell he's farther away than I thought.

I turn and see Dalton shielding his eyes, watching me. I pantomime that they're at least a kilometer away, and he motions that he'll stand guard for as long as he can see me. I'm zipping past the others, quietly calling to Jacob that I hear Anders . . . when Brady lurches out.

"I am not staying out here," Brady says. "If you're on the move, so am I."

I want to put my damn gun to his head. I might, too, if I could spare the time to slow down . . . and the time to chew him out . . . and the risk of being overheard by our sniper. I see Dalton watching from above. He gives a dismissive gesture, one I'd love to interpret as "Just shoot the son of a bitch," but I know better.

"Keep up," I say. "You want to try escaping again? That sniper isn't the only one in this forest with a gun."

"You don't need to keep reminding me," he grumbles as he jogs over.

When I glance back to Dalton, he puts a finger gun to his head and shakes his head, and I have to smile at that. By this point, we don't really give a shit if Brady is innocent. Killing him on principle seems like a fine idea.

He catches up and stays behind me. I'd rather he was in front, where I can watch him, but that won't help me find Anders and Diana quickly. I can no longer hear them. I'm moving at a slow jog, and Brady has the sense to do the same, making minimal noise.

Shortly after I start, I think I hear something, but it quickly goes quiet. I'm long out of Dalton's line of sight, unable to see more than the mountaintop over the trees. I'm mentally trying to pinpoint where the sound might have come from when I hear Diana, her voice harsh as she argues with Anders.

I'm not sure whether to breathe a sigh of relief that I hear her . . . or hiss in exasperation at her loudly bickering with him. Diana and Anders had a one-night stand after she arrived, and then I showed up and to her, it seemed that he suddenly turned his attentions my way. Not entirely true. Their affair had been a drunken one-nighter, which he regretted, realizing he might have taken advantage of her at a vulnerable time. But to have him hanging out with me a day after sharing her bed? Humiliating, and she hasn't forgiven him. I don't quite blame her. It's an awkward situation all around.

Now I'm just wishing they hadn't had the harebrained idea to team up and come find me. Why Diana? Even at our closest, I'd never have chosen her as a search-team partner.

"I am not—" she begins.

Anders answers, his voice pitched higher than normal, clearly feeling the strain of this pairing. I can't make out what he's saying, but it must be some variation on *Hell, yeah, you will, Di,* because she comes back with, "Absolutely not, you crazy—"

A hiss of pain cuts her short, and I stumble to a halt.

Will?

The question lasts only a split second. I know Will Anders, and it doesn't matter if he isn't *really* Will Anders, if he's a soldier named Calvin James, who shot his CO in cold blood. Anders would be the first person to call himself a killer, a monster. But even when I once suspected him of brutally murdering four residents, I'd struggled with my own conclusion. As naive as it sounded, I could not believe he'd done it. And he hadn't.

I know Will Anders. I also know Calvin James. I know exactly what happened, even if he doesn't understand it himself. Once I stood in front of a man I hated, pointed a gun at him, and pulled the trigger. I snapped. Anders did the same, spurred on by tragedy and rage and misprescribed medication.

When I hear Diana's words and that hiss of pain, I know that the other speaker is not Anders

"Casey!" Diana calls, and her companion doesn't stop her. "Casey? If you're out there, and you can hear me . . ." She pauses, as if expecting to be interrupted. "Run. Run like hell—"

A smack cuts her short. Whoever has her hostage told her to call to me. This just isn't the message he wanted imparted.

"Casey?" she shouts. "It's Brady's father. He's knocked out Will—"

Another *thwack,* hand against flesh. Then I hear Wallace talking to Diana, his voice clearer now as he tells her to stop it, he hasn't hurt Anders, hasn't hurt her, stop being so melodramatic.

"And you think I'm fucked-up?" Brady mutters behind me. "He's holding your friend hostage, smacking her around, and telling her she's overreacting."

"So he *is* dangerous?" I say.

Brady stares at me. "Have you been listening to anything I said? He's killed at least five people. Tortured them. Watched them *die.* Oh, but he seems like such a nice guy." He jabs a finger in the direction the voices came from. "Does *that* seem like a nice guy? Of course he's fucking dangerous. He's going to kill your friend and—"

"Just checking," I say as I kick out his knee.

Brady drops, and I grab his arms with one hand, wrenching them up again as I put my gun at his head and plant my foot on his back.

"Wallace!" I shout. "It's Casey."

"What the fuck are you—?" Brady begins.

"You just confirmed he's dangerous. Which means he'll kill Diana and Will if he doesn't get what he wants. I'm going to guess what he wants is you."

Brady goes wild, struggling and snarling. I keep wrenching his arm and warning him to stop. There's a crack as his wrist breaks. He howls in pain.

"You bitch. You—"

"Shhh," I say. "I can't hear your daddy."

I push Brady's face into the dirt and shout, "Wallace?"

"Yes . . ." The reply comes slow, tentative.

"You've got something I want," I say. "I'm going to guess I have something you want, too."

"If it's that sadistic bastard my wife whelped, you would be correct, Detective."

"Then bring Diana and follow the sound of my voice."

I keep Brady pinned, muffling his rage as I scan the treetops, all too aware of the chance we're taking with this confrontation. The chance that our voices will tell our sniper friend exactly where to find us.

Wallace eventually appears, Diana in the lead, a knife at her back.

"He ambushed us," she says. "Knocked out Will."

I mouth to ask if there are others. Anders and Diana can't be the only searchers. But her gaze sweeps over the forest in a desperate look that tells me, yes, there are others, but they aren't close enough to come running.

"I just want what I came for," Wallace says. "I haven't killed anyone. I've only done what I had to. I need you to give me Oliver."

"But that was the deal, wasn't it?" I say. "So why the sudden need to force my hand, Gregory? To start hurting my people?"

"I know you have doubts, Casey. I've seen it in your face. In Sheriff Dalton's. You've spoken to Oliver, and whatever he has said, it's made you wonder if you've been misled. I don't blame you, which is why I'm doing my best *not* to hurt your people. But I can't take the chance that you won't use lethal force to stop Oliver if he escapes. The very fact he's still alive tells me I'm right. You'll let him run, and others will die."

"You son of a—" Brady begins.

I push the gun against the back of Brady's neck.

"Oliver here is telling a new story," I say. "One that says *you're* the monster. The serial killer."

"What?" Wallace's eyes round. "My God, Ollie, you *are* desperate. You're actually accusing me—"

"I caught you," Brady snarls. "With that boy. I followed you to where you were keeping him, and I saw what you'd done. What you were doing. You murdered him right in front of me. Slit his throat while he begged me to save him."

"You know, Ollie, I recognize that story. It sounds very familiar. Maybe because it did happen . . . only I was the one following you. I was the one who saw that poor kid." Wallace's voice rises. "And I was the one begging. Begging you to let him go as he sobbed, gagged and bound, covered in blood and filth. A boy. A teenage *boy*. You tortured him. Murdered him. I don't even want to know what else you'd done to him."

Brady struggles to get up from under me. "You bastard. You sick, sick bastard. Do you think I've forgotten what you did to me when I was his age? I kept my mouth shut because you said you'd kill my mother if I told her. Maybe I should have *let* you, if it meant stopping you before anyone else died."

Wallace looks at me. "He will say anything to get out of this, Casey."

"So will you," Brady spat.

Wallace keeps his gaze on me. "I know you're angry at me for threatening your friends. But I have done the minimum damage possible. Same as with that woman in the village. I just want to get Oliver out of here before he kills more people. However angry you are right now, Casey, the difference in our behavior should speak for itself. Oliver has murdered multiple people up here. I've knocked out two. I've threatened this woman and, yes, I've struck her in anger. Ask her if I've done more. Check to see if she's suffered even a bruise."

Diana gives a reluctant shake of her head.

"We have no actual proof Oliver killed anyone except Brent," I say, "and even Brent says the bullet was fired accidentally, during a fight."

Brady stops struggling.

"I won't know about Val until I retrieve her body," I say. "I saw no signs of trauma that couldn't have been inflicted by a fall. As for the settler massacre, I believe someone else was responsible."

"Some *other* random killer roaming the woods?" Wallace says. "I'm sorry, Detective. I realize Oliver is an attractive young man, and he can be charming—"

"Stop right there," I say.

Brady gives a harsh laugh. "Yeah, no, Greg. Don't even try that. She hates my fucking guts, whether I'm guilty or not. The only reason she isn't shooting me is that she's actually a damn fine cop, one who gives a shit about—"

"You, too," I say. "Enough. I don't want patronizing bullshit from him or bootlicking flattery from you."

"She's right," Diana says. "I've known Casey half my life. Don't insult her. Don't flatter her. She'll see through that crap and stomp you both like bugs."

"Just give me my stepson," Wallace says. "That's all you need to do. Hand him to me, and I will lead you to your deputy, and we'll all walk back to town. It's not as if I can hijack the plane and fly out on my own."

"He can do exactly that," Brady says. "He has a *fleet* of small planes, and he insists on flying them himself, like he insists on doing everything himself. Including murder."

Wallace sighs. "And here is the problem, Casey. Lies. His endless lies. I don't know how to fly. I don't own any planes. If I did, why would Phil have brought me? Oliver is spouting nonsense. He'll say whatever it takes to make you doubt me."

And so they go, accusing one another and protesting their innocence, leaving me feeling like the therapist for the most dysfunctional family ever.

Except I'm not their therapist. I am their judge, jury, and, yes, executioner.

I can end this now. Decide who is lying and shoot him. I have Brady pinned under me, and Wallace is barely even bothering to hold the knife on Diana, too caught up in defending himself against his stepson's accusations.

All I have to do is decide who is telling the truth. Who is the real killer. Which is impossible, when I have nothing to go on but their say-so.

Maybe after all my years as a detective, my gut should tell me which one is guilty. But right now, it wants me to shoot both of them. It says they're both full of shit, and I don't think it's wrong. Neither is being completely honest. But one is a serial killer, and the other is just a garden-variety dangerous son of a bitch. One deserves death. One does not. And I have no idea which is which.

I catch Diana's eye. She's looking straight at me, tuning out father and son as she waits for me to resolve this, like I always do.

Casey to the rescue. Just trust Casey.

See how well that worked out for Val and Kenny.

I failed them. I will not fail Diana.

I could signal to her that she can jump aside and get free of Wallace, but that's a risk.

No more risks. No more being a homicide cop. I need to channel Dalton here. I am the guardian of those under my protection, and they are all that matters.

"He's yours," I say to Wallace.

Brady screeches, "What?"

"You'll escort him back to town," I say, "and I don't really give a damn what happens then."

Which is a lie. I have every intention of getting to the bottom of this. I just can't do it out here, with them raging at each other, drawing the attention of everyone around. And not while Anders lies unconscious and Kenny is in desperate need of medical attention. Just let me get them to town, and I'll figure out my next move there.

I haul Brady to his feet. When he resists, I squeeze his broken wrist. He howls . . . and a bullet hits the tree right beside Wallace's head.

Wallace spins. But he doesn't dive for cover. He grabs Diana, yanking her in front of him. When she tries to pull away, the knife flashes and blood sprays, and I forget Brady.

I run for Diana. Wallace holds her like a human shield. I knock her in the side, shoving her away. Wallace grabs my upper arm and yanks me into Diana's place. When I see the look on his face, I know what he is.

I finally know.

I swing my gun up. The idiot has forgotten I have it. He slashes with the knife, the blade aiming for my face. I wrench from his grasp.

"On the ground!" I say, gun barrel pressing up under his chin. "Get on the goddamn ground or—"

"You'll shoot?" Wallace says. "You haven't yet, Casey."

"Because I hadn't figured out which of you bastards is guilty. Now I have." I push the gun barrel in harder. "Do you notice which one I let escape? And which is at the end of my gun?"

"You're wrong. You—"

His whole body convulses so fast I'm sure it's a trick. I'm about to pull the trigger when I see Diana beside him, holding the knife, blood dripping from the blade. Wallace's mouth works. Then he topples.

I kick Wallace as he falls, and then I'm on him. He lies facedown on the ground, my gun to his head. Blood gushes from his side.

"I stabbed him," Diana says, and she's clutching the weapon in both hands. "I took the knife, and I stabbed him. He—"

"Get *down*," I say.

I look around, but there have been no more shots.

Brady is gone, and the sniper has stopped shooting.

That is no coincidence.

"It's your shooter, isn't it?" I say to Wallace. "You put someone out here to kill him. You paid the council to let you bring in an assassin."

Wallace gives a ragged chuckle. "You have seen too many movies, my dear. And Oliver was wrong. You're a lousy detective. You picked the wrong—"

"No, I did not. The minute that gun fired, you grabbed Diana to shield you. You stabbed—"

I look over sharply to see she's got her jacket off and is wrapping it around her arm.

"He sliced me good," she says. "You're going to need to give me a few stitches. I'm fine, though. Not that he gave a damn."

She's right. I saw Wallace's face when he pulled her to shield him. When he stabbed her. When he tried to stab me.

Backed into a corner, we cannot conceal our true selves. I saw his, and I still don't know exactly what we're dealing with here, but Gregory Wallace is not an innocent man.

I bind and gag him. Then I leave him where he lies, while Diana takes me to Anders.

FIFTY-NINE

When we arrive, Anders is conscious and struggling to get free from an old hemp rope tying him to a tree. His wrists are bloodied, and as much as I want to carefully tend to his injuries and Diana's, Kenny's situation is a much graver concern.

Our path takes us past Wallace. Diana offers to stay with him. I don't actually give a damn if *anyone* stays—he's not escaping those ties and if the cougar finds him and thinks he's a fine dinner, I'm okay with that. But I leave Diana behind, armed with a knife and a whistle.

When we set out again, Anders says, "Rough day?"

I'm not sure whether to laugh or cry. I think I do a little of both, and he puts his arm around my shoulders as we walk.

"Kenny was alive and stable when you left him," he says after I explain. "I'm not going to lie and say he'll be fine, but he was alive and he was stable. Also . . ." He glances over. "What happened to him wasn't your fault."

"He only came out here to clear his name."

"No, he comes out here all the time as a member of the militia. Odds are just as good that he could have been shot by this psycho sniper while just doing his job. You don't really feel guilty about him being out here. You feel guilty for thinking he was Brady's accomplice."

I nod.

"Lesson one in Rockton?" he says. "Trust no one. Except Eric. Well, trust him to not be a killer or a killer's accomplice. I know he has secrets, but I'm sure you already know those."

I glance over.

He shrugs. "I can tell. And I'm never going to push. That's his business. But I know his secret isn't *our* secret—that we've killed people. If you and I have that in our background, though, anyone could. Even Kenny. He was the most likely suspect for Brady's accomplice. So stop beating yourself up. I'll do whatever I can for him. Hopefully he'll be fine."

We walk a few more steps, and then he says, "There's more, isn't there? Something else happened out there."

"The sniper shot someone Eric knew, a hostile we . . ." I swallow. "A hostile might have helped. It was a misunderstanding. She ran into the forest. And there were others. Hostiles. Eric had to shoot them, and he tried to just wound them and . . . things got worse."

"Shit." He looks over. "And you?"

I shrug.

"Casey . . ."

"I shot one. Had to. Me or him. You know how—" I stop myself. There's a lightness in my voice. Forced casual, sardonic. *You know how it is. You were a soldier.* Which is not anything he needs to be reminded of.

"I do know," he says, brushing his shoulder against mine.

"I'm sorry. I didn't mean—"

He cuts me off with a quick embrace as we walk. "I do know. And it sucks every last goddamn time."

"I'm worried about Eric."

"I know you are."

"I'm also worried I may have . . ." I inhale. "He may have seen a side of me I'd rather he didn't."

"You mean the side that just told Wallace he's a piece of shit who deserves to be carved up and fed to the ravens?"

"Uh . . . possibly."

Anders laughs. "If you think Eric would be the least bit surprised by that, you are underestimating the man. You might try to hide that part, but you do a lousy job of it. Sorry. Wallace is alive, and you're doing everything you can to keep him that way until he can face his crimes. That's enough."

I look at him. "Is it too much? If only I'd killed Brady back in Rockton—"

"Yeah, don't even go there. You aren't that person. If we'd killed him then, yes, people would still be alive, but we had no way of knowing that, and we were right to suspect the council's story, considering Brady turned out to be innocent."

"Did he?"

Anders frowns at me. "You still have questions?"

Yes. Yes, I do.

We're halfway to the spot where I left Kenny with Dalton and Jacob when we hear the pound of feet on a nearby path.

"Brady," I say. "That's . . ."

When I trail off, Anders reaches into his pack and hands me his whistle. "Go on."

"No, I should—"

"You've done what you can for Kenny. I'm reasonably sure even I can't do any more until we get him back to Rockton. That's my real role here—the muscle to help make that happen. If I need a nurse, Eric does a fine job. You go get Brady."

"It might not be him."

"It is. Go."

I take off. As I jog along the path, I think.

So many questions.

And maybe, just maybe, an answer.

But for now, I will only say that I have questions. It seemed logical that the sniper works for Wallace. It might also seem logical that the sniper would stop shooting when Brady—his target—fled.

But that does not explain the fact that the first bullet was aimed at Wallace. That Wallace instinctively grabbed for a human shield.

Would you do that if you'd hired the man firing the gun? Of course not.

And if you did hire that man, and he saw you being taken captive, would he not turn his rifle on those attacking you? You can't collect payment if your client is dead.

When Diana and I went to free Anders, we left Wallace bound and gagged. And the sniper never returned to check on him, never returned to free him.

The sniper is not Wallace's man.

Yet Wallace is guilty.

I saw that mask slide from Gregory Wallace's face. I could say it was just the mask of civility falling away, like the hostiles in this forest, stripped of what passes for humanity when they are forced to fight for their lives.

That is bullshit.

Strip away my mask of civility, and you get someone who would shoot a man who left her to be beaten to death . . . and then blamed her for it. Someone who would have shot Wallace or Brady—not caring which was innocent—if it saved a friend.

What I saw in Wallace was more than my brand of darkness. It was evil.

When faced with danger, he pulled an innocent bystander into the path of the bullet.

Does that mean Wallace has done what Brady claims?

He could have. For now, I'll only say that. He is entirely capable of it.

As for Brady . . .

A theory. That's what I have. Now I need the man himself.

SIXTY

It's easy enough to sneak up on Brady. He hasn't transformed into a master woodsman. The problem has always been simply getting close enough to find him in this endless wilderness. Once I am, I can hear him, stopped to catch his breath. Those gasps cover my approach. Then I grab his broken wrist, still bound by my handcuff tie. He lets out a shriek, half pain, half surprise.

When he sees me, he deflates.

"Oh, come on, Detective," he says. "I'm starting to feel like that guy in *Les Miz,* chased by the cop who just won't give up, even when he knows the poor guy is innocent."

"Javert didn't know anything of the sort," I say. "And neither do I."

"Seriously?" He slumps, shaking his head, like I'm a patrol officer who pulled him over for speeding. Just a pain-in-the-ass cop, wasting the taxpayers' money trying to pin some silly little misdemeanor on him.

"I'm going to ask you again," I say. "How far do you think you'll get with your hands tied behind your back?"

"Does it matter?"

"Sure it does." I walk in front of him, my gun lowered. "A few years ago, I went to a party where they played a game called Would You Rather. It's supposed to be two equally shitty choices. Except the host didn't quite get the point and kept giving choices where there really was no choice at all. Like 'Would you rather take a bullet to the head or die of slow starvation in the forest?' Whatever fate you'd suffer out here is much worse than what your stepfather would do to you."

"Uh, did you miss the part where he's a fucking psychopath? He didn't shoot those people in the head. He tortured them."

"Yes, I'm sure being tied up and beaten wasn't—"

"Tied up and beaten? Is that your idea of torture? He cut them. He burned them. He pulled out their fingernails. Their teeth. He did the kind of things you see in movies, when they're trying to get spies to talk. Only he didn't want these people to talk. He wanted them to scream. To cry. To beg. To break."

"You got a good look then, at that boy you caught him with."

A heartbeat's pause before he plows on with, "Yes, yes, I did, Detective."

"And he molested you as a child."

A glimmer of relief as I move on, and he nods, "Yes."

"Tell me about that."

"What the hell is this? A therapy couch?"

"No, it's an interrogation room. You have accused your stepfather of molesting you. I've dealt with victims of that. I've had to interview them, lead them through it, and it was a horrible part of my job, but it was necessary to properly prosecute the offenders. So I know the stories. I know all the reactions a victim gives. Go on, Oliver. Convince me."

He starts to rage that he won't give me the satisfaction. That he won't play this bullshit game. Rage. Deflect. Rant.

I'm lying, of course. I have dealt with those victims. I have interviewed them. But there is no way in hell that I can tell a real accusation from a false one just by speaking to the accuser. Every response is different. I just want Brady to believe I can do it. He does, and so he says not one word about the abuse. He just rages at me until he finishes with, "You want me to talk about that? Put me in front of a real professional."

"With a lie detector?"

"Fuck you. My stepfather is a sadistic bastard, and whatever he did to me pales in comparison to what he did to his other victims."

I ease back. "I don't know. One could argue otherwise. I'm sure a defense attorney would. Gregory may not have molested you, but turning you into a killer? That's some seriously bad parenting."

"What? No. He's the killer. He's the one—"

"Yes, I suspect he is. You both are. Partners in crime, who turned on each other. How did it happen, Oliver? Not how he lured you into it. You're right—that's a story for a therapist, and I don't really care. I'm curious about the schism. The break. How did it come to this? Former partners, each desperately trying to pin the crimes on the other."

It takes three long seconds for him to say, "What the hell are you talking about?," and with that I know I've hit on the truth. The reason I couldn't pick a side. The solution that makes so much more sense than all the ones they've spouted.

Not a man trying to steal his stepson's inheritance. Not one trying to shield his wife from her son's horrible crimes. Not a young man who stumbled over his stepfather's horrible crimes.

Shared crimes. Shared blame. Equally shared? I don't give a damn.

"I've taken Wallace into custody," I say. "I'm doing the same with you. Eric will fly you both back down south and tie you up in a hotel room and place an anonymous call to the police."

"Sure, do that," Brady says. "And we'll tell them all about you and your town. Do you think you haven't given us enough information to pass on to the authorities? I know your name, Detective Casey Butler. I know his, Sheriff Eric Dalton. I know the names of a half dozen people in your town. I know I'm in Alaska—I've been here before, and I recognize the terrain. They will track you down and . . ."

He trails off, and I smile.

"Can't even finish that threat, can you?" I say. "They'll do what? We've given them two serial killers. You tell them that you were turned in by some secret prison camp in Alaska? Why would they care? And why would you presume they don't already know about us?"

He blinks at me.

"Turn around," I say. "And start walking—"

"Not so fast, Casey," a voice says behind me.

It's a familiar voice, but on hearing it, my heart skips.

Not possible. That is not . . .

I turn, and I see Dalton. But it wasn't his voice I heard. It was a woman's. Then I see Dalton's hands on his head, as he's prodded down the path by a woman.

"Hello, Casey," Val says. "You look surprised to see me."

"I—I saw your . . ." I don't finish. I will sound like a fool if I do, and I already feel the sting of my mistake.

But *how* was it a mistake?

I saw the bloat of her corpse. I know she was not alive.

Sharon, Dalton mouths, and with that, I understand.

Sharon. One of our winter dead. The woman who'd died of a heart attack last week. Whom we'd been burying when Brady arrived.

Sharon was not a perfect doppelgänger for Val. She was older. With longer hair. Heavier. Shorter. But none of that mattered for a water-bloated corpse floating facedown in the water. Cut the gray-streaked hair to Val's length. Dress her in Val's clothing. Put her corpse in the water and send it downstream, and even if we had managed to pull it out, between the rot and the bloat, it would have been hard to say it wasn't Val.

Benjamin Sanders had pulled that same trick with Nicole—found a dead hostile or settler and put her in Nicole's clothing and damaged the body enough that Dalton naturally concluded he'd found Nicole. Val knew we didn't have the equipment to test DNA, and that told her the trick might work again.

"Eric stopped to help me," Val says. "He couldn't resist, even when he considers me deadweight on your precious town. All I had to do was lie in his path, and he holstered his gun and raced over to help."

"And that's weakness to you, isn't it?" I say. "That he came to your aid, no questions asked, despite all the shit you've put him through."

"Put *him* through? I'm the one who's gone through hell in that god-forsaken town. Condemned to coexist with people who lack the IQ to carry on a proper conversation with me. Yet they all tried. Even you, Casey. Especially you. You had to try to help a poor fellow female, trapped in her home, cowering like a mouse. I wasn't cowering, you idiot. I was waiting. You said once that the council constructed a prison for me—made me too afraid to leave my house. No. I constructed it. It was my refuge, and you couldn't leave me well enough alone."

"Yeah," Dalton says. "We're all assholes for giving a shit."

My look warns him not to antagonize her. I'm all too aware of that gun at his back.

"You *should* have left me alone, Casey," she says. "But you couldn't. You had to dig and poke and prod. Destroy what little sanctuary I had. Rob me of what few allies I had."

"Allies?" I say. "You mean the council? Because I proved they set you up to be *raped*?"

"I was not raped." Her voice shakes along with the gun, and I give myself the same warning I gave Dalton. *Stop. Just stop.*

She continues, "I *escaped*. If you don't believe that's possible, it's because you didn't escape your attackers, Casey. You let them beat you. Let them almost kill you. Almost certainly let them rape you. You could not get away, so you cannot conceive of the possibility that another, stronger, smarter woman might have."

"Okay," I say, and it's a calm, even response, but she keeps shaking, wanting to fight, to defend herself, and I change the subject fast. "So you helped Oliver here. You ingratiated yourself with him, while pretending you were spying for us."

"And you bought it." She smiles. "You couldn't help yourself. Your pet project was showing signs of improvement. Joining the community. Making herself useful. I manipulated you into giving me access to him and you jumped at the chance."

"You brought supplies," I say. "Food. Weapons. That's why Oliver didn't bother retrieving my gun after he shot Brent. And you sent him *to* Brent. You knew Brent could lead you both to Jacob."

She says nothing. It doesn't matter. Not now.

Focus on the facts. On how this fills in the holes.

Brady attacked Brent because Val said Brent could get them a better hostage: Jacob. Who could also guide them out of the wilderness. And the companion Jacob saw with Brady? Val. From a distance, Jacob mistook her for a man. She brought those protein bars they shared, old stock she had access to. Brady had been so confident, he'd outright lied about it. Didn't even bother making up a story.

I have no idea what you're talking about, Detective.

Dalton jerks his chin toward Val, and it takes a moment to see what he's gesturing at—the rifle barrel poking over Val's collarbone, a gun slung at her back.

"You're the sniper," I say.

"Yes, I know my way around a gun, too, Casey," she says. "Did you presume I was too weak and timid? I told you I used to stay on my grandparents' farm. They had guns. I insisted on learning. I'm good at it—my aptitude for mathematics comes in handy with distance shooting. Of course, my grandparents didn't think it was a proper sport for a girl, so while they humored me as a child, I had to shoot in secret when I got older. Which was useful, as it turns out. Do you recall those boys who taunted me? Chased me? Tried to assault me? One died the month before he graduated from high school. Shot by a stray bullet in the forest. A careless hunter, it seems."

"And you shot Kenny," I say. "Who was no threat to you. Was never anything but respectful—"

"Respectful? He was a toad. Always trying to talk to me. Ask what he could do for me. I *know* what he wanted to do for me."

"So you shot him?"

"He was in the path of my actual target."

"Casey," Dalton says, when I don't respond. "You wanted to kill Casey. You felt threatened—"

"Threatened? By this *child*?" Val laughs. "No, Sheriff. I only wanted her out of the way. She stood between me and the one thing that really can get us out of this godforsaken wilderness."

"Him," I say. "Eric. Shooting him on our walk was accidental— you just wanted it to look as if someone was trying to assassinate Oliver. When Oliver couldn't get Brent to take him to Jacob, you decided Eric would do. He can guide you out. Keep you alive. You'd kill me and force him to help you escape."

"Now I don't need to kill you, so I won't. Proving I'm not threatened by you, Casey, I'll just borrow your lover for a week. If he gets us where we want to go, I'll set him free."

"And I'm supposed to trust you?"

"He's no threat to us once we escape, so why would we kill him?"

"Because you can. Because Oliver here is a sadistic—"

"It was Greg," Brady snarls. "He made me do it. He forced me to help him, and he said if I ever told anyone, he'd kill me."

"Which would be hard for him to do from a prison cell. He might have groomed you, Oliver, but that's only because he saw you for what you are—as much a narcissistic, sociopathic sadist as he is. And you, Val?"

I turn to her. "You felt like a prisoner in Rockton because you were. You weren't there by choice. Which means that farm boy isn't the only person you've killed. That's the thing about pulling a trigger. Either you're horrified and suffer a lifetime of guilt . . . or you realize it wasn't so bad after all. You tried to kill Kenny because he literally stood in your way. You tried to do the same to me because I figuratively blocked your path. You're no different than this psycho. Which means I can't trust you to let Eric go once he guides you out."

"I don't think you have a choice here, Casey. Drop to your knees with your head down or I'll put a bullet—"

I shoot her between the eyes.

I don't think about it. I cannot second-guess. I have my gun in my hand, and I have exactly one chance here, while she's talking, while she convinced she's won.

I swing my gun up, and I fire. I see her eyes. There is a moment there, a terrible moment, between her seeing the gun fire and death. A moment when she knows what has happened. A moment of horror that I will not forget.

Val drops to the ground.

"Holy shit," Brady says. "Holy—"

I point the gun at him, and he stops. I'm waiting for Dalton to tell me no, don't shoot Brady. But he says nothing. Does nothing. I glance back, and his face is ashen. He isn't in shock, though. He says nothing because he knows he doesn't need to. I had to shoot Val . . . and I don't have to shoot Brady.

"Start walking," I say to Brady.

"Hell, no. I am not—"

He stops talking. I think that means he's realized there's no point arguing. Then I see the blood blossoming on his chest.

His mouth works. He falls to his knees. And he topples face-first to the ground.

I spin, gun raised. That shot did not come from me. It did not come from Dalton. I didn't hear a gun fire, meaning it came from one with a suppressor. We don't have suppressors in Rockton.

Both of us turn, our guns raised, scanning the empty forest. Then I see a flash of motion. A killer in flight.

I tear off. Dalton passes me, but the gap is too wide, the killer dressed in camouflage, little more than a blur through the trees.

I let myself slow, gait smoothing as I squint at the shooter.

A slight figure. Narrow shoulders. Hips just as wide. It's a woman. She's fast and she's agile, and she knows how to move in the forest, racing down the path, leaping over obstacles, outrunning Dalton.

He shoots. The sound of that shot surprises me. It's wild, though. Intentionally wild—no matter what has happened, he's not aiming to bring down someone who shot a serial killer. He's just trying to get her attention. He does, and she glances over her shoulder, and I catch a flash of pale skin and light hair and a face I recognize.

Even from this distance, I recognize it.

She doesn't slow, though. And in trying to surprise her, Dalton got a shock himself, one that has him stumbling. Then she's around the corner, too far ahead to ever catch.

After a pause he heads back to me as I cover him. I *will* fire—if she turns and I see her gun trained on Dalton, I will shoot her.

She doesn't turn.

Dalton breaks into a jog and says, "Did you see . . . ?"

"I did."

"That was—"

"Petra."

We leave Val's and Brady's bodies behind. We cover them and mark the spot. Then we set out to Rockton.

"I killed Val," I say.

"You did what I couldn't. Last winter. With Benjamin."

He's looking straight ahead as we walk.

"I froze up," he says. "All I could see was Benjamin holding a knife on you, and I panicked. I should have shot him."

"No, you couldn't. If you had killed him, we'd have lost Nicole."

A few steps before he says, his voice low, "I didn't care. Not at that moment. I just froze."

"And I just reacted. I panicked. With another result."

He shakes his head. "You thought it through. Made a choice. I still regret not shooting Benjamin. I go over it and over it in my head. What if I lost you because I froze up? And now you'll second-guess making the opposite choice."

More quiet walking. Then he says, "We're both going to suffer. Wonder if we made the wrong decision. But I guess that's better than the alternative."

"Which is?"

"Not giving a shit." He looks back in the direction of the bodies. "Being like them."

SIXTY-ONE

We're nearing town when we meet Anders, pacing the path. He looks behind us and says, "You didn't find Brady."

"We did," I say. "Someone didn't want us bringing him back alive."

Anders swears. "The sniper."

I make a noise he can interpret as assent for now.

"How's Kenny?" I say, dreading the answer.

"Stable. That's all I can tell you. We got him back, and now we're getting the swelling down so Mathias and I can see the bullet. Unfortunately, that's not our biggest problem right now. Phil is ready to put Wallace on a plane and fly him out of here. I was giving you guys another sixty seconds before I stopped him at gunpoint."

We break into a jog, and I say, "Is Phil in on it? Or is this the council?"

"No idea. I told Phil what Wallace did. Told him you think he's the killer, not Brady. It seemed like he believed me. Then he starts packing. I say hell, no, not until you guys get back. He reminds me that, in Val's absence, he's in charge. I argued, but he ignored me. Acted like the walls were talking and then went to check the plane."

"Where is he now?"

"He ordered me to bring Wallace to the hangar. I told him to go fuck himself and came to see if you guys were nearby."

We head straight for the hangar. Anders tells us Jacob and Storm are fine. He managed to persuade Jacob to sneak into my old place through the back door, and he's recovering there.

We're nearing the hangar when we hear the plane start.

"Shit!" Anders says.

We're about twenty meters away when Phil appears, doing a last visual check of the runway.

"I'm taking the prisoner, Sheriff," he calls when he sees us.

"The hell you are," Dalton says.

"Actually, yes, I am, and while I know you need to bluster in front of Will and Casey, let's skip that part. Your protest is duly noted. But it doesn't change the fact that you are not in charge here. I can assure you, Mr. Wallace will be properly dealt with."

"We have a patient in urgent need—" I begin.

"And you have Dr. Atelier. Plus the sheriff's plane, should the council decide to extract Kenny."

"I want to talk to Wallace," I say. "I have questions that require answers."

"No, Casey, you have questions you would like answered, and you wish to stall me while you figure out how to stop me."

"I want to figure out how you can take him safely," I say. "He's a dangerous psychopath—"

"Yes, yes, I know," Phil says, as if I'm telling him Wallace might prove an annoying seatmate.

Dalton's gaze swings toward the hangar. Then he starts to run.

Phil holds his ground, saying, "If you physically try to stop me, Eric—"

Dalton swerves around the hangar instead, heading for the rear door. I follow, and Phil calls, "Whatever you two have in mind, it is a waste of time. If you attempt to stop me, there will be consequences. I would suggest, Casey, that you . . ."

I don't catch the rest, drowned out by the sound of the plane.

The back door to the hangar stands open.

Dalton circles into the trees to sneak up on the other side. Anders has joined us, and he gets into the trees, angled where he can cover me.

I swing through the doorway. There's a figure at the open passenger side. A small one wearing a hooded jacket. When I see her, there's a moment of confusion as complete as when I first spotted Val. Then it's like dominoes falling, connections made in an instant.

"Harper," I say. "Step away from the plane."

She turns and sees the gun. Hers starts to rise, but Anders barrels through, saying, "Drop the weapon!"

She looks toward the open main doors. Dalton appears there with his gun trained on her.

"Weapon down!" Anders barks. "Now!"

"Do as he says, hon." Wallace's muffled voice emerges from inside the plane. "They *will* shoot you."

She lowers her gun to the ground.

"Shit, it's just a kid," Anders says as he gets his first good look at her.

"A kid who murdered three of her fellow settlers. Including her own grandmother."

Harper just levels her gaze on me, and I've seen that look before, in teens I've arrested. Some cry. Some rage. Some just give me this look, a cold *So what?*

It's chilling enough when it's a kid I've arrested for breaking into a house. For this? "Chilling" does not begin to describe it.

I want to ask, "Why?" But I know better. I'll just see another look like I did when I arrested those kids, when I felt compelled to ask why, and they rolled their eyes like I was just another stupid grown-up, asking stupid questions.

The "why?" isn't about motive. It's more of a "how?" *How could you do such a thing?* That is a question Harper cannot answer. No one can.

"You said Albie wanted to go back and steal the horses," I say. "But your grandmother and the other man stopped him. You still wanted to do it, though. You told Albie that, after the others went to sleep, didn't you?"

"He acted like I was a little kid. He ignored me. I had a plan for getting the horses. He wouldn't listen. When I said I'd go myself, he threatened to whip me. *Whip* me. Then he said even if I stayed in camp, he was going to tell my grandmother. She'd have to tell Edwin, and I'd never get to go on another hunting trip again."

"So you waited until he went back to his guard post, snuck up, and slit his throat. Except the old man heard, so you had to kill him. And then your grandmother. She tried to get away. You couldn't let her. You chased her down and stabbed her."

"It was Albie's fault. He was going to tattle on me because I offered to *help* him get those horses."

"It wasn't the horses you wanted. It was the dog."

Her lip curls. "I don't care now. I don't need a dog. I'm going down south."

"And Mr. Wallace here is going to buy all the puppies you want, right? You really are a child, aren't you, Harper?"

She yanks a knife from her pocket. I just hold my gun on her.

She sneers. "You won't shoot me."

She reaches into the cockpit to cut the strap on Wallace's hand. I lunge to grab her, but a voice says, "I can't let you do that, Casey."

Phil's pointing a gun at me.

"She's a child," he says. "I know you're upset, but we can resolve this without violence."

Anders lets out a ragged laugh. "Please tell me you're part of this escape attempt. Because otherwise you're the biggest idiot alive."

He's not part of it. If Phil planned to spirit Wallace off to safety, Wallace wouldn't be letting Harper free him. She's cut the strap on his hands, and now she's pointing the knife at me as Wallace climbs into the pilot's seat.

"Guess you have your pilot's license after all," I say.

"Of course," Wallace says. "Harper?"

She backs into the passenger seat.

Phil comes around the side of the plane. "This is pointless, Gregory. You will be a hunted man. Don't take a child into that."

"Oh, for God's sake," I mutter. "You really are an idiot." I raise my gun. "Wallace? Get out of the plane."

Harper's hand swings up, and I'm thinking it's just the knife. It's not.

I backpedal. Phil grabs me as if I'm . . . I don't know. Fleeing? Out of the corner of my eye, I see Dalton lunge. Then Harper presses the button, and the pepper spray hits me full in the face. I double over, blinded. Phil howls in agony. Even Dalton curses, as stray particles hit him.

Anders shouts "Stop!" but he's the farthest away, unable to fire from his angle. I hear the door slamming, the plane rolling, Anders yells. A shot fires. Another, hitting metal. Then the engine roars as the plane takes off.

SIXTY-TWO

Wallace and Harper escape. Dalton goes to get our plane out, but Harper has cut wires in the engine. By the time he could fix it, they'd be gone.

The council claims they'll go after Wallace. I don't know if that's true. I don't think Phil does either. I don't bother asking him. I can barely get him to tell me what they've said. He walks out of that radio meeting and says, "I have to stay."

"Until they figure this out?" I ask.

A slow shake of his head, his gaze blank. "I don't know. I don't . . . They said this is my fault. So I stay."

At that moment, seeing the look on his face, if I could muster any sympathy for him, I would. But I can't. All I can think is *Not again.* Once more, we are saddled with a leader who does not want to be here. The council has learned nothing from Val.

I must talk to Petra. That is obvious, but my gut screams at the idea. It tells me I'm mistaken—that both Dalton and I were obviously mistaken. Petra? No. Never Petra. She's my friend.

Which doesn't mean shit, does it? Diana was my friend. Beth became my friend. Even Val had been inching toward something akin to friendship.

I can tell myself no, not Petra, but then I remember her on the back deck of the station, going after Jen. I remember the look in her eyes.

I tell Dalton that I want to do this alone.

I find Petra at home, working on a sketch, and she welcomes me in, as she always does, with a big smile, and again I tell myself I'm wrong. I must be wrong.

She starts to lead me inside, but I stay in her front entryway.

"I saw you in the forest."

"Ah."

That's what she says. It's all she says, and I feel anger surge, outrage, and yes, hurt.

"I saw you shoot Oliver Brady," I say.

"Are you sure?"

Are you sure?

Not a moment of surprise, just a cool semi-denial, a lackluster defense that cuts deeper than any feigned confusion.

The anger flares, white-hot, and I advance on her. She doesn't step back. She doesn't flinch. She just meets my gaze with a level stare.

"I saw you," I say, "Eric saw you. We were not mistaken."

She says nothing.

"I just told you that Oliver Brady is dead, and you didn't bat an eye. No one else in town knows. That alone proves you were there, Petra."

"I'm not denying I was there. I'm asking if you're sure I'm the one who shot him."

"You—"

"Am I your friend, Casey?"

It takes everything I have not to throw her against the wall, like she did to Jen.

"Don't you dare—" I begin.

"I'm not asking you to drop this because I'm a friend. I'm asking you to trust me because I'm a friend."

"Trust that you didn't kill—"

"Just trust me." She meets my gaze. "I am your friend. Yours. Eric's. Rockton's. Whatever happened out there wasn't a tragedy. It was cleanup."

"Who gave you the right—?"

"I'm not saying I shot Oliver Brady, Casey. I'm saying that it doesn't matter who did. Not really. He's dead, and that's what had to be done, and if you'd like to come in and discuss it . . ."

I turn and walk out.

This isn't over. This isn't like it was with Mathias, a resident who saw our predicament and solved it for us. Petra might play it that way, but it isn't the same. Even with Mathias, he is no "random resident," no ordinary citizen driven to act outside his nature.

This was an execution. An *ordered* execution. Otherwise, we have a resident who somehow found a gun and a silencer lying around and wandered into the forest in hopes of finding us, then saw and shot Brady to protect us. Despite the fact that, at that moment, he posed no threat.

Someone told Petra to kill Brady. And she did. Which means there is so much more to this—and to her.

Dalton doesn't know what to say about Petra. For now, there's no time to discuss it, much less pursue the matter. We have Kenny to worry about.

A bullet that close to the spine is a dangerous thing. Even moving him may have made the situation worse. To take him up in a plane and fly him to Whitehorse? We could do no more than pray we don't make things worse. We almost certainly will.

Dalton and I sit on the back porch of the clinic, after seeing Kenny and assessing the situation.

"Fuck," Dalton says. "I don't even know what to do."

"Is there any chance the council will fly in a surgeon?"

He shakes his head. "They can't even get us a doctor. Where the hell will they find a neurosurgeon?"

I take a deep breath. "April."

He looks over. "Your sister? Right, she's a neuroscientist, isn't she?"

"Yes, but she was a medical doctor first. She specialized in neuro-surgery. She didn't care for it, so she got her doctorate and went into research instead. Did I mention I come from a family of over-achievers?"

I give a wry smile. Dalton lays his hand on mine, and I realize I'm tugging a thread on my shirt, anxiously winding it around my finger.

"Are you sure you want to do that?" he says. "I know you and April . . ."

"I can try," I say. "For Kenny, I can try."

"Then let's go talk to the council."

TURN THE PAGE FOR A SNEAK PEEK AT
KELLEY ARMSTRONG'S NEXT NOVEL

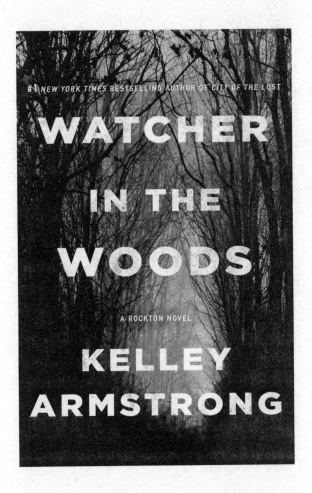

#1 *NEW YORK TIMES* BESTSELLING AUTHOR OF *CITY OF THE LOST*

WATCHER IN THE WOODS

A ROCKTON NOVEL

KELLEY ARMSTRONG

AVAILABLE FEBRUARY 2019

ONE

I have not seen my sister, April, in two years. Nine months ago, I called her before I fled to a hidden town in the Yukon, where people like me go to disappear. I didn't tell her where I was going. I only said that I had to leave, and she might not hear from me for a few years. Maybe I'm imagining it, but I thought I heard relief in her voice.

After our parents died, I would call before April's birthday, before Thanksgiving, before Christmas, and I'd suggest getting together. For the first year, she made excuses. Then she stopped bothering, and I stopped calling. I worked through every holiday and pretended it didn't matter. Of course it mattered.

Late last night, I called from a pay phone in Dawson City and told April that I needed her help, that a man's life depended on it. She hung up on me.

Now I'm outside the Vancouver hospital where she works. She's a neuroscientist, but also has her medical degree and consults on neurosurgery. According to her assistant, she's been here all night on an emergency call and should be leaving at any moment.

I'm standing by the parking garage. I've confirmed her car is inside. Now it's just a matter of waiting.

"Looks like good weather today," says a voice beside me.

I slant my gaze to a guy about four feet away. He's six feet tall, with light brown hair in a buzz cut. He's got a few days' worth of beard scruff, and he's wearing a ball cap, T-shirt, and shades. His leans against the building, paperback novel in hand.

"Didn't your mother ever tell you not to speak to strangers?" I say.

"Nah. She told strangers not to speak to me. And I won't be a stranger after you come back to my hotel room tonight."

I laugh. "Does that line ever work?"

"Never tried it." He lifts the shades. "I can offer further incentives, if you'd like."

"Like a room-service dinner?"

"Sure . . . eventually."

I slide over and lean my head against his shoulder before putting space between us again. Eric Dalton, the sheriff in Rockton, that hidden town where I've been living. Also the guy I've been living *with*. April doesn't know Dalton, so we're keeping that distance until I introduce him. Dalton can be a tad intimidating when he wants to be. And given the runaround I'm getting from April, he *really* wants to be.

"You could just wait at her place," he says.

"That would require knowing her address," I say. "She moved here a few years ago, and I only realized it when my birthday gift for her bounced back."

"Bitch."

I shrug. "Maybe I did something to piss her off."

"Yeah. It was definitely you, Casey. You're such a pain in the ass." He lifts his glasses again, so I don't miss his eye roll. "Your sister is a bitch, and if this wasn't Kenny's best chance, I'd say fuck it. If she doesn't want to know you, that's her loss."

I smile. "Thank you."

He starts to answer and then quickly lifts his book and murmurs, "I'm gonna guess that's her coming out now."

I look up. Dalton has never seen a photo of April, and if asked, I wouldn't have said there isn't much of a resemblance between us. Our mother was Filipino and Chinese; our father Scottish. April can pass for white where I cannot, and to me that has always meant that we look very different. She's a few inches taller than my five-two. Her skin is lighter. Her eyes are blue, their shape more Caucasian.

But we have the same straight dark hair, the same heart-shaped face, the same cheekbones and nose, all inherited from our mother. When I see April through Dalton's eyes, the similarities outweigh the differences. It's just that the differences have always loomed larger in my mind, wedged in by every acquaintance who met my sister and commented on the fact she "looked white."

It always seemed like one more way we were different. One more way that she was "better," and I feel a flare of outrage thinking that now. I am proud of my heritage. I wouldn't want to be able to "pass" for anything but what I am. Yet I cannot deny that when I was young, looking like April seemed better. Easier.

April spots me and slows. Her lips compress, and I am flung back to my childhood, seeing that same look from her every time I careened or bounced into a room. A moue of distaste for the wayward little sister who was always causing trouble, always disrupting April's orderly life. I'm only five years younger, but that gap always felt huge. Insurmountable.

"No," she says as she walks straight past me.

"I just want to talk."

"Did I say no last night?" April doesn't even glance over her shoulder. "Go back to . . ." She flutters a hand over her shoulder. "Wherever you went."

Dalton surges forward, but I stop him as I follow her into the garage. "I need your help, April."

"If you've frittered away your inheritance, I'm not lending you money."

If anyone else said this, I'd snap back a response. We both inherited seven figures from our parents, and mine has done nothing but grow since their death. Anyone who knows me—*at all*—wouldn't be surprised by this. Yet the person who should know me best is the one thinking I'd blow through a million bucks and come to her for a handout.

But I don't snap. I don't even feel the urge. With April, I am forever that little girl scrabbling up a mountain to get her attention. Forever trying to win her approval.

"I haven't touched my inheritance," I say evenly. "As I tried to explain on the phone, I need your medical assistance. For a friend who's been shot in the back."

She slowly pivots to stare at me. "What kind of trouble are you in, Casey?"

"None. Someone else—"

"A friend of yours has been shot, and you're coming to me instead of taking him to a hospital? Did you shoot him?"

I flinch. I can't help it. Thirteen years ago, I shot and killed a man. But April knows nothing of that, and it has nothing to do with the current situation.

Before I can answer, she turns away again. "Get this man to a hospital. Drop him off at the door if you need to. Then go away, Casey. Just . . ." Another hand flutter over her shoulder. "Go away again. Please."

Dalton strides past and plants himself in her path. "Your sister is talking to you. Turn the hell around and listen to her."

Her gaze flicks over him. Then she looks back at me. "Tell your fuck-toy to move, Casey."

"Hey!" I say my voice high, part outrage and part shock. My sister is never vulgar. Even the mention of sex usually has her flushing bright red.

She looks up at Dalton. "Yes, that's what you are. If you haven't realized it yet, take a tip from me. My sister doesn't date men. She just screws them."

"Huh," Dalton says. "Well, then I don't know who I've been living with for the past six months, but I guess it's not your sister. Or maybe I'm just special." He looks over at me. "Tell me I'm special."

I mouth an apology, but he dismisses it with a headshake. My sister isn't far off, as he knows. Until Dalton, I hadn't had a "boyfriend" since I was eighteen, and the reason for that had nothing to do with personal preference and everything to do with the fact that the guy I shot and killed *was* my last boyfriend.

April tries to walk around Dalton. He blocks her. He has his hands in his pockets, a clear signal that he will not physically stop her, but he's not about to let her pass him easily either.

"This isn't about me," he says. "It's about your sister. Who needs your help, and believe me, she wouldn't be here if she didn't."

April opens her mouth. Then a woman in a nurse's uniform enters the garage, and April straightens so fast I swear her spine crackles.

"Yes, I understand," she says, in her most businesslike voice. "Let's discuss this outside."

She leads us through a side door to a grassy area. It's empty, but she surveys it twice to be sure.

"If you wish to speak to me, I can spare . . ." She checks her watch. "Ten minutes. Then I have a salon appointment."

Dalton snorts a laugh before catching her expression. "Fuck, you're serious." He shakes his head. "Are you sure you two are related?"

"Yes, we are," April says coldly. "We simply don't share the same sense of responsibility."

"Yeah," Dalton says. "You could learn a few things from Casey."

She looks at me. "Please tell your guard dog he's using up your ten minutes."

I explain Kenny's situation, as fast as I can. I'm a homicide detective, but I grew up in a family of doctors and had been expected to take a career in medicine, so I know enough to give April a decent assessment of the damage and the treatment so far.

"You have doctors treating him," she says.

"No, we have me, plus an army veteran who received some medic training, and a psychiatrist with an MD but no on-job experience."

"This man needs a doctor. A hospital."

"The situation . . ." I glance at Dalton.

He nods, telling me to continue.

"The situation is not criminal," I say. "Let me clear that up right now. I've been working in a remote community. Very remote. We're more than willing to take the patient to a hospital, but he refuses to leave. He fears that if he goes, he won't be allowed back. The community is . . . a safe haven."

"Witness protection?"

"Something like that. It's complicated. That's all I can say, April. I am not asking you to do anything illegal. I wouldn't."

She's eased back, her guard still up but flexing. "I can't go on-site, Casey. I can recommend someone, but you really should get him to a hospital."

"We know that. And we aren't asking you to go on-site. Just consult. The two guys working with him are excellent medics. Steady hands. Steady minds." I force a tiny smile. "Which was always what Mom and Dad said made a good surgeon."

She flinches, and I realize maybe I shouldn't bring up our parents. She was always much closer to them than I was.

"We just need a consult," I say. "Lead them through the process of removing the bullet."

"Fine. We'll go to my place and video link them in."

"It's not a video link." I reach into my bag and hand her a satellite phone.

She stares at it. Then she looks at me. "You're kidding, right?"

"Our town *is* very remote." I pull pages from my bag. "But we have the medical equipment." I flip through the stack. "Here are photos and X-rays . . ."

She flips through them and then slows for a second pass before slapping the pages back into my hand.

"This can't be done by a satellite phone, Casey."

"It's that bad?"

"No, it's . . ." She throws up her hands. "It's actually *not* that bad. The problem is the location of the bullet. It's a tricky extraction, and I don't care how steady your psychiatrist's hands might be, you need someone on-site who knows what she's doing." She consults her cell phone. "I can give you three days. Possibly four."

"What?"

"It's Thursday. I was planning to work in the lab today and tomorrow, but that's not necessary. I need to be back for Tuesday, when I'm consulting on a surgery. You can have me until then."

TWO

I have no idea how we got from "I can't spare fifteen minutes for you, Casey," to "I'm yours for the next four days."

My sister is coming to Rockton, and I can't quite wrap my head around that.

Dalton made the call to let her come. Not a literal call—he didn't contact the council to ask permission. His excuse is that he has, and I quote, "no fucking idea what's going on with the council." That's true. The situation back in Rockton is stable, but we haven't had time post-chaos to reestablish procedures for dealing with the council.

Two weeks ago, the council sent us a serial killer for safekeeping. We aren't equipped for that, and he escaped. During the ensuing chase, Kenny got shot in the back, which is why we need April. We also lost our de facto town leader, Val. A few days ago, the council sent us Phil, who used to be our radio contact for communicating with them. That means we aren't sure who to call about bringing April back. Or, at least, it makes a very fine excuse.

There's an old saying about it being easier to ask for forgiveness than permission. That's what Dalton decides to do here. We don't trust the council to let us bring April in, and if we don't, Kenny will spend his life in a wheelchair. So, we'll sneak April into Rockton. She'll treat Kenny, and then we'll spirit her out of there. If we do this right, the only people who'll know are those who *have* to know—all people we trust.

We cannot tell April where she's going. In this, Dalton treats her like a new resident. She gets the usual spiel. Don't ask where you're going. Don't try to figure it out. Leave your cell phone and all electronics behind. Make one call to the person others will phone if they can't contact you. Tell him or her that you're taking the weekend off. I suggest she says she needs a stress break, an offline sabbatical. Dalton wouldn't understand the concept. April will.

She balks at leaving her tech behind. I explain that we don't have cellular or Wi-Fi access, and even recharging her batteries would mean plugging into a generator. She doesn't care. She argues that she needs her laptop, even if it's offline. I can tell Dalton's frustrated—we need to get her on a plane ASAP—but I work it out. She can take the laptop, nothing more.

We escort April to her condo to pack. She doesn't much like that either, but we're taking a huge chance here, one that could blow up with a slip of the tongue when she makes that call. I overhear it. It's brief, and I don't ask who she called. I have her put an auto-reply on her email and a message on her voice mail, explaining the offline weekend.

Then we're gone.

Rockton is in the Yukon. It might seem like it'd be wise to hide that—fly commercial into northern British Columbia, and then take a small plane. That's pointless, really. Knowing Rockton is in the Yukon is like only knowing a hotel is in Beijing. The exact place would be impossible to find.

Rockton is a wilderness town of two hundred, hidden by both technological and structural camouflage. The Yukon is roughly the size of Texas with a population of thirty-five thousand people. When Dalton first told me that, I thought he was misspeaking. He had to be. In a place that size, even tacking on a zero would make it sparsely populated. Dalton never misspeaks when it comes to facts. There are indeed thirty-five thousand people, two-thirds of them living in the capital of Whitehorse. The rest is wilderness. Glorious, empty, achingly beautiful wilderness.

As the plane begins its descent, I'm like a kid with my nose pressed against the glass. I see the mountains, the tallest still drizzled with snow. And I see trees, endless waves of green in more shades than I ever thought possible. Beside me, Dalton reaches for my hand. Across the aisle, April sees me staring out the window, and I catch her frowning reflection in it.

"What do you see?" she asks when I turn.

Home. That's what I want to say. I see the only place I've ever truly considered home. She'd grimace at that, so I only say, "We're in the Yukon."

There's no one in the seat beside her, and she leans to peer out her window for exactly two seconds before straightening with, "Trees."

"Yep," Dalton says. "That's what you get in a boreal forest."

She ignores him and opens her laptop to do some work. I think back to the first time I flew in. Even then, while I'd never consider myself outdoorsy, I'd been transfixed by the view. April has granted it only a fleeting glance, and with that, I'm five years old again, showing her an anthill or a turtle, waiting for a flicker of interest, and instead getting that two-second glance before she moves on.

We have a couple of hours before our connection to Dawson City, so I suggest popping into Whitehorse. Dalton's quick to agree— sitting in the tiny airport really isn't his idea of fun. April objects. It's only a two-hour wait. Leaving the airport is unwise. We'll need to go through security again. And really, what's the point?

"The point is that your sister wants a cookie," Dalton says. "And probably a cappuccino."

April stares, as if he's obviously kidding. He waves her to the exit and then prods her along, like a shepherd with a balking sheep.

I talk too much on the cab ride. I can't help it. I want April to see the incredible views and be stunned. To see the Yukon's "wilderness city" and be charmed. We go to the Alpine Bakery, and I know she's always been pro-organic, pro-natural foods, and I want her to be impressed at finding that here. I want her to get a cup of locally roasted coffee and a freshly baked cookie and relax.

Instead, she frets. Is it really safe to let the cab leave? Shouldn't we just grab my snack and go? My God, is that loaf of bread actually seven dollars?

"It's the north," I say. "Everything's expensive."

Dalton proceeds to buy a bag full of baked goods—bread and scones and cookies—and a few pounds of coffee. We get our snack and chat to an athletic senior couple who retired here after a chance visit. That is the story I hear, over and over, people who came to the Yukon for a work trip, for vacation, on a temporary placement, and never left.

The Yukon isn't an easy place to live—with long, dark winters that never seem to end—but it is a place that people *choose*. A place that seduces. I don't need my sister to be seduced, but I want her to see the magic. As Dalton and I talk to the couple, she picks at her scone and keeps checking her watch. We still have an hour to go— plenty of time for the five-kilometer drive to the airport and the nonexistent security line—but her anxiety is contagious and finally, with regret, I surrender to it.

The first time I came to Rockton, we drove from Whitehorse to Dawson City. Dalton and I have made that trip a couple of times since, when he needs supplies he can't get in Dawson. If he's picking up newcomers, he'll usually fly that leg, if only to avoid being in a car with a stranger for six hours. That's what we do today. We fly into the tiny Dawson airport, and then we head into the hangar, where our bush plane awaits.

"Are you going to be okay with a small plane?" I ask.

She stares, uncomprehending, and I remember my first walk to this hangar, when Dalton handed me a couple of pills. Mild antianxiety meds for the flight. The former town doctor had known my back- ground and sent the pills. I'd given Dalton a look not unlike April's, as I'd tried to figure out why anyone would think I needed medication.

"Your parents?" he'd said.

Because my parents died in a small plane crash. I'd been walking to a small plane without even thinking about that. Ashamed, I'd hur- ried to cover it up, to not be the cold bitch unaffected by the tragic death of her parents.

When April gives me that look, I realize she's not making the connection either. I won't make it for her. I won't put her through that discomfort. So I just say, "Bush planes aren't for everyone."

"If you're referring to Mom and Dad's crash, I am well aware of the statistical unlikelihood of perishing under the same circumstances. I am many times more likely to die in a car accident, and yet I don't see people swearing off motor vehicles when a loved one passes that way."

Sorry I mentioned it.

I want to mutter that, as I would have when I was young. Instead, I stick to my adult method of dealing with April: I ignore her.

As we fly, the noise of the plane makes conversation difficult. Dalton and I still manage it, mostly in gestures, him pointing out something in the forest or me doing the same. April doesn't say a word. By the time we touch down, I've forgotten she's even there, and I jump when she says, "Where are we?"

"Nowhere," I say. Then I grin at Dalton. "Everywhere."

April rolls her eyes. "I know I'm not supposed to ask for details. I simply didn't realize it was quite so . . ." A scrunch of her nose. "Remote."

"Yep," Dalton says. "That's why we warned you. No Wi-Fi. No cell service. We've got electricity, but it's strictly rationed."

"You'll be able to use whatever you need with Kenny, though," I say.

I haven't used his name before, and I expect her to comment. She only waits for the door to open.

As I help Dalton unload the plane, April wanders outside. I hear the thump of running footsteps and then a happy bark that makes me grin.

Storm must circle around April, wide enough that my sister doesn't notice a charging eight-month-old Newfoundland pup. The dog skids to a stop at my feet and dances with excitement until I give her the command. Then she jumps on me, front legs planted on my shoulders. After I hug her, she takes off to greet Dalton.

I step outside. April is about twenty feet away, at the edge of the clearing. I'm about to move away from the dark hangar when Anders jogs up behind April and pulls her into a hug.

"Didn't go well with your sister, huh?" he says.

April jumps like she's been knifed.

Anders falls back fast. "Shit. You're not . . ."

"Not the sister who allows strange men to hug her?" she snaps.

I jog out from the hanger.

"So you let strange men hug you?" Anders calls to me. "Guess that explains how you ended up with the sheriff."

I shake my head. "Will, this is my sister, April."

"Yeah, I figured that." He extends a hand. "Will Anders. Local deputy and the remaining third of the police force."

She gives his hand a perfunctory shake. Then she sees Storm and startles.

"Not a bear," Anders says. "Well, supposedly. Eric says she's some fancy purebred, but I'm still convinced someone conned our sheriff and sold him a black bear cub."

"She's a Newfoundland," I say, rubbing Storm's neck. "She's big, but she's well trained. You just need to watch out for flying fur and slobber."

"Isn't that . . ." April peers at her. "Didn't Aunt Becca's boyfriend have a dog like that?"

I light up in a grin. I can't help it. "He did. Nana—named after the Newfoundland in *Peter Pan*. I kinda fell in love with that dog, so Eric bought me this one."

She mutters something under her breath. It sounds like, "Of course, he did," but when I look up, she's only shaking her head.

"Her name's Storm," I say. "Because of . . ."

I rumple her white-streaked ear. April looks at me blankly.

"X-Men," Anders says. "Your sister is not afraid to let her geek flag fly. She's even got us playing D&D."

"Which was *your* idea," I say.

April stares at Anders. Admittedly, he is kind of stare-worthy. Her look, though, is pure confusion. If there's a stereotype of a guy who knows every rule in the D&D handbook, it is not Will Anders. He's six foot two, with a military buzz cut and a US Army tat on one bulging black bicep.

"Do you have an actual patient that I'm supposed to see?" April says finally.

"Casey and Will were waiting for me," Dalton says as he walks out of the hangar. "We have to sneak you into town, and I needed to put the plane to bed first. Now, let's talk about how we're going to do this."

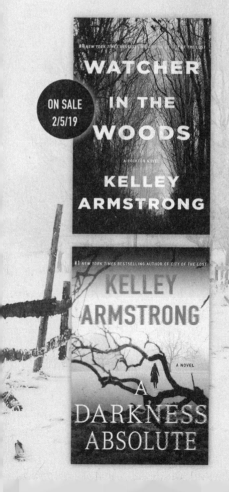

Woman
in the World
of Jesus

Evelyn
and
Frank Stagg

W THE WESTMINSTER PRESS
Philadelphia

Copyright © 1978 The Westminster Press

Scripture quotations from the Revised Standard Version of the Bible are copyrighted 1946, 1952, © 1971, 1973 by the Division of Christian Education of the National Council of the Churches of Christ in the U.S.A., and are used by permission.

First edition

Published by The Westminster Press ®
Philadelphia, Pennsylvania

PRINTED IN THE UNITED STATES OF AMERICA

9 8 7 6 5 4 3 2 1

Library of Congress Cataloging in Publication Data

Stagg, Evelyn, 1914–
  Woman in the world of Jesus.

  Bibliography: p.
  Includes index.
  1. Woman (Theology)—Biblical teaching.
  2. Jesus Christ—Attitude toward women.
  I. Stagg, Frank, 1911–   joint author
  II. Title
  BS2545.W65S72   261.8'34'12   77–28974
  ISBN 0–664–24195–6

Contents

Preface   7

Introduction   9

Part I: The World Into Which Jesus Came   13

Chapter 1: The Jewish World   15
Chapter 2: The Greek World   55
Chapter 3: The Roman World   79

Part II: Jesus and Woman   101

Chapter 4: The Manner of Jesus   102
Chapter 5: The Teaching of Jesus   126
Chapter 6: The Risen Christ and Woman   144

Part III: The Early Church and Woman   161

Chapter 7: Paul and Woman   162
Chapter 8: The Domestic Code and Woman   187
Chapter 9: Woman in the Synoptic Gospels
    and Acts   205
Chapter 10: Woman in the Johannine Writings   234

Conclusion   253

Continued

Notes   259

Bibliography   271

Index of Passages Cited   279

Index of Authors   291

Preface

This book is coauthored by husband and wife. It has been in the making for some years, with a serious move toward its actualization beginning in the fortieth year of their marriage (m. August 19, 1935). Design and research were a joint effort. Primary sources were read and reread independently and then assessed jointly as to relevance and meaning. Secondary sources were consulted freely but kept subordinate.

The first draft of the manuscript was articulated by the husband, tested unit by unit in joint review and revision. The final editing was the work of the wife, a major task requiring the judicious cutting of over two hundred pages of typescript. Demonstrations of perspectives on woman and her status reflected in the vast body of Jewish, Greek, and Roman literature could have been extended almost ad infinitum except for the realities of publication. It was her difficult task to achieve a proper tension between the ideals of research and the practical limits of publication.

Special acknowledgment is due Professors Marvin E. Tate, E. Glenn Hinson, and R. Alan Culpepper, colleagues who read a portion each of the manuscript and shared out of their knowledge and insights. Of course, they are not responsible for limitations remaining in the book; but it is a better book because of their help. Also, deep appreciation is expressed for the patient and careful work of Jewell R. Burke, who typed the manuscript.

EVELYN AND FRANK STAGG

Introduction

The title of this book looks two ways: to woman as perceived in the world Jesus entered and to woman as perceived in the world Jesus came to create. The first task necessarily is to probe as deeply as possible into that ancient world to see how woman fared in it. The basic concern behind the book is to understand the intention of Jesus for woman, in which light the past performance of the church may be tested and directions for today may be sought.

To understand people, we need to see not only where they stand but the direction in which they are moving. We need to see them in the community or world of which they are a part, including the cultural and religious patterns around them. This holds for Jesus, Paul, and all others. Is one found to be moving with or against the currents of the world? This book intends to be written from a Christian perspective, and it intends to inquire into three primary questions: (1) How did woman fare in the world before Jesus—in standing, as seen by others, and as seen by herself? (2) How did Jesus see woman and relate to her? (3) How did the early church see woman and relate to her?

The heart of the book is Jesus, or such is the intention of the authors. The book will, we hope, somehow reach beyond the church in its influence, but it is addressed to the church itself. Currently the church is being compelled by forces which will not play out and by voices which will not be silenced to reassess its own attitudes and practices. The book is offered on the assumption that the New Testament, in particular the tradition centering in Jesus himself, remains for Christians our basic and authoritative witness as under the living God we seek direction for today.

We are a part of the church which Jesus founded and which has from the first struggled to understand him and to follow him. By all evidence his radicality (radical refers to "roots"; Jesus went to the roots of religion and life) puzzled friends and foes and met with resistance from both. He was once bodily evicted from his home synagogue by a Sabbath congregation so threatened by him that it sought to kill him. His own family and intimate followers at times seem to have doubted his sanity or wisdom. Various power structures set aside their deep differences long enough to crucify him. The early church both followed and failed him. At best, most of the church seems never to have followed except "afar off."

Strikingly enough, the four canonical Gospels place women first, in particular Mary Magdalene, at the empty tomb and see them as the primary witness to the resurrection. The Gnostic Gospel According to Thomas goes so far in another direction that its closing lines read:

> Simon Peter said to them [the risen Jesus and his disciples]: Let Mary go out from among us, because women are not worthy of Life. Jesus said: See, I shall lead her, so that I will make her male, that she too may become a living spirit, resembling you males. For every woman who makes herself male will enter the Kingdom of Heaven. (The Gospel According to Thomas, Logion 114)[1]

Somewhere between the example and teaching of Jesus and this second-century Gnostic Gospel the church has struggled—all the way from "Whoever does the will of God is my mother, and my brother, and my sister" and "In Christ there is no male and female" to commands to wear veils and keep silence and "women are not worthy of life."

That Jesus meant to preserve the intention of the Law and the Prophets (the Old Testament) is explicit in the claims of Mt. 5: 17–20. That he intended to correct his heritage is likewise explicit in the claims of the six antitheses of Mt. 5:21–48. The radical correctives of Jesus to his religious heritage are apparent throughout the Gospels, and there should be no surprise that this holds for what he did for woman. The Christian hermeneutic which sees Jesus as both respectful of his heritage and exercising a lordship over it is both compelled by the New Testament and viable to the piety today which esteems and cherishes all Scripture yet worships Christ the Lord above all. By the same token, Jesus must be Lord over his church, the one by whom it is to be measured and corrected today.

PART I

The World Into Which Jesus Came

Jesus, "born of a woman, born under the Law" (Gal. 4:4), was born into a Jewish world. That world in turn was bound up with a larger world and had been so throughout its long history. The Judaism of which Jesus was a part had been for centuries in touch with the non-Jewish world from Egypt to Canaan, from Babylon to Rome: Egyptian (the Pharaohs), Canaanite, Babylonian, Persian, Greek, Egyptian again (Ptolemaic), Syrian, and Roman. Although ethnic, cultural, and religious identities are traceable, there was never such isolation that any one of these was sealed off from the others.

Jesus was born into a home of Jewish piety (cf. Lk. 1–2; Mt. 1–2). He participated customarily in the synagogue services of his people (Mk. 1:21; 3:1; 6:1f.; Lk. 4:16–30; *et passim*). He visited the Temple in Jerusalem many times, according to John's Gospel. He drew heavily from the Jewish scriptures, and he knew something of the oral tradition of the Jews (Mt. 15:2–20). He interacted with the piety and culture of Galilee, Judea, Samaria, and Decapolis. Although he seems to have had limited exposure beyond his Jewish world, his Jewish world itself was in significant interaction with the non-Jewish world.

The early church was cradled in Judaism, nurtured from its Scriptures, and worshiped in synagogues and the Temple in Jerusalem. The church soon penetrated the larger world, first through Jewish synagogues throughout the Mediterranean region and next through the inclusion of non-Jews in its fellowship. By the time the New Testament had been written, Christianity already had moved out into the larger, Gentile world and was itself becoming prevailingly Gentile. To understand New Testament perspectives on woman, it is necessary to consider both the differences within the following of Jesus and the nature of the larger world, both Jewish and non-Jewish, which was its matrix.

Chapter 1

THE
JEWISH WORLD

In seeking to isolate Jewish perspectives on woman, we shall study the Old Testament, the Jewish Apocrypha and Pseudepigrapha, the Dead Sea Scrolls, Philo of Alexandria, the first-century Jewish historian Josephus, and the Mishnah.

The Old Testament as we perceive it here is the Hebrew Scripture of ancient Judaism. This was foundational to its subsequent literature. It also was the first Bible of the earliest Christians. The Apocrypha and Pseudepigrapha must be included, but with certain cautions. They are Jewish writings, some pre-Christian and some reaching into the Christian era. These "outside books" do not represent "normative Judaism" any more than they represent "normative Christianity." But they do say something about those who produced them and those who preserved them.

The Dead Sea Scrolls belong incontestably to this study. These writings were sacred to a significant movement within the piety of Judaism in the time of Jesus. Although it is not proper to speak here or elsewhere of "normative Judaism," these writings are extremely significant. They were sufficiently precious to the community at Qumran that they were hidden in caves along the western shore of the Dead Sea, apparently to secure them from the oncoming Roman Tenth Legion as it swept through the Jordan valley in A.D. 68, fortunately to be recovered in 1947 and since. Inclusion of Philo and Josephus is not arbitrary. Philo is the chief extant source for the highly influential Hellenistic Judaism of Alexandria and a contemporary with Jesus. Philo did not speak for all Jews, but he spoke for some. On one occasion he led a powerful Jewish delegation to Rome in behalf of Jewish rights. Josephus is the

unparalleled Jewish historian of the first century, and his massive
works include some significant pronouncements about women.

The Mishnah poses a special problem. Because of its own claims
to preserve ancient Jewish traditions, it cannot be ignored. Yet,
because of inherent problems in the Mishnah, it must be used with
caution for any understanding of Judaism before A.D. 70.

There is no implication here that the total perspective or spirit
of a people is reflected in its extant literature. There is no way to
hear from all the people of any culture or religion of any period.
We do have extensive writings from ancient people, and they must
be heard. Furthermore, it is to be recognized that woman may have
fared better in actuality than would seem to be implied by the
literature of a given time. She may have commanded more respect
and affection than extant writings imply. Once more, there is no
implication that ancient perspectives have come down unmodified
among the heirs to ancient literature or tradition. To say no more,
the stability of the Jewish home and the highly favorable status of
the Jewish woman today are solid facts not to be forgotten in the
studies before us. Sometimes the people are ahead of their leaders,
and many women may have fared better in their world than in the
writings of their time.

THE OLD TESTAMENT

The status of woman in the Old Testament is not uniform, for
various perspectives are found there. The tension appears at the
outset in the distinct creation narratives of Genesis 1–2, and it is
traceable in both the private and the public life of woman. Over all
there is a decided male orientation and male bias, but never completely so or unchallenged by other motives.

The Creation Narratives

First of all, there are at least two creation narratives in Genesis,
woman having equality with man in one (1:24–30) but subordinated to man in the other (2:7–25). These two perspectives have
competed in both Judaism and Christianity, one or the other being

foundational in how woman is perceived. Since attitudes and life patterns for many to this day have their roots in these stories, they must be probed in depth at the outset of this work.

Scholars are generally agreed that the two stories derive from originally independent sources, a Priestly (P) account in 1:1–2:4a (and ch. 5) and a Yahwist (J) or Yahwist-Elohist (J-E) account in 2:4b–25.[1] The Priestly account in ch. 1 is thought to be later than the Yahwist account in ch. 2. It is thought that the J source received its present form around 950 B.C. and the E source a century or two later, whereas the P source grew out of the Babylonian exile and was composed around 538–450 B.C.[2] Apparently in the final redaction, the Priestly creation narrative is made a prologue not only to Genesis but to the whole Pentateuch or Hexateuch, this perspective being dominant at the time, at least for the Priestly school. That this perspective favorable to woman did not prevail in later Judaism or even in later Priestly circles does not negate the fact that at one important juncture, at least, there was a Jewish-Priestly view that accorded woman equal dignity with man.

Whatever may be said for these source theories, there are in fact two creation narratives in Genesis 1–5, with two distinct perspectives on woman. Whichever narrative is made foundational has far-reaching implications for all one's understanding of the origin, rights, responsibilities, and roles of woman. We shall see later that Jesus built upon the creation narrative of ch. 1 (borrowing from the "rib" narrative only 2:24, itself possibly an appendix to the narrative in ch. 2 and clearly dignifying woman), whereas Paul and other followers built upon the narrative in ch. 2. It is thus extremely important to compare the two stories as options confronting Jesus, his early followers, and also us.

Many attempts have been made to disprove any subordination of woman to man in the story in Genesis 2. One of the highly cogent interpretations is that of Phyllis Tribble, who finds woman in the story fully man's equal and in a sense actually superior.[3] She may be correct, but the exegesis seems forced. Woman, indeed, is esteemed in the story, and there is no apparent intention of putting her down. Woman is intelligent and free to make decisions, and she

exercises more initiative than man, however misdirected. But in
this story, man does have priority. He is created first, and woman
is created from him and for him. Although negative implications
far beyond its intention have been read into the story, no sound
exegesis can overcome the priority it gives man. Were the story
reversed, man created second and as a helper to woman, is it likely
that it would be seen as egalitarian?

In this story, God first made man (Gen. 2:7) and later made all
the lower animals and finally woman to relieve man's aloneness
and to be a helper or companion to him (v. 18). This is the rib
narrative, in which woman was made from a rib taken from the
side of man (vs. 21–22). In v. 23 she is called "woman" (*'ishshah*)
because she was taken out of man (*'ish*). Even in the assonance of
the Hebrew terms employed here woman is subordinated to man,
just as the English word "woman" is derived from "man"—"wif-
man" in Old English (see any standard English dictionary). The
same male bias is reflected in the English word "female," a word
dependent upon the prior word "male." It is difficult to find any
language free of such male bias.

The story in Gen. 2:7–25 probably intends to explain the powerful drive of the sexes toward each other, a drive stronger than that
which binds one to father and mother and which is not fulfilled
until the two again become "one flesh" (v. 24).[4] Westermann sees
Gen. 2:24 as an appendix to the Yahwistic creation narrative,
added as "an aetiological explanation of the attraction of the sexes
for each other, which brings about separation from home and
parents."[5] He sees the verse as concerned to show the power
wielded by "the basic longing and searching for each other by those
who are in love." He adds, "The strongest bonds, even those binding one to one's parents' house, are loosed by this power."[6]

There may be a trace here of an earlier time of matriarchal
culture, for it is said that a man leaves father and mother and
cleaves to his wife.[7] In patriarchal Israel the pattern was the reverse. Normally the woman left her parents to live with her husband or his family. Although a trace of an earlier matriarchal
pattern may thus be reflected here, the concern of the passage is
otherwise. The story is etiological, i.e., concerned to answer a

question, here the question of "the extremely powerful drive of the sexes to each other."⁸

Although the rib narrative subordinates woman to man, even it holds out some corrective in its reference to marriage. In marriage *"they* become one flesh" (2:24).⁹ Yet a trace of subordination lingers, for this is the union of "the man" *(hā'ādhām)* and his wife *('ishtō).* It is not "the woman" and her husband. Thus in this creation narrative, woman is second to man, created for him as his helper. They are equal, but to paraphrase George Orwell's *Animal Farm,* "He is more equal than she."

In the creation narrative of Gen. 1:26–30 there is no subordination, unless this be inferred from the listing of "male" before "female" in v. 27. In v. 26 the Hebrew term *'ādhām* is used generically, for male and female or "the human race." It is not a proper name for an individual, as in 5:3.¹⁰ Both are created together: "male and female he created them." Sexual distinction is here seen as a creation of God. This is of far-reaching implication. Gen. 1:27, "he created *them,*" excludes the idea that man originally was created "androgynous," i.e., one self as both male and female, only later to be divided into separate sexes.¹¹ In this Priestly story, both sexes are created simultaneously. In this perspective, "man," i.e., the human being, was created heterosexual, male and female; and they were so created as to find fulfillment in relationship with each other. The complementary nature of the relationship is original to humankind in the Priestly narrative.

The concept of "the image of God" (Gen. 1:26–27; 5:1f.) looks two ways, for it says something about God as well as about humanity. The Priestly narrative consistently has it that it was as "male and female" that "man" was created in the likeness or image of God. The concept of "image of God" does not appear in the rib story. The Priestly narrative implies femininity in God as much as masculinity—no more and no less. It is as "male and female" that "man" is in the image of God. One may ask, What does it mean to ascribe femininity to God? The obvious answer is, Exactly what it means to ascribe masculinity to God. Scripture does not discuss or even explicitly consider the "sexuality" of God, and it is precarious for us to do so. One does not have to think of God as "androgynous"; neither does one need to supply some female deity to balance a male deity. It is enough to hold that, according to the Priestly narrative, "male and female" belong equally and originally to humanity and that something in God himself has provided both femininity and masculinity to the only creature made in his likeness or image.

The Priestly story of creation is concerned with the human commission as well as origin. Both "male and female" are created in the image of God, and in that relationship both are assigned "dominion" over all else that God has made (Gen. 1: 26–30). The commission to "be fruitful and multiply" and to "have dominion" over all else in creation is given "to them" jointly. The Hebrew imperatives are second person plural, as male and female are addressed. Dominion presumably is to be exercised as God exercises it, creatively and not exploitively or destructively.

The Priestly narrative continues in Genesis 5, where again it is affirmed, "Male and female he created them, and he blessed them and named them Man when they were created" (v. 2). Adam here becomes a proper name (v. 3), but the basic idea of the creation of "Man" as male and female is retained.

It is not implied here that the perspective of the Priestly account in Gen. 1:27–2:4a prevails in the Pentateuch, much less in the Old Testament as a whole. It did not prevail among later priests, who became less prophetic in function and increasingly cultic, excluding women from priestly service, although women had participated in such prophetic and judicial ministries as belonged originally to the priesthood. Even ch. 5, which preserves the nonsubordinating perspective "he created them male and female" (v. 2), proceeds to give a male-oriented genealogy (vs. 3–32). Fathers and their firstborn sons are featured, with the recurrent "other sons and daughters" following as an addendum. No mention is made of the wives of the men (Adam, Seth, Enosh, *et al.*), and the daughters remain nameless (as do sons other than the firstborn).[12]

The Decalogue

The Decalogue in Exodus 20 (and Deut. 5:7–21) may further serve to illustrate that the male-oriented perspective tended to dominate in the Old Testament, despite the prominence given the nonsubordinating Priestly story. The male orientation of the Ten Commandments is seen in their being addressed to the male (in part due to the almost universal male orientation of language itself, a phenomenon not without significance). Hebrew verbs and pronouns in second person masculine singular make this clear, as in "your God" (Ex. 20:2). On the other hand, the Fourth Commandment makes no distinction between honor to be given "your father and your mother" (v. 12). This high respect for mothers as well as for fathers is maintained throughout the Old Testament. However, except for v. 12, the Decalogue is male-oriented throughout. A man is not to covet any of his neighbor's property—house, wife, male or female slave, ox or ass, or "anything that is his neighbor's" (v. 17; also Deut. 5:21). In this perspective, wife along with other properties belongs to her husband. It apparently never occurred to anyone to warn wives: "Do not covet your neighbor-woman's husband, ox, or ass." The commandment about the Sabbath involves daughters and maidservants, but even here the commandment is addressed to man.

Spoils of Battle

Male orientation and double standard are inescapable in the account of Moses' orders with respect to conquered Midianites: "Now therefore, kill every male among the little ones, and kill every woman who has known man by lying with him. But all the young girls who have not known man by lying with him, keep alive for yourselves" (Num. 31:17f.). In Deuteronomy, the recognized spoils of battle included beautiful women: "When you go forth to war against your enemies . . . and see among the captives a beautiful woman, and you have desire for her and would take her for yourself as wife . . ." (Deut. 21:10f.). The Hebrew soldier was permitted to keep her, but if later he had no delight in her he could release her but not sell her for money, for he had "humiliated her" (v. 14). If a man raped a virgin, he must pay the father fifty shekels of silver and take her as wife with no right to divorce her, "because he had violated her" (22:29).

Veils and Seclusion

Although there developed a strict practice of secluding women by veils and confinement to the house (never absolute), there was an earlier period when girls were not veiled and when they moved freely in public life, looking after sheep (Gen. 29:6), drawing water (Gen. 24:13; 1 Sam. 9:11), gleaning in the fields (Ruth 2:2f.), visiting in other houses (Gen. 34:1), and talking with men (Gen. 24: 15–21; 29:11f.; 1 Sam. 9:11–13).[13]

The Family

It was within the family that the women in Israel were most honored and influential. Although the Decalogue included a man's wife among his possessions, she gained great respect and influence upon the birth of her first child, especially if it was a boy (Gen. 16:4; 29:31–30:24).[14] Even here much is left to be desired, for the mother's status was something earned through providing an heir and not something already there by virtue of her personhood. On the other hand, it is not to be overlooked that there were barren wives who were loved and respected by their husbands and the community despite their barrenness. Proverbs 1:8 admonishes a son not to reject his mother's teaching. Proverbs 31:10–31 eulogizes the ideal wife, even though her recognized role was one of hard labor for her family, beginning before daybreak each day. This high respect for woman as mother, with the negative factors just observed, seems to be maintained consistently in Israel.

There is no more beautiful story in the Old Testament than that of Ruth. Here her role is the traditional one of wife, and the story is male-oriented to its closing lines, an all-male family lineage (Ruth 4:18–22). Throughout the story Ruth and Naomi are esteemed and loved, presented with tenderness and respect. Nonetheless, the male orientation remains. It is explicit in the blessing given by "the people who were at the gate, and the elders" (4:11a). The blessing is in three parts: (1) upon the woman who is coming into Boaz' house "like Rachel and Leah, who together built up the house of Israel"; (2) upon Boaz, that he may prosper and be renowned in Bethlehem; and (3) upon the house of Boaz, that it be blessed with children (4:11b–12). This is not to rob the story of its beauty. It is to observe that even in the tenderest of scenes, male domination remains.[15]

The high regard in which mothers were held is reflected in Isaiah's use of a mother's love for her child as a model for God's unfailing love for his people (Isa. 49:15; 66:13).

Not to be overlooked is The Song of Solomon, in which the love of a man and a woman for each other is expressed with fullest freedom and intensity. The woman's love is as intense and impassioned as the man's. Without a trace of embarrassment, each describes the beauty of the other's body and craves it. It is not mere sensuality, but the sensual is affirmed by each as good. Man and woman are equal in this poem, and to reduce it to allegory, as has been done, is arbitrary and with no support from the book itself.

In regard to marriage, divorce, and penalties for adultery, it is difficult to escape the conclusion that the subordination of woman as in the rib narrative of creation (Gen. 2:7–25) prevailed over the equality of "male and female" implied in the Priestly narrative of Genesis 1:27–30. It seems that it was customary for parents to arrange the marriage of their children, often at a very early age, with little choice left to sons or daughters. There are some instances in which the personal rights of a daughter were respected. For example, Abraham sent his servant to his kinspeople to find a wife for Isaac, and he selected Rebekah (Gen. 24), but her wishes were not ignored. Her brother Laban and their widowed mother consented, but they left the final decision to Rebekah. It is said of Reuel, a Midianite priest, that "he gave Moses his daughter Zipporah" (Ex. 2:21). Either she was not consulted or the story is telescoped. However, there is no ambiguity as to Caleb's bargaining off his daughter without according her the freedom to choose or give consent. Caleb promised: "Whoever smites Kiriath-sepher, and takes it, to him will I give Achsah my daughter as wife" (Josh. 15:16).

Beyond betrothal, the marriage relationship normally was biased in favor of the male. A bride, if challenged, must submit proof of her virginity at the time of her marriage, but no such requirement was considered for the groom (cf. Deut. 22:13–21). If a bride's virginity was not established, the townspeople were to take her to her father's door and there stone her to death for her "crime against Israel" (v. 21). Adultery was a crime against a husband's rights, so if a man were caught having relations with another man's wife, both were to be stoned (v. 22).

The double standard favoring the husband over the wife was acute in "the law in cases of jealousy" (Num. 5:11–31). Even where there was no prior proof of her infidelity, a wife could be put to a cultic test (supposedly able to validate or invalidate her faithfulness!) in cases where "the spirit of jealousy" came upon a husband (vs. 14, 30). She was "under her husband's authority" (vs. 19, 29). There was no comparable "law of jealousy" to protect the suspecting wife. The double standard appears further in the rule that a woman is rendered unclean twice as long for giving birth to a girl as to a boy (Lev. 12:2, 5). Though it is not explained, presumably the newborn girl was thought to be defiled by her mother and to be herself a defiling agent.

By Deuteronomic law a husband could divorce his wife, although there was no agreement among subsequent interpreters as to the grounds for it. The ambiguous cause cited is that there be found in the wife "some indecency" (Deut. 24:1). "Some indecency" could be construed as anything from burning the bread to adultery. It may be argued that the intention in divorce initially was to give some measure of protection to a wife, at least giving her legal release from obligations to her husband. However, divorce did operate in terms of male bias, whatever the original intention. Even the restrictions upon a husband's power to divorce a wife were male-oriented, concessions that only modified male domination. For example, on two grounds a man forfeited forever any right to divorce a woman: if he falsely accused an innocent wife of unchastity (22:13–19), or if he forced a virgin. In the latter case he was required to pay the father fifty shekels of silver, marry the girl, and "he may not put her away all his days" (vs. 28f.).

On the happier side, although there was clear provision for divorce in the Old Testament, it must not be overlooked that there was also a strong protest against it.[16] The strong statement in Malachi is not isolated, but represents a deep current in ancient Israel: "Let none be faithless to the wife of his youth. 'For I hate divorce, says the LORD the God of Israel' " (Mal. 2:15f.). This positive view is reflected today in the stability of Jewish marriages.

In the Old Testament, marriage was originally monogamous (cf. Gen. 2:21–24; 7:7) but moved from Lamech's two wives (Gen. 4:19) to Solomon's vast harem (1 Kings 11:1–3). The most common marriage pattern in Israel was monogamous, but many men had as many wives and concubines as they could support. There is no record of an Israelitess with two or more husbands at a time.[17]

The laws of inheritance favored the male. Daughters inherited only where there was no male heir (Job 42:13–15 is exceptional), as in the case of the daughters of Zelophehad (Num. 27:1–8); but even here, should these daughters marry outside their father's tribe, the inheritance would revert to their father's tribe (36:1–9). A widow did not inherit in her own right. A childless widow had two options: remaining in her husband's family through levirate marriage (Deut. 25:5–10) or returning to her father (Gen. 38:11; Lev. 22:13; Ruth 1:8).[18]

Inequities

Inequity between male and female obtained even in the matter of slavery. In the ancient world, slavery was widely practiced. Among pagans in the Greco-Roman world, a slave possessed no rights at all. The owner had absolute authority over the slave as his property. In Israel, there were controls, and a Hebrew slave was granted basic human rights, with some traces of a dual standard between male and female. A Hebrew male slave was automatically freed after serving six years, but a female came under a different set of rules (Ex. 21:1–11). A man could sell his daughter as a slave (v. 7). She was protected against various abuses (vs. 8–11), but there was no provision for her automatic release after serving for six years.

There are records of a most degrading use of a daughter by her father or a wife by her husband. On one occasion, a Levite from Ephraim recovered his concubine from Bethlehem, and on the way home he found hospitality for the night in Gibeah (Judg. 19). The gruesome story of his using his concubine to protect himself defies imagination. (See also Judg. 21:12, 21 for the fate of over four hundred virgins captured to replenish the Benjaminites.)

The using of Abishag in a futile attempt to generate heat in the dying body of David is told matter-of-factly (1 Kings 1:1–4). To the contemporaries the procedure seemed to pose no problem. In fact, this probably was seen as a sign of honor and power for the girl, a perspective more problematic today. Even Abraham used Sarah his wife to shield himself from what he thought was danger to his life, twice passing her off as his sister, thus letting another man have her on loan (Gen. 12:10–20; 20). There is some evidence for a recognized practice of calling one's wife one's sister (cf. S. of Sol. 4:9–5:2), but the story implies that Abraham was not offering Sarah a higher protective role but was seeking to deceive for his own safety.

Stereotype

Prevalent in the ancient literature is the stereotype of woman in unbecoming character, and roles often stigmatized with an epithet. Infidelity to God is to be an adulteress, not an adulterer. Epithets abound such as "the loose woman" and her "smooth words" (Prov. 2:16; 5:3), "noisy" and "wanton" (9:13), "contentious" (21:9, 19; 25:24). A beautiful woman without discretion is "like a gold ring in a swine's snout" (11:22). A contentious woman is "a continual dripping on a rainy day" (27:15). It is assumed that women are cowardly or full of fear. Egyptians are scorned when it is said that they "will be like women, and tremble with fear" (Isa. 19:16; cf. Jer. 50:37; 51:30). Abimelech's male chauvinism comes out when, upon being mortally wounded by a woman who dropped an upper millstone on his head, he asked his armor-bearer to kill him, lest men say, "A woman killed him" (Judg. 9:54). On the other hand, a woman could be of "good understanding and beautiful" (1 Sam. 25:3), and it was "a wise woman" who counseled Joab (2 Sam. 20:16).

Public Roles

Although the Old Testament is prevailingly male-oriented, this never becomes absolute. Recurrently, it is a woman who emerges in a time of crisis to lead and preserve Israel. Even in normal times, various public roles were open to women in Israel: judges, prophetesses, queens, army commanders, and worship leaders. These appear, but no priestesses in Israel! Why?

Moses was spared as a baby through the devotion, courage, and wisdom of his mother and sister. The prophetess Miriam, Aaron's sister, led all the women in a celebration of Israel's deliverance at the Red Sea, and her brief song belongs to the hymnody of the Old Testament (Ex. 15:20f.). Even Miriam failed to escape an apparent discrimination, for she was singled out for suffering (became leprous and banished from the camp for seven days) when she and Aaron rebuked Moses (Num. 12).

"Woman power" emerged as Deborah, prophetess and judge in Israel, summoned and commanded Barak and, with the assistance of the woman Jael, delivered the Israelites from the Canaanite general Sisera; and the song of Deborah has a major place in the hymnody of Israel (Judg. 4–5). Mixed in with the glorification of Deborah is a further reflection of the exploitation of woman as the mother of Sisera speculates as to why her son was not returned from battle: "Are they not finding and dividing the spoil?—a maiden or two for every man?" (5:30). Athaliah, mother of Judah's king Ahaziah, ruled for six years in the place of her son following his death, albeit with high-handed methods for which she was hated (2 Kings 11). The prophetess Huldah was sought out for her counsel by Hilkiah the priest and the king's ministers and she was a major force in Jewish reforms (2 Kings 22:14–19). King Saul appealed to a woman medium of Endor for help in a time of crisis (1 Sam. 28:7–25). Isaiah was married to a prophetess (Isa. 8:3).

The Book of Esther

The book of Esther claims special attention. Probably a late writing, it embodies some strong perspectives both favorable and unfavorable to woman. Its intention clearly is to glorify Esther as savior of Israel in dire crisis. Male bias appears in a setting that seems to be totally oblivious to that bias. Alongside the leitmotiv, the woman Esther as savior of Israel, is another strong motive: the subordination of woman to man, including unquestioning obedience of a wife to her husband.

The book is much debated as to origin and date, critical judgments ranging from the late Persian period to the Hellenistic (second or third centuries B.C.).[19] It does not attribute its motives to God. In fact, it contains no mention of God and is secular throughout. Scholars debate its intention, whether historical, fictional, or historical novel. Whatever its origin or intention, problems outside the task of this study, the book did find a secure place in the canon for Jews and Christians (but it alone of Old Testament writings is not found among the Dead Sea Scrolls), and it does reflect the perspectives on woman of some significant community. It is a part of the world Jesus entered.

Ahasuerus (Xerxes), who reigned from India to Ethiopia, made a six-month feast for all the princes, army chiefs, and other power figures of the empire, followed by a seven-day feast for the people of Susa, the capital. All was lavish, as this worldly king was showing off all the worldly splendor of his kingdom. On the seventh day of the feast, when the king's heart was merry with wine, he thought of yet another status symbol in his lavish holdings: his beautiful wife, the Queen Vashti! He summoned her to his banquet in order to have her display her beauty to his drunken guests. Vashti did the unpardonable: she disobeyed her husband's orders. She is the bad girl of the story for refusing to be exhibited before drinking men as a sex object. The king called in the "wise men who knew the times" (Esth. 1:13), and their consensus was that Vashti must be punished, "for this deed of the queen will be made known to all women, causing them to look with contempt upon their husbands" (v. 17). Vashti's position must be given to another, since all women are to give honor to their husbands, high and low (vs. 19–20).

Esther replaced Vashti as queen, but only after a yearlong elimination beauty contest throughout the empire. The rest of the story is its chief point: how Esther's influence over the king saved her stepfather Mordecai and all the Jews from the schemes of the wicked Haman and turned the tables on him.

As to perspectives on woman, the story is unambiguous. Vashti is bad because she will not obey her husband's orders to exhibit her beauty in public. The issue was closed: a wife must unquestionably obey her husband. Esther is the good woman and the heroine. She let her physical beauty be exploited for the king's sensual pleasure and vanity, and she used it as bargaining power in saving her people, enabling them to slaughter thousands instead of being slaughtered.

No Priestess in Israel

There is not a trace of a priestess in Israel. Two facts make this striking: (1) there were priestesses alongside priests in the ancient pagan world and (2) women in Israel were recognized in such major public roles as prophetess, judge, ruler, and hymnodist. Why exclusion from this one role? What impingement does this have on present-day understandings and patterns for ministry? Are criteria that had developed long ago for "sacred" rites that were performed around an altar by "holy" men now imposed upon Christian ministry that has its center elsewhere?

According to a widely held view, the exclusion of women from the priesthood in Israel may have been due to the long struggle between Yahwism and the fertility religions. It is theorized that the presence of sacred prostitutes in the fertility cults could have prejudiced the case for priestesses in the worship of Yahweh. There are complications to consider in this theory. In the fertility religions there were not only gods and goddesses and priests and priestesses; there were also both male and female prostitutes. The fertility cults were concerned with the ongoing of life: children, animal offspring, and crops. Baal (god of rain, storm, and fertility) emerged as one of the most powerful of the gods, and he was the arch foe to Mot (god of drought and death). Anath was sister-consort to Baal. In the fertility religions males, divine and human, were as deeply involved as females. So it is not apparent how the exclusion of priestesses in Israel would of itself overcome the threat of the fertility cults. In all likelihood, the struggle with the fertility religions did have something to do with the exclusion of women from priestly roles in Judaism, but probably there were other motivating factors.

A possible clue to one factor in the exclusion of woman from the Jewish priesthood is menstruation.[20] The menstrual period rendered a woman "unclean" and rendered "unclean" everything she touched (Lev. 15:19–33). This of itself could exclude a woman from the priesthood, since she would be "unclean" for about one fourth of the time. This is not a line of evidence that can be documented, but it is plausible and accords with perspectives and practices relating to "holiness" codes. Other ministries—the prophetic, judging, ruling—were on another basis. Divine calling, personal gifts, moral and ethical concern, and competence for the task were the criteria for other ministries. Women in Israel participated in these ministries, even if in a limited sense. The priesthood gravitated toward shrine-centered or altar-centered cultic concerns, more so in later than earlier years. "Defilement" could occur apart from moral, ethical, or attitudinal considerations. To touch the wrong thing or wrong person, or to experience an emission or a flow of blood could render one "unclean." Men were vulnerable to many "defilements," but women were even more vulnerable because of their "period" and because of childbirth, the latter defiling for a mother but not for a father.

There is clear evidence that once a major function of the priests in Israel was the teaching of the Law, their function around the altars gaining force later. In Deuteronomy, roles of teacher and judge are assigned to the Levitical priests (Deut. 17:8f.; 21:5). Teaching and ritual service appear side by side in a commission given to Levi: "They shall teach Jacob thy ordinances, and Israel thy law; they shall put incense before thee, and whole burnt offering upon thy altar" (33:10). Second Chronicles looks back upon a time when priests were teachers, bemoaning the loss: "For a long

time Israel was without the true God, and without a teaching
priest, and without law" (2 Chron. 15:3). Malachi is witness to the
function of the priest as medium of revelation and as teacher: "For
the lips of a priest should guard knowledge, and men should seek
instruction from his mouth, for he is the messenger of the LORD
of hosts" (Mal. 2:7). He rebukes the priests before him for failing
the people in this responsibility (v. 8). The same tradition appears
in Jeremiah: "For the law shall not perish from the priest, nor
counsel from the wise, nor the word from the prophet" (Jer. 18:18).
A shift toward a ritual emphasis alongside teaching appears in
instructions to Aaron: "You are to distinguish between the holy
and the common, and between the unclean and the clean; and you
are to teach the people of Israel all the statutes which the LORD
has spoken to them by Moses" (Lev. 10:10f.). Increasingly, priestly
duties gravitated to the altar: "And you shall attend to the duties
of the sanctuary and the duties of the altar, that there be wrath no
more upon the people of Israel" (Num. 18:5). Whereas there were
many shrines and altars, centralizing forces eventually turned all
cultic worship to one central shrine in Jerusalem (cf. Deut. 12:
5–14).

The Qumran community was both priestly-dominated and
Torah-centered. The founder was known as "the Teacher of Righ-
teousness." The most significant remains from this community are
the scrolls recovered from surrounding caves. These Jewish priests
yet saw themselves as mediums of revelation and as teachers of the
Law. Their chief rivals in the teaching role were the Pharisees, a
lay-oriented movement concerned to apply the Law to the whole
of Israel, bringing all Israel under cultic regulations for holiness.[21]
The Pharisees ruled against women teachers, and their code of
holiness would certainly be adverse to any idea of a woman priest.
Women had been excluded from the priesthood before the
Pharisaic rise to power, but the Pharisees' bias could only confirm
a pattern already set.

Both the increasing emphasis upon priestly ministry in relationship with altars and cultic holiness and the Pharisaic thrust would
make it increasingly difficult for woman to be admitted to the
priestly role. The prophetic-teaching-judging roles of earlier times

were open to some women. But women in Israel were kept at a distance from the center of holiness (as at the Temple, where women were denied access to the court of the Jewish men, the Holy Place, and the Holy of Holies). Menstruation and childbearing belong to the rationale that excluded them. In a man's world, a woman's period has, indeed, been her curse.

The above may bear upon the present-day question of "women in ministry." Exclusion of a woman from "ordination" to a pulpit-pastoral or other "Torah"-oriented ministry simply because she is a woman may well be an unwitting application of priestly-ritual practices of the past. To a Word-oriented ministry women in Israel were admitted long before "holiness' was concentrated at a central shrine and preserved by cultic rituals. Jesus rejected all cultic criteria for purity, internalizing clean and unclean in terms of the moral, ethical, personal. It compounds confusion not only to set aside Jesus' criteria for purity, but, in the case of a woman, to impose the cultic-priestly rules of a time now past upon the prophetic-teacher role of ministering the Word of God. Is the church today imposing upon women the cultic, ritual "holiness" code for altar-centered priestly ministry even where the ministry now under consideration is Word-centered and person-centered? If so, this may well be an "Olympic" record in ecclesiastical *non sequitur.*

THE APOCRYPHA AND PSEUDEPIGRAPHA

There were current in the time of Jesus many Jewish writings that finally were excluded from the Hebrew Bible when its canon was closed sometime after the destruction of Jerusalem in A.D. 70. These writings were then banned by the rabbis, and it was through Christians that many of them survived. Some of these writings are commonly ascribed to Pharisees. Neusner challenges the ascription of Pharisaic origin to any of these writings, holding it to rest on "shaky assumptions."[22] But it is unwarranted to dismiss this body of literature out of hand.[23] The problem of origin is compounded by the fact that fragments of some of these writings were found among the Dead Sea Scrolls (presumably belonging to Qumranite Essenes), including fragments of Tobit, Ecclesiasticus, the Epistle of Jeremiah, Jubilees, Enoch, and the Testaments of the Twelve Patriarchs.[24] They also leave some recognizable traces in the New Testament (cf. 1 Peter 3:19f.; 2 Peter 2:4; Jude 9f., to cite the most obvious).

Second Maccabees

In 2 Maccabees, written in the century before the birth of Jesus, is the story of the martyrdom of seven brothers and their mother, slain by order of the Syrian king Antiochus Epiphanes (2 Macc. 7). These were among the most honored in the Jewish piety which resisted Syrian tyranny. Offered their freedom if they would only eat the swine's flesh set before them, they accepted torture and death rather than violate their laws or their conscience. The sons were strong, but the mother was yet stronger, unflinching in the face of martyrdom and sustaining her sons in their trial. The story clearly intends to praise this noble woman. It also betrays an apparently unconscious male chauvinism: "Full of noble spirit and nerving her weak woman's heart with the courage of a man, she exhorted each of them [her sons]" (7:21).[25] Even a woman's courage must here be construed as "manly."

The Book of Judith

Written probably earlier but not later than the beginning of the first century of the Christian era, the Book of Judith is in two parts. The first part pictures a national crisis as Israel is threatened by the Assyrian king Nebuchadnezzar and his general Holofernes. Backed by a vast army of infantry and cavalry, Holofernes appeared about to bring Jerusalem to its knees in surrender. The second part is about Judith, widow of Manasses, who volunteered her service and promised to deliver her nation from the Assyrians. The leaders at Jerusalem put the fate of the whole nation in her hands, not even requiring that she divulge her plan. She overcame Holofernes with her beauty, taking care all the while discreetly to preserve her purity and piety, even to the extent of eating only her own clean food and rejecting that of the Assyrians. Having gotten

Holofernes drunk, she cut off his head and escaped with it. Upon
discovering their beheaded general, the Assyrians fled in panic and
disarray. The Jews were saved and the high priest personally
blessed Judith (15:8). Obviously, the writer sensed no problem in
the fact that it is as a sex object that Judith brings about the
downfall of Holofernes and his army. The book closes with a song
of praise, sung by Judith and all the people. It includes these lines:

> The Almighty Lord brought them [the Assyrians] to nought
>   by the hand of a woman.
> For their mighty one did not fall by young men,
> Neither did sons of the Titans smite him,
> Nor did high giants set upon him:
> But Judith the daughter of Merari made him weak
>   with the beauty of her countenance
>
>   (Judith 16:6–7).

The Book(s) of Adam and Eve

This work is Jewish in origin and from the first century of the
Christian era,[26] probably before the destruction of the Temple in
A.D. 70.[27] Its present form contains some Christian interpolations.
It is strongly ascetic, possibly Gnostic. It relates evil primarily to
lust (*Vita* xix.3). Eve assumes the full blame for sin and its consequences upon everyone (iii.1; xviii.1, *et passim*). Paradise was
segregated before the Fall, one section for males and one for
females (xxxii). (This makes one wonder how Eve then could have
influenced Adam's fall.) Celibacy is essential to saintliness. Eve is
consistently subordinated to Adam. Not only was it she who first
fell into sin, but she was less effective than Adam in penitence.
Adam anticipated this in saying, "Thou canst not do so much as
I, but do only so much as thou hast strength for" (vi.1). Eve was
supposed to tremble in the presence of her husband, and the
archangel Joel reminded Adam of his authority: "Thus saith the
Lord; I did not create thy wife to command thee, but to obey; why
art thou obedient to thy wife?" (*Slavonic Vita* xxxii.1).

The Book of Enoch

This is probably the most influential of the pre-Christian pseudepigrapha. It is composite, representing many authors and periods of time, with no unity in its teaching. One of its best-known passages is chs. 6–11, a story of the fall of angels, who defiled themselves with women, thus producing a race of giants. The "Watchers of heaven" are severely denounced for having "left the high, holy, and eternal heaven, and lain with women," thus having "defiled" themselves with "the daughters of men" (15:3). There seems to be a clear allusion to the Book of Enoch in Jude 6, "the angels which left their own habitation," and in 1 Peter 3:19–21 and 2 Peter 2:4f. Paul's concern that women be veiled when they pray or prophesy was somehow "because of the angels" (1 Cor. 11:10). This probably is a reflection of the idea found in Enoch that the angels were vulnerable to the beauty of woman and that an un-veiled woman would be an inviting target. The veil was a symbol of the husband's authority over his wife and its absence would imply her availability to another.

The Sibylline Oracles

On the positive side for recognizing woman in a dominant role is the ancient work known as the Sibylline Oracles. As it stands, the work is a composite of old and new oracles compiled by Jewish and Christian writers between about 160 B.C. and the fifth century of the Christian era or later.[28] The sybils, of course, were women. The Sibylline Oracles exercised considerable influence upon early Christians as well as Jews. Augustine had no trouble believing that the Erythraean (or Cumaean) sibyl prophesied in the times of the founding of Rome (or at the time of the Trojan War): "This sibyl of Erythrae certainly wrote some things concerning Christ."[29] He further asserted, "We might even think she ought to be reckoned among those who belong to the city of God."[30]

The name "sibyl" seems to be from the Greek *sibylla,* meaning "the counsel of God." The Greek components seem to be *sios,* the ancient Aeolian and Dorian spelling for *theos* (God), and *boulē* (counsel). It was not uncommon in various ancient cultures to believe that divine oracles were spoken through old women (cf. the woman of Endor, who, according to 1 Sam. 28:7–25, conjured up Samuel to speak to King Saul).

Although a low view of woman is traceable in much of the ancient world, there is this solid evidence of a recognition in the pre-Christian and early Christian Greco-Roman world that woman could be the medium of divine revelation, "a prophetess of the Mighty God" (*Sibyl. Ora.* III.818; IV.4–6). The extensive influence of the sibyl (or sibyls) attests to this. Augustine had such high regard for the sibyl of Erythrae that he even credited her with having employed some centuries before the birth of Jesus the acrostic on *ichthus* (the Greek word for "fish"), meaning "Jesus Christ the Son of God, the Savior."[31] Augustine had an extremely low or even vulgar view of sex,[32] yet he had no difficulty in seeing woman as capable of the highest service of God. He is not alone in this positive affirmation of woman alongside much that subordinated her to man. The very production of the Sibylline Oracles by Jews and Christians and their preservation attest to this. Recurrently in Judaism a woman may be a prophetess (as in early Christianity) but not a priestess. Strangely enough, cultic-priestly criteria tended to crowd woman out from the prophetic function too.

THE DEAD SEA SCROLLS

The scrolls recovered from eleven caves along the west bank of the Dead Sea since 1947 do not contain much that speaks explicitly to the subject of woman. This in itself may be significant. They are free of misogyny and seem not deliberately to denigrate woman. Possibly their strongest negative witness is to the near-dispensability of woman from their community and certainly from the holy wars of liberation which they anticipated. Expected was a glorious future triumph over their wicked enemies, achieved through a holy army of men from which were to be excluded all boys, women, and the physically imperfect, as is spelled out in The Scroll of the War Rule:

And no young boy and no woman shall enter their camps when they leave Jerusalem to go into battle until their return.

And no lame man, nor blind, nor crippled, nor having in his flesh some incurable blemish, nor smitten with any impurity in his flesh, none of these shall go with them into battle. They shall all be volunteers for the battle and shall be perfect in spirit and body and prepared for the Day of Vengeance.

And no man who is in a state of uncleanness because of his flux on the day of battle shall go down with them; for the angels of holiness shall accompany their armies. And there shall be a space of about two thousand cubits between all their camp and the site of the (retiring) place, and nothing shameful nor ugly shall be visible in the surroundings of all their camp. (VII.3b–7)[33]

Exclusion of women, boys, and others from the end-time war, "The War of the Sons of Light Against the Sons of Darkness," was on "holiness" grounds as culticly understood. There were women and children among the 930 valiant persons who held out at Masada for three years until their mass suicide in A.D. 73. These doubtless included Essenes, but this was not a typical holy war army. These were refugees from the Roman onslaught that destroyed Jerusalem in A.D. 70.

The people who hid the scrolls in the caves near the Dead Sea are thought to have been those of the community at Qumran, apparently Essene. This community was dominantly but not exclusively male, as both literary and archaeological evidences indicate. The Qumranites seem to have been the major community of a larger Essene sect, other communities being scattered about.[34] The Qumran community itself was formed for men, and any attachment of women seems to have been highly restrictive. Female skeletons found in some graves establish the presence of some women at Qumran, although the main cemetery was laid out primarily for males.

It is generally considered that marriage was practiced at Qumran as a practical necessity for survival but that the decided preference was for celibacy. Allowance must be made for possible variation in the Essene movement from place to place and from time to time.

Philo unequivocally declared: "Of the Essenes, none takes a wife" (*Hypothetica* 11.14; our trans.). Philo's misogyny is so pronounced that his judgment is suspect. In his *Hypothetica* (Apology for Judaism), he describes the Essenes as removing the chief threat to their communal life by banning marriage and requiring perfect continence. "Indeed, no Essaean takes a woman because women are selfish, excessively jealous, skilful in ensnaring the morals of a spouse and in seducing him by endless charms" (11.14).[35] Philo doubtless was wrong about the Essenes as totally rejecting marriage, and he goes far beyond anything implied in the scrolls themselves as to Essene feeling about women.

Josephus, whose chauvinism is barely restrained, recognizes more than one order of Essenes, with different practices as to marriage, reporting:

> Marriage they disdain, but they adopt other men's children, while yet pliable and docile, and regard them as their kin and mould them in accordance with their own principles. They do not, indeed, on principle, condemn wedlock and the propagation thereby of the race, but they wish to protect themselves against women's wantonness, being persuaded that none of the sex keeps her plighted troth to one man. (*War* II.viii.2; Loeb)

Josephus may well be correct in reporting both marrying and nonmarrying Essenes.

The scrolls, unfortunately, do not remove all ambiguity. That marriage was recognized is unmistakable, but whether normative or exceptional is uncertain. The Damascus Document (=the Zadokite Document) bears on this subject:

> And if they live in camps according to the rule of the land and take a wife and beget children, they shall walk in obedience to the Law, and according to the ordinance concerning [pledges], according to the rule of the Law; according to that which He said, *Between a man and his wife, and between a father and his child.* (VII.6b–9a. Cf. variation in Ms. B, I.2b–5.)

Recognizing the complexities and ambiguities of both literary and archaeological evidence, Frank Cross assumes the presence of both married and unmarried Essenes, concluding: "This area of

Essene life can best be understood, not by positing a sect of marrying Essenes alongside a celibate sect, but by recognizing an ambiguous attitude toward marriage integral to the structure of the Essene faith."[36] Essene emphasis upon continence may well have related more to a holy war code than to a depreciation of marriage itself.

The Damascus Document shows strong compassion for widows and orphans, with explicit obligations imposed upon the community. Members of the covenant are to keep themselves free of "the unclean riches of iniquity" gotten "by robbing the goods of the Sanctuary, or by stealing from the poor of His people to make of widows their prey and to murder the fatherless" (VI.15–17). On the other hand, a husband's authority over his wife and a father's over his daughter were assumed:

> Concerning the oath of a woman. As for that which he sai[d, *It is for*] *her husband to annul her oath,* let no husband annul the oath (of his wife) without knowing whether it should be fulfilled or annulled. If this oath is of a kind to violate the Covenant, let the husband annul it and let him not fulfil it. And likewise for the father of the woman. (XVI.10–12; Ms. B)

Dupont-Sommer sees here a modification of the authority of husbands and fathers as laid down in Numbers 30, the ordinance here limiting such right to annul a woman's vow only if the vow violated the Covenant.[37]

Further light on some Jewish perspective on woman may come from the surviving fragments of a scroll found in cave I and given the name the Genesis Apocryphon, with stories featuring Lamech and Abraham. Written in Aramaic, this work may have originated about 100 B.C. In the Genesis Apocryphon, Lamech is startled by the awesome appearance of a son born to his wife. The child has such transcendent marks that Lamech concludes that the child must not be his own but rather one conceived by one of the angels known as "the Watchers." Thereupon he went directly to his wife for verification: "Then I, Lamech, hastened and went to Bath-Enosh [my] wife, and I said to her . . . tell me [in truth] and with no lies" (II.3–6). In a tradition in which the witness of a woman was suspect or rejected, this is a significant turn. Moreover, Bath-

Enosh was equal to the occasion, more than holding her ground, as Lamech reports it: "Then Bath-Enosh my wife spoke to me with much heat" (II.8f.). Not until she saw a changed expression in Lamech's face did Bath-Enosh change her own outraged tone, having "mastered her emotion" (II.13). In the Genesis Apocryphon, Lamech later appeals to Enoch through Methuselah for "certainty," but only after appealing to his wife for verification.

The only book belonging to the Hebrew Bible (our Old Testament) not found among the Qumran scrolls is Esther. Why it is missing can only be a guess. Whether there was a deliberate rejection is not known. Esther was a Jewish heroine, memorialized in the Feast of Purim. She was also exploited in the story as a sex object. That any of this had anything to do with the absence of the book from the extant scrolls is unknown.

The Dead Sea Scrolls are free from the snide remarks and denigrating of woman found in much of the literature before, during, and after the period of the Essenes. There is no blaming of Eve for the human predicament. There are no slurs or epithets. There are no charges that woman is inherently inferior to man morally, intellectually, emotionally, or otherwise. Woman is not eulogized, and she is seldom brought into central focus. At crucial points, as in holy war, she is almost dispensable. There is in this no necessary implication of ascetically based rejection of woman. The key to community patterns may be the holy war code and priestly understanding of cultic purity. The community was oriented toward the expected "messianic" war between the sons of light and the sons of darkness. A part of the holiness required for such was a husband's refraining from sexual relationship with his wife. A near parallel may be seen in Uriah's refusal to sleep with his wife Bathsheba, even at David's insistence, while his fellow soldiers were encamped for battle (2 Sam. 11:11). There was no necessary rejection of woman, marriage, or sex as such at Qumran. There were some positive attitudes toward woman, yet it cannot be overlooked that focus was upon "sons" of light and darkness, not daughters.

PHILO OF ALEXANDRIA

The wide diversity in ancient Judaism, already observed in various expressions, included the perspectives of Philo of Alexandria, a contemporary of Jesus. Philo was infatuated with Greek philosophy, especially that of Plato. He interacted with Greek and other authors, and saw himself as a philosopher. He was first of all a devout Jew, recognizing the Pentateuch as foundational in revelation, and often applying the allegorical method of interpretation to the Pentateuch.

Although Philo by no means spoke for all Jews, he was unmistakably a devout Jew of wide influence. He lived in Egypt and not Palestine, but his perspectives must be considered as a significant part of the world, primarily the Jewish world, into which Jesus came.

Philo saw woman in a role strictly secondary to man, inferior and subordinate. The key to his understanding of man and woman is to be found in his view of their origins,[38] with particular attention to what he held to be the superiority of mind, which he called male, over sense perception (knowing through the five senses), which he called female. Throughout his extant writings he associates male-mind-active-superior-good, and he associates female-sense (sense perception)-passive-inferior-bad. He shows some concern for vindicating Jewish justice to women, to virgin daughters, captured girls, and wives; but even these passages betray the male orientation of the world he knows and approves. As is true in all Judaism, Philo stands solidly for the honoring of father and mother *(Spec. Leg.* II. 225–248 *et passim).*

Philo makes a distinction between the two creation stories in Genesis, seeing the first one as referring to the ideal man (in the Platonic sense) and the second to the empirical man. He writes, "There are two types of men; the one a heavenly man, the other an earthly" *(Leg. All.* I.31; II.4).[39] The heavenly man is seen as "made in the image of God," the earthly as "moulded" out of clay.

The rib story of creation lends itself to Philo's highly imaginative allegorizing, and from it he derives his mind-male and sense-female scheme. Somehow, "it was requisite that the creation of mind should be followed immediately by that of sense-perception, to be a helper and ally to it," so we are "rational beings," who partake of mind capable of discourse as well as of the faculty of "receiving sense-perceptions" (*Leg. All.* II.24f.). From Gen. 2:22, with the help of allegory, Philo proves that "the most proper and exact name for sense-perception is 'woman' " (II.38f.). Arguing from such observations that an object appears before the eye before there is seeing, he terms sense perception passive, whereas mind is active. Applied to the sexes, this means to him that "the man shows himself in activity and the woman in passivity" *(ibid.).* This presupposition is used widely today in distinguishing between man and woman, usually with no reference to Philo.

In Judaism generally, there always was recognition of the role of great women in the life of the people. Philo can find room for this and for identifying some women at least with both sense perception and "virtues," though he does warn that this "divine mystery" is for "the initiated" alone "whose ears are purified" (*Cher.* 40–52). Although he recalls that "we hold that woman signifies in a figure sense-perception," he contends that "the helpmeets" of Abraham, Isaac, Jacob, and Moses "are called women, but are in reality virtues" (41). He builds upon the observation that though it is said that "Adam knew his wife," such a phrase is not used for certain great men in the Pentateuch. The wives of these latter, unlike Eve, are "virtues" who received seed directly from God, though their offspring were borne to their husbands and not to God, who is complete and needs none. This "holy mystery" may be some modification of Philo's low view of woman, whereby the association is that of sense perception, woman, passivity, inferiority, and badness; but the modification is slight at best. What he is affirming is some kind of virginal birth in which a select wife is a "virtue" in that she is found "pregnant through no mortal agency" (47).

In a discourse on the justice of God, Philo maintains that "equality, the nurse of justice," is approved throughout by Moses and that equality appears in all that God does, as in creation, where he gave day and night, light and darkness. He then writes, "Equality too divided the human being into man and woman" (*Quis Her.* 164). However, he stops short of affirming full equality, adding, "two sections unequal indeed in strength, but equal as regards what was nature's urgent purpose, the reproduction of themselves in a third person" *(ibid.).* Commenting on Gen. 1:27, he seems to see the two in equality, but he does not pursue what would seem to have been a significant departure. Prevailingly, the story in Genesis 2 is followed.

Philo takes pride in the fact that all Jews know their laws. Each seventh day they provide hours of instruction in them, so that none need to seek out an authority and none can hide behind ignorance. But "they" apparently implied men, the women not coming directly under such formal instruction. Women could depend upon men for guidance: "The husband seems competent to transmit knowledge of the laws to his wife, the father to his children, the master to his slaves" (*Hypothetica* 7.14).

The dominance of husband over wife is assumed by Philo in explaining why the high priest is not to marry a widow, but only a virgin, it being simply that he must be free to "mould" her and "instruct" her without interference from the influence of a former husband. Thus, a high priest is to take only "a virgin who is innocent of marriage" (not even previously betrothed), one who is like "a sheet of wax levelled to show clearly the lessons to be inscribed upon it" (*Spec. Leg.* I.106)![40]

The subordination of woman may be illustrated in the matter of vows: "Virgins and wives are not allowed full control of their vows by the law" (*Spec. Leg.* II.24). Philo explains that this gives a father authority over his daughter and a husband over his wife as to whether their oaths are to hold or to be canceled.

The idea that by nature women are best suited to indoor life and men to outdoor life is explicit in Philo. A woman should avoid the streets, where she falls under the gaze of men, and she should time her visits to the temple when most people have gone home *(ibid.).* Apparently it did not occur to Philo that one might ask why women, whom he saw as bad, would not be safe among men, whom he saw as good.

Philo is proud of the superiority of the Hebrew moral code over

that of other nations, especially in matters of sex, and much that
he writes about continence and fidelity to marriage is of highest
quality. Dishonoring "by violence a woman widowed" and the
"corruption of a maiden" are criminal offenses, but they are
deemed "less serious" than the crime committed in adultery (*Spec.
Leg.* III.64f.). For Philo the magnitude of the crime of adultery
relates to the number of families injured, but always this centers
on encroachment upon a husband's rights.

In a more positive direction, Philo shows some concern for
humaneness to daughters and fairness to wives and to girls captured in war. If a priest's daughter marries one who is not a priest
and then is widowed, either by divorce or death of her husband,
and is without children, she is to be permitted to return to her
father. But if there were sons or daughters, the widowed mother
must take her place with her children, "For sons and daughters
belong to the house of the male parent and carry with them into
it the mother also" (*Spec. Leg.* I.130).

Philo points to strict laws protecting innocent wives from un-
scrupulous husbands who seek to rid themselves of unwanted wives
by falsely charging them with unfaithfulness. Husbands found to
have thus falsified their wives are made to pay monetary fines,
suffer the degradation of stripes, and are compelled to continue the
marriage, "if, that is, the women can bring themselves to consort
with such persons" (*Spec. Leg.* III.80–82).

The laws offered some protection to girls captured in war, but
Philo would perpetuate old patterns in the Mosaic law: "If you find
among the booty a comely woman for whom you feel a desire, do
not treat her as a captive, and vent your passion on her, but in a
gentler spirit pity her for her change of lot and alleviate her misfor-
tunes by changing her condition for the better in every way" (*Virt.*
110). She is to be given thirty days for mourning the loss of family,
and then she is to be received as a wife and not a harlot (111f.).
Philo praises the generosity of the man who proves to be so considerate of the captured girl. He seems to sense no problem with the
capture itself.

Philo cannot be faulted for having been born into a world that
was male-oriented, but his extensive writings indicate that he did

little to redress any inequities and much to further them. He tried
to make nature, logic, and religion serve to validate male domination.

THE WRITINGS OF JOSEPHUS

The Jewish historian Josephus wrote several books, some quite
massive, toward the end of the first Christian century. He attempted a comprehensive history of the Jews and dealt with many
of their customs and teachings. A considerable number of women
of prominence enter the story. Additionally, many passages speak
directly to the status and role of woman.

Josephus is more restrained than many of his day, but he definitely reflects a male bias, consciously or not. He begins his history
of the Jews by selecting the rib account of creation, with its implications (*Antiquities* I.i.2). The animals were created "male and female" (1), but man was created male, female later being derived
from male. Josephus writes further that God punished Adam "for
yielding to a woman's counsel" (4).

Josephus can be positive, as when he refers to "a certain wise
and intelligent old woman" who saved a city besieged by Joab
(*Antiq.* VII.xi.8; cf. 2 Sam. 20:16).[41] Likewise, he pictures Roman
soldiers at the fall of the Jewish fortress Masada (A.D. 73) as
amazed at the strength of the woman who spoke for the seven
survivors: "But it was with difficulty that they listened to her,
incredulous of such amazing fortitude" (*War* VII.ix.2).

A stereotype for woman is recurrent throughout these writings,
as the "womanly" character is referred to in negative terms. Numerous such allusions appear in the *Antiquities of the Jews.* Josephus comments upon Potiphar's wife after she failed to seduce
Joseph that "this method of avenging herself for so grievous a
slight and of accusing him in advance seemed to her alike wise and
womanly" (*Antiq.* II.iv.5). Josephus comments on Mariamne's suspicion of Herod: "And when in women's fashion she and, even
more so, Alexandra [the mother] affected not to believe his statements" (XV.iii.6). Of another woman he writes, ". . . the things
that Antipater's mother had said to certain people in the frivolous

way of a woman" (XVII.v.6). Josephus reports that slow collection of taxes incensed Gaius, "who called it womanly weakness to be so slow in collecting the money.... Gaius would give him women's words and such as had quite obscene connotations" (XIX.i.5).

In the *War of the Jews* the picture is somewhat muddled. Queen Alexandra, successor to her husband Alexander Jannaeus, is praised, though it seems to be implied that frailty belongs to woman: "For this frail woman firmly held the reins of government, thanks to her reputation for piety" (*War* I.v.1).

Josephus points up the well-defined moral code governing relationships between men and women. In his defense against Apion he writes:

> The Law recognizes no sexual connections, except the natural union of man and wife, and that only for the procreation of children. Sodomy it abhors, and punishes any guilty of such assault with death. It commands us, in taking a wife, not to be influenced by dowry, not to carry off a woman by force, nor yet to win her by guile and deceit, but to sue from him who is authorized to give her away the hand of one who is not ineligible on account of nearness of kin. (*Against Apion* II.24. Cf. Lev. 18:6ff. See further *Antiq.* III.xii.1; IV.viii.23; and *Apion* I.7f.)

Although there are several considerations here for the rights of the woman, the passage is male-oriented. It is addressed to the male, not the female.

Josephus may have known women in the stereotype of weakness, but he also was aware of Alexandra's (Mariamne's mother) rebellion against discrimination. When Herod sought to curtail her influence by putting her under surveillance, he writes of her:

> All this gradually made her wild with rage and caused hatred to grow in addition, for she had a full share of womanly pride and resented the supervision that came from his suspicion, and she thought anything was better than to be deprived of her freedom of action and to live the rest of her life in slavery and fear in spite of appearing to have honour. (*Antiq.* XV.iii.2)

In another direction, Josephus includes a long story in which it is argued that woman is the strongest of all (*Antiq.* XI.iii.1–10). The story centers around Zorobabelos (Zerubbabel) and Darius, the Persian king who provided for the Jews to return to Jerusalem from Babylonian exile. At a banquet given for many distinguished guests, Darius had each of his three bodyguards deliver a discourse on what is greatest of all: wine, kings, or women. Zorobabelos began this way:

> Wine and the king, whom all obey, are, to be sure, very strong, but greater in power than these are women. For it is a woman who brings a king into the world, and it is women who bear and bring up those who plant vines which produce wine. In short, there is nothing which we do not get from them. For it is they who weave our clothes for us, and it is through them that the affairs of the household receive due care and attention. And it is impossible for us to be separated from women. (*Antiq.* XI.iii.5)

This perspective on woman does not agree with what appears to be that of Josephus himself. Here the discourse on woman is simply a part of a larger story in which the superior wisdom of Zerubbabel gains for him the backing of Darius and the privilege of rebuilding the Temple in Jerusalem.

Josephus gives considerable attention to the family, including sections on the laws of divorce. He is explicit that Jewish law did not permit a woman to divorce her husband, cases like that of Herod's sister Salome being exceptional. The Herodian family was powerful enough to sit loose to Jewish laws when it suited them, for they answered ultimately to the Romans and not to the Jews.

Josephus is familiar with the much-debated question of the grounds of divorce, whether "for whatever cause" or adultery alone (*Antiq.* IV.viii.23; cf. Mt. 19:3). Like Philo, he points up a positive consideration for a girl captured in war and taken by a Hebrew as wife. Although the man cannot have it all his way, the major options are his, not hers.

The question of witnesses recognized in court bears significantly on the question of the status of woman. Josephus seems to stand alone in explicitly affirming that women were excluded as witnesses in Jewish courts:

> Put not trust in a single witness, but let there be three or at least two, whose evidence shall be accredited by their past lives. From women let

no evidence be accepted, because of the levity and temerity of their sex. (*Antiq* IV.viii.15)

There seems to be no evidence in the Pentateuch or elsewhere for the absolute exclusion of women's testimony. From the Old Testament and other Jewish literature may be cited incidents where a woman spoke up for herself, and she could even sue that her husband divorce her; but there is no clear evidence that as a third party, a woman's testimony was accepted in a Jewish court for or against another.

There is unambiguous evidence in Josephus for a graded segregation at the Temple in Jerusalem, with women near the bottom in privilege. This is spelled out in Josephus' defense of Judaism against Apion:

> All who ever saw our temple are aware of the general design of the building, and the inviolable barriers which preserved its sanctity. It had four surrounding courts, each with its special statutory restrictions. The outer court was open to all, foreigners included; women during their impurity were alone refused admission. To the second court all Jews were admitted and, when uncontaminated by any defilement, their wives; to the third male Jews, if clean and purified; to the fourth the priests robed in their priestly vestments. The sanctuary was entered only by the high-priests, clad in the raiment peculiar to themselves. (*Apion* II.8)

Even the gates were segregated, for women could enter "the women's court" only through the south and north gates, and they could not "pass by way of their own gate beyond the partition wall" (*War* V.v.2).

THE MISHNAH

Any employment of the Mishnah to recover Jewish teaching or practice before A.D. 70 is hazardous, yet it may not be neglected. The Mishnah is a body of rabbinical tradition which took its present shape in stages beginning at Jamnia (Yavneh) sometime after the destruction of Jerusalem and its Temple in A.D. 70 and which

was promulgated around A.D. 200.[42] It consists of sixty-three sections, or "tractates," grouped under six major divisions, the third
of which is entitled *Nashim,* "Women." In *Nashim* and other
divisions of the Mishnah are numerous rulings with respect to
women: betrothal, marriage, divorce, vows, inheritance, defilement, etc.

Two acute problems confront any use of the Mishnah for an
understanding of Judaism before A.D. 70. To what extent do the
formulations in the Mishnah preserve pre-70 tradition? What is the
relationship between the rabbis who formulated the Mishnah and
pre-70 Pharisees? The Mishnah itself affirms a basic continuity,
ascribing much of its tradition to the houses of Shammai and Hillel
and other pre-70 Jewish scholars. Jacob Neusner in particular has
challenged widely held positions on the Mishnah, but even
Neusner concedes that in these traditions "we may even gain a
perspective on part of pre-70 historical Pharisaism," especially as
relates to the last half century before the destruction of the Temple.[43]

Basic to the perspective of the Mishnah was man's authority
over woman. A Jewish girl was under the control of her father until
she came under the control of her husband:

> The father has control over his daughter [under twelve and a half years]
> as touching her betrothal whether it is effected by money, by writ, or
> by intercourse; and he has the right to aught found by her and to the
> work of her hands, and [the right] to set aside her vows, and he receives
> her bill of divorce; but he has not the use of her property [inherited]
> during her lifetime. (*Ket.* 4.4)[44]

The point is well made that a man's authority over a woman
does not necessarily imply that she was considered his property,[45]
but the distinction is not so clear as may be desired. It cannot be
escaped that the Mishnah tractate *Kiddushin* (Betrothals) begins
with a series of five areas of acquirements: woman, Hebrew bondman, Canaanitish bondman, large and small cattle, and property
(*Kid.* 1.1–5). If this does not imply that woman is the property of
man, the literary structure at least reflects no sensitivity to the
feelings of woman. The male orientation is obvious. It may be

recalled that the Decalogue (Ex. 20:17) lists a man's wife along with his manservants, maidservants, ox, and ass.

The section on Betrothals begins with a parallel to *Ket.* 4.4 in the declaration that "by three means is a woman acquired and by two means she acquires her freedom. She is acquired by money or by writ or by intercourse" (*Kid.* 1.1). The two means by which a woman could acquire her freedom were divorce or the death of her husband. The Hebrew bondmaid did have the advantage that she gained her freedom at twelve years and a day (*Kid.* 1.2).

The normal age for betrothal of a girl was between twelve and twelve and a half years, although there were betrothals and marriages at an earlier age.[46] It was at marriage that definite authority passed to the husband, including power "to revoke her vows" and such responsibility as "her maintenance," *ketubah* (i.e., marriage settlement), and her ransom should she be taken captive (*Ned.* 10.5; *Ket.* 4.7–9). A man controlled the earnings of his wife (*Yeb.* 10.1) and even what was found by minor sons and daughters or by his wife (*Baba Metzia* 1.5).

The Mishnah made the bearing of children a duty: "No man may abstain from keeping the law *Be fruitful and multiply,* unless he already has children: according to the School of Shammai two sons, according to the School of Hillel, a son and a daughter, for it is written, *Male and female created he them*" (*Yeb.* 6.6). The passage continues: "If he married a woman and lived with her ten years and she bore no child, it is not permitted him to abstain." Presumably he was to divorce her and acquire a new wife. The passage further affirms, "The duty to be fruitful and multiply falls on the man but not on the woman," but R. Johanan b. Baroka (ca. A.D. 120–140) said, "Of both it is written, 'And God blessed them and said unto them, Be fruitful and multiply.'" Rules were laid down governing the mutual obligations of husband and wife in the conjugal relationship, even to the minimum frequency (*Ket.* 5.6–7; *Git.* 4.5; *Eduy.* 1.13; 4.10. In this light, see 1 Cor. 7:5f.).

The "works which the wife must perform for her husband" included grinding flour, baking bread, washing clothes, cooking food, nursing her child, making ready her husband's bed, and

Chapter 2

THE
GREEK WORLD

The distinction between Jews and non-Jews in the world of Jesus is real, beyond any doubt. However, to see these as the proverbial "East" and "West," the twain never meeting, would be grossly mistaken. Jew and non-Jew constantly met, interacted, resisted each other, and inevitably influenced each other. Roman Hellenism, a blend of Rome and Greece and much else thrown in, dominated the Mediterranean world in the time of Jesus; and after Alexander, Greek had become the international language.

GREEK LITERATURE (9TH TO 5TH CENTURY B.C.)

Homer (9th century B.C.)

Homer and Hesiod stand at the head of extant Greek literature, about the ninth and eighth centuries respectively. Homer was a major source for Greek drama and other Greek expression. His *Iliad* is a poetic description of an episode in the nine-year siege of Troy, after Paris had seduced Helen and taken her from the home of his host Menelaus in Sparta to his own home in Troy. The *Odyssey* is a sequel about Odysseus' long return journey from Troy to Ithaca. Homer is a master storyteller. His gods and goddesses are humanlike, with both sexes having a variety of virtues and vices. The heroes and heroines likewise are a complex of virtues and vices, neither sex excelling the other in either. Homer knows conventional roles for men and women, war being the business of men and the home the center of a woman's life; but roles are not absolute. Women sometimes take leadership roles, and goddesses enter into battle as readily as gods. Zeus is a henpecked husband, but when pushed too far he can put Hera in her place. Recurrently it surfaces that a main incentive in war is to take as booty the captured wives and daughters of the enemy. The "crime" that aroused the Greeks against the Trojans was not the seduction of another's wife, this being a common practice, but the violation of the code of hospitality, betraying the trust of a host (*Iliad,* Bk. III).[1] Homer is not misogynous, but neither does he challenge chauvinism and stereotype. He is primarily a storyteller, not a prober as were the later dramatists who reworked his plots and characters.

The double standard for men and women prevails in Homer, yet women are far from being helpless property. They are not silenced nor ever completely subordinated. This is true especially for the more gifted and advantaged. Helen's beauty ensures her a basic security and respect despite her own shameful acts and the fall of Troy to the Greeks.

Although the world that Homer knows is male-oriented and male-dominated, his freedom from misogyny and any doctrinaire denigration of woman seems to be bound up with a "universalism" found later in some of the dramatists who drew heavily upon his poems. The true stature of Homer is reflected in his ability to transcend not only the distinction between Greek and Trojan but also that between man and woman. Never does Homer achieve in some great epigram anything like Paul's "not any Jew nor Greek, not any slave nor free, not any male and female" (Gal. 3:28), but he approximates this perspective in his tales of human suffering.

Hesiod (8th century B.C.)

Hesiod is highly significant for ancient perspectives on woman. He is negative in his view of woman, seeing her as the agent of evil, or even, in another version, as the embodiment of evil. His hostility comes to focus in the myth of Pandora (the all-endowed), which he includes in his two great epic poems, *Works and Days* and *Theogony*. Through this myth, Hesiod explains how evil and toil came upon mankind, and the woman Pandora is the cause. According to *Works and Days,* Prometheus had angered Zeus by stealing for men the fire which the latter had hidden. For being outwitted, Zeus promised revenge: "But I will give men as the price for fire an evil thing in which they may be glad of heart while they embrace their own destruction" (57f.).[2] He then laughed and gave order that from a mix of earth and water "a sweet, lovely maidenshape" be formed, vested with human voice and strength, and attractively adorned. He further commanded "to put in her a shameless mind and a deceitful nature" (67). When she was so fashioned and adorned and there was put within her "lies and crafty words and a deceitful nature" (79), Zeus "called this woman Pandora," because all who dwelt on Olympus "gave each a gift," presumably each god contributing something to her makeup.[3] The gift was sent to Epimetheus. Until now men had lived on earth free from worry, toil, pain, and sickness, but Pandora opened the jar (box) and all was changed for the worse: "But the woman took off the great lid of the jar with her hands and scattered all these and her thought caused sorrow and mischief to man" (94f.). Only Hope remained, but countless plagues were thus let loose upon men.

For Hesiod, then, the myth of Pandora is more than an accounting for the entrance of toil and ills upon man, though it is that. It likewise is an indictment of woman not only as the instrument of evil *(Works and Days)* but as evil itself *(Theogony)*. Unlike Eve, Pandora did not fall. Zeus made her evil as a snare and punishment to man.

Semonides of Amorgos (7th century B.C.?)

Semonides was a master of iambic verse, and some of his work has survived for nearly twenty-seven hundred years, but his scorn for woman rivals that of Hesiod. Extant is a satire on women in which he holds that God made various types, some from "the long-bristled swine," some from "the wicked fox," some from the dog, some from earth, some from the sea, some from "the ashen-colored and much beaten ass," another from "a dainty steed with flowing mane . . . who turns aside from servile work and toil," another from the ape, and finally one from the bee.[4] The last is praised because she "often has given birth to children fair and famed." She does not sit among the women and "hold converse of scandals bold," and she is a "boon of grace" from Zeus to men. Stylistically brilliant, the poem heaps charge upon charge against women as filthy, evil, loud, ugly, lazy, vain, etc. To Semonides, woman is "this greatest evil."

Sappho of Lesbos (ca. 600 B.C.)

By a strange irony, the sixth and early fifth centuries B.C. proved to be a great age for women in art and literature, despite a segregating tendency in Ionia and the legislation in Athens to restrict the freedom of women.[5] Poetesses were many and exercised far-reaching influence. Of all these poetesses, however, Sappho of Lesbos stands out as one of the most gifted.[6] Her poems seem to have been numerous, but only about two hundred fragments survive. Even so, the power of her lyrics is inescapable. Her magic was in her selection of words out of everyday speech and her arrangement of these words in Greek sentences in such order as to provide music of expression, intriguing ambiguity, deep feeling, and often profound insight. It is little wonder that those who became her disciples included Catullus, Horace, Ovid, and poets down to the modern period.

The lyrical force of Sappho's Greek verses cannot be fully captured in translation, but even so it may be felt. Groden sees one fragment as probably portraying a bride, a blushing girl likened to a ripened apple and her high social and moral standing symbolized by its position at the tip of the topmost bough, yet more desirable because elusive:

> . . . like the sweet-apple
> that has reddened

at the top of a tree,
at the tip of the topmost bough,
and the apple pickers
missed it there—no, not missed, so much
as could not touch.

(Groden, pp. xviii, 52)

Her words have music but also insight, as in the line: "and when-ever I am good to people, they're the ones who hurt me most of all" (Groden, p. 8). Again, "To have beauty is to have only that, but to have goodness is to be beautiful too" (*ibid.*, p. 29). Anyone engaged in pastoral care would like to hear Sappho further relative to that fragmentary line, "Am I still carrying a torch for my virginity?" (*ibid.*, p. 55). Or, "Childhood, my childhood, where are you going when you leave me?" (*ibid.*, p. 62). We would like to hear what went with the tortured line, "Pain penetrates me drop by drop" (Barnard, #61).

Variously assessed, Sappho will not be silenced. She unmistak-ably was a person of stature, and she lived in a Greek world that did not deny her the right to be.

The Laws of Gortyn (mid-5th century B.C.)

In the nineteenth century there was recovered a mural inscrip-tion which provides a part of what is known as the laws of Gortyn on the island of Crete, one of the foundations to the Greek tradition known to us.[7] This represents a mid-fifth century B.C. reformation of the laws of Crete, its fullest treatment being that of family relations and inheritance. At the very time the rights of women were being restricted in Athens, women were gaining a better legal status in Crete. The reforms restricted the power to dispose of women's property, strengthening the case for wives and daughters against that of husbands, fathers, sons, and uncles, and freeing an heiress from the compulsion of marrying a near kinsman to keep the inheritance within the family.

Athena Nike

Unlike the practice in Judaism, the Greeks accepted the role of priestesses as well as of priests. This may be documented from a stele with an inscription dating about 450–447 B.C., with instructions about the architecture of the temple for Athena Nike and the salaries of the priestesses to serve there.[8]

Goddesses were as prominent as gods among the Greeks. The male god Zeus may have been supreme, yet Athena was the central shrine in both the Erechtheum and the Parthenon at the heart of the Acropolis in Athens.

Together with the prominence of goddesses alongside gods and the recognition of priestesses alongside priests were evidences of male priorities in the family.

Herodotus (484?–425 B.C.)

Known as "the father of history," Herodotus declared at the outset of his nine-book work that he wrote in order that time not blot out the memory of the past, his particular interest being in the "great and marvelous deeds done by the Greeks and foreigners," i.e., the Greek and Persian wars (I.1).[9] He traveled far and wide and heard many stories reflecting the life-styles and customs of various people, and he claims to have reported them as he heard them.

Reading through Herodotus one encounters generally a male orientation, with woman more often subordinated than not and often exploited. He was quite pleased with a custom in Illyria.

> Once a year in every village all the maidens as they came to marriageable age were collected and brought together into one place, with a crowd of men standing around. Then a crier would stand up and offer them for sale one by one, first the fairest of all; and then when she had fetched a great price he put up for sale the next comeliest, selling all the maidens as lawful wives. Rich men of Assyria who desired to marry would outbid each other for the fairest; the commonalty, who desired to marry and cared nothing for beauty, could take the ill-favored damsels and money therewith; for when the crier sold all the comeliest,

he would put up her that was least beautiful, or crippled, and offer her to whosoever would take her to wife for the least sum. . . . The money came from the sale of the comely damsels, and so they paid the dowry of the ill-favored and the cripples. (I.196)

As an alternative to prostitution, this offered something; but Herodotus seems oblivious to implications of the total situation and practice—women sold in public auction!

Herodotus does find temple prostitution "the foulest Babylonian custom" (I.199). As he reports it, this custom compelled every woman in the land once in her life to sit in the temple of Aphrodite until she had intercourse with some stranger.

Herodotus in the fifth century B.C. reports a measure of freedom enjoyed by Egyptian women somewhat paralleling that reported by Theocritus in the third century B.C. He reports that in Egypt "the women buy and sell, the men abide at home and weave" (II.35). A discrimination obtained in that daughters against their wills were compelled to support their parents, but sons were not. Egypt had both gods and goddesses, and women actively participated in cultic rites alongside men (II.59f.). Women in Egypt could hold the highest office, as was true of the famed Cleopatra just before the birth of Jesus. However, the rule was male domination, Herodotus reporting only two queens in the Egyptian priestly records of 330 kings (II.100).

A case for fidelity to monogamous marriage, though compromised under pressure for an heir, appears in Herodotus' story of Anaxandrides, king of Sparta (V.39–41). The king was happily married to his sister's daughter, but she had borne him no children. The magistrates of Sparta demanded that he send away his barren wife and wed another to ensure the royal line. Anaxandrides' reply would be a credit to any culture or age: "And you are no good counsellors, when you bid me send away the wife I have, who is void of offence against me, and take another to my house; I cannot consent to it."

Herodotus has highest praise for Artemisia, a woman who led a significant part of the Persian force against Greece (VII.99). She was a widow with a small son and was under no necessity to enter actively into the campaign, except from her own "high-hearted valour." She was the governor of the men of Halicarnassus, Cos, Nioyrus, and Calydnon; and her five ships were reported to be among the best in the whole Persian fleet. Herodotus reports that of all the allies of Xerxes, Artemisia gave the king the best counsel, though he did not always follow it (VIII.69). This high praise of this woman is marred by one stereotype, to the implication of which Herodotus seems to be oblivious. She is characterized as being of "high-hearted valour" *(andrēinēs),* Greek for "manly." Again, when Xerxes sought to praise Artemisia for her courage and skill in naval battle, he said, "My men have become women, and my women men" (VIII.88). Athenian pride was severely bruised by the fact that "a woman should come to attack Athens," and an enormous prize was offered anyone who could capture her alive (VIII.93). Her escape was a further bruising of the male ego.

War has always meant plunder for the victors, and woman has been one of the chief victims of this male sport. Herodotus can matter-of-factly report the rewards heaped upon Greek warriors after their victory over the Persians at Plataeae. They received gifts, but to Pausanias, Greek leader in battle, was given "tenfold of every kind, women, horses, talents, camels, and all other things likewise" (IX.81). This lumping together of women with horses, talents, and camels comes under no censure. By contrast is the outrage of John the Seer, who depicted the same depraved traffic of the "Harlot City" in marketing all kinds of commodities along with "the bodies and souls of people" (Rev. 18:12f.).

THE GREEK DRAMA

Nowhere in the ancient world is there deeper probing into human existence, individual and social, than in the Greek plays, especially in the tragedies of Aeschylus, Sophocles, and Euripides; and in these, woman commands a central part of the stage. In a lighter vein, the comedies of Aristophanes and Menander, too, probe into basic questions of the nature, rights, and role of woman.

Aeschylus (ca. 513/12 to 456/55 B.C.)

The father of the Greek tragedy is Aeschylus.[10] He built upon the legends of Homer and his successors, oral tradition, and the earlier cultic dramas. With Aeschylus begins a new dimension in Greek interpretation of human existence. He wrote in trilogies, only one of which survives intact: *Agamemnon, The Libation Bearers,* and *The Eumenides* (all produced in 456 B.C.). The plays trace a chain of murders within the family, each intending to right a wrong, but each opening the door to new tensions, conflicts, and wrongs. Aeschylus struggles with the problem not so much of right against wrong but of what was seen as right against right, hate embedded in love, the web of entanglements in the complexities of human existence, tangled motivation, the outworking of moral law, deep-seated and angry passions, self-destruction in self-serving, the power of destiny or fate, the law of sin and its consequences, and, in particular, "the god of war, money changer of dead bodies" (*Agamemnon,* 438).

No character in Aeschylus' trilogy is stronger than Clytemnestra: sister of Helen of Troy; wife of Agamemnon; mother of Iphigenia, Electra, and Orestes; then wife of Aegisthus. Her life is as tangled as her motives. She hates Agamemnon for sacrificing their daughter at what he understood to be the will of the gods; yet after murdering him she seems to reflect a latent love as she tries to moderate angry passions: "No more violence. Here is a monstrous harvest and a bitter reaping time. There is pain enough already. Let us not be bloody now" (*Agamemnon,* 1654–1656). Blaming all on "fate," she concludes, "We could not do otherwise than we did . . . broken as we are by the brute heel of angry destiny" (1658–1660). She cannot put the deed out of mind, however, and it haunts her even in her dreams (*The Libation Bearers,* 524f.). With her mother-resentment was apparently a sense of guilt, for she had taken Aegisthus as lover while her husband Agamemnon fought at Troy.

Rejecting the established rule that it is man who chooses his mate, she, like her sister Helen, declared her independence of any "womanly" status or role, choosing her consort. In so doing, she ended up with a "womanish" man in the cowardly Aegisthus (*Agamemnon,* 1625), and she could not shake off all sense of guilt. Explaining her action to her son Orestes: "Destiny had some part in it, my child" (*The Libation Bearers,* 909), and "It hurts women to be kept from their men, my child" (920). The motive of jealousy enters too, as she sees Cassandra, whom Agamemnon brought home as a trophy and companion from Troy. Her jealousy is only thinly veiled under her expressed scorn for Cassandra, whom she publicly humiliates as captive slave and barbarian: "I have no leisure to stand outside the house and waste time on this woman" (*Agamemnon,* 1055), but the time she gives belies her boast.

Aeschylus does not ask his audience to love Clytemnestra or to approve her actions. He does not defend her murders or her relationship with Aegisthus, "this wickedly mated man" (*Agamemnon,* 1319). Aeschylus does present her as one who openly rejects a neat distinction between roles for men and women. But Clytemnestra goes beyond this. She makes claims in her own right, not merely that of an absent husband. When she describes the wifely role as "watchdog of the house" (607) she has no intention of so limiting her role. Somewhat enigmatically she dissociates herself from Agamemnon's wife: "Speak of me never more as the wife of Agamemnon" (1498f.). Here she may mean only that she is not guilty of her husband's death, serving only as an instrument for destiny or justice. But the line may well intend also to be a declaration of her independence. She is herself, no man's wife.

A most amazing play is *The Persians,* staged in Athens in 472 B.C., eight years after the Persian invasion of Greece was turned back at Salamis. The play is about this decisive battle between Greece and Persia, viewed from the Persian side. There is no gloating over Persia's fall. It is unparalleled outside the Greek plays (see Euripides below) that Aeschylus and the Athenians could with such empathy for their fallen foes depict in drama a war which, had it gone the other way, would have meant their own bondage: "They threaten to yoke in servitude Hellas" (50). Aeschylus wants his Athenian audience to identify with the pathos of a fallen foe: "Athens hateful to her foes. Recall how many Persians widowed vain, and mothers losing sons" (286–289).

But what about woman in *The Persians*? A major motive is to depict the suffering of war, and Aeschylus dwells more upon the anxieties, fears, privations, and sorrows of those back home, in particular the women: "And parents and wives counting the days tremble at lengthening time" (62–64). Athenians are made to feel with the Persians "when the crowds of women cry" (119). The aged Queen Atossa in particular is portrayed throughout the play in terms of her deep feelings for family and people. She falls short of truest greatness when against such massive ruin the torment with "the deepest pang" for her is the dishonor of her son, beaten in battle (845–851), but at least Aeschylus has deep feeling for this mother of the man who tried to enslave Greece. Aeschylus feels for all people: "Nations wail their native sons, who by Xerxes stuffed up hell" (922f.). Here may be the secret to Aeschylus' respect for woman; he is a universalist, with concern for all humanity. To him personal liberty is dearer than life. In the context of those two concepts—universality and personal freedom—the personhood of woman must be acknowledged.

Sophocles (496?–?406 B.C.)

The second of the great Greek tragedists, Sophocles reflects some significant perspectives on woman, although this was not for him a primary subject. His overriding concern and struggle was with human suffering: its meaning, the question of innocence and guilt, and the backdrop or overarching will of the gods.[11] He sees suffering resulting both from one's choices and from forces beyond oneself. One's sin as guilt is bound up with conscious choice. Ultimately, however, the gods "form this immovable background to human suffering and heroism."[12]

In *Oedipus at Colonus,* Sophocles paints the king as self-willed, stubborn, vindictive, impulsive, complaining, even though to be pitied because of fate: "These things are in the hands of God" (1781). His sons are like their father, scheming and fighting for the throne from which he was banished; but the daughters, Antigone and Ismene, remain true, strong, and self-giving throughout. Antig-

one especially is a tower of strength and an embodiment of devotion (445–449). She remains passionately loyal to father and brothers even at their worst. She pleads that they be open to one another,
forgiving, and that they turn from strife to peace. Sophocles is not
crusading for woman's rights; but, whatever the motive, the great
characters are more often than not those of woman, not man. The
stereotype shines through, even though it seems not to be a Sopho-
clean motive, when virtues are "manly" and weakness is "womanly." When the old, blind, and exiled Oedipus is cared for by his
daughter but not his sons, he concludes: "And [they] are not girls,
but men, in faithfulness" (1369). In Sophocles the women are often
"manly" and the men "womanly" (cf. 337–343 for stereotype). The
labels linger, but the reality does not support the stereotype.

Women play a part in all of Sophocles' plays, except for *Philoc-
tetes;* but we may single out *The Women of Trachis* (430–420 B.C.)
for special attention. Deianira, wife of Heracles, dominates the
stage for much of the play, her husband dominating the closing
part. Although he is the "hero," acclaimed by all as "the best of
all men on earth" (811f.), she is in personal qualities by far the
stronger and more attractive. Both suffer much through misin-
formed or ill-advised good intentions and from "the will of the
gods," but it is Deianira who accepts undeserved suffering graciously, unselfishly, and with great courage. She is grateful for her
husband, worrying for his safety, as he is gone much of the time.
She is candid but not bitter as she says of him: "We have had
children now, whom he sees at times, like a farmer working an
outlying field, who sees it only when he sows and when he reaps"
(31–33). Apprehensive when she has not heard from him for over
a year, she confesses, "I leap up from pleasant sleep in fright
. . . terrified to think I may have to live deprived of the one man
who is finest of all" (175–177). When finally a group of captive
women, including a beautiful young girl named Iole, appear at her
house, sent for her keeping by her absentee husband, she receives
them graciously, even though her suspicions are soon confirmed
about the intended role for Iole. Deianira is hurt deeply that her
husband has fought a war on false pretenses to wrest a new bride
from an unwilling father, but she has no spite or hatred for husband

or Iole (436–469). She tries to save her marriage, with resultant suffering for her husband, but the latter was not intended.

Heracles, by contrast, has no charity for Deianira as he reacts violently in his misery, evoking the gods to punish his wife and all his enemies. Concern for his own needs or wishes overrides all else. A strong note of misogyny comes from his lips: "A woman, a female, in no way like a man, she alone without even a sword has brought me down" (1061–1063). Ironically, he brands as "womanly" his own breakdown:

> Pity me, for I seem pitiful to many others, crying and sobbing like a girl, and no one could ever say that he had seen this man act like that before. Always without a groan, I followed my painful course. Now in my misery I am discovered a woman. (1070–1075)

Recurrently in Sophocles, it is the man and not the woman who proves to be "womanly"!

Euripides (d. 406 B.C.)

Euripides was a powerful voice for the voiceless: "barbarians," slaves, and women in particular. In 438 B.C. he presented the play *Alcestis,* and it is difficult to imagine a more powerful portrayal of woman.[13] Alcestis, the beautiful wife of Admetus, king of Pherae in Thessaly, is a tower of strength, a model in devotion or even sacrificial love, and a redeeming force in the life of her husband and others about her. The plot forms around an agreement by which the Fates of Death will spare Admetus when his hour comes and take instead Alcestis, who has volunteered to be his substitute. Apollo had brought about the arrangement when he found that his young friend Admetus was afraid to die. The Fates agreed to accept a substitute if such would agree in advance to die for him at the appointed hour. Admetus pleaded in vain with parents, other kin, and friends, for none would agree to die for him. Alcestis then volunteered to take his place in his hour of death. She did it out of her love for him and, apparently, because of her respect for the honorable role of wife. In her words as death drew near, "I, honouring thee, am setting thee in place before mine own soul to see this light, am dying, unconstrained to die for thee" (282–284).[14] Knowing that if she had been widowed, she would have a choice in remarriage, she yet preferred to give her life in order to spare him, rather than live without him and have their children be bereft of their father (285–288). She asked no "full requital" and knew that there was no such for the preciousness of life. Her request was that after her death he not marry another to her dishonor and to the hurt of the children. She pleaded only, "For these thy babes thou loveth no less than I, if that thine heart be right" (303f.). Euripides does not share the perspective found elsewhere that love for children belongs more to woman than to man. Alcestis loved them more than life, but so could Admetus if his heart were right.

The qualities in Alcestis transformed Admetus from a selfish coward into a strong man who preferred to die instead of his wife, or with her, and who wanted no life apart from her: "Thou alone living wast mine; and dead, mine only wife shalt thou be called: nor ever in thy stead shall bride Thessalian hail me as her lord" (328–331).[15] Alcestis so lifted the whole household—husband, children, and servants—that a servant could speak for all, "We have all perished, and not she alone" (825). The story is given a happy ending, as Hercules ambushes death and brings Alcestis back to life, but Euripides does not let this happy outcome in any way enter into the motive of Alcestis or Admetus. She went to her death thinking it final, and he firmly held to his new character and commitments when he thought that he would never see her again. It was a woman who excelled, yet there is no hint here that the qualities esteemed are male or female.

Hecuba (ca. 425 B.C.) is generally considered the first of Euripides' Trojan War plays, but its central theme is Hecuba herself, queen of the fallen Troy. This is a depth study of her character as she experiences the sufferings of a fallen city. Alongside Hecuba is her daughter Polyxena, sacrificed by the demand of Achilles as "a gift of honour for his tomb."[16] The first part of the play is about Polyxena, portrayed as going to her martyrdom with awesome qualities of character and spirit (341–378; 548–552). She can accept death but not slavery: "Never! — I will yield up this light from free eyes" (367). Her dying words would grace any martyr's lips:

> O Argives, ye which laid my city low,
> Free-willed I die: on my flesh let no man
> Lay hand: unflinching will I yield my neck.
> But, by the Gods, let me stand free, the while
> Ye slay, that I may die free; for I shame
> Slave to be called in Hades, who am royal.
>
> (Loeb, 547–552)

The Athenian Euripides never portrayed for his Athenian audience a Greek more noble than this vanquished Trojan nor a man more noble than this woman. Here humanity transcends both nationalism and sexual difference.

The second part of the play depicts Hecuba as she gets her revenge upon Polymestor, the king of Thrace who for gold killed her young son Polydorus, whom she had entrusted to Polymestor for safekeeping during the Trojan War. Hecuba stood up under the loss of the noble Polyxena, but when she learned of the death of her last child and only hope, her bitterness was such that she turned to cold-blooded vengeance, preferring vengeance over freedom (756f.). She tricked Polymestor and put him to a torturous and humiliating death. Euripides does not condone the cold fury of Hecuba, but he does put her consuming passion for revenge in the context of the larger depravity of men who slaughter for power, glory, gold, and revenge. Side by side he portrays the heroic in Polyxena and the cold fury of Hecuba. Qualities good and evil, beautiful and ugly belong to humanity, neither male nor female, Greek nor "barbarian" having exclusive rights to either.

Across the millennia, there may be few who have so boldly presented the case of woman, whatever the shortcomings of Euripides. His perspectives were offered the world which heavily impinged upon Jew and Christian, whatever the influence. It appears that Euripides was a Greek who struggled to be a citizen of the world, a man who struggled with the claims of non-Greek against Greek and of woman against man. Though he may never have worked it all out, he struggled with a feeling for the humanity which transcends the limits of nationality or sex. After all, is not this a basic perspective in all overcoming of racism, sexism, nationalism, or provincialism otherwise?

Aristophanes (ca. 448–380 B.C.)

Botsford and Sihler make the bold claim that Aristophanes in his comic play *Lysistrata* (411 B.C.) addressed the subject of woman's rights, "the first known piece of literature to do so."[17] This may be true, yet it may be exaggerated. Some have seen Aristophanes as an out-and-out reformer, others as simply an entertainer concerned only to make his audience laugh. The likelihood is that a complex of motives was at work in his plays.

The play is a powerful one in which on a Greek stage in Athens at the end of the fifth century B.C. women were portrayed as taking over the affairs of Athens and Sparta, ending a war that men seemed determined to perpetuate. Determined to end the war among the Greeks, Lysistrata rallied the women of Athens behind her plan, and she enlisted Lampito to do the same in Sparta. The women captured the Acropolis, locked out the men, already having covenanted to deny sex to their husbands until they turned from war to peace. The women themselves resisted Lysistrata's plan, not because they desired peace less than she but because they as normal women were as strongly sexed as men (Aristophanes does not hedge here). Under Lysistrata's unrelenting drive the women held out, using all their charms to excite the men but denying them fulfillment. Finally the men became so desperate that they capitulated, sex winning out over war.

A long dialogue between a magistrate of Athens and Lysistrata is not only clever and humorous, but the play brings into focus some significant issues. He demands of Lysistrata a reason for "this silly disturbance" of seizing the Acropolis (486f.).[18] She responds, "Keeping the silver securely in custody, lest for its sake ye continue the war." The magistrate finds it incredible that women could manage the budget: "You, women, you be the treasurers?" Lysistrata reminds him that women manage the economy of the household. "O, that is different," he retorts. She asks simply, "Why is it different?" When the magistrate protests that the money was "required for the fighting," she answers, "Well, but the fighting itself isn't requisite" (497). When the magistrate complains that now all is lost, Lysistrata rubs salt into his wounds by assuring him, "We will deliver you . . . whether you like it or not, we'll deliver you." So distraught is the magistrate that he can manage only to say, "Impudent hussy!" So it goes on and on. Lysistrata outwits him at every point and does so with poise and humor.

The magistrate's moment of truth comes when Lysistrata informs him of a mighty reversal: "Shift for the future our parts and our characters: you as the women in silence obey; we as the men, will harangue and provide for you; then shall the State be triumphant again, then shall we do what is best for the citizens" (526–528). Such for him would be "a shameful reproach and unbearable!"

Whatever the motive of Aristophanes, at least his play put the question of woman's rights and capabilities on the agenda twenty-five hundred years ago. Few writings before or since have given the subject so forceful an airing as done in this brilliant and "raunchy" play. If Aristophanes was concerned for woman's rights, he was moving against the stream, for Athens, including Plato, was moving the other way.

Menander (343/42 to 292/91 B.C.)

Only a few of the plays that Menander wrote have survived, and these are incomplete. Enough remains to disclose something of the status of women and the attitudes toward them in late fourth-century Greece. *The Epitrepontes* ("The Arbitrants"), the most nearly complete of the extant plays, features Pamphila, daughter of a well-to-do Athenian. She was brought up in seclusion, seemingly like all Athenian girls of means, and her father persisted even after her marriage in trying to exercise control over her. When he thought that her husband, Charisius, had been untrue to her, he sought to compel her to return to his home. Whether he was concerned most for his daughter or the dowry he had provided at her marriage is left in question (885, 866f.). That considerable freedom was granted single girls is implied from the Tauropolia, an annual all-night festival for girls, attended also by men. Though chaperoned, the monitoring was lax enough that Charisius had been able to separate Pamphila from the party long enough to get her pregnant (234–240).

Menander's strongest line supportive of the personhood of woman appears in Pamphila's protest to her father when the latter undertook to manage her affairs, even to the point of terminating her marriage to Charisius, whom both at the time thought to be untrue to her. Refusing to follow blindly her father's orders and insisting upon reasons for her being "rescued" by him, she says: "Necessary for my own good perhaps, but that's what you must make me see. Otherwise you'd be, not a father dealing with his daughter, but a master with his slave" (498f.).[19] Her strength of character is further displayed in her resolve to stay by her marriage even when she mistakenly thinks her husband to be untrue to her (637–646).

GREEK WRITERS (5TH TO 3D CENTURY B.C.)

Xenophon (434?–?355 B.C.)

Xenophon and Plato are often compared as to their attitudes toward women. Plato is represented as holding to the equality of men and women, and Xenophon viewing them as equals but with different gifts calling for different roles.[20] This is close to the truth about Xenophon but not about Plato. Plato called for equal "use" of women and men and accordingly for equal education, but he consistently affirmed that women were inferior to men. Xenophon's views were much more favorable to woman than Plato's, despite a latent male bias.

Xenophon praised Lycurgus, legislator of Sparta, for proposing equal diet and education for boys and girls. His concern was utilitarian, that girls be prepared to produce better offspring, and he saw the bearing of children as the highest function of a free woman (*Constitution of the Lacedaemonians,* I).[21] He saw men and women as having different capacities, calling for different roles; but his male bias comes through as he says, "Even in the matter of self-control, the males are stronger than the nature of females" (II).

It is in *Oeconomicus* ("Economics," i.e., management of a household or an estate) that Xenophon reveals most fully his perspective on woman. He has Socrates discuss the subject with Critobulus, the conversation turning to the case of Ischomachus, a man called "a gentleman" "by men, women, citizens and strangers alike" (VI.17).[22] Socrates relates a long conversation that he had with Ischomachus as to how he achieved the beauty and goodness by which he is universally acclaimed. Ischomachus credits his success to his partnership in marriage, by which he and his wife in a complementary relationship developed their gifts and estate together, he managing the outdoors and she the indoors (VII.3,13,16 *et passim*).

He explains to Socrates how it was that he was free to devote his energies to matters outside the home, accomplishing there the many achievements that won for him the name "gentleman." It was because his wife had achieved so fully in her sphere of management, that of the household from within. This was no accident, for Ischomachus had been a good teacher and she a good learner. The foundation for success was laid in his having acquired her at an early age: "She was not yet fifteen years old when she came to me, and up to that time she had lived in leading-strings, seeing, hearing, and saying as little as possible" (VII.5). Her parents had trained her to work with wool and to control her appetite, and that was a sufficient base (6). Ischomachus began training his wife early: "Well, Socrates, as soon as I found her docile and sufficiently domesticated to carry on conversation . . ." (10).

Xenophon is clear as to the mutuality proper to marriage as well as difference in complementary roles prescribed by nature or "the gods." He has Ischomachus say to his wife: "For it seems to me, dear, that the gods with great discernment have coupled together male and female, as they are called, chiefly in order that they may form a perfect partnership in mutual service" (VII.18). Nature is seen to dictate vocational differences: "And since both the indoor and the outdoor tasks demand labour and attention, God from the first adapted the woman's nature, I think, to the indoor and man's to the outdoor tasks and cares" (22). Even woman's role in nourishing infants is explained in terms of God's having "meted out to her a larger portion of affection for new-born babies than to the man" (24). Again, as the protector of the household "stores," "God meted out a larger share of fear to the woman than to the man" as he gave to man "a larger share of courage" (25). Having different aptitudes, "they have the more need of each other, and each member of the pair is the more useful to the other, the one being competent where the other is deficient" (28).

The chauvinism remains throughout, but it is tempered with deep respect. Although Ischomachus never relinquishes the role of teacher to his wife, he can with apparent joy and pride say to her:

> But the pleasantest experience of all is to prove yourself better than I am, to make me your servant; and, so far from having cause to fear that as you grow older you may not be honoured in the household, to feel confident that with advancing years, the better partner you prove to me and the better housewife to our children, the greater will be the honour paid to you in our home. For it is not through outward comeliness that the sum of things good and beautiful is increased in the world, but by the daily practice of the virtues. (VII.42–43a)

Whatever the lack, Xenophon at least undertook a serious assessment of the relationship between man and woman. He is free of the scorn for woman found far and wide. He finds essential meaning in sexual difference and in the complementary relationship, and he makes room for woman as "partner" and not necessarily as "junior partner."

Plato (427?–347 B.C.)

As seen above, it has been said that Plato recognized the equality of woman with man,[23] but this is not true. Plato advocated education for women, but he did this on utilitarian grounds, concerned to get from women the maximum service to the state. He emphatically declared woman to be inferior to man in all respects. His male bias is explicit and unrelieved.

In *The Republic,* Plato ascribed to Socrates the perspective which he adopted as his own, that men and women should have the best possible education for the good of the state, holding that despite some exceptions women generally are inferior to men (*Republic* V.449–471).[24] Socrates argues that just as there are male and female sheep dogs to guard the flock, so women as well as men should be guardians of the state. He holds that "there is no special faculty of administration in a state which a woman has because she is a woman, or which a man has by virtue of his sex," each sex having "the gifts of nature" alike; yet he adds, "but in all of them a woman is weaker than a man" (V.455de).

In *Laws* and *Critias,* Plato contends that women should be trained for war as well as for other services to the state. He argues that if for no other reason women, like birds, should be able to fight for their young, as when the men are away in a foreign war (*Laws* VII.814ab).

In *Timaeus,* Plato seems to cover the origin and nature of almost everything in the universe, including the origin of women. How seriously he wants to be taken may be debated, but a Platonic low is reached in this:

> On the subject of animals, then, the following remarks are offered. Of the men who came into the world, those who were cowards or led unrighteous lives may with reason be supposed to have changed into the nature of women in the second generation. (*Timaeus* 90c)

Thus man is prior to woman, and woman comes not from a "rib" but from cowardly and unrighteous men!

Woman fares no better in *Laws* than in *Timaeus,* for here she is found innately immoral. The Athenian stranger in the dialogue argues for "law and order in the state," contending in particular the mistakenness of "leaving the women unregulated by law" (*Laws* VI.780de). He refers to "that part of the human race which is by nature prone to secrecy and stealth on account of their weakness—I mean the female sex—has been left alone by the legislator as hopelessly undisciplined, which is a mistake" (VI.781a).

Women and eunuchs are found to be bad educators for children, for they fail to discipline them (*Laws* III.694–695a). Even mothers are seen as a threat to the character of their children: "The character of the son begins to develop when he hears his mother complaining that her husband has no place in the government, of which the consequence is that she has no precedence among other women . . . adding all the other complaints . . . which women are so fond of rehearsing" (*Republic* VIII.549cd).

Aristotle (384–322 B.C.)

Plato's most famous student may have departed from his teacher in some ways, but in no significant way does he modify Plato's low view of woman. More serious than his male chauvinism is Aristotle's failure to see the worth of personhood as such. It is here that Plato and Aristotle fall woefully behind Aeschylus and Euripides, who seriously struggled with the questions of freedom, dignity, and justice for all people.

Aristotle elevated the state (ironically the city-state, which obviously had had its day) above lesser communities (i.e., the family) and the individual. He applied here his method of analysis which runs through all his treatises, that "a compound should always be resolved into the simple elements or least parts of the whole" (*Politics* I.1).[25]

Aristotle saw the state as made up of households, and he has his own domestic code, a complete household consisting of slaves and freemen: "the first and least parts of a family are master and slave, husband and wife, father and children" (*Politics* I.3). He sees the slave as "property," as "a kind of instrument," "an instrument for maintaining life," "a living possession," slaves as "instruments of production," etc. (I.4).

One key to Aristotle's ability to relegate much of humanity to a subhuman status is his principle of "rule," which he finds throughout nature (Jesus elevated the principle of servanthood above rulership). Aristotle "on grounds both of reason and of fact" contends: "For that some should rule, and others be ruled is a thing not only necessary but expedient; from the hour of their birth, some are marked out for subjection, others for rule" (*Politics* I.5).

As to family rule, Aristotle is explicit: "A husband and father rules over wife and children, both free; but the rule differs, the rule over children being a royal, over wife a constitutional rule"

(*Politics* I.12). Acknowledging exceptions in nature, he yet contends that "the male is by nature fitter for command than the female" and that between male and female "the inequality is permanent" *(ibid.)*. Aristotle raises the question as to whether women and children "have virtues" (I.13). In an arbitrary way, despite his assumed logic, he pontificates about male and female, master and slave, parent and child. He explains, "For the slave has no deliberative faculty at all; the woman has, but it is without authority, and the child has, but it is immature" *(ibid.)*. He declares further, "The courage of a man is shown in commanding, of a woman in obeying" *(ibid.)*. He concludes his domestic code with a position already taken by Plato, "Women and children must be trained by education with an eye to the state" *(ibid.)*. This is utilitarian in purpose, not a recognition of the dignity, worth, or freedom of woman.

As will be seen later, there was a widely employed "domestic code" *(Haustafel)* among early Christians, as reflected in the parallels in Eph. 5:22–6:4; Col. 3:18–4:1; 1 Tim. 5:1–6:2; Titus 2:1–10; and 1 Peter 3:1–9. Whatever the limitations there, they belong to another world and another perspective as compared with Aristotle. Plato and Aristotle both reflected much of their world's perspective on woman, and they belonged far more to the problem than to the answer. They failed even to measure up to the best in their own Greek tradition.

Theocritus (fl. ca. 270 B.C.)

A Greek poet of the third century B.C., Theocritus, who lived both in Syracuse and Alexandria, portrayed the common people, and his *Idyl* XV throws light on women in Alexandria, Egypt. Gorgo and Praxinoë were apparently middle-class, with slave-girl attendants, and they went together to see a festival following the marriage of Ptolemy Philadelphus (ca. 266 B.C.). They are pictured as somewhat lighthearted, now blaming in a free but not too serious mood a stupid husband for his blunders or jealousy, picking at one another in the security of mutual acceptance, chattering constantly, yet knowledgeable about the larger world. One of the entertainers at the festival is a woman singer who exceeds Gorgo's expectations: "Praxinoë, the woman is cleverer than we fancied! Happy woman to know so much, thrice happy to have so sweet a voice."[26]

This is a far cry from restrictions upon Jewish and other women who were to be seen as little as possible. The poet is male, but for what his poetry is worth, he does not depict the Greek woman in Alexandria as confined to the house, gagged as to speech in public, or feeling sorry for herself. The "griping" sounds more like the universal pastime of all men and women of all times. As far as it goes, the work of Theocritus implies considerable freedom to middle-class women in Alexandria at this time.

GREEK TO GRECO-ROMAN

The Greeks continued to be a significant people throughout the period of our concern, i.e., into the Christian era; but by the second century B.C., Rome was the political power to which eventually the whole Mediterranean world was compelled to bow. Rome's rise began in the third century B.C., and by 197 B.C. Rome had liberated Greece from the Macedonian threat and had formed a protective alliance with Greece. Already Rome had come under the spell of Greek culture, including its literature. Such was the mixture of two cultures that "Greco-Roman" describes the result. Breaking off here in our tracing of woman's position as reflected in Greek literature, we turn now to the considerably Grecianized (Hellenized) Roman world.

Chapter 3

THE
ROMAN WORLD

Describing the Roman world is not a simple task, even though the undertaking is limited, as here, to woman in it. Rome dominated the whole world known to Jesus and his earliest followers, but Rome itself was greatly shaped by the Greeks. To sort out all the currents that flowed through the Greco-Roman world into which Jesus was born is beyond the scope of this book. Intended is some portrayal of the Roman woman as to her role and status, and as she is seen through Roman eyes.

The drama of Plautus and Terence took its model in the New Comedy of Menander, not that of Aristophanes. Its concern was not to challenge established ways of life, although there is occasional moralizing, but to entertain a theater audience with a reflection of its own ways, leaving the audience comfortable in its prosperity and security.[1] Their plays are set usually in Athens, and their characters bear Greek names, but basically it is Roman life that is pictured. Edith Hamilton observes that under Roman rule no one could write anything defamatory of Rome or laugh directly at its citizens.[2] Thus is found a reason for a setting outside Italy.

The Roman family is sharply etched: the authoritarian father; the "matronly" mother; the son who, when compelled to choose between duty to parents or love for wife or mistress, chooses the former; the daughter whose whole life is subject to arrangement by father or husband. Yet the picture is not that unambiguous. The Roman woman had her own power and influence within the home and knew how to use it on occasion. In the home the wife is sufficiently powerful that the "henpecked" husband appears for the first time in literature. The double standard for men and women is generally recognized, providing for roaming husbands, courtesans, winking at "discreet and occasional" affairs of husbands, but with uncompromised chastity for the wife. For the young it was a rather permissive society. There is hugging and kissing galore throughout the plays, and premarital sex is commonplace. Although parents arranged marriages, young people also "fell in love" and would move heaven and earth to free themselves for marriage. Many marriages were arranged by parents, and here the dowry was a fixed item, in effect the purchase of a husband for a bride. Dowry-based marriages are usually pictured as loveless, especially in the later years. The dowry gave the wife virtual control over the dependent husband, and he saw himself as having been robbed of his freedom.

Plautus (254?–184 B.C.)

With the comic plays of Plautus we have our first direct expression of Roman life through a Roman writer.[3] Since comedy serves its purpose only as it reflects the life-style of its audience, it may be assumed that these plays do tell us something of Roman ways, perspectives, and values of the time.

Amphitryon is a rather simple play featuring the dirty tricks of the gods Jupiter and Mercury played upon a Theban family. Amphitryon, commander in chief of the Theban army, is deeply devoted to his wife, Alcmena, and his first concern upon returning from a successful campaign is to get home to his wife, share with her the glory and rewards of victory, and be with her again. She is equally devoted to him, living for his return. Even the mean tricks of the gods, who pose as Amphitryon and his slave Sosia, are not strong enough to overcome completely the love that binds Amphitryon and Alcmena, even though the confusion of it all drives them to desperation.

Prized above all else in a Roman wife was that she be chaste. This was nonnegotiable. There was more than that expected of her, of course. For our understanding of the Roman wife of the period, the quiet words of Alcmena are most significant:

Personally I do not feel that my dowry is that which people call a dowry, but purity and honour and self-control, fear of God, love of parents, and affection for my family, and being a dutiful wife to you, sir, lavish of loving-kindness and helpful through honest service. (*Amphitryon* II.839–842)

Alongside the model matron Plautus also knows the wife who actually rules the roost, especially when the money in the family is her inheritance. The henpecked husband appears in such a play as *The Comedy of Asses*. Demaenetus lived in dread of his wife (I.16–22), having yielded to her the real headship of the family by accepting an overriding dowry to begin with: "Sold myself! Gave up my authority for a dowry!" (I.87). His ultimate humiliation comes when his wife, finally alerted to his two-timing manner, drags him by the ear out of a courtesan's house in plain view of their son, slaves, and acquaintances.

In *The Comedy of Asses*, Artemona is chaste and the de facto head of the household, but she is not in any sense a strong or beautiful character. Her power is in her purse, and her domination is over a weasel husband, Demaenetus. The other women in the play are likewise lacking in nobility, especially Cleareta in her determination to secure herself financially by offering her daughter Philaenium to the man with the most cash. The two young people in the play, typically, are madly in love with each other, but there is nothing to indicate more than sexual attraction. As usual in the Roman plays, "love" is for the young, with no trace of it in the typical aged couple. Demaenetus would "rather drink bilge water" than kiss his wife (V.895); and as to love, he tells their own son, "Love her? I? I love her now for not being near" (V.900).

Some trace of patriarchal domination lingers even in the dishonest and weak Demaenetus, in his son's yielding to his father that he share a night with his son's girl. The son is not happy with the arrangement, but he yields, recognizing a son's duty to his father. Dolefully yet "faithfully" he gives his filial love and his girl to his father: "Ah yes, father, I give you both, as a son should" (V.836).

Roman plays laugh at woman in a way not done in the Greek plays, despite the presence in the latter of lines unfavorable to woman. The stereotype is far more pronounced and unrelieved in Roman plays.

A daughter was fully dependent upon her parents, and her obedience to mother or father was expected. In *The Persian* the attractive and highly intelligent and articulate daughter of the "parasite" Saturio boldly and tactfully seeks to dissuade her father from some of his shady business dealings, but never does she challenge his right to command her, even if it is to be used by him in some deception (III.329–399). When Saturio charges her with impertinence, the daughter replies, "No, I'm not, sir, and I don't hold it impertinent to give my father good advice, young though I am." She further warns him, "Father, dishonour is deathless; it goes on living even when you think it's dead." And again to her father, "And any girl or woman is certainly bad if she holds her peace when she sees things going wrong." For all her courage and conviction, she will not disobey her father. When Saturio, impatient to get on with his dishonest scheme, demands threateningly, "Do you intend to obey your father's orders, or not?" the answer is predictable: "I do."

Terence (185–159 B.C.)

Six plays of Terence come down to us, written by a young man who died at age twenty-six. All six plays center in family life, with major attention given the love life of the young. Fathers are the heads of the families, most of them authoritarian but with their own problems and, on occasion, vulnerable to intimidation by wife or son. Mothers are totally absent from some of the plays, and wives normally are subordinate to their husbands. Young men are girl-crazy, and to Terence premarital sex is almost the rule. Whatever the conduct of the young people, their marriages are to be arranged by or sanctioned by their fathers.

In *The Mother-in-Law,* Terence presents family roles clearly etched. Pamphilus was in love with Bacchis, a courtesan, but his father, Laches, wanted him to marry Philumena. Terence thus characterizes Laches and the times: ". . . talking just the strain of all fathers, how he was old and had only that one son and wanted

a protection for his old age" (I.115ff.). Pamphilus struggles between two claims, "whether to listen more to duty or to love"
(I.122).⁴ The outcome of the son's yielding to his father's will is
predictable. Later Pamphilus reflects, "I couldn't for a moment
bring myself to refuse the wife that my father thrust upon me"
(II.293ff.).

Pamphilus went through the wedding but did not consummate
it, "either that night or the next" (I.136f.). After the wedding he
continued his relationship with Bacchis, although "she at once
became much more unamiable and mercenary," now that he was
no longer her own (I.15–60). It was a man's world, in which a
husband's roaming was normal but in which a wife was expected
to be chaste. Philumena simply made the best of a bad situation:
"In the true spirit of a gentlewoman, retiring and modest, his wife
put up with her husband's unpleasantness and outrages and concealed his affronts" (I.164f.). Gradually Pamphilus shifted his love
from Bacchis to his loyal wife.

Parental claim upon children is seen to extend into the married
lives of the latter. When Pamphilus mistakenly thinks that his
wife's pregnancy is by some other man, he retains some sense of
loyalty to her; but his primary concern is to protect his parents
from any shame: "I will do what I can [for my wife] consistently
with my duty to my parents, for I ought to respect my father before
my love" (III.445ff.). If he must choose between wife and mother,
Pamphilus concludes, "Now my filial respect urges me to prefer the
happiness of my mother" (III.481).

The Mother-in-Law reflects little consistency as to moral standards. Phidippus, father of Philumena, found no problem in his
daughter's marrying a young man who had a mistress. In fact, he
went so far as to say that he would have distrusted his son-in-law
had he too abruptly broken with his mistress. It is "more reasonable for us to wink at it" than make an issue of such a matter, so
long as the husband is "discreet and occasional" in his visits with
his mistress, he argues (IV.550ff.).

The ever-present double standard appears here. Philumena was
pregnant, unknowingly by her husband, who had raped her in the
dark, neither recognizing the other. The infidelity of a woman was

a crime so great that Philumena's secret was carefully guarded, lest the wrath of offended men fall upon her. The offending male was secure unless he had encroached upon another male's rights.

Throughout, Terence worked with plays borrowed from Greece, and he retained Greek names for persons and places. Since a comedy must reflect the life of the audience, it follows that what is reflected is Roman family life, not Greek. That the plays were played and that they have survived, really as the foundation to modern European drama, implies that they must have fairly well represented Roman life.

Cicero (106–43 B.C.)

Marcus Tullius Cicero was an orator, lawyer, statesman, and prolific writer. He was a major figure in the history of Rome from its decline as a republic to the rise of Octavian. Cicero was close to and critical of the formation of the famous triumvirate of Crassus, Pompey, and Caesar, rejecting an invitation to join the three. He was routinely host or dinner guest to the power figures of the century: Pompey, Caesar, Brutus, Cassius, Anthony, et al. Cleopatra, whom he detested, once lived across the river from him. His personal ups and downs varied with those of Rome: once consul of the republic, exiled in the early 50's, caught between the clashing ambitions of Pompey and Caesar, and finally executed by the twenty-year-old Octavian, who was subsequently the "Augustus Caesar" when Jesus was born.

From the hundreds of extant letters of Cicero much light is thrown upon woman in the Roman world in the century before the birth of Jesus. Caution must be observed lest the world of Cicero be equated with the Roman world itself. Cicero's whole adult life was lived in the inner circle of the power structures of Roman society: political, economic, military, social. Cicero loved the "simple life," which to him was freedom to move at will into the center of the stage of public life or retreat to his town house or his many suburban, village, country, or seashore villas, with lictors, couriers, and slaves to run his daily errands and protect his privacy. Cicero's world is not to be confused with that of the masses of people, yet

Cicero does represent a significant part of the real Roman world into which Jesus came.

Cicero was a true scholar, and he has left us many major essays, addresses, and books in philosophy, politics, and morals. Additionally, he was a most prolific letter writer, hundreds of such extant letters having been written to his bosom friend Atticus, his alter ego to whom he bared his mind and heart on almost every area of his life, public and private, from 68 B.C. until shortly before his execution in 43 B.C. Although basically candid and often devastatingly open in his public speech and writing, Cicero could be diplomatic and almost manipulative of power figures. So the real Cicero is not always apparent in such public statements. However, in his letters to Atticus he often sent a copy of a letter or speech with its language of diplomacy and with it what he really thought and felt. These letters, then, though just a part of what is extant from Cicero, represent Cicero's most unguarded thought and feeling.[5]

In Cicero's Roman world women had a rather secure and meaningful place within the home, and they were not excluded from public life. Government belonged almost exclusively to men, though Cleopatra, powerful queen of Egypt (69–30 B.C.), is not to be discounted; and Servilia seems to have controlled the Empire's corn market in 44 B.C. Cleopatra and Servilia were more exceptional than normal, but there was place for them as for Paul's merchant friend Lydia from Thyatira (Acts 16:14).

Cicero's letters contain no trace of misogyny. Cicero almost always sends his greetings to Pilia, wife of Atticus, and to Attica, his daughter. He sends greetings from Terentia, his wife of many years and mother of the pride and joy of his life, his own daughter, Tullia. There is not a trace of bias for a son against a daughter as found in the Jewish world and in much of the pagan world. Infanticide would have been unthinkable to Cicero and Atticus, both of whom lavished their love upon their daughters, almost to the point of worshiping them. The famous papyrus letter a generation later (1 B.C.) in which a husband wrote his expecting wife his instructions, to the effect that if she bore a son, she was to keep it but if a daughter, to "expose" it, i.e., put her out to die,[6] is to be taken at face value. To many, girl babies were not wanted, and husbands in the pagan world could legally commit unwanted baby girls to death. But Cicero and Atticus represent a world far removed from this. When Attica was born (50 B.C.) Cicero wrote Atticus, "I am glad you take delight in your baby daughter, and have satisfied yourself that a desire for children is natural" (VII.2). Cicero and Atticus even enjoy representing it as though their little daughters are in complete command of them. Cicero writes: "Your tiny daughter has done me a favor in ordering you earnestly to send me her greetings" (V.1). Of his own daughter he playfully writes: "My little darling, Tullia, keeps asking for your promised present and duns me as though I were answerable for you. But I am going to deny my obligation rather than pay up" (I.8).

Marriages were negotiated by parents, but in Cicero's circle the feelings of sons and daughters were considered. Tullia was engaged more than once, and she participated in decisions affecting her life. When Tullia married Dolabella, Cicero took it in stride, although his preference would have been otherwise:

> While in my province I show Appius every honour, suddenly I find myself father-in-law of Dolabella his accuser. You invoke heaven's benison. So say I, and you I know are sincere. Believe me, it was the last thing I had expected. . . . I understand that my women folk are highly pleased with the young man's obliging and courteous temper. As for the rest, don't pick holes in him. (VI.6)

Subsequently, Cicero was supportive of his daughter's choice: "My son-in-law is agreeable to me, to Tullia, and to Terentia. He has any amount of native charm or shall I say culture: and that is enough" (VII.3).

As often among advantaged Romans, Tullia's marriage ended in divorce. In marriage, a dowry went with the bride to the husband, but there were controls as to its use. The dowry was paid in three installments, and in the event of divorce a settlement was made in favor of the one not initiating the divorce. If the wife divorced her husband, any remaining installments were to be paid, unless she could prove that he had been guilty of misconduct. If the husband initiated the divorce, he was to refund the dowry.

Cicero's marriage to Terentia finally ended in divorce. For the most part he gave her fullest respect, including her greetings in his letters and recognizing her rights and responsibilities in decision-making. Gradually the marriage lost its love, and eventually the relationship became sufficiently strained to admit his suspicions of her dishonesty (XI.24). We do not hear her side.

The many marital failures reflected in the letters of Cicero do not imply misogyny nor a low view of woman. They reflect a breakdown in human relationships, with offenses on both sides. Cicero himself knows how to plead with women in his family but not to command them (VII.14).

Catullus (ca. 84 to ca. 54 B.C.)

Poets do not speak for or to all people, but they do represent a significant part of their world. Valerius Catullus' thirty or so years fell in that significant period when Rome was moving from a republic toward imperial rule. The consuming theme of his poetry, though there are others, is that of love between a man and a woman. His poetry throws considerable light on perspectives on woman and her status, at least in a part of the Roman world in the century before the Christian era.[7] The most intense and moving poetry extant from Catullus is addressed to or is about his "Lesbia," his name for the famous or infamous Clodia, a beautiful and radically independent member of the powerful Claudian family and also wife of the Consul Metellus Celer (60 B.C.). For some time Clodia and Catullus carried on an intense relationship, inspiring his most beautiful poems. However, Clodia soon betrayed him in favor of numerous other lovers, and his subsequent poetry reflects his passionate effort to win her back and finally his bitter disillusionment with her and women in general.

While their relationship was firm, Catullus' poetry was winged with song. Although Catullus loved Lesbia as a person, not just as a sex object, and sought to win her love, not command it, the physical was unashamedly extolled:

Let us live, my Lesbia, and love, and value at one farthing all the talk of crabbed old men.

Suns may set and rise again. For us, when the short light has once set, remains to be slept the sleep of one unbroken night.

Give me a thousand kisses, then a hundred, then another thousand, then a second hundred, then yet another thousand, then a hundred. Then, when we have made up many thousands, we will confuse our counting, that we may not know the reckoning, nor any malicious person blight them with evil eye, when he knows that our kisses are so many. (*Poems* V)[8]

To Catullus, love was to be won, not coerced: "Farewell, my mistress; now Catullus is firm; he will not seek you nor ask you against your will" (*Poems* VIII). When his cause became yet more hopeless, Catullus cried out to his friend, "O, Caelius, my Lesbia, that Lesbia, Lesbia whom alone Catullus loved more than himself and all his own, now in the cross-roads and alleys serves the filthy lusts of the descendants of lordly-minded Remus" (LVIII). Finally, in utter despair and bitterness Catullus seemingly stereotypes all women: "The woman I love says that there is no one whom she would rather marry than me, not if Jupiter himself were to woo her. Says; —but what a woman says to her ardent lover should be written in wind and running water" (LXX).

Catullus maintains no true stereotype of men or women, but he does reach out desperately for a love that binds a man and a woman to each other, and he sinks into despair when such love is betrayed on either side.

Despite his personal disappointment and bitter disillusionment in his affair with Clodia, Catullus was able to write beautiful epithalamia (nuptial songs and poems to a bride and groom), these providing the best literary witness to the Roman marriage ceremonial of the time. The songs trace the ceremonial steps in which bride and groom were brought from betrothal to the marriage chamber. They make explicit such customs as the transfer of authority over the girl from her parents to the groom, the feigned reluctance of the bride to surrender her virginity to her husband, the eagerness of each for the other, the parts played by attendants to bride and groom, the careful carrying of the bride across the threshold lest some hostile spirit be aroused, the surrender of bachelor freedom for the bride alone, and the anticipation of a son to bear such likeness to his father that the bride's chastity be validated.

Indeed, it may be said that the marriage poems of Catullus do have a heavy erotic strain, but the unabashed sensual dimension is never simply that. There is no degrading of woman or sex. The approach is human, personal, and holistic.

Tibullus (54?–?18 B.C.)

Albius Tibullus was probably the purest of the Roman elegiac poets of his time. His themes were Roman, and he was committed to Roman life in simplest expression, even though he was a Roman of equestrian family. He despised war and also the greed that sent men across land and sea in quests for riches and glory. His poetry esteems the simple life content with a cozy fire in winter and the shade of a tree and flow of a stream in summer. These simple joys were to be shared with one to love and by whom to be loved. For Tibullus that was enough. He could leave to fools or worse the chasing of defeated armies, victory parades, trophies from conquest, whether merchandising or war. Of love and the simple things of life Tibullus sang, and his poems always sing and soar.

Tibullus was sensual but not a mere sensualist. Like Catullus, he unabashedly rejoiced in the sexual dimensions of love, but woman was more than a sex object for him. Sex for sale was to him an anomaly. He rejoiced in the physical beauty of a woman but never as an animal. A woman's love was to be won, not gained by contract or coercion. His own life goals are explicit:

> I ask not for the riches of my sires or the gains which garnered harvests brought to my ancestors of yore. A small field's produce is enough—enough if I may sleep upon my bed and the mattress ease my limbs as heretofore. What delight to hear the winds rage as I lie and hold my love safe in my gentle clasp; or, when the stormy South Wind sheds the chilling showers, to follow the road of untroubled sleep, the rain my lullaby! This be my lot; let him be rightly rich who can bear the rage of the sea and the dreary rain. Ah, sooner let all the gold and all the emeralds perish from the world than any maiden weep for my departings. (I.i.41–50)[9]

To the theme of the preference of love and the simple life at home over conquest afar Tibullus often returns:

> That man was iron who, when thou mightest have been his, chose rather to follow war and plunder. Let him chase Cilicia's routed troops before him, and pitch his marital camp upon captured ground; let folk gaze upon him as he sits his swift charger, from head to foot a tissue of silver and gold, if only with thee, my Delia, I may put the oxen in the yoke and feed my flock on the familiar hill; and, so my young arms may hold thee fast, I shall find soft slumber even on the rugged earth. (I.ii.65–74)

In the poetry of Tibullus woman is never presented as a public figure, and this may be significant. On the other hand, Tibullus has no attraction whatever to a public life for himself or anyone. If he sees woman only in the role of lover, wife, or homemaker, it is because he prizes no other life. For war, so much a part of the Rome he knew, he had undisguised scorn: "Who was the first discoverer of the horrible sword? How savage was he and literally iron! Then slaughter and battles were born into the world of men: then to grisly death a shorter road was opened" (I.x.1–4). With war he links gold and the highly coveted products of culture for which men fight: "This curse of precious gold; nor were there wars when the cup of beechwood stood beside men's food. There were no citadels, no palisades, and void of care the flock's commander courted sleep with his sheep of divers hue around him" (I.x.7–10). In the generation just before the birth of Jesus a voice from within the circle of highest Roman advantage with lyric beauty sang out loud and clear of love and of woman. And he did so in a manner that puts him in a world above much of the crudity of men of privilege who should have known better. Jesus went far beyond and above Tibullus, but between them was more affinity than might be expected, just as there was a mighty chasm between Jesus and many who should have been his spiritual kin but who were not— not at least in perspectives on woman.

Propertius (49?-?15 B.C.)

Propertius throws considerable light upon at least the advantaged stratum of Roman society during the time of Augustus.[10] Woman in the world that Propertius knew moved about quite freely and had considerable control over her own life.

Propertius' own Cynthia, his mistress for at least five years, dominated much of his life and was for much of his poetry his major inspiration. He was attracted to her both for her physical beauty and for her literary inclination as well as for her gifts in dance and song. His respect for her judgment is explicit:

> I marvel not only at comeliness of form, nor if a woman boasts glorious ancestry. Be it rather my joy to have read my verse as I lay in the arms of a learned maid and to have pleased her pure ears with what I write. When such bliss hath fallen to my lot, farewell the confused talk of the people; I will rest secure in the judgment of my mistress. (II.xii.9–14)

Propertius attests to the power of a woman over a man, sometimes gladly and sometimes in protest: "Why marvellest thou that a woman sways my life and drags my manhood captive beneath her rule?" (III.xi.1–3). After breaking with Cynthia he writes, "For five years I had the heart to be thy faithful slave" (III.xxv.3). Reacting to Cynthia's infidelity to him, Propertius finds woman's record to be such: "Sooner shalt thou have power to dry the waters of the deep and pluck down the lofty stars with mortal hand, than bring it to pass that our maids should refuse to sin" (II.xxxii.49–51).

Stereotype of woman appears in Propertius' charge of greed: "Ye ask, wherefore the greed of women makes their love so costly, and wherefore our empty coffers cry out that Venus has been their bane" (III.xiii.1f.). Stung by the competition of rich lovers who came with expensive gifts whereas he had only his poetry to offer, Propertius charges, apparently with considerable truth, that women tended to give their favors to the rich. He did see expensive gifts as the corrupter of women. But he went beyond this. At the very time Augustus was leading the Romans to world domination and prosperity, Propertius warned: "I will speak out; and may my country find me a true seer! Rome is being shattered by her own prosperity" (III.xiii.59f.).

In Propertius we hear a pagan who lived in Rome just before the birth of Jesus. His poetry is free of misogyny, though his frustrated love often lashes out bitterly. Although he reflects clearly the lovers who fight and sometimes make up, making irresponsible charges in their changing moods, there is here no such low view of woman as found elsewhere so widely. There is no hint that woman is inferior to man, intellectually or morally or otherwise. There is here no unwillingness to relate to a woman as a person in the fullest sense, as a peer in the arts and literature included.

Vergil (70–19 B.C.)

Publius Vergilius Maro is best known for his *Aeneid,* the Roman counterpart to Homer's *Odyssey.* In this epic, Vergil traces the career of Aeneas, the Trojan who lays the foundation for Rome and the Empire over which Augustus presided as Vergil composed the *Aeneid* (30–19 B.C.). Vergil was contemporary with Augustus (63 B.C.–A.D. 14), and he was his ardent supporter as Octavian became Augustus in 27 B.C., the first Emperor of Rome. The *Aeneid* is a classic representative of civil religion, its explicit and unrelenting theme being the divine ordination that in Aeneas a new Trojan-Latin race be founded, the beginning of Rome. This was "manifest destiny," the divine compulsion that Rome be so founded.

In the *Aeneid* woman holds a prominent place, with her own dignity, power, and freedom. There is no misogyny, no denigration of woman, and relatively little stereotype. There are conventional roles as normative, yet these may be crossed or transcended. Women can be good or bad in the *Aeneid,* but so may men. Never are women expected to remain silent, stay indoors, be veiled, or become second-class. Women and men appear together in the epic as belonging alike to the human scene and sharing alike the agonies, joys, and frustrations of life.

Some of the strongest characters in the *Aeneid* are women, reflecting for the most part traits that are human, neither male nor female in particular. Dido is a dominant figure through Books I-IV. She had led some Phoenicians in the founding of a new state at Carthage, and she is queen in fact as in name. Her people in Carthage recognize her as "the key to the creation of her state" (I, p. 20)[11]. Vergil pauses to register a point, "And who was the leader of this enterprise? Dido, a woman!" (p. 16). Dido was not only the esteemed founder and leader of her people, but she for years remained uncompromisingly faithful to Sychaeus, her first husband, "whose single infidelity was with death" (p. 75). Only the power of the goddess Venus can overcome Dido's fidelity to vows made to a now deceased husband. Venus does bring her son Aeneas and Dido together, stranded alone in a cave in which they took refuge from a violent thunderstorm. Even so, it was only after an agonizing struggle that Dido yields to the claims of a new love:

> Yes! I feel again some trace of love's first fires!
> But oh! Let the earth gape open to its core,
> Let God Almighty dash me with thunderbolts
> To the darkness, the blank of hell, to uttermost night,
> Before I lie with another man and break
> My vows to the man I married. He has my heart,
> It is his to hold, it is his alone—let him keep it
> There in the tomb.
>
> (IV, p. 76)

With Venus at work behind the scenes, Dido finally yielded: "Her chastity melted in a furnace of desire and she made up her mind" *(ibid.)*. Once her mind was made up, this strong and free-spirited woman gave herself voluntarily to Aeneas as her master, prepared to risk the loss of her people's loyal support as the price for her Aeneas. It was a shattering blow to her when suddenly and unannounced Aeneas and his Trojans sailed away from Carthage, intending to abandon Dido without a word. Discovering the move, Dido pleaded desperately that he remain and then as she saw that "All, all is gone," she "fumed," called him traitor, and evoked a curse upon him, finally seeking escape in suicide (pp. 83–93). The gamut of thoughts and feelings attributed to Dido are human, not those of a particular sex. At no point does Vergil denigrate her. It is Destiny which rules, Jupiter's overriding will that Aeneas move on to his "Roman inheritance."

Of the many great women in the *Aeneid,* Camilla stands out in a role not conventional yet by no means singular for women in the world known to Vergil. This warrior maid, adored leader of the Volscian cavalry, was the bravest and most skillful of the allies of Turnus, the Italian rival to the aspirations of Aeneas. Hers was no idle boast as she volunteered to lead the fight against Aeneas and the invading Trojans: "O Turnus, if the brave may fitly feel confident of themselves I am confident. I offer therefore boldly to oppose the Trojan cavalry forces and I myself will ride alone against the Etruscan horsemen, let my hand strike the first blow of the perilous battle" (XI, p. 260). Turnus proudly responded, "You are to be in joint command with me!" *(ibid.).* With the choice of "Italy's daughters" about her—"Larina, Tulla and Tarpeia"—she devastated the opposing cavalry, only falling at last to the arrow shot from ambush by a cowardly man who did not dare enter the open fight. Although Camilla fought with "one breast laid bare for ease in the fight" (p. 264), it was not to her beauty but to her weapons that the men fell in open battle.

Vergil is neither a woman libber nor a woman hater. Men and women are people in his epic poem. They are both different and alike. Although there are traces of stereotype (cf. pp. 90, 157, 205), although beautiful girls are known as coveted prizes in war or bribes for favors (cf. pp. 9, 102, 199), and although it is recognized that it is a father's "right" to give his daughter in marriage to whom he chooses (X, p. 225), these traces of discrimination are by far overshadowed by the larger scene in which men and women meet and compete in terms of their own individual gifts and inclinations. Fate, Destiny, and the gods and goddesses have the final say, but within these limits are the human qualities which wear no sexist label.

Ovid (43 B.C. to A.D. 17)

About A.D. 8, Jesus at age twelve was taken to the Temple at Jerusalem (Jesus was born not later than 4 B.C., our present calendar being off at least four years). In that same year Publius Ovidius Naso was banished from Rome by the Emperor Augustus, chiefly because of a book he had written on *The Art of Love (Ars Amatoria)*. Ovid was also charged with some minor act which offended Augustus, the precise nature of which is unknown to us. This now unknown "error" was only the occasion for the banishment, for the emperor had for some years resented Ovid's *The Art of Love,* this work being in direct conflict with "reforms" instituted by Augustus. Ovid's poem probably tells us much about Roman society in the days of Augustus, especially a side of it which Augustus wished to suppress.

Ars Amatoria is extremely erotic, offering instruction in almost everything relating to winning, enjoying, and keeping a lover. Two of its three books offer instruction to men, but its third book is addressed to women seeking to win a man. Especially was it offensive to Augustus because it not only reflected erotic patterns but *taught* them.

That *Ars Amatoria* spoke both to and for Roman society can hardly be doubted, else the action of Augustus is hardly understandable. Had Ovid's book enjoyed little influence or had it not reflected Roman life to any considerable degree, it is not likely that Augustus would have found it a threat calling for Ovid's banishment.

Ovid was never strictly sensual. For him sex was empty unless experienced as fully by the woman as the man. With other Roman poets of the time, he had no use for harlotry. To buy sex like potatoes could hardly please any poet. Even with a lover the enjoyment, even "frenzy," must be mutual or the act empty. For Ovid a woman was not something to be used even in love or marriage. For all his sensuality, this Roman pagan who wrote during the early childhood of Jesus went far in recognizing the personhood of woman alongside that of man:

> Let both man and woman feel what delights them equally. I hate embraces which leave not each outworn; that is why a boy's love [a novice?] appeals to me but little. I hate her who gives because she must, and who, herself unmoved, is thinking of her wool [a woman's chore].

Pleasure given as a duty has no charms for me; for me let no woman
be dutiful. (II.682–688)[12]

Ovid esteemed the woman of culture far above the one who only
bartered her body for the expensive gifts of her suitors. With
Propertius, he protested "the age of gold." He idealized the woman
of such literary inclination and competence that she would respond
more to the lover who came with poetry than with gold. He de-
plored it that many would turn away Homer in favor of a barbarian
who came with expensive gifts:

Poems are praised, but costly gifts are sought; so be he wealthy, even
a barbarian pleases. Now truly is the age of gold: by gold comes many
an honour, by gold is affection gained. Though you come, Homer, and
all the Muses with you, if you bring nothing, Homer, out you go!
(II.275–280)

The third book of *The Art of Love* is addressed to woman. It
gives a comprehensive treatment of cosmetics, clothes, hair styles,
removal of unsightly hair from the legs, whitening the teeth, fresh-
ening the breath, on occasion working hard to appear as being
casual in hairdo or dress, and mastering all the seductive arts. Ovid
then turns to culture as most important in the art of love. He
encourages women to become skilled with lyre and harp and to
know the best of literature. The sensual, sordid, and all that understandably would arouse the ire of Augustus is there, explicitly there
in its erotic and sometimes almost pornographic expression. Yet
significantly there is likewise a recognition of woman as equally
with man a human being, a person in her own right. Ovid obviously
requires redemption; but for all his lack, is not Ovid more redeem-
able than the Augustus who banished him?

Ovid gave major space to the enhancement of physical beauty
and high priority to culture for woman, but he did not overlook
the importance of character, whatever may have been his limited
understanding of that. Even in his poem *On Painting the Face* he
stresses the priority of character:

Think first, ye women, to look to your behaviour. The face pleases
when character commends. Love of character is lasting; beauty will be

ravaged by age, and the face that charmed will be ploughed by wrinkles. The time will come, when it will vex you to look at a mirror, and grief will prove a second cause of wrinkles. Goodness endures and lasts for many a day, and throughout its years love securely rests thereon. (43–50)[13]

He could have gotten this from Sappho, who wrote, "To have beauty is to have only that, but to have goodness is to be beautiful too."[14]

Ovid's own family life offers further light on the status of woman in his time. He was thrice married, his first two marriages soon ending in divorce. His third marriage, into "one of the oldest and most respected families of Rome, the Fabii,"[15] seems to have been one of love. It held firm until his death, despite his last decade in banishment. At his banishment he persuaded his wife to remain in Rome and work for his freedom, which she faithfully did, though without success.

Then there was Perilla, his precious daughter (or stepdaughter?) by his third wife. Perilla was a lyric poetess in her own right, and she was highly regarded as such by Ovid. She had from nature her own "rare dower of native wit" (*Tristia* VII.13f.) which Ovid himself had recognized in her when she was a little girl and had cultivated as her "guide and comrade" *(duxque comesque).* Although she may properly prize her physical beauty, what matters is beyond this: "In brief we possess nothing that is not mortal except the blessings of heart and mind" (*Tristia* VII.43f.).

Of Ovid's many writings, yet two more may be consulted for perspectives on woman and her status in the Roman world at the very time Jesus was born into it. In *The Amores,* Ovid is explicit as to those for whom he writes:

For my readers I want the maid not cold at the sight of her promised lover's face, and the untaught boy touched by passion till now unknown; and let some youth who is wounded by the same bow as I am now, know in my lines the record of his own heart's flame, and, long wondering, say: "From what tatler has this poet learned, that he has put in verse my own mishaps?" (II.i.5–10)[16]

For him the sensual expression is always prominent, and he knows no symbol for marriage so serviceable as "the bed." But in *The Amores,* as well as elsewhere, love is far more than sex. He detests prostitution, both the purchase and sale of sex, whether in prostitution as such or in courtship or marriage where another is "bought" by gifts whatever. To Ovid the motive behind the deed was primary: " 'Tis not the giving but the asking of a price, that I despise and hate. What I refuse at your demand, cease only to wish, and I will give!" (I.x.63f.).

The Heroides, based chiefly on Greek sources, consists of "letters" written by legendary lovers to one another, most of them by the heroine. Of course, they are not real letters and they all come from the pen of Ovid. The work does reflect significant attitudes, status, and behavior patterns relating to women. There is some familiar stereotype of both sexes, traces of a double standard, and also strong evidence for considerable freedom and influence enjoyed by woman. In all these poems woman's normal role is seen as being that of lover or wife. She is for the most part self-respecting, self-reliant, often seizing the initiative in her own affairs, and both bold and articulate in speaking out for herself. There is never a hint that she should remain silent or submissive, although it is not uncommon for a "heroine" to offer herself in a subordinate or submissive role if only she may claim her lover for herself alone.

Oenone is a woman wronged and deeply hurt, Paris having abandoned her for Helen of Troy, pleading with him for his return to her. She fights desperately to win back her husband from Helen, but throughout she remains unbowed and proud. She is a strong person who will not be cowed, ignored, or silenced. She chides Paris, "Will you read my letter through? or does your new wife forbid?" (V.1). She reminds him that he was without distinction when she whose "hands are such as the sceptre could well beseem" took him as husband (77–88). She is not dazzled by him or Priam's court in Troy. She shames him for his broken vows to her and his betrayal of a host's confidence. Helen is a "Greek heifer" who can only ruin him, his homeland, and his family (117f.), for the Helen who betrayed husband will betray others: "By no art may purity once wounded be made whole; 'tis lost, lost once and for all"

(103f.). For all her free spirit, Oenone bows at last to love, appealing to Paris as the one alone who can heal her wound: "I come with no Danai [Greeks], and bear no bloody armour—but I am yours, and I was your mate in childhood's years, and yours through all time to come I pray to be!" (156–158). Oenone cannot be subdued but she can submit.

Despite the apparent freedom of first-century B.C. Roman woman, the age-old double standard is there too. When marriage vows are betrayed it almost always is on the male side, although there are striking examples of the opposite. Again, it is woman and not man who pays the price for transgressing established lines.

A striking example in *The Heroides* is that of Canace and Macareus, sister and brother whose love for each other took them beyond what a brother and sister should be to each other (XI.21–32). Although the infatuation and consent were mutual, it was she and not he from whom the heavy penalty was exacted by a male-oriented system. Their father "ordered his little grandchild thrown to the dogs and birds" (83), and through a guard ordered his daughter's suicide: "Aeolus sends this sword to you . . . and bids you know from your desert what it may mean" (94f.). Infanticide for an unwanted baby and suicide required of a daughter who had transgressed—these were patterns not invented by the poet. Ovid, pagan poet that he was, here and in all *The Heroides* makes the reader identify and suffer with Canace and others of her sex who know the injustices of the double standard. Most significant is Ovid's understanding of the love that seeks first the good of the other person and knows how to forgive even when deeply hurt.

Anticipation of forgiving and sheltering love struggles for expression in this Roman poet. What we like to call *agapē* was struggling for expression in Ovid's "Dido to Aeneas." Though deeply hurt, the Queen of Carthage says of Aeneas:

> 'Tis true he is an ingrate, and unresponsive to my kindnesses, and were I not fond I should be willing to have him go; yet, however ill his thought of me, I hate him not, but only complain of his faithlessness, and when I have complained I do but love more madly still. (VII.27–30)

Dido's motives are mixed, some quite unworthy, but the nobler feelings at least have their place alongside the meaner ones.

Ovid groped his way somewhere between sensuality and some nobler motives, but he struggled with sentiments and perspectives short of, yet reaching out toward redeeming love. Significantly, he placed his best lines in the mouths of women.

PART II

Jesus and Woman

Whatever else may be said of Jesus, he was not conventional. Both continuity and discontinuity with his past and his contemporaries seem to have characterized him. He was like yet unlike. He was "born of a woman, born under the Law" (Gal. 4:4). Jesus was a Jew. He was nurtured in a Jewish home of piety; he went by custom on the Sabbath Day to the synagogue; he worshiped at the Temple; and he drew heavily upon the Jewish scriptures. The continuity is unmistakably there. His followers remembered him as saying, "Salvation is from the Jews" (Jn. 4:22).

With this is also radical discontinuity. Jesus was bodily evicted from his home synagogue (Lk. 4:16–30). He was crucified by the Romans and his own people (Mk. 15 and par.; 1 Thess. 2:15). His own family seemed not to have understood him or to have been fully supportive during his lifetime (Mk. 3:31–32; par.). Even the inner circle of the Twelve lagged behind and sometimes openly opposed him, even at crucial points (cf. Mk. 8:27–38; par.). Jesus crossed conventional lines well established in his day, and his people from the first struggled between the pull of his own example and teaching and that of the world of which they also were a part.

Three chapters, with some inevitable overlap, will be devoted to "Jesus and Woman." Chapter 4 will seek to trace his manner with woman. Chapter 5 will probe into his teachings that bear upon woman. Chapter Six will examine the two main traditions of Jesus' resurrection, one centering in Cephas and men (1 Cor. 15:1–7) and the other in Mary Magdalene and women (the four Gospels). Related to this is the role of woman in proclamation and instruction.

Chapter 4

THE MANNER
OF JESUS

The four canonical Gospels are our almost exclusive source for an answer to the question of the manner in which Jesus related to women. No other New Testament writing makes any direct approach to this subject. There are extant Gnostic gospels and the second-century *Protevangelium of James.*[1] They portray a world quite different from that of the canonical Gospels. Each of these sources will be examined.

No credible scholar today holds that the canonical Gospels are verbatim recordings of Jesus' words or televised pictures of his actions. Even a casual comparison of Synoptic parallels discloses the fact that the same saying or event could be reported variously, whether due to different sources or interests. What we have in the Gospels are concerns to characterize Jesus as to his manner and intention, not to supply audiovisual tape recordings. We believe that through the variants shines a dominant person who is sufficiently recognizable even though he must be seen today through the eyes of others and heard today through the ears of others. The "criterion of discontinuity,"[2] his striking dissimilarity to both Jewish and early Christian piety, encourages this confidence. Jesus is the one who shines through the Gospels yet remains the one all of us keep trying to make nearer our image lest he make us in his image. "Lord, I believe, help thou my unbelief" (Mk. 9:24) is a proper cry for us all.

JESUS AND HIS MOTHER

The canonical Gospels offer only one story about the boyhood of Jesus, Luke's story about the boy Jesus in the Temple in Jerusalem (Lk. 2:41-52). According to this story "his parents" went up to Jerusalem each year to the Feast of the Passover (v. 41). This feast celebrated God's deliverance of Israel from Egyptian bondage in the time of Moses; and it kept alive the nation's hopes that God would again intervene to deliver his people, in Jesus' time from Roman rule. For such deliverance the Qumranites were firmly confident, assured that God would send "the Anointed of Aaron and Israel" (The Scroll of the Rule IX.11; cf. The Rule Annexe II.11-22) to cleanse and free his people. In The Scroll of the War Rule is described the imminent war between the Sons of Light, the Essenes, and the Sons of Darkness, in which the "Kittim," presumably Romans, would be destroyed and God's people ushered into an eternal rule of light and justice.

There is no evidence to link Jesus or his family with Qumran, but hopes expressed there must have been shared more widely in the piety of Judaism. That the family of Jesus shared in current national hopes or associated them with the Passover celebration is nowhere explicit. If so, this may serve as a clue to the family's position regarding Jesus' vocation (cf. Jn. 2:1-11; 7:1-9; Mk. 3: 31-35 par.; Gal. 2:12; Acts 21:17-25). The family on occasion seemed to push Jesus toward some public role and on others sought to restrain him. It could have been that there was a fundamental difference between the stance of Jesus and his family on the manifest destiny of the nation, the family being more traditional and Jesus envisioning a new community transcending national lines.

Joseph and Mary did take along the twelve-year-old Jesus on their annual pilgrimage to the Passover (which could be celebrated only in Jerusalem). At age twelve a Jewish boy was within a year of his *bar mizvah*, full responsibility as a son of the Law. At the conclusion of the feast "his parents" started their return journey homeward, leaving Jesus behind as they thought that he was somewhere in the caravan with kinsmen or acquaintances (Lk. 2:44).

Mary's eager search for her missing boy implies her deep concern, and her reproach upon finding him is a normal parental reaction (v. 48). Luke gives his first clue as to some tension between Jesus and Mary not so much in her normal parental reproach but in the lad's reply to her: "Why were you [pl.] seeking me; did you not know that it was morally necessary *(dei)* for me to be about the things of my Father?" (v. 49). Jesus respected Mary and Joseph and submitted to their parental authority (v. 51a), and his maturation continued with no further mention of tension (v. 52).

John 2:1–11 has a striking parallel to Luke's story about the boy and his mother in the Temple, despite the great difference between the stories. Both stories imply strong bonds between Jesus and his mother but also tension and distance. Jesus and his disciples were among the invited guests at a wedding feast in Cana of Galilee, and apparently Mary had a relationship with the hosting family close enough that she knew about the shortage of the wine and felt some obligation in the matter. She reported the matter to Jesus, presumably expecting him to do something about it or even prompting him to do so. Apparently Jesus heard it as the latter. His reply seems curt: "What to me and to you, woman; not yet has my hour come" (v. 4). The term "woman" is respectful but formal.

The heart of the matter is in the enigmatic question, *Ti emoi kai soi,* "What [is there between] me and you?" Neither here nor elsewhere does Jesus renounce the mother-son relationship as such, but here as in Luke 2:49 he declares his vocational independence of his mother. In Luke the mother's love is not to interfere with his Father's business. In John he has an "hour" to meet, and Mary can neither hasten nor hinder it. In fact, she has no understanding of his "hour," which far from the easy joy of wine and a wedding feast will prove to be both his suffering and his glory (cf. Jn. 2:4; 7:30; 8:20; 12:23, 27; 13:1; 17:1). His vocation was his own to understand, to follow, and to fulfill. Within its proper limits, the relationship of mother and son was honored to the last (Jn. 19:26f.), but this relationship was not permitted to encroach upon his own right and responsibility to identity. He was himself; she must be herself.

It is demonstrable in the Gospels that Jesus did have high regard for the personhood of those whom he met. We may have one key to this in Jesus' assertion of his own individual personhood, even when pushed by his nearest and dearest, including his own mother. Jesus was prepared to be true to himself, whatever the cost in terms of being misunderstood, resented, feared, hated, or crucified—including the risk of a rupture of relationship with even his mother. Is this the other side of the coin of self-denial (Mk. 8:34–38; Jn. 12:23–33)? Can there be any meaningful self-denial without self-affirmation? What "self" is there to deny if it is not first affirmed? Moreover, it may follow that Jesus could not really affirm Mary, any woman, or any person if he did not affirm himself. Significantly, Jesus included "love yourself" in his reaffirmation of the great commandment to love God with one's whole being and the like commandment to "love neighbor as yourself" (Mk. 12:29–31).[3]

That Jesus did not reject Mary nor she forsake him is attested by their encounter at the cross (Jn. 19:25–27). Mary was there! Whatever her misunderstanding, disappointment, shame, or fear—she was there. Jesus saw her and committed her to the care of one of his closest disciples, "Woman, behold your son. . . . Behold your mother" (vs. 26f.).

All four Gospels indicate a strained relationship between Jesus and his family. John 7:5 says explicitly, "Not even his brothers believed on him." The Synoptics tell of the appearance of his mother and brothers (no mention that the sisters were present) (Mk. 3:31–35; Mt. 12:46–50; Lk. 8:19–21). Mark has it that "They sent to him, calling him." Matthew softens it, "seeking to speak with him." Luke has it that because of the crowd they were not able to reach Jesus and that it was reported to him, "Your mother and your brothers stand outside, wishing to see you." Their motive or intention is not explained. The tradition is more interested in the far-reaching reply of Jesus: "My mother and my brothers are those hearing and doing the word of God" (Lk. 8:21). Matthew has it, "Whoever may do the will of my Father in heaven, this one is my brother and sister and mother" (Mt. 12:50). In the radicality of this sweeping claim Jesus transcends all stereotype, all claims to advantage, even the ties of natural family as he affirms a new basis for family. Inclusion in his family has nothing to do with the accidents of birth (racial, ethnic, sex, or whatever). In Jesus' answer is total disregard for cultic rites so precious to religion, Jewish and Christian, rituals cherished and defended by those from whom Jesus came and, deny it not, by many in the family he formed, from the earliest days until now.

It probably does not do justice to Jesus to say that he was a "woman liberator." He came to liberate the human being. Jesus both denied and affirmed his mother, in such a way as to offer her the personal identity that does not belong to the moment or the circumstance but to eternity.

THE WOMAN BENT DOUBLE

A story in Luke 13:10–17 may well serve to dramatize what Jesus more than any other has done for woman. He saw a woman bent over and unable to stand erect. He freed her from her infirmity, enabling her to stand up straight. This story has to do with a physical restoration, but it may well point to something far more significant than the immediate reference. In a real sense, Jesus has enabled woman to stand up with a proper sense of dignity, freedom, and worth.

It is striking that Jesus referred to this woman as "a daughter of Abraham" (v. 16). Elsewhere we hear of "children of Abraham" (Mt. 3:8; Lk. 3:8; Jn. 8:39), "seed of Abraham" (Jn. 8:33; Rom. 9:7; 11:1; Gal. 3:29), and "sons of Abraham" (Gal. 3:7), but here only in the New Testament do we hear of "a daughter of Abraham." Jesus not only enabled the woman to stand erect, but he spoke of her as though she belonged to the family of Abraham just as did the "sons" of Abraham.

Jesus healed this woman on the Sabbath Day and in connection with his preaching in "one of the synagogues." The "ministry of touch" was employed by Jesus for various persons, including lepers (Mk. 1:41) and the bier upon which a corpse lay (Lk. 7:14). Jesus touched this woman. He gave her priority over the day, the Sabbath, and over his own security. The ruler of the synagogue rebuked Jesus for healing on the Sabbath, but Jesus stood firm in his action and exposed the inconsistency of his opponents who did not hesitate to lead an ox or an ass to water on the Sabbath (13:15). Here is a basic clue to understanding Jesus. The personal, whether God or a human being, always took priority for him over things and over religion itself. A woman was a person, that first. Jesus the "Liberator" said to this crippled woman, "Woman, you are released from your infirmity!" (v. 12).

A WIDOW OF NAIN

The Gospels clearly ascribe to Jesus two miracles of raising persons from the dead, and in both stories the dead are restored to women. Of Jairus' daughter Jesus said, "The child did not die but is sleeping" (Mk. 5:39; Mt. 9:24; Lk. 8:52). Jesus restored to a widow of Nain her only son (Lk. 7:11–17) and to Mary and Martha their brother Lazarus (Jn. 11:1–44). In each case the compassion of Jesus for the grief-stricken women is stressed.

Jesus was moved with compassion for the widow of Nain, her sorrow being double, for the dead boy was "the only son to his mother" (Lk. 7:12). A corpse was the most defiling thing of all as measured by Jewish cultic holiness, but Jesus "touched the bier" (v. 14). Upon raising the boy from the dead, "He gave him to his mother," responding to a woman's grief.

A WIDOW'S OFFERING

The moving story of a poor widow's casting of "two copper coins" ("two mites," KJV) into the Temple treasury appears in Mk. 12:41–44 and Lk. 21:1–4. This story does not necessarily reflect directly upon Jesus' attitude toward woman, for its chief point is to esteem sacrificial giving over a contribution out of one's surplus. As Jesus observed, he saw the sizable gifts of many rich people and then a poor widow's gift of "two copper coins," something like a penny in American money. By secular standards her gift was as nothing compared to the large contributions of others.

Jesus declared that the widow had given more than all the others combined. They gave out of their abundance or surplus. What the poor widow gave was her self—"all her living." It was food out of her mouth. Paul L. Stagg has described this kind of giving as "wholeness in giving" as contrasted with "fragmentary giving—money but not self, a fixed part of one's money but not the responsible use of all."[4] The intention of the story is to focus on the personal dimension in meaningful giving. Women had only limited access to the Temple in Jerusalem, but Jesus found the most praiseworthy piety and sacrificial giving not in the rich contributors (or in the priestly custodians of cultic "holiness") but in a woman.

A WOMAN WHO ANOINTED JESUS' FEET

Luke alone tells about the anointing of Jesus' feet by a woman acknowledged to be a sinner (Lk. 7:36–50). Another story appears in the other three Gospels, in which a woman in Bethany anointed Jesus' head with very costly ointment shortly before his death (Mk. 14:3–9; Mt. 26:6–13; Jn. 12:1–8). Scholars are not agreed as to the relationship of these stories, some seeing them as historically distinct and some seeing them as doublets, two versions of the same story. The problem of the "anointing" stories as well as the whole question of the identity and relationship of the "Marys" in the Gospels are beyond the scope of this book. That there are some unsolved problems is acknowledged in fairness to the evidence as one question preoccupies us, How did Jesus relate to women?

With acknowledged reservations, we shall treat the stories as distinctly two and not doublets. (See pp. 120f.)

In the Lucan story Jesus was an invited dinner guest in the home of a Pharisee, at a formal meal in which host and guests reclined on couches with their feet extended out from the table. All at the table were men (cf. masculine participle in Lk. 7:49, "those reclining together"). In the course of the meal a woman from the town known as "a sinner" (vs. 37, 39, 47f.) entered the room and anointed Jesus' feet both with her tears and with some ointment.

The woman planned to anoint Jesus with ointment, having acquired an alabaster box of ointment for the purpose upon learning that Jesus was in the Pharisee's house (v. 37). That her tears fell upon his feet and that she wiped them with her hair probably was unplanned and unanticipated even by her. She entered to express her gratitude to Jesus, and the tears may have come unanticipated out of the emotion of the moment.

It is not explicit whether Jesus had encountered this particular woman before. It could be that the woman only knew of Jesus' openness toward her kind, forgiving and redeeming. Either she personally had encountered already his forgiveness or she had come to know his attitude toward sinners. What her sin was is not disclosed. Women of the time had few options, and it is most likely that her sin was the familiar one of prostitution. Had she been an adulteress, a wife who had been unfaithful to her husband, she would have been stoned. In a male-oriented world, prostitutes were despised as sinners, but men could retain their respectability even though they patronized prostitutes.

When Jesus permitted the woman to express her love as she did, the host scorned Jesus for it, saying to himself that were Jesus a prophet (a prophet's function was chiefly discernment, not just predicting) he would know what kind of woman she was and would not let her touch him. Such touching would "defile" one and render one ritually unclean. Jesus showed his prophetic power of discernment by reading his host's mind and exposing it.

The grammar of Lk. 7:47 permits the understanding that the woman was forgiven because she loved much. The context requires the opposite, and the grammar permits it. Jesus' point is that the woman's obviously great love is evidence that she knew herself to have been forgiven much. Her love for Jesus resulted from her sense of being forgiven.

This story at minimum reflects the manner of Jesus with one sinful woman. Probably it reflects a manner so widely expressed and so widely recognized among sinners that this particular sinner had the courage to publicly express her love for one who saw her not as a sex object to be exploited but a person to accept as having worth.

A WOMAN WHO TOUCHED JESUS' GARMENT

The ministry of touch is not a modern invention or discovery, though it may be a rediscovery for some. The ancients knew it.

Jesus practiced it, sometimes touching the "untouchables" and letting them touch him. Among the things considered defiling, disqualifying one for the rituals of religion, was an issue of blood, especially menstruation or hemorrhage. One such woman found the courage in a crowd to force her way up to him, approaching from behind, and to touch his garment (Mk. 5:27; par.). She had been plagued with a flow of blood for twelve years, no one being able to heal her. When she touched Jesus' garment, the flow stopped. Jesus turned and asked who touched him. The disciples tried to brush aside the question, protesting that in such a crowd no individual could be singled out. Jesus refused to let it go at that. Though moved by crowds (cf. Mt. 9:36–38), he was highly sensitive to the individual (and knew the difference between elbows and fingertips). He pressed his inquiry until the woman identified herself and declared to the crowd the blessing that had come to her. He thus treated her not only as having worth but as responsible. Jesus did not rebuke her for what by the cultic code of holiness would have been her defilement of him. Rather he relieved her of any sense of guilt for her seemingly rash act and said, "Daughter, your faith has saved you; go in peace!" (Mk. 5:34). Shalom! Peace is well-being under God's rule.

What drew this woman to Jesus? Her faith was not unmixed with fear and possibly superstition, but her impressions of Jesus were such that she pressed through the crowd until she touched him. Something about Jesus gave her the courage to touch his garment. He did not condemn her for it; he blessed her for it. He called her "Daughter." He sent her on her way in peace. Jesus did nothing to change a woman's period or its related physical problems, but he did remove the "stigma" or "curse" imposed upon it by religion in the ancient world.[5]

A WOMAN REBUKED

One mark of insecurity is the fear of taking a negative stance. The feeling of security frees one to agree or disagree. Jesus could do either. In the scenes preserved in the Gospels he almost always takes a positive stance toward woman, and he never denigrates womanhood as such. On occasion he does dissociate from some stance taken by a woman, as seen above even in relation to his own mother. So it was on one occasion as he was addressed laudably by an unnamed woman in a crowd (Lk. 11:27-28).

Luke reports that as Jesus was speaking on one occasion a woman from the crowd lifted her voice and cried out, "Blessed [is or be] the womb that bore you and the breasts that nursed you." Whether this reflects an early disposition toward exalting Mary to a special place in the church may only be debated.

Whatever the woman's motive, Jesus did give her a curt answer: "On the contrary *(menoun),* blessed are those hearing the word of God and observing it." Compliance with the word of God makes one blessed, not motherhood as such, even the mothering of Jesus. There is no denigrating of motherhood in the manner or teaching of Jesus, but neither does Jesus succumb to the unreflecting sentimentality that exalts motherhood as such.

Here as elsewhere, Jesus affirmed personhood, giving it its worth apart from sexuality or other distinctions. This parallels the emphasis in his affirming as his "brother," "sister," and "mother" anyone who does the will of God (Mk. 3:35; par.). This is no incidental point. This is the heart of Jesus' perception of persons. Ethnic, racial, cultic, sexual, and other distinguishing factors were secondary to him. Personhood was primary. Only by self-exclusion is one not included.

A WOMAN CAUGHT IN ADULTERY

The story appearing in most Bibles as Jn. 7:53-8:11 does not seem to have been original to the Gospel of John or any other New Testament writing. It is absent from the two oldest copies of the Gospel of John known to us. The Bodmer Codex known as Papyrus 66 is an early third-century copy of John, written in Greek on papyrus with pen and ink; and it knows nothing of this story. Papyrus 75 is older and better preserved, dating from between A.D. 175 and 225 and including both Luke and John. It does not have this story. It is likewise omitted from other ancient manuscripts in Greek, many on vellum, as well as from various ancient versions

and extant writings of early church fathers. Some manuscripts have
the story after John 7:52, one after John 7:36, some after John
21:24, and some after Luke 21:38. Some manuscripts which contain the story place an asterisk with it to indicate its problematic
origin.[6]

By all evidences this story circulated outside the canonical Gospels for a time and then found a home at various places within the
Gospel of John and in some manuscripts of Luke. Eventually it was
accorded a more secure home following John 7:52 and came thus
into the first printed editions of the Greek New Testament (A.D.
1516) and thus into English translations beginning with Tyndale
(1525). Already it was in the Latin versions, including the Vulgate
(fourth century) and the Wycliffe Bible which was translated from
the Vulgate. Whether or not the story is historical cannot be determined. It rings true to what otherwise is known about Jesus (cf. Mt.
21:31f.), and it is hardly a story that the church would have invented. It could be historical, a story that first lived outside the
canonical Gospels. It is included here for study but with full acknowledgment of its uncertain origin. Either the story does preserve an actual occurrence or it reflects the way Jesus was remembered by at least some in the church (cf. Mt. 21:31f.).

The story has its setting in the Temple in Jerusalem as Jesus was
teaching, with a crowd gathered around him. Some scribes and
Pharisees interrupted the teaching as they brought in a woman who
had been taken in the very act of adultery. They stood her before
Jesus, declared the charge, reminded him of Moses' command that
such women be stoned, and then asked, "What do you say?" The
story adds that they were seeking to "try" Jesus, so that they might
have some accusation against him. Presumably, they had reason to
believe that he would say something not supportive of the recognized law for adulteresses, else their move was pointless.

For a time Jesus said nothing in reply. He stooped down and
wrote with his finger on the ground. It is idle to speculate what he
wrote, for there is no hint in the text. Whatever may have moved
Jesus to his first action, it gave the woman opportunity to see the
real motives at work. Her accusers were after Jesus, not just her.
She was to them a worthless object to be used in trapping Jesus.

She had at least one thing in common with Jesus—they were opposed by the same people.

After a time Jesus stood up and said to the accusers: "Let the one among you who is without sin cast the first stone." He then stooped down again and wrote on the ground. In his answer Jesus did not condone adultery. He compelled them to judge themselves and find themselves guilty—of this sin and/or others. None could pass the test, and they slipped out one by one, beginning with the eldest. Only when Jesus and the woman were left alone did he address her. He asked her a simple question, "Woman, where are they? Did no one condemn you?" Her reply was brief: "No one, Lord."

Jesus' final word to the woman was one of affirmation and commission: "Neither do I condemn you; go, from now on sin no more." Jesus did not condone adultery. He did not indulge her sin. In directing her to sin no longer he acknowledged that she had sinned, and he turned her in a new direction. Her accusers probably could only make her bitter and defiant. The one who did not accuse her provided her with the only real encouragement to own her sin and turn from it.

In this story Jesus rejected the double standard and turned the judgment upon the male accusers. His manner with this sinful woman was such that she found herself challenged to a new self-understanding and a new life.

A SYROPHOENICIAN WOMAN

The story in Mk. 7:24–30 and its parallel in Mt. 15:21–28 is unlike any other in the canonical Gospels. There is a near approach in Jn. 12:20–36, where some Greeks come to see Jesus and thus plunge Jesus into deep agony. Interestingly, the Syrophoenician woman is likewise introduced as "Greek." In the Marcan and Matthean story, Jesus appears to be harsh toward the woman as he first denies her request for help for her daughter; and he also appears to be condescending and denigrating of her as he says, "First let the children be fed, for it is not fitting to take the bread of the children and throw it to the dogs" (Mk. 7:27). In context "the children" seem to be Jews and "the dogs" Gentiles.[7]

Equally noteworthy in this story is the way Jesus appears to be bested in repartee with the Syrophoenician woman. Elsewhere in the Gospels, Jesus uniformly prevails over his opponents. Here the woman has the better of it in her reply, "Sir, even the dogs under the table eat from the children's crumbs" (Mk. 7:28). Jesus then responded positively to the woman, "because of this word" (v. 29). Whatever else the story may imply, it has it that a foreign woman comes out victorious and vindicated.

The story is about "a woman" who is further identified as "a Greek, a Syrophoenician by race" (vs. 25f.). The point is not that she is a woman but that she is Gentile, not Jewish. "Dogs" was an epithet of the day for Gentiles. The problem of the story is not so much that Jesus seems harsh toward a woman but that he appears on the side of Jewish contempt for Gentiles. In both Mark and Matthew non-Jews are likened to "dogs," and a woman deeply concerned for her daughter's condition is brushed off until she herself prevails in the repartee with Jesus.

Both Mark and Matthew hold Jesus in highest possible esteem. Each Evangelist had options in materials selected, and each could edit or redact any story or saying reported. Why then was the story included? Since it was included, why was it permitted to let Jesus appear both harsh to a disadvantaged person and also to be bested in repartee? Several possible explanations may be explored.

One possibility is that Jesus was instructing his disciples, first assuming a familiar Jewish stance toward aliens and then abandoning it as its unfairness was exposed. In Matthew especially, but also in Mark, the story may serve as an object lesson for prejudiced disciples as a barrier is broken down between Jew and Gentile.

A second interpretation focuses upon the woman herself, seeing Jesus' intention to test the woman's faith. Both Mark and Matthew have it that Jesus said, "It is not fitting *(kalon)* to take the children's bread and throw *(balein)* it to the dogs." To her firm faith Jesus then responded positively. The woman's faith had been severely tested and vindicated. Jesus' parting word to her is one of affirmation and acclaim.

A third interpretation focuses on Jesus himself, seeing a deep struggle within Jesus as he struggled between the claims of both Jew and Gentile upon himself. There is no evidence that Jesus ever turned away from his own people, even though he had an openness to Jews who were outside accepted circles (publicans, sinners, harlots), though he went out of his way to affirm Samaritans between whom and Jews were strong feelings of mutual animosity, and though he looked beyond his nation to all nations in his concern. With this universal perspective and concern, Jesus had a deep commitment to his own immediate kin. Jesus saw his mission to include the world; but he was deeply committed to a mission to and through Israel, not around Israel.

With increasing resistance and hostility from his own people, and with a commitment beyond Israel, Jesus' agony apparently was intensified. Why not go directly to the larger world? Why not abandon Israel? This he could not do. Somehow he must have it both ways, give himself unreservedly to Israel and yet also to the world. The coming of a Greek woman, a Syrophoenician (Matthew calls her a Canaanitess), intensified the trauma. With increasing hostility from his own people, why not respond to this outsider's appeal? Why not go now to the Gentile world, abandoning Israel? The story by this interpretation, then, sees a real struggle within Jesus himself in the claims of two worlds upon him.

As to the manner of Jesus with women, one further observation may be made from this story. The radical alternative to discrimination may be uncritical deference. Although a minor note in the Gospels, here and there it is shown that Jesus did not substitute uncritical deference for prejudice against woman. He related to women as persons with worth and dignity. In this story as elsewhere, Jesus is seen as capable of a critical stance toward woman and respectful of her self-affirmation as she boldly counters his own remarks.

THE WOMAN AT THE WELL IN SAMARIA

The long story about Jesus and a woman of Samaria found in Jn. 4:1–42 is highly significant for understanding Jesus in several relationships: Samaritans, woman, the sinful. In talking openly with this woman Jesus crossed a number of lines which normally would have separated a Jewish teacher (cf. "Rabbi" in v. 31) from such a person as this woman of Samaria.

The story centers in Jesus' encounter with a woman of Samaria at Jacob's well near Sychar. Jesus did two things that were highly unconventional and astonishing for his cultural-religious situation: he as a man talked theology openly with a woman, and he as a Jew asked to drink from the ritually unclean bucket of a Samaritan. If to this is added the awkwardness of the woman's marital record, five former husbands and now living with a man who was not her husband, the whole incident is remarkable, indeed.

While Jesus' disciples went into the town to secure food, Jesus rested at the well, apparently exhausted (Jn. 4:6). As he waited there alone a woman of Samaria came to draw water, and Jesus asked her for a drink of water. Her surprise at being so approached by a Jew evoked her astonished reply, "How is it that you being a Jew ask from me to drink, being a Samaritan woman?" A parenthetical observation is made, whether by the woman or by John is not clear: "For Jews do not use [vessels] with Samaritans" (v. 9). The familiar rendering, "For Jews have no dealings with Samaritans," is misleading and untrue to the Greek text. The Greek verb means "to use with," and here it alludes to the cultic code of purity that forbade a Jew to eat or drink from a vessel of a non-Jew, considered ritually unclean.[8] Jews did have dealings with Samaritans, buying and selling and otherwise.

Equally significant was Jesus' crossing of barriers between himself as a man and this Samaritan as a woman. This is what astonished the disciples most upon their return to the well: "They were marveling that he was talking with a woman" (Jn. 4:27). The Greek text does not say "the woman"; it reads "a woman." It was a marvel to the disciples to see a man talking to a woman in public —any woman. As seen in Chapter 1, a man in the Jewish world did not normally talk with a woman in public, even with his own wife. For a rabbi (v. 31) to discuss theology with a woman was yet more unconventional.

In keeping with a pattern already observed, Jesus did not defer to a woman simply because she was a woman. On the one hand,

Jesus did not hesitate to ask of the woman that she let him drink from her vessel. On the other hand, he did not hesitate to offer her a drink of another kind from a Jewish "bucket" as he said to her, "Salvation is of the Jews" (Jn. 4:22). Salvation was coming to this Samaritan woman from the Jews, and Jesus did not hesitate to say so. As a Samaritan she needed to be able to drink from a Jewish vessel, and Jesus no more sanctioned Samaritan prejudice against Jew than Jewish prejudice against Samaritan.

Here again, the key to Jesus' stance is found in his perceiving persons as persons. In the stranger at the well he saw a person primarily—not primarily a Samaritan, a woman, or a sinner. She was not required to cease to be a woman or a Samaritan, but she was by the very manner of Jesus challenged to become a person first of all.

The closing note of the story is a portrayal of the evangelized as having become an evangelist. The woman introduced her community to "a man" whom they came to acclaim as "the Savior of the world" (Jn. 4:42). Jesus liberated this woman and awakened her to a new life in which not only did she receive but also gave. She became a part of the liberating thrust, a catalyst for releasing a community of persons from a closed provincialism to a fellowship opened to the world. She brought "many Samaritans" to faith (v. 39). If the men in John 1 were the first "soul winners," this woman was the first "evangelist" in John's Gospel.

MARY AND MARTHA

Luke and John attest to a close relationship between Jesus and the sisters Mary and Martha. They are featured in three major stories: (1) a tension between the two sisters over roles (Lk. 10:38–42); (2) grief at the death of their brother Lazarus, followed by his being raised (Jn. 11:1–44); and (3) the anointing of Jesus by Mary (explicitly in Jn. 12:1–8; presumably in Mk. 14:3–9; Mt. 26:6–13). Numerous details in the stories remain unclear, but there is a solid tradition that Jesus had very close ties with these two women.

Kitchen and Study

Luke alone relates the story of tension between Martha and
Mary on an occasion of a visit of Jesus to their home. While
Martha prepared the meal, Mary sat at the feet of Jesus and "she
was hearing his word" (Lk. 10:39). Martha became distracted over
the big thing she was making over serving the meal. Finally she
gave vent to her feelings, stood over Jesus (apparently seated or
reclining), and protested: "Lord, is it not a care to you that my
sister has abandoned me alone to serve? Speak to her that she help
me." Jesus then chided Martha for being so distracted and troubled
over many things, when only one thing was necessary (What? A
single dish? The word of God?). He then affirmed Mary in her
choice of "the good part" which would not be taken from her.

Mary's choice was not a conventional one for Jewish women.
She sat at the feet of Jesus and was listening to "his word." Both
the posture and the reference to Jesus' "word" seem to imply
teaching, religious instruction. Jewish women were not permitted
to touch the Scriptures; and they were not taught the Torah itself,
although they were instructed in accordance with it for the proper
regulation of their lives. A rabbi did not instruct a woman in the
Torah. Not only did Mary choose the good part, but Jesus related
to her in a teacher-disciple relationship. He admitted her into "the
study" and commended her for the choice. A Torah-oriented role
for women was not unprecedented in Israel as was seen in Chapter
1, but the drift had been away from it. First, women were excluded
from the altar-oriented priestly ministry, then the exclusion encroached upon the Word-oriented ministry for women. Jesus re-
opened the Word-ministry for woman. Mary was at least one of his
students in theology.

The story vindicates Mary's rights to be her own person. It
vindicates her right to be Mary and not Martha. It vindicates a
woman's right to opt for the study and not be compelled to be in
the kitchen. It would go beyond the story's intention to deny
Martha the right to opt for the hostess or homemaker role, even
though Jesus accorded a higher value to Mary's choice of "the
word" than Martha's choice of the meal. Jesus did not make the

two exclusive. He established his own priorities in declaring, "Man shall not live by bread alone, but by every word proceeding out through the mouth of God" (Mt. 4:4). In this he followed Deut. 8:3 and the solid Jewish understanding of the holistic nature of the human being, created out of the dust of the earth and yet in the image of God (Gen. 1:26f.; 2:7), so created as to require both bread and word.[9] Martha needed to be reminded of the priority of word over bread.

Luke's story of Jesus in the home of Martha and Mary puts him solidly on the side of the recognition of the full personhood of woman, with the right to options for her own life. In "socializing" with both sisters and in defending Mary's right to a role then commonly denied a Jewish woman, Jesus was following his far-reaching principle of human liberation.

The Grieving Sisters

Chapter 11 in the Gospel of John is about the raising of Lazarus from four days in the tomb. The central figure, however, is Jesus, identified as the resurrection and the life. The sisters Mary and Martha come in prominently in the story, with further evidence as to Jesus' relationship with them. When their brother became ill they sent for Jesus. For some undisclosed reason, Jesus did not arrive until Lazarus was in his fourth day of death. The grieving sisters met Jesus, Martha first and then Mary. Jesus raised Lazarus and then proclaimed himself as the resurrection and the life.

Why Jesus delayed his arrival until after Lazarus had died is not disclosed. Martha was first to meet with Jesus upon his arrival, she going outside the village (Jn. 11:30) to meet him when she heard that he had come, Mary remaining in the house (v. 20). There may have been a gentle reproach in her voice as Martha said to Jesus, "Lord, had you been here my brother would not have died." She hastened to express full confidence that God would grant whatever he asked. In their exchange about the resurrection and Jesus' identity, Martha reflected cogency beyond that required for preparing and serving a meal (cf. Jn. 11:21–27). Apparently Martha and not just Mary had benefited from the study.

Mary remained in the house until Jesus called for her, sending word by Martha (Jn. 11:28–30). Upon receiving the message, Mary quickly arose and went to meet Jesus, falling at his feet (Mary is at the feet of Jesus in every appearance in John's Gospel) and repeating the words already used by Martha: "Lord, had you been here my brother would not have died" (v. 32). Seeing Mary and her friends weeping, Jesus was deeply moved. When invited to come and see where Lazarus had been laid, Jesus burst into tears *(edakrusen)*. The Jews standing by understood this as reflecting Jesus' love for Lazarus, "See how he loved him" (v. 36).

What evidence there is for one sister being stronger than the other or at least normally taking the lead role may favor Martha. At the tomb it was she who protested rolling away the stone, fearing embarrassment to the family because of the condition of the body (Jn. 11:39). Balancing this is the final word about many of the Jews being persuaded to faith, identified as "those coming to Mary" (v. 45). Each sister had her identity and prominence. Jesus had close ties with each as with their brother. There is not a hint that the love which bound all four to one another was sexist. The strongest case is for theirs as a close relationship as persons, with neither denial of sexual difference nor preoccupation with it. Here were persons of two sexes whose mutual respect, friendship, and love carried them through experiences of tension, grief, and joy. Apparently Jesus was secure enough to develop such a relationship with two sisters and their brother without fear for his reputation. He could oppose them without the fear of chauvinism. That Jesus had much to do with the liberation and growth of Martha and Mary is not to be doubted. That he received meaningfully from them seems clearly implied in the stories about the relationship.

The Anointing at Bethany

We have noted already the problem of relating the anointing of Jesus by a "sinful woman" (Lk. 7:36–50) and his being anointed in Bethany (Mk. 14:3–9; Mt. 26:6–13; Jn. 12:1–8). The Gospels do offer the stories as having to do with two separate anointings, and we shall view them accordingly, with full acknowledgment of problems. In all the variants some firm lines do appear with respect to differences between Martha and Mary along with the close ties binding together Jesus, the two sisters, and their brother.

It is only John who identifies Mary with the anointing in Bethany, the woman remaining unnamed in Mark and Matthew. Jesus called her act a "beautiful deed." He assured this story of a woman's sacrificial love a place in the gospel wherever preached. Although it is not explicit that Mary actually anticipated Jesus' death, this may be implied. At least her beautiful deed gave Jesus needed support as he approached his awaited hour. Our New Testament professor when we were seminary students, W. Hersey Davis, used to suggest that of all those close to Jesus the first to catch on that he really meant what he said about his coming death were Judas and Mary, the former betraying him and the latter anointing him. This well could be so. Whatever her understanding of what was ahead, she ministered to him in no common way.

In this story Martha has another way of serving, as in Luke's nonanointing narrative. It need not follow that she loved Jesus less than did Mary. It could be that this manner of serving was "her thing." In any case, here were two sisters, inseparable as far as the stories go, each her own person, however different. In his last, difficult days Jesus was ministered to by each, one "practically" (serving a meal) and one lavishly (anointing him).

WOMEN WHO MINISTERED WITH JESUS

Luke alone supplies the datum that there were many women who not only benefited personally from Jesus' ministry but who ministered to him and with him, even to accompanying him and the Twelve on evangelistic journeys (Lk. 8:1–3). Most prominent among these is Mary Magdalene, to whom special attention will be given in Chapter 6.

Luke 8:1–3 consists of only one long sentence in the Greek text, although usually broken down into smaller units in English translation. There are three main focal points in the sentence: Jesus, the Twelve, and certain women. Jesus is described as on the move through cities and towns, preaching the Kingdom of God, evangel-

izing, and being attended by the Twelve and certain women whom
he had healed. The Twelve are mentioned as being with Jesus, but
of them nothing more is said here. The chief motive of the paragraph seems to be to bring certain women, of whom there were
"many," into focus, representing them as recipients of healing at
different levels of need and as actively participating with Jesus and
the Twelve in their crusades, with special reference to their monetary support. Luke indicates that there were many of them and that
these included women prominent in the public life of the state as
well as in the church.

Two categories of healing are specified: evil spirits and infirmities. It was currently a general practice to ascribe various mental
and emotional disturbances to "demons," "evil spirits," or "unclean spirits." This understanding of various human ills was prevalent in the pagan world as well as in late Judaism. Symptoms and
conditions now termed some form of neurosis or psychosis were
then theologically assessed as "demon possession." This is a whole
study in itself and not the central concern of this book.[10] Briefly
stated, Jesus nowhere to our knowledge denied the objective reality
of "demons," nor did he debate the question as such. Whether
accommodation to current understanding or his own perception of
forces behind human ills, Jesus did deal directly with the resultant
phobias, suicidal mania, schizophrenia, guilt, alienation, and other
physical, emotional, and mental disturbances. He liberated and
humanized people who otherwise were being enslaved or destroyed
by forces within themselves and in society.

According to Luke, Jesus healed many women of "evil spirits
and infirmities." In addition to acute problems attributed to "demons" or "spirits," there were physical problems that were especially burdensome to women. Any issue of blood was "defiling,"
rendering one socially unfit, and such problems were aggravated
for woman because of her "period." Luke here does not specify the
particular nature of the "evil spirits and infirmities" from which
these women had been healed, except for Mary Magdalene, from
whom he says "seven demons" had been cast out. Presumably
these "many" women had been healed of various illnesses, physical, emotional, and mental. With no specific data on Mary Magda-

lene's "seven demons," it is idle to speculate. What is significant is that women whose conditions were subject to scorn and penalty found in Jesus a liberator who not only enabled them to find health but whom he dignified as full persons by accepting their own ministries to himself and the Twelve.

Three women are named, "Joanna" and "Susanna" in addition to Mary Magdalene. Joanna is identified as "the wife of Chuza, Herod's steward." This probably is a reference to Herod Antipas, one of the sons of Herod the Great and tetrarch over Galilee. Popular notions have identified Mary Magdalene as the "sinful woman" in Lk. 7:36–50, but Luke does not even hint at this.

It is significant that women did have an open and prominent part in the ministry of Jesus. Luke's word for their "ministering" is widely used in the New Testament. Its noun cognate, *diakonos,* may be rendered "minister," "servant," or "deacon" (the latter in Rom. 16:1 for Phoebe and in the pastoral letters). The passage before us implies that Jesus attracted to his movement a large number of women, ranging from some in desperate need to some in official circles of government.

TWELVE AND NO WOMEN

That the Twelve were all men is indicated in each of the four listings in the New Testament (Mk. 3:13–19; Mt. 10:1–4; Lk. 6: 12–16; Acts 1:13). The names vary in the four lists, but the male identity is uniform. Why were the Twelve all men? This is the strongest single evidence against a clear breakthrough on the part of Jesus in the recognition of the full equality of women with men. Apostleship was a role distinction, and a primary one in the early church. Why men only? The New Testament gives no clear answer, and there are optional assessments, including the one above, that at this point even in the example of Jesus there is not a complete overcoming of male bias.

Several considerations may be placed alongside this one. Jesus advanced various principles that went beyond their immediate implementation. For example, he clearly repudiated the Jew-Samaritan antipathy, affirming not only his own Jewish kin but also the Samaritan. Even so, there are no Samaritans among the Twelve. Hence, no more may be read into Jesus' not having included women in the Twelve than in his not having included Samaritans in the Twelve. He affirmed both woman and Samaritan as persons with fullest right to identity, freedom, and responsibility; but for some undisclosed reason he included neither in the circle of the Twelve.

It may have been that custom here was so entrenched that Jesus simply stopped short of fully implementing a principle that he made explicit and emphatic: "Whoever does the will of God is my brother, and sister, and mother" (Mk. 3:35). If restriction to Jewish men was deliberate, the explanation is more difficult. One explanation may relate to the apparently symbolic intention of the number twelve. The disciples who are known as "the twelve apostles" had purpose beyond any merely symbolic significance, yet it is difficult to escape the conclusion that there was some reason behind the selection of precisely twelve, no more and no less. The most obvious reason for this would be the offering of a parallel to the twelve patriarchs or twelve tribes of Israel, each headed by a son of Jacob. The Twelve could dramatize both the continuity with national Israel and the discontinuity which looked beyond national Israel to a new fellowship inclusive of any who would come by faith. The continuity with the Israel out of which Jesus came would be expressed by the selection of a new set of "patriarchs," men out of national Israel. Discontinuity and enlargement to include "children of faith" instead of restriction to "children of flesh" could have been dramatized by inclusion of women, Samaritans, and Gentiles in the Twelve; but for the time this may have been an ideal awaiting its time of actualization.

However the restriction of the Twelve to Jewish men is to be accounted for, Jesus did introduce far-reaching principles, which bore fruit even in a former rabbi who at least in vision could say, "There is not any Jew nor Greek, not any slave nor free, not any male and female; for ye all are one in Christ Jesus" (Gal. 3:28). Further, the inclusion of "many" women in the traveling company of Jesus represents a decisive move in the formation of a new community. The Twelve are men, but even at this point women "minister" to them.

This is not to dismiss the restriction of the Twelve to male Jews as necessarily without male bias. The explanation nearest at hand is that Jesus began where he was, within the structures of Judaism as he knew it in his upbringing. His closest companions initially may have been Jews, men, and men of about his own age. He began there but he did not stop there. The thrust was outward, increasingly inclusive and not restrictive. Even in the early stages of his mission, women were becoming deeply involved at the power center of Jesus' movement.

As a concluding caveat, the logic which from the male composition of the Twelve would exclude women from high office or role in the church would likewise exclude the writers and most of the readers of this book, for there were no non-Jews among the Twelve. Unless one would argue that "apostolic succession" (however adapted) is for Jews only, it cannot be for men only.

Chapter 5

THE TEACHING
OF JESUS

Although related, Jesus' discernible manner and his explicit teaching provide two major avenues to an understanding of his attitude toward woman.

DISCOURSE ADDRESSED TO MEN

The Gospels report the public discourse of Jesus in the masculine gender, addressed to men and not women. Of course, there are instances where Jesus spoke directly to women, as in the case of his mother, Mary and Martha, the woman at Jacob's well, *et al.* Greek has three grammatical genders: masculine, feminine, and neuter. There are distinct masculine and feminine forms for the definite article, pronouns, and other parts of speech. In public addresses reported in the Gospels, Jesus addresses his hearers as "ye" and refers to them as "they," and these pronouns are in the masculine gender. In various other ways the public discourses are male-oriented as to grammatical gender.

What does this imply? Is the male address due to Jesus himself? Does Jesus simply use male-oriented forms of public address as he inherited them, with no intended slight to woman? Does the prominence of the masculine gender reflect the perspective of the men who wrote the Gospels and shaped the traditions behind them?

The Matthean Sermon on the Mount (Mt. 5–7) serves well to illustrate the male orientation of public addresses ascribed to Jesus. The Beatitudes bear the masculine stamp throughout (likewise in Luke). The key term *makarioi* ("blessed," "happy," or "fortunate") is in the masculine gender. The masculine gender is used for "the poor," "the ones mourning," "the meek," and all the others described. The pronoun "they" is invariably masculine in the Beatitudes. In the pericope[1] about anger, the warnings and instructions concern one's "brother" (Mt. 5:22–24). Those who love their enemies as well as their friends are "sons" of their "Father in heaven" (vs. 43–48). The Model Prayer is not only addressed to "our Father," but "our debtors" are designated in the masculine gender. The "speck" and the "beam" are in the eyes of brothers. Masculine articles and adjectives are used for "those" who merely say "Lord, Lord!" and those commended for doing the will of God (7:21–23). The instructions for church discipline relate to the erring "brother" (18:15). The "many" who are "called" and the "few" who are "chosen" appear in masculine gender. And so it is found throughout the Gospels.

On the other side, appeal could be made to Jesus' avoidance of either masculine or feminine usage in pointing to a little child as exemplifying greatness in the Kingdom (Mk. 9:33–37; Mt. 18:1–5; Lk. 9:46–48). The term *paidion* is neuter, so it cannot be known whether Jesus selected a little boy or a little girl to make his point. But too much is not to be made of this, for although child may refer to boy or girl, the remarks following fall back into the conventional language which is male-oriented: "Whoever [*hos* is masculine in gender] receives one of such little children in my name receives me" (Mk. 9:37). The form of address is as though to males only *(hos)*, but it is unlikely that such restriction is intended.

Examples of the dominance of the masculine gender in discourses ascribed to Jesus could be multiplied. Does this male-oriented language imply bias or insensitivity? Of course, one must allow for the possibility that this form of address goes back to Jesus himself. Possibly it reflects that redaction of the church. It conforms to the then current patterns in public address. Even in Luke-Acts, where special sensitivity to woman seems to appear (see below Chapter 9), the addressees are masculine in the public speeches. Peter addresses "Men, Jews, and all those dwelling in Jerusalem," all terms being masculine in gender (Acts 2:14; also v. 22). Those hearing and crying out, "Men, brethren, what shall we do?" are all masculine (v. 37). Were there no women in the audience? In Athens, Paul addressed "Men, Athenians" (17:22), even though notable women are reported among his converts (v. 34).

Special pleading for Jesus may be our disposition here, but in the absence of any explicit denigration of woman on his part and in the light of his deliberate and radical affirmation of woman in his manner and teaching, it is tempting to see the heavy hand of traditional language here. To our knowledge, Jesus left nothing that he himself had written. His words reach us only through the writings of others. Language itself, the Greek of the New Testament as well as modern English, incorporates a strong male bias difficult to overcome. That Jesus was highly sensitive to the personhood of woman is compelling, whatever may be the reason for the male orientation of much of the diction ascribed to him.

LOOKING UPON A WOMAN IN LUST

Jesus spoke directly to the matter of reducing a woman to a sex object. In the Sermon on the Mount he charged that it is to "commit adultery in his heart" for a man "looking upon a woman for the purpose of lusting after her" (Mt. 5:28). The passage is concerned first of all with the guilt of the man, but it has implications for Jesus' respect for woman as being more than a sex object.

The force of Jesus' teaching is best felt when it is examined against its historical background, both in the Jewish world and in the Greco-Roman world. The Seventh Commandment in the Decalogue reads, "You shall not commit adultery" (Ex. 20:14). Like the Beatitudes of Jesus, these commandments are addressed to men, whatever the implication of that. As seen in Chapter 1, adultery in Judaism was a sin against the rights of a man. For any man, single or married, to have sexual relations with another man's wife was ruled adultery. For a single woman to have sexual relations with a married man was not considered adultery, as in the case of a prostitute. Judah was not censured for going in to one whom he thought to be a prostitute, only when it turned out that she was his daughter-in-law; it was the pregnant Tamar who almost suffered being stoned to death (Gen. 38:12–26). David's sin was seen as against Uriah, from whom he stole Bathsheba (2 Sam.

12:9). Harlotry was sinful, but it applied only to a woman. A man did not bear the same stigma as the harlot he visited. Rape was a crime, primarily against the father whose daughter was raped. Adultery was not a crime against a woman but the crime of a wife and some man against her husband.

Jesus extended the understanding of adultery in two directions: (1) it could be committed against a woman and (2) it could be committed in the heart even if not given overt expression. The latter implication is invariably found in Jesus' teaching, but the former has not been sufficiently recognized.

In terming the lustful look adultery Jesus did not confuse temptation with adultery. He was tempted in all points as we are, but he did not sin (Heb. 4:15). Jesus' humanity was real (not Docetic), and he experienced the physical appetites, drives, and emotions native to human existence. Nothing is said about a sexual drive, but this is implied in the affirmation (not negative confession) that in "every thing" Jesus was tempted in the manner we are. Temptation is not sin. Temptation is the normal tension that occurs when something that belongs to the givenness of our nature is confronted by options before us. Sin and guilt arise at the point of consent.

Jesus rejected the idea that one is guiltless unless he overtly commits adultery. The "lustful look" is that if and only if it represents intention: "the one looking at a woman to desire her." Another misconception is to assume that Jesus meant to say that the lustful look is as bad as the overt act. It surely is not as harmful to the woman; she is less harmed by being ogled than raped. Jesus does not imply that if one is to look in lust, he may as well go all the way. He makes one point here: to look with a view to adultery is of itself an adulterous act. The locus at which sin arises and at which it must be conquered is within the human heart.

But another primary implication is embedded in the teaching of Jesus on the subject of the adulterous heart and lustful look. Jesus sees woman in terms of her rightful personhood and not just as a sex object. In much of Jewish literature, canonical and noncanonical, woman is an object at man's disposal or for man's use or pleasure. In much of the Greek literature woman is despised, ridiculed, and denigrated. This is explicit as early as Hesiod and

Semonides of Amorgos and prominent in the benighted rationales of Plato and Aristotle, though already seriously reassessed in the drama of Aeschylus and Euripides. Although woman fares better in Roman perspective, even there she often is little more than a sex object. The Roman literature even here offers some balance, for it recognizes in woman the same sexual drives as in man, sex being a basic preoccupation on both sides.

Jesus declared that a man could commit adultery against a woman (Mt. 5:28)! A man may commit adultery against *any* woman, even one who has no husband. This was innovative. Apart from the primary concern to internalize sin, this text represents woman as having rights in her own right. She is not a thing to be used. To look upon a woman with a view to lust is to commit adultery *against her (emoicheusen autēn),* not just against her husband. This represents a major breakthrough alongside others in the radicality of Jesus (cf. Mk. 2:17; 2:27f.; 3:35; 7:15; etc.). In all the radicality of Jesus runs one fundamental perspective, the priority of the personal over all else.

Nowhere is Jesus remembered as warning a woman not to look with lust upon a man. This may be understood as overlooking a woman's own sexuality. That a woman had the same sexual drive as a man is explicit in Roman drama and poetry. In the Jewish world, apparently, a woman's sexual drive was overlooked or considered taboo in discussion. It was a man's world, and the abuses were so overwhelming on the male side that Jesus made his assault directly upon the injustice and inequity as he found it. That a woman is as capable of committing adultery in her heart against a man, reducing him to a sex object, is a conclusion requiring no debate.

That Jesus nowhere is represented as critical of woman as woman is significant. He rejected his mother's interference and he challenged other women on occasion, but not womanhood as such. This does not imply that he was oblivious to the fact that in woman are all the virtues and vices found in man. It is that here, as in the case of the poor and the alien, he championed the disadvantaged against the advantaged, the abused against the abusers. Had the shoe been on the other foot, man suffering discrimination in a woman-oriented world, another approach would have been required.

DIVORCING AN INNOCENT WIFE

Divorce was a man's prerogative in the Jewish world. In the Roman world a woman could divorce her husband. A Jewish woman could sue, asking a court to compel her husband to give her a divorce (see Chapter 1). Jesus took two bold stands in relation to divorce: (1) he appealed to God's original provision for marriage but not for divorce and (2) he championed the rights of the faithful wife, her right not to be divorced. According to Mk. 10:12 Jesus took yet a third position as he accorded a wife the same rights and responsibilities in divorce as a husband, a contemporary Roman but not Jewish position.

In the first of two major passages in Matthew in which Jesus speaks directly to the issue of divorce, Mt. 5:31f., the subject is restricted to the injustice of a husband who divorces an innocent wife. The injunction quoted from Deut. 24:1 is male-oriented: "Whoever puts away his wife, let him give her a bill of divorce." In its original form the requirement offered the woman a legal document showing that her former husband had relinquished his claims upon her. This gave her some freedom for rebuilding her own life. But Jesus rejected this. No bill of divorce could really safeguard her from continuing damage. This is the point of his "But I say to you."

The declaration of Jesus about such divorce is difficult to preserve in translation: "But I say to you that every one putting away his wife except for the cause of fornication makes her to be victimized as an adulteress [passive voice in Greek], and whoever marries the woman who is put away is made adulterous [middle or passive voice]" (Mt. 5:32).[2] Most translations ignore the passive voice of the Greek infinitive and translate it, "makes her commit adultery." This is untenable. How would the fact of being divorced make one commit adultery? This is usually answered by saying that the passage assumes that she remarries, but that is neither affirmed nor required by the text (see Today's English Version for this forcing of the text). What Jesus says is that any innocent woman who is divorced is "made adulterous," i.e., she is treated as though she were an adulteress. She is victimized in being cast out, as an adulteress is cast out. The bill of divorce is supposed to distinguish her from a real adulteress, for the latter would be cast out without a bill of divorce, but Jesus gives no real value to this distinction. He stresses what the innocent wife and the guilty wife share in common—both are cast out. An innocent wife's right is the right to be retained and respected. Her rights are not preserved by the bill of divorce which her husband gives her. He has in fact degraded her and exposed her to continuing injustice.

Jesus in this passage is dealing with one situation alone, that in which an innocent wife is caused to suffer by a husband who thinks himself to be a righteous man because he has given his wife the "protection" of a bill of divorce.

To indicate the extent of the damage done by the husband who puts away his innocent wife, Jesus traced it to any subsequent marriage of the wife. Anyone marrying her is "made adulterous." This would seem to mean that the new husband suffers the same injustice suffered by the deposed innocent wife. Both come under society's stigma. Even today in a much freer society this holds true (e.g., just ask a divorced person in certain vocations if this affects one's getting a job). Jesus here challenges the injustice of a man's world where a husband thinks that it is his right to put away his wife, even if innocent.

If one thinks it an overtranslation to render the phrase in Mt. 5:32, "makes her to be victimized as an adulteress," this may be compared with the parallel grammar in v. 28, "he commits adultery against her." In v. 28 the case is that of a man who looks with lust upon a woman who may not even know that she is being ogled —yet the Greek reads literally, "he adulterates her." The guilty man treats the woman as an adulteress, but this does not mean that she is actually that. He has made her that in his own mind. So in v. 32, the woman is victim and not a guilty agent.

DIVORCE AND REMARRIAGE

There are three other passages in the Gospels where Jesus is quoted on the subject of divorce (Mk. 10:1–12; Mt. 19:1–12; Lk. 16:18). Matthew and Mark are in such close parallel that they undoubtedly intend to report the same response of Jesus to his questioners, yet there are significant differences between them. Luke stands apart, with one verse in no apparent relationship with its context.

One thing common to all passages ascribed to Jesus is the absence of the double standard that discriminated against woman. Also, there is a strong affirmation of marriage as a union between a man and a woman not to be broken by mankind. God's will from the beginning makes no provision for divorce, the latter being a concession made later to human hardness of heart. According to Matthew, Jesus allowed divorce and remarriage to the innocent party where the spouse had been unfaithful. In Mark there is evidence that Jesus recognized that a wife had the same right to divorce her husband that a husband had to divorce his wife; but Jesus warns wife equally with husband against an adulterous act against that one's spouse.

Luke's report of Jesus' teaching on divorce is brief and unambiguous: "Every one putting away his wife and marrying another commits adultery, and the one marrying the woman put away from her husband commits adultery" (Lk. 16:18). This makes no provision for remarriage following divorce. It could be argued that here God's original and unconditioned will for the permanency of marriage is declared, whereas elsewhere Luke traces God's redeeming love as he offers new life against whatever background of failure or brokenness (cf. Lk. 15). However, Luke does not modify the position of Jesus in this context.[3]

Significant for our purpose is the fact that the Lucan passage is a judgment upon the male offender against marriage. No explicit indictment is made of woman, whatever may be implied. Contrary to the male bias that prevailed, Jesus weights the judgment against the man who remarries after divorcing his wife and the man who marries a divorced woman.

Why Luke introduces 16:18 into this context is not readily apparent, for nothing else in the context refers to marriage or divorce. His opponents had just mocked Jesus for his warnings as to the wrong way of relating to money. In reply, Jesus said, "You are those justifying yourselves before men, but God knows your hearts," God counting abominable what such men esteem (v. 15). Jesus then applied the principle to other areas, including divorce (v. 18).

In Lk. 16:18, then, the subject of divorce comes in only incidentally, as an illustration of man's self-justification, calling good what God called evil. The passage clearly opposes divorce. Significantly, it is the male offender who is censured. Most striking is the fact that Jesus charges a man as committing adultery against a woman, contrary to the male orientation, which found adultery to be a sin against some man's rights.

The treatment of divorce in Mt. 19:1–12 is generally recognized to be later than that in Mk. 10:1–12, Mark being a primary source to Matthew.[4] Although there are other variations between the two Evangelists, the chief difference is between Mark's representation of the Pharisees as asking Jesus "if it is lawful for a husband to divorce a wife" (Mk. 10:2) and Matthew's having them ask "if it is lawful for a man to put away his wife for any cause" (Mt. 19:3). Many see Matthew not only as reflecting the debate between the strict position of the school of Shammai and the liberal position of the school of Hillel, but also as reducing the stricter demand in Mark to accommodate it to the limitations and practical necessities of the continuing church.

Mark 10:1–12 does appear to be more primitive than its Matthean parallel, although this has been contested.[5] Probably more striking in Mark than the absence of the "except" clause is Mark's recognition of a woman's power to divorce her husband. In Roman society a wife could divorce a husband, but this did not hold true among Jews except in the case of royal persons, like the Herods, who were more Roman than Jewish. Did Mark simply ascribe to Jesus a Roman practice, reflecting Mark's situation and not actually that of Jesus? This is the conclusion of many scholars and the basis upon which some have argued that at this point Matthew is more primitive than Mark. However, a case can be made both for the priority of Mark and for his not having read back into the teaching of Jesus a position found only outside Judaism.

It is possible that in Mk. 10:12 ("And if she [the wife] having put away her husband should marry another, she commits adultery") the position is actually that of Jesus himself (cf. 1 Cor. 7:10f.). If so, Jesus has gone beyond Jewish perspective and practice and looked upon the wife as upon the husband, both under the same restrictions and under the same judgment in the event of divorce and remarriage. In Mk. 10:11 a husband is seen as capable of committing adultery against his wife, though it is not clear whether "against her" refers to the wife he divorces or the one he next marries. In v. 12 a wife is seen as having power to divorce her husband, and she is judged as committing adultery if she then marries another man. Whatever the harshness here, at least there is no double standard for husbands and wives.

Most significant in both Matthew and Mark is the fact that Jesus appealed to God's will in creation, building upon the Priestly narrative in Gen. 1:27; 5:2, where male and female are created together and for one another, with no subordination as in the rib passage. From the creation narrative in Genesis 2, Jesus drew only v. 24, probably an appendix to the rib narrative, this verse stressing the equality of male and female as in marriage the two become one flesh. Thus Jesus not only took a firm stand for the unbreakable character of marriage in the original will of God but he made no place for the subordination of one to the other in marriage. Where there is failure, he found husband and wife equally responsible.

"EUNUCHS" FOR THE KINGDOM OF HEAVEN

Matthew alone has the rather enigmatic pericope about "eunuchs." This follows a long passage on the subject of divorce (cf. Mt. 19:1–12). The disciples apparently were awed by the heavy demand of Jesus concerning marriage, for Jesus ascribed divorce to a concession to man's hardness of heart, reminding his disciples that "the Creator from the beginning made them male and female" and that marriage was a union so strong that it was intended to override ties as strong as even that of a son for his parents (vs. 4f.). Jesus then added that what God has united is not to be separated by man (v. 5). To this strict ruling of Jesus the disciples replied: "If the case of a man is thus with a woman, it is better not to marry" (v. 10). The response is strictly male-oriented. Why should a man get into a marriage from which he cannot be released? A marriage so conceived seemed to them to be too great a price to pay for its worth.

Jesus in turn expanded the question. He introduced the subject of eunuchs, presumably as representing the alternative to marriage. He spoke of three kinds of eunuchs: those who are eunuchs from birth, those who are made eunuchs by men, and those who make eunuchs of themselves for the sake of the Kingdom of Heaven. Those who are eunuchs from birth presumably are persons who are born impotent or incapable of sexual practice. The second group, those made eunuchs by men, are those literally castrated so as to be made suitable to their master's needs. The third group, those making themselves eunuchs for the sake of the Kingdom of Heaven, presumably are persons who commit themselves to the celibate life, with no necessary practice of actual castration.[6]

So understood, Jesus offered two options: marriage or celibacy. He did not relieve the heavy demand upon marriage. What he did was to point to the single life as equally demanding. Jesus did not command marriage or the single life. He did not denigrate either. This is implied in a play on words in his concluding remark: "Let the one who is able to make room [for it] make room *(chōrein chōreitō)."* One must consider the high demands of marriage; one likewise must consider the high demands of the single life. His respect for individuality and for the individual choice in this matter accords with such respect everywhere in his manner and teaching.

If by eunuchs for the Kingdom's sake Jesus referred to the option of the single life, it is to be recognized that this relates in his teaching to vocation. There is no hint here of the asceticism that perceives the material in general and sex in particular as evil. This is vocationally based celibacy and not ascetic-based avoidance of marriage or sex. Apparently Jesus opted for the single life and did so on vocational grounds. He offered this to his followers as a viable option alongside that of marriage.

SEXUALITY IN HEAVEN

The subject of sex in heaven receives scant attention in Scripture, but it is met directly in one Synoptic passage (Mk. 12:18–27; Mt. 22:23–33; Lk. 20:27–40). The Synoptic parallels are almost identical, but with some Lucan amplification. The teaching of Jesus on the subject is set against the background of a Sadducean attempt to embarrass Jesus. Although the question of sexuality as such is not explicit, Jesus is represented as teaching that marriage will not take place in heaven, there being no need for it.

The Sadducees did not believe in resurrection, and they had what apparently was a stock joke in the form of a story, calculated to ridicule the Pharisaic position, held also by Jesus. The apocryphal story was that of a woman married to seven brothers in succession, as according to the Levirate law (Gen. 38:8; Deut. 25:5) each time she was widowed another of her husband's brothers took her to wife. They asked, then, whose wife would she be in the resurrection, since the seven had her. Jesus replied that they understood neither the Scriptures nor the power of God (Mk. 12:24). He affirmed that when the dead arise they (men) neither marry nor are they (women) given in marriage, explaining that they are "as angels in the heavens" (v. 25), presumably like angels in that they do not marry.

Luke varies from Mark and Matthew with a more direct approach to the question of marriage in heaven. Strikingly, "The sons of this age marry and are given in marriage" (Lk. 20:34). The familiar pattern is for men to marry and women to be given in marriage, but Luke has Jesus describe "sons" as given in marriage as well as marrying. "The sons of this age" are the unrighteous. Probably "sons" is a term used here for men and women, but the masculine term is the one used. The masculine term is also used for those in heaven, but apparently the term here implies men and women. The terminology is male-oriented. On the other side it pictures sons as "given in marriage" or "not given in marriage." Of those found worthy of the coming age and the resurrection Jesus says, "they neither marry nor are given in marriage." An explanation follows which possibly is implied in Mark/Matthew but which is explicit in Luke: "For neither are they able to die any more, for they are equal with angels, and they are sons of God, being sons of the resurrection" (Lk. 20:36). Here the point at which "the sons" are compared with angels is unambiguous; they cannot die anymore. They are further described as sons of God, sons of the resurrection. Apparently it is the deathlessness of those in heaven which makes marriage no longer in order. This is not further explained, but it is hard to escape the conclusion that marriage here is related to childbearing (cf. Gen. 1:28); and since there is no more dying there is no longer need for reproduction.

Neither here nor elsewhere are family units envisioned in heaven. Presumably the ideal of one inclusive and sublimated family is implied, as anticipated in the claim of Jesus, "Whoever does the will of God, this one is my brother and sister and mother." At least the latter passage sees all the faithful without discrimination or subordination of one sex to the other.

JESUS' TRUE FAMILY

Passing attention has been given to the Synoptic pericope involving Jesus' identification of his true family. It will now be approached more directly (Mk. 3:31–35; Mt. 12:46–50; Lk. 8:19–21).

There are only minor verbal differences among the three Synoptics in this story. Mark reports that his mother and his brothers were standing outside the house where he was teaching and that they "sent to him, calling him" (Mk. 3:31). Matthew has it that as Jesus was speaking with the crowds his mother and brothers were standing outside "seeking to speak with him" (Mt. 12:46). Luke reports that Jesus' mother and brothers came but were unable to reach Jesus because of the crowd, it then being reported to Jesus: "Your mother and your brothers are standing outside wishing to see you" (Lk. 8:19f.). The Synoptics say nothing of the family's intention beyond this, but the response of Jesus seems to imply a strained relationship of some nature. Presumably his mother and brothers were attempting to intervene in what Jesus was doing, whether because they were unsympathetic with the direction of his life, or that they were fearful for his well-being, or whatever.

Jesus' reply to the quest of his mother and brothers belongs to the most significant of all sayings ascribed to Jesus: "Whoever does the will of God, this one is my brother and sister and mother" (Mk. 3:35). The Lucan version reads, "My mother and brothers are those hearing the word of God and doing it" (Lk. 8:21). All three Evangelists have only the mother and brothers present, the sisters not present. In Mark and Matthew, Jesus' reply makes "sister" explicit alongside "mother" and "brother." Luke does not include "sisters" in Jesus' reply, probably not because of any insensitivity to the importance of sisters but because the sisters were not present and not alluded to in the report to Jesus. Note that he does not add "my father."

Implied in Jesus' identification of his true family is possibly the most important principle of all in recognizing the worth of woman or anyone else. Natural ties of flesh, ethnic identity, sexual identity, cultic distinction, etc., are purely secondary and not the basis or criterion for the true family. Personhood and faith/obedience to God are primary and sufficient. So seen, Jesus was not a "woman liberator" any more than a "Samaritan liberator" or "Gentile liberator." He was a human liberator. Persons matter. Personhood matters immediately and ultimately.

Here again Jesus' peace with himself and his sense of security was such that he could address a stern word to or concerning his natural mother or brothers or sisters. The battle against stereotype, discrimination, or prejudice is not yet won as long as relationships are such that preferential treatment must be given lest one be liable to some charge of chauvinism, racism, or whatever. The fullness of love, respect, and acceptance opens the way for honesty and integrity in address, even when the word that must be spoken must bear a measure of judgment.

WOMAN'S RIGHT TO THE STUDY

We have no tradition in the Gospels in which Jesus discussed as such the subject of woman's right to study, discuss, or teach the Law, but much may be implied in the way he talked with Mary and then defended her choice of hearing his word as over against Martha's concern with serving the meal.

In Lk. 10:38–42 are two statements by Jesus, both to Martha, first chiding Martha for being distracted and for troubling about many things, and then commending Mary's better choice: "Martha, Martha, you are distracted and troubled concerning many things, but one thing is needed; for Mary chose the good part which shall not be taken away from her."

There is a text-critical problem in Lk. 10:42, for in the manuscripts there are several variant readings to the one now generally accepted, "but one thing is needed." Among the alternate readings are these: "few things are needed or one," "few things are needed," and the absence of any reference to "one thing is needed." Although far from certain, probably the reading offered in the above paragraph is to be adopted, v. 42 beginning with the simple statement, "but one thing is needful" (a possible allusion to the Great Commandment).

What is this "one thing" which is needful? Jesus could have meant simply that one dish of food was sufficient, there being no need for a meal so elaborate as to cause distraction and troubling in the serving. More likely, the "one thing" needful relates to "the good part" which Mary had chosen. If so, it was the hearing of Jesus' word. What Mary had chosen "will not be taken away from her." This would apply to benefaction derived from hearing Jesus' word, not from eating a meal, however elaborate.

It does not follow that Jesus denied meaning to what Martha was doing. He often referred to meals and eating in a positive way. He was accused by his opponents as a "glutton and winebibber," doubtless with exaggeration, but there is no tradition that anyone accused him of ascetic practice or disdain for eating. Martha was chided first of all for what she was letting the serving of a meal do to her. Instead of being in charge of the meal, the meal was in charge of Martha. She was making too much of something to which, by every evidence, Jesus himself was not indifferent.

The positive side of Jesus' response to Martha is in what he said about Mary's choice of the "one thing" that was needful, the part that would not be taken from her. Jesus made our concern that others have food a primary matter, with implications for the Final Judgment (Mt. 25:31–46); but he warned against our preoccupation with food or other material needs for ourselves. Jesus provided bread for others, but he also warned that one does not live by bread alone. Food meets a temporal need, but "his word" meets an eternal need. Mary chose the "study" as over against the kitchen. Jesus related to her in a role that a rabbi normally would have restricted to men. Jesus commended Mary's choice and affirmed such choice as eternally significant. This story does not take Mary into the further role of teacher, but it does affirm her as a proper student of the word. Elsewhere, as seen above and as to be seen below, Jesus did enlist women in some ministry of the word.

WOMB AND WORD

In Lk. 11:27–28 is the story of an unnamed woman's eulogy of the womb that bore Jesus and the breasts which nursed him, followed by a terse reply from Jesus. While Jesus was speaking, a woman lifted up her voice from out of the crowd and said to him, "Blessed [is or be] the womb that bore you and the breasts that nursed you." To this Jesus replied, "Rather, blessed are those hearing the word of God and keeping it." In the story of Mary and Martha the choice was between food and word. Here it is between womb and word. Jesus no more despised motherhood than he did meals, but he gave priority to the word of God over both. Significantly, he addressed women in each of these instances, commending one and correcting another.

It may be debated as to whether there is in this story reflection of a growing cult of Mary or not. By the second century there was a strong interest in "the holy family," with special attention to Mary, as reflected in the *Protevangelium of James.*[7] By that time stories were developing supportive of "the immaculate conception" of Mary (she having a miraculous birth) and her "perpetual virginity." Already in Matthew and Luke are the virginal birth stories, but with nothing in the direction of the *Protevangelium* (a pseudonym ascribed to James, the brother of Jesus, and presuming to be the "first" or "proto" Gospel). There are some passages in the Gospels which, whether by deliberate intention or not, exercise some control over what is to be made of Mary and the brothers and sisters of Jesus (cf. Mk. 3:31–35; Mt. 12:46–50; Lk. 8:19–21; Jn. 2:4; 7:1–9).

The unnamed woman's acclaim of the womb that bore Jesus and the breasts that succored him may have been the use of traditional language with no special reference to Mary. Apparently the woman intended to express her feeling about Jesus, even though she did so in terms of his mother. Whether the expression was her own coinage or traditional, it does eulogize or draw upon a tradition eulogizing motherhood. The terse reply of Jesus is a corrective to an undue focus upon the role of woman in childbearing. Woman's highest glory is not in bearing and nursing babies, however important and praiseworthy that may be.

Jesus shifted the eulogy from womb to word. It may be a proper deduction from the passage to understand Jesus as according to woman a higher function and blessedness than motherhood, even though he esteemed that. In the world Jesus knew, woman's vocation was primarily related to the womb. Jesus did respect the roles of wife and mother, but he perceived woman as more than womb. She, as well as man, may be a hearer and doer of the word of God.

TEN MAIDENS

One of Jesus' parables of the Kingdom of Heaven is that of the ten maidens, five foolish and five wise (Mt. 25:1–13). The parable cannot justly be construed as chauvinistic, for the wise disciples who are prepared for Christ's return are typified in this parable by maidens. In fact, neither wisdom nor folly is given a sexual identity. He could speak of "foolish virgins" with no apparent fear of being considered chauvinistic. He could speak of "wise virgins" with no necessary concern at the moment with woman's liberation. These were persons, subject to the strengths and weaknesses characteristic of the human race.

Jesus was capable of speaking to or about woman without apparent prejudice or preferential protection. So it was with his mother, Martha, and others. In the give-and-take of relationships with them, he accorded them the dignity of persons with whom he could agree or disagree, whom he could commend or censure, hold up as an example of folly or wisdom. That he employed the language of the day, male-oriented as it was, is attested in the traditions ascribed to him. Of utmost importance is the fact that there is no tradition indicating that Jesus in any way denigrated woman as woman. In his manner, his personal relationships, and in his teachings is compelling evidence that his basic assessment of any person was in terms of personal qualities that have no sexual identity. He knew persons, some Jews and some not, some adult and some children, some men and some women. Without denying the distinctions that were real, he affirmed the personhood that was common to all.

Chapter 6

THE RISEN CHRIST AND WOMAN

The most significant affirmation of woman in the New Testament may well be found in the tradition made prominent in all four Gospels that women were the ones to find the tomb of Jesus empty; that according to Mark and Luke the announcement of Jesus' resurrection was first made to women; that according to Matthew and John, Jesus actually appeared first to women (in John to Mary Magdalene alone); and that according to all four Gospels women were commissioned to inform Peter and the other apostles as to the most fundamental tenet of the Christian faith, that Jesus is not dead but risen!

For most readers of the Gospels the stories are taken at face value, leaving no doubt as to the priority of women in knowing and proclaiming this foundational fact to Christian faith. But for critical scholarship the matter is not that simple. Most critical scholars give priority to the male-oriented tradition preserved in 1 Cor. 15:1–7 and seriously challenge the empty tomb tradition.

The Problem

The basic problem before us is the apparent tension between the empty tomb tradition of the four Gospels giving priority to women and the appearance tradition of 1 Cor. 15:1–7 giving exclusive attention to men. Along with this is the further problem of extensive differences in the empty tomb tradition appearing in the four Gospels. Is there a basic empty tomb tradition underlying the four versions with their many variants as they appear in the four Gospels? How early is this tradition? How dependable? What is the relationship between the empty tomb tradition of the Gospels and the Cephas *et al.* tradition of First Corinthians? Which has priority? These are the basic questions for this chapter.

Critical scholarship is almost unanimous in giving priority to the tradition preserved in 1 Cor. 15:1–7, concentrated upon the appearance of the risen Christ to Cephas (Peter), the Twelve, above five hundred brethren at once, James (the brother of Jesus), all the apostles, and last of all to Paul. It is the contention of this book that on critical grounds this whole question needs to be reassessed, as indeed it has been by many critical scholars. The empty tomb tradition with its focus upon the involvement of women is not to be written off as secondary or unreliable. It is as deeply embedded in the traditions of the church as any other, and it must be reckoned with in all seriousness.

There is much that is "self-validating" about the empty tomb tradition. The fact is that the Gospels preserve the tradition even though it required defense and was not the witness upon which the church rested its case. Why then was it preserved? The most obvious answer is that it could not be ignored. From another direction, why would a male-oriented church invent a women-oriented tradition, especially if already there was an older and established one, such as the one that Paul received and transmitted to the Corinthians by the early fifties?

If, as we hope to show, the Gospels are credible in their recognition that knowledge of Jesus' resurrection was first communicated to women and that they were commissioned to inform the apostles of this all-important event, we have in this the strongest possible affirmation of woman. Whereas others found woman not qualified or authorized to teach, the four Gospels have it that the risen Christ commissioned women to teach men, including Peter and the other apostles, the basic tenet of the Christian faith! Strange that woman's right to teach or preach has been challenged by a church which, according to the Gospels, was first informed by women that Jesus is not among the dead but among the living.

There can be no doubt that the resurrection of Jesus is foundational to New Testament faith. The earliest apostolic preaching stressed this.[1] The book of Acts makes this apparent (cf. Acts 1:22;

2:32; 3:15; 4:10; *et passim*). Paul made the gospel stand or fall with
the fact of Jesus' resurrection (1 Cor. 15:12–19). He declared that
if Christ is not risen, our faith is vain and our preaching vain.
Elsewhere he stresses the primacy of the resurrection (1 Thess.
4:14; Rom. 10:9; Eph. 5:14). The book of Revelation knows Jesus
as the one who died and who is alive forevermore (Rev. 1:18).

WOMEN AND THE EMPTY TOMB

No one of the four Gospels gives an inclusive or definitive story
of the resurrection of Jesus or his appearances, but there is one
point at which all four converge, in telling (with variations) about
the visit of certain women to the tomb (Mk. 16:1–8; Mt. 28:1–8;
Lk. 24:1–12; Jn. 20:1–13).

Agreements and differences appear in the four Gospels in their
treatment of the women and the empty tomb, as E. L. Bode has
demonstrated.[2] Agreements in all four Gospels include (1) emphasis upon the first day of the week, (2) prominence of Mary Magdalene, and (3) attention to the stone that had closed the tomb.
Differences have to do with (1) the precise time of the visit of the
women to the tomb, (2) the number and identity of the women, (3)
the purpose of the visit, (4) the appearance of the messenger(s),
angelic or human, (5) the message of the angel(s) or man (men),
and (6) the response of the women. This combination of significant
agreements and differences seems to imply a basic tradition and
additionally some independent traditions.

Variants in the Empty Tomb Tradition

As the empty tomb tradition stands in its four variant forms in
the Gospels, the differences are so many and so great that there is
no hint of collusion or late construction. Examination in some
depth of these differences will bear out this conclusion.[3]

1. Although each Evangelist has it that the women visited the
tomb on or at "the first day of the week" (Mk. 16:2; Mt. 28:1; Lk.
24:1; Jn. 20:1), they differ as to the precise time. Mark has it "the
sabbath being past," "very early on the first day of the week," that

they came to the tomb, "the sun having risen" (Mk. 16:1f.). Matthew has it on "the evening of the sabbath, as the first day was drawing on" (Mt. 28:1). Luke has the visit of the women to the tomb to be on the first day of the week "at early dawn" (Lk. 24:1). John also locates the visit to the tomb on the first day of the week, Mary Magdalene coming "early, it yet being dark" (Jn. 20:1).

2. The same degree of difference holds for a second area of variants, the number and identity of women visiting the empty tomb. Mark names Mary Magdalene, Mary (mother?) of James, and Salome (Mk. 16:1). Matthew lists Mary Magdalene and "the other Mary" (Mt. 28:1). Luke names Mary Magdalene, Joanna, Mary of James, and "the rest" (*hai loipai* is feminine), implying two or more other women (Lk. 24:10). John refers to Mary Magdalene alone as visiting the tomb (Jn. 20:1).

3. The four Evangelists do not even present a clear, unambiguous purpose for the women's visit to the tomb, a third area of variation. Mark is explicit that with spices bought after the Sabbath the women came to anoint the body (Mk. 16:1). Luke seems to imply the same purpose (Lk. 24:1). Matthew reports only that they came "to see the tomb" (Mt. 28:1). John gives no explanation of Mary Magdalene's visit to the tomb.

4. A fourth point of variance in the empty tomb tradition has to do with the messengers who addressed the women. In Mark, the women enter the tomb and then see "a young man seated at the right, clothed in a white robe" (Mk. 16:5). Matthew reports that "an angel of the Lord" came down from heaven, rolled the stone away, and sat upon it (Mt. 28:2). He further reports that the angel's appearance was like lightning and his clothing white as snow (v. 3). Luke has it that the women entered the open tomb and that as they were perplexed about not finding the body there, "two men stood by them in dazzling clothing" (Lk. 24:4). John tells of two visits made by Mary Magdalene to the tomb, one before and one after telling Peter and the beloved disciple about the stone being rolled away. On the second visit, after Peter and his fellow disciple had gone, Mary looked into the tomb and saw "two angels in white," one sitting at the head and one at the feet where the body of Jesus had lain (Jn. 20:12).

5. There is less divergence in the message given the women at the empty tomb. In Mark the "young man" commissions them to tell Jesus' "disciples and Peter" that he will go before them into Galilee where they will "see him" just as he had told them (Mk. 16:6f.). Matthew has basically the same description, concluding with the commission that "the angel" gives them (Mt. 28:7). Significantly, in Matthew, Jesus himself appears to the women and personally commissions them to go to his disciples and tell them that they will see him in Galilee (v. 10). In Luke the "two men" chide the women for looking for the living among the dead, reminding them that Jesus had told them while yet in Galilee of his coming death and his resurrection "on the third day" (Lk. 24:5–7). John reports of the "two angels" only that they ask Mary Magdalene why she is weeping (Jn. 20:13). He then reports that Jesus himself appeared to Mary and commissioned her to go to his "brethren" and say to them, "I am ascending to my Father and your Father and my God and your God" (v. 17).

6. A sixth point of divergence is in the response of the women. The Gospel of Mark breaks off at 16:8, the various endings found in many manuscripts apparently being later scribal additions.[4] As it stands, the women say nothing since they are overcome by fear. In Matthew they went quickly from the tomb "with fear and great joy" and ran to tell Jesus' disciples (Mt. 28:8). Luke in 24:9 reports that the women remembered the promise Jesus had made in Galilee and that they returned from the tomb and "told all these things to the Eleven and all the rest [*tois loipois* is masculine]." John reports that Mary Magdalene upon finding the stone removed ran and told Simon Peter and the disciple "whom Jesus loved" (Jn. 20:2) and that upon being sent by the risen Jesus she said to his disciples, "I have seen the Lord," telling them the things Jesus had spoken to her (v. 18).

A Basic Empty Tomb Tradition

When all these divergences are considered as a whole, they are quite impressive. All attempts at harmonization are forced. What does clearly emerge is a basic tradition about certain women (or

Mary Magdalene alone) visiting the tomb after the Sabbath, finding it empty, and being deeply moved by what they experienced there. On the other hand, the Gospels no more than Paul rest the case for the resurrection of Jesus on the empty tomb or the witness of the women. In Mark there is no report of the women to the disciples. In Matthew there is no explicit report that the women spoke to the disciples, but this may be inferred.

Luke has it that the women did report "to the Eleven and the rest" (men), but in terms of what all of them, the women and the men, had heard Jesus himself foretell when they were together in Galilee (Lk. 24:9). Luke is emphatic that the witness of the women was not believed: "But these words appeared before them [the apostles] as idle, and they disbelieved them." The "them" of v. 11 is feminine in gender; the apostles disbelieved the women.

John describes Mary Magdalene as first telling "Simon Peter and the other disciple whom Jesus loved" about the empty tomb (Jn. 20:2). At that point Mary herself had only concluded that the body had been removed and placed elsewhere (v. 2b). These two disciples were convinced only by the evidence, not by Mary's word. Only the direct appearance of Jesus to Mary convinced her that he was alive (v. 16). Under Jesus' commission she did report to Jesus' "brothers," i.e., "the disciples" (masculine): "I have seen the Lord!" (vs. 17f.). The sequel demonstrates that none believed upon her report but only when they themselves saw Jesus, Thomas in particular demanding such evidence (vs. 19–29).

Significance of the Empty Tomb Tradition

What then does this imply for the part played by women in connection with the resurrection of Jesus? Paul has nothing to say about women as witnesses to an empty tomb or the risen Lord. The Gospels make this prominent, yet they are careful to show that the church's faith in the resurrection did not rest upon the fact of an empty tomb or upon the witness of women. This makes all the more significant the fact that all four Gospels were compelled to deal with this tradition, giving it great prominence and at the same time subordinating it to Jesus' appearance to his disciples. Accord-

ing to this underlying tradition, not invalidated by its many secondary variants, the risen Lord did choose to appear first to women
(or a woman) and commission them (her) to proclaim this most
important fact to the disciples, including Peter and the other apostles.

"The First Day of the Week" vs. "On the Third Day"

The four Gospels agree in linking the empty tomb tradition and
the visit(s) of the women on "the first day of the week" (Mk. 16:1f.;
Mt. 28:1; Lk. 24:1; Jn. 20:1). Luke 24:6 reaches back to another
tradition, that of instructions given by Jesus while yet in Galilee,
foretelling his suffering, death, and promised rising "on the third
day." "On the third day" belongs to the tradition preserved in 1
Corinthians 15. Two traceable traditions appear, then, one with
"on the first day of the week" linked to the empty tomb tradition
and one with "on the third day" linked to the tradition of the
appearance of Jesus to his disciples. Evidence here may be found
supporting the independence of the empty tomb tradition from the
appearance tradition preserved by Paul.

A strong tradition employing the phrase "on the third day"
appears in four groups of texts: predictions of Jesus' resurrection;
the sign of Jonah; rebuilding the Temple; and Jesus' "fulfilment"
in Jerusalem.[5]

The Synoptic Gospels ascribe to Jesus three predictions of his
death and his resurrection "on the third day" or "after three days."
Mark uses the phrase "after three days" (Mk. 8:31; 9:31; 10:34).
Matthew follows Mark, with a change to "on the third day" (Mt.
16:21; 17:23; 20:19); but in Mt. 27:63f. two expressions occur side
by side in the words of the high priests and Pharisees to Pilate:
"after three days" and "until the third day." Luke's phrase is close
to that of Matthew (Lk. 9:22; 18:33; 24:7, 46). Only in Matthew
is "the sign of Jonah" related to the entombment of Jesus, where
just as Jonah was in "the belly of the fish three days and three
nights" so Jesus was to be "in the heart of the earth three days and
three nights" (Mt. 12:40). John links "three days" with the rebuilding of "the temple" (Jn. 2:19) and the resurrection of Jesus (v. 22).

Echoes of this are heard in Mk. 14:58; 15:29; Mt. 26:61; 27:40. In the enigmatic reply of Jesus to Herod Antipas, Jesus spoke of his work "today and tomorrow," adding the promise "on the third day I shall be perfected" (Lk. 13:32). This probably refers to his resurrection. If so, it adds to the strong "third day" tradition in the Gospels linked to Jesus' resurrection but not to the empty tomb tradition.

Christian Worship on the First Day of the Week

Nowhere in the New Testament are we told explicitly why Christian worship centers on the first day of the week instead of on the Jewish sabbath, the seventh day.[6] The earliest Christians were Jews as was Jesus, and they worshiped in the synagogues, so on the seventh day. Traces of the almost universal practice of Christians in making the first day of the week the special day of worship can be found in the New Testament. The only explicit mention of "the Lord's day" in the New Testament is in Rev. 1:10. First Corinthians 16:1–4 prescribes a gathering of a collection "according to the first of the week" (v. 2). According to Jn. 20:19, Jesus appeared to his disciples on "the evening of that day, the first day of the week." Again Jesus appeared to them, this time with Thomas present, "eight days later," which by counting a part of a day a full day may imply the Sunday following (v. 26). The most likely reason for special celebration of the first day of the week by Christians is found in the tradition that Jesus arose on that day. It is the empty tomb tradition connected with the women which consistently stresses "the first day of the week."

Paul himself seemingly knew of the practice of special worship on the first day of the week (cf. 1 Cor. 16:1–4; Acts 20:7), but this is not stressed in the appearance tradition in 1 Corinthians 15, where the phrase is "on the third day" and not on "the first day of the week."

To summarize, Sunday or the first day of the week as a special day for Christian worship is apparently grounded on the tradition that Jesus arose on the first day of the week. This tradition is bound up with the tradition which knew women to have been the first to discover the empty tomb. The tradition that located Jesus' resurrection "on the third day" or "after three days" had separate history, and it is the one upon which Paul built. Neither the Gospels nor Paul rested the church's faith in the resurrection in the empty tomb or the women's witness, but this tradition is early and strong. Paul neither affirmed nor denied it. He may not have known it, but probably he just ignored it. The Gospels preserve it but rest their case finally on the appearance of the risen Christ to men. There is no solid evidence to challenge successfully the historical trustworthiness of the tradition about the women and the empty tomb, even though that tradition may have been problematic in a male-oriented church addressing its message to a male-dominated world.

THE RESURRECTION TRADITION IN ACTS

The book of Acts makes much of the witness borne to the resurrection of Jesus, especially in words ascribed to Peter and Paul. Acts is closely related to the Gospel of Luke, the two books now commonly referred to as Luke-Acts. Luke acknowledged his dependence upon various sources, written and oral (Lk. 1:1–4); and in Luke-Acts appear two distinct and independent traditions, traceable apparently to his sources, the Gospel of Luke preserving both traditions and the book of Acts including only the "third day" tradition featuring the appearances of Jesus to men (yet with a trace of "the first day of the week" tradition in Acts 20:7).

A Successor to Judas

When a replacement for Judas was sought, that one's qualifying credentials were clearly spelled out by Peter as he addressed the one hundred and twenty as "Men, brothers" (Acts 1:16). Where were the women from Galilee so prominent in Luke's account of the death, burial, and resurrection of Jesus (cf. Lk. 23:49, 55f.; 24:1–12, 21–24)? It is difficult to believe that those women who followed Jesus from Galilee to Jerusalem and who stood by when few had the courage and/or commitment to do so would not now be present. Women do reappear in the story shortly (cf. Acts 6:1). Two men were presented, and from these two Matthias was selected (1:23–26). So far as the credentials stressed are concerned, having accompanied Jesus in his work and being able to witness to his being alive, certain women who followed him from Galilee to the cross and who were first to learn of the empty tomb and his being alive would have been prime candidates. Mary Magdalene would have qualified as one who could have testified to his resurrection. But these were women in a world that did not grant credibility to a woman's witness.

Sermons in Acts

Sermons attributed to Peter and Paul in Acts do not allude to women as even in an unofficial capacity giving their witness to the living Lord. In his sermon on the Day of Pentecost, Peter makes the resurrection paramount, declaring: "This Jesus God raised up, of whom all we are witnesses" (Acts 2:32). The "all we" is masculine. Again, after the healing of a lame man at the Temple, Peter preached to "the people" who gathered, addressing them as "Men, Israelites" (masculine terms), crediting the miracle to "the Author of life . . . whom God raised from the dead" (3:15). To this he added, "of which [or "of whom"] we are witnesses" (v. 15b). Greek grammar here leaves ambiguous whether or not women are included. In the sermon ascribed to Peter in the home of Cornelius the witnesses to the resurrection are unambiguously male.

In Acts 13:16–41 is recorded a sermon ascribed to Paul, preached in a synagogue in Antioch of Pisidia. As in all apostolic preaching, the death and resurrection of Jesus is central. This tradition knows about the "tomb" (v. 29); but there is no reference to its being empty, and there is no reference to women as witnesses to the living Christ.

The conclusion is inescapable from Luke-Acts that an empty tomb and appearance to women tradition was more widely known than employed in the early church. The apostolic preaching in Acts is male-oriented.

THE TRADITION PAUL RECEIVED

In 1 Cor. 15:3–7, written perhaps around A.D. 53, Paul reminds the Corinthians that he had "delivered" to them a tradition that he himself had "received":

> that Christ died for our sins according to the Scriptures, and that he was buried, and that he has been raised on the third day according to the Scriptures, and that he appeared to Cephas, afterward to the Twelve, after that he appeared to above five hundred brothers at one time, out of whom the majority (masculine gender) remain until now, but certain ones have fallen asleep; after that he appeared to James, after that to all the apostles. (1 Cor. 15:3–7)

Paul then adds himself to the list of those to whom Jesus had appeared: "And last of all, as to one untimely born, he appeared to me also" (v. 8).

The Early Fifties. Paul's first mission to Corinth began probably in the fall of A.D. 50 or the spring of A.D. 51 and continued for about eighteen months (cf. Acts 18:1–18), and at that time he "delivered" to the Corinthians an already well-established tradition about the death of Jesus and his appearance to various men.

The tradition that Paul "received" and also transmitted in the early fifties made no reference to the empty tomb or to women. It is strictly a male-oriented tradition. This agrees with the solid evidence elsewhere that the early church built its case upon the witness of men, not women. On the other hand, there are traces even in Paul of a knowledge of the empty tomb tradition.

To Cephas "First"? Nothing in 1 Corinthians precludes the tradition preserved in the four Gospels about women and the open tomb. Paul did not quote the tradition he received as saying "to Cephas *first*" (1 Cor. 15:4). No textual variant reads "first." The tradition may imply "first" but it does not say that. Nothing in the syntax of the Greek sentence requires the implication "to Cephas first."

He Was Buried. On the positive side, there are traces in 1 Corinthians 15 of a possible knowledge of the tradition about the tomb and that of "the first day of the week" associated with it. The tradition Paul received affirmed that Jesus "was buried" (1 Cor. 15:4).

That Paul tended to link the ideas of "burial" and "resurrection," as is done in the tradition he received (1 Cor. 15:4), is supported in both Romans and Colossians.

In Col. 2:12 is a close parallel to the passage in Romans: "having been entombed (buried) together with him in baptism, in which also ye were raised together through the faith that is in the energizing of God, the One having raised him out of the dead ones." Here again "raised" is set over against "buried" or "entombed." It requires strong evidence or argument to overcome the seeming implication that resurrection has something to do with the tomb and not just with Jesus. The miracle implied is not just that the disciples' faith was revived; the implication is that something first happened to Jesus in his bodily existence and that one result was that the tomb was left empty.

Holistic View. Paul's own holistic view of personhood implies that he would think of resurrection not in some spiritualized, ghostly sense (a "soul" in the Greek sense) but as bodily. The very thought of "absence from the body" (a common idea in the pagan world) was repelling to Paul (2 Cor. 5:1–5); but what the New Testament claims about Jesus' resurrection is not an exact parallel to what it implies concerning our resurrection. Resurrection for us is a transformation of the body from one kind to another, the present body returning to dust. The New Testament represents the resurrection of Jesus as unique, it being the raising up of the body which was entombed, there also at some point being its transformation.

Why Silence About Empty Tomb? If Paul knew of the empty tomb tradition, as seems evident, it can only be surmised why he did not mention it. The most likely reason was that, along with the rest of the church, he stressed only the appearances to men as the "official" witness of the church.

On the Third Day. The tradition that Paul received and passed on to the Corinthians in the early fifties contains the highly significant phrase "on the third day" (1 Cor. 15:4). Not only does this phrase distinguish this tradition from the empty tomb tradition that employed another phrase, "the first day of the week"; but it implies something for the nature of what occurred. The tradition that Paul transmitted has to do with resurrection and not just immortality. By resurrection Paul means nothing less than a bodily resurrection.

Paul speaks of various appearances of Jesus, to Cephas and many others as well as to himself; but he speaks of only one act of Jesus' being raised—"on the third day." Paul is speaking of more than a sense of the divine presence or a sense of Christ's presence. He does not refer to an empty tomb, but he speaks of a resurrection that necessarily concerns a body that had been entombed and was raised.

Resurrection and Immortality. It is a common error to confuse two distinct ideas, that of resurrection and that of immortality.[7] Resurrection has to do with body. In fact, it is a redundancy to say "bodily resurrection." There is no resurrection except bodily. Immortality is an ancient and widely held pagan idea having to do with "soul," the latter understood as the original, essential, and immortal self. There was an ancient dualism that made a sharp distinction between soul and body, or spirit and matter. In an old pagan view, death liberates soul (or spirit encased in soul) from the body, allowing it to return to its original home of pure spirit.

Paul shared in the holistic view of "man" (the human being) set forth in Gen. 2:7. A "soul" (*psychē* in Greek) is a "self" (cf. Lk. 12:19; Acts 2:41). Paul's doctrine in 1 Corinthians 15 is that of resurrection, contending for both continuity and discontinuity between the body "sown" and the body "raised" (1 Cor. 15:35–41). Paul's point is to insist upon an actual resurrection, first for Jesus and then for his followers. He recognized that in resurrection some significant change would be wrought in the body, but the "spiritual body" was indeed "body." Just as there is both continuity and discontinuity between a seed sown and the plant produced (v. 37), so there is both continuity and discontinuity between the body now and that in resurrection.

The First Day of the Week. There is in 1 Corinthians further evidence that Paul may have known of the empty tomb tradition, in his instructions about the gathering of a fund, to be pursued regularly "on the first day of the week" (1 Cor. 16:2). This seems to imply a practice of special assembly on "Sunday," or the first day of the week. There is no other clue to the setting apart of Sunday as a day of worship except that of Jesus' resurrection on that particular day.

Last of All. When Paul speaks of Christ as having appeared to Cephas, various others, and himself, he means far more than simply an awareness of a divine presence. Paul did not say "to Cephas *first,*" but he did say, "last of all *(eschaton de pantōn)* . . . he appeared to me also" (1 Cor. 15:8). If Paul meant no more than a sense of Christ's presence, he had no right to say "last of all." Christians to this day claim a sense of that presence. Jesus promised his disciples that where two or three were gathered in his name he would be present (Mt. 18:20). The view that understands "resurrection" as something that happened to the faith of the church rather than to Jesus simply does not do justice to the claims of the Gospels or Paul. The Gospels are explicit that Jesus was raised *before* anyone believed it. The resurrection caused the faith; the faith of the church did not produce the "resurrection." So it is with Paul's witness.

No Women Included? Did Paul know nothing of appearances of the risen Christ to women? He neither affirms nor denies this. In 1 Corinthians it is quite clear that Paul is not comfortable with the witness of women (see Chapter 7). The witness of a woman was not recognized in Jewish courts. Paul and the tradition he follows seem concerned with the "official" witness of men. He not only says nothing about the women which the Gospels report to have found the tomb empty and to have received from Jesus or his messengers the assurance that he was alive, but neither does Paul allude to the presence of women among the "above five hundred brothers" to whom Jesus appeared "at one time" (1 Cor. 15:6).

Paul could have known of an empty tomb tradition involving women despite the fact of his total silence on the subject, just as he transmitted a tradition about "above five hundred brethren" with no mention of women. The strictly male listing in 1 Corinthians 15 by no means settles the question thrust upon us by the empty tomb tradition so deeply embedded in the four Gospels.

According to the Scriptures. Another line of evidence indicating the independence from one another of the Gospels' empty tomb tradition and that preserved in 1 Corinthians 15 has to do with the phrase "according to the Scriptures." The tradition that Paul received and transmitted to the Corinthians included the affirmation: "Christ died for our sins according to the Scriptures . . . and he has been raised on the third day according to the Scriptures" (1 Cor. 15:3f.). What Scriptures? Paul does not say. There is a near parallel in Lk. 24:46, where the risen Christ appeared to his disciples and interpreted the events in which they then were caught up in terms of "Moses and the Prophets and Psalms" (v. 44), their way of designating what we know as "the Old Testament." Verse 46 reads, "And he said to them, Thus it has been written, the Christ to suffer and to arise from the dead on the third day."

Thus Paul and Luke preserve a tradition that links the Scriptures, the death of Jesus, and the resurrection on the third day. The Lucan passage is not a part of the empty tomb tradition which he shares with the other three Gospels. When Paul wrote 1 Corinthians around A.D. 53 it is not likely that he was alluding to Lk. 24:46, for in all probability none of the Gospels had taken its written shape that early.[8] By "according to the Scriptures," Luke clearly refers to the Old Testament (v. 44). Probably this also is what Paul intends by "according to the Scriptures" (1 Cor. 15:3f.). The same appearance tradition stands behind Lk. 24:46 and 1 Cor. 15:1–7, and it is independent of the empty tomb tradition.

The only other trace of the tradition linked with "according to the Scriptures" is in Mt. 12:40, "Just as Jonah was in the belly of the fish three days and three nights, thus shall the Son of man be in the heart of the earth three days and three nights." It is true that neither phrase appears here, "according to the Scriptures" or "on the third day"; but there is at least a near equivalence to these phrases in the reference to Jonah and the three days and nights in the fish or earth.

Probably the tradition behind Lk. 24:44–46 and 1 Cor. 15:1–7 looks back to what Bode calls "the general Old Testament motif, which is enforced by midrash and targum, that the third day is the day of divine salvation, deliverance and manifestation."[9]

There are then a number of lines of evidence with cumulative force distinguishing the empty tomb tradition in the Gospels and the appearance to men tradition behind Luke 24 and 1 Corinthians 15. The empty tomb tradition features women, "the first day of the week," the stone rolled away, heralds at or in the tomb (man or men or angel or angels), with no reference to "according to the Scriptures." The tradition shared by Luke and Paul stresses "according to the Scriptures," "the third day," and appearances of Jesus to men. The empty tomb tradition lived on because it was so early, so deeply embedded, and so widely known that it could not be ignored by the Gospels, even though Paul avoided it, building upon another and more convenient tradition.

SUMMARY

The empty tomb tradition with central place given to woman at the very foundations of Christian faith and witness is not to be dismissed as late, secondary, or legendary. It has a secure place within the four Gospels and has apparent traces elsewhere in the New Testament, including the writings of Paul. On critical grounds it is credible. That Jesus appeared first to women or a woman after his resurrection is a tradition to be taken in all seriousness. Why Jesus first appeared to Mary Magdalene and other women is a matter of judgment. This may be explained in terms of their initiative; they were there at the tomb! Not at all to be discounted is also the initiative of Jesus. The tradition has it that he took the initiative to appear to Peter, James, Paul, and others. Why may it not be that he chose to appear first to a woman or to a number of women? Whereas John the Baptist's disciples buried him (Mk. 6:29), Jesus' male disciples fled, leaving the burial to others. Women, however, had some role in the burial of Jesus. They affirmed him in his darkest hour. Did Jesus have his reasons for choosing thus to affirm them?

PART III

The Early Church and Woman

This part, which consists of four chapters, will attempt to trace the position of woman in the early church through the New Testament period. This will take us up to the "patristic" period but not into it. We leave to others the task of tracing the status of woman beyond the period covered by the New Testament, roughly the first century.

To be acknowledged is the debate over the distinction between the New Testament period and the patristic (Clement, Ignatius, Polycarp, *et al.*). However, we cannot go into the question of canon and are content here to follow what has been largely the consensus of the church since Athanasius in a festal letter in A.D. 367 listed as canonical precisely the twenty-seven writings known generally now as the New Testament.

Chapter 7

PAUL
AND WOMAN

Known as "Saint" Paul to millions for nearly two millennia, this man from Tarsus has also been denounced both from within and from without the church from his own lifetime until now. He has been described as "a man of conflict,"[1] and this could apply both to his inner tensions and to his deep involvement in the most intense struggles of the church (2 Cor. 11:28).

In the struggle today for woman's rightful place in the church and in the world, no one is more controversial than Paul. Is he on the side of woman's liberation, or is he a major barrier to such liberation? Was Paul a misogynist? Was he at least a male chauvinist? Many so understand Paul. His most ardent defenders find that they do, indeed, have to defend him against the charge of chauvinism. It is not proper to sweep aside problems as though they were not there, nor is it fair to Paul to overlook factors that at least make his course of action more understandable. Probably four areas of tension are discernible: tension within Paul himself; tension between vision and implementation; tension within the situation in the churches, with the threat of legalism on the one hand and libertinism on the other; and tension between personhood and roles in the structures of church and society.

Paul saw himself as a runner still straining toward "the mark" of his high calling, being pulled forward by "the upward calling of God in Christ Jesus" (Phil. 3:12–14). Paul was a follower of Jesus Christ; and like all followers, he fell short of the one whom he was following. Grounded in the theology that with God there is no partiality among persons (Rom. 3:22, 29), Paul yet belonged to the human race which never shakes off completely its heritage and

which suffers the universal fallibility of compromising its most
cherished ideals. Scripture shows Moses, David, Peter, and others
of God's servants to have fallen short of ideals to which they were
committed. So it is with us all. "Lord, I believe; help thou my
unbelief." (Mk. 9:24.) Paul is most fairly judged by the direction
in which he is moving, not by the point of his progress alone.

PAUL'S NONSUBORDINATING VISION (GAL. 3:28)

Galatians is Paul's "freedom manifesto." Its ideals come to
expression elsewhere in Paul's writings, but in Galatians the theme
is proclaimed most directly and forcefully. In this letter Paul rejects bondage to the Mosaic law in favor of the freedom for which
Christ freed us (Gal. 5:1). He scorns any compromise of this hard-
won freedom. The cultic rite of circumcision is not to be imposed
upon anyone who knows the liberty of living by faith out of the
goodness of God (3:11–14). Our common humanity and oneness
in Christ are not to be obscured by such secondary distinctions as
ethnic identity, legal status, or sexuality, for "there is not any Jew
nor Greek, not any slave nor free, not any male and female; for ye
all are one in Christ Jesus" (v. 28).

If this is taken at face value, the whole question is settled as to
the dignity, worth, freedom, and responsibility of woman. This text
does not deny the reality of sexual difference any more than it
denies the reality of distinctions that are ethnic (Jew and Greek)
or legal (slaves and free persons). There are such distinctions, but
"in Christ" these are transcended. Sexual difference is a fact and
an important one, with relevance in human existence; but so far as
our being "in Christ" is concerned, being male or female is not a
proper agenda item. The phrase "in Christ" implies one's personal
relationship with Jesus Christ; but it also implies one's being in the
family of Christ. To be in Christ is to be in the church, the body
of Christ (1 Cor. 12:12f.; Rom. 12:5). For those "in Christ" or in
the church, the body of Christ, it is irrelevant to ask if one is Jew
or Gentile, slave or free, male or female. Those are distinctions
traceable to physical birth or legal code. Being "in Christ" is of
another character and another origin. One is "in Christ" by the

personal faith which is openness to him and his people: "All ye are sons of God through the faith that is in Christ Jesus" (Gal. 3:26).

Even in his great freedom manifesto Paul does not escape the male orientation of language, describing as "sons" (v. 26) those among whom there is "not any male and female" (v. 28).

Galatians 3:28 brings into sharp focus three distinctions which are to be transcended in Christ: ethnic (Jew and Greek), legal (slave and free), and sexual (male and female). In this letter Paul was most concerned with the Jew-Gentile relationship, as was true of his ministry in general. This probably was the most controversial issue within the early church and the one for which Paul suffered most. It is the issue that finally separated synagogue and church, Judaism and Christianity. This is the struggle traced in the book of Acts and reflected throughout Paul's letters.[2] In Luke-Acts is traced the movement of Christianity from the piety of Judaism (Lk. 1–2) to its status as a world movement, outside the structures of Judaism. Acts shows Paul to have been in the thick of this struggle for freedom from ethnic or legal restrictions upon the people of Christ. His letters verify this as a focal point in Paul's preaching and struggles. This is a major concern in Galatians. The issue between Jew and Gentile was the compelling one behind Paul's momentous decision at Corinth (Acts 20:1–6) to turn back from plans to undertake a mission to Spain by way of Rome in favor of a hazardous mission to Jerusalem, bearing a collection of money by which he hoped to unite the Gentile givers and the Jewish receivers (cf. 1 Cor. 16:1–4; 2 Cor. 8–9; Rom. 15:14–33; Acts 20–28).[3]

There is no apparent reason why Paul should not have applied the same logic and rebuke to any discrimination on the basis of difference in legal status (slave or free) or on the basis of sexual difference (male or female). His strongest protest against denying full brotherhood to a Christian slave appears in the letter to Philemon. In that letter, Paul pleaded for Onesimus, a runaway slave whom he was returning to his owner. Paul acknowledged the legal claims which the master had upon his slave; but he appealed to a higher claim, that of kinship within the family of Christ. He affirmed Onesimus as his "child" (Philemon 10) whom he had "begotten"; but he also affirmed him as his "brother beloved" (v. 16). Paul so identified with Onesimus that whatever happened to Onesimus happened to himself; in receiving Onesimus, Paul himself would be received (v. 17). Paul pleaded with the owner, commonly thought to be Philemon but possibly Archippus,[4] to receive Onesimus as a brother and not as a slave. Beyond any doubt, Paul operated here on the principle that "in Christ" there is "not any slave nor free." There is no evidence that Paul normally crusaded for the rights of slaves as he did for the full dignity and freedom of Gentiles, but at least in Philemon he measured up to that standard.

The third focus of Paul's "no Jew nor Greek; not any slave nor free; not any male and female" did not fare so well in practice as the first two foci. Measured by his own background and contemporary perspectives and practices, Paul made amazing progress even in implementation; but measured by his own vision in Gal. 3:28, much remained to be done in closing the gap between ideal and practice. It is as unjust to Paul to stress only the gap and forget the progress as it is untrue to recognize in Paul no lag between the "mark" of his "upward calling" and the point of his compliance or progress. With all fairness to Paul, it remains that he did not carry through as fully with respect to nondiscrimination between male and female as he did with respect to Jew and Gentile or even slave and free.

One significant passage in Romans would logically have far-reaching implications supportive of Paul's vision in Galatians, even though it makes no reference to male and female.

In Rom. 12:3–8 the focal point is that of "charismatic gifts" within the church as the body of Christ (v. 6). Just as in a physical body there are many members with their different functions, "thus the many of us are one body in Christ, individually members of one another" (v. 5). At this point Paul turns to charismatic gifts, with a play upon the Greek word for "grace" *(charismata kata charin)*. *Charis* is the Greek word for grace, and *charismata* are simply gifts of God's grace. Any gift of grace is "charismatic," hence there are no noncharismatic children of God. Eternal life itself is *charisma* (6:23). In 12:6–8 *charismata* include prophecy (preaching), ministry, teaching, comforting or exhortation, contributing money, presiding or administration, and acts of mercy. The list is not exhaustive, simply illustrative.

Paul's point is that *charismata* are indeed gifts of grace. As gifts they are not to be occasions for personal pride, jealousy, or competitiveness. Moreover, they are responsibilities, not favors. These gifts are to be exercised. The possession of a gift carries with it the obligation to employ it. If one has the charismatic gift of preaching, that one is to preach; if the charismatic gift of teaching, that one is to teach; etc. The basic criterion, then, for any form of ministry is to have the God-given gift for it! The question is, Can a "preacher" preach? Can a "teacher" teach? Can an "administrator" administrate? These charismatic gifts are seen here not as being special privileges but as carrying special obligations.

Suppose this principle were applied within the church? Is it relevant or proper to raise the question of sexual identity with respect to ministry? Suppose a woman has the gift of preaching? the gift of teaching? the gift of administering? Although Rom. 12:3–8 says nothing explicitly about women in ministry, its principle and logic are inescapable: the possession of a gift from God's grace carries with it the obligation that it be exercised within the church and in the service of the church and that the church allow the gifted person to exercise the gift. Romans 12:3–8 thus is as significant as is the explicit affirmation of Gal. 3:28: "There is not any Jew nor Greek, not any slave nor free, not any male and female; for ye all are one in Christ Jesus."

IMPLEMENTING THE VISION

Problems are much easier solved at the conference table or on the drawing boards than in the life situations in which they exist. War, poverty, disease, discrimination, injustice to minorities, and countless other problems have been "overcome" in great declarations. After all, do we not have it in black and white that "all men are created equal" and that all have the right to life, liberty, and the pursuit of happiness? A great church conference in Jerusalem, under the leading of such giants as Paul, Peter, James, and Barnabas, put it into writing that cultic practices like circumcision, a priority item for some zealous persons, were not to be imposed upon Gentiles (Acts 15); but the struggle went on in the church then, and in various shapes the same struggle has continued until this day, as some group is always imposing its cultic patterns on some other. So it was with Paul's vision as expressed in Gal. 3:28 and supported in Rom. 12:3–8. Working it out in life situations is another matter.

First Thessalonians

This possibly is Paul's earliest letter, although a case can be made for the priority of Galatians. Few would dispute the view that both 1 Thessalonians and Galatians are early, whichever may be the earlier.

In 1 Thessalonians, Paul addresses his readers as "brothers" and refers to Christians generally in like manner, employing the term no less than eighteen times. He never includes "sisters" among his addressees. He knows his readers as "sons of light" and as "sons of the day" (1 Thess. 5:5), not as "daughters." To a point this can be accounted for as no more than the utilization of a language and literary form of address which is itself already male-oriented and not in particular chargeable to Paul. We have seen that the Gospels represent Jesus as employing terms of address in the masculine gender. Further, in the pejorative references to "those who sleep" (v. 7) and "the idlers" (v. 14; also 2 Thess. 3:2, 6), the terms are masculine in gender. So far, too much is not to be read into semantics, except as it reflects on the male domination behind the formation of language itself.

The serious evidence in 1 Thessalonians as it bears on Paul's perspective and practice with respect to woman appears chiefly in 4:1–8. Paul's admonitions are to men, and in this passage the restricted perspective is more than a matter of semantics:

> For this is the will of God, your holiness, that ye abstain from fornication, that each one of you know how to obtain [ktasthai can mean "to buy" or "to possess"] his own vessel [skeuos seems here to refer to wife]

in holiness and honor, not in the passion of lust like pagans who do not
know God; that no one transgress or overreach his brother in this
matter. (1 Thess. 4:3–6)

The concern here is for holiness, presumably in relationship with
acquiring or possessing a wife. The term *skeuos* literally employed
designates some kind of vessel (cf. Mk. 3:27; 11:16; Lk. 8:16). It
is used in the New Testament metaphorically for persons, with no
necessary implication of dishonor or disparagement. Paul is a
"chosen vessel" to bear God's name to the whole world (Acts
9:15). In 1 Thess. 4:4 "vessel" could refer to one's own self, but this
is not likely. Probably the reference is to a wife, as in 1 Peter 3:7,
where designating the wife "the weaker vessel" is explicit.

Not only the language, but the perspective itself is male, with
no word addressed to woman. Not only is the wife referred to as
a vessel, the term admittedly not of itself denigrating, but the
warning is against transgressing upon the rights of another man,
a "brother's" rights as they relate to a woman (1 Thess. 4:6). The
passage intends moral and ethical progress beyond that practiced
by the "pagan"; but it does not consider in any discernible way the
personhood, dignity, and rights of woman herself. The only approach in the letter to any expressed feeling for woman is in Paul's
likening himself to a "nurse" caring for "her" children (2:7).

First Corinthians

In no letter under Paul's name are his feelings more visible than
in 1 Corinthians, written around A.D. 53, probably earlier than his
other extant letters, except for the Thessalonian letters and Galatians. In assessing Paul's thought and feeling as reflected in this
letter, we must keep in mind two conditioning factors: (1) much
that is in the letter is in reply to a letter to Paul from the Corinthians (1 Cor. 7:1), which means that they set much of the agenda,
the issues not necessarily being priority ones for Paul, and (2) the
letter is concerned for the most part with a specific situation, about
as much pagan as Christian. Paul here did not have the luxury of

setting forth an ideal; he was hard pressed to bring some order out of near chaos.

Probably what most accounts for Paul's seeming change of direction as he moves from the concerns of Galatians to those of 1 Corinthians is the rise of a new problem, that of the throwing off of all restraints by some at Corinth who saw themselves as "spiritual" (1 Cor. 3:1–3). These "pneumatics" seized upon Paul's doctrine of freedom, but they applied it in ways which Paul disapproved. Apparently seeing themselves as above sin, they could even accept incest without shame (5:1f.). They apparently boasted that for themselves all things were "lawful" (6:12). They boasted of having "knowledge" *(gnōsis),* but it only "puffed up" instead of building up (8:1). They insisted upon personal freedom and rights even to the hurt of weaker brethren (chs. 8–10). In their exercise of what they considered their personal rights and freedom, they caused confusion and disorder in their public services (chs. 11–14).

Apparently Paul saw at Corinth a misapplication of freedom and sought to curb it. It may have been that women and slaves, in particular, were making the most of their freedom "in Christ," extending it into all the structures of church and society in a way which Paul thought to threaten those structures. Against this, he called for contentment with the life in which one was called: "Let each remain in the calling in which he was called" (1 Cor. 7:20). Paul played down the matter of one's status (vs. 19, 22), and he repeated the injunction to remain in the calling in which one was called (vs. 20, 24). This is the context in which his restrictions upon woman are given. Apparently fearing the abuse of freedom, he prescribed certain restraints, the heaviest falling upon women.

Although 1 Corinthians contains some of the passages that seem to be extremely prejudiced against woman, there are also some that are positive. The letter begins with a recognition of "those of Chloe" (1 Cor. 1:11), presumably family or employees of a woman named Chloe. In the closing part of the letter Paul conveys greetings from "Aquila and Prisca, with the church in their house" (16:19). At least, Prisca shares equally with her husband in recognition. In 5:1 it is the man who is censured for an incestuous relationship with his father's wife. In some situations such a woman would have been stoned to death. The warnings in 5:9ff. and 6:9–11 are against immoral men, with no allusion to immoral women. In 6:15–20 it is bodily union with a prostitute which is condemned, but there is some ambiguity in the full implication of the passage. It is addressed to men, not women, as the likely offenders. That men require such stern warning may imply their poorer record; but on the other hand, the ideal of the body as the temple of the Holy Spirit (v. 19) is set forth in male perspective.

Conjugal Rights (1 Cor. 7:1–7). At 7:1 Paul picks up a letter from the Corinthians and responds to questions that they have raised. The first concerns the question as to whether or not a Christian should marry, with special attention to conjugal rights within marriage. It is a solid plus for perspective on woman that Paul insists upon a wife's conjugal claims upon her husband as exactly those of husband's claims upon wife. Also significant is the fact that Paul addresses the wife as directly as the husband, which is contrary to the usual pattern of addressing men and instructing women indirectly. Throughout this passage, duties between husband and wife are mutual and reciprocal; and there is no subordinating of one to the other.

Despite these positives, the passage begins with a double negative, an apparently dim view of marriage and the question approached from male perspective: "It is not good *(kalon)* for a man to touch a woman" (1 Cor. 7:1). The Greek *kalon* may have a moral reference, but it does not normally carry this force, *agathos* being the more usual word for moral goodness. *Kalon* normally implies what is "fitting." Paul seems not to imply that there is anything morally wrong in marriage, but he clearly favors the single life. Apparently it was upon vocational grounds and in view of his eschatological expectation of an early return of Jesus that Paul so strongly favored refraining from marriage. He does not share the Gnostic view that marriage or sex is evil; but even so, this is a concession to marriage, not the affirmation of marriage found elsewhere.

The phrase "to touch a woman" presumably alludes to sexual

relationship. Nothing is said here about it being well for a woman not "to touch a man." The real problem arises in a concession to marriage as an escape from the threat of "fornication" (1 Cor. 7:2). To begin with, marriage itself has never been a fail-safe cure to fornication. If this is the only basis upon which the Corinthians can hear, that is one thing; if this is the basis for marriage itself, that is something else. At least, Paul recognizes that women have sexual needs as well as men (v. 2).

The "likewise" in v. 3 is highly significant. Here is the recognition that a wife has the same conjugal claim upon a husband as does the husband upon wife. This was by no means a widely recognized principle. Each *owes* sexual fulfillment to the other spouse. Each spouse has a certain "authority" over the other's body (v. 4). To deny conjugal fulfillment on either's part is to "defraud" the other (v. 5). Abstention between husband and wife is to be by "agreement" and only for a "season," with a view to its resumption (v. 5b).

The question of abortion was not raised between Paul and the Corinthians or elsewhere in his writings, but this passage does imply something for this current debate. Paul is explicit that a wife does not have authority independent of her husband over her own body, just as the husband does not have authority independent of the wife over his body. Contextually, the issue is that of sexual fulfillment. The principle would seem to extend to other dimensions of the relationship. It would seem that in a pregnancy resulting from mutual consent, both parties have a claim upon what together they have produced.

Paul closed this passage with the observation that he was offering a "concession" and not a "command" (1 Cor. 7:6). Whether this relates to the whole paragraph or only its last point is unclear. Presumably he meant marriage itself as the concession. Interestingly, he terms it "a *charisma* from God," whether one's *charisma* be for marriage or for the single life.

The Unmarried and Widows (1 Cor. 7:8–9, 39–40). Precisely what Paul means by "unmarried" is difficult to pin down. It seems that he can use the term for anyone, man or woman, who has lost a spouse by death or divorce and who has not remarried.

With less assurance than is to be desired, we conclude that in 1 Corinthians 7, Paul uses "unmarried" for man or woman who has lost a spouse, whether by separation or death; and by "virgin" he can refer to the never-married, man or woman; although except for v. 25 the feminine article restricts the usage to women.

What is most significant for our purpose is the extent to which Paul in 1 Corinthians 7 treats men and women with equity. We have seen this already with respect to conjugal rights (1 Cor. 7:3). He seemingly extends this to the options of remaining single, getting married, and separation or divorce.

In 1 Cor. 7:8 "the unmarried [m.] and widows" clearly refers to men and women once with but now without a spouse, whether by separation/divorce or death of the spouse. In any case, in vs. 8–9 he prefers that the unmarried (the widowed or separated) remain thus; but he acknowledges that the demands of the unmarried life may be too great for most. He concedes that in their case it is "better to marry than to burn," presumably "to burn" in lust. As in v. 2, the motive suggested for marriage, avoidance of fornication or lust, leaves much to be desired and offers no fail-safe alternative.

In 1 Cor. 7:39–40, Paul resumes the subject of vs. 8–9, offering his "judgment" to widows, conceding a widow's right to remarry in the event of her husband's death, provided it be "in the Lord," i.e., that she marry another Christian; but in his "judgment" she will be happier should she remain unmarried. Paul thinks that he also has in this judgment "the spirit of God" (v. 40). The widows, of course, have not been heard from here. Important to our investigation is Paul's respect for a woman's right to exercise her own option as to whether to remarry or remain unmarried.

The Married and Divorce (1 Cor. 7:10–16). This unit divides into two parts, with a command from "the Lord" (vs. 10–11) and Paul's own advice as to mixed marriages, where a Christian is married to an unbeliever (vs. 12–16).

Paul begins to give a charge to "those having married," then he corrects himself: "not I but the Lord." Although "those having married" is masculine, the charge is directed to woman: "a wife not to be separated from her husband." Should she be separated, she is to remain "unmarried" or be reconciled to her husband. Possibly the language simply is realistic about the legal status of husband and wife with respect to divorce. At least in the Jewish world, only the husband could actually divorce, the wife only sue to be divorced. Paul is careful to speak here of the wife as being separated but the husband as putting aside his wife. On the other hand, in 1 Cor. 7:13 the wife is told not to divorce her unbelieving husband if he is content to live with her. In the final analysis this whole passage does seem to accord the wife rights and responsibilities parallelling those of the husband.

In 1 Cor. 7:12–16, Paul ventures his own judgment as to a mixed marriage of believer and unbeliever. The admonitions are addressed understandably to the believers and not to the unbelievers. They are encouraged to preserve a marriage to the unbeliever, if the unbelieving spouse is content to continue the marriage. The problem under consideration may be that arising where the marriage had taken place before either was a believer. Some at Corinth seem to have feared that it was a sin to continue such a marriage and that children born to such a union would be "unclean." Paul assures them that for the believer such a mixed marriage is holy, having been sanctified by the believer. The failure of one spouse does not imply guilt for the other nor rob the marriage of the holiness it holds for the believer. The same holds for children born to that union. They are "sanctified" by the believing parent.

Paul closes the discussion of this issue of a mixed marriage by warning the believer, wife or husband, that it may not be possible to save the mixed marriage. Considering pagan practices of the day, infanticide included, it is understandable that a believer's marriage to a pagan could become unworkable. If the unbelieving spouse "separates himself," then "let him separate." Treating husband and wife equitably, Paul concludes: "The brother or the sister is not enslaved in such cases" (1 Cor. 7:15a).

Concerning Virgins (1 Cor. 7:25–35). Paul's phrase, "concerning virgins," is uncertain as to precise reference; and it is strongly debated today. It is by no means certain that "virgins" here refers to women alone. The term is used in Rev. 14:4 for men, and it is used a number of times outside the New Testament for males.[5] Matthew Black argues forcefully from context, from early Christian practice, and from patristic interpretation of this passage that it probably intends to include males as well as females among "the virgins" addressed.[6] Contextual factors incline us to believe that Paul here includes men as well as women in the "virgins" addressed.

Paul admonishes his readers to make no new move as to their marital status. If married, seek no release from marriage. If unmarried, do not seek marriage. This actually is addressed to man: "Have you been bound to a wife; do not seek release. Have you been released from a wife; do not seek a wife" (1 Cor. 7:27). Paul lays down no rule, only admonition. He clearly stays aloof from ascetic-based celibacy. In this passage, as elsewhere, he urges the unmarried status in view of his expectation of the End, believing that "the season is wound up" (v. 29), i.e., that the time will soon come when ordinary pursuits of life will no longer be in effect (vs. 29–31; cf. Mk. 12:25). The abstention from marriage which he recommends, then, is eschatological and vocational, not ascetic.

Although men and women fare equally under these admonitions, there remains a male orientation, at least in the form of address. Apparently there is here a strong thrust toward nondiscrimination between men and women, but old patterns of thought and speech persist even when made obsolete by new perspective.

To Give in Marriage or Not (1 Cor. 7:36–38). This is a much-debated passage, scholars being divided as to whether "the virgin" whose marriage is under consideration is a daughter whose father may or may not give her in marriage or the betrothed of a man who may or may not consummate the marriage with her. Verse 38 seems decisive, where the idea is that of giving in marriage, a father's prerogative, rather than marrying, a groom's function. The phrase is *ho gamizōn,* "the one giving in marriage," rather than *ho gamōn,* "the one marrying." If the reference is to an engaged couple, Paul's advice is that the man not consummate the marriage with his betrothed, although he allows either choice. Such "marriages" were practiced later in the piety of some Christians, but it is not likely that this is what Paul is advising at Corinth. Probably it is advice to the father of a virgin of marriageable age. If there are no prior commitments requiring his giving his daughter in marriage and she is equal to the decision, Paul advises that the father not give her in marriage. If circumstances favor the giving of her in marriage, Paul approves that. He concludes that the father giving his virgin daughter in marriage does well, but the one who does not does better.

Whichever is the intention of this passage, some male orientation is reflected. Paul addresses the man, whether a father or a groom-to-be. The initiative rests with the man. If a father, we have here the ancient custom by which a father gives his daughter to the groom. Presumably, this was the social practice at Corinth.

Covering a Woman's Head (1 Cor. 11:2–16). In all Paul's writings, this passage is one of the least favorable to woman; and it is extremely difficult to reconcile with much of Paul's own writings, to go no farther.[7] The passage subordinates wife to husband (or woman to man; *gynē* means "woman" or "wife" and *anēr* means "man" or "husband"), requires that a woman be veiled when she prays or prophesies, and forbids a man the wearing of a head covering when he prays or prophesies or long hair at any time. Paul insists that a woman wear a head covering when she prays or prophesies, presumably in public worship. As a *reductio ad absurdum,* Paul argues that if a woman is to be unveiled she may as well have her hair shorn or her head shaved (v. 6). Apparently, he assumes that no one would defend a Christian woman's shearing her hair or shaving her head. However, the demand is for the veil or head covering; and this is tied to a "hierarchy" in which God is the head of Christ, Christ the head of man, and man the head of woman (v. 3).

Paul's basic appeal seems to be to creation, and he seemingly draws something from each of the two creation narratives in Genesis 1–2. From the rib account in Genesis 2 he draws the teaching of the subordination of woman to man. Man's being "the glory of

God" (1 Cor. 11:7) may be based upon the story in Genesis 1; but in that story male and female are created together, and both are created in the image of God (Gen. 1:26–27). Neither creation story in Genesis speaks of woman as "the glory of man." Of course, the story in Genesis 2 has it that woman was created for man, made from a rib from man's side. We have seen above that Jesus built upon the nonsubordinating story in Genesis 1; Paul builds primarily upon the subordinating story in Genesis 2, with seemingly some adaptation from the story in Genesis 1. Paul is not comfortable with this subordination of woman to man, somewhat modifying it in 1 Cor. 11:11–12.

Jesus internalized good and evil, giving priority to values that were personal, moral, and ethical. For the most part, Paul follows in this pattern (cf. Gal. 1:6–9; 2:3, 11–14; 3:1–6; 4:9–11; 6:12–16; Rom. 2:28–29; 14:13–14; Eph. 2:11; Col. 2:8, 16–23; Phil. 3:2–11; *et passim*). It is difficult to see how the requirement of a veil differs from the cultic and legal "works" (like circumcision) which elsewhere Paul found to be empty or actually opposed to the faith in which one lives out of the goodness of God (Gal. 3:11; Rom. 1:17).

1 Corinthians 11:10 is quite enigmatic, where the importance of a woman's being veiled is "because of the angels." The best clue to the intention here comes from Jewish interpretation of Gen. 6:4. It was understood that angels had intercourse with women and that from them giants were born (cf. Enoch 6–11; 15:3). Presumably, the warning in 1 Cor. 11:10 is that angels would be tempted by a woman who did not wear the veil that signaled her husband's authority over her.[8]

Apparently not confident that the Corinthians would be convinced by his appeal to creation or the warning about the angels, Paul next appealed to the Corinthians' own judgment: "Judge this among yourselves; Is it fitting for a woman to pray to God unveiled?" (1 Cor. 11:13). To this appeal, he adds that of nature: "Does not nature itself teach you that if a man wears his hair long it is a dishonor to him?" (v. 14). It is not apparent how nature teaches this. Finally Paul turned from all these arguments, seeking to silence any "contentious" person with the reminder that the churches had no "such custom," presumably no such custom as a man praying with head covered or a woman praying with it uncovered.

The problems here are many. What is Paul's authority or source for the hierarchy: God, Christ, man, woman? How does he utilize the two creation stories in Genesis? What importance is there to a head covering in worship? Are veils binding upon women today? What about the subordination of woman (or wife) to man (or husband)? What about the angels? What about the teaching of nature? Is "custom" (1 Cor. 11:16) binding upon Christian conscience? With all these problems there are some implications of positive significance. Paul does discuss the role of women in "praying and prophesying." This can hardly be other than in public worship. "Prophecy" is some form of inspired preaching. Apparently Paul did recognize the right of women to participate thus in public worship. Even the subordination implied for woman is something with which he really is not comfortable, as evidenced by his balancing statement: "Moreover, neither is woman apart from man nor man apart from woman in the Lord; for just as woman is out of man, thus also man is through woman, and all things are from God" (vs. 11–12). Whatever the problem of correlating perspectives of Galatians and 1 Corinthians, the letters are probably best understood as struggles on two different fronts, Galatians concerned for freedom and 1 Corinthians for order.

Silence for Women in Church (1 Cor. 14:34–35). In a context concerned with orderliness in church worship appears this passage enjoining women to silence in church:

> Let women be silent in church, for it is not permitted for them to speak; but let them be subordinate, just as the law says. If they wish to learn anything, let them inquire at home from their husbands, for it is a shame for a woman to speak in church. (1 Cor. 14:34–35)

One attempt at easing this passage is to connect it with "speaking in tongues." True, it appears in a long section, chs. 12–14, concerned primarily with the problem of "tongues"; but this injunction is against speaking in church as such, with special attention to teaching. As it stands, this passage imposes total silence upon women in church.

There are two major problems of correlation with Paul's writing elsewhere. It is not apparent how this exclusion of woman can be reconciled with the gospel proclaimed in Gal. 3:28, "There is . . . not any male and female; for ye all are one in Christ Jesus." Closer at hand, it is not apparent how the command to silence can be workable in relationship with the "praying and prophesying" as recognized in 1 Cor. 11:5, where a woman is not forbidden to pray or prophesy, only required to wear a veil in so doing. The clash between these two injunctions is unrelieved if both passages stand. Adding to the difficulty is the surprising appeal in 1 Cor. 14:34b, "just as the law says." Presumably "the law" is the Mosaic law, but there is no reading in the Old Testament to which this clearly refers. Genesis 3:16 affirms the husband's rule over his wife, but there is no requirement of silence there. Probably synagogue patterns are reflected, where active participants were male only. Yet more important than the elusiveness of the law intended is the very fact that in Paul's name there should be the imposition of the law upon the churches. In Galatians and elsewhere, Paul took a strong and impassioned stand against imposing the law, in particular in its ritual expressions, upon the church. The perspective of Galatians appears to be incompatible and irreconcilable with the silencing of women by an appeal to "the law."

It is altogether possible that 1 Cor. 14:34–35 is a gloss by a scribal hand, introduced into the letter after it left Paul's hands. No known manuscript omits these verses, but a number of manuscripts have these verses after 14:40. These are witnesses to an early text type known as Western (including the Greek mss. D G 88*; the Old Latin mss. ar, d, e, f, g; and the church fathers Ambrosiaster and Sedulius Scotus). The manuscripts having vs. 34–35 after v. 40 are not as impressive as those having the verses after v. 33, but they are not insignificant. It is altogether possible that this passage was entered as a scribal gloss in the margin of an early manuscript and from there was moved into the text at two different places by subsequent scribes. This could have happened so early that no manuscript survives without the gloss, but its early "floating" nature is reflected in its appearing at two different places in extant manuscripts, after v. 33 in most manuscripts but after v. 40 in some early witnesses.

There is nothing which a priori rules out vs. 34–35 as a non-Pauline gloss. There are thousands of variants in Biblical manuscripts, so there are textual disturbances. Most of these are quite early. The internal evidence is the strongest possible for questioning this passage as coming from Paul. It poses a number of insuperable problems in the face of Pauline position in this very letter, to say nothing of its clash with the basic stance of Galatians. At the very least, Paul deserves the benefit of the doubt.

Summary. What, then, is to be concluded as to Paul's perspective on woman as reflected in 1 Corinthians? It is mixed. There are some strong affirmations of woman, and there are some subordinating passages, even omitting 1 Cor. 14:34–35. His openness toward woman is far beyond that of his probable upbringing. The fact that he can worship in public service with women, recognizing their right to pray and prophesy; his recognition of woman's equality in conjugal and other rights; and his willingness to address women directly as responsible persons in the church are all factors on the positive side of one moving in the direction of the implementation of a revolutionary vision, that "in Christ" there is "no male and female."

Romans

Possibly the most influential of all Paul's letters, that to the Romans, has little to say directly on the subject of woman. (See above for the significance of Rom. 12:6–8.) In this letter, Paul was concentrating on the overriding problem of the relationship of "Jew and Greek" under God. That God does not show partiality between male and female is as inescapable from the thesis of Romans as that he does not show partiality between Jew and Gentile. Paul did not extend the application accordingly in Romans, but it is there for extension.

An Analogy from Marriage (Rom. 7:1–6). Marriage forms one analogy employed by Paul to illustrate the break between the old life in sin and the new life in Christ. The passage may be so read as to imply some subordination of woman, for a wife is described as subordinate to her husband. The Greek word for "married woman" is literally "woman under man *(hypandros)."* The passage speaks of the wife as bound to the husband as long as he lives, released when he dies. Probably no intended slight is to be inferred; but it probably follows that this is another in the endless chain of examples of language itself as carrying a deeply embedded male bias.

Romans 16. The chapter begins significantly: "I commend to you Phoebe our sister, being a deacon *(diakonon)* of the church in Cenchreae" (v. 1). There is no term "deaconess" (as in RSV) here or elsewhere in the New Testament. Phoebe was a "deacon." Of course, the term "deacon" was employed for anyone engaged in any form of ministry *(diakonia).* Among those called "deacon" in the New Testament are included anyone who serves (Mt. 20:26), the servants who drew the water at the Cana wedding (Jn. 2:5), political rulers (Rom. 13:4), Christ (Rom. 15:8), Apollos and Paul (1 Cor. 3:5), and Timothy (1 Thess. 3:2). The term gradually acquired a technical usage for a specific church office (1 Tim. 3:8, 12; 4:6). Just what is its force when applied to Phoebe is uncertain. Possibly she was a "deacon" in the official sense of that term. Paul affirms her as "a helper" of many, including himself (Rom. 16:2). This passage cannot be used as a proof text clinching the argument for women "deacons," but it is solidly on the side of acknowledging the partnership of women in the work of the church.

A second woman of prominence in Romans 16 is Prisca. Significantly, she and her husband are listed as "Prisca and Aquila" (cf. reverse in Acts 18:2; but Priscilla first in Acts 18:18, 26; Aquila first in 1 Cor. 16:19; Prisca first in 2 Tim. 4:19). Both are Paul's "fellow workers in Christ" (Rom. 16:3). Both "risked their necks" for Paul, and for them Paul and all the Gentile churches give thanks (v. 4). A church meets in "their" house (v. 5).

Other women, otherwise unknown to us, are recognized in this chapter. A certain "Mary" has worked hard among the readers. The sisters Tryphaena and Tryphosa have "labored in the Lord," and "the beloved Persis" had "worked hard in the Lord" (v. 12). Paul knows the mother of Rufus as his own (v. 13). He sends greetings to "Julia" and to the sister of Nereus. There is no chauvinism here. Men and women are honored alike as servants of Christ. But alas, even in this letter so positive toward woman, the male orientation of language has its say: "I beg you, brethren . . ." (v. 17).

Philippians

Almost buried in the fourth and final chapter of Philippians is Paul's appeal to Euodia and Syntyche "to be of the same mind in the Lord" (Phil. 4:2). With this is an appeal to some anonymous "true yokefellow" to help these women, presumably to work through their differences. Paul recalls the fact that these women once worked together with himself as well as with Clement and his other co-workers (v. 3). These women have had an important role in the life and work of the church; and what now seems at stake is not only their personal welfare but the health of the church itself.

When the letter as a whole is considered, the significance of the appeal to and for Euodia and Syntyche is enhanced.[9] Although known ever since John A. Bengel (d. 1752) as the "joy letter" ("the sum of the epistle is 'I rejoice; rejoice ye' "), there is far more to it than that. Throughout the letter is an undercurrent of apprehension for the unity of the church. Chiefly Paul has appealed to "the mind" which was in Christ Jesus, pleading that this be "the mind" which governs their fellowship (Phil. 2:1–11). It probably is not by chance that his appeal to Euodia and Syntyche is that they be of the same "mind" in the Lord, the word being cognate to that used of the "mind" of Christ.

Whatever be "the hidden agenda" behind the Philippian letter, it is clear that Paul approaches the matter of the two women with respect, deep concern, and consummate tactfulness. There is no hint that they be "silenced," subordinated, rebuked, or treated in any way except with full respect for their personhood. One further nuance may be found in Paul's appeal to his true yokefellow. The word for "help" (Phil. 4:3) is literally "take hold together with these women." The matter was not to be taken out of their hands. Ultimately they had to bear the responsibility for working through their problem, as the direct appeal to each implies. They needed to have someone "take hold together with them" but not take over for them. Whatever chauvinism may linger in Paul, he was no chauvinist who made this appeal to Euodia, Syntyche, and the true yokefellow.

ORDINATION AND MINISTRY

For much of the church the question of ordination to ministry for women is settled by the restriction "the husband of one wife" found in 1 Tim. 3:12 and Titus 1:6. To many this Pauline proof text seems sufficient to exclude all women, for traditionally a woman does not have a wife.

But the matter is not so simple. If the simplistic approach is to be followed, there are many proof texts that may be cited. Galatians 3:28 taken alone would settle the matter in another direction, ruling out sexual distinction as relevant. Further, if ordination is to be restricted to "the husband of one wife," Paul himself would seem to be excluded, for he seems to imply that he was without spouse when he wrote 1 Cor. 7:7; and he clearly preferred that all single persons remain single (vs. 25–38). Excluded by this test also would be John the Baptist, Jesus, and all unmarried persons.

The intention of the restriction "husband of one wife" is unclear in 1 Tim. 3:12 and Titus 1:6. The passage may be directed against celibacy, divorce, polygamy, or remarriage under any circumstances. Neither the grammar nor the context removes the ambiguity. Among some in the early church there was special honor accorded those who remained unmarried after the death of a spouse. A widow was not to be "enrolled" as such unless she was past sixty and "wife of one husband" (1 Tim. 5:9). Remarriage following the death of a spouse was permitted, but remaining unmarried seems to have been viewed with higher esteem. This may be the intention behind the criterion, "husband of one wife."

In truth, we do not know to what it was addressed. Dogmatic application so as to exclude women from ordination is to imply an understanding of the expression which actually is beyond the competence of any interpreter today.

The whole question of ordination is unclear in the New Testament. The English noun "ordination" does not appear in the KJV, and the verb "to ordain" translates no less than a dozen different Greek words. There is no one Greek word in the New Testament which dominates as the word for "ordination." There is not one uniform intention in the many appearances of the English word "ordain" in the New Testament. Greek words that may be rendered "ordain" include the following: *diatassō*, "to arrange" (1 Cor. 7:17; 9:14; Gal. 3:19); *kataskeuazō*, "to prepare" (Heb. 9:6); *krinō*, "to decide" (Acts 16:4); *horizō*, "to mark off" (Acts 10:42; 17:31); *proorizō*, "to mark out before" (1 Cor. 2:7); *tassō*, "to set in order" (Acts 13:48; Rom. 13:1); *kathistēmi*, "to place or set" (Titus 1:5; Heb. 5:1; 8:3); *poieō*, "to appoint" (Mk. 3:14); *tithēmi*, "to place" (Jn. 15:16; 1 Tim. 2:7); *cheirotoneō*, "to elect by stretching out the hand" (Acts 14:23); *ginomai*, "to become" (Acts 1:22). All of these Greek words appear in English translations current today as "ordination"! This means that in the Greek New Testament there is no such firm idea of "ordination" as is implied by the English word. The idea is far more fluid in the Greek Testament than in English usage. In the New Testament anything "ordered" is a form of ordination.

Imposition of hands is a familiar practice in the New Testament, but its origin and purpose are unclear. Were "ordination" and "laying on of hands" bound to one another? Were hands placed upon a person for a lifelong ministry or for a particular ministry of a restricted nature? Did the whole church place hands upon certain ones, or was this done by a "presbytery"? There are no clear answers to these questions. In Acts 6:6 hands are laid upon seven men selected to administer a relief fund. "They" can relate to the apostles or to the congregation as having laid hands upon the seven. In Acts 13:3 hands are laid upon Paul and Barnabas as they are about to embark on a missionary journey. Greek syntax leaves ambiguous who laid hands upon these two, either three of the five "prophets and teachers" listed in v. 1 or, as is probable, the whole church in Antioch. Why would three of the prophets and teachers lay hands upon two of their own number? Was this laying on of hands an "ordination"? Were Paul and Barnabas thus being ordained? If an ordination, was it a first ordination or an additional one? They already were among the prophets and teachers, and for some years they had been engaged in ministry. The term "ordination" is not employed here, but these two were being commissioned to a ministry. Apparently the whole church laid hands upon them in recognition of God's appointment of them to a particular mission. In Acts 8:16f. hands are laid upon certain Samaritans, but there is nothing in the context about ordination or ministry.

The pastoral epistles may reflect a more formalized practice of ordination than elsewhere in the New Testament. Timothy is reminded of his having had hands laid upon him by a presbytery (1 Tim. 4:14). He is told not to lay hands quickly upon any man (5:22). It is not clear whether this latter relates to ordination or restoration of a wayward member. In 2 Tim. 1:6, Paul refers to his own hands as having been laid upon Timothy, with no mention of other hands. The plain truth is that the whole matter of laying on of hands and ordination is unclear in the New Testament. Possibly what is reflected is a fluid state, moving from maximum freedom and variety toward more formalized practice. Where did it begin, and where does it properly end, and by what authority do we find our direction? Jesus appointed twelve apostles, a unique group; and otherwise we see little if any trace of his having organized anything. He created a movement; structures gradually emerged to meet practical needs.

Another gray area is that between "ministry" and "deacons" in the New Testament. In English and in common practice of the church there is generally a clear distinction between "ministers" and "deacons," especially where ordination obtains. This implies a clearer and more formal pattern than is traceable in the Greek New Testament. In fact, the distinction breaks down for the most part in the Greek New Testament. The Greek word most often rendered "ministry" is *diakonia,* simply a cognate of *diakonos,* which may be rendered "minister" or "deacon." The Greek word *diakonos* appears as a technical term in 1 Tim. 3:8, 12, designating an office alongside that of "bishop" and/or "presbyter" (1 Tim. 3:1; cf. Titus 1:5, 7, for interchange of "bishop" and "presbyter"). Even here the term is not firmly fixed, for Timothy is a *diakonos* (1 Tim. 4:6). Another ambiguity appears in 1 Tim. 3:11, where *gynaikas* can mean "wives" or "women," i.e., wives of deacons or women as deacons.

Outside the pastoral epistles the term *diakonos* is so fluid that it may be used for anyone who serves in any capacity. The servants at the Cana wedding who were sent by Mary to draw water are called "deacons" (Jn. 2:5). The king in Rom. 13:4 is called "God's *diakonos* unto good." Any follower of Jesus is a *diakonos* (Mk. 9:35; 10:43). Christ himself is called *diakonos* (Rom. 15:8). Paul refers to himself as *diakonos* (1 Cor. 3:5; Eph. 3:7; Col. 1:23). Paul called Apollos a *diakonos* (1 Cor. 3:5). Paul called Phoebe a *diakonos* (Rom. 16:1). She is called a "deacon," not a "deaconess" (this term not appearing in the New Testament). It is interesting that Eph. 4:11 specifies that Christ gave to the church apostles, prophets, evangelists, pastors, and teachers, with no mention of "deacons," even though Paul has just termed himself a *diakonos* (3:7). The list probably is not intended to be exhaustive, and it probably reflects a rather fluid structuring within the church. The passage does recognize certain ministers charged with equipping all the saints (the whole church) for ministry. There are special ministries but no provision for nonministering saints.

Nothing decisive emerges from New Testament evidence as to "husband of one wife" or "wife of one husband," "ordination," laying on of hands, "ministry," and "deacons." Terms are employed variously, and practices are more open than structured and formalized. At best, church structures and forms are in the making in the New Testament and not finalized. There is in the Pauline writings no clear case for the ordination of a woman to a special ministry (possibly implied with respect to Phoebe as a "deacon" in Rom. 16:1 and also in 1 Tim. 3:11), but Paul in various letters recognized ministry as pertaining to the whole church. In Rom. 12:2-8 he made the point that charismatic gifts (preaching, teaching, giving, comforting, administration, etc.) obligate one to exercise the gift. So understood, the basic criterion for ministry in any form is having the gift for it by God's grace. In Eph. 4:11–16 the living Christ is seen as providing equipping ministries to prepare all the saints for ministry. The pastoral epistles do not unambiguously exclude women from special ministries. Galatians 3:28 affirms a principle that makes ethnic, legal, and sexual distinctions irrelevant to being "in Christ." This clearly has a soteriological reference; it would seem logically to have the same implication for ministry.

Chapter 8

THE DOMESTIC CODE
AND WOMAN

Four Pauline letters have been reserved for study in this chapter along with 1 Peter. This was justified on the assumption of an underlying Domestic Code reflected in Col. 3:18–4:1; Eph. 5:22–6:9; 1 Peter 2:13–3:7; Titus 2:1–10; and 1 Tim. 2:1ff., 8ff.; 3:1ff., 8ff.; 5:17ff.; 6:1f. This code is thought to have been developed to meet the needs for order within the churches and in the domestic and civil structures of society. The main focus of the Domestic Code is upon husband/wife, parent/child, and master/slave relationships, a format we have encountered above in Aristotle (*Politics* I.3) and Philo (*Hyp.* 7.14). Our concern is with its implications for woman.

Serious study of the New Testament Domestic Code *(Haustafel)* began with Martin Dibelius in 1913,[1] with a wide range of studies in the years since.[2] This chapter will draw heavily upon the Tübingen dissertation by James E. Crouch.[3] Crouch finds in Col. 3: 18–4:1 the earliest traceable form of the Christian code, further developments being found in Ephesians, the pastorals, and 1 Peter (as well as in early patristic literature: 1 Clement, Polycarp, Didache, and Barnabas). He concludes that the Domestic Code was developed to meet the threat of a form of "enthusiasm" such as appeared within the churches threatening to undermine the basic structures of society. Women and slaves, in particular, would find in their Christian freedom that which they sought to extend to relationships outside the church as well as within it.

In Crouch's view, the early Christians found in Hellenistic Judaism a code which they adapted and Christianized for their purpose. The form of the code in which reciprocal social duties are stressed (husband/wife, parent/child, master/slave) is traced to Judaism's own Oriental background, with its strong moral/ethical demand but also with a low view of woman.

One may ask why the Domestic Code with its restraints upon women, children, and slaves appears in what is generally recognized as the Pauline tradition. It may be a seeming irony that the Domestic Code in the New Testament is linked to the apostle who fought so openly and who suffered such personal sacrifice for freedom and equity for Jew and Greek, bond and free, male and female.

At bottom is probably to be seen the perennial tension between freedom and order. Freedom is ever at the risk of its abuse in terms of permissiveness, disorder, anarchy, or chaos. The twin threats of legalism and libertinism are ancient and recurrent. Various books of the New Testament reflect this ongoing struggle for a proper relationship between law and grace, gift and demand, freedom and responsibility.[4] This situation apparently became acute in the early churches, with Paul at the center of this battle.

Paul's first major battle was with legalism, as certain "Judaizers" or people of "the circumcision" (cf. Acts 10:45; 11:2; Gal. 2:12; Titus 1:10) sought to impose circumcision upon Gentile converts to Christianity (Acts 15:1, 5; Gal. 6:12). Paul saw circumcision as implying more than submission to an initiation rite; it implied obligation to the whole Law (Gal. 5:3). He took a firm stand, resisting any effort to impose Jewish cultic rites upon Gentile believers (Acts 15; Gal. 2:3). What mattered to him was "a new creation" (Gal. 6:15); and "in Christ" there is "not any Jew nor Greek, not any slave nor free, not any male and female" (3:28).

The hard-won victory for freedom, especially for Gentiles, opened up a new front on which Paul had to do battle, that of libertinism. To some of Paul's hearers, being freed from "the Law" was an invitation to anti-nomianism, the rejection of all restraint, especially on the part of those seeing themselves as "the spiritual ones." Women and slaves, who had suffered under the heaviest restraints, would understandably make the most of their new freedom "in Christ." Paul in 1 Corinthians struggled with what to him was an abuse of freedom and a threat to order and continued the effort on a reduced scale in Romans. The issue continued, and it is strongly reflected in the five letters before us.

There is more to be considered than such situations as at Corinth. There was in Paul himself a strong "nomistic" strain. He emphasized salvation as the gift of God's grace rather than a reward for human works. But Paul fought as hard on the other front, and he was deeply concerned for the quality of life found in the Christian community. He held firmly to the beliefs that the Law was from God and that its intention was to be accomplished. Paul's nomistic strain met head on the antinomian impulse which arose chiefly in the Gentile churches. The restraints employed in meeting this threat of moral anarchy spilled over into various human relationships and were even extended into the areas of roles in church and manner of dress.

If this reconstruction of the origin and intention of the New Testament Domestic Code is correct, it at least makes more understandable the tension between the freedom proclaimed in Galatians and the restraints later imposed upon women in letters in the Pauline tradition. There was Paul's own nomistic strain alongside his clarion call to freedom. There was the threat to order and structures as well as to moral/ethical values. There was the already established tradition in Jewish Christianity, with its heritage in paraenetic instructions and regulations. It was not a simple situation in which one man single-handedly imposed male chauvinism upon Gentile churches. Whatever be the difficulty today in getting it all together, it may at least help to see the development of the Domestic Code in its historical matrix.

COLOSSIANS 3:18–4:1

Although duties are reciprocal in this early formation of the Domestic Code the heaviest demands fall upon wives, children, and slaves. Wives are asked to subordinate themselves to their husbands (Col. 3:18), children are to obey their parents (v. 20), and slaves are to obey their masters (v. 22). Husbands are to love their wives (v. 19), fathers (*pateres* may include both parents here) are to avoid exasperating their children (v. 21), and masters are to be just and equitable toward their slaves, knowing that they too face a master in heaven (4:1).

The subordination of woman to man in the Colossian Domestic Code may be anticipated in the way the new humanity in Christ expressed in Gal. 3:28 is modified in Col. 3:11. In Galatians, for those "in Christ" there is "not any Jew nor Greek, not any slave nor free, not any male and female." In Colossians there is a near parallel, but "not any male and female" is dropped from the pattern. There is a strong appeal for a new quality of life among those who have "died together with Christ" and "raised together with Christ" (Col. 2:20–3:17). The "old humanity" with its practices is to be stripped off in favor of the "new humanity" (3:9f.). This new humanity is in "the image of the one creating," and described as "where there is not any Greek and Jew, circumcision and uncircumcision, barbarian, Scythian, slave, free person, but [where] Christ is all things and in all" (v. 11). The idea is the same as in Gal. 3:28, but "not any male and female" gives way to not any "barbarian, Scythian." This may be without motive, but it is hard to believe that it represents no more than stylistic variation. Concerns that called forth the Domestic Code probably account for the omission.

Although the subordination of wife to husband follows the familiar pattern found in contemporary Judaism, there is some softening of it here. First, woman is addressed directly as a responsible person. Next, she is asked to assume voluntarily a role subordinate to that of her husband. The husband is not told to subordinate his wife to himself, and she is not told to obey her husband.

It is a common misrepresentation to trace to Paul or to New Testament Domestic Code the requirement that wives obey their husbands. This demand was introduced into marriage vows for much of the church; but its New Testament support is found only in 1 Peter 3:6, and there only by implication from Sarah's obedience to Abraham. The Domestic Code requires obedience of children and slaves, not of wives. Addressing wives directly, Col. 3:18 at most commands wives to subject themselves to their husbands. The verb is imperative and in the middle voice. The wife is to be the acting agent in the subordination, not the passive object. This contrasts sharply with Philo, who explained: ". . . because the male is more complete, more dominant than the female, closer akin to causal activity, for the female is incomplete and in subjection and belongs to the category of the passive rather than the active" (*Spec. Leg.* I.200). It is when measured by the manner of Jesus and by the vision of Gal. 3:28 that the restriction is most problematic.

The parallel of Col. 3:18 and 1 Cor. 14:34 is apparent, both requiring the wife's subordination to the husband; but the Corinthian "as the law says" has as its Colossian counterpart, "as is fitting in the Lord." In Chapter 7 we observed the extreme difficulties in 1 Cor. 14:34–35, with the possibility of a scribal gloss. The Colossian phrase "in the Lord" is more understandable in the light of problems apparent in the early churches. The Domestic Code seems to counter with the restriction that even for one "in Christ" (here, "in the Lord") there are restrictions to be observed in the structures of society.

The best that can be made for role subordination within structures of society is that they are functionally normal and hardly escapable. Wherever two or more persons relate, there are differing roles and these normally assume some subordinating pattern. This is true in government, business, sports, and in most of life. Many of these roles are arbitrary and are subject to exchange. It is when subordination is seen as rooted in nature, when it is coercive, and when permanent and irreversible that it becomes a most serious threat to personal values.

Freedom, too, can pose its own threats. The long overdue gains in woman's liberation probably pose a major threat today to marriage. It is one thing, and we believe a right thing, to recognize the full personhood of woman. The personhood of woman, as of man, implies her right to develop as fully as possible her individual potential. Should two individuals marry, their becoming one flesh does not mean both become husband or both become wife; it means ideally that each contributes to the fulfillment of the other as a person. This is an attainable goal within marriage, with one vocation or two vocations within the marriage. Obviously, there are hazards in either pattern. Where there is only one vocation within a marriage, there is the danger of the subordination of one spouse to the other. Where there are two vocations, there is the danger of two separate ways, two persons remaining two and never becoming one.

Any idea of subordination of one to the other as an inherent right or as a dictate of nature or custom is to be rejected, but one cannot write off all role subordination as in itself necessarily destructive to or incompatible with equal dignity and freedom of persons united in marriage or in other structures of society.

There is some implication for woman in the second part of the Colossian Domestic Code, where "children" then "fathers" are addressed. Children are to obey their "parents," no distinction being made between the authority of father and mother over the child. Parental authority is recognized, assuming that parental responsibility is necessary to its fulfillment. Such authority is not assigned one spouse over another.

In Col. 3:21 "fathers" are addressed, but probably in this context both parents are intended. Actually, either parent may so abuse a child. Even so, some bias is reflected, if only semantic. Parents are never addressed as "mothers."

In the third unit of the Domestic Code, slaves are to obey in all things their masters "according to flesh" (Col. 3:22). The far-reaching principle here is that being "in Christ" does not free one from the claims of society and its institutions but gives added responsibility, the one "in Christ" being answerable to the high claims of Christ. The Domestic Code does not at this point apply this principle to the wife, but it may be in the background.

The Domestic Code in Colossians does not challenge existing structures; rather it upholds them. To a point, the Domestic Code conforms to two current expectations: that the wife be subordinate to the husband and that the husband give the same love to his wife expected of any husband.[5] The chief advance is in addressing the wife directly as one responsible for the regulating of her own role as wife.

EPHESIANS 5:22–6:9

Ephesians is generally considered later than Colossians and dependent upon it. The Domestic Code here follows the basic structure of that in Colossians (wives/husbands; children/fathers; slaves/masters), but it is more extensively Christianized and more deeply embedded contextually in the letter.

A major addition to the Ephesian form of the Domestic Code is found at the outset in Eph. 5:21: "being subject to one another in reverence for Christ." Before anything is said about wives submitting themselves to their husbands, each one in the church is instructed to submit to each other "in reverence for Christ."

Behind the phrase "in the fear of Christ" or "in reverence for Christ" may be a trace of the problem in the churches giving rise to the Domestic Code. As seen, the sense of freedom "in Christ" probably posed the new problem of rejection of all authority; and here, as elsewhere, the plea is made that "in Christ" calls for voluntary submission to one another rather than the assertion of independence of one another. In any event, what is said to wives, children, and slaves is in principle first directed to all Christians.

There is no verb in Eph. 5:22, so one must be inferred from context. There is nothing here to imply "obey." Contextually, the injunction to wives is to subject themselves "to their own husbands as to the Lord." The phrase "as to the Lord" is probably emphatic. This looks to the principle governing all Christian submission. Any submission or service rendered another is to be expressive of one's submission to Christ. The quality put into a marital or other relationship is to be one worthy of Christ. Again, being "in Christ" is not to serve as an escape from obligation to others but to be the principle for voluntary self-giving at the highest standard.

Another dimension is introduced into the principle "as to the Lord" (Eph. 5:22) when in vs. 23–24 a fixed order is established: "as the church is subject to Christ, thus also the wives to their husbands in everything." This picks up the idea of a hierarchy in which Christ is head of the church and the husband head of the wife (cf. 1 Cor. 11:2–16). This is made explicit in v. 23, but there the letter's overriding concern with the church leads to the soteriological emphasis upon Christ as "himself the savior of the body," i.e., "the church." Ephesians, then, goes beyond Colossians in appealing to nature, not just redemption, as setting an order in which the husband is head of the wife. There is no explicit appeal to the rib story of creation, but its perspective seems to lie behind the Ephesian Domestic Code.

Ephesians goes beyond Colossians as to the love with which husbands are to love their wives. In Colossians there is no hint as to any love other than that which any husband is expected to have for his wife. In Ephesians it is explicit that the husband's love for his wife is to be modeled after that of Christ for the church, a self-giving or self-sacrificing love (Eph. 5:25). Further, the identity of husband and wife is to be such that in loving her he really loves himself. Appeal is made to Gen. 2:24. This verse, unlike the rib story to which it is attached, is not subordinating. It affirms that in marriage "the two become one flesh."

The Domestic Code in Ephesians, then, goes beyond that in Colossians in several ways. It has been further Christianized. It heightens the love by which husband and wife are to be united. It places heavier demand upon the husband, enjoining him to love his wife in the manner Christ loved the church. But it also goes beyond Colossians in fixing the wife's subordination to the husband. Like Colossians, Ephesians addresses the wives directly, calling upon them as responsible persons to subject themselves to their husbands. It softens this by putting it in the context of an inclusive claim upon all Christians, that they all be subjected to one another. With all this, the husband is declared to be the head of the wife in an order that is fixed. This in turn is softened by appeal to Gen. 2:24, but again the code is weighted in favor of the husband by the closing injunction that the wife revere her husband (Eph. 5:33). In various ways, then, the Ephesian Domestic Code inclines toward equality of husband and wife, but the husband remains "more equal" than the wife.

In the second of the trilogy of relationships, that of children and parents (Eph. 6:1–4), roles do change; and the very two persons who were "wife" and "husband," the former subordinated to the latter, now are "parents," with no subordination one to the other. Children are to obey their "parents," with no hint as to priority of one parent over the other in parental authority. Appeal is made to the Fifth Commandment: "Honor your father and your mother" (cf. Ex. 20:12). Following the pattern in Colossians, there is in Eph. 6:4 a male bias in some respect, where "fathers" are enjoined not to exasperate their children but rather to nurture them in the discipline of the Lord.

The Ephesian Domestic Code follows through on the pattern of that in Colossians, the third pair in the trilogy being "slaves" and "masters" (Eph. 6:5–9). As in Colossians, slaves as well as children are commanded to obey. Also, the quality of obedience is to be determined by one's relationship to Christ, not to parent or master to whom obedience is due.

FIRST PETER 2:13–3:7

An overriding concern of 1 Peter is to strengthen and guide Christians through a situation of oppression if not actual persecution. The term "Christian" appears in 1 Peter 4:16 (found elsewhere in the New Testament only in Acts 11:26; 26:28), and here it is to be a name under which one may both suffer and glorify God.[6] Suffering is a recurrent theme throughout the letter, and Christians are to accept it as something to be expected by any follower of the suffering Christ (4:12–14). Courage is to be derived from the remembrance of Christ's own triumphant death and resurrection and the assurance of a final, eschatological victory (1:3–9; 4:7; 5:10f.). With the call to courage is the call to holiness: "As the one having called you is holy, be ye yourselves holy in all your manner of life" (1:15). There is no motive, as in later Domestic Code, to avoid trouble by satisfying the expectations of society. The motive is that they be found true and thus silence any who would accuse them of wrongdoing and that their good deeds might be seen to the glory of God (2:11f.).

The tension between freedom and order, a probable factor in the rise of the Christian Domestic Code, is explicit in 1 Peter 2:13–17.

Freedom in Christ is not to be used as a cloak for evil nor to escape from obligations to the social order. All Christians are called on to be subject to ruling powers, whether emperor or governor (v. 13). This is to be done "because of the Lord," i.e., precisely because one is under the Lordship of Christ. Anarchy is rejected in favor of an ordered society, and civil government is seen as ordained by God as a deterrent to evil and in the interest of good (vs. 13f.; cf. Rom. 13:1–7). There is a play on the terms for "free persons" *(eleutheroi)* and slaves *(douloi)* in 1 Peter 2:16. Precisely as "free persons" are we to give ourselves in submission to constituted authority; and we are not to use our freedom as a cloak for evil (libertinism or antinomianism), for we are "slaves" of God.

In 1 Peter 2:17 there is a summary as to Christian attitude toward all persons: "Honor all persons; love the brotherhood [feminine article]; fear God; honor the emperor." It is against this Christian disposition to be submissive and to respect all persons that the Domestic Code is to be read in 1 Peter. Servants and wives are not alone in submission.

The Domestic Code proper in 1 Peter comes to focus on household servants (1 Peter 2:18–25), wives (3:1–6), and husbands (v. 7). Whatever problems for perspectives today, the basic motives are positive. Household servants are admonished to give service which properly reflects their own quality of existence, not that of their masters. Wives are called to such deportment as may by their very example bring conversion to husbands who disobey the spoken word. Husbands are asked to be considerate of their wives and to honor them.

Those addressed in 1 Peter 2:18 are "household servants," the term *doulos* (slave) not appearing here. They are asked to be submissive to their masters and to offer this "in all respect." Such service is to be given the "harsh" as well as the "good and gentle." In suffering for right, they follow the example of Christ. Strength for such suffering is to be found where Christ found it, in trusting in the One who judges righteously.

Wives likewise are admonished to be subject or subordinate to their husbands (1 Peter 3:1), that in their manner they may win over disobedient husbands to Christ. Husbands who had disobeyed "the word" may be won apart from the word as they look upon the "holy manner of life" of their wives. As elsewhere in the Domestic Code, a contrast is drawn between outer adornment and inner beauty. What are found redeeming are not the braiding of hair, costly jewels, or display of wardrobe, but those qualities of the inner self so precious to God, "a gentle and quiet spirit." Appeal is made to the example of "the holy women" of old who put their trust in God and who were submissive to their husbands. Sarah is singled out for her example, and here only in the New Testament is the term "obey" employed for wives in relationship with their husbands. Even here, Christian wives are not actually told to obey their husbands, although this implication lurks in the citation: "as Sarah obeyed Abraham, calling him lord" (v. 6). Women who follow such example are "her children." So there are "children of Sarah" as well as the frequently mentioned "children of Abraham"!

Husbands are called upon to "live together" with their wives "according to knowledge" (1 Peter 3:7). It is the duty of the husband to become enlightened as to how to relate to his wife. He is to have an informed sensitivity to her as a person. He is to remember that she is a "joint heir of the gift of life."

Traditional language, and presumably perspective, enters right at the point of the appeal to enlightened sensitivity to the wife. She is referred to as "the weaker vessel." The writer does not specify the nature of this weakness. The concluding motive is likewise male-oriented, addressed to the husbands: "in order that your prayers not be hindered." Whatever the problems here, the Petrine Domestic Code intends to respect the wives. It likewise reflects limits of the community out of which it came.

TITUS 2:1–10

Titus probably is earlier than 1 Timothy, and they will be studied in that order. The Domestic Code in Titus seems to be less advanced than that in 1 Timothy, but its form varies considerably from that in Colossians and Ephesians. In Titus the sequence is: older men, older women, young women, young men, slaves. None is addressed directly; Titus himself is instructed as to how to instruct these men and women.

The "sound doctrine" with which Titus 2:1–10 is concerned has to do with life-style, not beliefs as such. This version of the Domestic Code calls for attitudes and conduct that are a credit to "the word of God" (v. 5), such as will "adorn the teaching of God our Savior" (v. 10). There is concern for moral and ethical values, and there is throughout a strong emphasis upon the kind of deportment that will avoid discredit from without and win respect for the community and its message. This latter is applied especially to wives and slaves.

Older men are to be "temperate, serious, sensible, sound in faith, in love, in endurance" (Titus 2:2). Younger men are to be "sensible" or "self-controlled"; and Titus himself is to be an example in all "good works," and in his teaching to be of such integrity, seriousness, and sound speech as to leave opponents with nothing bad to say about the church (vs. 7f.).

Older women are likewise to be in deportment such as is "priestly-proper." There are no priestesses in Judaism or Christianity, but here at least a sacred or priestly term describes conduct expected of "older women." The idea may be that of "reverence" (RSV) or the "holy life" (TEV). On the negative side, they are not to be slanderers or slaves to much wine (Titus 2:3). On the positive side, they are to be "teachers of what is fitting"; but this teaching seems to be restricted to young women. There is no hint that the older women teach men of any age. What they are to teach has to do with domestic matters. They are to teach young women to love their husbands and their children and to be "sensible, pure, domestic, good, and submissive to their husbands" (vs. 4f.).

The deportment which "older women" are to teach the "young women" has as a basic motive the reputation of the church in society. This is explicit: "in order that the word of God not be slandered" (Titus 2:5b). The same motive is applied to Titus' manner of teaching (v. 8) and to the deportment of slaves (v. 10). This strengthens the conclusion that the Domestic Code was developed not only for order within the church but with a view to the church's reputation before the outside world. Behind the Domestic Code is a strong motive for satisfying the expectations of society—its values, customs, and structures.

There can be no doubt but that the Domestic Code in Titus sees woman in a domestic role. The only teaching assigned to older women has to do with teaching younger women in domestics. It is explicit that young women are to be "submissive" to their husbands. This may imply "obedience," but it is not explicit. There is no excuse for rendering *hypotassomenas* "obey" as in the TEV (Titus 2:5) (*hypakouein* is the word for "obey," as for children and slaves in Eph. 6:1, 5; Col. 3:20, 22).

Slaves are to be submissive (doubtless implying obedience) to their masters (Titus 2:9f.). There is no reciprocal word to masters. Whereas in Colossians and Ephesians the appeal was to the expectations of Christ, here it is to the expectations of society.

Further evidence of concern for meeting the expectations of society, and possibly also of some rebellion on the part of Christians, is found in Titus 3:1ff., where all are to be reminded "to be submissive to rulers and authorities, to be obedient, ready for every good work, to slander no one, to avoid fighting, to be gentle, and to show gentleness to all men." This is not encouragement to the prophetic ministry which challenges the values and ways of the world. It is not an encouragement to tension with the world. This is not mere expediency, for strong appeal is made to personal qualities unlike those of the world; but the focus here is not upon changing the world. For the sharpest tension with the world one must turn to Jesus, not the church even at its best.

FIRST TIMOTHY

First Timothy is largely the Domestic Code. In form it does not follow the simple trilogy of Colossians (wives/husbands, children/fathers, slaves/masters), but it prescribes a code of conduct for women and slaves as well as for various others in the church. The letter reflects not a crusading church out to change the world at any risk but a church intent upon living in peace with its world. It is not enough to please God and satisfy conscience; the church must take care that it have the respect of the outside world. At no point is the church seen as in the book of Revelation to be in necessary tension with the world, a church prepared for martyrdom but not for surrender.

The whole epistle is under "the order of God our Savior and Jesus Christ our hope" (1 Tim. 1:1). Those teaching contrary doctrines are to be ordered to stop (vs. 3, 5). To Timothy is entrusted a "charge" or "command" which he is to impose upon the church, these words becoming his "weapons" that he might "fight the good fight" (v. 18). The "good fight" is that for order within the church and peace with the world. Envisioned here is a piety within the church that does not arouse the hostility of the world.

Women come in for considerable attention in 1 Timothy. They are not included in instructions to "men everywhere" who are "to pray," lifting up hands in prayer "without anger or argument" (1 Tim. 2:8). It is doubtful that women are really excluded from prayer, but they are not mentioned here. Whereas men are instructed as to proper manner in prayer, women are instructed as to proper dress and deportment in general (vs. 9–15). Attention is given first to proper dress as unassuming, modest, and simple. Fancy hairdos, costly jewelry, and costly clothes are to be shunned. Instead, a woman's adornment is to be in her good works. Even though the weight probably falls on good works as her true beauty, the prescription banning attention to cosmetics is a part of the writer's concern.

The next restriction upon the Christian woman is more severe: silence and submission. The Domestic Code has now reached a new stage in restriction upon woman. The writer lays it down as law, based upon creation and history. For him it is not simply a matter of custom; it is something inherent in nature that woman be subordinate to man and that she not teach a man or have any authority over a man. Addressing Timothy, he commands that a woman learn "in quietness and in all submission" (1 Tim. 2:11). The next rule is absolute: "I do not permit a woman to teach, neither to exercise authority over a man; rather she is to remain quiet" (v. 12). Presumably, it is in church that she is to remain silent, with no permission to teach. Nowhere is she to have authority over a man.

The writer bases his position on Genesis, appealing to the rib narrative of creation and the story of the fall of Adam and Eve. He makes two points: (1) Adam was created before Eve and (2) it was Eve and not Adam who was deceived and broke God's law (1 Tim. 2:13f.). Nothing is made of the creation narrative in Genesis 1, that in which "male and female" are created together, both in the image of God, and both given dominion over all else in creation (Gen. 1:26f.). As seen above, Jesus built upon the nonsubordinating narrative; 1 Timothy follows the Pauline tradition of building upon the rib narrative.

Woman is disqualified from teaching by appeal to the story of the fall into sin in Genesis 3. The writer finds Eve to be both vulnerable to deception and also guilty of transgression. The passage here is explicit that "Adam was not deceived" (1 Tim. 2:14), but it is not explained under what circumstances he sinned. Presumably, he knew what he was doing when he disobeyed God. Somehow this qualifies Adam but not Eve to teach, men but not women.

Most enigmatic is 1 Tim. 2:15: "She shall be saved through childbearing, if they [sic] continue in faith and love and holiness with modesty." In the New Testament "salvation" can refer to anything from recovery from sickness to salvation from sin. Only context can clarify intention, for the word itself is used in various ways. If this verse intends salvation from sin, it is a singular view in the New Testament. Elsewhere there is no promise of salvation by the procreation of children or teaching that a woman must have children in order to be saved. Surely the passage does not intend to exclude childless women from salvation. If a distinction is made here between salvation in its usual soteriological sense (i.e., from sin) and salvation simply as fulfillment, probably it is the latter sense that is intended here. This may intend to say that a woman finds her personal fulfillment, or vocational fulfillment, not in teaching but in the home. Implied here may be what is explicit in 5:14, where young widows are admonished to marry, bear children, and rule their households.

There can be no doubt as to the writer's commitment to marriage and homemaking as the proper vocation for women. He rejects the gnosticizing opposition to marriage, linking it with the "good" which God created (1 Tim. 4:1–5). He is explicit as to young widows: "I will, therefore, young widows to marry, to bear children, to rule the household, to give opponents no occasion or cause to revile us" (5:14). Apparently society expected this role of woman, and the writer prescribes it.

Women are discussed in a passage dealing with qualifications for "deacons" (1 Tim. 3:8–13). It is not clear whether these "women" are wives of the deacons or holders of a similar office (the Greek word can mean either "woman" or "wife"). Since women are strictly forbidden to teach or have authority over a man (2:11), the reference here probably is to wives of "deacons." The phrase "married only once," employed for "bishops" (3:2) and "deacons" (v. 12), is not to serve as a proof text to exclude women from either office. To begin with, the intention of the phrase is ambiguous. It could have to do with forbidding the single life, polygamy, remarriage after divorce, or a second marriage under any circumstance. A strong case can be made for the last option, for in the early church it was considered among some to be exceptionally virtuous not to remarry even after the death of a spouse. The same phrase is used for the widow who is eligible for being placed on the church roll for widows; she must be at least sixty years of age and one who has not been married more than once (5:9). "Married only once," then, was a distinction in piety within the early church, applied to women as well as men. In 3:2, 12 the phrase does not necessarily intend to exclude women from office; rather it probably stresses what was considered a mark of piety, as when applied to widows in 5:9.

A problem is left unresolved in 1 Timothy when widows qualify for being "enrolled as a widow" only if above sixty and not "married more than once" (1 Tim. 5:9); yet "younger widows" are encouraged to marry (v. 14), thus disqualifying themselves from being "enrolled as widows" should they be widowed again when past sixty. This seems to subject the younger widows to most difficult options. Close examination of the text discloses two motives for wanting the younger widows to marry, one moral (v. 11) and one economic (v. 16). The Domestic Code reflects the judgment that the younger widows would find their sexual drives ("grow wanton" in RSV) too strong for a life of continence, so marriage was seen as the escape from this moral threat. The other motive was that, by their marrying, the church would not be financially "burdened" by having on its hands a young woman with possibly years yet to live.

In a culture where few women engaged in remunerative work, a widow's livelihood would be a serious problem. The church recognized its responsibility for the welfare of widows, but the recommendations worked out in the Domestic Code are stringent. First, relatives of the widow are to accept this obligation. Then, if there are no relatives, the church is to accept the care of the widow only if she is sixty years of age, married only once, exemplary in conduct, and of good reputation. The Domestic Code sees two problems in the church's undertaking the financial care of younger widows—one is the longtime burden on resources of the church; the other is the temptation of a young widow who has no obligation to a husband to grow lax and even destructive in her life. So, younger widows are admonished to marry, even though this could pose for them a problem if again widowed.

The Domestic Code in 1 Timothy, then, has been extended to cover life as a whole for the Christian community. In fact, the church itself is seen as a family, where "an older man" is to be exhorted as a father, "younger men" treated like brothers, "older women" like mothers, and "younger women" like sisters (1 Tim. 5:1f.). Individual families are to have their own integrity, the church not taking over their responsibilities (cf. vs. 4–8). On the other hand, the whole church is under a domestic code that governs order within the church and within the home.

SUMMARY

The Domestic Code seems clearly to represent the direction in which the church was moving from the fifties or sixties onward, from a rather fluid life-style to a more structured and ordered one, from a great excitement about its freedom "in Christ" to an increasing concern for what appeared to be abuse of freedom in two directions: in the moral threat of permissiveness and in the threat to structures within and outside the church. For much of its history the church has imposed rather strict limits upon women, and this disposition seems best understood in terms of factors that gave rise to the Domestic Code. Paul himself was a great exponent of freedom, and his fight for freedom reached its highest expression known to us in Galatians. As early as 1 Corinthians and Romans, in the middle fifties, we see strong indications of antinomianism and also resistance to authority. Paul turns to this new problem in these letters. From Colossians onward the problem of order somewhat overshadows the concern for freedom in the Pauline churches. Despite the unparalleled impulse in Jesus toward dignity and liberation for all persons, including women, and despite Paul's own early commitment to the overcoming in Christ of all partialities, various ones have come out on the short end of freedom, even within the church. In part, the roots of this are found early in the concern for order, and they have continued to bear their fruits.

Chapter 9

WOMAN IN THE SYNOPTIC GOSPELS AND ACTS

The intention of this chapter is to trace perspectives on woman in the Synoptic Gospels and Acts. Synoptic relationships themselves have not been solved and probably never will be. We are assuming the priority of Mark over Matthew and Luke, with full recognition that this is far from established. It seems to be the best working hypothesis thus far advanced, but it leaves much unexplained. In this view, Matthew and Luke independently of each other both used Mark as a basic source, with yet another source in common (Q for *Quelle*), and each having considerable material found nowhere else. We assume that John appeared later than the Synoptics and reflects a later stage in Christian development, but that it contains early and historically accurate traditions which developed independently of the Synoptics.

More important to our investigation are the relative dates of the Gospels as over against the Pauline letters. It is almost universally recognized that Paul's letters are among the earliest of the New Testament writings, appearing from the early fifties into the early sixties, the Gospels appearing from the late sixties into the early nineties. If so, a major interest for us is the greater freedom accorded woman in the Gospels than in the epistles. The Gospels know nothing of the rules and regulations imposed upon women in 1 Corinthians and in the letters containing the Domestic Code. If the Gospels were written after the epistles, the pattern calls for explanation. One possibility is that there were widely separated currents or traditions within the early church, one reflected in the Pauline letters and the code and the other in the Gospels.

Another possibility (our persuasion) is that the four Evangelists and the sources with which they worked faithfully preserve the stance of Jesus even though the four Gospels appeared later than the letters and even though the Evangelists and their sources took considerable liberty in shaping the tradition in various forms. No source or Evangelist attributed to Jesus the imposition of anything like the rules and regulations found in the Domestic Code or even in 1 Corinthians. The Gospels represent Jesus as fully committed to freedom and personhood, resting the responsibility for that freedom upon the person and not "shielding" or "safeguarding" it by rules. Apparently, the stance of Jesus was so emphatic and unambiguous that no one could ascribe to him any backing away from freedom, even though freedom carried with it the dangers of being perversely used. Significantly, Paul and the Domestic Code do not ascribe to Jesus any of their rules as to veils, silence for woman, subordination of wife to husband, and the like. These rules are absent from the Gospels and Acts, and in the letters they are not traced to Jesus.

John A. T. Robinson has just added another major challenge from critical ranks to the "assured results" of critical scholarship, contending that there is no compelling evidence for dating any Gospel later than A.D. 60 or any New Testament writing later than A.D. 70.[1] He sees all four Gospels and Acts as coming in some form from possibly before A.D. 40 and not later than the early sixties, with the Pauline letters appearing from A.D. 50 to 58. If the Gospels are this early, their primitive perspective is more readily understandable.

Much in the four Gospels does seem to be more primitive in perspective and development than much found in the letters of Paul or letters thought to be under Pauline influence. This is true for soteriology (salvation). Forgiveness and salvation are presented more directly and with less sophistication in the Gospels than in the letters.[2] As to ecclesiology, the development of church order and structures is far simpler in the Gospels than in the letters. Significantly for our study, the Gospels know nothing about rules or restraints worked out for women, children, and slaves as special classes within the church. In the Gospels and Acts there are no regulations for women's hairdos, cosmetics, jewelry, or dress. They know nothing about imposing silence upon women or their being unfit for teaching. They know nothing about woman being created to be subordinate to man or being more susceptible to temptation or deception. How can this be, if the Gospels and Acts actually are written after the Pauline letters and after at least the early stages of the Domestic Code?

Robinson's *Redating the New Testament* would put the whole matter in a simpler light, dating the Gospels and Acts much earlier than is done generally in critical study. As tempting as is this reconstruction, we do not see it as sufficiently compelling to displace the generally held view that the Gospels are in fact later in reaching at least their present form than are the letters of Paul.

Unlike Part II, the focus in this chapter will not be on Jesus himself but on the movement that he created as traced in the Synoptic Gospels and Acts. It is to be admitted that it is most difficult to distinguish between Jesus and those upon whose witness we are dependent for our knowledge of his manner, his words, and his deeds; but this is an important task, however precarious. The attempt to get at the motives of the author of a Gospel is called redaction criticism. Its basic assumption is that the author was a theologian and that his hand and his intention are somewhat distinguishable from the materials with which he worked, his own perspective and motive being discernible. The book of Acts is included here because of its close relationship with the Gospel of Luke. Consensus is so great among scholars that for a half century these two writings have been known as Luke-Acts, two volumes of one continuing work.[3]

To state more simply the task of this chapter, it is to try to understand how Mark, Matthew, and Luke looked upon woman and how woman fared in the church as they knew it. How well did the church for whom these wrote preserve the disposition of Jesus? Chapter 10 will investigate the perspective in the Johannine writings (the Gospel of John, the letters of John, and the Revelation). It is hoped that these two chapters, along with the preceding chapters on Paul and the Domestic Code, will disclose directions taken at different times in different situations within the churches and throw some light on how we got where we are in a movement

begun by Jesus and with some help as to how we may proceed from
here.

THE GOSPEL OF MARK

Women appear prominently in a dozen major scenes in Mark's
rather brief Gospel. The first woman to appear is Simon's mother-
in-law (Mk. 1:30f.). Entering the home of Simon and Andrew, with
James and John, Jesus was told that Simon's mother-in-law was
sick of a fever. Jesus went to her, took her by the hand, and raised
her up. The fever left her, and she "ministered" to them, presumably preparing a meal for them, although this is not specified. The
story is told so simply that motives or attitudes are not explicit.
There certainly is not a trace of denigration of woman. That she
"ministered" to them may imply her relegation to household duties
only, but to "minister" is a test of greatness and true discipleship
in Mark (9:35; 10:43, 45; 15:41). The pericope may even have as
its motive the teaching that salvation at any level is to lead to
service to others. Although the relationship is identified, mother-
in-law to Simon, nothing is made explicitly of the fact that she was
a woman. In this story being a woman is a nonissue.

Mark shares with all Biblical writers the employment of a male-
oriented language, without amending it. Even one who sews
patches on garments and who knows not to sew unshrunk cloth on
an old garment is masculine in Mk. 2:21. The bias is embedded in
the language, and it is employed with no apparent sensitivity to this
as a problem. The same may hold for Mark's report of the five
thousand whom Jesus fed as "men" (*andres* is the term for adult
males). Women and children were not counted here (6:44).

Mother. Mark preserves the highly significant story of the coming of Jesus' mother and brothers (Mk. 3:31–35), apparently to
take him out of the limelight, they possibly sharing with "those
around him" the fear that he was "beside himself" (v. 21). There
is no implication of a negative attitude here toward Mary because
she is a woman; for Jesus' brothers are linked with her, with no
suggestion but that they have the same feeling toward Jesus. Sexu-

ality is a nonissue here. If there is a trace of evidence for feeling either way, it is positive, appearing in the addition of "my sister" in Jesus' affirmation of his true family, only his mother and brothers being mentioned elsewhere in the story. Matthew retains "my sister" with Mark, Luke omitting the reference.

Daughter. Two women appear in the blending of two stories, the healing of Jairus' daughter and the healing of a woman with an issue of blood (Mk. 5:21–43). As related, the stories are linked in their occurrence, the woman's healing having taken place while Jesus was on his way to Jairus' home. There is another linkage, whether deliberate or not being undetermined. Both healed ones are called "daughter." Jairus, a synagogue ruler, made an impassioned appeal: "My little daughter is near death." After the woman with hemorrhage had touched Jesus' garment and then been identified, she fell with fear and trembling at his feet, apparently expecting a severe rebuke for her deed (v. 33). When she had "told him all the truth," he replied: "Daughter, your faith has saved you; go in peace and be healed from your scourge" (v. 34). Jesus called "daughter" one whom the cultic holiness code called "unclean." Mark or his source brought into one combined story two "daughters," one the little daughter of a synagogue ruler and the other a grown woman suffering from "the curse." It may be too much to claim that Mark or his source thus deliberately affirmed both a little girl in a world that preferred boys and a hemorrhaging woman in a world that counted such unclean and defiling; but the stories are there, and both are designated by a term used in affection and implying worth. At the least, there is no room for misogyny or denigration of woman in these stories. Their atmosphere is in another world from that concerned with veils, silence, subordination, etc. The stories must say something about Jesus and Mark.

A Wicked Woman. One woman in Mark's Gospel is portrayed in lurid colors: Herodias the wife of Herod Antipas and formerly the wife of his brother Philip (Mk. 6:17). Mark lays upon her the guilt for the beheading of John the Baptist. According to Mark, John had told Herod that it was not lawful for him to take his brother's wife. Herod put John in jail, but it was Herodias who engineered his death. She nursed her "grudge" against John until an occasion arose which she was able to exploit. Literally, she "had it in" for John (v. 19). Herodias' daughter danced before Herod and his guests at a birthday banquet, and Herod was so pleased that he promised her anything she asked, up to the half of his kingdom. Prompted by her mother, she asked for the head of John on a platter. Herod was grieved but yielded to his wife's pressure. John was beheaded, and the severed head was given to the daughter who in turn delivered it to Herodias, that she might gloat over it. There is not a more gruesome story in Mark's Gospel, and a woman plays the most gruesome part of all.

What is to be made of this story? First of all, there were such women in the ancient world, just as there were such men. The story in no way implies that "women are like that." Herodias is not painted as wicked because she is a woman. There are ruthless men in Mark's Gospel. Apparently Mark tells the story this way because this is how he understands it. Herodias is not only cruel; she is powerful. Herod is weak and Herodias mean, but this is not because one is a man and the other a woman. They are people to Mark, and each is vulnerable to the weaknesses and evils of humanity.

A Greek Woman's Daughter. The difficulties of the story in Mk. 7:24–30 have been considered above (Chapter 4). It is significant that Mark included a story that could reflect adversely on Jesus. At first, Jesus seems to be extremely harsh toward the woman who appealed to him in behalf of her "little daughter." The woman's complete devotion to her little daughter, her willingness to be humbled in pleading for help, and her cleverness in repartee with Jesus paint her in a good light. The story closes with Jesus' affirmation of this Greek woman of Syrophoenicia. Why does Mark include such a story? Its effect surely is to commend and esteem the woman whether or not Mark's deliberate intention.

Divorce. In a passage on divorce (Mk. 10:1–12) a religious perspective on woman is exposed, rejected, and given a different turn.

Jesus was asked if it were lawful "for a man to divorce a woman" (v. 2). Apart from the issue of divorce, there is present in the question a male bias so deep that the piety out of which it came reflected no sensitivity to it. In the Jewish world men divorced women, not the reverse. Jesus built upon another base, appealing to the Priestly narrative in Genesis 1 rather than the rib narrative in Genesis 2: "From the beginning, male and female He made them," adding to this the nonsubordinating appendix to the story in Genesis 2, "For this cause a man shall leave his father and mother and shall be joined to his wife, and the two shall become one flesh" (Gen. 2:24). Equality of man and woman in creation and in marriage is affirmed here. Mark quotes Jesus as branding it adultery against a woman to divorce one and marry another (Mk. 10:11). This is revolutionary. Jesus addressed a piety that thought of adultery as an offense against a husband's rights; Jesus applied it to a woman's rights. Next, Mark quotes Jesus as saying it to be adulterous if a woman divorces her husband and marries another man (v. 11b). It recognizes the same rights and same responsibilities for men and women in marriage. There is not a hint of a double standard here, except in the opponents' initial question.

Whose Wife? In Mk. 12:18–27 is a Sadducean story calculated to embarrass Jesus or anyone believing in resurrection. They recited what probably was one of their stock stories about a woman married in turn to seven brothers, and then posed their question: "In the resurrection, of which of them shall she be wife, for the seven had her as wife" (v. 23). The male bias is obvious. Whose wife? They all had her. It would never have occurred to them to ask, "Which of the seven will be her husband, for she had all seven?"

Widows. Mark has sequentially a saying of Jesus sympathetic with widows (Mk. 12:40) and a story exemplifying a poor widow as the giver most esteemed (vs. 41–44). Their proximity may be without significance, but it is interesting that two such strong affirmations of widows should appear side by side. In Mark the "little people" are consistently more perceptive and righteous than the powerful and ambitious. In the former story Jesus scorned the piety that makes long prayers yet "devours the houses of widows." This alludes to the "pious" who divorce their religion from their business standards. Many a widow has been beaten out of her house by some shrewd dealer who knows how to stay within the letter of the law yet manage to take over another's property, in this case her very shelter.

In the second reference Jesus praised a poor widow who gave all she had, although but two small coins. In so doing, she gave herself. The money did not come out of a surplus but out of what she had for daily bread. One widow's shelter was taken over by a man who prayed long prayers. Another widow gave her daily bread as an expression of her devotion. Why is it that in Gospels which are written relatively late, years after many of the epistles, and in which, according to scholarly judgment, they tell us more about the Evangelists and the early church than about Jesus, we have such an accumulation of such sayings and stories? The most credible answer is that Jesus must have been like that, and the Evangelists and their traditions dared not represent Jesus otherwise. But the evidence mounts in another direction. Mark must have had some sympathy for the perspective attributed to Jesus.

The Pregnant and Those Nursing Babies. Mark 13 is known as "the little apocalypse"; and it describes two catastrophic events, one to occur in the lifetime of the generation (*genea,* Mk. 13:30), and another at the "end" (*to telos,* v. 7) of the age. In describing the one that his generation would experience, presumably the destruction of Jerusalem in A.D. 70, Jesus showed special compassion for the pregnant women and nursing mothers who would have to flee their homes in those difficult days (v. 17). The immediate subject had to do with the fate of a nation and its great city and temple, but Jesus was not forgetful of those for whom it would have special sufferings, including those carrying unborn babies and those nursing babies. If Mark wrote during the crisis of the Jewish-Roman War, he presumably shared the feeling. One will have to look elsewhere for male chauvinism; it is not in this logion whether it belongs to Jesus, Mark, or his source.

A Beautiful Deed. Mark relates the story of an unnamed woman who anointed Jesus' head while he was at the table in the home of Simon the leper in Bethany (Mk. 14:3–9). Some persons there were indignant that such costly ointment was "wasted" instead of being sold and the money given to the poor. Jesus reminded them that the poor are with us always, implying presumably that if they really were interested in the poor they would have ample opportunity to give to them. These indignant men (masculine gender) were vehemently reproaching the woman. Jesus cut them off by saying, "Let her alone" (v. 6). He then proceeded to call what she had done "a beautiful deed." She had bestowed the costly ointment upon him, for him; but Jesus designated it a memorial to her. Again, a woman is seen as exemplary in sacrificial service. The villains in the story are men, evidenced by their insensitivity to the woman, to the poor who are still there if they care to help them, and to Jesus, whose death is anticipated not by the men about him but by this woman. However one relates this story to Jesus himself, it must be seen as another Marcan selection. It must say something about Mark also and about those who preserved the tradition.

Frightened by a Maid. Tradition has it that Mark was a spokesman for Peter, an early tradition that can be neither proved nor disproved. That Peter was held high in the esteem of all the Evangelists and the early church hardly requires defense. But Peter's failings are not concealed in the Gospels, Acts, or letters of Paul. In this story he is so frightened by a maid's identification of him as a follower of Jesus that he swore that he did not even know Jesus. By the time Mark wrote, Peter had a secure place in the affection and esteem of the church, and women were being brought under rather severe restraints. Mark represents some current within the church which was able to live with a story in which the great apostle was frightened by a maid and in which a maid's word was true at a point where Peter's was false. If tradition is correct and Peter was Mark's source, it says something positive about Peter, a man who was both weak and strong.

From Galilee to the Cross and the Empty Tomb. Not until his story of the crucifixion of Jesus does Mark disclose the fact that a great number of women had followed Jesus in Galilee, ministering to him there, and that they followed him all the way to the cross (Mk. 15:40f.). Three of these women are named: Mary Magdalene, prominent in each of the four Gospels; another Mary known as the mother of James the younger and of Joses; and Salome. James and Joses must have had some prominence in the early church to account for their mother being so identified. Additionally, Mark reports that there were "many others" of the women who came up from Galilee to Jerusalem with Jesus (v. 41). The nature of their "ministering" to him is not specified. They not only looked on as Jesus was on the cross, but the two Marys "were looking on" to see where Jesus was buried (v. 47), something the disciples apparently were afraid to do. All three of these women went to the tomb soon after the sun had risen on the first day of the week, taking spices which they had bought to anoint the body. They expected to find the stone in place, for they wondered how they would be able to roll it from the opening in the tomb. They found the tomb open, entered it, saw a "young man" seated on the right side and dressed in a white robe (an angel?), and were amazed. They were informed by the messenger that Jesus was risen and they were commissioned to tell "his disciples and Peter" that he would precede them into Galilee and that they would see him there as he had told them. The women were so shaken with amazement and fear that they went out from the tomb and said nothing to anyone (Mk. 16:8). Mark's Gospel breaks off at this point (or ends here).

The story gives women the primary place in loyalty to Jesus to the last. They followed him in some numbers from Galilee to Jerusalem, having ministered to him in Galilee. Some remained nearby at the crucifixion, watched to see the place of the burial, and were back at the tomb following the Sabbath. They knew about the empty tomb and received the word of the resurrection before any of the apostles or men followers of Jesus. They were commissioned to give the disciples and Peter the greatest news ever proclaimed. How Mark intends that his closing word be understood is not clear. That the women were frightened he makes explicit. He raises not a doubt as to their devotion or loyalty, and he shows them to have great courage through the darkest hours. If the original ending is lost, it doubtless holds the answer to our questions. If Mk. 16:8 is the intended ending, possibly Mark is saying that belief in the resurrection did not rest on the empty tomb or the witness of the women; but this would leave unanswered the question of just how this came about. Whatever the answer to our questions, the women come out better than the men in the closing scenes of Mark's Gospel. In fact, throughout Mark's Gospel women except for Herodias consistently show up in a good light. Even though there are passages highly significant in their portrayal of women, it is when the dozen or so are considered together that Mark's positive attitude toward woman is best appreciated.

THE GOSPEL OF MATTHEW

Matthew's perspective on woman may be examined in terms of what he does with Marcan material and by the enrichment of his Gospel by use of other sources. Our investigating Matthew before Luke does not imply that Matthew is earlier than Luke. It simply is more convenient to reserve Luke for investigation along with Acts.

Matthew's Use of Mark. Matthew omits very little of Mark, only nine passages of any length. Of these only one passage is about a woman, the story of the poor widow's offering (Mk. 12:41–44). There is nothing in Matthew's Gospel to indicate that he would have found this beautiful Marcan story problematic. Thematic arrangement and space needs for the great amount of new material he worked in probably account for his omissions of some Marcan material.

In material common to Matthew and Mark, there are numerous modifications, some strictly stylistic and some in content. There is no indication that Matthew was uncomfortable with Mark's positive attitude toward woman. There may be some revisions even more favorable to woman. In the story of the miracle of the feeding he adds "apart from women and children" (Mt.

14:21) to Mark's "five thousand men" (Mk. 6:44).

Matthew heightened the dramatic effect of Mark's story of the Greek woman who appealed to Jesus to heal her daughter (Mk. 7:24–30; Mt. 15:21–28). He introduces the part of Jesus' disciples, who impatiently say to Jesus, "Send her away, because she cries after us." Matthew also adds Jesus' word about being sent only to "the lost sheep of the house of Israel," to which the woman replied: "Lord, help me!" Picking up Mark's lines about the little children and the little dogs and the woman's cogent remark, Matthew heightens Jesus' reply by adding: "O woman, great is your faith!" Mark's story is sympathetic with the woman and puts her in good light, but the Matthean additions give her yet greater stature, especially in the character of her spirit over that of the impatient disciples and in Jesus' commendation of her.

Matthew modifies Mark's treatment of divorce, giving the whole discussion a somewhat different turn (Mk. 10:1–12; Mt. 19:1–12). He omits the Marcan reference to a woman's divorcing a man, possibly to avoid what is generally thought to be a Roman but not Jewish practice. Instead, Matthew gives attention to the question of divorce "for any cause," and he recognized "fornication" as grounds for divorce. He retains the Marcan focus upon the nonsubordinating creation narrative as well as the blending of the nonsubordinating Gen. 2:24 with it, thus supporting the oneness of husband and wife both in creation and marriage. Male bias appears in the disciples' protest that it is better not to marry than to be bound by a marriage, a Matthean addition to Mark; but the disciples' protest is discredited. Matthew has Jesus stress the high demands of the single life alongside those of the married life (Mt. 19:10–12).

Matthew amends Mark's story of the selfish request of James and John for places of honor in Jesus' Kingdom (Mk. 10:35–45), introducing the idea that it was their mother who approached Jesus with the request (Mt. 20:20–28). He does not carry through on this, for Jesus' reply was directly to James and John, "Ye do not know what ye ask . . ." (v. 22). Probably Matthew has no disposition to cast the mother in a bad light but to remove some of the offense from the apostles.

Another Matthean addition to Mark is in the story of the triumphal entry of Jesus into Jerusalem. Matthew inserts a quotation from Isaiah and Zechariah, "Say to the daughter of Zion, behold your king comes to you, meek and riding upon an ass, even upon a colt the foal of an ass" (Mt. 21:5). Jerusalem is "the daughter of Zion" or, if William F. Stinespring is correct, "Daughter Zion" (Zion as daughter).[4] In either case, neither Matthew nor his source finds it awkward to liken God's people to a daughter, whether Jerusalem be seen as "daughter of Zion" or "Daughter Zion."

Matthew adds to the Marcan story of Jesus before Pilate the attempt of Pilate's wife to dissuade him from action against Jesus. While Pilate was sitting on the judges' bench, his wife sent to him saying, "Let there be nothing between you and that righteous man, for I suffered many things this day in a dream because of him" (Mt. 27:19). Pilate is weak, allowing himself to be pressured into action he knows to be wrong; but his wife is wise and strong enough to counsel a better course for her husband. There probably here is no deliberate motive to address the issue of woman, but it clearly follows that in this passage Matthew has no prejudice against woman. Matthew's point is not to contrast male and female but good and evil.

It is precarious to compare Matthew and Mark with respect to what happened after the tomb was found open, for Mark's Gospel breaks off at Mk. 16:8. Whether there was a now lost ending which told of an appearance of Jesus to the women is not known (vs. 9–20 are spurious). What is clear is that Matthew does report that the risen Jesus appeared to Mary Magdalene and another Mary, commissioning them to take to his disciples a most important message: "Do not be afraid; go and proclaim to my brethren that they go into Galilee, and there they shall see me" (Mt. 28:10). Matthew has it, then, that the men receive instruction through women and that women saw the risen Jesus before any of the men. Again, this probably is not intentionally corrective of misogyny or the denigration of woman; but it obviously is free of any prejudice against woman, and it accords woman the highest place in the earliest proclamation of the most important tenet in the Christian faith—Jesus is alive!

Non-Marcan Material in Matthew. There is considerable material in Matthew with no parallel in Mark, some of this shared with Luke and some alone in Matthew. Of this large amount of material, a few passages have implications for the Matthean attitude toward woman. There is a marriage feast that a king made for his son, with no reference to a bride (Mt. 22:1–14). This correctly reflects the social practice of the day, and telling the story without acknowledging the male bias may be significant. Were there supporting evidence for a chauvinistic attitude in Matthew, more could be made of this passage. Probably the story simply serves its parabolic intention, reflecting actual custom, with no disposition to sanction (or judge) the social practice of the day. In another parable there are five foolish virgins; but these are matched by five wise virgins, so a case for bias cannot be made here (25:1–13).

Three non-Marcan passages in Matthew have more significance for Matthew's perspective on woman, the first being the genealogy with which he begins and the second being the virginal birth story which follows this. In both stories women are portrayed as human, with qualities good and bad, strong and weak. There is no stereotype of woman in either story. Both stories are by far more positive toward woman than negative. In the Matthean genealogy, four women besides Mary appear. This in itself is noteworthy, for Jewish genealogies were male as a glance at the "beget" chapters of the Old Testament will show. These four women (Tamar, Rahab, Ruth, and the wife of Uriah) were non-Jewish and women of sin or suffering, yet their place in this genealogy is one of honor.[5] Matthew may imply that in Christ there is place for the Gentile, the sinner, the suffering, and the disadvantaged; but he offers no explanation for their inclusion. Whatever his motive, it is positive toward these women and, apparently, toward women in general.

Like Luke, Matthew features a virginal birth story, the two being somewhat different. Matthew is positive toward Mary, although he does not eulogize her (Mt. 1:18–25). The story is concerned with the divine origin of Jesus (vs. 18–25) as well as with his human origin (vs. 1–17).

In the Matthean Sermon on the Mount there is a strong protest against the reduction of woman to a sex object (Mt. 5:27–30). True, the passage is directed against the male exploitation, exposing as de facto adultery the looking upon a woman with a view to lust. The pericope does reflect a strong sensitivity to the worth of woman. Adultery is something that can be practiced against a woman, not just against a man's property rights.

It probably would be too much to conclude that Matthew consciously sought to rectify attitudes toward woman, but it is quite convincing that his attitude was positive. Although the Gospel of Matthew probably dates from after A.D. 70, years after the status and role of woman had become a major agenda item in many churches, there is not a hint of such concerns as went into the making of the Domestic Code.

THE GOSPEL OF LUKE

Women have a prominent place in the Gospel of Luke. Featured there are Elizabeth, Mary, Anna, the widow of Serepta, the widow of Nain, a sinful woman who anointed Jesus, the many women who accompanied Jesus on his preaching missions, the woman who touched his garment, Mary and Martha, a woman whom Jesus rebuked, a crippled woman, a widow before a judge, a widow who gave two mites, some women at the burial of Jesus, and women at the open tomb. That Luke had a special interest in woman is hardly to be doubted. It does not follow that this was his overriding theme, for Luke had many strong interests; and the overriding theme of Luke-Acts seems to be the tracing of the Christian movement from its Jewish origins to its liberation from ethnic, cultural, cultic, and other restraints so that the gospel could be preached unhindered to any willing to hear it.[6] Luke had a special interest in the poor, in Samaritans, and in any who were disadvantaged. His concern for the dignity and liberation of woman seems to have been a part of a larger concern for human dignity and liberation.

Luke's Use of Mark. Luke's treatment of Marcan materials reflects little if any detectable difference in the attitudes of the two Evangelists toward women. There is no denigration of woman in either. There is no trace of misogyny on the part of any one of the

Evangelists. The Gospels do reflect the fact of discrimination against women, but such is not the perspective of the Evangelists themselves. Their most obvious insensitivity to woman is their employment of traditional, male-oriented language, as when even beatitudes are in the masculine gender.

On the negative side, Luke drops from Mark's story of the healing of Peter's mother-in-law the phrase "taking her hand" (Mk. 1:30–31; Lk. 4:38–39). This probably is merely stylistic and without motive otherwise. In Jesus' declaration of his true family as those who do God's will, Luke dropped Mark's inclusion of "my sister" along with "my mother" and "my brother" (Mk. 3:35; Lk. 8:19–21). This again may be stylistic, for only the mother and brothers were present in this scene.

Luke drops altogether Mk. 10:1–12, a passage on divorce, where Mark refers to a woman divorcing her husband, normally considered a Roman but not a Jewish practice. This passage speaks both for and against woman, recognizing her equal rights with man and also her equal guilt. Omission of the story here may have been to save space for something else, but the motive cannot be determined.

Luke retains a number of Marcan passages highly favorable to woman. He alone retains Mark's woe upon those "devouring widow's houses" despite their outward show of piety in making long prayers (Mk. 12:40; Lk. 20:47). Both Luke and Matthew retain Mark's blending of the stories of the healing of Jairus' daughter and the woman with an issue of blood (Mk. 5:21–43; Lk. 8:40–56; Mt. 9:18–26). Some stylistic agreements of Matthew and Luke against Mark (e.g., Mt. 9:20; Lk. 8:44) may reflect a non-Marcan source (Q) with the same story. No tradition or Evangelist makes Jesus a misogynist or has him denigrating woman or indifferent to her needs. This perspective attributed to Jesus is preserved at the very time the church was moving in the direction of imposing restraints upon woman's freedom (see Chapters 7 and 8).

Luke alone follows Mark in retaining the beautiful story of the widow's giving of her two mites (Mk. 12:41–44; Lk. 21:1–4). The high praise is for sacrificial giving, the giving of oneself in giving one's very livelihood; but it is a woman who is singled out for such high praise. The story reflects not only Jesus' deep feeling for this widow but also the faithfulness of Mark and Luke in preserving this perspective at a time when widows did not always fare too well even within the church. Both Luke and Matthew retain Mark's report of Jesus' recognition of the special hardships borne by women in times of war, as he pictures in the terrible days ahead the flight of the pregnant and those nursing babies (Mk. 13:17; Lk. 21:23; Mt. 24:19).

Luke omits the Marcan story of the anointing of Jesus by an unnamed woman in Bethany (Lk. 14:3–9), but he has a similar story and one even more significant in relationship with woman (7:36–50). The story in Luke and one in John 12:1–8 may be variants of the Marcan (and Matthean) story. Either Luke has opted for another version of the Marcan story (which he knew) or he has selected a similar but different story. The woman whom Luke describes as having anointed Jesus was known as a "sinner" (v. 37). The Lucan story shows the sympathy and respect Jesus had for woman and also for a sinner who is open to help and grateful for it. Here a sinful woman is praised above a self-righteous Pharisee. The story (or stories) preserved in various forms in the Gospels reflects nothing of the reduction of woman to a subordinate status as seen in the later Pauline literature and in the Domestic Code. Again, the Gospels are later in formation than letters in the Pauline tradition, but they preserve a more primitive Christian perspective on woman. Luke himself does not subordinate woman, and none of the four Gospels ascribes to Jesus perspectives or courses already adopted in churches when these Gospels were written.

All four Gospels relate Peter's failure at the trial of Jesus, and each reports that a maiden was instrumental in compelling Peter to take some public stand with respect to Jesus. In the well-known story Luke adds a touch that may be simply stylistic or a deliberate accentuation of the fact that it was before a woman that Peter was humbled: "I do not know him, woman!" (Lk. 22:57). Here again, in Gospels formulated years after certain churches already had worked out subordinating formulas for women in the church, Jesus is denied by the leader of the apostles, and a woman's word is exhibited as true alongside an apostle's word exposed as false. All

four Gospels give women an extremely important place in the story
of the death, burial, and resurrection of Jesus. Women come out
far better than men in the story. There is no record that any woman
sought the death of Jesus. In each of the Gospels women stand by
as Jesus hung on the cross; they were attentive to the tomb, being
last there on the evening of his burial and first there on the morning
of his resurrection. Some are named and some were designated as
those having followed him to Jerusalem from Galilee. Luke does
not heighten the role of women over Mark's account unless it is in
his having the women speak directly to the apostles, giving them
the risen Lord's message which had been communicated to them
by two messengers (angelic) at the open tomb (Lk. 24:1–10). The
men, by contrast, are presented as disbelieving long after the
women are convinced that Jesus was alive (vs. 11, 22–24, 36–42).

Non-Marcan Material in Luke. Like Matthew, Luke has a
wealth of enriching material beyond that derived from Mark. Some
of this non-Marcan material is shared with Matthew, but much of
it is Luke's alone. Included are passages that clearly reflect a
positive view of woman. The first two chapters of Luke reflect the
deep piety of Judaism and the early church, and women are as
prominent in this piety as men. Stories about a widow of Nain, the
great love of a woman who knew herself forgiven, Mary's choice
of "the better part," the healing of the crippled woman, a woman
sweeping the house for a lost coin, and a widow pleading her case
before an unjust judge are some of the Lucan stories found nowhere
else.

Luke opens his Gospel with materials not found elsewhere. His
stylistically beautiful preface (Lk. 1:1–4) does not anticipate the
prominence he gives women in Luke-Acts, for it is exclusively
male.

Elizabeth is introduced with Zechariah. He is of the priestly
order of Abijah, but she is of the "daughters of Aaron." As to piety,
"both were righteous before God" (Lk. 1:6). Being childless had
been her "shame among men" (v. 25). The "shame" or "reproach"
always fell upon the wife, not the husband, when the marriage was
childless. Some manuscripts ascribe the Magnificat (vs. 46–55) to

Elizabeth, though most attribute it to Mary. Whichever, it is to a woman that this beautiful song of praise is ascribed. There is not in the hymnody of the church a song more beautiful or theologically profound than this which Luke ascribes to a woman, whether Mary or Elizabeth. There is not in this Gospel the slightest hesitation to accord to a woman so high a place in the articulation of the faith and worship of the people of God. Of lesser note, even in the naming of the forerunner to Jesus, a woman is the speaker (vs. 57–66). Of course, Zechariah was speechless at the time; but when he regained his voice, he simply confirmed that Elizabeth was right when she corrected those who assumed that the baby would bear the name of his father, saying: "He shall be called John."

What is known as the "virgin birth" is that, but probably Luke's real concern is with the "miraculous conception" or the divine origin of Jesus. Better yet, the story stresses the divine gift. When told that she would bear a son, Mary's question was, "How shall this be, since I do not know a man?" (Lk. 1:34). The answer came back, "With God nothing is impossible" (v. 37). Mary could not of herself produce a son, but God was able to give her one. Mary is not worshiped or adored in the Gospel of Luke, but she is esteemed and respected. She receives gentler treatment than Zechariah for a similar offense. When promised a son, Zechariah asked, "How shall I know this?" (v. 18). Gabriel informed Zechariah that he would be speechless until the fulfillment of the promise, "because you did not believe my words" (v. 20). When Mary asked her question, she was given further assurance and explanation. Unless deference itself is here a form of discrimination, the mother of Jesus fared better than the father of John the Baptist.

Among the people of piety featured by Luke was the prophetess Anna (Lk. 2:36–38). She was a widow, either eighty-four years of age or widowed for eighty-four years. She had spent her life at the Temple, worshiping through fastings and prayers day and night. She was there when Jesus was presented in the Temple, and "she spoke concerning him to all those awaiting the redemption of Jerusalem." Anna engaged in a form of preaching. In this she stood in an ancient tradition in Israel; for though women were excluded from the priesthood, many did participate in the ministry of the word. Luke knows this tradition and reports it in both his volumes as continuing in the early church.

Luke alone reports on the boyhood of Jesus, describing a visit he made to the Temple at age twelve (Lk. 2:41–52). Reference is made to "his parents" (v. 41) and to his "father" (v. 48), but the story centers in Jesus and his mother. In this story Mary overshadows her husband, speaking for him as well as herself. The twelve-year-old son stood his ground, respectfully but firmly, as he reminded his mother of a higher claim that he must answer (v. 49). The story maintains a careful balance between the claims of the individual and the family, the claims of parent and child, the claims of human parents and the ultimate claims of the heavenly Father. There are no rules such as were developed in the Domestic Code; there is the principle of freedom and responsibility in their ongoing tension.

There is not a woman in the Lucan genealogy (Lk. 3:23–38). In this respect it is traditional. This taken alone might imply male bias on the part of Luke. Of course, it is a male bias that ancient genealogies were male; and it may reflect some insensitivity on Luke's part that he has not modified this pattern. Evidence of Luke's positive attitude toward woman is so strong elsewhere, that caution may be exercised here. Luke's likely motive in his version of the genealogy of Jesus is to stress the universal, tracing Jesus' human origin to Adam, the head of the human race.

There is hardly a more touching story than that of the raising of the widow's son at Nain (Lk. 7:11–17). The story itself is moving, but Luke's manner of narrating it must say something for his own understanding of Jesus and for his sensitivity to the plight of a woman who has lost both her husband and her only son. After his reference to the great crowd around Jesus, Luke introduces the woman, carefully bringing out the pathos of her situation. As Jesus was approaching the gate of the city, "Behold, there was being borne out one who had died, an only son to his mother, and she was a widow." Luke brings it out that in all that crowd, Jesus had eyes for one in particular, the bereaved woman: "The Lord seeing her was moved with compassion for her and he said to her, Stop weeping." Jesus then "touched the bier" (v. 14). He touched what was considered most defiling of all by cultic standards of holiness. After reviving the son, "He gave him to his mother" (v. 15). The compassion of Jesus for the woman is explicit; that of Luke is apparent in the tender manner in which he tells the story. This is far removed from the misogyny of many cited earlier in our study, from the arbitrary "logic" of Plato and Philo, from the buffoonery of Semonides and others who made their little jokes, and even from the codes concerned with special restrictions upon woman. Both Jesus and Luke belonged to another world.

We have seen already that though Luke dropped Mark's story of an anointing of Jesus by a woman in Bethany (Mk. 14:3–9), he more than compensates by including one not found elsewhere, the story of a sinful woman who anointed Jesus and whose grateful love was held up as exemplary of the piety which excels that of the Pharisee who could not conceal his contempt for Jesus for letting himself be touched by this "manner of a woman" one who "is a sinner" (Lk. 7:36–49). Luke feels secure in describing a Savior unafraid to be touched by this woman. He is comfortable in presenting her as embodying genuine faith, love, and piety.

Luke alone preserves the pericope that tells of the important role played by women during the ministry of Jesus (Lk. 8:1–3). True it is that this datum comes out in the Marcan passion narrative, followed there by both Matthew and Luke (Mk. 15:43); but only Luke features it in the body of his narrative of the ministry of Jesus. He names Mary Magdalene, Joanna, the wife of Chuza, Herod's steward, and Susanna, adding "and many others." Luke alone specifies that they ministered to Jesus and the Twelve "out of their possessions" (Lk. 8:3). They helped finance the mission of Jesus and the Twelve, but this does not imply that their ministry was limited to this.

Mary and Martha are prominent otherwise, but only Luke tells about the tension that arose between them in the presence of Jesus (Lk. 10:38–42). The primary intention of the story is to point to the priority of "the word" over a meal. Martha's was a proper role, but Mary had chosen the better part in giving priority to "hearing his word."

Another story unique to Luke is that of a woman whom Jesus found "bent over and not able to stand up at all" (Lk. 13:10–17). Luke brings out the pathos of the woman's impairment, for she had been in that condition for "eighteen years." Luke tells the story in such a masterful way that he brings out not only her burden and Jesus' tender compassion but also the sharp contrast between religious people who cared more for the Sabbath Day than for a woman's condition and Jesus' willingness to override any cultic value, here the Sabbath, in favor of human need.

Luke 15 comes close to being Luke's Gospel in brief. It proclaims God's joy over the recovery of any one sinner who was lost. Luke develops this through three powerful parables: a shepherd who recovered a lost sheep, a woman who recovered a lost coin, and a father who recovered a lost son. Although the third of these parables is obviously the climactic one, with the prodigal son and his elder brother typifying respectively the "tax gatherers and sinners," with whom Jesus had the habit of eating, and the "Pharisees and their scribes," who rebuked Jesus for doing it (Lk. 15:1f.), the other two parables are given status alongside this great one. Luke does not hesitate to liken God's joy to that of the woman any more than to that of the shepherd or the father.

A final Lucan distinctive is the parable of a widow pleading her case before a harsh judge (Lk. 18:1–8). Her case seemed to be hopeless, but she pressed it until she prevailed. This woman serves as a model in the faith which endures under seemingly hopeless odds. Luke alone ascribes to Jesus this story making exemplary the strength and courage of a woman.

THE BOOK OF ACTS

Known in early manuscripts as "Acts" or "Acts of [the] Apostles," this book is addressed to "Theophilus" and looks back upon "the first book" which the author made, almost certainly the Gospel of Luke. Jesus is the continuing theme, with special attention to that impulse which began with him in the heart of Jewish piety and reached within a few decades into the heart of the larger world, crossing geographical, ethnic, and cultic lines in the process. What was at stake was the worth of every person over the provincialism and exclusiveness which tends to warp culture and even religion. Acts ends with its final word in the Greek text shouting its victory, "unhindered!"[7]

Women have some prominence in Acts, but they are less prominent there than in the Gospel of Luke. It is hard to escape the conclusion that Jesus' followers gave less room to women than did Jesus. But what about Luke? Since he authored both books, an even hand might be expected from him. This is complicated by the fact that he used sources, and faithfulness to these sources in the Gospel and Acts could somewhat override Luke's own feelings. Also, the situations and movements that Luke describes in the two volumes had their own character and tone, leaving their marks on the final product. These factors do not account fully for the final effect, for Luke did exercise options in selection of materials, in his arrangements, and to some extent in style.

Acts is more male-oriented than the Gospel of Luke. The terms "men," "brothers," "fathers," dominate even in situations where there must have been the presence of women. Instances throughout Acts are almost too numerous to require listing. Although in the Gospel those who stood by most faithfully at the cross and at the tomb were women, in Acts at the ascension of Jesus the "two men dressed in white" (angels?) address men: "Men of Galilee . . ." (Acts 1:11). That there were women among the believers remaining in Jerusalem is explicit: "All these were continuing steadfastly with one accord in prayer with the women and Mary the mother of Jesus and his brothers" (v. 14). Those Jews dwelling in Jerusalem were "godly men" (2:5). When Peter addressed the people on the Day of Pentecost, they were "Men, Jews, and all those dwelling [masculine] in Jerusalem" (v. 14). The Scripture which he quoted to interpret the outpouring of the Spirit upon the disciples included women with men in the reception of the Spirit and in preaching:

> And it shall be in the last days, says God, I shall pour out from my Spirit upon all flesh, and your sons and your daughters will prophesy, and your young men shall see visions and your old men shall dream dreams, and upon my manservants and upon my maidservants in those

days shall I pour out from my Spirit, and they shall prophesy. (Acts 2:17f. Cf. Joel 2:28–32)

The text from Joel quoted by Peter gives equal place to women with men, but the sermon on Pentecost is formally addressed to men only: "Men, Israelites" (Acts 2:22); "Men, brothers" (v. 29); "Men, brothers" (v. 37). A subsequent sermon at the Temple is addressed to "Men, Israelites" (3:12) and "brothers" (v. 17). The same pattern is ascribed to Paul (13:16, 26; 15:36; 17:22; 22:1).

The male orientation of the church surfaces at key points. When the one hundred and twenty were called upon to seek out a successor to Judas, they not only were addressed as "men, brothers" (Acts 1:16); but the replacement must be from among "the men" who had accompanied Jesus from his baptism to his resurrection (vs. 21f.). Possibly no women were in the following from the very first; but some were prominent in his service in Galilee (Lk. 8:1–3; 23:49) and were at the cross and open tomb. There were women who could have witnessed to the resurrection. When a committee was chosen to administer the fund for widows, only men were considered (Acts 6:3). There was no shortage of women believers (5:14). Later, women had suffered along with men under the persecutions of Saul of Tarsus (8:3). A woman like Dorcas may have added perspective and expertise to a committee responsible for caring for widows. Dorcas apparently served as an unofficial committee of one in Joppa, and at her death "all the widows" crowded around Peter to show him the clothing Dorcas had made for them (9:39).

The conference in Jerusalem called to settle the question of requirements for Gentile converts was male-oriented. The big issue was circumcision, and that itself was an initiation rite pertaining only to men. There was a form of circumcision for women in some pagan cultures, but there is no trace of it in Judaism or the early church. The assembled church in Jerusalem was addressed as "brothers" (Acts 15:13), and so was the letter sent from the conference to the Gentile churches: "The apostles and the elders, brothers, to all the brothers among the Gentiles in Antioch, Syria, and Cilicia, greetings" (v. 23). Even Paul's proposal to Barnabas was worded with a male bias: "Returning, let us visit the brothers in each of the cities in which we preached the word of the Lord, to see how they are" (v. 36). This may be traditional language, and clearly women were present among groups termed "brothers"; but the male bias in the language was not overcome. Was this Luke's insensitivity? What we saw in his Gospel makes this difficult to believe. Was he faithful to his sources and to the tone of the movement he traces? Possibly something of all this is true.

Although women may be slighted in the male character of much of the language employed in Acts and in the procedures of the church, that is the extent of any bias. There is nothing in Acts which intends to put women down. There is not a trace of misogyny or of intentional denigration of woman. On the other hand, there is much which is positive; although it may not come up to the high standard of materials closer to Jesus. Acts may well show that Jesus' followers are at best just that, followers who rarely if ever really keep up with him.

The first woman to be singled out for prominence in Acts is Sapphira, and she came under the heaviest of censure (Acts 5: 1–11). There is not a hint that her failings were due to her being a woman. All her faults are present in her husband, Ananias; and Acts knows other women who are exemplary at the very points where Sapphira failed. It is significant that in Acts women can be painted as good or bad, sacrificial or self-serving, strong or weak. That Sapphira is in the story along with Dorcas and Lydia not only adds to the credibility of Acts but speaks for its disposition to represent people as people and not in stereotypes.

Acts reflects a deep concern for widows. The discrimination alleged in Acts 6:1 was not against widows as such but against Greek-speaking Jewish Christians. There is nothing about an official roll for widows with age and other requirements such as were worked out in the Domestic Code (cf. 1 Tim. 5:9f.). Apparently need was the criterion. There is no exclusion of "younger widows" with the admonition that they marry (vs. 11–15). The situation in Acts seems to be more primitive and less structured than that reflected in the Domestic Code. In Joppa the only ministry to widows described was spontaneous and unofficial.

Acts makes allusion to a number of women, some distinguished, who were believers (Acts 17:4, 12). In Antioch of Pisidia there were some "devout women of high standing" whom the opponents of Paul and Barnabas succeeded in stirring up against the apostles (13:50). There is no implication that these women were more vulnerable to such manipulation than men, for "leading men" were likewise enlisted in driving the apostles out of town. Among the most notable Christian women in Acts is Lydia, a merchant from Thyatira whom Paul and his companions met in Philippi (16: 11–15). She already was one who "worshiped God" and was in a Jewish place of prayer on the Sabbath Day when Paul found her. Apparently, there was no Jewish synagogue in the Roman colony of Philippi, but some women met for prayer on the Sabbath. Upon becoming a Christian, Lydia opened her home to the missionaries, persuading them to accept her hospitality. Luke no doubt sees her as a major force in laying the foundations for the church in Philippi.

In another vein, Luke tells the story of "a slave girl" in Philippi whom certain men were exploiting for financial gain (Acts 16: 16–24). The story is made incidental to a larger story of the arrest and deliverance of the missionaries and the conversion of a Philippian jailer, but Luke so tells the story that the reader's sympathies are with the girl. Those who exploited her are the villains, and they are men.

Priscilla is prominent in Acts (18:2, 26) as in the Pauline epistles (1 Cor. 16:19; Rom. 16:3; 2 Tim. 4:19). Aquila and his wife Priscilla are first introduced in terms of his birth in Pontus and their being forced out of Italy along with other Jews because of an expulsion edict by the Emperor Claudius. Significantly, they become "Priscilla and Aquila" when they meet Apollos, a Jew come from Alexandria to Ephesus and a Christian. Apollos is described as "an eloquent speaker" with a "thorough knowledge of the Scriptures" and one who had been "instructed in the way of the Lord" and who taught with great "enthusiasm" (Acts 18:24–26). For all this, Apollos yet required help. When Priscilla and Aquila heard him, they "took him to themselves and set forth to teach him more accurately the way of God" (v. 26). With no sense of embarrassment or its being an impropriety, Luke tells about a woman instructing a man in theology. Apollos was no ordinary man. Luke first gave him a major buildup. He was a gifted and experienced teacher/preacher of the gospel to whom Priscilla and Aquila gave a "postgraduate" course of study. There is no hint here or elsewhere in Acts that a woman should be subordinate, be silent, and not teach a man. Either Luke is free of any disposition to deny woman a ministry of the word, or he is so honest with his sources and the situation he describes that his own feelings are submerged.

Artemis was the goddess of Ephesus and was worshiped in the Roman province of Asia and in "all the world" (Acts 19:24–27). Luke gives extended coverage to a crisis situation that developed in Ephesus related to Artemis. There is no hint that Artemis was condemned by Christian conscience because she was a female deity; it was because she was seen as false and because of the idolatry connected with her.

In an almost incidental way, Luke mentions four single daughters of Philip the evangelist and identifies them as "prophesying" (Acts 21:9). The term employed for these women is one for preaching. Some scholars see "prophecy" to be a special form of preaching, but it is preaching nonetheless. This datum is given as a part of the larger story of Paul's last-recorded visit to Jerusalem. The passing reference is tantalizing. How many other women of the time were preachers? Luke shows no interest in pursuing this subject. He refers to the vocation of these four single women without sense of embarrassment or the need to explain, as though this was so accepted that it called for no apology.

The last women to be named in Acts are Drusilla, Jewish wife of the Roman governor Felix (Acts 24:24), and Bernice, sister to Drusilla and King Herod Agrippa II (25:13, 23). Were Luke a misogynist or chauvinist, he could have a field day here with these two sisters, for in character and record they were open to scorn. Bernice, especially, was vulnerable to barbs. She had been married and divorced several times, and she was now living with her brother, rumors being that they were living in incest. Luke has nothing to say of all this. Any implication of censure of these women is not because they are women but because they are allied with Felix and Agrippa, before whom Paul was made to appear in chains.

What, then, may we conclude from Acts? There is a heavy use of traditional language that bears a male bias. Whether traceable to Luke himself or his sources is difficult to determine. There is no trace of conscious or intended denigration of woman. There are indications that already there are patterns in the church which in later development come to expression in the Domestic Code, but there also is abundant freedom to women for ministries of various kinds, including teaching and preaching. Acts is free of stereotype, there being no implication that qualities of character follow sexual lines. Qualities of goodness and evil, strength and weakness, courage and fear belong to human existence with no bias for one sex or the other. Luke himself seems to be positive in his attitude toward woman, but in Acts this is not an issue as such.

SUMMARY

The Synoptic Gospels and Acts take us at least to around A.D. 60, the time of Paul's arrival in Rome. Few scholars would date any of these writings so early. A more likely span is from around A.D. 65 for Mark to a decade or two beyond that for Matthew and Luke, with Acts somewhat later than Luke. Compared with 1 Corinthians and the five letters containing the Domestic Code (Colossians, Ephesians, 1 Peter, Titus, and 1 Timothy) woman's status as reflected in the Synoptics and Acts is amazingly free. There is no discernible disposition to place limits upon women. There are reflections of the bias of traditional language, and traditional roles play some part. There is no reference to the rib narrative of creation. There is no suggestion that woman is to be subordinate to man. The apostles, the Seven in Acts, and official leaders generally are male. On the other hand, there is no exclusion of women from teaching or preaching; there is rather an affirmation of woman's right to the study of the word and the ministry of the word. Homemaking is normative for woman, but there is no restriction of woman to this vocation. There is no hint that she is to be silent in church, and there are no directives as to her cosmetics or wardrobe.

That in the Synoptic Gospels woman occupies such a place of dignity and freedom is probably to be attributed to the Gospels' fidelity to Jesus. The view that the Gospels tell us much about the church but little about Jesus is a dogma that has little in its support. For all the freedom exercised by the Evangelists and their sources, they apparently do retain an authentic picture of Jesus. Nothing that already has developed in the churches leading to various codes for conduct obscures the strong lines that belong to Jesus of Nazareth, liberator of the human being, and in particular liberator of woman. The Evangelists not only preserve Jesus' perspective on woman, but they seem to be comfortable with it.

Acts intends to describe the church beyond the ministry of Jesus and does so. Certain patterns already affect woman's roles within the church, but there is in Acts nothing approaching the Domestic Code. Either our dating of New Testament writings is out of order or Acts discloses the fact that the restraints imposed upon woman in the Pauline tradition were not universally applied in the churches. Luke-Acts is seemingly beyond 1 Corinthians in date, to go no farther, and restrictions upon woman explicit in this letter are unknown to Luke-Acts.

Chapter 10

WOMAN IN THE JOHANNINE WRITINGS

Five writings in the New Testament are commonly ascribed to John, brother of James and son of Zebedee. Authorship of these writings has been disputed from as early as the second century, and the debate continues unabated. More secure by far than the question of authorship are the affinities among these writings, justifying their consideration as a "Johannine corpus." Differences are there, too, in style as well as perspective, between the Gospel of John and the Revelation to John. Dionysius of Alexandria about the middle of the third century assigned these writings to two different men named John, John the Elder of Ephesus and John the Apostle, even though the historicity of "John the Elder" remains unestablished.[1] More recently it has been argued that the Gospel and the letters come from different authors, the Johannine letters coming from the "Presbyter" of Asia around A.D. 96–110.[2] A credible case can be made for a "School of John," a group of followers of the apostle John (cf. Jn. 21:24; 1 Jn. 5:18, 19), from whom came these writings which are both alike and unalike.[3]

No attempt is made here to resolve the centuries' old problem of the authorship of these writings. Because they are customarily grouped and because of their affinities along with their differences, these five writings will be the base for this chapter. All five are generally considered to be as late as the closing decade of the first century, some scholars putting them earlier and some later; and this makes them significant to our study. If indeed this late, they represent a period decades later than 1 Corinthians and later than at least most of the letters containing the Domestic Code. Also, they belong to a community or situation considerably unlike that of the Synoptic Gospels and Acts. These Johannine writings, as will be seen, seem to be as free of any disposition to make a special class of women and the imposition of restraints upon their freedom as are the Synoptics and Acts. If true, this does add up to a significant picture: traditions as distinct as the Synoptics and the Johannine corpus, both later in formation than at least some of the letters in the Pauline tradition, are free of the restraints upon women made explicit and formal in the Domestic Code.

THE GOSPEL OF JOHN

One will look in vain in the Fourth Gospel for a single trace of any disposition to make a special class of women or to formulate rules designed for women only. There is no hint of a dress code for women or ground rules governing their speech. There is no reminder of Eve's subordination to Adam or of her vulnerability to deception. There is a special group of disciples known as "the twelve" (Jn. 6:67–71; 20:24), and these are male. Except for the Twelve, who did occupy a unique place in the following of Jesus, there are no class distinctions among those around Jesus. Some of his closest companions were women. The Evangelist's own attitude is positive, with no hint of inferiority, weakness, or fixed status dictated by creation, nature, the Fall, or custom. Issues prominent in the Pauline tradition as they relate to women are unnoticed in the Gospel of John.

The great passages in the Gospel of John featuring women have been examined at close range in Part II, and that need not be repeated here. To assess the Evangelist's perspective on woman or that of his traditions and community, we need only to see the overall picture. As significant as what is not there, as observed above, is the cumulative force of the stories featuring the woman of Samaria (Jn. 4); Mary and Martha at the death of their brother (ch. 11); an anointing of Jesus by Mary (ch. 12); the women at the cross (ch. 19); and above all, the primacy of Mary Magdalene in the appearances of the risen Jesus (ch. 20). The author is explicit in affirming the selective principle which he followed, having known far more than he included (20:30f.; 21:25). Since by his own

statement much was left out, what he included must have had for
him primary significance. Although the intention of this Gospel is
to tell us about Jesus, it must also tell us much about the author
and the traditions upon which he drew.

In the first Cana miracle (Jn. 2:1–11) John does not blunt the
seemingly curt reply of Jesus to his mother: "What to me and to
you, woman; not yet has my hour come" (v. 4). He reports the
same distance between Jesus and his brothers over the same issue
of his "hour" (v.4) or "kairos," i.e., his "time" (7:6). John is harder
on the brothers, "Not even his brothers believed on him" (v.5).
Either he shows some deference to Jesus' mother, or the distance
between Jesus and his mother was actually less than that between
Jesus and his brothers. Probably the latter is the case, and John is
painting the picture as it actually is, not even applying to Mary the
inverted discrimination of deference. He does report that after the
Cana wedding, where there is some tension between Jesus and
Mary, Jesus went down to Capernaum and remained there many
days with his mother, brothers, and disciples (2:12). However, at
the cross Mary was present but the brothers were not (19:25–27).
John seems to imply in his Gospel that Mary did not really understand her son, yet her love for him and faithfulness to him never
wavered. Jesus refused to let Mary determine his course, yet he
affirmed her in her own right from first to last. From the cross he
made provision for her, giving her to the care of "the disciple whom
he loved" (vs. 26f.). His brothers in the flesh were not there; but
for Jesus a "soul brother" was there who could be a "son" to Mary
and Mary a "mother" to him.

Assuming the historicity of these stories, they tell much about
Jesus. The very telling of the stories and the way they are told show
us much about John and/or the tradition upon which he draws.
Somewhere in the Christian community there was a sensitivity
toward woman which could be both respectful and honest, devoted
but not patronizing. There is here not a trace of overt chauvinism.
There are traces of the heavy hand of male orientation which
plagues most of us even when we purpose to have nothing of it, in
language itself, if not otherwise. Such traces are found in John. A
case in point is the charge: "Not even his brothers believed in him"

(Jn. 7:5). What about the sisters? Although attested in the Synoptics, there is no mention in John of sisters in the family of Jesus. John mentions that a sister to Jesus' mother was at the cross (19:25), but sisters to Jesus are unknown or unacknowledged. Like Mark and Luke, John reports that Jesus fed five thousand adult males, only Matthew having remembered that there were women and children there, too. These are negative factors, not without significance; but they do not approach the deliberate and overt means employed elsewhere in subjugating woman to man.

As seen in Part II, the encounter of Jesus with a woman of Samaria (Jn. 4:1–42) puts beyond any doubt his radical rejection of established patterns of discrimination, including that against woman. The way the story is told reflects the sympathetic stance of the narrator. The story is told with a keen sense for the dramatic, with careful attention to tension, suspense, and surprise. Jesus went through Samaria, crashing through conventional barriers of various sorts; but it is John who holds this up as a moral necessity (v. 4). Jesus did some astonishing things, but it is the Evangelist, or his source, who makes the point: "And at this point his disciples came, and they were marveling that he was talking with a woman" (v. 27). The story is about Jesus primarily, but John is the one who concludes the long story by observing that it was "because of the word of the woman" that many of these Samaritans believed on Jesus (v. 39). Even though John's very last remark in the long story is to the effect that having heard Jesus directly for themselves the villagers no longer are dependent upon her word, it is acknowledged that they were dependent upon her at the first (v. 42). With dramatic skill, the storyteller moves the Samaritan woman from a very shady character to one of great stature. Next to Jesus, she dominates the story. Whoever composed this narrative appears to be free of any cultural or theological hang-up that is uncomfortable with having a woman become a foremost "minister of the word." The community out of which and to which this Gospel was addressed was evidently expected to be receptive to this perspective.

Not to be pressed, but in the same vein as the above, is John's reference to "the parents" in the story of the healing of a man born blind (Jn. 9). At one point, Jesus' critics tried to discredit him by denying the miracle outright. They called in "the parents" of the man and asked them to testify to the facts in the case (vs. 18–23). A woman's witness was not normally accredited in Jewish circles. In this story no priority is given to either parent; the terms "father" and "mother" are not employed. Four times in six verses "the parents" are mentioned; and the testimony is "theirs," not "his" or "hers." This stylistic detail may be without significance; but if it implies anything, it is on the side of a positive attitude toward woman.

John's seventh sign, the raising of Lazarus (Jn. 11), is the climax to the first part of the book, "the Book of Signs"[4]; and the heart of its message clearly is in the claim of Jesus, "I am the resurrection and the life" (v. 25). In brief, the story can be told in a sentence: Jesus raised Lazarus. But John gives great prominence to Mary and Martha throughout the story. Jesus dominates the story, but otherwise the sisters command the center of the stage. The locale is "the city of Mary and Martha" (v. 1). Lazarus is identified in terms of his sisters, more notable than he. A subsequent story of Mary's anointing of Jesus (ch. 12) is anticipated in a way that implies that the readers are expected already to know about Mary (11:2). One of the most surprising lines is that immediately following the raising and unbinding of Lazarus: "Many of the Jews therefore, those having come to Mary and having seen what things he did [grammatically, it could be "what things she did"], believed on him" (v. 45). This does not ascribe to Mary the direct role of evangelist ascribed to the woman of Samaria, but it at least couples her name directly with the conversion of many of the Jews to Jesus. This may not be the intention of the verse, but its author apparently is not afraid of that implication.

John 12:1–8 parallels Mk. 14:3–9 (Mt. 26:6–13) in the story of an anointing of Jesus in Bethany. In Mark and Matthew the woman is anonymous, but in John it is Mary who anoints Jesus. It is not likely that John followed Mark as a source, but there are some striking parallels, one being their almost verbatim agreement in Jesus' defense of his benefactor against attack: "Let her alone" (Jn. 12:7; Mk. 14:6). The only difference is in number, "ye" in Mark and "you" (sing.) in John. The phraseology apparently belongs to the tradition and not to the Evangelist.

If anything, John heightens the role of women at the death and resurrection of Jesus (Jn. 19:25–27; 20:1–18). Not at a distance, but alongside the cross were his mother, his mother's sister, and Mary Magdalene (punctuation makes it uncertain whether there were three or four women there, whether "Mary the wife of Clopas" is also "his mother's sister" or not). The "disciple whom Jesus loved" was there near Jesus' mother (19:26), but otherwise the male following was absent. John's highest tribute to a woman comes in the climactic chapter of his whole Gospel, where Mary Magdalene shares much of the stage with the risen Lord (20:1–18). Her single-hearted devotion even when it appeared that all was lost is portrayed in her manner and words. John tells the story primarily to proclaim the central fact that Jesus is alive; but the story is told in such a way that the reader identifies with Mary and has a warm feeling toward her. To top it all, John has her stand before the disciples before any one of them had seen Jesus and say to them, "I have seen the Lord!" (v. 18). This woman was the bearer of the risen Lord's most important message to the men nearest Jesus.

We are not overlooking the story of the adulterous woman brought to Jesus. Although appearing in the Gospel of John in many Bibles, this story is not original to John or Luke, although it appears at different places in each of these Gospels in some manuscripts. Whatever the origin of the story, it represents both the double standard of men traditionally and Jesus' exposure of this sham along with his redemptiveness toward sinners. The story reflects the positive stance toward woman for whoever may have formulated it or preserved it.

THE FIRST LETTER OF JOHN

This letter is a favorite with many because of its forceful teaching on love. It likewise has probably the clearest exposition of *koinōnia* in the New Testament. Amazingly, there is no reference to woman in the letter (no persons are named). There is not one unambiguous reference to a mother, wife, sister, or daughter.

If our count is correct, there are 89 Greek terms in 1 John which are masculine in gender and which unambiguously refer to males (excluding reference to deity). These terms include nouns, pronouns, adjectives, and participles. Brothers, singular or plural, are addressed or alluded to 12 times, fathers twice, young men twice, and "beloved ones" five times. The readers are addressed as "children" 13 times, but the Greek terms are neuter in grammatical gender, applicable to male or female. Since there are in the letter no unambiguously female references, it is likely that the "children" are perceived as masculine.

Participles abound in 1 John as designations of various ones, good and bad. By our count, there are 41 such participles appearing in the masculine gender (counting only those unambiguously masculine). All are male: the one saying, the one keeping, the one loving, the one hating, the one doing, the one denying, the one confessing, the one straying, the one having, the one abiding, the one having been begotten, the one sinning, the one fearing, the one believing, the one conquering. The good and bad are male.

John warns about "many false prophets" (1 Jn. 4:1), all of whom are masculine. The "murderer" is masculine (3:15). "The liar" is male (2:22; 4:20). There is not just one "antichrist" but rather there are many "antichrists" (2:18, 22; 4:3), all masculine. On the other hand, "the righteous one" too is masculine (3:7). Good and evil for the writer do not follow sexual lines, for both kinds are masculine.

What is to be made of this massive array of masculine references in this letter? Probably much may be ascribed to traditional language, where a term in one gender intends to include both sexes. If so, the language itself is heavily biased, and its bias is not overcome in this letter. But more than this appears. Terms like "fathers" and "young men" with no reference to "mothers" or "young women" reflect more than the bias of traditional language. The writer does seem to think in terms of a male audience or readership. This is especially true in a carefully composed, poetic address:

I write to you, children,
    because sins have been forgiven you because of his name.
I write to you, fathers,
    because ye know the one from the beginning.

> I write to you, young men,
>> because ye have conquered the evil one.
> I wrote to you, children,
>> because ye know the Father.
> I wrote to you, fathers,
>> because ye know the ones from the beginning.
> I wrote to you, young men,
>> because ye are strong
>> and the word of God abides in you
>> and ye have conquered the evil one.
>
>> (1 Jn. 2:12–14)

The male orientation here is impossible to escape, even though the word for "children" *(teknia)* is of neuter gender. This poem, along with the addresses as "beloved ones" (masculine) in 2:7; 3:21; 4:1, 7, 11, takes us into a male world.

It does not follow that the writer is intentionally or consciously biased toward males. There is no overt discrimination against women. There is no implication that evil begins with women. The problem is that women are left out completely, so far as explicit mention is concerned. Here probably is a classic case of male bias so deeply ingrained in culture that it lives on with no conscious motive. What is not apparent is the "prophetic" stance of one like Jesus who constantly moved against ingrained bias. We have seen in Chapter 2 that Jesus, too, employed male-oriented language, or he is so represented (he himself wrote nothing); but on every hand in the manner and teaching of Jesus are his radical protests against discrimination. It is not just male-oriented language which is to be considered; with it are to be sought the presence or absence of compensating factors.

First John seems to have had as one of its primary tasks the refutation of a gnosticizing tendency in which one claimed sinless perfection yet lived on in sin. John denied outright the theory of some that they were above sin (1 Jn. 1:8, 10). He exposed the sinful practices of these pseudo-spirituals, protesting that sin does not go on unchecked in one abiding in Christ (3:6, 9). These and other difficult problems clearly are the primary concerns of the author. His concern is not with equity between men and women. This to some extent may account for inattention to women.

First John is anonymous, but it has never belonged other than to the Johannine tradition. Its date and place of writing are unknown. It is generally considered to have originated around the end of the first century, probably in the East.[5]

THE SECOND LETTER OF JOHN

This letter is anonymous, but the writer does identify himself as "the elder." Attention to the test of love and warning as to "the antichrist" are marks of affinity with 1 John. The threat of apostasy, actually separating from the writer's community, is explicit in both letters. Both letters warn against false teachings, and both stress that which is "from the beginning." Both see truth as something to do or in which to walk, not just something to believe. Both seem to resist a Docetic or a Gnostic threat. Both affirm the humanity as well as the deity of Christ, one "come in the flesh." The two letters, then, at least seem to represent the same basic Christian tradition.

Unlike 1 John, this letter does have a feminine reference. The letter is addressed to "the elect lady and her children" (2 Jn. 1, 5). The "elect lady" seems to be the church and "her children," the individual members. The grammatical gender of "children" is neuter, but the church is perceived here as womanly. The church is not explicitly the "bride" of Christ here, but that idea may be in mind, just as it is implied but not explicit in Eph. 5:22–33. In Rev. 21:9 the "New Jerusalem" is explicitly "the bride, the wife of the Lamb"; and the reference is obviously to Christ and his church. Probably "the elect lady" of 2 John is to be understood in this direction. The Greek word for "church" is feminine, making it an easy transition to "lady."

The language of this brief letter is for the most part male-oriented. "Those knowing the truth" are masculine at least in grammatical gender (v. 1). The "many erring ones," "those not confessing Jesus Christ" as "coming in flesh," are masculine as to grammatical gender. Even "the antichrist" is masculine (v.7). Both "the progressive one" (apparently self-styled) who departs and "the one remaining in the teaching" are masculine (v. 9). The one to be denied acceptance because of his false teaching is masculine (v. 10), and the one who violates this warning is likewise masculine (v. 11).

The letter closes with greetings from "the children of your elect sister," apparently one church greeting another, each represented by the writer as a woman. The letter has nothing in it that is overtly biased toward either sex. The language for the most part is masculine, but the model for the church addressed and the one associated with the writer is feminine. The most likely implication is that the male/female relationship is a nonagenda item in this little letter.

THE THIRD LETTER OF JOHN

Like the letter just reviewed, this one is from one who identifies himself as "the elder." The plural "we" (3 Jn. 12) is reminiscent of John 21:24, where others are associated in some way with the writer. Traditionally this letter, although anonymous, is attributed to John. It has no direct concern with the place of woman in the church, and it offers little to our study.

There are a few stylistic patterns reflecting the male bias of language used, if not also of the writer. "The one doing good" and "the one doing evil" are both cast in the masculine gender (v. 11). "The friends" who join in sending greetings are male, and those who "by name" are to receive greetings are male (v. 15). If there is chauvinism in the letter, it is not overt but in the omission of any reference to women in the church.

THE BOOK OF REVELATION

This book is not anonymous, for the writer identifies himself as "John" (Rev. 1:1, 4, 9; 22:8). He is "servant" of God or of Jesus Christ (1:1), and he is "brother" and "partner" with his readers in "affliction and kingdom and endurance in Jesus" (1:9). The intention of the book is to inspire the readers to remain faithful to Jesus Christ as they are threatened from within by some corrupting movement, apparently Gnostic,[6] and from without by the power structures of the world.[7] The writer sees church and world, headed respectively by Christ and Satan, in a final and decisive struggle.[8] The people of God are called to holiness and uncompromising faithfulness to Christ, warned of imminent martyrdom and assured of final triumph. Women and men play important roles within this book, and it is instructive for our purpose.

On the negative side is the massiveness of male-oriented language throughout Revelation. It is not unrelieved, as is the case in 1 John; but its heavy hand nonetheless is felt by any reflective reading. Exhaustive citing will not be attempted, but some of the examples may be noted. The opening sentence declares that God gave "the revelation of Jesus Christ" so that it might be shown "to his servants" (*tois doulois* being masculine). Masculine participles are employed throughout for characterizing people. An all-male cast is at least grammatically envisioned in "the one reading" and "those hearing and keeping" the things written in this book (Rev. 1:3), for the masculine gender is used. The recurrent phrase, "the one(s) conquering," is masculine (2:7, 11, 17, 26; 3:5, 12, 21). The triumphant martyrs for Christ are masculine (6:11) as are the 144,000 (7:4) and the innumerable multitude of Christ's people (v. 9). But this same male-oriented language is used for the evil as well as for the good. Those who pierced Jesus are set forth in masculine gender (1:7). In fact all "those dwelling upon the earth" are male so far as the masculine gender of language employed is concerned (8:13; 11:10). Obviously, the masculine gender in linguistic usage does not intend to exclude women. The language is conventional, and John employs it.

More significant for perspective is the casting of men and women in certain roles in Revelation. There is the woman "Jezebel" at Thyatira (Rev. 2:20), the name itself since the days of Elijah a byword and an epithet. Then there is "the great harlot" (17:1), "Babylon, the great, the mother of harlots" (v. 5). The world's evil is epitomized in this harlot whose destruction is celebrated in a long dirge (18:1–19:4). From these two, the reader could easily conclude that John was a misogynist; but this would be to misunderstand him. The new Jerusalem, the Holy City, likewise is portrayed as a woman, being none other than "the bride, the wife of the Lamb" (21:9). In ch. 12 a "woman" represents the people of God before the birth of Jesus and following. The woman in this chapter plays a dual role as the mother of Jesus Christ and also as the persecuted church. Clearly, then, woman in Revelation does not stand for evil. Woman can symbolize the worst or the best. There is no stereotype.

Another strong line of evidence in Revelation is in the writer's employment of men for both good and evil. The riders of the four horses are men, leaving bloodshed, famine, and death wherever they go (Rev. 6:1–8). The men who impose the dilemma of idolatry or death upon people are caricatured as a "beast" out of the sea and a "beast" out of the earth (ch. 13). It by no means follows that John sees all men as beastly. He employs a wide range of imagery to depict reality; and both men and women are painted in the most lurid or beautiful colors. John is not a woman hater, and he is not a hater of men. For him, good and evil do not follow sexual lines.

John's perception of good and evil is moral/ethical. He is not world-hating, although he can picture the world as beastly. He is not a Gnostic with dualism that despises the material. He can depict the Harlot City dressed out in all her costly garments and jewelry, and she is gaudy. He can portray the Holy City as adorned with the same jewelry, and she is pure and beautiful. To John the material is not evil; materialism is evil. The same principle applies to his understanding of men and women. Neither is good or evil, wise or foolish, strong or weak as such. Either is capable of any degree of good or evil. He sees each as choosing a way of life. Fates are not imposed; they are chosen. Character is not something given by nature; it is achieved. Beastly people are guilty, responsible for their condition, life-styles, and destiny. A refrain in the book is the incredible refusal of the wicked to repent even when warnings and opportunities abound (cf. Rev. 9:20; 16:9). Men and women are what they are by their own response to the options before them. The book closes on this assumption, with its open invitation to any who will to come and to drink freely of "the water of life" (22:17). True, the masculine gender appears even in this great invitation; but surely it is not the intention of John to hang out a "For Men Only" sign at the gates of heaven. The language remains male-oriented to the end of the book; the perspective is intensely moral and personal, without stereotype of men or women.

It is not to be overlooked that the book of Revelation is a form of drama. It is highly poetic, employing colors, shapes, sounds, smells, movement, animals, numbers, and whatever is at hand to create moods and communicate ideas. As observed in Chapter 2 in Greek drama, the dramatis personae, or cast of players, includes all sorts. All kinds of lines are placed in the mouths of the characters in the drama; and all kinds of sentiments, motives, and deeds are ascribed to them. The writer's own perspectives are not represented by all the lines in the play. His perspectives are to be derived from the way he influences the reader to identify with or feel antipathy toward what is in the drama. So it is with Revelation. When it comes to men and women, the writer causes us to have antipathy for certain men and women but also to identify with certain men and women. In this is a major evidence that he is not a chauvinist but rather a careful student of humanity as it is.

The first woman to be featured in Revelation is "the woman Jezebel" (Rev. 2:20). It is not likely that there was a woman in the church at Thyatira actually named "Jezebel." This probably is John's epithet for her. The very term is used in scorn; and it may be more than redundancy that she is called "the *woman* Jezebel." Any Jezebel would be a woman. What cautions against reading too much into the phrase is that the book does not elsewhere imply that women tend to be like Jezebel. The censure is against a particular woman at Thyatira and not against women in general. This woman is seen further as one "calling herself a prophetess." There is no necessary implication that she is censured because of her claim to this role within the church. She is censured because she is false, misleading the people of God. John represents "the son of God" as saying to the church: "I have against you that you permit the woman Jezebel, the one calling herself a prophetess, both to teach and to lead astray my servants to commit fornication and to eat things sacrificed to idols" (v. 20). This seems to imply that it was a recognized practice in John's time for a woman to prophesy and teach in the churches. There is no challenge to this function. It is the abuse and not the practice that is rebuked.

The "fornication" with which "the woman Jezebel" was corrupting the church at Thyatira may have been sexual immorality,
but the term is used often for the worship of other gods. The issue
about eating "things sacrificed to idols" may go beyond simply
buying meat for home use from markets supplied by what was left
from animals sacrificed to pagan gods. The whole animal was not
burned, only a token part, the rest being sold through the markets.
A deeper involvement would be actual participation in a pagan
feast, itself an act of idolatry. Stern warning is given that such
practice must stop. There is not a word to the effect that a woman
not prophesy or teach, neither is it implied that women who
prophesy or teach tend to corrupt others.

John is not harsher with the false prophetess "Jezebel" than
with the "false prophet" in Rev. 16:13. Under the symbolism of the
"sixth bowl," John portrays an unholy trinity of "dragon" (Satan),
"the beast" (idolatrous state), and "false prophet" (civil religion as
lackey of the state). He shows his scorn for the false prophet, the
mark of whom is his subservience to the power structures of the
world, by charging that from his mouth and the mouths of his
unholy companions come "three unclean spirits like frogs." The
false prophetess and the false prophet have in common as their
abominable sin that they speak not for God but for false gods,
leading men to give themselves to other than the true God. The
issue is not between man and woman; it is between true and false
prophethood.

The 144,000 who are secure under "the seal of the living God"
are all males (Rev. 7:1–8). If this is intended to be taken in a literal
sense, the implications are amazing. The amazement is heightened
if the further description of the 144,000 is taken literally. All are
Israelites, "twelve thousand from each tribe of the sons of Israel"
(v. 4). The tribes are named, Dan being omitted with Manasseh
substituting for Dan (v. 6). Not explained is how there can be
twelve thousand distinct groups from Joseph and Manasseh, father
and son. The 144,000 appear in 14:1–5 with further description:
"These are they who did not defile themselves with women, for
they are virgins" (v. 4). We have seen above (Chapter 7) that in the
New Testament the term "virgin" may be used on occasion to

include men as well as women (cf. 1 Cor. 7:25). The "virgins" here are male, it being specified that they have "not defiled themselves with women." They also are ones in whose mouths there has not been found a lie; and they are "blameless" (Rev. 14:5). If the martyrs in 20:1–6 are identical with the 144,000 as seems true but not explicit, there are additional marks. These are all martyred by decapitation (v. 4). There is no hint that one descriptive mark is to be taken more literally or less literally than any other. Presumably, John does not expect literally to limit the saints made secure by the seal of the living God to males only, Israelites by ethnic identity, virgins, men who have never lied, blameless men, and martyrs by decapitation.

To literalize the book of Revelation is to trivialize it. Its message is to be taken seriously, but to literalize everything is to rob it of its seriousness. The number 144,000 is doubtless a symbolic number, symbolizing the totality and completion of God's people. All of his own are under his protecting seal. They are not literally "branded" on their foreheads, and they are not literally confined to twelve thousand from each tribe of Israel. It is not likely that for a calendar limit of one thousand years, there will be only 144,000 Israeli, "virgin" men reigning with Christ.

If symbolic usage is recognized in Revelation, there still remains the question of precisely what is implied in John's reference to men who are "virgins," men who had not "defiled themselves with women." Taken at face value, the passage seems to imply an ascetic bias, the sexual relationship being seen as evil. The problem with this is that it does not stand up elsewhere in the book. Fornication is condemned, but marriage is not. In fact, the book moves to a high point in its picture of the readying of "the bride, the wife of the Lamb" (Rev. 21:9). If marriage were viewed as sinful, it is not understandable that John lets it serve as the model for the union of Christ and his people. There is too much that is positive in Revelation about woman and about marriage to let this one passage so swing the verdict as to make him an ascetic.

R. H. Charles concluded that this passage on "virgins" is an interpolation made by an ascetic scribe after John's time.[9] This is possible; but without any external support for it, the conjecture from strictly internal evidence is precarious. Caird proposes this to be modeled after the Deuteronomic regulations for holy war (cf. Deut. 20; 23:9f.).[10] We concede that we find no fully satisfactory accounting for the passage, though Caird's interpretation may be the best. Except for this passage, John seems to be free of the idea that women are a source of defilement; but there lurks somewhere behind the phraseology this very idea. If this is an interpolation, all is clear. If original, some tension remains with the overall tone of the book.

The woman in the twelfth chapter of Revelation is a major figure in the entire book, and she commands a high place of honor. It is at this point that the book turns directly to the coming of Christ into the world, his triumph over Satan, and the continuing victories for his people. The "woman" who first signifies the people from whom Christ came is described as "clothed with the sun, the moon under her feet, and upon her head a victory crown of twelve stars" (Rev. 12:1). Through this imagery Israel as the "mother" of Jesus Christ is glorified; but it is no small tribute to woman that she should be the model for the human origins of Christ. It is she who bears the child who is such a threat to Satan that he does all he can to destroy the child. The woman then symbolizes the persecuted yet triumphant church, whom Satan also tries in vain to destroy or corrupt. Satan fails again, and in anger he dashes off to make war against "the rest of her seed" (v. 17). There is no asceticism here to prevent John from representing this glorious "woman" as bearing other children.

The "great harlot" in Rev. 17:1–19:4 is "the world," in kaleidoscopic fashion seen "spiritually" as "Sodom and Egypt, where their Lord was crucified" (11:8) and also "Babylon" (14:8; 7:5). The immediate reference probably was to Rome, then ruled by the self-styled "god" Domitian; but for John "the harlot city" probably is "the world" anywhere with its complex of power structures (civil, religious, military, and economic) bidding for the worship of mankind. John both scorns this "harlot" and stands in awe of her. He is a knowledgeable and astute observer who understands the awesome power the world has over mankind. He is no provincial; he knows his world with all its charms. He is no culturally deprived or frustrated loser who can only cry "sour grapes." John has all the marks of an advantaged person, as his wide knowledge of his world implies. He is a highly imaginative person, with amazing descriptive power. He chooses a "woman" to depict the world with its awesome power to compete with God himself for the hearts of men. This is not misogyny. He can use woman likewise in portraying the opposite to the world.

The long dirge portraying the fall of "Babylon" is followed by the appearance of "the new Jerusalem." Just as the world apart from God is portrayed as "the harlot city," so are the people of God portrayed as "the holy city." From Rev. 19:5 on, John through various symbols depicts and celebrates the ultimate victory of Christ and his people, those who like him have found life through death. The celebration begins with an announcement of a marriage:

> Hallelujah! For the Lord our God, the Almighty, reigns.
> Let us rejoice and let us be glad,
> And let us give the glory to him,
> Because the marriage of the Lamb has come,
> And his wife has made herself ready;
> And it was granted to her that she be clothed in pure white linen,
> For the linen is the righteous works of the saints.
>
> (Rev. 19:6–8)

Grammatically, the "blessed ones" who are "the ones invited to the marriage supper of the Lamb" (v. 9) are male (masculine gender). This of itself seems to imply male bias, as though all the saints were men; but the church itself is depicted as "woman." Neither usage, symbol or male-oriented, traditional language, is to be taken alone. John is not really biased for male or female. Only one with highest regard for woman and for marriage could picture the glorious triumph of Jesus and his people thus.

With this kaleidoscopic range and flexibility, John is able to move from the model of a marriage to that of a glorious city, "the new Jerusalem" (Rev. 21:9–22:5). One of the seven angels promises to show him "the bride, the wife of the Lamb" (21:9). He then is shown "the holy city Jerusalem coming down out of heaven from

God, having the glory of God" (vs. 10f.). Utilizing many of the same raw materials out of which he had pictured "the harlot city," John now portrays the magnificence of "the holy city." Both are presented under the model of a woman. Both are pictured in terms of the materials of the world. The difference is moral, ethical, personal. To him the world is not evil as such. The material is not evil as such. Woman is not evil as such. Good and evil, beauty and ugliness, and the holy and the unholy have to do with what comes from the heart. The world can be evil, brutish, and ugly. It can be good, gentle, and beautiful. So it is with man. So it is with woman. In keeping with this perception of man and woman, the book closes with a call to decision—to drink freely from the water of life (22:17).

SUMMARY

The Johannine writings are sufficiently different in style and in perspective to make their common authorship problematic. More defensible than single authorship is the theory of a Johannine school, out of which could come just such a combination of affinities and differences as characterize these writings. That all five date from near the end of the first century is likely. That all are later than 1 Corinthians, the earliest New Testament writing to make an issue of woman's place in the church, and probably later than most if not all of the writings containing the Domestic Code is probable. If so, the Johannine writings attest along with the Synoptic Gospels and Acts to the fact that in much of the church tradition in the last decades of the first century the issue of woman was not so acute as in the Pauline tradition.

In the Gospel of John the attitude toward woman is strongly positive. The presence of the Twelve and the male orientation of language are the two factors negative toward woman. Compensating for this is the prominence accorded women in the Gospel, this including recognition of woman's personhood, rights, freedom, and responsibility. Women are prominent at crucial junctures in the ministry of Jesus, and Mary Magdalene occupies a place of highest privilege and honor relative to the risen Christ. John's

Gospel contains no restrictions imposed upon woman as such.

The three letters are also free of overt subordination of woman. Traditional language with its male bias is used unchallenged. First John makes no direct reference to women. Second John does use "lady" as its model for the churches. There is little pro or con in these letters to imply that woman was an issue in the churches involved.

The book of Revelation retains unchallenged the male-oriented language found almost universally. Other than this, it seems to be biased neither for nor against woman. Virtues and vices are matters of moral choice and not the dictates of sexual identity. Woman can represent the harlotry of the world or the people of God as the bride of Christ. Likewise, men are found as both beastly and saintly. Neither the material, nor sex, nor marriage is seen as inherently good or evil. To John human character and destiny are matters of choice, as throughout the book persons are addressed as morally capable and responsible in the presence of far-reaching options. In brief, the Johannine corpus seems to reflect a vigorous Christian community near the end of the first century in which woman had considerable freedom and responsibility and in which there is no traceable issue of the status and role of woman.

CONCLUSION

The world Jesus entered was prevailingly male-oriented and male-dominated. For the most part, men dominated in all power structures: civil, economic, military, religious. However, it was not a monolithic world. There were competing ideals, perspectives, and patterns in life. Positive and negative factors appear here and there in various places, times, and cultures. "Exceptions" have the habit of challenging "rules." Even so, by no means could it be called a woman's world. The evidences make it difficult not to call it a man's world into which Jesus was born.

The Scriptures upon which Jesus was nurtured and from which he drew until his last hours on the cross, our Old Testament, pose the problem at the outset through two creation narratives, one nonsubordinating in its perspective of male and female as created together in the image of God and given dominion together over all else in creation (Gen. 1) and the other subordinating woman to man, a helper created second from man's rib (Gen. 2). These two perspectives competed in the literature and life of Judaism, the rib perspective gaining ascendancy over the nonsubordinating view, definitely prevailing at the time of Jesus' birth. Despite Jesus' own reversal of this trend as he built upon the Priestly story in Genesis 1 along with the nonsubordinating appendix to the rib story (Gen. 2:24), the early church struggled between Jesus' own liberating stance and the impulse to limit woman's freedom, with increasing restraints in the later letters of Paul and the churches in the Pauline tradition.

A problem awaiting more adequate study is that of the relationship between the ministry of the Word and the ministry of the altar, for women in ministry today may suffer as much from confusion here as anywhere else. There were prophetesses and judges in Israel but no priestesses, even though there were priestesses as well as priests in the pagan cults. The Jewish priesthood seems originally to have been a ministry of the Word of God and continued to remain such in the priestly cult of the Essenes at Qumran through the time of Jesus; but for much of Judaism the priesthood gravitated increasingly toward the cultic rites carried out at the Temple in Jerusalem, where "holiness" was a primary concern and where it was measured by such cultic criteria as included freedom from an issue of blood. Menstruation would of itself exclude women from the priesthood where such perspectives prevailed. To what extent did such cultic criteria for holiness play a part in excluding women from the priesthood in Judaism? Has this confusion of ministries of Word and altar carried over into the church?

The world into which Jesus came was not just Jewish; it was Greco-Roman-Oriental. Much of Greek culture had poured into Jewish and Roman life, as well as into the whole Mediterranean world and beyond. The Greeks had their own competing perspectives on woman. Strong chauvinism and sometimes misogyny surface from Hesiod to Plato and Aristotle, despite redeeming impulses in Homer and the poetic genius of Sappho and other women and despite the brilliant probings of the Greek dramatists into the issues of human justice and freedom, especially the plays of Aeschylus and Euripides, and, in another vein, those of Aristophanes.

Rome ruled the world Jesus knew. Rome had been conquered culturally by the Greeks whose armies they had defeated. Rome added her own ingredients to the mix, and woman fared differently in Roman society. Much of the Roman literature reflects for woman far greater freedom and responsibility than among the Jews and Greeks. Although seemingly more egalitarian, Roman society did not necessarily harvest a higher quality of human existence out of her fairer distribution of freedom. There, as elsewhere, freedom carries no assurance of its responsible use.

There are both continuity and discontinuity between Jesus and the world he entered, just as there are both continuity and discontinuity between Jesus and the church which followed him. Building upon Gen. 1:26–31; 2:24, Jesus in his manner and his teaching accorded woman the dignity, freedom, and responsibility of a human being. He was not a woman's liberator. He was a liberator, concerned to set free any person with the courage to receive freedom. He was found repeatedly on the side of the disadvantaged: women, "sinners" among the Jews, aliens, Samaritans, the poor, the lame, the lepers, the blind, the deaf, and those suffering any privation or bondage. By love's law of compensation, he favored the unfavored. Jesus crashed through many barriers as he related to women as persons. He freely socialized with women, without a hint that he feared for his reputation. He talked openly with women, contrary to established custom and accepted teaching. He accepted the services of women, and he honored women with a primary role in proclaiming his resurrection from the dead.

As to structures in ministry, Jesus appointed only the Twelve. There is not a trace of structure otherwise in terms of "offices," "orders," "ordination," or organization. The Twelve were men, the strongest evidence for male bias, if it is found anywhere in Jesus. Presumably the Twelve were patterned on the twelve patriarchs upon whom Israel was founded. The Twelve probably served as a sign for the reconstitution of Israel which Jesus proposed to bring about. If the Twelve did serve in this symbolic manner, it is understandable that they were all men and that they were all Jews, patterned after the twelve patriarchs of Israel. The Twelve are unique in the New Testament. Except for Judas they had no replacements. They are not a model for subsequent ministry.

If the fact that the Twelve were all males excludes women from Christian ministry, it must be considered that they also were all Jews. Does this exclude all non-Jews from Christian ministry? It is sounder to see the Twelve as a sign for reconstituted "Israel," with no necessary implications of bias in Jesus and no necessary implications for the shape of Christian ministry today. The church in its wholeness, the body of Christ, is the extended Twelve, if that model is to be retained.

Apart from the Twelve, women as well as men joined Jesus in his ministry. He commissioned all his followers to ministry, and he declared ministry to human need to be the basic criterion for the

Final Judgment of all (Mt. 25:31–46). There is no trace of "ordina-tion" for anyone during the ministry of Jesus. If anyone had first honor in announcing his resurrection, the basic tenet in the Chris-tian faith, it was Mary Magdalene.

The movement toward structures, orders, and restraining rules began after Jesus, by the best evidence of the New Testament. There is only one ministering body, Christ's body which we all are. Ministry is thus grounded by privilege and obligation in being in the body of Christ and in having received the *charismata* (gifts of grace) from God's Spirit. To this point, there is nothing about orders or ordination.

Freedom has its perils, and those struck with unusual force at Corinth. Some of Paul's hearers interpreted freedom as license, with libertine or antinomian directions. In 1 Corinthians are early traces of restraining rules, especially relating to wives and women in general. In later developments, from Colossians through the pastoral epistles, there gradually took shape an elaborate domestic code and church "orders." Even so, orders and structures were somewhat fluid. Initially, the concerns seem to have been for meet-ing human needs (the appointment of the seven to supervise a fund for the needy, a "role" for eligible widows, etc.) and the safeguard-ing of order and structures in the face of freedom perversely used. Probably the church has never been as fully committed to freedom as Jesus. Jesus never divorced freedom from responsibility, but he dared to offer freedom even though he knew that we can use it perversely. The church has tended to trust controls more than freedom, and it seems that woman has suffered disproportionately in the result.

Probably the major danger today in our awakening concern for the freedom and rights of woman is precisely where Paul encoun-tered it—the threat to morals and to structures. Freedom is more easily claimed and proclaimed than exercised responsibly. It seems to us that a true following of Jesus Christ compels us to recognize the full personhood of woman. Paul did not misunderstand Jesus as he affirmed that "in Christ" there is no male and female any more than Jew or Greek, bond or free (Gal. 3:28). With a partial recovery today of this perspective on woman is its obvious threat to structures, in particular the family. It seems to us that this right of woman to personhood must be affirmed, but this is not to be done with indifference to marriage and the home. Marriage itself has its own claims, and these claims place the freedom of both husband and wife under certain limits. Marriage necessarily obtains in the creative tension in which two become one and yet, paradoxically, remain two. Individual personhood remains, and two persons give themselves in such commitment to each other that they are one though yet two.

The place of woman in ministry within the church is an issue that will not go away. It is on the agenda, and it rightly will remain there. How the church will settle it and in what spirit remains to be seen. It seems to us that the moving of God's Spirit among his people is to be recognized here. Belatedly but surely, the strikingly positive stance of Jesus toward woman is demanding recognition today.

There are solid Biblical bases for a full recognition of the freedom and responsibility of woman in ministry and the freedom of God's Spirit to bestow the gifts for ministry upon men and women alike. Of course, the matter can be proof-texted either way. There are oft-quoted texts to exclude women from ministry; but from the Priestly narrative of the creation with male and female commissioned together to creative dominion over all creation to the risen Christ's commissioning of Mary Magdalene to inform doubting apostles that he was not dead but alive we have solid Biblical basis for not only woman's privilege in ministry but her responsibility for it. The Biblical basis is found in our being together the body of Christ, his ministering body. It is found in our transcending as persons the accidents of birth (ethnic and sexual) as well as the orders of society (legal and cultic) by our being "in Christ." It is found in the *charismata* of God's grace, the very possession of a gift for ministry being the obligation to its exercise.

The question of "ordination" for women is not to be divorced from the question of ordination as such. In truth, the whole question of "orders," "ordination," and laying on of hands is unclear in the New Testament. Except for the appointment of "the Twelve," we have nothing from Jesus as to any of these. His concern was not with structures or forms but with life: God, you, and others bound together by love, trust, acceptance, commitment. The early church as visible in the New Testament was moving toward more structures. This movement was concerned with safeguarding freedom from abuse and for implementing the various tasks of the church. Even so, throughout the period covered by the New Testament, the church remained quite fluid and open in this respect.

Awaiting further study is the problem of the possible influence of the Roman Empire upon licensing and ordination in the church. There were licensed religions in the Empire, others having no legal rights or protection and subject to suppression by the state. To what extent did licensing and ordination become important within the church against this background, Christianity itself having been unlicensed until Constantine? Whatever the case there, the church itself developed the pattern of not only licensing its ministries but excluding those whom it did not license. The church in its various confessional forms has a record of excluding from ministry those not having its "ordination." Preachers as late as in colonial America were jailed by state churches because they preached without a license. Separatist or free-church groups resorted to their own licensing and ordaining of ministers, affirming now their freedom not from a Roman Empire but from some church or state-church body. Ecumenical endeavors to this day find as a major roadblock the dispute over who has the right to ordain to the ministry. How much of this whole matter has deeper roots in the practices of the Roman Empire, from which happily the church gained its freedom, than from Jesus?

Hardened structures, fixed orders, and rules belong more to the developing church than to the movement at its rise. The church today may opt for hardened structures, thus favoring its later stages, or it may opt for more openness to the moving of God's Spirit and its own earliest flexibility. It seems to us that the greater our openness to the manner and teaching of Jesus, the greater the freedom and the responsibility of woman (and all others) in the gifts and the demands of him who is the head of his body, the church.

Notes

Introduction
1. *The Gospel According to Thomas,* Coptic text established and translated by Antoine Guillaumont and others, p. 57.

PART I

Chapter 1. The Jewish World
1. Claus Westermann, *Creation,* tr. by John J. Scullion, pp. 5–7, concludes: "The Old Testament presents not one but many Creation accounts." He finds the recognition of two separate creation accounts in Genesis 1:1–2:4a (Priestly Code, sixth-fifth centuries B.C.) and 2:4b–24 with chapter 3 (an older Yahwist, tenth-ninth centuries B.C.) to be "one of the most important and most assured results of the literary-critical examination of the Old Testament" (p. 6). Westermann notes further that the study of the history of tradition, recognizing a long oral tradition behind written sources, now recognizes "that in Israel there were not just two accounts of Creation . . . but a long series extending through the whole history of the tradition" *(ibid.).* See also Gerhard von Rad, *Genesis, A Commentary,* rev. ed., pp. 24–28, and S. H. Hooke, "Genesis," *Peake's Commentary on the Bible,* p. 179.

2. Cf. H. H. Rowley, "The Literature of the Old Testament," *Peake's Commentary on the Bible,* pp. 87f., and von Rad, *op. cit.,* p. 25. See E. A. Speiser, *Genesis,* The Anchor Bible, pp. 9f., for the view that both accounts derive from a body of antecedent traditions, with evidence for Mesopotamian connections seen in parallels between "the so-called Babylonian Creation Epic, or *Enūma eliš,*" and Genesis. See further James B. Pritchard (ed.), *Ancient Near Eastern Texts Relating to the Old Testament,* 2d ed., pp. 60–72.

3. Phyllis Tribble, "Woman in the Old Testament," *The Interpreter's*

Dictionary of the Bible, Supplementary Volume, pp. 905f. See also William E. Hull, "Woman in Her Place: Biblical Perspectives," *Review and Expositor,* Vol. LXXII (Winter 1975), No. 1, pp. 13ff., for a nonsubordinating interpretation. This informative and cogent essay appears in an issue under the theme "Woman and the Church."

4. See Von Rad, *op. cit.,* pp. 84f.

5. Westermann, *op. cit.,* p. 87.

6. *Ibid.,* p. 88.

7. Roland de Vaux, *Ancient Israel,* Vol. 1, *Social Institutions,* pp. 19f., finds that the matriarchate was somewhat common in primitive societies, especially in relation to small-scale cultivation. This does not mean that the mother exercised authority over the family but that lineage was traced through the mother, the child thus belonging to the mother's family and social group. Pastoral civilization tended to be patriarchal, and so was the Israelite family from the time of our earliest documents, according to de Vaux.

8. Von Rad, *op. cit.,* pp. 84f.

9. English translations from the Old Testament are from the *Revised Standard Version* (1952). Unless otherwise indicated, translations from the Greek New Testament are our own.

10. John Skinner, *A Critical and Exegetical Commentary on Genesis,* The International Critical Commentary, pp. 32f.

11. See Von Rad, *op. cit.,* p. 60.

12. There may be evidence here and elsewhere in the Old Testament for a *fratriarchate,* i.e., authority and property passed on from brother to brother, but none for a *sororiarchate,* i.e., the eldest sister as head of the family. Cf. de Vaux, *op. cit.,* p. 19.

13. de Vaux, *op. cit.,* p. 30.

14. See de Vaux, *op. cit.,* p. 39.

15. For a comparison with Ugaritic custom in marriage blessing, one may see Simon B. Parker's informative study, "The Marriage Blessing in Israelite and Ugaritic Literature," *Journal of Biblical Literature,* Vol. 95 (March 1976), No. 1, pp. 23–30.

16. Israel Abrahams, *Studies in Pharisaism and the Gospels,* rev. ed. pp. 68f.

17. See de Vaux, *op. cit.,* pp. 19–61.

18. *Ibid.,* p. 54.

19. Cf. Robert Gordis, "Studies in the Esther Narrative," *Journal of Biblical Literature,* Vol. 95 (March 1976), No. 1, pp. 43f.

20. This section was written before the public announcement of the

significant study by Janice Delaney, Mary Jane Lupton, and Emily Toth, *The Curse: A Cultural History of Menstruation*. Also unnoticed until this section was written is J. B. Segal, "Popular Religion in Ancient Israel," *Journal of Jewish Studies*, Vol. XXVII (Spring 1976), No. 1, pp. 1–22, with a similar stress upon "menstrual periods" as a major factor in excluding women in Israel from religious ceremonial (p. 5). Intriguing but not documented is his claim: "A male infant was circumcised on the eighth day after birth because he was affected by his mother's uncleanness during the first seven days after the delivery; the eighth day was the first on which he could be approached by the male who carried out the ceremony" (pp. 5f.).

21. Cf. Jacob Neusner, *Understanding Rabbinic Judaism from Talmudic to Modern Times*, pp. 12–15, and his *From Politics to Piety: The Emergence of Pharisaic Judaism*, p. 83.

22. Jacob Neusner, *The Rabbinic Traditions About the Pharisees Before 70*, Part III, p. 364.

23. Neusner, *From Politics to Piety*, p. 4.

24. Cf. A. Dupont-Sommer, *The Essene Writings from Qumran*, tr. by G. Vermes, pp. 295–305.

25. Quotations are from R. H. Charles, *The Apocrypha and Pseudepigrapha of the Old Testament*, 2 vols.

26. *Ibid.*, Vol. II, pp. 126f.

27. C. C. Torrey, *The Apocryphal Literature*, pp. 132f.

28. Charles, *The Apocrypha and Pseudepigrapha*, Vol. II, pp. 368f.

29. Augustine, *The City of God*, tr. by Marcus Dods, with Introduction by Thomas Merton, p. 628.

30. *Ibid.*, p. 630.

31. *Ibid.*, pp. 628f.

32. *Ibid.*, pp. 466f. Augustine argued against the view that women would be raised as men in heaven, affirming that "the sex of woman is not a vice, but nature" (p. 839) and that the woman is "a creature of God even as the man" (p. 840). Cf. *The Gospel of Thomas* 99.16–28 for the Gnostic view that there is no place for a female in the Kingdom of God, where Jesus must turn even Mary into male to qualify her for the Kingdom!

33. Quotations are from A. Dupont-Sommer, *The Essene Writings from Qumran*.

34. For options and the possibility that the Essenes known to Philo, Josephus, the Elder Pliny, and Hippolytus represent a later development of the community represented by the Qumranites, see H. H. Rowley, *The Zadokite Fragments and the Dead Sea Scrolls*, pp. 82f.

35. Philo, cited in Dupont-Sommer, *op. cit.,* p. 27.

36. Frank Moore Cross, Jr., *The Ancient Library of Qumran and Modern Biblical Studies,* rev. ed., p. 98.

37. Dupont-Sommer, *op. cit.,* p. 162, fns. 4 and 5.

38. Research on fetal development gives no support to Philo. Money and Ehrhardt conclude, "Until about the sixth week after conception, the embryo does not begin to differentiate sexually" *(Man & Woman, Boy & Girl,* p. 36). Gilman finds "that all embryos begin as 'female,' male development being contingent on a subtle process of hormonal triggering mechanisms" ("The Militant Madonna," *The Feminist Papers,* pp. 257f., ed. by Alice S. Rossi).

39. Philo is cited from F. H. Colson and G. H. Whitaker (trs.), *Philo,* The Loeb Classical Library,

40. Philo's further remark about mind to the effect that "unblemished and purged, as perfect virtue purges, it is itself the most religious of sacrifices and its whole being is highly pleasing to God" *(ibid.)* is interesting in comparison with his contemporary Paul's injunction in Rom. 12: 1-2.

41. Josephus is cited from H. St. J. Thackeray, Ralph Marcus, Allen Wikgren, and Louis H. Feldman (trs.), *Josephus,* The Loeb Classical Library.

42. Following the destruction of Jerusalem a quasi-political rabbinical academy was established at Yavneh, a coastal town in Palestine, founded by Yohanan b. Zakkai and his disciples Eliezer b. Hyrcanus and Joshua b. Hananiah (A.D. 70-ca. 125). After the Jewish-Roman war of 132–135 the academy was reestablished in the Galilean town of Usha (A.D. 140), where work continued until the publishing of the Mishnah. Cf. Neusner, *From Politics to Piety,* pp. xi-xiii, 97–141.

43. Neusner, *The Rabbinic Traditions,* p. 318. For a distinction between Pharisees and rabbis and the view that there was a "transition from Pharisaism to rabbinism, or the union of the two" in the time of Eliezer ben Hyrcanus (ca. A.D. 80–120), see Jacob Neusner (ed.), *Understanding Rabbinic Judaism from Talmudic to Modern Times,* pp. 11–19.

44. All citations from the Mishnah are from Herbert Danby (tr.), *The Mishnah* (Oxford University Press, 1933).

45. Cf. de Vaux, *op. cit.,* p. 27.

46. Joachim Jeremias, *Jerusalem in the Time of Jesus,* tr. by F. H. and C. H. Cave, p. 365. Although this section is based directly on the Mishnah, the work of Jeremias was extremely helpful in isolating pertinent passages.

47. *Ibid.,* pp. 359, 361.

48. *Ibid.,* p. 360.

49. Isaiah Sonne, "Synagogue," *The Interpreter's Dictionary of the Bible* (Abingdon Press, 1962), Vol. R-Z, p. 486.

Chapter 2. The Greek World

1. Homer, *The Iliad,* tr. by Samuel Butler and ed. by Louise R. Loomis.

2. Hesiod is cited from Hugh G. Evelyn-White (tr.), *Hesiod, the Homeric Hymns, and Homerica,* new and rev. ed., The Loeb Classical Library.

3. Friedrich Solmsen, *Hesiod and Aeschylus,* pp. 78f., fn. 12.

4. Tr. by E. G. Sihler in George W. Botsford and Ernest G. Sihler (eds.) *et al., Hellenic Civilization,* pp. 188–191.

5. Botsford and Sihler, *op. cit.,* pp. 15f.

6. See assessment of optional views by Mary Barnard, *Sappho, A New Translation,* 95–102. Also, for some erotic expression in the relationships implied by the poems, see Suzy Q. Groden (tr.), *The Poems of Sappho,* p. xii.

7. This review of the Gortynian laws as they related to women's rights is drawn solely from Botsford and Sihler, *op. cit.,* pp. 275–288.

8. Botsford and Sihler, *op. cit.,* p. 350, citing E. L. Hicks and G. H. Hill, *Manual of Greek Historical Inscriptions,* No. 37; and E. S. Roberts and E. A. Gardner, *Introduction to Greek Epigraphy,* No. 4.

9. Herodotus is cited from A. D. Godley (tr.), *Herodotus,* The Loeb Classical Library.

10. Acknowledged here is heavy dependence upon the introduction to Aeschylus, and the Greek tragedy as such, by Richmond Lattimore (tr.), *Aeschylus I,* The Complete Greek Tragedies, ed. by David Grene and Richmond Lattimore, pp. 1–35. Translations from Aeschylus are from this work, compared at points with the Greek text found in H. Weir Smyth (tr.), *Aeschylus,* The Loeb Classical Library.

11. Cf. David Grene, "Introduction," *Sophocles I,* The Complete Greek Tragedies, ed. by David Grene and Richmond Lattimore, pp. 1–8.

12. *Op. cit.,* II, p. 74. Sophocles is cited from Grene and Lattimore (eds.), *op. cit.*

13. Euripides has been charged with a "notorious misogyny" (cf. Whitney J. Oates and Eugene O'Neill, Jr., *The Complete Greek Drama,* Vol. II, p. 863), but at worst the evidence is mixed. There is no apparent hatred of woman in *Alcestis* or even in *Medea.* It is true that Aristophanes in *The Thesmophoriazusae* represents the Athenian women as up in arms over Euripides' insults to their sex, but Aristophanes was capable of misrepresenting a contemporary, as he did to Socrates in *The Clouds,* where

of all things he accuses Socrates of impiety and dishonesty. There is little surprise that he could as unjustly charge Euripides with misogyny. Euripides develops all kinds of characters, ascribing beauty and strength as well as meanness and weakness to each sex alike (cf. *Hecuba* 1180–1183 and 1184–1187).

14. Arthur S. Way (tr.), *Euripides,* The Loeb Classical Library.

15. "Lord" translates *anēr,* "man" or "husband."

16. Philip Vellacott, *Euripides: Medea and Other Plays,* p. 9. Unless otherwise indicated, quotations from *Hecuba* follow Vellacott's translation.

17. Botsford and Sihler, *op. cit.,* p. 340.

18. Aristophanes is cited from Benjamin Bickley Rogers (tr.), *Aristophanes,* The Loeb Classical Library.

19. Translated by L. A. Post in Oates and O'Neill, *op. cit.,* p. 1163. Line numbers are from Loeb.

20. Cf. E. R. Goodenough, *An Introduction to Philo Judaeus,* p. 166, who misleadingly says that Philo in his low view of woman "shows his popular rather than Greek philosophical background, for Plato and the Stoics alike had been emphasizing the equal value of women." Goodenough here unfortunately follows E. Geiger, *Philon in Alexandria als sozialer Denker* (Stuttgart, 1932), pp. 42f. Plato repeatedly rejects the equality of women with men, arguing only for equal education for utilitarian purposes.

21. Botsford and Sihler, *op. cit.,* p. 132.

22. Quotations from *Economics* are from E. C. Marchant (tr.), *Xenophon: Memorabilia and Oeconomicus,* The Loeb Classical Library.

23. Cf. Goodenough, *op. cit.,* p. 166.

24. Plato is cited from Benjamin Jowett (tr.), *The Dialogues of Plato,* 4th ed.

25. Aristotle is cited from Louise R. Loomis (ed.), *Aristotle: On Man in the Universe,* based on translations by John Henry MacMahon *(Metaphysics),* William Ogle *(Parts of Animals),* James E. C. Welldon *(Nicomachean Ethics),* Benjamin Jowett *(Politics),* and Samuel Henry Butcher *(Poetics).*

26. Botsford and Sihler, *op. cit.,* p. 661.

Chapter 3. The Roman World

1. Edith Hamilton, *The Roman Way,* p. 20.

2. *Ibid.,* p. 23.

3. Plautus is cited from Paul Nixon (tr.), *Plautus,* The Loeb Classical Library.

4. Terence is cited from John Sargeaunt (tr.), *Terence,* The Loeb Classical Library.

5. Cicero is cited from E. O. Winstedt (tr.), *Cicero: Letters to Atticus,* The Loeb Classical Library. Citations are by book and letter number.

6. Cf. W. H. Davis, *Greek Papyri of the First Century,* pp. 1f. The instruction reads, "If of all things you bear a child, if it is a male, let it alone (live); if it is a female, cast it out." Cf. *P. Oxy.* IV.744, "Letter of Hilarion to his wife Alis."

7. James Davies, *Catullus, Tibullus, and Propertius,* Ancient Classics for English Readers, p. 15.

8. F. W. Cornish (tr.), "The Poems of Gaius Valerius Catullus," *Catullus, Tibullus, and Pervigilium Veneris,* The Loeb Classical Library, pp. 7f.

9. J. P. Postgate (tr.), "Tibullus," *Catullus, Tibullus, and Pervigilium Veneris,* p. 195.

10. Propertius is cited from H. E. Butler (tr.), *Propertius,*.

11. Patric Dickinson (tr.), *The Aeneid,* pp. 306f. Quotations from *The Aeneid* are from this book. Because lines are not numbered in the version followed here, *The Aeneid* is cited by book number (Roman numeral) and page number (Arabic) in Dickinson's translation.

12. Quotations from *The Art of Love* are from J. H. Mozley (tr.), *Ovid: The Art of Love and Other Poems,* rev. ed., The Loeb Classical Library.

13. Mozley (tr.), *op. cit.*

14. Groden (tr.), *op. cit.,* p. 29.

15. Grant Showerman (tr.), *Ovid: Heroides and Amores,* The Loeb Classical Library, p. 3.

16. Quotations from *The Amores* and *The Heroides* are from Showerman (tr.), *op. cit.* (1931).

PART II

Chapter 4. The Manner of Jesus

1. See Edgar Hennecke and Wilhelm Schneemelcher (eds.), *New Testament Apocrypha,* Eng. tr. by R. McL. Wilson, Vol. I, pp. 370–388.

2. Cf. Norman Perrin, *Rediscovering the Teaching of Jesus,* pp. 39f. Following Rudolf Bultmann, *History of the Synoptic Tradition,* tr. by John Marsh (Harper & Row, Publishers, 1963), p. 205, Perrin finds that a tradition most likely goes back to Jesus when it can be shown that it

comes from neither the church nor Judaism.

3. See Frank Stagg, *Polarities of Man's Existence in Biblical Perspective,* pp. 179–191, for fuller study of "self affirmed and self denied."

4. Paul L. Stagg, "An Interpretation of Christian Stewardship," *What Is the Church?* ed. by Duke K. McCall, p. 148.

5. See Delaney, Lupton, and Toth, *The Curse: A Cultural History of Menstruation,* for a tracing of attitudes, beliefs, and practices relating to menstruation and for the authors' assessments. The book brings together considerable factual data and critical assessments along with some inadequately documented reports and some opinions that hardly lend themselves to verification.

6. See any standard commentary on the Gospel of John. For full evidence, see The United Bible Societies' *Greek New Testament, in loc.,* or Bruce M. Metzger, *A Textual Commentary on the Greek New Testament,* pp. 219–222.

7. The Greek word for "dogs" here is the diminutive form, which may somewhat soften the statement, but even so the harshness may be felt.

8. Cf. David Daube, "Jesus and the Samaritan Woman: The Meaning of *sugchraomai,"* *Journal of Biblical Literature,* Vol. 69 (June 1950), No. 2, pp. 137–147.

9. See Frank Stagg, *Polarities of Man's Existence in Biblical Perspective,* pp. 45–74.

10. Recommended is Ragnar Leivestad, *Christ the Conqueror,* and Frank Stagg, *New Testament Theology,* pp. 21–23, and *Polarities of Man's Existence in Biblical Perspective,* pp. 131–134.

Chapter 5. The Teaching of Jesus

1. "Pericope" is a technical term used in Biblical study for a small unit of tradition, saying or narrative.

2. R. C. H. Lenski, *The Interpretation of St. Matthew's Gospel,* pp. 230–235.

3. The authors' own position is that the question of divorce and remarriage is best approached in terms of the ideal and the individual case as it is found. The clear teaching of Jesus is that God's will from the beginning provides for marriage but not divorce. This is the ideal. Although there is no Scriptural proof text for it, the principle of redemption seems best to apply to any situation of human failure, including failure in marriage. Where there is acknowledgment of failure and openness to a new quality of existence, it would seem that forgiveness and rebuilding of life

are within the provision of God's redemptive grace so clearly embodied and taught by Jesus.

4. This is contested by William R. Farmer, *The Synoptic Problem.* Although cogently argued on critical grounds, Farmer's thesis of Marcan dependence upon Matthew fails to answer many questions, most notably why anyone would have deleted so much Matthean material to produce Mark. Enrichment of Marcan material by Matthean requires no defense.

5. Cf. R. H. Charles, *The Teaching of the New Testament on Divorce,* pp. 85ff., and B. H. Streeter, *The Four Gospels, A Study of Origins,* p. 259.

6. See Matthew Black, *The Scrolls and Christian Origins,* p. 85, for linkage between the concepts of "virgin" and "eunuch" in Syriac, Hebrew, and other usage.

7. Cf. Hennecke and Schneemelcher (eds.), *New Testament Apocrypha,* Vol. I, pp. 374–388.

Chapter 6. The Risen Christ and Woman

1. Cf. C. H. Dodd, *The Apostolic Preaching and Its Developments.* Dodd may have pressed his claims unduly, but the basic contention of this book is valid.

2. Acknowledged here is heavy dependence upon Edward Lynn Bode, *The First Easter Morning: The Gospel Accounts of the Women's Visit to the Tomb of Jesus,* pp. 5–24. This is a careful analysis of the Biblical materials and interaction with current critical literature on the subject.

3. Cf. Bode, *op. cit.,* pp. 6–18, whom we follow here.

4. William R. Farmer, *The Last Twelve Verses of Mark,* argues for a more favorable assessment of Mk. 16:9–20, but the case for this or other extant endings beyond 16:8 is unconvincing. Either the Gospel of Mark ended with 16:8 or the original ending is lost.

5. Cf. Bode, *op. cit.,* pp. 105–126. Again, heavy dependence upon Bode is acknowledged. His own dependence upon many scholars is acknowledged in his footnotes.

6. In the Epistle to the Hebrews (4:1–11) the whole life in Christ is seen as the Christian "sabbath." The first day of the week is nowhere in the New Testament termed "sabbath." Presumably "the Lord's day" came to be an alternate designation for "the first day of the week" (cf. Rev. 1:10).

7. Cf. Oscar Cullmann, *Immortality of the Soul or Resurrection of the Dead? The Witness of the New Testament,* for clear analysis.

8. The whole question of the dating of the Gospels and their relationship to one another remains unsettled, and some scholars would date all

four Gospels before A.D. 70. We doubt that any of the four Gospels predates 1 Corinthians, but see Chapter 9 on "redating."

9. Cf. Bode, *op. cit.*, p. 125.

PART III

Chapter 7. Paul and Woman

1. Cf. Donald W. Riddle, *Paul, Man of Conflict: A Modern Biographical Sketch.*

2. Cf. Frank Stagg, *The Book of Acts: The Early Struggle for an Unhindered Gospel,* for development of this understanding of the purpose and message of Acts. See also his "The Unhindered Gospel," *Review and Expositor,* Vol. LXXI (Fall 1974), No. 4, pp. 451–462.

3. Cf. Malcolm O. Tolbert, "Life Situation and Purpose of Romans," *Review and Expositor,* Vol. LXXIII (Fall 1976), No. 4, pp. 391–399, for development of this theme.

4. Cf. John Knox, *Philemon Among the Letters of Paul,* rev. ed., for argument. See also Ray F. Robbins, "Philemon," *The Broadman Bible Commentary,* pp. 377f., for a more cautious assessment of Knox's theory.

5. Cf. Walter Bauer, *"Parthenos,"* A *Greek-English Lexicon of the New Testament and Other Early Christian Literature,* tr. by William F. Arndt and F. Wilbur Gingrich, p. 632.

6. Cf. Black, *The Scrolls and Christian Origins,* pp. 83–88. C. K. Barrett, *The First Epistle to the Corinthians,* Harper's New Testament Commentaries, pp. 172–174, takes issue with Black's conclusions. For further evidence that *parthenoi* could refer to men as well as women, see Hans Conzelmann, *First Corinthians,* tr. by James W. Leitch, Hermeneia—A Critical and Historical Commentary on the Bible, pp. 130–132.

7. See William O. Walker, Jr., "1 Corinthians 11:2–16 and Paul's Views Regarding Women," *Journal of Biblical Literature,* Vol. 94 (March 1975), No. 1, pp. 94–110, for a strong case against the originality of this whole passage. This conclusion could be correct, but the contingencies are so great that we opt for the harder task of working with the text as it is.

8. See Barrett, *op. cit.,* pp. 253f., for alternate interpretations.

9. Cf. Frank Stagg, "Philippians," *The Broadman Bible Commentary,* pp. 182f., *et passim,* for life situation and purpose behind Philippians.

Chapter 8. The Domestic Code and Woman

1. Martin Dibelius, *An die Kolosser, Epheser, an Philemon,* Handbuch zum Neuen Testament.

2. For an extensive exploration of massive paraenetic materials in the Epistles, see E. G. Selwyn, "On the Inter-relation of 1 Peter and Other New Testament Epistles," in E. G. Selwyn (ed.), *The First Epistle of St. Peter,* Essay II, pp. 365–466.

3. James E. Crouch, *The Origin and Intention of the Colossian Haustafel.*

4. Cf. Frank Stagg, *Polarities of Man's Existence in Biblical Perspective,* pp. 120–142, 164–178.

5. Crouch, *op. cit.,* pp. 111–114.

6. Cf. Willi Marxsen, *Introduction to the New Testament,* tr. by Geoffrey Buswell, pp. 232–238, and Francis W. Beare (ed.), *The First Epistle of Peter,* pp. 9–19.

Chapter 9. Woman in the Synoptic Gospels and Acts

1. John A. T. Robinson, *Redating the New Testament,* pp. 352f., *et passim.*

2. Cf. Frank Stagg, "Salvation in Synoptic Tradition," *Review and Expositor,* Vol. LXIX (Summer 1972), No. 3, pp. 355–367.

3. Cf. Henry J. Cadbury, *The Making of Luke-Acts,* 2d ed. See also Leander E. Keck and J. Louis Martyn (eds.), *Studies in Luke-Acts* (Abingdon Press, 1966).

4. William F. Stinespring, "No Daughter of Zion: A Study of the Appositional Genitive in Hebrew Grammar," *Encounter,* Vol. 26 (Spring 1965), No. 2, 133–141.

5. Cf. Marshall D. Johnson, *The Purpose of the Biblical Genealogies,* Society for New Testament Studies, Monograph Series 8, for view that Jewish tradition had already in Midrashim on the Old Testament exonerated these women and that Matthew draws upon this heritage.

6. Cf. Frank Stagg, *The Book of Acts,* pp. 1–18.

7. For tracing of this theme in Acts, see Frank Stagg, "The Unhindered Gospel," *Review and Expositor,* Vol. LXXI (Fall 1974), No. 4, pp. 451–462. Major theories of the purpose of Acts and the most pertinent literature on the subject are reviewed here.

Chapter 10. Woman in the Johannine Writings

1. Cf. W. G. Kümmel, *Introduction to the New Testament,* rev. ed. tr. by Howard Clark Kee, pp. 330; and Marxsen, *op. cit.,* pp. 234–246, 442–445, 469–472.

2. C. H. Dodd, *The Johannine Epistles,* The Moffatt New Testament Commentary, pp. lxvi-lxxi.

3. Cf. R. Alan Culpepper, *The Johannine School: An Evaluation of the Johannine-School Hypothesis Based on an Investigation of the Nature of Ancient Schools,* Society of Biblical Literature Dissertation Series 26.

4. Cf. William E. Hull, "John," *The Broadman Bible Commentary,* pp. 199f., 227–324. See also Robert T. Fortna, *The Gospel of Signs: A Reconstruction of the Narrative Source Underlying the Fourth Gospel,* Society for New Testament Studies, Monograph Series 11.

5. Marxsen, *op. cit.,* p. 264.

6. Cf. Barclay M. Newman, Jr., *Rediscovering the Book of Revelation,* who sees Gnosticism as the sole problem.

7. Cf. G. B. Caird, *The Revelation of St. John the Divine,* Harper's New Testament Commentaries, for both internal and external threats.

8. Carl E. Braaten, *Christ and Counter Christ,* captures this central message of the Revelation.

9. R. H. Charles, *A Critical and Exegetical Commentary on the Revelation of St. John,* The International Critical Commentary, Vol. II, pp. 8f.

10. Caird, *op. cit.,* pp. 178ff.

Bibliography

Abrahams, Israel, *Studies in Pharisaism and the Gospels,* rev. ed. KTAV Publishing House, 1967.

Aeschylus, *Aeschylus,* tr. by H. Weir Smyth. The Loeb Classical Library. Harvard University Press, 1946.

———, *Aeschylus I,* tr. by Richmond Lattimore. The Complete Greek Tragedies, ed. by David Grene and Richmond Lattimore. Washington Square Press, 1973.

Aristophanes, *Aristophanes,* tr. by Benjamin Bickley Rogers. The Loeb Classical Library. 3 vols. G. P. Putnam's Sons, 1924.

Aristotle, *On Man in the Universe,* ed. by Louise R. Loomis. Walter J. Black, 1943.

Augustine, *The City of God,* tr. by Marcus Dods, with Introduction by Thomas Merton. Random House, 1950.

Barrett, C. K., *The First Epistle to the Corinthians.* Harper's New Testament Commentaries. Harper & Row, Publishers, 1968.

Bauer, Walter, *"Parthenos," A Greek-English Lexicon of the New Testament and Other Early Christian Literature,* tr. by William F. Arndt and F. Wilbur Gingrich. The University of Chicago Press, 1957.

Beare, Francis W., "Greek Religion and Philosophy," *The Interpreter's Dictionary of the Bible.* Abingdon Press, 1962.

——— (ed.), *The First Epistle of Peter.* The Macmillan Co., 1947.

Black, Matthew, *The Scrolls and Christian Origins.* Charles Scribner's Sons, 1961.

Bode, Edward Lynn, *The First Easter Morning: The Gospel Accounts of the Women's Visit to the Tomb of Jesus.* Rome: Biblical Institute Press, 1970.

Botsford, George W., and Sihler, Ernst G. (eds.), *Hellenic Civilization, with Contributions from William L. Westermann and Others,* tr. by E. G. Sihler. Columbia University Press, 1915.

Braaten, Carl E., *Christ and Counter Christ.* Fortress Press, 1972.

Cadbury, Henry J., *The Making of Luke-Acts,* 2d ed. 1927. London: S.P.C.K., 1958.

Caird, G. B., *The Revelation of St. John the Divine.* Harper's New Testament Commentaries. Harper & Row, Publishers, 1966.

Catullus, *Catullus, Tibullus, and Pervigilium Veneris,* "The Poems of Gaius Valerius Catullus," tr. by F. W. Cornish. The Loeb Classical Library. G. P. Putnam's Sons, 1913.

Charles, R. H., *The Apocrypha and Pseudepigrapha of the Old Testament.* 2 vols. Oxford: At the Clarendon Press, 1913.

————, *A Critical and Exegetical Commentary on the Revelation of St. John.* 2 vols. The International Critical Commentary. Edinburgh: T. & T. Clark, 1920.

————, *The Teaching of the New Testament on Divorce.* London: Williams & Norgate, 1921.

Cicero, *Cicero: Letters to Atticus,* tr. by E. O. Winstedt. The Loeb Classical Library. 3 vols. Harvard University Press, 1912.

Conzelmann, Hans, *First Corinthians,* tr. by James W. Leitch. Hermeneia —A Critical and Historical Commentary on the Bible. Fortress Press, 1975.

Cross, Frank Moore, Jr., *The Ancient Library of Qumran and Modern Biblical Studies,* rev. ed. Doubleday & Co., 1961.

Crouch, James E., *The Origin and Intention of the Colossian Haustafel.* Göttingen: Vandenhoeck & Ruprecht, 1972.

Cullmann, Oscar, *Immortality of the Soul or Resurrection of the Dead? The Witness of the New Testament.* The Macmillan Co., 1958.

Culpepper, R. Alan, *The Johannine School: An Evaluation of the Johannine-School Hypothesis Based on an Investigation of the Nature of Ancient Schools.* Society of Biblical Literature Dissertation Series 26. Scholars Press, 1975.

Daube, David, "Jesus and the Samaritan Woman: The Meaning of *sugchraomai,*" *Journal of Biblical Literature,* Vol. 69 (June 1950), No. 2, pp. 137–147.

Davies, James, *Catullus, Tibullus, and Propertius.* Ancient Classics for English Readers. J. B. Lippincott Co., 1884.

Davis, W. Hersey, *Greek Papyri of the First Century.* Harper & Brothers, 1933.

Delaney, Janice; Lupton, Mary Jane; and Toth, Emily, *The Curse: A Cultural History of Menstruation.* E. P. Dutton & Co., 1976.

de Vaux, Roland, *Ancient Israel*, Vol. 1, *Social Institutions*. McGraw-Hill Book Co., 1965.

Dibelius, Martin, *An die Kolosser, Epheser, an Philemon*. Handbuck zum Neuen Testament. Tübingen, 1913.

Dodd, C. H., *The Apostolic Preaching and Its Developments*. Willett, Clark & Co., 1937.

————, *The Johannine Epistles*. The Moffatt New Testament Commentary. Harper & Brothers, 1946.

Dupont-Sommer, A., *The Essene Writings from Qumran*, tr. by G. Vermes. Oxford: Basil Blackwell, 1961.

Euripides, *Euripides*, tr. by Arthur S. Way. The Loeb Classical Library. 4 vols. Harvard University Press, 1912.

Farmer, William R., *The Last Twelve Verses of Mark*. Cambridge: At the University Press, 1974.

————, *The Synoptic Problem*. The Macmillan Co., 1964.

Fortna, Robert T., *The Gospel of Signs: A Reconstruction of the Narrative Source Underlying the Fourth Gospel*. Society for New Testament Studies, Monograph Series 11. Cambridge: At the University Press, 1970.

Goodenough, E. R., *An Introduction to Philo Judaeus*. Yale University Press, 1940.

Gordis, Robert, "Studies in the Esther Narrative," *Journal of Biblical Literature*, Vol. 95 (March 1976), No. 1, pp. 43–58.

Guillaumont, Antoine, and others (trs.), *The Gospel According to Thomas*. Coptic text established and translated. Harper & Row, Publishers, 1959.

Hadas, Moses, and McLean, John, *Euripides: Ten Plays*. Bantam Books, 1960.

Hamilton, Edith, *The Greek Way*. W. W. Norton & Co., 1930, 1943. Discus Books published by Avon, 1973.

————, *The Roman Way*. W. W. Norton & Co., 1932. Discus Books published by Avon, 1973.

Hennecke, Edgar, and Schneemelcher, Wilhelm (eds.), *New Testament Apocrypha*, Vol. I, Eng. tr. ed. by R. McL. Wilson. The Westminster Press, 1963.

Herodotus, *Herodotus*, tr. by A. D. Godley. The Loeb Classical Library. 4 vols. G. P. Putnam's Sons, 1920.

Hesiod, *Hesiod, the Homeric Hymns, and Homerica*, tr. by Hugh G. Evelyn-White, new and rev. ed. The Loeb Classical Library. Harvard University Press, 1936.

Hicks, E. L., and Hill, G. H., *Manual of Greek Historical Inscriptions,* new ed. Oxford, 1901.

Homer, *The Iliad,* tr. by Samuel Butler; ed. by Louise R. Loomis. Walter J. Black, 1942.

Hooke, S. H., "Genesis," *Peake's Commentary on the Bible.* Thomas Nelson & Sons, 1962.

Hull, William E., "John," *The Broadman Bible Commentary.* The Broadman Press, 1970.

———, "Woman in Her Place: Biblical Perspectives," *Review and Expositor,* Vol. LXXII (Winter 1975), No. 1, pp. 5–17.

Jeremias, Joachim, *Jerusalem in the Time of Jesus,* tr. by F. H. and C. H. Cave. Fortress Press, 1969.

Johnson, Marshall D., *The Purpose of the Biblical Genealogies.* Society for New Testament Studies ,Monograph Series 8. Cambridge: At the University Press, 1969.

Josephus, Flavius, *Josephus,* tr. by H. St. J. Thackeray, Ralph Marcus, Allen Wikgren, and Louis H. Feldman. The Loeb Classical Library. 9 vols. Harvard University Press, 1926–1965.

Knox, John, *Philemon Among the Letters of Paul,* rev. ed. Abingdon Press, 1951.

Kümmel, Werner G., *Introduction to the New Testament,* rev. ed. tr. by Howard Clark Kee. Abingdon Press, 1975.

Leivestad, Ragnar, *Christ the Conqueror.* The Macmillan Co., 1954.

Lenski, R. C. H., *The Interpretation of St. Matthew's Gospel.* The Wartburg Press, 1943.

Marxsen, Willi, *Introduction to the New Testament,* tr. by Geoffrey Buswell. Fortress Press, 1968.

Metzger, Bruce M., *A Textual Commentary on the Greek New Testament.* United Bible Societies, 1971.

Mishnah, The, tr. by Herbert Danby. Oxford University Press, 1933.

Money, John, and Ehrhardt, Anke A., *Man & Woman, Boy & Girl: Differentiation and Dimorphism of Gender Identity from Conception to Maturity.* The John Hopkins University Press, 1972.

Neusner, Jacob, *From Politics to Piety: The Emergence of Pharisaic Judaism.* Prentice-Hall, 1973.

———, *The Rabbinic Traditions About the Pharisees Before 70.* Leiden: E. J. Brill, 1971.

———, *Understanding Rabbinic Judaism from Talmudic to Modern Times.* KTAV Publishing House, 1974.

Newman, Barclay M., Jr., *Rediscovering the Book of Revelation*. Judson Press, 1968.

Oates, Whitney J., and O'Neill, Eugene G., Jr. (eds.), *The Complete Greek Drama*. 2 vols. Random House, 1938.

Ovid, *The Art of Love and Other Poems*, tr. by J. H. Mozley, rev. ed. The Loeb Classical Library. Harvard University Press, 1939.

————, *Heroides and Amores*, tr. by Grant Showerman. The Loeb Classical Library. 1921. Reprint. G. P. Putnam's Sons, 1931.

Parker, Simon B., "The Marriage Blessing in Israelite and Ugaritic Literature," *Journal of Biblical Literature*, Vol. 95 (March 1976), No. 1, pp. 23–30.

Perrin, Norman, *Rediscovering the Teaching of Jesus*. Harper & Row, Publishers, 1967.

Philo, *Philo*. 10 vols. Vols. I–V, tr. by F. H. Colson and G. H. Whitaker; Vols. VI–IX, tr. by F. H. Colson; Vol. X, tr. by F. H. Colson and Index by J. W. Earp. The Loeb Classical Library. Harvard University Press, 1949.

Plato, *The Dialogues of Plato*, tr. by Benjamin Jowett. 4th ed. 4 vols. Oxford: Clarendon Press, 1953.

Plautus, *Plautus*, tr. by Paul Nixon. The Loeb Classical Library. 5 vols. Harvard University Press, 1916–1938.

Pritchard, James B. (ed.), *Ancient Near Eastern Texts Relating to the Old Testament*, 2d ed. Princeton University Press, 1955.

Propertius, *Propertius*, tr. by H. E. Butler, The Loeb Classical Library. The Macmillan Co., 1912.

Riddle, Donald W., *Paul, Man of Conflict: A Modern Biographical Sketch*. Abingdon-Cokesbury Press, 1940.

Robbins, Ray F., "Philemon," *The Broadman Bible Commentary*. The Broadman Press, 1971.

Roberts, E. S., and Gardner, E. A., *Introduction to Greek Epigraphy*. 2 vols. Cambridge: At the University Press, 1887, 1905.

Robinson, John A. T., *Redating the New Testament*. The Westminster Press, 1976.

Rossi, Alice S. (ed.), *The Feminist Papers from Adams to de Beauvoir*. Columbia University Press, 1973.

Rowley, H. H., "The Literature of the Old Testament," *Peake's Commentary on the Bible*. Thomas Nelson & Sons, 1962.

————, *The Zadokite Fragments and the Dead Sea Scrolls*. Oxford: Basil Blackwell, 1952.

Sappho, *Poems,* tr. by Suzy Q. Groden. The Bobbs-Merrill Co., 1966.

———, *Sappho, A New Translation,* by Mary Barnard. University of California Press, 1958.

Segal, J. B., "Popular Religion in Ancient Israel," *Journal of Jewish Studies,* Vol. XXVII (Spring 1976), No. 1, pp. 1–22.

Selwyn, E. G. (ed.), *The First Epistle of St. Peter.* London: Macmillan and Co., 1947.

Skinner, John, *A Critical and Exegetical Commentary on Genesis.* The International Critical Commentary. Charles Scribner's Sons, 1925.

Solmsen, Friedrich, *Hesiod and Aeschylus.* Cornell University Press, 1949.

Sonne, Isaiah, "Synagogue," *The Interpreter's Dictionary of the Bible.* Abingdon Press, 1962.

Sophocles, *Sophocles I,* The Complete Greek Tragedies, ed. by David Grene and Richmond Lattimore. Washington Square Press, 1972.

Speiser, E. A., *Genesis,* The Anchor Bible. Doubleday & Co., 1964.

Stagg, Frank, *The Book of Acts: The Early Struggle for an Unhindered Gospel.* The Broadman Press, 1955.

———, *New Testament Theology.* The Broadman Press, 1962.

———, "Philippians," *The Broadman Bible Commentary.* The Broadman Press, 1971.

———, *Polarities of Man's Existence in Biblical Perspective.* The Westminster Press, 1973.

———, "Salvation in Synoptic Tradition," *Review and Expositor,* Vol. LXIX (Summer 1972), No. 3, pp. 355–367.

———, "The Unhindered Gospel," *Review and Expositor,* Vol. LXXI (Fall 1974), No. 4, pp. 451–462.

Stagg, Paul L., "An Interpretation of Christian Stewardship," *What Is the Church?* ed. by Duke K. McCall. The Broadman Press, 1958.

Stinespring, William F., "No Daughter of Zion: A Study of the Appositional Genitive in Hebrew Grammar," *Encounter,* Vol. 26 (Spring 1965), No. 2, pp. 133–141.

Streeter, B. H., *The Four Gospels, A Study of Origins.* London: Macmillan, 1924.

Terence, *Terence,* tr. by John Sargeaunt. The Loeb Classical Library. 2 vols. The Macmillan Co., 1913.

Tibullus, *Catullus, Tibullus, and Pervigilium Veneris,* "Tibullus," tr. by J. P. Postgate. The Loeb Classical Library. G. P. Putnam's Sons, 1913.

Tolbert, Malcolm O., "Life Situation and Purpose of Romans," *Review and Expositor,* Vol. LXXIII (Fall 1976), No. 4, pp. 391–399.

Torrey, C. C., *The Apocryphal Literature.* Yale University Press, 1945.

Tribble, Phyllis, "Woman in the Old Testament," *The Interpreter's Dictionary of the Bible, Supplementary Volume.* Abingdon Press, 1976.

Vellacott, Philip, *Euripides: Medea and Other Plays.* Penguin Books, 1963.

Vergil, *The Aeneid,* tr. by Patric Dickinson. Mentor Books, The New American Library, 1961.

von Rad, Gerhard, *Genesis, A Commentary,* rev. ed. The Westminster Press, 1972.

Walker, William O., Jr., "1 Corinthians 11:2–16 and Paul's Views Regarding Women," *Journal of Biblical Literature,* Vol. 94 (March 1975), No. 1, pp. 94–110.

Westermann, Claus, *Creation,* tr. by John J. Scullion. Fortress Press, 1974.

Xenophon, *Memorabilia and Oeconomicus,* tr. by E. C. Marchant. The Loeb Classical Library. G. P. Putnam's Sons, 1923.

Index
of Passages Cited

OLD TESTAMENT

Genesis

1 176,
    201, 211, 253
1–2 . . . . . 16, 175
1:1–2:4a 17,
    259n
1–5 17
1:24–30 16
1:26–27 19,
    119, 176, 201
1:26–30 . . . 19, 20
1:26–31 255
1:27 19,
    43, 135
1:27–30 23
1:27–2:4a. 20
1:28 138
2 . . . . . . 43, 135,
    176, 211, 253
2:4b–24 . . . . 259n
2:4b–25 17
2:7 . . . . . 18, 119,
    156
2:7–25 16,
    18, 23
2:18 18
2:21–22 18
2:21–24 25

2:22 42
2:24 . . . 17, 18, 19,
    135, 194, 211,
    216, 253, 255
3 201
3:16 178
4:19 25
5:1f. 19
5:2 . . . . . 20, 135
5:3 . . . . . . 19, 20
5:3–32 20
7:7 25
12:10–20 26
12:20 26
16:4 22
24 23
24:13 22
24:13ff. 52
24:15–21 22
29:6 22
29:11f. 22
29:31–30:24 . . . 22
34:1 22
38:8 137
38:11 25
38:12–26 128

Exodus

2:16 52
2:21 23

15:20f. 27
20 21
20:12 195
20:14 128
20:17 50
21:1–11 25
21:7 25
21:8–11 25

Leviticus

10:10f. 31
12:2, 5 24
15:19–33 30
18:6ff. 46
22:13 25

Numbers

5:11–31 24
5:14, 30 24
5:19, 29 24
12 27
18:5 31
27:1–8 25
31:17f. 21
36:1–9 25

Deuteronomy

5:7–21 21
8:3 119
12:5–14 31

17:8f. 30
20 249
21:5 30
21:10f. 21
21:14. 22
22:13–19 24
22:13–21 24
22:21. 24
22:28f. 25
22:29. 22
23:9f. 249
24:1 . . . . 24, 51,
                        131
25:5 137
25:5–10 25
33:10. 30

Joshua
15:16. 24

Judges
4–5 27
5:30 27
9:54 27
19 26
21:12, 21. 26

Ruth
1:8 25
2:2f. 22
4:11a 23
4:11b–12 23
4:18–22 22

1 Samuel
9:11 22
9:11–13 22
25:3 27
28:7–25 . . . 27, 36

2 Samuel
11:11 40
12:9 128
20:16. . . . . 27, 45

1 Kings
1:1–4 26
11:1–3 25

2 Kings
11 27
22:14–19 27

2 Chronicles
15:3 31

Esther
1:13 28
1:17 28
1:19–20 29

Job
42:13–15 25

Proverbs
1:8 22
2:16 26
5:3 26
11:22. 26
21:9 26
25:24. 26
27:15. 26
31:10–31 22

Song of Solomon
4:9–5:2 26

Isaiah
8:3 27

19:16. 26
49:15. 23
66:13. 23

Jeremiah
18:18. 31
50:37. 26
51:30. 26

Joel
2:28–32 228

Malachi
2:7 31
2:8 31
2:15f. 25

JEWISH APOCRYPHA
AND
PSEUDEPIGRAPHA

2 Maccabees
7:21 33

Judith
16:6–7 34

Book(s) of Adam and
        Eve
    Vita
    iii.1; vi.1; xviii.1;
        xix.3; xxxii . 34
    Slavonic Vita
    xxxii.1 34

The Book of Enoch
6–11 35
15:3 35

Sibylline Oracles
III. 818 36
IV. 4–6. 36

NEW TESTAMENT

Matthew
1–2. 13
1:1–17 218
1:18–25 218
3:8 106
4:4 119
5–7. 126
5:17–20 10
5:21–48 10
5:22–24 127
5:27–30 218
5:28 128,
            130, 132
5:31f. 131
5:32 . . . . 131, 132
5:43–48 127
7:21–23 127
9:18–26 220
9:20 220
9:24 107
9:36–38 110
10:1–4 123
12:40. 150
12:46. 138
12:46–50. . . . 105,
            138, 142
12:50. 105
14:21. 216
15:2–20 13
15:21–28. . . . 113,
                216
16:21. 150
17:23. 150
18:1–5 127

18:15. 127
18:20. 157
19:1–12 . . 133, 134,
            135, 216
19:3 . . . . 47, 134
19:4f. 136
19:5 136
19:10. 136
19:10–12. 216
20:19. 150
20:20–28. 216
20:22. 216
20:26. 180
21:5 217
21:31f. 112
22:1–14 218
22:23–33. 137
24:19. 221
25:1–13 . . 142, 218
25:31–46. . 141, 256
26:6–13 108,
        117, 120, 238
26:61. 151
27:19. 217
27:40. 151
27:63f. 150
28:1 146,
            147, 150
28:1–8 146
28:2 147
28:3 147
28:7 148
28:8 148
28:10. . . . 148, 217

Mark
1:21 13
1:30f. . . . 208, 220
1:41 106
2:17 130

2:21 208
2:27f. 130
3:1 13
3:13–19 123
3:14 183
3:27 168
3:31 138
3:31–32 101
3:31–35 103,
            105, 138,
            142, 208
3:35 . . . 111, 124,
        130, 139, 220
5:21–43 . . 209, 220
5:27 110
5:33 209
5:34 . . . . 110, 209
5:39 107
6:1f. 13
6:17 209
6:19 210
6:29 160
6:44 . . . . 208, 216
7:15 130
7:24–30 113,
            210, 216
7:25f. 114
7:27 113
7:28 114
7:29 114
8:27–38 101
8:31 150
8:34–38 105
9:24 . . . . 102, 163
9:31 150
9:33–37 127
9:35 208
9:37 127
10:1–12 . . 133, 134,
        210, 216, 220

10:2 . . . . 134, 211
10:11 . . . 135, 211
10:12 . . . 131, 135
10:34 150
10:35–45 216
10:43 208
10:45 208
11:16 168
12:18–27 . . 137, 211
12:23 211
12:24 137
12:25 . . . 137, 174
12:29–31 105
12:40 . . . 211, 220
12:41–44 107,
   211, 215, 220
13 212
13:17 . . . 212, 221
13:30 212
14:3–9 . . 108, 117,
   120, 213, 225,
   238
14:6 . . . . 213, 238
14:13 52
14:58 151
15 101
15:29 151
15:40f. 214
15:41 . . . 208, 214
15:43 225
15:47 214
16:1f. . . . 147, 150
16:1–8 146
16:2 146
16:5 147
16:6f. 148
16:8 . . . 148, 214,
   215, 217
16:9–20 217

Luke
1–2 . . . . . 13, 164
1:1–4 . . . 152, 222
1:6 222
1:18 223
1:20 223
1:25 222
1:34 223
1:37 223
1:46–55 222
1:57–66 223
2:36–38 223
2:41 . . . 103, 224
2:41–52 . . 103, 224
2:44 103
2:48 . . . 104, 224
2:49 . . . 104, 224
2:51a 104
2:52 104
3:8 106
3:23–38 224
4:16–30 . . 13, 101
4:38–39 220
6:12–16 123
7:11–17 . . 107, 224
7:12 107
7:14 106,
   107, 225
7:15 225
7:36–49 225
7:36–50 108,
   120, 123, 221
7:37 . . . 108, 221
7:37, 39, 47f. . . 108
7:47 109
7:49 108
8:1–3 121,
   225, 228
8:3 225
8:16 168

8:19f. 138
8:19–21 105,
   138, 142, 220
8:21 . . . 105, 139
8:40–56 220
8:44 220
8:52 107
9:22 150
9:46–48 127
10:38–42 52,
   117, 140,
   225
10:39 118
10:42 140
11:27–28 . . 111, 141
12:19 156
13:10–17 . . 106, 226
13:12 107
13:15 107
13:16 106
13:32 151
14:3–9 221
15 . . . . . 133, 226
15:1f. 226
16:15 134
16:18 . . . 133, 134
18:1–8 226
18:33 150
20:27–40 137
20:34 137
20:36 138
20:47 220
21:1–4 . . . 107, 220
21:23 221
21:38 112
22:57 221
23:49 . . . 152, 228
23:55f. 152
24 159

24:1 146,
        147, 150
24:1–10 222
24:1–12 . . 146, 152
24:4 147
24:5–7 148
24:6 150
24:7 150
24:9 . . . . 148, 149
24:10. 147
24:11. . . . 149, 222
24:21–24. 152
24:22–24. 222
24:36–42. 222
24:44. 158
24:44–46. 159
24:46. . . . 150, 158

John
2:1–11 103,
        104, 236
2:4 104,
        142, 236
2:5 . . . . . 180, 185
2:12 236
2:19 150
2:22 150
4 235
4:1–42 . . . 115, 237
4:4 237
4:6 116
4:7 52
4:9 116
4:22 . . . . 101, 117
4:27 52,
        116, 237
4:31 116
4:39 . . . . 117, 237
4:42 . . . . 117, 237

6:67–71 235
7:1–9 . . . . 103, 142
7:5 105,
        236, 237
7:6 236
7:30 104
7:36 112
7:52 112
7:53–8:11 111
8:20 104
8:33 106
8:39 106
9 237
9:18–23 238
11 119,
        235, 238
11:1 238
11:1–44 . . 107, 117
11:2 238
11:20. 119
11:21–27. 119
11:25. 238
11:28–30. 120
11:30. 119
11:32. 120
11:36. 120
11:39. 120
11:45. . . . 120, 238
12 . . . . . 235, 238
12:1–8 . . 108, 117,
        120, 221, 238
12:7 238
12:20–36. 113
12:23. 104
12:23–33. 105
12:27. 104
15:16. 183
17:1 104
19 235
19:25. 237

19:25–27. . . . 105,
        236, 239
19:26. 239
19:26f. 104,
        105, 236
20 235
20:1 146,
        147, 150
20:1–13 146
20:1–18 239
20:2 . . . . 148, 149
20:2b 149
20:12. 147
20:13. 148
20:16. 149
20:17. 148
20:17f. 149
20:18. . . . 148, 239
20:19. 151
20:19–29 149
20:24. 235
20:26. 151
20:30f. 235
21:24 112,
        234, 243
21:25. 235

Acts
1:11 227
1:13 123
1:14 227
1:16 . . . . 152, 228
1:21f. 228
1:22 . . . . 145, 183
1:23–26 153
2:5 227
2:14 . . . . 127, 227
2:17f. 228
2:22 . . . . 127, 228
2:29 228

2:32 . . . . 146, 153

2:37 . . . . 127, 228

2:41 156

3:12 228

3:15 . . . . 146, 153

3:15b 153

3:17 228

4:10 146

5:1–11 229

6:1 . . . . . 153, 229

6:3 228

6:6 183

8:3 228

8:16f. 184

9:15 168

9:39 228

10:42 183

10:45 188

11:2 188

11:26 195

13:1 184

13:3 183

13:16 228

13:16–41 153

13:26 228

13:29 153

13:48 183

13:50 230

14:23 183

15 . . . . 167, 188

15:1 188

15:5 188

15:13 228

15:23 229

15:36 . . . 228, 229

16:4 183

16:11–15 230

16:16–24 230

17:4 230

17:12 230

17:22 . . . . 128, 228

17:31 183

17:34 128

18:1–18 154

18:2 . . . . 180, 230

18:18 180

18:24–26 230

18:26 180,
                   230

19:24–27 231

20–28 164

20:1–6 164

20:7 . . . . 151, 152

21:9 231

21:17–25 103

22:1 228

24:24 231

25:13 231

25:23 231

26:28 195

Romans

1:17 176

2:28–29 176

3:22 162

3:29 162

6:23 165

7:1–6 180

9:7 106

10:9 146

11:1 106

12:2–8 185

12:3–8 165,
                   166, 167

12:5 . . . . 163, 165

12:6 165

12:6–8 . . . 165, 179

13:1–7 196

13:1 183

13:4 . . . . 180, 185

14:13–14 176

15:8 180

15:14–33 164

16 180

16:1 123,
                   180, 185

16:2 180

16:3 . . . . 180, 230

16:4 180

16:5 180

16:12 181

16:13 181

16:17 181

1 Corinthians

1:11 169

2:7 183

3:1–3 169

3:5 . . . . 180, 185

5:1 169

5:1f. 169

5:9ff. 170

6:9–11 170

6:12 169

6:15–20 170

6:19 170

7 172

7:1 . . . . 168, 170

7:1–7 170

7:2 . . . . 171, 172

7:3 . . . . 171, 172

7:4 171

7:5 171

7:5b 171

7:5f. 50

7:6 171

7:7 182

7:8 172

7:8–9 . . . . 171, 172

7:9 169

7:10f.... 135, 172
7:10–16 172
7:12–16 .. 172, 173
7:13 173
7:15a....... 173
7:17 183
7:20 169
7:22 169
7:24 169
7:25 .... 172, 248
7:25–35 173
7:25–38 182
7:27 174
7:29 174
7:29–31 174
7:36–38 174
7:38 174
7:39–40 .. 171, 172
7:40 172
8–10 169
8:1 169
9:14 183
11–14 169
11:2–16 52,
        175, 193, 268n
11:3 175
11:5 178
11:6 175
11:7 176
11:10.... 35, 176
11:11–12.. 176, 177
11:13....... 176
11:14....... 176
11:16....... 177
12–14 177
12:12f....... 163
14:33.... 178, 179
14:34....... 191
14:34–35.... 177,
        178, 179, 191

14:34b 178
14:40 178
15 ... 150, 151,
    155, 156, 158, 159
15:1–7 .. 101, 144,
        145, 158, 159
15:3f....... 158
15:3–7 154
15:4 154,
            155, 156
15:6 158
15:8 .... 154, 157
15:12–19..... 146
15:35–41..... 156
15:37....... 157
16:1–4 ... 151, 164
16:2 .... 151, 157
16:19...... 169,
            180, 230

2 Corinthians
5:1–5....... 155
8–9........ 164
11:28...... 162

Galatians
1:6–9....... 176
2:3 ..... 176, 188
2:11–14 176
2:12 .... 103, 188
3:1–6....... 176
3:7........ 106
3:11 176
3:11–14 163
3:19 183
3:26 164
3:28 .. 56, 124, 163,
    164, 166, 182, 186,
    188, 190, 191, 256
3:29 106

4:4 ..... 13, 101
4:9–11 176
5:1 163
5:3 188
6:12 188
6:12–16 176
6:15 188

Ephesians
2:11 176
3:7 185
4:11 185
4:11–16 186
5:14 146
5:21 193
5:22 193
5:22–33 242
5:22–6:4 77
5:22–6:9 187
5:23–24 193
5:25 194
5:33 194
6:1 199
6:1–4....... 194
6:4 195
6:5 199
6:5–9....... 195

Philippians
2:1–11 181
3:2–11 176
3:12–14 162
4:2 181
4:3 ..... 181, 182

Colossians
1:23 185
2:8 176
2:12 155
2:16–23 176

2:20–3:17 190
3:9f. 190
3:11 190
3:18 . 189, 190, 191
3:18–4:1 77,
                187, 189
3:19 189
3:20 . . . 189, 199
3:21 . . . . 189, 192
3:22 . 189, 192, 199
4:1 190

1 Thessalonians
2:7 168
2:15 101
3:2 180
4:1–8 167
4:3–6 168
4:4 168
4:6 168
4:14 146
5:5 167
5:7 167
5:14 167

2 Thessalonians
3:2 167
3:6 167

1 Timothy
1:1 200
1:3 200
1:5 200
1:18 200
2:1ff. 187
2:7 183
2:8 200
2:8ff. 187
2:9–15 200
2:11 . . . 200, 202

2:12 200
2:13f. 201
2:14 201
2:15 201
3:1 185
3:1ff. 187
3:2 202
3:8 . . . . 180, 185
3:8ff. 187
3:8–13 202
3:11 185
3:12 180,
        182, 185, 202
4:1–5 202
4:6 . . . . 180, 185
4:14 184
5:1f. 203
5:1–6:2 77
5:4–8 203
5:9 . . . . 182, 202
5:9f. 229
5:11 202
5:11–15 229
5:14 . . . 201, 202
5:16 202
5:17ff. 187
5:22 184
6:1f. 187

2 Timothy
1:6 184
4:19 . . . 180, 230

Titus
1:5 . . . . 183, 185
1:6 182
1:7 185
1:10 188
2:1–10 77,
        187, 197, 198

2:2 198
2:3 198
2:4f. 198
2:5 . . . . 198, 199
2:5b 198
2:7f. 198
2:8 198
2:9f. 199
2:10 198
3:1ff. 199

Philemon
10 164
16 165
17 165

Hebrews
4:15 129
5:1 183
8:3 183
9:6 183

1 Peter
1:3–9 195
1:15 195
2:11f. 195
2:13–3:7 . . 187, 195
2:13 196
2:16 196
2:17 196
2:18–25 196
3:1–6 196
3:7 196
2:18 196
3:1 196
3:1–9 77
3:6 . . . . 190, 197
3:7 . . . . 168, 197
3:19f. 33

3:19–21 35
4:7 195
4:12–14 195
4:16 195
5:10f. 195

2 Peter
2:4 33
2:4f. 35

1 John
1:8 241
1:10 241
2:7 241
2:12–14 241
2:18 240
2:22 240
3:6 241
3:7 240
3:9 241
3:15 240
3:21 241
4:1 . . . . . 240, 241
4:3 240
4:7 241
4:11 241
4:20 240
5:19 234

2 John
1 242
5 242
7 242
9 243
10 243
11 243

3 John
11 243

12 243
15 243

Jude
6 35
9f. 33

Revelation
1:1 243
1:3 244
1:4 243
1:7 244
1:9 243
1:10 151
1:18 146
2:7 244
2:11 244
2:17 244
2:20 . . . . 244, 246
2:26 244
3:5 244
3:12 244
3:21 244
6:1–8 245
6:9 244
6:11 244
7:1–8 247
7:4 . . . . . 244, 247
7:5 249
7:6 247
8:13 244
9:20 245
11:8 249
11:10 244
12:1 249
12:17 249
13 245
14:1–5 247
14:4 . . . . 174, 247
14:5 248

14:8 249
16:9 245
16:13 247
17:1 244
17:1–19:4 249
17:5 244
18:1–19:4 244
18:12f. 62
19:5 250
19:6–8 250
19:9 250
20:1–6 248
20:4 248
21:9 242,
            245, 248,
                250
21:9–22:5 250
21:10f. 251
22:8 243
22:17 . . . . 245, 251

DEAD SEA SCROLLS

Damascus Document
I. 2b–5 (Ms.B) . 38
VI. 15–17 39
VII. 6b–9a. . . . 38
XVI. 10–12
    (Ms. B) . . . 39

Genesis Apocryphon
II. 3–6 39
II. 8f. 40
II. 13 40

Scroll of the Rule
IX. 11 103

Rule Annexe
II. 11–22 103

Scroll of the War Rule
VII. 3b–7 37

MISHNAH

Aboth
1.5 52

Baba Metzia
1.5 50

Berakoth
7.2 53

Eduyoth
1.12 52
1.13 50
4.10 50

Gittin
4.5 50
9.10 51

Hagigah
1.1 53

Ketuboth
1.10 52
2.1 52
4.4 . . . . . . 49, 50
4.7–9 50
5.5 51
5.6–7 50
6.1 51
7.6 51
9.4 53

Kiddushin
1.1 50
1.1–5 49

1.2 50
1.7 53
4.12 52

Nedarim
4.3 53
9.9 51
10.5 50

Shebuoth
4.1 53

Taanith
4.8 53

Yebamoth
6.6 50
10.1 50
14.1 51
15.2 52
16.7 53

**CLASSICAL, HELLE-
NISTIC, AND OTHER
ANCIENT WRITINGS**

Aeschylus
  Agamemnon
  438 63
  607 64
  1055 64
  1319 64
  1498f. 64
  1625 64
  1654–1656 . . . 63
  1658–1660 . . . 63
  Libation Bearers
  524f 63
  909 64
  920 64

Persians
  50 64
  62–64 65
  119 65
  286–289 65
  845–851 65
  922f. 65

Aristophanes
  Lysistrata
  486f. 70
  497 70
  526–528 71

Aristotle
  Politics
  I.1 76
  I.3 76
  I.4 76
  I.5 76
  I.12 77
  I.13 77

Athena Nike. . . 60

Augustine
  City of God
  XVIII.23 . 35, 36
  XXII.17. . . 261n

Catullus
  Poems 88

Cicero
  Letters to Atticus
  I.8 86
  VI.1 86
  VI.6 86
  VII.2 86

VII.3 86
VII.14 87
XI.24 87

Euripides
 Alcestis
282–284 68
285–288 68
303f. 68
328–331 68
825 68
 Hecuba
341–378 68
367 68
547–552 69
548–552 68
756f. 69

Herodotus
 *Greek and Persian
   Wars*
I.1 60
I.196 61
I.199 61
II.35 61
II.59f. 61
II.100 61
V.39–41 61
VII.99 61
VIII.69 62
VIII.88 62
VIII.93 62
IX.81 62

Hesiod
 Works and Days
57f. 57
67 57
79 57
94f. 57

Homer
 Iliad . 55, 56, 263n
 Odyssey . . 55, 92

Josephus
 Against Apion
I.7f. 46
II.8 48
II.24 46
 Antiquities
I.i.2 45
II.iv.5 45
III.xii.1 46
IV.viii.15 . . . 48
IV.viii.23 . 46, 47
VII.xi.8 45
XI.iii.1–10 . . . 46
XI.iii.5 47
XV.iii.2 46
XV.iii.6 45
XVII.v.6 . . . 46
XIX.i.5 46
 War of the Jews
I.v.1 46
II.viii.2 38
V.v.2 48
VII.ix.2 45

Laws of Gortyn . 59

Menander
 Epitrepontes
234–40 72
498f. 72
637–646 72
866f. 71
885 71

Ovid
 Amores

I.x.63f. 98
II.i.5–10 97
 Art of Love
II.275–280 . . 96
II.682–688 . . 96
 Dido to Aeneas
VII.27–30 . . . 99
 Heroides
V.1 98
V.77–88 98
V.103f. 99
V.117f. 98
V.156–158 . . . 99
XI.21–32 . . . 99
XI.83 99
XI.94f. 99
 *On Painting the
   Face*
43–50 97
 Tristia
VII.13f. 97
VII.43f. 97

Philo
 De Cherubim
40–52 42
41 42
47 42
 Hypothetica
7.14 43
11.14 38
 Legum Allegoria
I.31 41
II.4 41
II.24f. 42
II.38f. 42
 *Quis Rerum Divina-
   rum Heres*
164 43
 De Specialibus Legi-

bus
I.106.   43
I.130.   44
I.200.   191
II.24.   43
II.225–248 . .   41
III.64f.   44
III.80–82 . . .   44
De Virtutibus
110   44
111f.   44

Plato
Laws
III.694–695a .   75
VI.780de . . .   75
VI.781a   75
VII.814ab. . .   75
Republic
V.449–471. . .   75
V.455de   75
VIII.549cd . .   76
Timaeus
90c.   75

Plautus
Amphitryon
II.839–842 . .   81
The Comedy of Asses
I.16–22   81
I.87   81
V.836   81
V.895   81
V.900   81
The Persian
III.329–399 . .   82

Propertius
II.xii.9–14. . .   91
II.xxxii.49–51.   91

III.xi.1–3 . . .   91
III.xiii.1f. . . .   91
IIIxiii.59f. . . .   92
III.xxv.3. . . .   91

Protevangelium of James 102, 141–142

Sappho
Extant Fragments
.   58–59

Semonides of Amorgos . . .   57–58

Sophocles
Oedipus at Colonus
337–343. . . .   66
445–449. . . .   67
1369.   66
1781.   65
Women of Trachis
31–33   66
175–177. . . .   66
436–469. . . .   66
811f.   66
1061–1063. . .   67
1070–1075. . .   67

Terence
Mother-in-Law
I.15–60   83
I.115ff.   83
I.122.   83
I.136f   83
I.164f.   83
II.293ff.   83
III.445ff. . . .   83
III.481.   83
IV.550ff.   83

Theocritus
Idyl XV . .   77, 78

Thomas, Gospel Acc. to
Logion   114, 261n

Tibullus
I.i.41–50. . . .   89
I.ii.65–74 . . .   90
I.x.1–4.   90
I.x.7–10   90

Vergil
Aeneid
I, p. 16   93
I, p. 20   93
I, p. 75   93
IV, p. 76 . . .   93
IV, pp. 83–93.   93
X, p. 225 . . .   94
XI, p. 260. . .   94
XI, p. 264. . .   94

Xenophon
Constitution of the Lacedaemonians
I   72
II   73
Oeconomicus
VI.17   73
VII.3   73
VII.5   73
VII.6   73
VII.10.   73
VII.13.   73
VII.16.   73
VII.18.   73
VII.22.   73
VII.24.   74
VII.25.   74
VII.28.   74
VII.42–43a . .   74

Index of Authors

Abrahams, I., 260n

Barnard, M., 263n
Barrett, C. K., 268n
Bauer, W., 268n
Black, M., 174, 267n, 268n
Bode, E. L., 146, 159, 267n
Botsford, G. W., and Sihler, E. G., 263n, 264n
Braaten, C. E., 270n
Bultmann, R., 265n

Cadbury, H. J., 269n
Caird, G. B., 249, 270n
Charles, R. H., 248, 261n, 267n, 270n
Conzelmann, H., 268n
Cross, F. M., 38, 262n
Crouch, J. E., 187, 269n
Cullmann, O., 267n
Culpepper, R. A., 270n

Daube, D., 266n
Davies, J., 265n
Davis, W. H., 265n
Delaney, J.; Lupton, M. J.; and Toth, E., 261n, 266n
de Vaux, R., 260n, 262n
Dibelius, M., 268n
Dickinson, P., 265n
Dodd, C. H., 267n, 269n

Dupont-Sommer, A., 39, 261n, 262n

Farmer, W. R., 267n
Fortna, R. T., 270n

Godley, A. D., 263n
Goodenough, E. R., 264n
Gordis, R., 260n
Grene, D., 263n
Groden, S. Q., 58, 263n, 265n

Hamilton, E., 79, 264n
Hennecke, E., and Schneemelcher, W., 265n, 267n
Hooke, S. H., 259n
Hull, W. E., 260n, 270n

Jeremias, J., 262n
Johnson, M. D., 269n
Jowett, B., 264n

Keck, L. E., and Martyn, J. L., 269n
Knox, J., 268n
Kümmel, W. G., 269n

Lattimore, R., 263n
Leivestad, R., 266n
Lenski, R. C. H., 266n

Marchant, E. C., 264n
Marxsen, W., 269n, 270n
Metzger, B. M., 266n
Money, J., and Ehrhardt, A. A., 262n

Neusner, J., 32, 49, 261n, 262n
Newman, B. M., Jr., 270n

Oates, W. J., and O'Neill, E., Jr., 263n, 264n
Orwell, G., 19

Parker, S. B., 260n
Perrin, N., 265n
Pritchard, J. B., 259n

Riddle, D. W., 268n
Robbins, R. F., 268n
Robinson, J. A. T., 206, 207, 269n

Rossi, A. S., 262n
Rowley, H. H., 259n, 261n

Segal, J. B., 261n
Selwyn, E. G., 269n
Skinner, J., 260n
Solmsen, F., 263n
Sonne, I., 263n
Speiser, E. A., 259n
Stagg, F., 266n, 268n, 269n
Stagg, P. L., 108, 266n
Stinespring, W. F., 217, 269n

Tolbert, M. O., 268n
Torrey, C. C., 261n
Tribble, P., 17, 259n

Vellacott, P., 264n
Von Rad, G., 259n, 260n

Walker, W. O., Jr., 268n
Westermann, C., 18, 259n, 260n